### The critics on T. H. White's
## THE ONCE AND FUTURE KING

"A gay, warm, sad, glinting, rich, mystical, true and beautiful tapestry of human history and human spirit. Read it and laugh. Read it and learn. Read it and be glad you are human."
— Minneapolis *Tribune*

"Intensely contemporary and pungent . . . not only better . . . and richer for being a retelling, it is also more original . . . In fact, there is everything in this great book."
— *Saturday Review*

". . . should be enormously popular and become one of the curious classics of English literature."
— David Garnett

T.H. WHITE

# THE ONCE AND FUTURE KING

BERKLEY BOOKS, NEW YORK

For J. A. J. A.

This Berkley book contains the complete
text of the original hardcover edition.
It has been completely reset in a type face
designed for easy reading, and was printed
from new film.

THE ONCE AND FUTURE KING

A Berkley Book / published by arrangement with
G. P. Putnam's Sons

PRINTING HISTORY
G. P. Putnam's Sons edition published 1965
Berkley edition / July 1966
Thirty-fourth printing / January 1981

ISBN: 0-425-05076-9

A BERKLEY BOOK ® TM 757,375
Berkley Books are published by Berkley Publishing Corporation,
200 Madison Avenue, New York, New York 10016.
PRINTED IN THE UNITED STATES OF AMERICA

# Contents

*Incipit Liber*
*Primus*

# THE
# SWORD
# IN
# THE
# STONE

*She is not any common earth*
*Water or wood or air,*
*But Merlin's Isle of Gramarye*
*Where you and I will fare.*

# 1

*On Mondays, Wednesdays and Fridays it was Court* Hand and Summulae Logicales, while the rest of the week it was the Organon, Repetition and Astrology. The governess was always getting muddled with her astrolabe, and when she got specially muddled she would take it out of the Wart by rapping his knuckles. She did not rap Kay's knuckles, because when Kay grew older he would be Sir Kay, the master of the estate. The Wart was called the Wart because it more or less rhymed with Art, which was short for his real name. Kay had given him the nickname. Kay was not called anything but Kay, as he was too dignified to have a nickname and would have flown into a passion if anybody had tried to give him one. The governess had red hair and some mysterious wound from which she derived a lot of prestige by showing it to all the women of the castle, behind closed doors. It was believed to be where she sat down, and to have been caused by sitting on some armour at a picnic by mistake. Eventually she offered to show it to Sir Ector, who was Kay's father, had hysterics and was sent away. They found out afterwards that she had been in a lunatic hospital for three years.

In the afternoons the programme was: Mondays and Fridays, tilting and horsemanship; Tuesdays, hawking; Wednesdays, fencing; Thursdays, archery; Saturdays, the theory of chivalry, with the proper measures to be blown on all occasions, terminology of the chase and hunting etiquette. If you did the wrong thing at the mort or the undoing, for instance, you were bent over the body of the dead beast and smacked with the flat side of a sword. This was called being bladed. It was horseplay, a sort of joke like being shaved when crossing the line. Kay was not bladed, although he often went wrong.

When they had got rid of the governess, Sir Ector said; "After all, damn it all, we can't have the boys runnin' about all day like hooligans—after all, damn it all? Ought to be havin' a first-rate eddication, at their age. When I was their age I was doin' all this Latin and stuff at five o'clock every mornin'. Happiest time of me life. Pass the port."

Sir Grummore Grummursum, who was staying the night because he had been benighted out questin' after a specially long run, said that when he was their age he was swished every mornin' because he would go hawkin' instead of learnin'. He attributed to this weakness the fact that he could never get beyond the Future Simple of Utor. It was a third of the way down the left-hand leaf, he said. He thought it was leaf ninety-seven. He passed the port.

Sir Ector said, "Had a good quest today?"

Sir Grummore said, "Oh, not so bad. Rattlin' good day, in fact. Found a chap called Sir Bruce Saunce Pité choppin' off a maiden's head in Weedon Bushes, ran him to Mixbury Plantation in the Bicester, where he doubled back, and lost him in Wicken Wood. Must have been a good twenty-five miles as he ran."

"A straight-necked 'un," said Sir Ector.

"But about these boys and all this Latin and that," added the old gentleman. "Amo, amas, you know, and runnin' about like hooligans: what would you advise?"

"Ah," said Sir Grummore, laying his finger by his nose and winking at the bottle, "that takes a deal of thinkin' about, if you don't mind my sayin' so."

"Don't mind at all," said Sir Ector. "Very kind of you to say anythin'. Much obliged, I'm sure. Help yourself to port."

"Good port this."

"Get it from a friend of mine."

"But about these boys," said Sir Grummore. "How many of them are there, do you know?"

"Two," said Sir Ector, "counting them both, that is."

"Couldn't send them to Eton, I suppose?" inquired Sir Grummore cautiously. "Long way and all that, we know."

It was not really Eton that he mentioned, for the College of Blessed Mary was not founded until 1440, but it was a place of the same sort. Also they were drinking Metheglyn, not port, but by mentioning the modern wine it is easier to give you the feel.

"Isn't so much the distance," said Sir Ector, "but that giant What's-'is-name is in the way. Have to pass through his country, you understand."

"What is his name?"

"Can't recollect it at the moment, not for the life of me. Fellow that lives by the Burbly Water."

"Galapas," said Sir Grummore.

"That's the very chap."

"The only other thing," said Sir Grummore, "is to have a tutor."

"You mean a fellow who teaches you."

"That's it," said Sir Grummore. "A tutor, you know, a fellow who teaches you."

"Have some more port," said Sir Ector. "You need it after all this questin'."

"Splendid day," said Sir Grummore. "Only they never seem to kill nowadays. Run twenty-five miles and then mark to ground or lose him altogether. The worst is when you start a fresh quest."

"We kill all our giants cubbin'," said Sir Ector. "After that they give you a fine run, but get away."

"Run out of scent," said Sir Grummore, "I dare say. It's always the same with these big giants in a big country. They run out of scent."

"But even if you was to have a tutor," said Sir Ector, "I don't see how you would get him."

"Advertise," said Sir Grummore.

"I have advertised," said Sir Ector. "It was cried by the *Humberland Newsman and Cardoile Advertiser.*"

"The only other way," said Sir Grummore, "is to start a quest."

"You mean a quest for a tutor," explained Sir Ector.

"That's it."

"Hic, Haec, Hoc," said Sir Ector. "Have some more of this drink, whatever it calls itself."

"Hunc," said Sir Grummore.

So it was decided. When Grummore Grummursum had gone home next day, Sir Ector tied a knot in his handkerchief to remember to start a quest for a tutor as soon as he had time to do so, and, as he was not sure how to set about it, he told the boys what Sir Grummore had suggested and warned them not to be hooligans meanwhile. Then they went hay-making.

It was July, and every able-bodied man and woman on the estate worked during that month in the field, under Sir Ector's direction. In any case the boys would have been excused from being eddicated just then.

Sir Ector's castle stood in an enormous clearing in a still more enormous forest. It had a courtyard and a moat with pike in it. The moat was crossed by a fortified stone bridge which ended half-way across it. The other half was covered by a wooden drawbridge which was wound up every night. As soon as you had crossed the drawbridge you were at the top of the village street—it had only one street—and this extended for about half a mile, with thatched houses of wattle and daub on either side of it. The street divided the clearing into two huge fields, that on the left being culti-vated in hundreds of long narrow strips, while that on the right ran down to a river and was used as pasture. Half of the right-hand field was fenced off for hay.

It was July, and real July weather, such as they had in Old England. Everybody went bright brown, like Red In-dians, with startling teeth and flashing eyes. The dogs moved about with their tongues hanging out, or lay panting in bits of shade, while the farm horses sweated through their coats and flicked their tails and tried to kick the horse-flies off their bellies with their great hind hoofs. In the pasture field the cows were on the gad, and could be seen galloping about with their tails in the air, which made Sir Ector angry.

Sir Ector stood on the top of a rick, whence he could see what everybody was doing, and shouted commands all over the two-hundred-acre field, and grew purple in the face. The best mowers mowed away in a line where the grass was still uncut, their scythes roaring in the strong sunlight. The women raked the dry hay together in long strips with wooden rakes, and the two boys with pitchforks followed up on either side of the strip, turning the hay in-wards so that it lay well for picking up. Then the great carts followed, rumbling with their spiked wooden wheels, drawn by horses or slow white oxen. One man stood on top of the cart to receive the hay and direct operations, while one man walked on either side picking up what the boys had prepared and throwing it to him with a fork. The cart was led down the lane between two lines of hay, and was loaded in strict rotation from the front poles to the back, the man on top calling out in a stern voice where he wanted each fork to be pitched. The loaders grumbled at the boys for not having laid the hay properly and threatened to tan them when they caught them, if they got left behind.

When the wagon was loaded, it was drawn to Sir Ector's

rick and pitched to him. It came up easily because it had been loaded systematically—not like modern hay—and Sir Ector scrambled about on top, getting in the way of his assistants, who did the real work, and stamping and perspiring and scratching about with his fork and trying to make the rick grow straight and shouting that it would all fall down as soon as the west winds came.

The Wart loved hay-making, and was good at it. Kay, who was two years older, generally stood on the edge of the bundle which he was trying to pick up, with the result that he worked twice as hard as the Wart for only half the result. But he hated to be beaten at anything, and used to fight away with the wretched hay—which he loathed like poison—until he was quite sick.

The day after Sir Grummore's visit was sweltering for the men who toiled from milking to milking and then again till sunset in their battle with the sultry element. For the hay was an element to them, like sea or air, in which they bathed and plunged themselves and which they even breathed in. The seeds and small scraps stuck in their hair, their mouths, their nostrils, and worked, tickling, inside their clothes. They did not wear many clothes, and the shadows between their sliding muscles were blue on the nut-brown skins. Those who feared thunder had felt ill that morning.

In the afternoon the storm broke. Sir Ector kept them at it till the great flashes were right overhead, and then, with the sky as dark as night, the rain came hurling against them so that they were drenched at once and could not see a hundred yards. The boys lay crouched under the wagons, wrapped in hay to keep their wet bodies warm against the now cold wind, and all joked with one another while heaven fell. Kay was shivering, though not with cold, but he joked like the others because he would not show he was afraid. At the last and greatest thunderbolt every man startled involuntarily, and each saw the other startle, until they laughed away their shame.

But that was the end of the hay-making and the beginning of play. The boys were sent home to change their clothes. The old dame who had been their nurse fetched dry jerkins out of a press, and scolded them for catching their deaths, and denounced Sir Ector for keeping on so long. Then they slipped their heads into the laundered shirts, and ran out to the refreshed and sparkling court.

"I vote we take Cully and see if we can get some rabbits in the chase," cried the Wart.

"The rabbits will not be out in this wet," said Kay sarcastically, delighted to have caught him over natural history.

"Oh, come on. It will soon be dry."

"I must carry Cully, then."

Kay insisted on carrying the goshawk and flying her, when they went hawking together. This he had a right to do, not only because he was older than the Wart but also because he was Sir Ector's proper son. The Wart was not a proper son. He did not understand this, but it made him feel unhappy, because Kay seemed to regard it as making him inferior in some way. Also it was different not having a father and mother, and Kay had taught him that being different was wrong. Nobody talked to him about it, but he thought about it when he was alone, and was distressed. He did not like people to bring it up. Since the other boy always did bring it up when a question of precedence arose, he had got into the habit of giving in at once before it could be mentioned. Besides, he admired Kay and was a born follower. He was a hero-worshipper.

"Come on, then," cried the Wart, and they scampered off toward the Mews, turning a few cartwheels on the way.

The Mews was one of the most important parts of the castle, next to the stables and the kennels. It was opposite to the solar, and faced south. The outside windows had to be small, for reasons of fortification, but the windows which looked inward to the courtyard were big and sunny. The windows had close vertical slats nailed down them, but no horizontal ones. There was no glass, but to keep the hawks from draughts there was horn in the small windows. At one end of the Mews there was a little fireplace and a kind of snuggery, like the place in a saddle-room where the grooms sit to clean their tack on wet nights after fox-hunting. Here there were a couple of stools, a cauldron, a bench with all sorts of small knives and surgical instruments, and some shelves with pots on them. The pots were labelled Cardamum, Ginger, Barley Sugar, Wrangle, For a Snurt, For the Craye, Vertigo, etc. There were leather skins hanging up, which had been snipped about as pieces were cut out of them for jesses, hoods or leashes. On a neat row of nails there were Indian bells and swivels and silver varvels, each with Ector cut on. A special shelf, and

the most beautiful of all, held the hoods: very old cracked
rufter hoods which had been made for birds before Kay
was born, tiny hoods for the merlins, small hoods for tier-
cels, splendid new hoods which had been knocked up to
pass away the long winter evenings. All the hoods, except
the rufters, were made in Sir Ector's colours: white leather
with red baize at the sides and a bunch of blue-grey plumes
on top, made out of the hackle feathers of herons. On the
bench there was a jumble of oddments such as are to be
found in every workshop, bits of cord, wire, metal, tools,
some bread and cheese which the mice had been at, a
leather bottle, some frayed gauntlets for the left hand,
nails, bits of sacking, a couple of lures and some rough
tallies scratched on the wood. These read: Conays 1 1 1 1
1 1 1 1, Harn 1 1 1, etc. They were not spelled very well.

Right down the length of the room, with the afternoon
sun shining full on them, there ran the screen perches to
which the birds were tied. There were two little merlins
which had only just been taking up from hacking, an old
peregrine who was not much use in this wooded country
but who was kept for appearances, a kestrel on which the
boys had learned the rudiments of falconry, a spar-hawk
which Sir Ector was kind enough to keep for the parish
priest, and, caged off in a special apartment of his own at
the far end, there was the tiercel goshawk Cully.

The Mews was neatly kept, with sawdust on the floor to
absorb the mutes, and the castings taken up every day.
Sir Ector visited the place each morning at seven o'clock
and the two austringers stood at attention outside the door.
If they had forgotten to brush their hair he confined them
to barracks. They took no notice.

Kay put on one of the left-hand gauntlets and called
Cully from the perch—but Cully, with all his feathers
close-set and malevolent, glared at him with a mad marigold eye and refused to come. So Kay took him up.

"Do you think we ought to fly him?" asked the Wart
doubtfully. "Deep in the moult like this?"

"Of course we can fly him, you ninny," said Kay. "He
only wants to be carried a bit, that's all."

So they went out across the hay-field, noting how the
carefully raked hay was now sodden again and losing its
goodness, into the chase where the trees began to grow, far
apart as yet and parklike, but gradually crowding into the
forest shade. The conies had hundreds of buries under

these trees, so close together that the problem was not to find a rabbit, but to find a rabbit far enough away from its hole.

"Hob says that we must not fly Cully till he has roused at least twice," said the Wart.

"Hob does not know anything about it. Nobody can tell whether a hawk is fit to fly except the man who is carrying it.

"Hob is only a villein anyway," added Kay, and began to undo the leash and swivel from the jesses.

When he felt the trappings being taken off him, so that he was in hunting order, Cully did make some movements as if to rouse. He raised his crest, his shoulder coverts and the soft feathers of his thighs. But at the last moment he thought better or worse of it and subsided without the rattle. This movement of the hawk's made the Wart itch to carry him. He yearned to take him away from Kay and set him to rights himself. He felt certain that he could get Cully into a good temper by scratching his feet and softly teasing his breast feathers upward, if only he were allowed to do it himself, instead of having to plod along behind with the stupid lure. But he knew how annoying it must be for the elder boy to be continually subjected to advice, and so he held his peace. Just as in modern shooting, you must never offer criticism to the man in command, so in hawking it was important that no outside advice should be allowed to disturb the judgment of the austringer.

"So-ho!" cried Kay, throwing his arm upward to give the hawk a better take-off, and a rabbit was scooting across the close-nibbled turf in front of them, and Cully was in the air. The movement had surprised the Wart, the rabbit and the hawk, all three, and all three hung a moment in surprise. Then the great wings of the aerial assassin began to row the air, but reluctant and undecided. The rabbit vanished in a hidden hole. Up went the hawk, swooping like a child flung high in a swing, until the wings folded and he was sitting in a tree. Cully looked down at his masters, opened his beak in an angry pant of failure, and remained motionless. The two hearts stood still.

# 2

*A good while later, when they had been whistling* and luring and following the disturbed and sulky hawk from tree to tree, Kay lost his temper.

"Let him go, then," he said. "He is no use anyway."

"Oh, we could not leave him," cried the Wart. "What would Hob say?"

"It is my hawk, not Hob's," exclaimed Kay furiously. "What does it matter what Hob says? He is a servant."

"But Hob made Cully. It is all right for us to lose him, because we did not have to sit up with him three nights and carry him all day and all that. But we can't lose Hob's hawk. It would be beastly."

"Serve him right, then. He is a fool and it is a rotten hawk. Who wants a rotten stupid hawk? You had better stay yourself, if you are so keen on it. I am going home."

"I will stay," said the Wart sadly, "if you will send Hob when you get there."

Kay began walking off in the wrong direction, raging in his heart because he knew that he had flown the bird when he was not properly in yarak, and the Wart had to shout after him the right way. Then the latter sat down under the tree and looked up at Cully like a cat watching a sparrow, with his heart beating fast.

It was well enough for Kay, who was not really keen on hawking except in so far as it was the proper occupation for a boy in his station of life, but the Wart had some of the falconer's feelings and knew that a lost hawk was the greatest possible calamity. He knew that Hob had worked on Cully for fourteen hours a day to teach him his trade, and that his work had been like Jacob's struggle with the angel. When Cully was lost a part of Hob would be lost too. The Wart did not dare to face the look of reproach which would be in the falconer's eye, after all that he had tried to teach them.

What was he to do? He had better sit still, leaving the lure on the ground, so that Cully could settle down and come in his own time. But Cully had no intention of doing this. He had been given a generous gorge the night before, and he was not hungry. The hot day had put him in a bad temper. The waving and whistling of the boys below, and their pursuit of him from tree to tree, had disturbed his never powerful brains. Now he did not quite know what he wanted to do, but it was not what anybody else wanted. He thought perhaps it would be nice to kill something, from spite.

A long time after that, the Wart was on the verge of the true forest, and Cully was inside it. In a series of infuriating removes they had come nearer and nearer, till they were further from the castle than the boy had ever been, and now they had reached it quite.

Wart would not have been frightened of an English forest nowadays, but the great jungle of Old England was a different matter. It was not only that there were wild boars in it, whose sounders would at this season be furiously rooting about, nor that one of the surviving wolves might be slinking behind any tree, with pale eyes and slavering chops. The mad and wicked animals were not the only inhabitants of the crowded gloom. When men themselves became wicked they took refuge there, outlaws cunning and bloody as the gore-crow, and as persecuted. The Wart thought particularly of a man named Wat, whose name the cottagers used to frighten their children with. He had once lived in Sir Ector's village and the Wart could remember him. He squinted, had no nose, and was weak in his wits. The children threw stones at him. One day he turned on the children and caught one and made a snarly noise and bit off his nose too. Then he ran into the forest. They threw stones at the child with no nose, now, but Wat was supposed to be in the forest still, running on all fours and dressed in skins.

There were magicians in the forest also in those legendary days, as well as strange animals not known to modern works of natural history. There were regular bands of Saxon outlaws—not like Wat—who lived together and wore green and shot with arrows which never missed. There were even a few dragons, though these were small ones, which lived under stones and could hiss like a kettle.

Added to this, there was the fact that it was getting dark.

The forest was trackless and nobody in the village knew what was on the other side. The evening hush had fallen, and the high trees stood looking at the Wart without a sound.

He felt that it would be safer to go home, while he still knew where he was—but he had a stout heart, and did not want to give in. He understood that once Cully had slept in freedom for a whole night he would be wild again and irreclaimable. Cully was a passager. But if the poor Wart could only mark him to roost, and if Hob would only arrive then with a dark lantern, they might still take him that night by climbing the tree, while he was sleepy and muddled with the light. The boy could see more or less where the hawk had perched, about a hundred yards within the thick trees, because the home-going rooks of evening were mobbing that place.

He made a mark on one of the trees outside the forest, hoping that it might help him to find his way back, and then began to fight his way into the undergrowth as best he might. He heard by the rooks that Cully had immediately moved further off.

The night fell still as the small boy struggled with the brambles. But he went on doggedly, listening with all his ears, and Cully's evasions became sleepier and shorter until at last, before the utter darkness fell, he could see the hunched shoulders in a tree above him against the sky. Wart sat down under the tree, so as not to disturb the bird any further as it went to sleep, and Cully, standing on one leg, ignored his existence.

"Perhaps," said the Wart to himself, "even if Hob does not come, and I do not see how he can very well follow me in this trackless woodland now, I shall be able to climb up by myself at about midnight, and bring Cully down. He might stay there at about midnight because he ought to be asleep by then. I could speak to him softly by name, so that he thought it was just the usual person coming to take him up while hooded. I shall have to climb very quietly. Then, if I do get him, I shall have to find my way home, and the drawbridge will be up. But perhaps somebody will wait for me, for Kay will have told them I am out. I wonder which way it was? I wish Kay had not gone."

He snuggled down between the roots of the tree, trying to find a comfortable place where the hard wood did not stick into his shoulder-blades.

"I think the way was behind that big spruce with the spike top. I ought to try to remember which side of me the sun is setting, so that when it rises I may keep it on the same side going home. Did something move under that spruce tree, I wonder? Oh, I wish I may not meet that old wild Wat and have my nose bitten off! How aggravating Cully looks, standing there on one leg as if there was nothing the matter."

At this there was a quick whirr and a smack and the Wart found an arrow sticking in the tree between the fingers of his right hand. He snatched his hand away, thinking he had been stung by something, before he noticed it was an arrow. Then everything went slow. He had time to notice quite carefully what sort of an arrow it was, and how it had driven three inches into the solid wood. It was a black arrow with yellow bands round it, like a wasp, and its cock feather was yellow. The two others were black. They were dyed goose feathers.

The Wart found that, although he was frightened of the danger of the forest before it happened, once he was in it he was not frightened any more. He got up quickly—but it seemed to him slowly—and went behind the other side of the tree. As he did this, another arrow came whirr and frump, but this one buried all except its feathers in the grass, and stayed still, as if it had never moved.

On the other side of the tree he found a waste of bracken, six foot high. This was splendid cover, but it betrayed his whereabouts by rustling. He heard another arrow hiss through the fronds, and what seemed to be a man's voice cursing, but it was not very near. Then he heard the man, or whatever it was, running about in the bracken. It was reluctant to fire any more arrows because they were valuable things and would certainly get lost in the undergrowth. Wart went like a snake, like a coney, like a silent owl. He was small and the creature had no chance against him at this game. In five minutes he was safe.

The assassin searched for his arrows and went away grumbling—but the Wart realized that, even if he was safe from the archer, he had lost his way and his hawk. He had not the faintest idea where he was. He lay down for half an hour, pressed under the fallen tree where he had hidden, to give time for the thing to go right away and for his own heart to cease thundering. It had begun beating like this as soon as he knew that he had got away.

"Oh," thought he, "now I am truly lost, and now there is almost no alternative except to have my nose bitten off, or to be pierced right through with one of those waspy arrows, or to be eaten by a hissing dragon or a wolf or a wild boar or a magician—if magicians do eat boys, which I expect they do. Now I may well wish that I had been good, and not angered the governess when she got muddled with her astrolabe, and had loved my dear guardian Sir Ector as much as he deserved."

At these melancholy thoughts, and especially at the recollection of kind Sir Ector with his pitchfork and his red nose, the poor Wart's eyes became full of tears and he lay most desolate beneath the tree.

The sun finished the last rays of its lingering good-bye, and the moon rose in awful majesty over the silver tree-tops, before he dared to stand. Then he got up, and dusted the twigs out of his jerkin, and wandered off forlorn, taking the easiest way and trusting himself to God. He had been walking like this for about half an hour, and sometimes feeling more cheerful—because it really was very cool and lovely in the summer forest by moonlight—when he came upon the most beautiful thing that he had seen in his short life so far.

There was a clearing in the forest, a wide sward of moonlit grass, and the white rays shone full upon the tree trunks on the opposite side. These trees were beeches, whose trunks are always more beautiful in a pearly light, and among the beeches there was the smallest movement and a silvery clink. Before the clink there were just the beeches, but immediately afterward there was a knight in full armour, standing still and silent and unearthly, among the majestic trunks. He was mounted on an enormous white horse that stood as rapt as its master, and he carried in his right hand, with its butt resting on the stirrup, a high, smooth jousting lance, which stood up among the tree stumps, higher and higher, till it was outlined against the velvet sky. All was moonlit, all silver, too beautiful to describe.

The Wart did not know what to do. He did not know whether it would be safe to go up to this knight, for there were so many terrible things in the forest that even the knight might be a ghost. Most ghostly he looked, too, as he hoved meditating on the confines of the gloom. Eventually the boy made up his mind that even if it were a ghost, it would be the ghost of a knight, and knights were bound by their vows to help people in distress.

"Excuse me," he said, when he was right under the mysterious figure, "but can you tell me the way back to Sir Ector's castle?"

At this the ghost jumped, so that it nearly fell off its horse, and gave out a muffled baaa through its visor, like a sheep.

"Excuse me," began the Wart again, and stopped, terrified, in the middle of his speech.

For the ghost lifted up its visor, revealing two enormous eyes frosted like ice; exclaimed in an anxious voice, "What, what?"; took off its eyes—which turned out to be horn-rimmed spectacles, fogged by being inside the helmet; tried to wipe them on the horse's mane—which only made them worse; lifted both hands above its head and tried to wipe them on its plume; dropped its lance; dropped the spectacles; got off the horse to search for them—the visor shutting in the process; lifted its visor; bent down for the spectacles; stood up again as the visor shut once more, and exclaimed in a plaintive voice, "Oh, dear!"

The Wart found the spectacles, wiped them, and gave them to the ghost, who immediately put them on (the visor shut at once) and began scrambling back on its horse for dear life. When it was there it held out its hand for the lance, which the Wart handed up, and, feeling all secure, opened the visor with its left hand, and held it open. It peered at the boy with one hand up—like a lost mariner searching for land—and exclaimed, "Ah-hah! Whom have we here, what?"

"Please," said the Wart, "I am a boy whose guardian is Sir Ector."

"Charming fellah," said the Knight. "Never met him in me life."

"Can you tell me the way back to his castle?"

"Faintest idea. Stranger in these parts meself."

"I am lost," said the Wart.

"Funny thing that. Now I have been lost for seventeen years.

"Name of King Pellinore," continued the Knight. "May have heard of me, what?" The visor shut with a pop, like an echo to the What, but was opened again immediately. "Seventeen years ago, come Michaelmas, and been after the Questing Beast ever since. Boring, very."

"I should think it would be," said the Wart, who had never heard of King Pellinore, nor of the Questing Beast, but he felt that this was the safest thing to say in the circumstances.

"It is the Burden of the Pellinores," said the King proudly. "Only a Pellinore can catch it—that is, of course, or his next of kin. Train all the Pellinores with that idea in mind. Limited eddication, rather. Fewmets, and all that."

"I know what fewmets are," said the boy with interest. "They are the droppings of the beast pursued. The harborer keeps them in his horn, to show to his master, and can tell by them whether it is a warrantable beast or otherwise, and what state it is in."

"Intelligent child," remarked the King. "Very. Now I carry fewmets about with me practically all the time.

"Insanitary habit," he added, beginning to look dejected, "and quite pointless. Only one Questing Beast, you know, so there can't be any question whether she is warrantable or not."

Here his visor began to droop so much that the Wart decided he had better forget his own troubles and try to cheer his companion, by asking questions on the one subject about which he seemed qualified to speak. Even talking to a lost royalty was better than being alone in the wood.

"What does the Questing Beast look like?"

"Ah, we call it the Beast Glatisant, you know," replied the monarch, assuming a learned air and beginning to speak quite volubly. "Now the Beast Glatisant, or, as we say in English, the Questing Beast—you may call it either," he added graciously—"this Beast has the head of a serpent, ah, and the body of a libbard, the haunches of a lion, and he is footed like a hart. Wherever this beast goes he makes a noise in his belly as it had been the noise of thirty couple of hounds questing.

"Except when he is drinking, of course," added the King.

"It must be a dreadful kind of monster," said the Wart, looking about him anxiously.

"A dreadful monster," repeated the King. "It is the Beast Glatisant."

"And how do you follow it?"

This seemed to be the wrong question, for Pellinore began to look even more depressed.

"I have a brachet," he said sadly. "There she is, over there."

The Wart looked in the direction which had been indicated with a despondent thumb, and saw a lot of rope wound round a tree. The other end of the rope was tied to King Pellinore's saddle.

"I do not see her very well."

"Wound herself round the other side, I dare say. She always goes the opposite way from me."

The Wart went over to the tree and found a large white dog scratching herself for fleas. As soon as she saw the Wart, she began wagging her whole body, grinning vacuously, and panting in her efforts to lick his face, in spite of the cord. She was too tangled up to move.

"It's quite a good brachet," said King Pellinore, "only it pants so, and gets wound round things, and goes the opposite way. What with that and the visor, what, I sometimes don't know which way to turn."

"Why don't you let her loose?" asked the Wart "She would follow the Beast just as well like that."

"She goes right away then, you see, and I don't see her sometimes for a week.

"Gets a bit lonely without her," added the King, "following the Beast about, and never knowing where one is. Makes a bit of company, you know."

"She seems to have a friendly nature."

"Too friendly. Sometimes I doubt whether she is really chasing the Beast at all."

"What does she do when she sees it?"

"Nothing."

"Oh, well," said the Wart. "I dare say she will get to be interested in it after a time."

"It is eight months, anyway, since we saw the Beast at all."

The poor fellow's voice had grown sadder and sadder since the beginning of the conversation, and now he definitely began to snuffle. "It is the curse of the Pellinores," he exclaimed. "Always mollocking about after that beastly Beast. What on earth use is she, anyway? First you have to stop to unwind the brachet, then your visor falls down, then you can't see through your spectacles. Nowhere to sleep, never know where you are. Rheumatism in the winter, sunstroke in the summer. All this horrid armour takes hours to put on. When it is on it's either frying or freezing, and it gets rusty. You have to sit up all night polishing the stuff. Oh, how I do wish I had a nice house of my own to live in, a house with beds in it and real pillows and sheets. If I was rich that's what I would buy. A nice bed with a nice pillow and a nice sheet that you could lie in, and then I would put this beastly horse in a meadow and tell that beastly brachet to run away and play, and throw all this beastly armour out of the window, and let the beastly Beast go and chase himself—that I would."

"If you could show me the way home," said the Wart craftily, "I am sure Sir Ector would put you up in a bed for the night."

"Do you really mean it?" cried the King. "In a bed?"

"A feather bed."

King Pellinore's eyes grew round as saucers. "A feather bed!" he repeated slowly. "Would it have pillows?"

"Down pillows."

"Down pillows!" whispered the King, holding his breath. And then, letting it out in one rush, "What a lovely house your gentleman must have!"

"I do not think it is more than two hours away," said the Wart, following up his advantage.

"And did this gentleman really send you out to invite me in?" (He had forgotten about the Wart being lost.) "How nice of him, how very nice of him, I do think, what?"

"He will be pleased to see us," said the Wart truthfully.

"Oh, how nice of him," exclaimed the King again, beginning to bustle about with his various trappings. "And what a lovely gentleman he must be, to have a feather bed!

"I suppose I should have to share it with somebody?" he added doubtfully.

"You could have one of your own."

"A feather bed of one's very own, with sheets and a pillow—perhaps even two pillows, or a pillow and a bolster—and no need to get up in time for breakfast! Does your guardian get up in time for breakfast?"

"Never," said the Wart.

"Fleas in the bed?"

"Not one."

"Well!" said King Pellinore. "It does sound too nice for words, I must say. A feather bed and none of those fewmets for ever so long. How long did you say it would take us to get there?"

"Two hours," said the Wart—but he had to shout the second of these words, for the sounds were drowned in his mouth by a noise which had that moment arisen close beside them.

"What was that?" exclaimed the Wart.

"Hark!" cried the King.

"Mercy!"

"It is the Beast!"

And immediately the loving huntsman had forgotten everything else, but was busied about his task. He wiped his spectacles upon the seat of his trousers, the only accessible piece of cloth about him, while the belling and bloody cry arose all round. He balanced them on the end of his long nose, just before the visor automatically clapped to. He clutched his jousting lance in his right hand, and galloped off in the direction of the noise. He was brought up short by the rope which was wound round the tree—the vacuous brachet meanwhile giving a melancholy yelp— and fell off his horse with a tremendous clang. In a second he was up again—the Wart was convinced that the spectacles must be broken—and hopping round the white horse with one foot in the stirrup. The girths stood the test and he was in the saddle somehow, with his jousting lance between his legs, and then he was galloping round and round the tree, in the opposite direction to the one in which the brachet had wound herself up. He went round three times too often, the brachet meanwhile running and yelping the other way, and then, after four or five back casts, they were both free of the obstruction. "Yoicks, what!" cried King Pellinore, waving his lance in the air, and swaying excitedly in the saddle. Then he disappeared into the gloom of the forest, with the unfortunate hound trailing behind him at the other end of the cord.

# 3

*The boy slept well in the woodland nest where he* had laid himself down, in that kind of thin but refreshing sleep which people have when they begin to lie out of doors. At first he only dipped below the surface of sleep, and skimmed along like a salmon in shallow water, so close to the surface that he fancied himself in air. He thought himself awake when he was already asleep. He saw the stars above his face, whirling on their silent and sleepless axis, and the leaves of the trees rustling against them, and he heard small changes in the grass. These little noises of footsteps and soft-fringed wing-beats and stealthy bellies drawn over the grass blades or rattling against the bracken at first frightened or interested him, so that he moved to see what they were (but never saw), then soothed him, so that he no longer cared to see what they were but trusted them to be themselves, and finally left him altogether as he swam down deeper and deeper, nuzzling into the scented turf, into the warm ground, into the unending waters under the earth.

It had been difficult to go to sleep in the bright summer moonlight, but once he was there it was not difficult to stay. The sun came early, causing him to turn over in protest, but in going to sleep he had learned to vanquish light, and now the light could not rewake him. It was nine o'clock, five hours after daylight, before he rolled over, opened his eyes, and was awake at once. He was hungry.

The Wart had heard about people who lived on berries, but this did not seem practical at the moment, because it was July, and there were none. He found two wild strawberries and ate them greedily. They tasted nicer than anything, so that he wished there were more. Then he wished it was April, so that he could find some birds' eggs and eat those, or that he had not lost his goshawk Cully, so that the hawk could catch him a rabbit which he would cook by rubbing two sticks together like the base Indian. But he had lost Cully, or he would not have lost himself, and probably the sticks would not have lighted in any case. He decided that he could not have gone more than three or four miles from home, and that the best thing he could do would be to sit still and listen. Then he might hear the noise of the haymakers, if he were lucky with the wind, and he could hearken his way to the castle by that.

What he did hear was a faint clanking noise, which made him think that King Pellinore must be after the Questing Beast again, close by. Only the noise was so regular and single in intention that it made him think of King Pellinore doing some special action, with great patience and concentration—trying to scratch his back without taking off his armour, for instance. He went toward the noise.

There was a clearing in the forest, and in this clearing there was a snug cottage built of stone. It was a cottage, although the Wart could not notice this at the time, which was divided into two bits. The main bit was the hall or every-purpose room, which was high because it extended from floor to roof, and this room had a fire on the floor whose smoke came out eventually from a hole in the thatch of the roof. The other half of the cottage was divided into two rooms by a horizontal floor which made the top half into a bedroom and study, while the bottom half served for a larder, storeroom, stable and barn. A white donkey lived in this downstairs room, and a ladder led to the one upstairs.

There was a well in front of the cottage, and the metallic noise which the Wart had heard was caused by a very old gentleman who was drawing water out of it by means of a handle and chain.

Clank, clank, clank, went the chain, until the bucket hit the lip of the well, and "Drat the whole thing!" said the old gentleman. "You would think that after all these years of study you could do better for yourself than a by-our-lady well with a by-our-lady bucket, whatever the by-our-lady cost.

"By this and by that," added the old gentleman, heaving his bucket out of the well with a malevolent glance, "why can't they get us the electric light and company's water?"

He was dressed in a flowing gown with fur tippets which had the signs of the zodiac embroidered over it, with various cabalistic signs, such as triangles with eyes in them, queer crosses, leaves of trees, bones of birds and animals, and a planetarium whose stars shone like bits of looking-glass with the sun on them. He had a pointed hat like a dunce's cap, or like the headgear worn by ladies of that time, except that the ladies were accustomed to have a bit of veil floating from the top of it. He also had a wand of lignum vitae, which he had laid down in the grass beside him, and a pair of horn-rimmed spectacles like those of King Pellinore. They were unusual spectacles, being without ear pieces, but shaped rather like scissors or like the antennae of the tarantula wasp.

"Excuse me, sir," said the Wart, "but can you tell me the way to Sir Ector's castle, if you don't mind?"

The aged gentleman put down his bucket and looked at him.

"Your name would be the Wart."

"Yes, sir, please, sir."

"My name," said the old man, "is Merlyn."

"How do you do?"

"How do."

When these formalities had been concluded, the Wart had leisure to look at him more closely. The magician was staring at him with a kind of unwinking and benevolent curiosity which made him feel that it would not be at all rude to stare back, no ruder than it would be to stare at one of his guardian's cows who happened to be thinking about his personality as she leaned her head over a gate.

Merlyn had a long white beard and long white moustaches which hung down on either side of it. Close inspecpection showed that he was far from clean. It was not that he had dirty fingernails, or anything like that, but some large bird seemed to have been nesting in his hair. The Wart was familiar with the nests of Spar-hark and Gos, the crazy conglomerations of sticks and oddments which had been taken over from squirrels or crows, and he knew how the twigs and the tree foot were splashed with white mutes, old bones, muddy feathers and castings. This was the impression which he got from Merlyn. The old man was streaked with droppings over his shoulders, among the stars and triangles of his gown, and a large spider was slowly lowering itself from the tip of his hat, as he gazed and slowly blinked at the little boy in front of him. He had a worried expression, as though he were trying to remem-

ber some name which began with Chol but which was pronounced in quite a different way, possibly Menzies or was
it Dalziel? His mild blue eyes, very big and round under
the tarantula spectacles, gradually filmed and clouded
over as he gazed at the boy, and then he turned his head
away with a resigned expression, as though it was all too
much for him after all.

"Do you like peaches?"

"Very much indeed," said the Wart, and his mouth began to water so that it was full of sweet, soft liquid.

"They are scarcely in season," said the old man reprovingly, and he walked off in the direction of the cottage.

The Wart followed after, since this was the simplest
thing to do, and offered to carry the bucket (which seemed
to please Merlyn, who gave it to him) and waited while
he counted the keys—while he muttered and mislaid them
and dropped them in the grass. Finally, when they had got
their way into the black and white home with as much
trouble as if they were burgling it, he climbed up the ladder after his host and found himself in the upstairs room.

It was the most marvellous room that he had ever been
in.

There was a real corkindrill hanging from the rafters,
very life-like and horrible with glass eyes and scaly tail
stretched out behind it. When its master came into the
room it winked one eye in salutation, although it was
stuffed. There were thousands of brown books in leather
bindings, some chained to the book-shelves and others
propped against each other as if they had had too much
to drink and did not really trust themselves. These gave out
a smell of must and solid brownness which was most secure. Then there were stuffed birds, popinjays, and maggot-
pies and kingfishers, and peacocks with all their feathers
but two, and tiny birds like beetles, and a reputed phoenix
which smelt of incense and cinnamon. It could not have
been a real phoenix, because there is only one of these at
a time. Over by the mantelpiece there was a fox's mask,
with GRAFTON, BUCKINGHAM TO DAVENTRY, 2
HRS 20 MINS written under it, and also a forty-pound
salmon with AWE, 43 MIN., BULLDOG written under
it, and a very life-like basilisk with CROWHURST OT-
TER HOUNDS in Roman print. There were several boars'
tusks and the claws of tigers and libbards mounted in
symmetrical patterns, and a big head of Ovis Poli, six live

grass snakes in a kind of aquarium, some nests of the solitary wasp nicely set up in a glass cylinder, an ordinary beehive whose inhabitants went in and out of the window unmolested, two young hedgehogs in cotton wool, a pair of badgers which immediately began to cry Yik-Yik-Yik-Yik in loud voices as soon as the magician appeared, twenty boxes which contained stick caterpillars and sixths of the puss-moth, and even an oleander that was worth sixpence —all feeding on the appropriate leaves—a guncase with all sorts of weapons which would not be invented for half a thousand years, a rod-box ditto, a chest of drawers full of salmon flies which had been tied by Merlyn himself, another chest whose drawers were labelled Mandragora, Mandrake, and Old Man's Beard, etc., a bunch of turkey feathers and goose-quills for making pens, an astrolabe, twelve pairs of boots, a dozen purse-nets, three dozen rabbit wires, twelve corkscrews, some ants' nests between two glass plates, ink-bottles of every possible colour from red to violet, darning-needles, a gold medal for being the best scholar at Winchester, four or five recorders, a nest of field mice all alive-o, two skulls, plenty of cut glass, Venetian glass, Bristol glass and a bottle of Mastic varnish, some satsuma china and some cloisonné, the fourteenth edition of the Encyclopaedia Britannica (marred as it was by the sensationalism of the popular plates), two paint-boxes (one oil, one water-colour), three globes of the known geographical world, a few fossils, the stuffed head of a cameleopard, six pismires, some glass retorts with cauldrons, bunsen burners, etc., and a complete set of cigarette cards depicting wild fowl by Peter Scott.

Merlyn took off his pointed hat when he came into this chamber, because it was too high for the roof, and immediately there was a scamper in one of the dark corners and a flap of soft wings, and a tawny owl was sitting on the black skull-cap which protected the top of his head.

"Oh, what a lovely owl!" cried the Wart.

But when he went up to it and held out his hand, the owl grew half as tall again, stood up as stiff as a poker, closed its eyes so that there was only the smallest slit to peep through—as you are in the habit of doing when told to shut your eyes at hide-and-seek—and said in a doubtful voice:

"There is no owl."

Then it shut its eyes entirely and looked the other way.

"It is only a boy," said Merlyn.

"There is no boy," said the owl hopefully, without turning round.

The Wart was so startled by finding that the owl could talk that he forgot his manners and came closer still. At this the bird became so nervous that it made a mess on Merlyn's head—the whole room was quite white with droppings—and flew off to perch on the farthest tip of the corkindrill's tail, out of reach.

"We see so little company," explained the magician, wiping his head with half a worn-out pair of pyjamas which he kept for that purpose, "that Archimedes is a little shy of strangers. Come, Archimedes, I want you to meet a friend of mine called Wart."

Here he held out his hand to the owl, who came waddling like a goose along the corkindrill's back—he waddled with this rolling gait so as to keep his tail from being damaged—and hopped down to Merlyn's finger with every sign of reluctance.

"Hold out your finger and put it behind his legs. No, lift it up under his train."

When the Wart had done this, Merlyn moved the owl gently backward, so that the boy's finger pressed against its legs from behind, and it either had to step back on the finger or get pushed off its balance altogether. It stepped back. The Wart stood there delighted, while the furry feet held tight on his finger and the sharp claws prickled his skin.

"Say how d'you do properly," said Merlyn.

"I will not," said Archimedes, looking the other way and holding tight.

"Oh, he *is* lovely," said the Wart again. "Have you had him long?"

"Archimedes has stayed with me since he was small, indeed since he had a tiny head like a chicken's."

"I wish he would talk to me."

"Perhaps if you were to give him this mouse here, politely, he might learn to know you better."

Merlyn took a dead mouse out of his skull-cap—"I always keep them there, and worms too, for fishing. I find it most convenient"—and handed it to the Wart, who held it out rather gingerly toward Archimedes. The nutty curved beak looked as it if were capable of doing damage, but Archimedes looked closely at the mouse, blinked at the

Wart, moved nearer on the finger, closed his eyes and leaned forward. He stood there with closed eyes and an expression of rapture on his face, as if he were saying Grace, and then, with the absurdest sideways nibble, took the morsel so gently that he would not have broken a soap bubble. He remained leaning forward with closed eyes, with the mouse suspended from his beak, as if he were not sure what to do with it. Then he lifted his right foot —he was right-handed, though people say only men are— and took hold of the mouse. He held it up like a boy holding a stick of rock or a constable with his truncheon, looked at it, nibbled its tail. He turned it round so that it was head first, for the Wart had offered it the wrong way round, and gave one gulp. He looked round at the company with the tail hanging out of the corner of his mouth —as much as to say, "I wish you would not all stare at me so"—turned his head away, politely swallowed the tail, scratched his sailor's beard with his left toe, and began to ruffle out his feathers.

"Let him alone," said Merlyn. "Perhaps he does not want to be friends with you until he knows what you are like. With owls, it is never easy-come and easy-go."

"Perhaps he will sit on my shoulder," said the Wart, and with that he instinctively lowered his hand, so that the owl, who liked to be as high as possible, ran up the slope and stood shyly beside his ear.

"Now breakfast," said Merlyn.

The Wart saw that the most perfect breakfast was laid out neatly for two, on a table before the window. There were peaches. There were also melons, strawberries and cream, rusks, brown trout piping hot, grilled perch which were much nicer, chicken devilled enough to burn one's mouth out, kidneys and mushrooms on toast, fricassee, curry, and a choice of boiling coffee or best chocolate made with cream in large cups.

"Have some mustard," said the magician, when they had got to the kidneys.

The mustard-pot got up and walked over to his plate on thin silver legs that waddled like the owl's. Then it uncurled its handles and one handle lifted its lid with exaggerated courtesy while the other helped him to a generous spoonful.

"Oh, I love the mustard-pot!" cried the Wart. "Wherever did you get it?"

At this the pot beamed all over its face and began to strut a bit, but Merlyn rapped it on the head with a tea-spoon, so that it sat down and shut up at once.

"It is not a bad pot," he said grudgingly. "Only it is in-clined to give itself airs."

The Wart was so much impressed by the kindness of the old man, and particularly by the lovely things which he possessed, that he hardly liked to ask him personal ques-tions. It seemed politer to sit still and to speak when he was spoken to. But Merlyn did not speak much, and when he did speak it was never in questions, so that the Wart had little opportunity for conversation. At last his curiosity got the better of him, and he asked something which had been puzzling him for some time.

"Would you mind if I ask you a question?"

"It is what I am for."

"How did you know to set breakfast for two?"

The old gentleman leaned back in his chair and lighted an enormous meerschaum pipe—Good gracious, he breathes fire, thought the Wart, who had never heard of tobacco—before he was ready to reply. Then he looked puzzled, took off his skull-cap—three mice fell out—and scratched in the middle of his bald head.

"Have you ever tried to draw in a looking-glass?" he asked.

"I don't think I have."

"Looking-glass," said Merlyn, holding out his hand. Immediately there was a tiny lady's vanity-glass in his hand.

"Not that kind, you fool," he said angrily. "I want one big enough to shave in."

The vanity-glass vanished, and in its place there was a shaving mirror about a foot square. He then demanded pencil and paper in quick succession; got an unsharpened pencil and the *Morning Post;* sent them back; got a foun-tain pen with no ink in it and six reams of brown paper suitable for parcels; sent them back; flew into a passion in which he said by-our-lady quite often, and ended up with a carbon pencil and some cigarette papers which he said would have to do.

He put one of the papers in front of the glass and made five dots.

"Now," he said, " I want you to join those five dots up to make a W, looking only in the glass."

The Wart took the pen and tried to do as he was bid.

"Well, it is not bad," said the magician doubtfully, "and in a way it does look a bit like an M."

Then he fell into a reverie, stroking his beard, breathing fire, and staring at the paper.

"About the breakfast?"

"Ah, yes. How did I know to set breakfast for two? That was why I showed you the looking-glass. Now ordinary people are born forwards in Time, if you understand what I mean, and nearly everything in the world goes forward too. This makes it quite easy for the ordinary people to live, just as it would be easy to join those five dots into a W if you were allowed to look at them forwards, instead of backwards and inside out. But I unfortunately was born at the wrong end of time, and I have to live backwards from in front, while surrounded by a lot of people living forwards from behind. Some people call it having second sight."

He stopped talking and looked at the Wart in an anxious way.

"Have I told you this before?"

"No, we only met about half an hour ago."

"So little time to pass?" said Merlyn, and a big tear ran down to the end of his nose. He wiped it off with his pyjamas and added anxiously, "Am I going to tell it you again?"

"I do not know," said the Wart, "unless you have not finished telling me yet."

"You see, one gets confused with Time, when it is like that. All one's tenses get muddled, for one thing. If you know what is *going* to happen to people, and not what *has* happened to them, it makes it difficult to prevent it happening, if you don't want it to have happened, if you see what I mean? Like drawing in a mirror."

The Wart did not quite see, but was just going to say that he was sorry for Merlyn if these things made him unhappy, when he felt a curious sensation at his ear. "Don't jump," said the old man, just as he was going to do so, and the Wart sat still. Archimedes, who had been standing forgotten on his shoulder all this time, was gently touching himself against him. His beak was right against the lobe of the ear, which its bristles made to tickle, and suddenly a soft hoarse voice whispered, "How d'you do," so that it sounded right inside his head.

"Oh, owl!" cried the Wart, forgetting about Merlyn's troubles instantly. "Look, he has decided to talk to me!"

The Wart gently leaned his head against the smooth feathers, and the tawny owl, taking the rim of his ear in its beak, quickly nibbled right round it with the smallest nibbles.

"I shall call him Archie!"

"I trust you will do nothing of the sort," exclaimed Merlyn instantly, in a stern and angry voice, and the owl withdrew to the farthest corner of his shoulder.

"Is it wrong?"

"You might as well call me Wol, or Olly," said the owl sourly, "and have done with it.

"Or Bubbles," it added in a bitter voice.

Merlyn took the Wart's hand and said kindly, "You are young, and do not understand these things. But you will learn that owls are the most courteous, single-hearted and faithful creatures living. You must never be familiar, rude or vulgar with them, or make them look ridiculous. Their mother is Athene, the goddess of wisdom, and, although they are often ready to play the buffoon to amuse you, such conduct is the prerogative of the truly wise. No owl can possibly be called Archie."

"I am sorry, owl," said the Wart.

"And I am sorry, boy," said the owl. "I can see that you spoke in ignorance, and I bitterly regret that I should have been so petty as to take offence where none was intended."

The owl really did regret it, and looked so remorseful that Merlyn had to put on a cheerful manner and change the conversation.

"Well," said he, "now that we have finished breakfast, I think it is high time that we should all three find our way back to Sir Ector.

"Excuse me a moment," he added as an afterthought, and, turning round to the breakfast things, he pointed a knobbly finger at them and said in a stern voice, "Wash up."

At this all the china and cutlery scrambled down off the table, the cloth emptied the crumbs out of the window, and the napkins folded themselves up. All ran off down the ladder, to where Merlyn had left the bucket, and there was such a noise and yelling as if a lot of children had been let out of school. Merlyn went to the door and shouted, "Mind, nobody is to get broken." But his voice was entirely drowned in shrill squeals, splashes, and cries of "My, it is cold," "I shan't stay in long," "Look out, you'll break me," or "Come on, let's duck the teapot."

"Are you really coming all the way home with me?" asked the Wart, who could hardly believe the good news.

"Why not? How else can I be your tutor?"

At this the Wart's eyes grew rounder and rounder, until they were about as big as the owl's who was sitting on his shoulder, and his face got redder and redder, and a breath seemed to gather itself beneath his heart.

"My!" exclaimed the Wart, while his eyes sparkled with excitement at the discovery. "I must have been on a Quest!"

# 4

*The Wart started talking before he was half-way* over the drawbridge. "Look who I have brought," he said. "Look! I have been on a Quest! I was shot at with three arrows. They had black and yellow stripes. The owl is called Archimedes. I saw King Pellinore. This is my tutor, Merlyn. I went on a Quest for him. He was after the Questing Beast. I mean King Pellinore. It was terrible in the forest. Merlyn made the plates wash up. Hallo, Hob. Look, we have got Cully."

Hob just looked at the Wart, but so proudly that the Wart went quite red. It was such a pleasure to be back home again with all his friends, and everything achieved.

Hob said gruffly, "Ah, master, us shall make an austringer of 'ee yet."

He came for Cully, as if he could not keep his hands off him longer, but he patted the Wart too, fondling them both because he was not sure which he was gladder to see back. He took Cully on his own fist, reassuming him like a lame man putting on his accustomed wooden leg, after it had been lost.

"Merlyn caught him," said the Wart. "He sent Archimedes to look for him on the way home. Then Archimedes told us that he had been and killed a pigeon and was eating it. We went and frightened him off. After that, Merlyn stuck six of the tail feathers round the pigeon in a circle, and made a loop in a long piece of string to go round the feathers. He tied one end to a stick in the ground, and we went away behind a bush with the other end. He said he would not use magic. He said you could not use magic in Great Arts, just as it would be unfair to make a great statue by magic. You have to cut it out with a chisel, you see. Then Cully came down to finish the pigeon, and we pulled the string, and the loop slipped over the feathers and caught him round the legs. He was angry! But we gave him the pigeon."

Hob made a duty to Merlyn, who returned it courteously. They looked upon one another with grave affection, knowing each other to be masters of the same trade. When they could be alone together they would talk about falconry, although Hob was naturally a silent man. Meanwhile they must wait their time.

"Oh, Kay," cried the Wart, as the latter appeared with their nurse and other delighted welcomers. "Look, I have got a magician for our tutor. He has a mustard-pot that walks."

"I am glad you are back," said Kay.

"Alas, where did you sleep, Master Art?" exclaimed the nurse. "Look at your clean jerkin all muddied and torn. Such a turn as you gave us, I really don't know. But look at your poor hair with all them twigs in it. Oh, my own random, wicked little lamb."

Sir Ector came bustling out with his greaves on back to front, and kissed the Wart on both cheeks. "Well, well, well," he exclaimed moistly. "Here we are again, hey? What the devil have we been doin', hey? Settin' the whole household upside down."

But inside himself he was proud of the Wart for staying out after a hawk, and prouder still to see that he had got it, for all the while Hob held the bird in the air for everybody to see.

"Oh, sir," said the Wart, "I have been on that quest you said for a tutor, and I have found him. Please, he is this gentleman here, and he is called Merlyn. He has got some badgers and hedgehogs and mice and ants and things on this white donkey here, because we could not leave them behind to starve. He is a great magician, and can make things come out of the air."

"Ah, a magician," said Sir Ector, putting on his glasses and looking closely at Merlyn. "White magic, I hope?"

"Assuredly," said Merlyn, who stood patiently among the throng with his arms folded in his necromantic gown, while Archimedes sat very stiff and elongated on the top of his head.

"Ought to have some testimonials," said Sir Ector doubtfully. "It's usual."

"Testimonials," said Merlyn, holding out his hand.

Instantly there were some heavy tablets in it, signed by Aristotle, a parchment signed by Hecate, and some typewritten duplicates signed by the Master of Trinity, who could not remember having met him. All these gave Merlyn an excellent character.

"He had 'em up his sleeve," said Sir Ector wisely. "Can you do anything else?"

"Tree," said Merlyn. At once there was an enormous mulberry growing in the middle of the courtyard, with its luscious blue fruits ready to patter down. This was all the more remarkable, since mulberries only became popular in the days of Cromwell.

"They do it with mirrors," said Sir Ector.

"Snow," said Merlyn. "And an umbrella," he added hastily.

Before they could turn round, the copper sky of summer had assumed a cold and lowering bronze, while the biggest white flakes that ever were seen were floating about them and settling on the battlements. An inch of snow had fallen before they could speak, and all were trembling with the wintry blast. Sir Ector's nose was blue, and had an icicle hanging from the end of it, while all except Merlyn had a ledge of snow upon their shoulders. Merlyn stood in the middle, holding his umbrella high because of the owl.

"It's done by hypnotism," said Sir Ector, with chattering teeth. "Like those wallahs from the Indies.

"But that'll do," he added hastily, "that'll do very well. I'm sure you'll make an excellent tutor for teachin' these boys."

The snow stopped immediately and the sun came out—"Enough to give a body a pewmonia," said the nurse, "or to frighten the elastic commissioners"—while Merlyn folded up his umbrella and handed it back to the air, which received it.

"Imagine the boy doin' a quest like that by himself," exclaimed Sir Ector. "Well, well, well! Wonders never cease."

"I do not think much of it as a quest," said Kay. "He only went after the hawk, after all."

"And got the hawk, Master Kay," said Hob reprovingly.

"Oh, well," said Kay, "I bet the old man caught it for him."

"Kay," said Merlyn, suddenly terrible, "thou wast ever a proud and ill-tongued speaker, and a misfortunate one. Thy sorrow will come from thine own mouth."

At this everybody felt uncomfortable, and Kay, instead of flying into his usual passion, hung his head. He was not at all an unpleasant person really, but clever, quick, proud, passionate and ambitious. He was one of those people who would be neither a follower nor a leader, but only an aspiring heart, impatient in the failing body which imprisoned it. Merlyn repented of his rudeness at once. He made a little silver hunting-knife come out of the air, which he gave him to put things right. The knob of the handle was made of the skull of a stoat, oiled and polished like ivory, and Kay loved it.

# 5

Sir Ector's home was called The Castle of the Forest Sauvage. It was more like a town or a village than any one man's home, and indeed it was the village during times of danger: for this part of the story is one which deals with troubled times. Whenever there was a raid or an invasion by some neighbouring tyrant, everybody on the estate hurried into the castle, driving the beasts before them into the courts, and there they remained until the danger was over. The wattle and daub cottages nearly always got burned, and had to be rebuilt afterwards with much profanity. For this reason it was not worth while to have a village church, as it would constantly be having to be replaced. The villagers went to church in the chapel of the castle. They wore their best clothes and trooped up the street with their most

respectable gait on Sundays, looking with vague and dignified looks in all directions, as if reluctant to disclose their
destination, and on week-days they came to Mass and ves-
pers in their ordinary clothes, walking much more cheerfully. Everybody went to church in those days, and liked it.

The Castle of the Forest Sauvage is still standing, and you
can see its lovely ruined walls with ivy on them, standing
broached to the sun and wind. Some lizards live there now,
and the starving sparrows keep warm on winter nights in
the ivy, and a barn owl drives it methodically, hovering
outside the frightened congregations and beating the ivy
with its wings, to make them fly out. Most of the curtain
wall is down, though you can trace the foundations of the
twelve round towers which guarded it. They were round,
and stuck out from the wall into the moat, so that the archers could shoot in all directions and command every part
of the wall. Inside the towers there are circular stairs. These
go round and round a central column, and this column is
pierced with holes for shooting arrows. Even if the enemy
had got inside the curtain wall and fought their way into
the bottom of the towers, the defenders could retreat up the
bends of the stairs and shoot at those who followed them
up, inside, through these slits.

The stone part of the drawbridge with its barbican and the
bartizans of the gatehouse are in good repair. These have
many ingenious arrangements. Even if enemies got over the
wooden bridge, which was pulled up so that they could not,
there was a portcullis weighted with an enormous log which
would squash them flat and pin them down as well. There
was a large hidden trap-door in the floor of the barbican,
which would let them into the moat after all. At the other
end of the barbican there was another portcullis, so that
they could be trapped between the two and annihilated from
above, while the bartizans, or hanging turrets, had holes in
their floors through which the defenders could drop things
on their heads. Finally, inside the gatehouse, there was a
neat little hole in the middle of the vaulted ceiling, which
had painted tracery and bosses. This hole led to the room
above, where there was a big cauldron, for boiling lead or
oil.

So much for the outer defences. Once you were inside
the curtain wall, you found yourself in a kind of wide alley-
way, probably full of frightened sheep, with another complete castle in front of you. This was the inner shell-keep,

with its eight enormous round towers which still stand. It is lovely to climb the highest of them and to lie there looking out toward the Marches, from which some of these old dangers came, with nothing but the sun above you and the little tourists trotting about below, quite regardless of arrows and boiling oil. Think for how many centuries that unconquerable tower has withstood. It has changed hands by secession often, by siege once, by treachery twice, but never by assault. On this tower the look-out hoved. From here he kept the guard over the blue woods towards Wales. His clean old bones lie beneath the floor of the chapel now, so you must keep it for him.

If you look down and are not frightened of heights (the Society for the Preservation of This and That have put up some excellent railings to preserve you from tumbling over), you can see the whole anatomy of the inner court laid out beneath you like a map. You can see the chapel, now quite open to its god, and the windows of the great hall with the solar over it. You can see the shafts of the huge chimneys and how cunningly the side flues were contrived to enter them, and the little private closets now public, and the enormous kitchen. If you are a sensible person, you will spend days there, possibly weeks, working out for yourself by detection which were the stables, which the mews, where were the cow byres, the armoury, the lofts, the well, the smithy, the kennel, the soldiers' quarters, the priest's room, and my lord's and lady's chambers. Then it will all grow about you again. The little people—they were smaller than we are, and it would be a job for most of us to get inside the few bits of their armour and old gloves that remain—will hurry about in the sunshine, the sheep will baa as they always did, and perhaps from Wales there will come the ffff-putt of the triple-feathered arrow which looks as if it had never moved.

This place was, of course, a paradise for a boy to be in. The Wart ran about it like a rabbit in its own complicated labyrinth. He knew everything, everywhere, all the special smells, good climbs, soft lairs, secret hiding-places, jumps, slides, nooks, larders and blisses. For every season he had the best place, like a cat, and he yelled and ran and fought and upset people and snoozed and daydreamed and pretended he was a Knight, without stopping. Just now he was in the kennel.

People in those days had rather different ideas about the

training of dogs to what we have today. They did it more by love than strictness. Imagine a modern M.F.H. going to bed with his hounds, and yet Flavius Arrianus says that it is "Best of all if they can sleep with a person because it makes them more human and because they rejoice in the company of human beings: also if they have had a restless night or been internally upset, you will know of it and will not use them to hunt next day." In Sir Ector's kennel there was a special boy, called the Dog Boy, who lived with the hounds day and night. He was a sort of head hound, and it was his business to take them out every day for walks, to pull thorns out of their feet, keep cankers out of their ears, bind the smaller bones that got dislocated, dose them for worms, isolate and nurse them in distemper, arbitrate in their quarrels and to sleep curled up among them at night. If one more learned quotation may be excused, this is how, later on, the Duke of York who was killed at Agincourt described such a boy in his Master of Game: "Also I will teach the child to lead out the hounds to scombre twice in the day in the morning and in the evening, so that the sun be up, especially in winter. Then should he let them run and play long in a meadow in the sun, and then comb every hound after the other, and wipe them with a great wisp of straw, and this he shall do every morning. And then he shall lead them into some fair place where tender grass grows as corn and other things, that therewith they may feed themselves as it is medicine for them." Thus, since the boy's "heart and his business be with the hounds," the hounds themselves become "goodly and kindly and clean, glad and joyful and playful, and goodly to all manner of folks save to the wild beasts to whom they should be fierce, eager and spiteful."

Sir Ector's dog boy was none other than the one who had his nose bitten off by the terrible Wat. Not having a nose like a human, and being, moreover, subjected to stone-throwing by the other village children, he had become more comfortable with animals. He talked to them, not in baby-talk like a maiden lady, but correctly in their own growls and barks. They all loved him very much, and revered him for taking thorns out of their toes, and came to him with their troubles at once. He always understood immediately what was wrong, and generally he could put it right. It was nice for the dogs to have their god with them, in visible form.

The Wart was fond of the Dog Boy, and thought him very clever to be able to do these things with animals—for he could make them do almost anything just by moving his hands—while the Dog Boy loved the Wart in much the same way as his dogs loved him, and thought the Wart was almost holy because he could read and write. They spent much of their time together, rolling about with the dogs in the kennel.

The kennel was on the ground floor, near the mews, with a loft above it, so that it should be cool in summer and warm in winter. The hounds were alaunts, gaze-hounds, lymers and braches. They were called Clumsy, Trowneer, Phoebe, Colle, Gerland, Talbot, Luath, Luffra, Apollon, Orthros, Bran, Gelert, Bounce, Boy, Lion, Bungey, Toby, and Diamond. The Wart's own special one was called Cavall, and he happened to be licking Cavall's nose—not the other way about—when Merlyn came in and found him.

"That will come to be regarded as an insanitary habit," said Merlyn, "though I cannot see it myself. After all, God made the creature's nose just as well as he made your tongue.

"If not better," added the philosopher pensively.

The Wart did not know what Merlyn was talking about, but he liked him to talk. He did not like the grown-ups who talked down to him, but the ones who went on talking in their usual way, leaving him to leap along in their wake, jumping at meanings, guessing, clutching at known words, and chuckling at complicated jokes as they suddenly dawned. He had the glee of the porpoise then, pouring and leaping through strange seas.

"Shall we go out?" asked Merlyn. "I think it is about time we began lessons."

The Wart's heart sank at this. His tutor had been there a month, and it was now August, but they had done no lessons so far. Now he suddenly remembered that this was what Merlyn was for, and he thought with dread of Summulae Logicales and the filthy astrolabe. He knew that it had to be borne, however, and got up obediently enough, after giving Cavall a last reluctant pat. He thought that it might not be so bad with Merlyn, who might be able to make even the old Organon interesting, particularly if he would do some magic.

They went into the courtyard, into a sun so burning that the heat of hay-making seemed to have been nothing. It was baking. The thunder-clouds which usually go with hot weather were there, high columns of cumulus with glaring edges, but there was not going to be any thunder. It was too hot even for that. "If only," thought the Wart, "I did not have to go into a stuffy classroom, but could take off my clothes and swim in the moat."

They crossed the courtyard, having almost to take deep breaths before they darted across it, as if they were going quickly through an oven. The shade of the gatehouse was cool, but the barbican, with its close walls, was hottest of all. In one last dash across the desert they had reached the drawbridge—could Merlyn have guessed what he was thinking?—and were staring down into the moat.

It was the season of water-lilies. If Sir Ector had not kept one section free of them for the boys' bathing, all the water would have been covered. As it was, about twenty yards on each side of the bridge were cut each year, and one could dive in from the bridge itself. The moat was deep. It was used as a stew, so that the inhabitants of the castle could have fish on Fridays, and for this reason the architects had been careful not to let the drains and sewers run into it. It was stocked with fish every year.

"I wish I was a fish," said the Wart.

"What sort of fish?"

It was almost too hot to think about this, but the Wart stared down into the cool amber depths where a school of small perch were aimlessly hanging about.

"I think I should like to be a perch," he said. "They are braver than the silly roach, and not quite so slaughterous as the pike are."

Merlyn took off his hat, raising his staff of lignum vitae politely in the air, and said slowly, "Snylrem stnemilpmoc ot enutpen dna lliw eh yldnik tpecca siht yob sa a hsif?"

Immediately there was a loud blowing of sea-shells, conches and so forth, and a stout, jolly-looking gentleman appeared seated on a well-blown-up cloud above the battlements. He had an anchor tattooed on his stomach and a handsome mermaid with Mabel written under her on his chest. He ejected a quid of tobacco, nodded affably to Merlyn and pointed his trident at the Wart. The Wart found he had no clothes on. He found that he had tumbled off the drawbridge, landing with a smack on his side in the water. He found that the moat and the bridge had grown hundreds of times bigger. He knew that he was turning into a fish.

"Oh, Merlyn," he cried, "please come too."

"For this once," said a large and solemn tench beside his ear, "I will come. But in future you will have to go by yourself. Education is experience, and the essence of experience is self-reliance."

The Wart found it difficult to be a new kind of creature. It was no good trying to swim like a human being, for it made him go corkscrew and much too slowly. He did not know how to swim like a fish.

"Not like that," said the tench in ponderous tones. "Put your chin on your left shoulder and do jack-knives. Never mind about the fins to begin with."

The Wart's legs had fused together into his backbone and his feet and toes had become a tail fin. His arms had become two more fins—of a delicate pink—and he had sprouted some more somewhere about his stomach. His head faced over his shoulder, so that when he bent in the middle his toes were moving toward his ear instead of toward his forehead. He was a beautiful olive-green, with rather scratchy plate-armour all over him, and dark bands down his sides. He was not sure which were his sides and which were his back and front, but what now appeared to be his belly had an attractive whitish colour, while his back was armed with a splendid great fin that could be erected for war and had spikes in it. He did jack-knives as the tench directed and found that he was swimming vertically downward into the mud.

"Use your feet to turn to left or right," said the tench, "and spread those fins on your tummy to keep level. You are living in two planes now, not one."

The Wart found that he could keep more or less level by altering the inclination of his arm fins and the ones on his stomach. He swam feebly off, enjoying himself very much.

"Come back," said the tench. "You must learn to swim before you can dart."

The Wart returned to his tutor in a series of zig-zags and remarked, "I do not seem to keep quite straight."

"The trouble with you is that you do not swim from the shoulder. You swim as if you were a boy, bending at the hips. Try doing your jack-knives right from the neck downward, and move your body exactly the same amount to the right as you are going to move it to the left. Put your back into it."

Wart gave two terrific kicks and vanished altogether in a clump of mare's tail several yards away.

"That's better," said the tench, now out of sight in the murky olive water, and the Wart backed himself out of his tangle with infinite trouble, by wriggling his arm fins. He undulated back toward the voice in one terrific shove, to show off.

"Good," said the tench, as they collided end to end. "But direction is the better part of valour.

"Try if you can do this one," it added.

Without apparent exertion of any kind it swam off backward under a water-lily. Without apparent exertion—but the Wart, who was an enterprising learner, had been watching the slightest movement of its fins. He moved his own fins anti-clockwise, gave the tip of his tail a cunning flick, and was lying alongside the tench.

"Splendid," said Merlyn. "Let us go for a little swim."

The Wart was on an even keel now, and reasonably able to move about. He had leisure to look at the extraordinary universe into which the tattooed gentleman's trident had plunged him. It was different from the universe to which he had been accustomed. For one thing, the heaven or sky above him was now a perfect circle. The horizon had closed to this. In order to imagine yourself into the Wart's position, you would have to picture a round horizon, a few inches about your head, instead of the flat horizon which you usually see. Under this horizon of air you would have to imagine another horizon of under water, spherical and practically upside down—for the surface of the water acted partly as a mirror to what was below it. It is difficult to imagine. What makes it a great deal more difficult to imagine is that everything which human beings would consider to be above the water level was fringed with all the colours of the spectrum. For instance, if you had happened to be fishing for the Wart, he would have seen you, at the rim of the tea saucer which was the upper air to him, not as one person waving a fishing-rod, but as seven people, whose outlines were red, orange, yellow, green, blue, indigo and violet, all waving the same rod whose colours were as varied. In fact, you would have been a rainbow man to him, a beacon of flashing and radiating colours, which ran into one another and had rays all about. You would have burned upon the water like Cleopatra in the poem.

The next most lovely thing was that the Wart had no weight. He was not earth-bound any more and did not have to plod along on a flat surface, pressed down by gravity and the weight of the atmosphere. He could do what men have always wanted to do, that is, fly. There is practically no difference between flying in the water and flying in the air. The best of it was that he did not have to fly in a machine, by pulling levers and sitting still, but could do it with his own body. It was like the dreams people have.

Just as they were going to swim off on their tour of inspection, a timid young roach appeared from between two waving bottle bushes of mare's tail and hung about, looking pale with agitation. It looked at them with big, apprehensive eyes and evidently wanted something, but could not make up its mind.

"Approach," said Merlyn gravely.

At this the roach rushed up like a hen, burst into tears, and began stammering its message.

"If you p-p-p-please, doctor," stammered the poor creature, gabbling so that they could scarcely understand what it said, "we have such a d-dretful case of s-s-something or other in our family, and we w-w-w-wondered if you could s-s-s-spare the time? It's our d-d-d-dear Mamma, who w-w-w-will swim a-a-all the time upside d-d-d-down, and she d-d-d-does look so horrible and s-s-s-speaks so strange, that we r-r-r-really thought she ought to have a d-d-d-doctor, if it w-w-w-wouldn't be too much? C-C-C-Clara says to say so, Sir, if you s-s-s-see w-w-w-what I m-m-m-mean?"

Here the poor roach began fizzing so much, what with its stammer and its tearful disposition, that it became quite inarticulate and could only stare at Merlyn with mournful eyes.

"Never mind, my little man," said Merlyn. "There, there, lead me to your dear Mamma, and we shall see what we can do."

They all three swam off into the murk under the drawbridge, upon their errand of mercy.

"Neurotic, these roach," whispered Merlyn, behind his fin. "It is probably a case of nervous hysteria, a matter for the psychologist rather than the physician."

The roach's Mamma was lying on her back as he had described. She was squinting, had folded her fins on her chest, and every now and then she blew a bubble. All her children were gathered round her in a circle, and every time she blew they nudged each other and gasped. She had a seraphic smile on her face.

"Well, well, well," said Merlyn, putting on his best bedside manner, "and how is Mrs. Roach today?"

He patted the young roaches on the head and advanced with stately motions toward his patient. It should perhaps be mentioned that Merlyn was a ponderous, deep-beamed fish of about five pounds, leather coloured, with small scales, adipose in his fins, rather slimy, and having a bright marigold eye—a respectable figure.

Mrs. Roach held out a languid fin, sighed emphatically and said, "Ah, doctor, so you've come at last?"

"Hum," said the physician, in his deepest tone.

Then he told everybody to close their eyes—the Wart peeped—and began to swim round the invalid in a slow and stately dance. As he danced he sang. His song was this:

> Therapeutic,
> Elephantic,
> Diagnosis,
> Boom!
> Pancreatic,
> Microstatic,
> Anti-toxic,
> Doom!
> With a normal catabolism,
> Gabbleism and babbleism,
> Snip, Snap, Snorum,
> Cut out his abdonorum.
> Dyspepsia,
> Anaemia,
> Toxaemia.
> One, two, three,
> And out goes He,
> With a fol-de-rol-derido for the Five Guinea Fee.

At the end of the song he was swimming round his patient so close that he actually touched her, stroking his brown smooth-scaled flanks against her more rattly pale ones. Perhaps he was healing her with his slime—for all the fishes are said to go to the Tench for medicine—or perhaps it was by touch or massage or hypnotism. In any case, Mrs.

Roach suddenly stopped squinting, turned the right way up, and said, "Oh, doctor, dear doctor, I feel I could eat a little lob-worm now."

"No lob-worm," said Merlyn, "not for two days. I shall give you a prescription for a strong broth of algae every two hours, Mrs. Roach. We must build up your strength, you know. After all, Rome was not built in a day."

Then he patted all the little roaches once more, told them to grow up into brave little fish, and swam off with an air of importance into the gloom. As he swam, he puffed his mouth in and out.

"What did you mean by that about Rome?" asked the Wart, when they were out of earshot.

"Heaven knows."

They swam along, Merlyn occasionally advising him to put his back into it when he forgot, and the strange underwater world began to dawn about them, deliciously cool after the heat of the upper air. The great forests of weed were delicately traced, and in them there hung motionless many schools of sticklebacks learning to do their physical exercises in strict unison. On the word One they all lay still; at Two they faced about; at Three they all shot together into a cone, whose apex was a bit of something to eat. Water snails slowly ambled about on the stems of the lilies or under their leaves, while fresh-water mussels lay on the bottom doing nothing in particular. Their flesh was salmon pink, like a very good strawberry cream ice. The small congregations of perch—it was a strange thing, but all the bigger fish seemed to have hidden themselves—had delicate circulations, so that they blushed or grew pale as easily as a lady in a Victorian novel. Only their blush was a deep olive colour, and it was the blush of rage. Whenever Merlyn and his companion swam past them, they raised their spiky dorsal fins in menace, and only lowered them when they saw that Merlyn was a tench. The black bars on their sides made them look as if they had been grilled, and these also could become darker or lighter. Once the two travellers passed under a swan. The white creature floated above like a Zeppelin, all indistinct except what was under the water. The latter part was quite clear and showed that the swan was floating slightly on one side with one leg cocked over its back.

"Look," said the Wart, "it is the poor swan with the

deformed leg. It can only paddle with one leg, and the other side of it is hunched."

"Nonsense," said the swan snappily, putting its head into the water and giving them a frown with its black nares. "Swans like to rest in this position, and you can keep your fishy sympathy to yourself, so there." It continued to glare at them from up above, like a white snake suddenly let down through the ceiling, until they were out of sight.

"You swim along," said the tench, "as if there was nothing to be afraid of in the world. Don't you see that this place is exactly like the forest which you had to come through to find me?"

"Is it?"

"Look over there."

The Wart looked, and at first saw nothing. Then he saw a small translucent shape hanging motionless near the surface. It was just outside the shadow of a water-lily and was evidently enjoying the sun. It was a baby pike, absolutely rigid and probably asleep, and it looked like a pipe stem or a sea-horse stretched out flat. It would be a brigand when it grew up.

"I am taking you to see one of those," said the tench, "the Emperor of these purlieus. As a doctor I have immunity, and I dare say he will respect you as my companion as well —but you had better keep your tail bent in case he is feeling tyrannical."

"Is he the King of the Moat?"

"He is. Old Jack they call him, and some call him Black Peter, but for the most part they do not mention him by name at all. They just call him Mr. P. You will see what it is to be a king."

The Wart began to hang behind his conductor a little, and perhaps it was as well that he did, for they were almost on top of their destination before he noticed it. When he did see the old despot he started back in horror, for Mr. P. was four feet long, his weight incalculable. The great body, shadowy and almost invisible among the stems, ended in a face which had been ravaged by all the passions of an absolute monarch—by cruelty, sorrow, age, pride, selfishness, loneliness and thoughts too strong for individual brains. There he hung or hoved, his vast ironic mouth permanently drawn downward in a kind of melancholy, his lean clean-shaven chops giving him an American expression, like that of Uncle Sam. He was remorseless, disillusioned, logical, predatory, fierce, pitiless—but his great jewel of an eye was that of a stricken deer, large, fearful, sensitive and full of griefs. He made no movement, but looked upon them with his bitter eye.

The Wart thought to himself that he did not care for Mr. P.

"Lord," said Merlyn, not paying attention to his nervousness, "I have brought a young professor who would learn to profess."

"To profess what?" asked the King of the Moat slowly, hardly opening his jaws and speaking through his nose.

"Power," said the tench.

"Let him speak for himself."

"Please," said the Wart, "I don't know what I ought to ask."

"There is nothing," said the monarch, "except the power which you pretend to seek: power to grind and power to digest, power to seek and power to find, power to await and power to claim, all power and pitilessness springing from the nape of the neck."

"Thank you."

"Love is a trick played on us by the forces of evolution. Pleasure is the bait laid down by the same. There is only power. Power is of the individual mind, but the mind's power is not enough. Power of the body decides everything in the end, and only Might is Right.

"Now I think it is time that you should go away, young master, for I find this conversation uninteresting and exhausting. I think you ought to go away really almost at once, in case my disillusioned mouth should suddenly determine to introduce you to my great gills, which have teeth in them also. Yes, I really think you might be wise to go away this moment. Indeed, I think you ought to put your back into it. And so, a long farewell to all my greatness."

The Wart had found himself almost hypnotized by the big words, and hardly noticed that the tight mouth was coming closer and closer to him. It came imperceptibly, as the lecture distracted his attention, and suddenly it was looming within an inch of his nose. On the last sentence it opened, horrible and vast, the skin stretching ravenously from bone to bone and tooth to tooth. Inside there seemed to be nothing but teeth, sharp teeth like thorns in rows and ridges everywhere, like the nails in labourers' boots, and it was only at the last second that he was able to regain his own will, to pull himself together, to recollect his instructions and to escape. All those teeth clashed behind him at the tip of his tail, as he gave the heartiest jack-knife he had ever given.

In a second he was on dry land once again, standing beside Merlyn on the piping drawbridge, panting in his stuffy clothes.

# 6

One Thursday afternoon the boys were doing their archery as usual. There were two straw targets fifty yards apart, and when they had shot their arrows at one, they had only to go to it, collect them, and shoot back at the other, after facing about. It was still the loveliest summer weather, and there had been chicken for dinner, so that Merlyn had gone off to the edge of their shooting-ground and sat down under a tree. What with the warmth and the chicken and the cream he had poured over his pudding and the continual repassing of the boys and the tock of the arrows in the targets—which was as sleepy to listen to as the noise of a lawn-mower or of a village cricket match—and what with the dance of the egg-shaped sunspots between the leaves of his tree, the aged man was soon fast asleep.

Archery was a serious occupation in those days. It had not yet been turned over to Indians and small boys. When you were shooting badly you got into a bad temper, just as the wealthy pheasant shooters do today. Kay was shooting badly. He was trying too hard and plucking on his loose, instead of leaving it to the bow.

"Oh, come on," he said. "I am sick of these beastly targets. Let's have a shot at the popinjay."

They left the targets and had several shots at the popinjay—which was a large, bright-coloured artificial bird stuck on the top of a stick, like a parrot—and Kay missed these also. First he had the feeling of, "Well, I will hit the filthy

thing, even if I have to go without my tea until I do it."
Then he merely became bored.

The Wart said, "Let's play Rovers then. We can come
back in half an hour and wake Merlyn up."

What they called Rovers, consisted in going for a walk
with their bows and shooting one arrow each at any agreed
mark which they came across. Sometimes it would be a
molehill, sometimes a clump of rushes, sometimes a big
thistle almost at their feet. They varied the distance at
which they chose these objects, sometimes picking a target
as much as 120 yards away—which was about as far as
these boys' bows could carry—and sometimes having to
aim actually below a close thistle because the arrow always
leaps up a foot or two as it leaves the bow. They counted
five for a hit, and one if the arrow was within a bow's
length, and they added up their scores at the end.

On this Thursday they chose their targets wisely. Besides,
the grass of the big field had been lately cut, so that they
never had to search for their arrows for long, which nearly
always happens, as in golf, if you shoot ill-advisedly near
hedges or in rough places. The result was that they strayed
further than usual and found themselves near the edge of
the savage forest where Cully had been lost.

"I vote," said Kay, "that we go to those buries in the
chase, and see if we can get a rabbit. It would be more fun
than shooting at these hummocks."

They did this. They chose two trees about a hundred
yards apart, and each boy stood under one of them waiting
for the conies to come out again. They stood still, with
their bows already raised and arrows fitted, so that they
would make the least possible movement to disturb the
creatures when they did appear. It was not difficult for
either of them to stand thus, for the first test which they
had had to pass in archery was standing with the bow at
arm's length for half an hour. They had six arrows each
and would be able to fire and mark them all before they
needed to frighten the rabbits back by walking about to collect. An arrow does not make enough noise to upset more
than the particular rabbit that it is shot at.

At the fifth shot Kay was lucky. He allowed just the right
amount for wind and distance, and his point took a young
coney square in the head. It had been standing up on end
to look at him, wondering what he was.

"Oh, well shot!" cried the Wart, as they ran to pick it up.

It was the first rabbit they had ever hit, and luckily they had killed it dead.

When they had carefully gutted it with the hunting knife which Merlyn had given—to keep it fresh—and passed one of its hind legs through the other at the hock, for convenience in carrying, the two boys prepared to go home with their prize. But before they unstrung their bows they used to observe a ceremony. Every Thursday afternoon, after the last serious arrow had been shot, they were allowed to fit one more nock to their strings and to shoot the arrow straight up into the air. It was partly a gesture of farewell, partly of triumph, and it was beautiful. They did it now as salute to their first prey.

The Wart watched his arrow go up. The sun was already westing toward evening, and the trees where they were had plunged them into a partial shade. So, as the arrow topped the trees and climbed into sunlight, it began to burn against the evening like the sun itself. Up and up it went, not weaving as it would have done with a snatching loose, but soaring, swimming, aspiring to heaven, steady, golden and superb. Just as it had spent its force, just as its ambition had been dimmed by destiny and it was preparing to faint, to turn over, to pour back into the bosom of its mother earth, a portent happened. A gore-crow came flapping wearily before the approaching night. It came, it did not waver, it took the arrow. It flew away, heavy and hoisting, with the arrow in its beak.

Kay was frightened by this, but the Wart was furious. He had loved his arrow's movement, its burning ambition in the sunlight, and, besides, it was his best one. It was the only one which was perfectly balanced, sharp, tight-feathered, clean-nocked, and neither warped nor scraped.

"It was a witch," said Kay.

# 7

*Tilting and horsemanship had two afternoons a* week, because they were the most important branches of a gentleman's education in those days. Merlyn grumbled about athletics, saying that nowadays people seemed to think that you were an educated man if you could knock another man off a horse and that the craze for games was the ruin of scholarship—nobody got scholarships like they used to do when he was a boy, and all the public schools had been forced to lower their standards—but Sir Ector, who was an old tilting blue, said that the battle of Crécy had been won upon the playing fields of Camelot This made Merlyn so furious that he gave Sir Ector rheumatism two nights running before he relented

Tilting was a great art and needed practice. When two knights jousted they held their lances in their right hands, but they directed their horses at one another so that each man had his opponent on his near side. The base of the lance, in fact, was held on the opposite side of the body to the side at which the enemy was charging. This seems rather inside out to anybody who is in the habit, say, of opening gates with a hunting-crop, but it had its reasons For one thing, it meant that the shield was on the left arm, so that the opponents charged shield to shield, fully covered. It also meant that a man could be unhorsed with the side or edge of the lance, in a kind of horizontal swipe, if you did not feel sure of hitting him with your point. This was the humblest or least skilful blow in jousting.

A good jouster, like Lancelot or Tristram, always used the blow of the point, because, although it was liable to miss in unskilful hands, it made contact sooner. If one knight charged with his lance held rigidly sideways, to sweep his opponent out of the saddle, the other knight with his lance held directly forward would knock him down a lance length before the sweep came into effect.

Then there was how to hold the lance for the point stroke. It was no good crouching in the saddle and clutching it in a rigid grip preparatory to the great shock, for if you held it inflexibly like this its point bucked up and down to every movement of your thundering mount and you were practically certain to miss the aim. On the contrary, you had to sit loosely in the saddle with the lance easy and balanced against the horse's motion. It was not until the actual moment of striking that you clamped your knees into the horse's sides, threw your weight forward in your seat, clutched the lance with the whole hand instead of with the finger and thumb, and hugged your right elbow to your side to support the butt.

There was the size of the spear. Obviously a man with a spear one hundred yards long would strike down an opponent with a spear of ten or twelve feet before the latter came anywhere near him. But it would have been impossible to make a spear one hundred yards long and, if made, impossible to carry it. The jouster had to find out the greatest length which he could manage with the greatest speed, and he had to stick to that. Sir Lancelot, who came some time after this part of the story, had several sizes of spears and would call for his Great Spear or his Lesser Spear as occasion demanded.

There were the places on which the enemy should be hit. In the armoury of The Castle of the Forest Sauvage there was a big picture of a knight in armour with circles round his vulnerable points. These varied with the style of armour, so that you had to study your opponent before the charge and select a point. The good armourers—the best lived at Warrington, and still live near there—were careful to make all the forward or entering sides of their suits convex, so that the spear point glanced off them. Curiously enough, the shields of Gothic suits were more inclined to be concave. It was better that a spear point should stay on the shield, rather than glance off upward or downward, and perhaps hit a more vulnerable point of the body armour. The best place of all for hitting people was on the very crest of the tilting helm, that is, if the person in question were vain enough to have a large metal crest in whose folds and ornaments the point would find a ready lodging. Many were vain enough to have these armorial crests, with bears and dragons or even ships or castles on them, but Sir Lancelot always contented himself with a bare helmet, or a bunch of feathers which would not hold spears, or, on one occasion, a soft lady's sleeve.

It would take too long to go into all the interesting details of proper tilting which the boys had to learn, for in those days you had to be a master of your craft from the bottom upward. You had to know what wood was best for spears, and why, and even how to turn them so that they would not splinter or warp. There were a thousand disputed questions about arms and armour, all of which had to be understood.

Just outside Sir Ector's castle there was a jousting field for tournaments, although there had been no tournaments in it since Kay was born. It was a green meadow, kept short, with a broad grassy bank raised round it on which pavilions could be erected. There was an old wooden grandstand at one side, lifted on stilts for the ladies. At present the field was only used as a practice-ground for tilting, so a quintain had been erected at one end and a ring at the other. The quintain was a wooden Saracen on a pole. He was painted with a bright blue face and red beard and glaring eyes. He had a shield in his left hand and a flat wooden sword in his right. If you hit him in the middle of his forehead all was well, but if your lance struck him on the shield or on any part to left or right of the middle line, then he spun round with great rapidity, and usually caught you a wallop with his sword as you galloped by, ducking. His paint was somewhat scratched and the wood picked up over his right eye. The ring was just an ordinary iron ring tied to a kind of gallows by a thread. If you managed to put your point through the ring, the thread broke, and you could canter off proudly with the ring round your spear.

The day was cooler than it had been for some time, for the autumn was almost within sight, and the two boys were in the tilting yard with the master armourer and Merlyn. The master armourer, or sergeant-at-arms, was a stiff, pale, bouncy gentleman with waxed moustaches. He always marched about with his chest stuck out like a pouter pigeon, and he called out "On the word One—" on every possible occasion. He took great pains to keep his stomach in, and often tripped over his feet because he could not see them over his chest. He was generally making his muscles ripple, which annoyed Merlyn.

Wart lay beside Merlyn in the shade of the grandstand and scratched himself for harvest bugs. The saw-like sickles had only lately been put away, and the wheat stood in stooks of eight among the tall stubble of those times. The Wart still itched. He was also sore about the shoulders and had a burning ear, from making bosh shots at the quintain— for, of course, practice tilting was done without armour. Wart was pleased that it was Kay's turn to go through it now and he lay drowsily in the shade, snoozing, scratching, twitching like a dog and partly attending to the fun.

Merlyn, sitting with his back to all the athleticism, was practising a spell which he had forgotten. It was a spell to make the sergeant's moustaches uncurl, but at present it only uncurled one of them, and the sergeant had not noticed it. He absent-mindedly curled it up again every time Merlyn did the spell, and Merlyn said, "Drat it!" and began again. Once he made the sergeant's ears flap by mistake, and the latter gave a startled look at the sky.

From far off at the other side of the tilting ground the sergeant's voice came floating on the still air.

"Nah, nah, Master Kay, that ain't it at all. Has you were. Has you were. The spear should be 'eld between the thumb and forefinger of the right 'and, with the shield in line with the seam of the trahser leg. . . ."

The Wart rubbed his sore ear and sighed.

"What are you grieving about?"

"I was not grieving; I was thinking."

"What were you thinking?"

"Oh, it was not anything. I was thinking about Kay learning to be a knight."

"And well you may grieve," exclaimed Merlyn hotly. "A lot of brainless unicorns swaggering about and calling themselves educated just because they can push each other off a horse with a bit of stick! It makes me tired. Why, I believe Sir Ector would have been gladder to get a by-our-lady tilting blue for your tutor, that swings himself along on his knuckles like an anthropoid ape, rather than a magician of known probity and international reputation with first-class honours from every European university. The trouble with the Norman Aristocracy is that they are games-mad, that is what it is, games-mad."

He broke off indignantly and deliberately made the sergeant's ears flap slowly twice, in unison.

"I was not thinking quite about that," said the Wart. "As a matter of fact, I was thinking how nice it would be to be a knight, like Kay."

"Well, you will be one soon enough, won't you?" asked the old man, impatiently.

Wart did not answer.

"Won't you?"

Merlyn turned round and looked closely at the boy through his spectacles.

"What is the matter now?" he enquired nastily. His inspection had shown him that his pupil was trying not to cry, and if he spoke in a kind voice he would break down and do it.

"I shall not be a knight," replied the Wart coldly. Merlyn's trick had worked and he no longer wanted to weep: he wanted to kick Merlyn. "I shall not be a knight because I am not a proper son of Sir Ector's. They will knight Kay, and I shall be his squire."

Merlyn's back was turned again, but his eyes were bright behind his spectacles. "Too bad," he said, without commiseration.

The Wart burst out with all his thoughts aloud. "Oh," he cried, "but I should have liked to be born with a proper father and mother, so that I could be a knight errant."

"What would you have done?"

"I should have had a splendid suit of armour and dozens of spears and a black horse standing eighteen hands, and I should have called myself The Black Knight. And I should have hoved at a well or a ford or something and made all true knights that came that way to joust with me for the honour of their ladies, and I should have spared them all after I had given them a great fall. And I should live out of doors all the year round in a pavilion, and never do anything but joust and go on quests and bear away the prize at tournaments, and I should not ever tell anybody my name."

"Your wife will scarcely enjoy the life."

"Oh, I am not going to have a wife. I think they are stupid.

"I shall have to have a lady-love, though," added the future knight uncomfortably, "so that I can wear her favour in my helm, and do deeds in her honour."

A humblebee came zooming between them, under the grandstand and out into the sunlight.

"Would you like to see some real knights errant?" asked the magician slowly. "Now, for the sake of your education?"

"Oh, I would! We have never even had a tournament since I was here."

"I suppose it could be managed."

"Oh, please do. You could take me to some like you did to the fish."

"I suppose it is educational, in a way."

"It is very educational," said the Wart. "I can't think of anything more educational than to see some real knights fighting. Oh, won't you please do it?"

"Do you prefer any particular knight?"

"King Pellinore," he said immediately. He had a weakness for this gentleman since their strange encounter in the Forest.

Merlyn said, "That will do very well. Put your hands to your sides and relax your muscles. *Cabricias arci thuram, catalamus, singulariter, nominativa, haec musa.* Shut your eyes and keep them shut. *Bonus, Bona, Bonum.* Here we go. *Deus Sanctus, est-ne oratio Latinas? Etiam, oui, quare? Pourquoi? Quai substantivo et adjectivum concordat in generi, numerum et casus.* Here we are."

While this incantation was going on, the patient felt some queer sensations. First he could hear the sergeant calling out to Kay, "Nah, then, nah then, keep the 'eels dahn and swing the body from the 'ips." Then the words got smaller and smaller, as if he were looking at his feet through the wrong end of a telescope, and began to swirl round in a cone, as if they were at the pointed bottom end of a whirlpool which was sucking him into the air. Then there was nothing but a loud rotating roaring and hissing noise which rose to such a tornado that he felt that he could not stand it any more. Finally there was utter silence and Merlyn saying, "Here we are." All this happened in about the time that it would take a sixpenny rocket to start off with its fiery swish, bend down from its climax and disperse itself in thunder and coloured stars. He opened his eyes just at the moment when one would have heard the invisible stick hitting the ground.

They were lying under a beech tree in the Forest Sauvage.

"Here we are," said Merlyn. "Get up and dust your clothes.

"And there, I think," continued the magician, in a tone of satisfaction because his spells had worked for once without a hitch, "is your friend, King Pellinore, pricking toward us o'er the plain."

"Hallo, hallo," cried King Pellinore, popping his visor up and down. "It's the young boy with the feather bed, isn't it, I say, what?"

"Yes, it is," said the Wart. "And I am very glad to see you. Did you manage to catch the beast?"

"No," said King Pellinore. "Didn't catch the beast. Oh, do come here, you brachet, and leave that bush alone. Tcha! Tcha! Naughty, naughty! She runs riot, you know, what. Very keen on rabbits. I tell you there's nothing in it, you beastly dog. Tcha! Tcha! Leave it, leave it! Oh, do come to heel, like I tell you.

"She never does come to heel," he added.

At this the dog put a cock pheasant out of the bush, which rocketed off with a tremendous clatter, and the dog became so excited that it ran round its master three or four times at the end of its rope, panting hoarsely as if it had asthma. King Pellinore's horse stood patiently while the rope was wound round its legs, and Merlyn and the Wart had to catch the brachet and unwind it before the conversation could go on.

"I say," said King Pellinore. "Thank you very much, I must say. Won't you introduce me to your friend, what?"

"This is my tutor Merlyn, a great magician."

"How-de-do," said the King. "Always like to meet magicians. In fact I always like to meet anybody. It passes the time away, what, on a quest."

"Hail," said Merlyn, in his most mysterious manner.

"Hail," replied the King, anxious to make a good impression.

They shook hands.

"Did you say Hail?" inquired the King, looking about him nervously. "I thought it was going to be fine, myself."

"He meant How-do-you-do," explained the Wart.

"Ah, yes, How-de-do?"

They shook hands again.

"Good afternoon," said King Pellinore. "What do you think the weather looks like now?"

"I think it looks like an anti-cyclone."

"Ah, yes," said the King. "An anti-cyclone. Well, I suppose I ought to be getting along."

At this the King trembled very much, opened and shut his visor several times, coughed, wove his reins into a knot, exclaimed, "I beg your pardon?" and showed signs of cantering away.

"He is a white magician," said the Wart. "You need not be afraid of him. He is my best friend, your majesty, and in any case he generally gets his spells muddled up."

"Ah, yes," said King Pellinore. "A white magician, what? How small the world is, is it not? How-de-do?"

"Hail," said Merlyn.

"Hail," said King Pellinore.

They shook hands for the third time.

"I should not go away," said the wizard, "if I were you. Sir Grummore Grummursum is on the way to challenge you to a joust."

"No, you don't say? Sir What-you-may-call-it coming here to challenge me to a joust?"

"Assuredly."

"Good handicap man?"

"I should think it would be an even match."

"Well, I must say," exclaimed the King, "it never hails but it pours."

"Hail," said Merlyn.

"Hail," said King Pellinore.

"Hail," said the Wart.

"Now I really won't shake hands with anybody else," announced the monarch. "We must assume that we have all met before."

"Is Sir Grummore really coming," inquired the Wart, hastily changing the subject, "to challenge King Pellinore to a battle?"

"Look yonder," said Merlyn, and both of them looked in the direction of his outstretched finger.

Sir Grummore Grummursum was cantering up the clearing in full panoply of war. Instead of his ordinary helmet with a visor he was wearing the proper tilting-helm, which looked like a large coal-scuttle, and as he cantered he clanged.

He was singing his old school song:

"We'll tilt together
 Steady from crupper to poll,
 And nothin' in life shall sever
 Our love for the dear old coll.
 Follow-up, follow-up, follow-up, follow-up, follow-up
 Till the shield ring again and again
 With the clanks of the clanky true men."

"Goodness," exclaimed King Pellinore. "It's about two months since I had a proper tilt, and last winter they put me up to eighteen. That was when they had the new handicaps."

Sir Grummore had arrived while he was speaking, and had recognized the Wart.

"Mornin'," said Sir Grummore. "You're Sir Ector's boy, ain't you? And who's that chap in the comic hat?"

"That is my tutor," said the Wart hurriedly. "Merlyn, the magician."

Sir Grummore looked at Merlyn—magicians were considered rather middle-class by the true jousting set in those days—and said distantly, "Ah, a magician. How-de-do?"

"And this is King Pellinore," said the Wart. "Sir Grummore Grummursum—King Pellinore."

"How-de-do?" inquired Sir Grummore.

"Hail," said King Pellinore. "No, I mean it won't hail, will it?"

"Nice day," said Sir Grummore.

"Yes, it is nice, isn't it, what?"

"Been questin' today?"

"Oh, yes, thank you. Always am questing, you know. After the Questing Beast."

"Interestin' job, that, very."

"Yes, it is interesting. Would you like to see some fewmets?"

"By Jove, yes. Like to see some fewmets."

"I have some better ones at home, but these are quite good, really."

"Bless my soul. So these are her fewmets."

"Yes, these are her fewmets."

"Interestin' fewmets."

"Yes, they are interesting, aren't they? Only you get tired of them," added King Pellinore.

"Well, well. It's a fine day, isn't it?"

"Yes, it is rather fine."

"Suppose we'd better have a joust, eh, what?"

"Yes, I suppose we had better," said King Pellinore, "really."

"What shall we have it for?"

"Oh, the usual thing, I suppose. Would one of you kindly help me on with my helm?"

They all three had to help him on eventually, for, what

with the unscrewing of screws and the easing of nuts and bolts which the King had clumsily set on the wrong thread when getting up in a hurry that morning, it was quite a feat of engineering to get him out of his helmet and into his helm. The helm was an enormous thing like an oil drum, padded inside with two thicknesses of leather and three inches of straw.

As soon as they were ready, the two knights stationed themselves at each end of the clearing and then advanced to meet in the middle.

"Fair knight," said King Pellinore, "I pray thee tell me thy name."

"That me regards," replied Sir Grummore, using the proper formula.

"That is uncourteously said," said King Pellinore, "what? For no knight ne dreadeth for to speak his name openly, but for some reason of shame."

"Be that as it may, I choose that thou shalt not know my name as at this time, for no askin'."

"Then you must stay and joust with me, false knight."

"Haven't you got that wrong, Pellinore?" inquired Sir Grummore. "I believe it ought to be 'thou shalt'."

"Oh, I'm sorry, Sir Grummore. Yes, so it should, of course. Then thou shalt stay and joust with me, false knight."

Without further words, the two gentlemen retreated to the opposite ends of the clearing, fewtered their spears, and prepared to hurtle together in the preliminary charge.

"I think we had better climb this tree," said Merlyn. "You never know what will happen in a joust like this."

They climbed up the big beech, which had easy branches sticking out in all directions, and the Wart stationed himself toward the end of a smooth bough about fifteen feet up, where he could get a good view. Nothing is so comfortable to sit in as a beech.

To be able to picture the terrible battle which now took place, there is one thing which ought to be known. A knight in his full armour of those days, or at any rate during the heaviest days of armour, was generally carrying as much or more than his own weight in metal. He often weighed no less than twenty-two stone, and sometimes as much as twenty-five. This meant that his horse had to be a slow and enormous weight-carrier, like the farm horse of today, and that his own movements were so hampered by his burden of iron and padding that they were toned down into slow motion, as on the cinema.

"They're off!" cried the Wart, holding his breath with excitement.

Slowly and majestically, the ponderous horses lumbered into a walk. The spears, which had been pointing in the air, bowed to a horizontal line and pointed at each other. King Pellinore and Sir Grummore could be seen to be thumping their horses' sides with their heels for all they were worth, and in a few minutes the splendid animals had shambled into an earth-shaking imitation of a trot. Clank, rumble, thump-thump went the horses, and now the two knights were flapping their elbows and legs in unison, showing a good deal of daylight at their seats. There was a change in tempo, and Sir Grummore's horse could be definitely seen to be cantering. In another minute King Pellinore's was doing so too. It was a terrible spectacle.

"Oh, dear!" exclaimed the Wart, feeling ashamed that his blood-thirstiness had been responsible for making these two knights joust before him. "Do you think they will kill each other?"

"Dangerous sport," said Merlyn, shaking his head.

"Now!" cried the Wart.

With a blood-curdling beat of iron hoofs the mighty equestrians came together. Their spears wavered for a moment within a few inches of each other's helms—each had chosen the difficult point-stroke—and then they were galloping off in opposite directions. Sir Grummore drove his spear deep into the beech tree where they were sitting, and stopped dead. King Pellinore, who had been run away with, vanished altogether behind his back.

"Is it safe to look?" inquired the Wart, who had shut his eyes at the critical moment.

"Quite safe," said Merlyn. "It will take them some time to get back in position."

"Whoa, whoa, I say!" cried King Pellinore in muffled and distant tones, far away among the gorse bushes.

"Hi, Pellinore, hi!" shouted Sir Grummore. "Come back, my dear fellah, I'm over here."

There was a long pause, while the complicated stations of the two knights readjusted themselves, and then King Pellinore was at the opposite end from that at which he had started, while Sir Grummore faced him from his original position.

"Traitor knight!" cried Sir Grummore.

"Yield, recreant, what?" cried King Pellinore.

They fewtered their spears again, and thundered into the charge.

"Oh," said the Wart, "I hope they don't hurt themselves."

But the two mounts were patiently blundering together, and the two knights had simultaneously decided on the sweeping stroke. Each held his spear at right angles toward the left, and, before the Wart could say anything further, there was a terrific yet melodious thump. Clang! went the armour, like a motor omnibus in collision with a smithy, and the jousters were sitting side by side on the green sward, while their horses cantered off in opposite directions.

"A splendid fall," said Merlyn.

The two horses pulled themselves up, their duty done, and began resignedly to eat the sward. King Pellinore and Sir Grummore sat looking straight before them, each with the other's spear clasped hopefully under his arm.

"Well!" said the Wart. "What a bump! They both seem to be all right, so far."

Sir Grummore and King Pellinore laboriously got up.

"Defend thee," cried King Pellinore.

"God save thee," cried Sir Grummore.

With this they drew their swords and rushed together with such ferocity that each, after dealing the other a dint on the helm, sat down suddenly backwards.

"Bah!" cried King Pellinore.

"Booh!" cried Sir Grummore, also sitting down.

"Mercy," exclaimed the Wart. "What a combat!"

The knights had now lost their tempers and the battle was joined in earnest. It did not matter much, however, for they were so encased in metal that they could not do each other much damage. It took them so long to get up, and the dealing of a blow when you weighed the eighth part of a ton was such a cumbrous business, that every stage of the contest could be marked and pondered.

In the first stage King Pellinore and Sir Grummore stood opposite each other for about half an hour, and walloped each other on the helm. There was only opportunity for one blow at a time, so they more or less took it in turns, King Pellinore striking while Sir Grummore was recovering, and vice versa. At first, if either of them dropped his sword or got it stuck in the ground, the other put in two or three extra blows while he was patiently fumbling for it or trying to tug it out. Later, they fell into the rhythm of the thing more perfectly, like the toy mechanical people who saw wood on Christmas trees. Eventually the exercise and the monotony restored their good humour and they began to get bored.

The second stage was introduced as a change, by common consent. Sir Grummore stumped off to one end of the clearing, while King Pellinore plodded off to the other. Then they turned round and swayed backward and forward once or twice, in order to get their weight on their toes. When they leaned forward they had to run forward, to keep up with their weight, and if they leaned too far backward they fell down. So even walking was complicated. When they had got their weight properly distributed in front of them, so that they were just off their balance, each broke into a trot to keep up with himself. They hurtled together as it had been two boars.

They met in the middle, breast to breast, with a noise of shipwreck and great bells tolling, and both, bouncing off, fell breathless on their backs. They lay thus for a few minutes, panting. Then they slowly began to heave themselves to their feet, and it was obvious that they had lost their tempers once again.

King Pellinore had not only lost his temper but he seemed to have been a bit astonished by the impact. He got up facing the wrong way, and could not find Sir Grummore. There was some excuse for this, since he had only a slit to peep through—and that was three inches away from his eye owing to the padding of straw—but he looked muddled as well. Perhaps he had broken his spectacles. Sir Grummore was quick to seize his advantage.

"Take that!" cried Sir Grummore, giving the unfortunate monarch a two-handed swipe on the nob as he was slowly turning his head from side to side, peering in the opposite direction.

King Pellinore turned round morosely, but his opponent had been too quick for him. He had ambled round so that he was still behind the King, and now gave him another terrific blow in the same place.

"Where are you?" asked King Pellinore.

"Here," cried Sir Grummore, giving him another.

The poor King turned himself round as nimbly as possible, but Sir Grummore had given him the slip again.

"Tally-ho back!" shouted Sir Grummore, with another wallop.

"I think you're a *cad*," said the King.

"Wallop!" replied Sir Grummore, doing it.

What with the preliminary crash, the repeated blows on the back of his head, and the puzzling nature of his opponent, King Pellinore could now be seen to be visibly troubled in his brains. He swayed backward and forward under the hail of blows which were administered, and feebly wagged his arms.

"Poor King," said the Wart. "I wish he would not hit him so."

As if in answer to his wish, Sir Grummore paused in his labours.

"Do you want Pax?" asked Sir Grummore.

King Pellinore made no answer.

Sir Grummore favoured him with another whack and said, "If you don't say Pax, I shall cut your head off."

"I won't," said the King.

Whang! went the sword on the top of his head.

Whang! it went again.

Whang! for the third time.

"Pax," said King Pellinore, mumbling rather.

Then, just as Sir Grummore was relaxing with the fruits of victory, he swung round upon him, shouted "Non!" at the top of his voice, and gave him a good push in the middle of the chest.

Sir Grummore fell over backwards.

"Well!" exclaimed the Wart. "What a cheat! I would not have thought it of him."

King Pellinore hurriedly sat on his victim's chest, thus increasing the weight upon him to a quarter of a ton and making it quite impossible for him to move, and began to undo Sir Grummore's helm.

"You said Pax!"

"I said Pax Non under my breath."

"It's a swindle."

"It's not."

"You're a cad."

"No, I'm not."

"Yes, you are."

"No I'm not."

"Yes, you are."

"I said Pax Non."

"You said Pax."

"No, I didn't."

"Yes, you did."

"No, I didn't."

"Yes, you did."

By this time Sir Grummore's helm was unlaced and they could see his bare head glaring at King Pellinore, quite purple in the face.

"Yield thee, recreant," said the King.

"Shan't," said Grummore.

"You have got to yield, or I shall cut off your head."

"Cut it off then."

"Oh, come on," said the King. "You know you have to yield when your helm is off."

"Feign I," said Sir Grummore.

"Well, I shall just cut your head off."

"I don't care."

The King waved his sword menacingly in the air.

"Go on," said Sir Grummore. "I dare you to."

The King lowered his sword and said, "Oh, I say, do yield, please."

"You yield," said Sir Grummore.

"But I can't yield. I am on top of you after all, am I not, what?"

"Well, I have feigned yieldin'."

"Oh, come on, Grummore. I do think you are a cad not to yield. You know very well I can't cut your head off."

"I would not yield to a cheat who started fightin' after he said Pax."

"I am not a cheat."

"You are a cheat."

"No, I'm not."

"Yes, you are."

"No, I'm not."

"Yes, you are."

"Very well," said King Pellinore. "You can jolly well get up and put on your helm and we will have a fight. I won't be called a cheat for anybody."

"Cheat!" said Sir Grummore.

They stood up and fumbled together with the helm, hissing, "No, I'm not"—"Yes, you are," until it was safely on. Then they retreated to opposite ends of the clearing, got their weight upon their toes, and came rumbling and thundering together like two runaway trams.

Unfortunately they were now so cross that they had both ceased to be vigilant, and in the fury of the moment they missed each other altogether. The momentum of their armour was too great for them to stop till they had passed each other handsomely, and then they manœuvred about in such a manner that neither happened to come within the other's range of vision. It was funny watching them, because King Pellinore, having already been caught from behind once, was continually spinning round to look behind him, and Sir Grummore, having used the strategem himself, was doing the same thing. Thus they wandered for some five minutes, standing still, listening, clanking, crouching, creeping, peering, walking on tiptoe, and occasionally making a chance swipe behind their backs. Once they were standing within a few feet of each other, back to back, only to stalk off in opposite directions with infinite precaution, and once King Pellinore did hit Sir Grummore with one of his back strokes, but they both immediately spun round so often that they became giddy and mislaid each other afresh.

After five minutes Sir Grummore said, "All right, Pellinore. It is no use hidin'. I can see where you are."

"I am not hiding," exclaimed King Pellinore indignantly. "Where am I?"

They discovered each other and went up close together, face to face.

"Cad," said Sir Grummore.

"Yah," said King Pellinore.

They turned round and marched off to their corners, seething with indignation.

"Swindler," shouted Sir Grummore.

"Beastly bully," shouted King Pellinore.

With this they summoned all their energies together for one decisive encounter, leaned forward, lowered their heads like two billy-goats, and positively sprinted together for the final blow. Alas, their aim was poor. They missed each other by about five yards, passed at full steam doing at least eight knots, like ships that pass in the night but speak not to each other in passing, and hurtled onward to their doom. Both knights began waving their arms like windmills, anti-clockwise, in the vain effort to slow up. Both continued with undiminished speed. Then Sir Grummore rammed his head against the beech in which the Wart was sitting, and King Pellinore collided with a chestnut at the other side of the clearing. The trees shook, the forest rang. Blackbirds and squirrels cursed and wood-pigeons flew out of their leafy perches half a mile away. The two knights stood to attention while one could count three. Then, with a last unanimous melodious clang, they both fell prostrate on the fatal sward.

"Stunned," said Merlyn, "I should think."

"Oh, dear," said the Wart. "Ought we to get down and help them?"

"We could pour water on their heads," said Merlyn reflectively, "if there was any water. But I don't suppose they would thank us for making their armour rusty. They will be all right. Besides, it is time that we were home."

"But they might be dead!"

"They are not dead, I know. In a minute or two they will come round and go off home to dinner."

"Poor King Pellinore has not got a home."

"Then Sir Grummore will invite him to stay the night. They will be the best of friends when they come to. They always are."

"Do you think so?"

"My dear boy, I know so. Shut your eyes and we will be off."

The Wart gave in to Merlyn's superior knowledge. "Do you think," he asked with his eyes shut, "that Sir Grummore has a feather bed?"

"Probably."

"Good," said the Wart. "That will be nice for King Pellinore, even if he was stunned."

The Latin words were spoken and the secret passes made. The funnel of whistling noise and space received them. In two seconds they were lying under the grandstand, and the sergeant's voice was calling from the opposite side of the tilting ground, "Nah then, Master Art, nah then. You've been a-snoozing there long enough. Come aht into the sunlight 'ere with Master Kay, one-two, one-two, and see some real tilting."

# 8

*It was a cold wet evening, such as may happen even* toward the end of August, and the Wart did not know how to bear himself indoors. He spent some time in the kennels talking to Cavall, then wandered off to help them turn the spit in the kitchen. But there it was too hot. He was not forced to stay indoors because of the rain, by his female supervisors, as happens too frequently to the unhappy children of our generation, but the mere wetness and dreariness in the open discouraged him from going out. He hated everybody.

"Confound the boy," said Sir Ector. "For goodness' sake stop mopin' by that window there, and go and find your tutor. When I was a boy we always used to study on wet days, yes, and eddicate our minds."

"Wart is stupid," said Kay.

"Ah, run along, my duck," said their old Nurse. "I han't got time to attend to thy mopseys now, what with all this sorbent washing."

"Now then, my young master," said Hob. "Let thee run off to thy quarters, and stop confusing they fowls."

"Nah, nah," said the sergeant. "You 'op orf art of 'ere. I got enough to do a-polishing of this ber-lady harmour."

Even the Dog Boy barked at him when he went back to the kennels.

Wart draggled off to the tower room, where Merlyn was busy knitting himself a woollen night-cap for the winter.

"I cast off two together at every other line," said the magician, "but for some reason it seems to end too sharply. Like an onion. It is the turning of the heel that does one, every time."

"I think I ought to have some eddication," said the Wart. "I can't think of anything to do."

"You think that education is something which ought to

be done when all else fails?" inquired Merlyn nastily, for he was in a bad mood too.

"Well," said the Wart, "some sorts of education."

"Mine?" asked the magician with flashing eyes.

"Oh, Merlyn," exclaimed the Wart without answering, "please give me something to do, because I feel so miserable. Nobody wants me for anything today, and I just don't know how to be sensible. It rains so."

"You should learn to knit."

"Could I go out and be something, a fish or anything like that?"

"You have been a fish," said Merlyn. "Nobody with any go needs to do their education twice."

"Well, could I be a bird?"

"If you knew anything at all," said Merlyn, "which you do not, you would know that a bird does not like to fly in the rain because it wets its feathers and makes them stick together. They get bedraggled."

"I could be a hawk in Hob's mews," said the Wart stoutly. "Then I should be indoors and not get wet."

"That is pretty ambitious," said the old man, "to want to be a hawk."

"You know you will turn me into a hawk when you want to," shouted the Wart, "but you like to plague me because it is wet. I won't have it."

"Hoity-toity!"

"Please," said the Wart, "dear Merlyn, turn me into a hawk. If you don't do that I shall do something. I don't know what."

Merlyn put down his knitting and looked at his pupil over the top of his spectacles. "My boy," he said, "you shall be everything in the world, animal, vegetable, mineral, protista or virus, for all I care—before I have done with you—but you will have to trust to my superior backsight. The time is not yet ripe for you to be a hawk—for one thing Hob is still in the mews feeding them—so you may as well sit down for the moment and learn to be a human being."

"Very well," said the Wart, "if that's a go." And he sat down.

After several minutes he said, "Is one allowed to speak as a human being, or does the thing about being seen and not heard have to apply?"

"Everybody can speak."

"That's good, because I wanted to mention that you have

been knitting your beard into the night-cap for three rows now."

"Well, I'll be. . . ."

"I should think the best thing would be to cut off the end of your beard. Shall I fetch some scissors?"

"Why didn't you tell me before?"

"I wanted to see what would happen."

"You run a grave risk, my boy," said the magician, "of being turned into a piece of bread, and toasted."

With this he slowly began to unpick his beard, muttering to himself meanwhile and taking the greatest precautions not to drop a stitch.

"Will it be as difficult to fly," asked the Wart when he thought his tutor had calmed down, "as it was to swim?"

"You will not need to fly. I don't mean to turn you into a loose hawk, but only to set you in the mews for the night, so that you can talk to the others. That is the way to learn, by listening to the experts."

"Will they talk?"

"They talk every night, deep into the darkness. They say about how they were taken, about what they can remember of their homes: about their lineage and the great deeds of their ancestors, about their training and what they have learned and will learn. It is military conversation really, like you might have in the mess of a crack cavalry regiment: tactics, small arms, maintenance, betting, famous hunts, wine, women and song.

"Another subject they have," he continued, "is food. It is a depressing thought, but of course they are mainly trained by hunger. They are a hungry lot, poor chaps, thinking of the best restaurants where they used to go, and how they had champagne and caviare and gypsy music. Of course, they all come of noble blood."

"What a shame that they should be kept prisoners and be hungry."

"Well, they do not really understand that they are prisoners, any more than the cavalry officers do. They look on themselves as being dedicated to their profession, like an order of knighthood or something of that sort. You see, the membership of the mews is, after all, restricted to the raptors—and that does help a lot. They know that none of the lower classes can get in. Their screen perches don't carry blackbirds or such trash as that. And then, as to the hungry part, they are far from starving or that kind of hunger.

They are in training, you know, and like everybody in strict training, they think about food."

"How soon can I begin?"

"You can begin now, if you want to. My insight tells me that Hob has this minute finished for the night. But first of all you must choose what kind of hawk you would prefer to be."

"I should like to be a merlin," said the Wart politely.

This answer flattered the magician. "A very good choice," he said, "and if you please we will proceed at once."

The Wart got up from his stool and stood in front of his tutor. Merlyn put down his knitting.

"First you go small," said he, pressing him on the top of his head until he was a bit smaller than a pigeon. "Then you stand on the ball of your toes, bend at the knees, hold your elbows to your sides, lift your hands to the level of your shoulders, and press your first and second fingers together, as also your third and fourth. Look, it is like this."

With these words the ancient nigromant stood upon tiptoe and did as he had explained.

The Wart copied him carefully and wondered what would happen next. What did happen was that Merlyn, who had been saying the final spells under his breath, suddenly turned himself into a condor, leaving the Wart standing on tiptoe unchanged. He stood there as if he were drying himself in the sun, with a wingspread of about eleven feet, a bright orange head and a magenta carbuncle. He looked very surprised and rather funny.

"Come back," said the Wart. "You have changed the wrong one."

"It is this by-our-lady spring cleaning," exclaimed Merlyn, turning back into himself. "Once you let a woman into your study for half an hour, you do not know where to lay your hands on the right spell, not if it was ever so. Stand up and we will try again."

This time the now tiny Wart felt his toes shooting out and scratching on the floor. He felt his heels rise and stick out behind and his knees draw into his stomach. His thighs became quite short. A web of skin grew from his wrists to his shoulders, while his primary feathers burst out in soft blue quills from the ends of his fingers and quickly grew. His secondaries sprouted along his forearms, and a charming little false primary sprang from the end of each thumb. The dozen feathers of his tail, with the double deck-feathers in the middle, grew out in the twinkling of an eye, and all the covert feathers of his back and breast and shoulders slipped out of the skin to hide the roots of the more important plumes. Wart looked quickly at Merlyn, ducked his head between his legs and had a look through there, rattled his feathers into place, and began to scratch his chin with the sharp talon of one toe.

"Good," said Merlyn. "Now hop on my hand—ah, be careful and don't gripe—and listen to what I have to tell you. I shall take you into the mews now that Hob has locked up for the night, and I shall put you loose and unhooded beside Balin and Balan. Now pay attention. Don't go close to anybody without speaking first. You must remember that most of them are hooded and might be startled into doing something rash. You can trust Balin and Balan, also the kestrel and the spar-hawk. Don't go within reach of the falcon unless she invites you to. On no account must you stand beside Cully's special enclosure, for he is unhooded and will go for you through the mesh if he gets half a chance. He is not quite right in his brains, poor chap, and if he once grips you, you will never leave his grip alive. Remember that you are visiting a kind of Spartan military mess. These fellows are regulars. As the junior subaltern your only business is to keep your mouth shut, speak when you are spoken to, and not interrupt."

"I bet I am more than a subaltern," said the Wart, "if I am a merlin."

"Well, as a matter of fact, you are. You will find that both the kestrel and the spar-hawk will be polite to you, but for all sake's sake don't interrupt the senior merlins or the falcon. She is the honorary colonel of the regiment. And as for Cully, well, he is a colonel too, even if he is infantry, so you must mind your p's and q's."

"I will be careful," said the Wart, who was beginning to feel rather scared.

"Good. I shall come for you in the morning, before Hob is up."

All the hawks were silent as Merlyn carried their new companion into the mews, and silent for some time afterward when they had been left in the dark. The rain had given place to a full August moonlight, so clear that you could see a woolly bear caterpillar fifteen yards away out of doors, as it climbed up and up the knobbly sandstone of the great keep, and it took the Wart only a few moments for his eyes to become accustomed to the diffused brightness inside the mews. The darkness became watered with light, with silver radiance, and then it was an eerie sight which dawned upon his vision. Each hawk or falcon stood in the silver upon one leg, the other tucked up inside the apron of its panel, and each was a motionless statue of a knight in armour. They stood gravely in their plumed helmets, spurred and armed. The canvas or sacking screens of their perches moved heavily in a breath of wind, like banners in a chapel, and the rapt nobility of the air kept their knight's vigil in knightly patience. In those days they used to hood everything they could, even the goshawk and the merlin, which are no longer hooded according to modern practice.

Wart drew his breath at the sight of all these stately figures, standing so still that they might have been cut of stone. He was overwhelmed by their magnificence, and felt no need of Merlyn's warning that he was to be humble and behave himself.

Presently there was a gentle ringing of a bell. The great peregrine falcon had bestirred herself and now said, in a high nasal voice which came from her aristocratic nose, "Gentlemen, you may converse"

There was dead silence.

Only, in the far corner of the room, which had been netted off for Cully—loose there, unhooded and deep in moult —they could hear a faint muttering from the choleric infantry colonel. "Damned niggers," he was mumbling. "Damned administration. Damned politicians. Damned bolsheviks. Is this a damned dagger that I see before me, the handle toward my hand? Damned spot. Now, Cully, hast thou but one brief hour to live, and then thou must be damned perpetually."

"Colonel," said the peregrine coldly, "not before the younger officers."

"I beg your pardon, Mam," said the poor colonel at once. "It is something that gets into my head, you know. Some deep demnation."

There was silence again, formal, terrible and calm.

"Who is the new officer?" inquired the first fierce and beautiful voice.

Nobody answered

"Speak for yourself, sir," commanded the peregrine,

looking straight before her as if she were talking in her sleep.

They could not see him through their hoods.

"Please," began the Wart, "I am a merlin. . . ."

And he stopped, scared in the stillness.

Balan, who was one of the real merlins standing beside him, leaned over and whispered quite kindly in his ear, "Don't be afraid. Call her Madam."

"I am a merlin, Madam, an it please you."

"A Merlin. That is good. And what branch of the Merlins do you stoop from?"

The Wart did not know in the least what branch he stooped from, but he dared not be found out now in his lie.

"Madam," he said, "I am one of the Merlins of the Forest Sauvage."

There was silence at this again, the silver silence which he had begun to fear.

"There are the Yorkshire Merlins," said the honorary colonel in her slow voice at last, "and the Welsh Merlins, and the McMerlins of the North. Then there are the Salisbury ones, and several from the neighbourhood of Exmoor, and the O'Merlins of Connaught. I do not think I have heard of any family in the Forest Sauvage."

"It would be a cadet branch, Madam," said Balan, "I dare say."

"Bless him," thought the Wart. "I shall catch him a special sparrow tomorrow and give it to him behind Hob's back."

"That will be the solution, Captain Balan, no doubt."

The silence fell again.

At last the peregrine rang her bell. She said, "We will proceed with the catechism, prior to swearing him in."

The Wart heard the spar-hawk on his left giving several nervous coughs at this, but the peregrine paid no attention.

"Merlin of the Forest Sauvage," said the peregrine, "what is a Beast of the Foot?"

"A Beast of the Foot," replied the Wart, blessing his stars that Sir Ector had chosen to give him a First Rate Eddication, "is a horse, or a hound, or a hawk."

"Why are these called beasts of the foot?"

"Because these beasts depend upon the powers of their feet, so that, by law, any damage to the feet of hawk, hound or horse, is reckoned as damage to its life. A lamed horse is a murdered horse."

"Good," said the peregrine. "What are your most important members?"

"My wings," said the Wart after a moment, guessing because he did not know.

At this there was a simultaneous tintinnabulation of all the bells, as each graven image lowered its raised foot in distress. They stood on both feet now, disturbed.

"Your what?" called the peregrine sharply.

"He said his damned wings," said Colonel Cully from his private enclosure. "And damned be he who first cries Hold, enough!"

"But even a thrush has wings!" cried the kestrel, speaking for the first time in his sharp-beaked alarm.

"Think!" whispered Balan, under his breath.

The Wart thought feverishly.

A thrush had wings, tail, eyes, legs—apparently everything.

"My talons!"

"It will do," said the peregrine kindly, after one of her dreadful pauses. "The answer ought to be Feet, just as it is to all the other questions, but Talons will do."

All the hawks, and of course we are using the term loosely, for some were hawks and some were falcons, raised their belled feet again and sat at ease.

"What is the first law of the foot?"

("Think," said friendly little Balan, behind his false primary.)

The Wart thought, and thought right.

"Never to let go," he said.

"Last question," said the peregrine. "How would you, as a Merlin, kill a pigeon bigger than yourself?"

Wart was lucky in this one, for he had heard Hob giving a description of how Balan did it one afternoon, and he answered warily, "I should strangle her with my foot."

"Good!" said the peregrine.

"Bravo!" cried the others, raising their feathers.

"Ninety per cent," said the spar-hawk after a quick sum. "That is, if you give him a half for the talons."

"The devil damn me black!"

"Colonel, please!"

Balan whispered to the Wart, "Colonel Cully is not quite right in his wits. It is his liver, we believe, but the kestrel says it is the constant strain of living up to her ladyship's standard. He says that her ladyship spoke to him from her full social station once, cavalry to infantry, you know, and that he just closed his eyes and got the vertigo. He has never been the same since."

"Captain Balan," said the peregrine, "it is rude to whisper. We will proceed to swear the new officer in. Now, padre, if you please."

The poor spar-hawk, who had been getting more and more nervous for some time, blushed deeply and began faltering out a complicated oath about varvels, jesses and hoods. "With this varvel," the Wart heard, "I thee endow . . . love, honour and obey . . . till jess us do part."

But before the padre had got to the end of it, he broke down altogether and sobbed out, "Oh, please your ladyship. I beg your pardon, but I have forgotten to keep my tirings."

("Tirings are bones and things," explained Balan, "and of course you have to swear on bones.")

"Forgotten to keep any tirings? But it is your duty to keep tirings."

"I—I know."

"What have you done with them?"

The spar-hawk's voice broke at the enormity of his confession. "I—I ate 'em," wept the unfortunate priest.

Nobody said anything. The dereliction of duty was too terrible for words. All stood on two feet and turned their blind heads toward the culprit. Not a word of reproach was spoken. Only, during an utter silence of five minutes, they could hear the incontinent priest snivelling and hiccoughing to himself.

"Well," said the peregrine at last, "the initiation will have to be put off till tomorrow."

"If you will excuse me, Madam," said Balan, "perhaps we could manage the ordeal tonight? I believe the candidate is loose, for I did not hear him being tied up."

At the mention of an ordeal the Wart trembled within himself and privately determined that Balin should have not one feather of Balan's sparrow next day.

"Thank you, Captain Balin. I was reflecting upon that subject myself."

Balin shut up.

"Are you loose, candidate?"

"Oh, Madam, yes, I am, if you please: but I do not think I want an ordeal."

"The ordeal is customary."

"Let me see," continued the honorary colonel reflectively.

"What was the last ordeal we had? Can you remember, Captain Balan?"

"My ordeal, Mam," said the friendly merlin, "was to hang by my jesses during the third watch."

"If he is loose he cannot do that."

"You could strike him yourself, Mam," said the Kestrel, "judiciously, you know."

"Send him over to stand by Colonel Cully while we ring three times," said the other merlin.

"Oh, no!" cried the crazy colonel in an agony out of his remoter darkness. "Oh no, your ladyship. I beg of you not to do that. I am such a damned villain, your ladyship, that I do not answer for the consequences. Spare the poor boy, your ladyship, and lead us not into temptation."

"Colonel, control yourself. That ordeal will do very well."

"Oh, Madam, I was warned not to stand by Colonel Cully."

"Warned? And by whom?"

The poor Wart realised that now he must choose between confessing himself a human, and learning no more of their secrets, or going through with this ordeal to earn his education. He did not want to be a coward.

"I will stand by the Colonel, Madam," he said, immediately noticing that his voice sounded insulting.

The peregrine falcon paid no attention to the tone.

"It is well," she said. "But first we must have the hymn. Now, padre, if you have not eaten your hymns as well as your tirings, will you be so kind as to lead us in Ancient but not Modern No. 23? The Ordeal Hymn.

"And you, Mr. Kee," she added to the kestrel, "you had better keep quiet, for you are always too high."

The hawks stood still in the moonlight, while the sparhawk counted "One, Two, Three." Then all those curved or toothed beaks opened in their hoods to a brazen unison, and this is what they chanted:

Life is blood, shed and offered.
    The eagle's eye can face this dree.
To beasts of chase the lie is proffered:
    *Timor Mortis Conturbat Me.*


The beast of foot sings Holdfast only,
    For flesh is bruckle and foot is slee.

Strength to the strong and the lordly and lonely.
    *Timor Mortis Exultat Me.*


Shame to the slothful and woe to the weak one.
    Death to the dreadful who turn to flee.
Blood to the tearing, the talon'd, the beaked one.
    *Timor Mortis* are We.

"Very nice," said the peregrine. "Captain Balan, I think
you were a little off on the top C. And now, candidate, you
will go over and stand next to Colonel Cully's enclosure,
while we ring our bells thrice. On the third ring you may
move as quickly as you like."

"Very good, Madam," said the Wart, quite fearless with
resentment. He flipped his wings and was sitting on the extreme end of the screen perch, next to Cully's enclosure of
string netting.

"Boy!" cried the Colonel in an unearthly voice, "don't
come near me, don't come near. Ah, tempt not the foul
fiend to his damnation."

"I do not fear you, sir," said the Wart. "Do not vex
yourself, for no harm will come to either of us."

"No harm, quotha! Ah, go, before it is too late. I feel
eternal longings in me."

"Never fear, sir. They have only to ring three times."

At this the knights lowered their raised legs and gave
them a solemn shake. The first sweet tinkling filled the
room.

"Madam, Madam!" cried the Colonel in torture. "Have
pity, have pity on a damned man of blood. Ring out the old,
ring in the new. I can't hold off much longer."

"Be brave, sir," said the Wart softly.

"Be brave, sir! Why, but two nights since, one met the
duke 'bout midnight in a lane behind Saint Mark's Church,
with the leg of a man upon his shoulder: and he howled
fearfully."

"It is nothing," said the Wart.

"Nothing! Said he was a wolf, only the difference was a
wolf's skin was hairy on the outside, his on the inside. Rip
up my flesh and try. Ah, for quietus, with a bare bodkin!"

The bells rang for the second time.

The Wart's heart was thumping, and now the Colonel
was sidling toward him along the perch. Stamp, stamp, he

went, striking the wood he trod on with a convulsive grip
at every pace. His poor, mad, brooding eyes glared in the
moonlight, shone against the persecuted darkness of his
scowling brow. There was nothing cruel about him, no
ignoble passion. He was terrified of the Wart, not triumphing, and he must slay.

"If it were done when 'tis done," whispered the Colonel,
"then 'twere well it were done quickly. Who would have
thought the young man had so much blood in him?"

"Colonel!" said the Wart, but held himself there.

"Boy!" cried the Colonel. "Speak, stop me, mercy!"

"There is a cat behind you," said the Wart calmly, "or
a pinemarten. Look."

The Colonel turned, swift as a wasp's sting, and menaced
into the gloom. There was nothing. He swung his wild
eyes again upon the Wart, guessing the trick. Then, in the
cold voice of an adder, "The bell invites me. Hear it not,
Merlin, for it is a knell that summons thee to heaven or to
hell."

The third bells were indeed ringing as he spoke, and honour was allowed to move. The ordeal was over and the Wart
might fly. But as he moved, but as he flew, quicker than
any movement or flight in the world, the terrible sickles
had shot from the Colonel's plated legs—not flashed out,
for they moved too quick for sight—and with a thump,
with a clutch, with an apprehension, like being arrested
by a big policeman, the great scimitars had fixed themselves
in his retreating thumb.

They fixed themselves, and fixed irrevocably. Gripe,
gripe, the enormous thigh muscles tautened in two convulsions. Then the Wart was two yards further down the
screen, and Colonel Cully was standing on one foot with a
few meshes of string netting and the Wart's false primary,
with its covert-feathers, vice-fisted in the other. Two or
three minor feathers drifted softly in a moonbeam toward
the floor.

"Well stood!" cried Balan, delighted.

"A very gentlemanly exhibition," said the peregrine, not
minding that Captain Balan had spoken before her.

"Amen!" said the spar-hawk.

"Brave heart!" said the kestrel.

"Might we give him the Triumph Song?" asked Balin, re-
lenting.

"Certainly," said the peregrine.

And they all sang together, led by Colonel Cully at the top of his voice, all belling triumphantly in the terrible moonlight.

> The mountain birds are sweeter
>  But the valley birds are fatter,
> And so we deemed it meeter
>  To carry off the latter.
> We met a cowering coney
>  And struck him through the vitals.
> The coney was like honey
>  And squealed our requitals.
> Some struck the lark in feathers
>  Whose puffing clouds were shed off.
> Some plucked the partridge's nethers,
>  While others pulled his head off.
> But Wart the King of Merlins
>  Struck foot most far before us.
>   His birds and beasts
>   Supply our feasts,
>  And his feats our glorious chorus!

"Mark my words," cried the beautiful Balan, "we shall have a regular king in that young candidate. Now, boys, chorus altogether for the last time":

> But Wart the King of Merlins
>  Struck foot most far before us.
>   His birds and beasts
>   Supply our feasts,
>  And his feats our glorious chorus!

# 9

*"Well!" said the Wart, as he woke up in his own bed* next morning. "What a horrible, grand crew!"

Kay sat up in bed and began scolding like a squirrel. "Where were you last night?" he cried. "I believe you climbed out. I shall tell my father and get you tanned. You know we are not allowed out after curfew. What have you been doing? I looked for you everywhere. I know you climbed out."

The boys had a way of sliding down a rain-water pipe into the moat, which they could swim on secret occasions when it was necessary to be out at night—to wait for a badger, for instance, or to catch tench, which can only be taken just before dawn.

"Oh, shut up," said the Wart. "I'm sleepy."

Kay said, "Wake up, wake up, you beast. Where have you been?"

"I shan't tell you."

He was sure that Kay would not believe the story, but only call him a liar and get angrier than ever.

"If you don't tell me I shall kill you."

"You will not, then."

"I will."

The Wart turned over on his other side.

"Beast," said Kay. He took a fold of the Wart's arm between the nails of first finger and thumb, and pinched for all he was worth. Wart kicked like a salmon which has been suddenly hooked, and hit him wildly in the eye. In a trice they were out of bed, pale and indignant, looking rather like skinned rabbits—for in those days, nobody wore clothes in bed—and whirling their arms like windmills in the effort to do each other a mischief.

Kay was older and bigger than the Wart, so that he was bound to win in the end, but he was more nervous and imaginative. He could imagine the effect of each blow that was aimed at him, and this weakened his defence. Wart was only an infuriated hurricane.

"Leave me alone, can't you?" And all the while he did not leave Kay alone, but with head down and swinging arms made it impossible for Kay to do as he was bid. They punched entirely at each other's faces.

Kay had a longer reach and a heavier fist. He straightened his arm, more in self-defence than in anything else, and the Wart smacked his own eye upon the end of it. The sky became a noisy and shocking black, streaked outward with a blaze of meteors. The Wart began to sob and pant. He managed to get in a blow upon his opponent's nose, and this began to bleed. Kay lowered his defence, turned his back on the Wart, and said in a cold, snuffling, reproachful voice,

"Now it's bleeding." The battle was over.

Kay lay on the stone floor, bubbling blood out of his nose, and the Wart, with a black eye, fetched the enormous key out of the door to put under Kay's back. Neither of them spoke.

Presently Kay turned over on his face and began to sob. He said, "Merlyn does everything for you, but he never does anything for me."

At this the Wart felt he had been a beast. He dressed himself in silence and hurried off to find the magician.

On the way he was caught by his nurse.

"Ah, you little helot," exclaimed she, shaking him by the arm, "you've been a-battling again with that there Master Kay. Look at your poor eye, I do declare. It's enough to baffle the college of sturgeons."

"It is all right," said the Wart.

"No, that it isn't, my poppet," cried his nurse, getting crosser and showing signs of slapping him. "Come now, how did you do it, before I have you whipped?"

"I knocked it on the bedpost," said the Wart sullenly.

The old nurse immediately folded him to her broad bosom, patted him on the back, and said, "There, there, my dowsabel. It's the same story Sir Ector told me when I caught him with a blue eye, gone forty years. Nothing like a good family for sticking to a good lie. There, my innocent, you come along of me to the kitchen and we'll slap a nice bit of steak across him in no time. But you hadn't ought to fight with people bigger than yourself."

"It is all right," said the Wart again, disgusted by the fuss, but fate was bent on punishing him, and the old lady was inexorable. It took him half an hour to escape, and then only at the price of carrying with him a juicy piece of raw beef which he was supposed to hold over his eye.

"Nothing like a mealy rump for drawing out the humours," his nurse had said, and the cook had answered:

"Us hadn't seen a sweeter bit of raw since Easter, no, nor a bloodier."

"I will keep the foul thing for Balan," thought the Wart, resuming his search for his tutor.

He found him without trouble in the tower room which he had chosen when he arrived. All philosophers prefer to live in towers, as may be seen by visiting the room which Erasmus chose in his college at Cambridge, but Merlyn's tower was even more beautiful than this. It was the highest room in the castle, directly below the look-out of the great keep, and from its window you could gaze across the open field—with its rights of warren—across the park, and the chase, until your eye finally wandered out over the distant blue tree-tops of the Forest Sauvage. This sea of leafy timber rolled away and away in knobs like the surface of porridge, until it was finally lost in remote mountains which nobody had ever visited, and the cloud-capped towers and gorgeous palaces of heaven.

Merlyn's comments upon the black eye were of a medical nature.

"The discoloration," he said, "is caused by haemorrhage into the tissues (ecchymosis) and passes from dark purple through green to yellow before it disappears."

There seemed to be no sensible reply to this.

"I suppose you had it," continued Merlyn, "fighting with Kay?"

"Yes. How did you know?"

"Ah, well, there it is."

"I came to ask you about Kay."

"Speak. Demand. I'll answer."

"Well, Kay thinks it is unfair that you are always turning me into things and not him. I have not told him about it but I think he guesses. I think it is unfair too."

"It is unfair."

"So will you turn us both next time that we are turned?"

Merlyn had finished his breakfast, and was puffing at the meerschaum pipe which made his pupil believe that he breathed fire. Now he took a deep puff, looked at the Wart, opened his mouth to speak, changed his mind, blew out the smoke and drew another lungful.

"Sometimes," he said, "life does seem to be unfair. Do you know the story of Elijah and the Rabbi Jachanan?"

"No," said the Wart.

He sat down resignedly upon the most comfortable part of the floor, perceiving that he was in for something like the parable of the looking-glass.

"This rabbi," said Merlyn, "went on a journey with the prophet Elijah. They walked all day, and at nightfall they came to the humble cottage of a poor man, whose only treasure was a cow. The poor man ran out of his cottage, and his wife ran too, to welcome the strangers for the night and to offer them all the simple hospitality which they were able to give in straitened circumstances. Elijah and the Rabbi were entertained with plenty of the cow's milk, sustained by home-made bread and butter, and they were put to sleep in the best bed while their kindly hosts lay down before the kitchen fire. But in the morning the poor man's cow was dead."

"Go on."

"They walked all the next day, and came that evening to the house of a very wealthy merchant, whose hospitality they craved. The merchant was cold and proud and rich, and all that he would do for the prophet and his companion was to lodge them in a cowshed and feed them on bread and water. In the morning, however, Elijah thanked him very much for what he had done, and sent for a mason to repair one of his walls, which happened to be falling down, as a return for his kindness.

"The Rabbi Jachanan, unable to keep silence any longer, begged the holy man to explain the meaning of his dealings with human beings.

" 'In regard to the poor man who received us so hospitably,' replied the prophet, 'it was decreed that his wife was to die that night, but in reward for his goodness God took the cow instead of the wife. I repaired the wall of the rich miser because a chest of gold was concealed near the place, and if the miser had repaired the wall himself he would have discovered the treasure. Say not therefore to the Lord: What doest thou? But say in thy heart: Must not the Lord of all the earth do right?' "

"It is a nice sort of story," said the Wart, because it seemed to be over.

"I am sorry," said Merlyn, "that you should be the only one to get my extra tuition, but then, you see, I was only sent for that."

"I do not see that it would do any harm for Kay to come too."

"Nor do I. But the Rabbi Jachanan did not see why the miser should have had his wall repaired."

"I understand that," said the Wart doubtfully, "but I still think it was a shame that the cow died. Could I not have Kay with me just once?"

Merlyn said gently, "Perhaps what is good for you might be bad for him. Besides, remember he has never asked to be turned into anything."

"He wants to be turned, for all that. I like Kay, you know, and I think people don't understand him. He has to be proud because he is frightened."

"You still do not follow what I mean. Suppose he had gone as a merlin last night, and failed in the ordeal, and lost his nerve?"

"How do you know about that ordeal?"

"Ah, well, there it is again."

"Very well," said the Wart obstinately. "But suppose he had not failed in the ordeal, and had not lost his nerve. I don't see why you should have to suppose that he would have."

"Oh, flout the boy!" cried the magician passionately. "You don't seem to see anything this morning. What is it that you want me to do?"

"Turn me and Kay into snakes or something."

Merlyn took off his spectacles, dashed them on the floor and jumped on them with both feet.

"Castor and Pollux blow me to Bermuda!" he exclaimed, and immediately vanished with a frightful roar.

The Wart was still staring at his tutor's chair in some perplexity, a few moments later, when Merlyn reappeared. He had lost his hat and his hair and beard were tangled up, as if by a hurricane. He sat down again, straightening his gown with trembling fingers.

"Why did you do that?" asked the Wart.

"I did not do it on purpose."

"Do you mean to say that Castor and Pollux did blow you to Bermuda?"

"Let this be a lesson to you," replied Merlyn, "not to swear. I think we had better change the subject."

"We were talking about Kay."

"Yes, and what I was going to say before my—ahem!— my visit to the still vexed Bermoothes, was this. I cannot change Kay into things. The power was not deputed to me when I was sent. Why this was so, neither you nor I am able to say, but such remains the fact. I have tried to hint at some of the reasons for the fact, but you will not take them, so you must just accept the fact in its naked reality. Now please stop talking until I have got my breath back, and my hat."

The Wart sat quiet while Merlyn closed his eyes and began to mutter to himself. Presently a curious black cylindrical hat appeared on his head. It was a topper.

Merlyn examined it with a look of disgust, said bitterly, "And they call this service!" and handed it back to the air. Finally he stood up in a passion and exclaimed, "Come here!"

The Wart and Archimedes looked at each other, wondering which was meant—Archimedes had been sitting all the while on the window-sill and looking at the view, for, of course, he never left his master—but Merlyn did not pay them any attention.

"Now," said Merlyn furiously, apparently to nobody, "do you think you are being funny?

"Very well then, why do you do it?

"That is no excuse. Naturally I meant the one I was wearing.

"But wearing now, of course, you fool. I don't want a hat I was wearing in 1890. Have you no sense of time at all?"

Merlyn took off the sailor hat which had just appeared and held it out to the air for inspection.

"This is an anachronism," he said severely. "That is what it is, a beastly anachronism."

Archimedes seemed to be accustomed to these scenes, for he now said in a reasonable voice: "Why don't you ask for the hat by name, master? Say, 'I want my magician's hat,' not 'I want the hat I was wearing.' Perhaps the poor chap finds it as difficult to live backward as you do."

"I want my magician's hat," said Merlyn sulkily.

Instantly the long pointed cone was standing on his head.

The tension in the air relaxed. Wart sat down again on the floor, and Archimedes resumed his toilet, pulling his pinions and tail feathers through his beak to smooth the barbs together. Each barb had hundreds of little hooks or barbules on it, by means of which the barbs of the feather were held together. He was stroking them into place.

Merlyn said, "I beg your pardon. I am not having a very good day today, and there it is."

"About Kay," said the Wart. "Even if you can't change him into things, could you not give us both an adventure without changing?"

Merlyn made a visible effort to control his temper, and to consider this question dispassionately. He was sick of the subject altogether.

"I cannot do any magic for Kay," he said slowly, "except my own magic that I have anyway. Backsight and insight and all that. Do you mean anything I could do with that?"

"What does your backsight do?"

"It tells me what you would say is going to happen, and the insight sometimes says what is or was happening in other places."

"Is there anything happening just now, anything that Kay and I could go to see?"

Merlyn immediately struck himself on the brow and exclaimed excitedly, "Now I see it all. Yes, of course there is, and you are going to see it. Yes, you must take Kay and hurry up about it. You must go immediately after Mass. Have breakfast first and go immediately after Mass. Yes, that is it. Go straight to Hob's strip of barley in the open field and follow that line until you come to something. That will be splendid, yes, and I shall have a nap this afternoon instead of those filthy Summulae Logicales. Or have I had the nap?"

"You have not had it," said Archimedes. "That is still in the future, Master."

"Splendid, splendid. And mind, Wart, don't forget to take Kay with you so that I can have my nap."

"What shall we see?" asked the Wart.

"Ah, don't plague me about a little thing like that. You run along now, there's a good boy, and mind you don't forget to take Kay with you. Why ever didn't you mention it before? Don't forget to follow beyond the strip of barley. Well, well, well! This is the first half-holiday I have had since I started this confounded tutorship. First I think I shall have a little nap before luncheon, and then I think I shall have a little nap before tea. Then I shall have to think of something I can do before dinner. What shall I do before dinner, Archimedes?"

"Have a little nap, I expect," said the owl coldly, turning his back upon his master, because he, as well as the Wart, enjoyed to see life.

# 10

*Wart knew that if he told the elder boy about his* conversation with Merlyn, Kay would refuse to be condescended to, and would not come. So he said nothing. It was strange, but their battle had made them friends again, and each could look the other in the eye, with a kind of confused affection. They went together unanimously though shyly, without explanations, and found themselves standing at the end of Hob's barley strip after Mass. The Wart had no need to use ingenuity. When they were there it was easy.

"Come on," he said, "Merlyn told me to tell you that there was something along here that was specially for you."

"What sort of thing?" asked Kay.

"An adventure."

"How do we get to it?"

"We ought to follow along the line which this strip makes, and I suppose that would take us into the forest. We should have to keep the sun just there on our left, but allow for it moving."

"All right," said Kay. "What is the adventure?"

"I don't know."

They went along the strip, and followed its imaginary line over the park and over the chase, keeping their eyes skinned for some miraculous happening. They wondered whether half a dozen young pheasants they started had anything curious about them, and Kay was ready to swear that one of them was white. If it had been white, and if a black eagle had suddenly swooped down upon it from the sky, they would have known quite well that wonders were afoot, and that all they had to do was to follow the pheasant—or the eagle—until they reached the maiden in the enchanted castle. However, the pheasant was not white.

At the edge of the forest Kay said, "I suppose we shall have to go into this?"

"Merlyn said to follow the line."

"Well," said Kay, "I am not afraid. If the adventure was for me, it is bound to be a good one."

They went in, and were surprised to find that the going was not bad. It was about the same as a big wood might be nowadays, whereas the common forest of those times was like a jungle on the Amazon. There were no pheasant-shooting proprietors then, to see that the undergrowth was thinned, and not one thousandth part of the number of the present-day timber merchants who prune judiciously at the few remaining woods. The most of the Forest Sauvage was almost impenetrable, an enormous barrier of eternal trees, the dead ones fallen against the live and held to them by ivy, the living struggling up in competition with each other toward the sun which gave them life, the floor boggy through lack of drainage, or tindery from old wood so that you might suddenly tumble through a decayed tree trunk into an ants' nest, or laced with brambles and bindweed and honeysuckle and convolvulus and teazles and the stuff which country people call sweethearts, until you would be torn to pieces in three yards.

This part was good. Hob's line pointed down what seemed to be a succession of glades, shady and murmuring places in which the wild thyme was droning with bees. The insect season was past its peak, for it was really the time for wasps and fruit; but there were many fritillaries still, with tortoise-shells and red admirals on the flowering mint. Wart pulled a leaf of this, and munched it like chewing-gum as they walked.

"It is queer," he said, "but there have been people here. Look, there is a hoof-mark, and it was shod."

"You don't see much," said Kay, "for there is a man."

Sure enough, there was a man at the end of the next glade, sitting with a wood-axe by the side of a tree which he had felled. He was a queer-looking, tiny man, with a hunchback and a face like mahogany, and he was dressed in numerous pieces of old leather which he had secured about his brawny legs and arms with pieces of cord. He was eating a lump of bread and sheep's-milk cheese with a knife which years of sharpening had worn into a mere streak, leaning his back against one of the highest trees they had ever seen. The white flakes of wood lay all about him. The dressed stump of the felled tree looked very new. His eyes were bright like a fox's.

"I expect he will be the adventure," whispered Wart.

"Pooh," said Kay, "you have knights-in-armour, or drag-ons, or things like that in an adventure, not dirty old men cutting wood."

"Well, I am going to ask him what happens along here, anyway."

They went up to the small munching woodman, who did not seem to have seen them, and asked him where the glades were leading to. They asked two or three times before they discovered that the poor fellow was either deaf or mad, or both. He neither answered nor moved.

"Oh, come on," said Kay. "He is probably loopy like Wat, and does not know what he is at. Let's go on and leave the old fool."

They went on for nearly a mile, and still the going was good. There were no paths exactly, and the glades were not continuous. Anybody who came there by chance would have thought that there was just the one glade which he was in, a couple of hundred yards long, unless he went to the end of it and discovered another one, screened by a few trees. Now and then they found a stump with the marks of the axe on it, but mostly these had been carefully covered with brambles or altogether grubbed up. The Wart consid-ered that the glades must have been made.

Kay caught the Wart by the arm, at the edge of a clear-ing, and pointed silently toward its further end. There was a grassy bank there, swelling gently to a gigantic sycamore, upward of ninety feet high, which stood upon its top. On the bank there was an equally gigantic man lying at his ease, with a dog beside him. This man was as notable as the syca-more, for he stood or lay seven feet without his shoes, and he was dressed in nothing but a kind of kilt made of Lincoln green worsted. He had a leather bracer on his left forearm. His enormous brown chest supported the dog's head—it had pricked its ears and was watching the boys, but had made no other movement—which the muscles gently lifted as they rose and fell. The man appeared to be asleep. There was a seven-foot bow beside him, with some arrows more than a cloth-yard long. He, like the woodman, was the col-our of mahogany, and the curled hairs on his chest made a golden haze where the sun caught them.

"He is it," whispered Kay excitedly.

They went to the man cautiously, for fear of the dog. But the dog only followed them with its eyes, keeping its chin pressed firmly to the chest of its beloved master, and giving them the least suspicion of a wag from its tail. It moved its tail without lifting it, two inches sideways in the grass. The man opened his eyes—obviously he had not been asleep at all—smiled at the boys, and jerked his thumb in a direction which pointed further up the glade. Then he stopped smiling and shut his eyes.

"Excuse me," said Kay, "what happens up there?"

The man made no answer and kept his eyes closed, but he lifted his hand again and pointed onward with his thumb.

"He means us to go on," said Kay.

"It certainly is an adventure," said the Wart. "I wonder if that dumb woodman could have climbed up the big tree he was leaning against and sent a message to this tree that we were coming? He certainly seems to have been expecting us."

At this the naked giant opened one eye and looked at Wart in some surprise. Then he opened both eyes, laughed all over his big twinkling face, sat up, patted the dog, picked up his bow, and rose to his feet.

"Very well, then, young measters," he said, still laughing. "Us will come along of 'ee arter all. Young heads still meake the sharpest, they do say."

Kay looked at him in blank surprise. "Who are you?" he asked.

"Naylor," said the giant, "John Naylor in the wide world it were, till us come to be a man of the 'ood. Then 'twere John Little for some time, in the 'ood like, but mostly folk does put it back'ard now, and calls us Little John."

"Oh!" cried the Wart in delight. "I have heard of you, often, when they tell Saxon stories in the evening, of you and Robin Hood."

"Not Hood," said Little John reprovingly. "That bain't the way to name 'un, measter, not in the 'ood."

"But it is Robin Hood in the stories," said Kay.

"Ah, them book-learning chaps. They don't know all. How'm ever, 'tis time us do be stepping along."

They fell in on either side of the enormous man, and had to run one step in three to keep up with him; for, although he talked very slowly, he walked on his bare feet very fast. The dog trotted at heel.

"Please," asked the Wart, "where are you taking us?"

"Why, to Robin 'ood, seemingly. An't you sharp enough to guess that also, Measter Art?"

The giant gave him a sly peep out of the corner of his eye

at this, for he knew that he had set the boys two problems at once—first, what was Robin's real name, and second, how did Little John come to know the Wart's?

The Wart fixed on the second question first.

"How did you know my name?"

"Ah," said Little John. "Us knowed."

"Does Robin 'ood know we are coming?"

"Nay, my duck, a young scholard like thee should speak his name scholarly."

"Well, what is his name?" cried the boy, between exasperation and being out of breath from running to keep up. "You said 'ood."

"So it is 'ood, my duck. Robin 'ood, like the 'oods you'm running through. And a grand fine name it is."

"Robin Wood!"

"Aye, Robin 'ood. What else should un be, seeing as he rules 'em. They'm free pleaces, the 'oods, and fine pleaces. Let thee sleep in 'em, come summer, come winter, and hunt in 'em for thy commons lest thee starve; and smell to 'em as they brings forward their comely bright leaves, according to order, or loses of 'em by the same order back'ards: let thee stand in 'em that thou be'st not seen, and move in 'em that thou be'st not heard, and warm thee with 'em as thou fall'st on sleep—ah, they'm proper fine pleaces, the 'oods, for a free man of hands and heart."

Kay said, "But I thought all Robin Wood's men wore hose and jerkins of Lincoln green?"

"That us do in the winter like, when us needs 'em, or with leather leggings at 'ood 'ork: but here by summer 'tis more seasonable thus for the pickets, who have nought to do save watch."

"Were you a sentry then?"

"Aye, and so were wold Much, as you spoke to by the felled tree."

"And I think," exclaimed Kay triumphantly, "that this next big tree which we are coming to will be the stronghold of Robin Wood!"

They were coming to the monarch of the forest.

It was a lime tree as great as that which used to grow at Moor Park in Hertfordshire, no less than one hundred feet in height and seventeen feet in girth, a yard above the ground. Its beech-like trunk was embellished with a beard of twigs at the bottom, and where each of the great branches had sprung from the trunk the bark had split and was now discoloured with rain water or sap. The bees zoomed among its bright and sticky leaves, higher and higher toward heaven, and a rope ladder disappeared among the foliage. Nobody could have climbed it without a ladder, even with irons.

"You think well, Measter Kay," said Little John. "And there be Measter Robin, atween her roots."

The boys, who had been more interested in the look-out man perched in a crow's nest at the top of that swaying and whispering pride of the earth, lowered their eyes at once and clapped them on the great outlaw.

He was not, as they expected, a romantic man—or not at first—although he was nearly as tall as Little John. These two, of course, were the only people in the world who have ever shot an arrow the distance of a mile, with the English long-bow. He was a sinewy fellow whose body did not carry fat. He was not half-naked, like John, but dressed discreetly in faded green with a silvery bugle at his side. He was clean-shaven, sunburned, nervous, gnarled like the roots of the trees; but gnarled and mature with weather and poetry rather than with age, for he was scarcely thirty years old. (Eventually he lived to be eighty-seven, and attributed his long life to smelling the turpentine in the pines.) At the moment he was lying on his back and looking upward, but not into the sky.

Robin Wood lay happily with his head in Marian's lap. She sat between the roots of the lime tree, clad in a one-piece smock of green girded with a quiver of arrows, and her feet and arms were bare. She had let down the brown shining waterfall of her hair, which was usually kept braided in pigtails for convenience in hunting and cookery, and with the falling waves of this she framed his head. She was singing a duet with him softly, and tickling the end of his nose with the fine hairs.

"Under the greenwood tree," sang Maid Marian,
"Who loves to lie with me,
   And tune his merry note
   Unto the sweet bird's throat."

"Come hither, come hither, come hither," hummed Robin.

"Here shall he see
  No enemy
  But winter and rough weather."

They laughed happily and began again, singing lines alternately:

> "Who doth ambition shun
> And loves to lie in the sun,
> Seeking the food he eats
> And pleased with what he gets,"

then, both together:

> "Come hither, come hither, come hither:
> Here shall he see
> No enemy
> But winter and rough weather."

The song ended in laughter. Robin, who had been twisting his brown fingers in the silk-fine threads which fell about his face, gave them a shrewd tug and scrambled to his feet.

"Now, John," he said, seeing them at once.

"Now, Measter," said Little John.

"So you have brought the young squires?"

"They brought me."

"Welcome either way," said Robin. "I never heard ill spoken of Sir Ector, nor reason why his sounders should be pursued. How are you, Kay and Wart, and who put you into the forest at my glades, on this of all days?"

"Robin," interrupted the lady, "you can't take them!"

"Why not, sweet heart?"

"They are children."

"Exactly what we want."

"It is inhuman," she said in a vexed way, and began to do her hair.

The outlaw evidently thought it would be safer not to argue. He turned to the boys and asked them a question instead.

"Can you shoot?"

"Trust me," said the Wart.

"I can try," said Kay, more reserved, as they laughed at the Wart's assurance.

"Come, Marian, let them have one of your bows."

She handed him a bow and half a dozen arrows twenty-eight inches long.

"Shoot the popinjay," said Robin, giving them to the Wart.

He looked and saw a popinjay five-score paces away. He guessed that he had been a fool and said cheerfully, "I am sorry, Robin Wood, but I am afraid it is much too far for me."

"Never mind," said the outlaw. "Have a shot at it. I can tell by the way you shoot."

The Wart fitted his arrow as quickly and neatly as he was able, set his feet wide in the same line that he wished his arrow to go, squared his shoulders, drew the bow to his chin, sighted on the mark, raised its point through an angle of about twenty degrees, aimed two yards to the right because he always pulled to the left in his loose, and sped his arrow. It missed, but not so badly.

"Now, Kay," said Robin.

Kay went through the same motions and also made a good shot. Each of them had held the bow the right way up, had quickly found the cock feather and set it outward, each had taken hold of the string to draw the bow—most boys who have not been taught are inclined to catch hold of the nock of the arrow when they draw, between their finger and thumb, but a proper archer pulls back the string with his first two or three fingers and lets the arrow follow it—neither of them had allowed the point to fall away to the left as they drew, nor struck their left forearms with the bowstring—two common faults with people who do not know—and each had loosed evenly without a pluck.

"Good," said the outlaw. "No lute-players here."

"Robin," said Marian, sharply, "you can't take children into danger. Send them home to their father."

"That I won't," he said, "unless they wish to go. It is their quarrel as much as mine."

"What is the quarrel?" asked Kay.

The outlaw threw down his bow and sat cross-legged on the ground, drawing Maid Marian to sit beside him. His face was puzzled.

"It is Morgan le Fay," he said. "It is difficult to explain her."

"I should not try."

Robin turned on his mistress angrily. "Marian," he said. "Either we must have their help, or else we have to leave the other three without help. I don't want to ask the boys to go there, but it is either that or leaving Tuck to her."

The Wart thought it was time to ask a tactful question,

so he made a polite cough and said: "Please, who is Morgan the Fay?"

All three answered at once.

"She'm a bad 'un," said Little John.

"She is a fairy," said Robin.

"No, she is not," said Marian. "She is an enchantress."

"The fact of the matter is," said Robin, "that nobody knows exactly what she is. In my opinion, she is a fairy.

"And that opinion," he added, staring at his wife, "I still hold."

Kay asked: "Do you mean she is one of those people with bluebells for hats, who spend the time sitting on toadstools?"

There was a shout of laughter.

"Certainly not. There are no such creatures. The Queen is a real one, and one of the worst of them."

"If the boys have got to be in it," said Marian, "you had better explain from the beginning."

The outlaw took a deep breath, uncrossed his legs, and the puzzled look came back to his face.

"Well," he said, "suppose that Morgan is the queen of the fairies, or at any rate has to do with them, and that fairies are not the kind of creatures your nurse has told you about. Some people say they are the Oldest of All, who lived in England before the Romans came here—before us Saxons, before the Old Ones themselves—and that they have been driven underground. Some say they look like humans, like dwarfs, and others that they look ordinary, and others that they don't look like anything at all, but put on various shapes as the fancy takes them. Whatever they look like, they have the knowledge of the ancient Gaels. They know things down there in their burrows which the human race has forgotten about, and quite a lot of these things are not good to hear."

"Whisper," said the golden lady, with a strange look, and the boys noticed that the little circle had drawn closer together.

"Well now," said Robin, lowering his voice, "the thing about these creatures that I am speaking of, and if you will excuse me I won't name them again, is that they have no hearts. It is not so much that they wish to do evil, but that if you were to catch one and cut it open, you would find no heart inside. They are cold-blooded like fishes."

"They are everywhere, even while people are talking."

The boys looked about them.

"Be quiet," Robin said. "I need not tell you any more. It is unlucky to talk about them. The point is that I believe this Morgan is the queen of the—well—of the Good Folk, and I know she sometimes lives in a castle to the north of our forest called the Castle Chariot. Marian says that the queen is not a fairy herself, but only a necromancer who is friendly with them. Other people say she is a daughter of the Earl of Cornwall. Never mind about that. The thing is that this morning, by her enchantments, the Oldest People of All have taken prisoner one of my servants and one of yours."

"Not Tuck?" cried Little John, who knew nothing of recent developments because he had been on sentry.

Robin nodded. "The news came from the northern trees, before your message arrived about the boys."

"Alas, poor Friar!"

"Tell it how it happened," said Marian. "But perhaps you had better explain about the names."

"One of the few things we know," said Robin, "about the Blessed Ones, is that they go by the names of animals. For instance, they may be called Cow, or Goat, or Pig, and so forth. So, if you happen to be calling one of your own cows, you must always point to it when you call. Otherwise you may summon a fairy—a Little Person I ought to have said—who goes by the same name, and, once you have summoned it, it comes, and it can take you away."

"What seems to have happened," said Marian, taking up the story, "is that your Dog Boy from the castle took his hounds to the edge of the forest when they were going to scombre, and he happened to catch sight of Friar Tuck, who was chatting with an old man called Wat that lives hereabouts—"

"Excuse us," cried the two boys, "is that the old man who lived in our village before he lost his wits? He bit off the Dog Boy's nose, as a matter of fact, and now he lives in the forest, a sort of ogre?"

"It is the same person," replied Robin, "but—poor thing—he is not much of an ogre. He lives on grass and roots and acorns, and would not hurt a fly. I am afraid you have got your story muddled."

"Fancy Wat living on acorns!"

"What happened," said Marian patiently, "was this. The

three of them came together to pass the time of day, and one of the hounds (I think it was the one called Cavall) began jumping up at poor Wat, to lick his face. This frightened the old man, and your Dog Boy called out, 'Come here, Dog!' to make him stop. He did not point with his finger. You see, he ought to have pointed."

"What happened?"

"Well, my man Scathelocke, or Scarlett, as they call him in the ballads, happened to be woodcutting a little way off, and he says that they vanished, just vanished, including the dog."

"My poor Cavall!"

"So the fairies have got them."

"You mean the People of Peace."

"I am sorry.

"But the point is, if Morgan is really the Queen of these creatures, and if we want to get them away before they are enchanted—one of their ancient Queens called Circe used to turn the ones she captured into hogs—we shall have to look for them in her castle."

"Then we must go there."

# 11

*Robin smiled at the elder boy and patted him on the* back, while the Wart thought despairingly about his dog. Then the outlaw cleared his throat and began to speak again.

"You are right about going there," he said, "but I ought to tell you the unpleasant part. Nobody can get into the Castle Chariot, except a boy or girl."

"Do you mean you can't get in?"

"You could get in."

"I suppose," explained the Wart, when he had thought this over, "it is like the thing about unicorns."

"Right. A unicorn is a magic animal, and only a maiden can catch it. Fairies are magic too, and only innocent people can enter their castles. That is why they take away people's children out of cradles."

Kay and Wart sat in silence for a moment. Then Kay said: "Well, I am game. It is my adventure after all."

The Wart said: "I want to go too. I am fond of Cavall."

Robin looked at Marian.

"Very well," he said. "We won't make a fuss about it, but we will talk about plans. I think it is good of you two to go, without really knowing what you are in for, but it will not be so bad as you think."

"We shall come with you," said Marian. "Our band will come with you to the castle. You will only have to do the going-in part at the end."

"Yes, and the band will probably be attacked by that griffin of hers afterwards."

"Is there a griffin?"

"Indeed there is. The Castle Chariot is guarded by a fierce one, like a watch dog. We shall have to get past it on the way there, or it will give the alarm and you won't be able to get in. It will be a terrific stalk."

"We shall have to wait till night."

The boys passed the morning pleasantly, getting accustomed to two of Maid Marian's bows. Robin had insisted on this. He said that no man could shoot with another's bow any more than he could cut with another's scythe. For their midday meal they had cold venison pattie, with mead, as did everybody else. The outlaws drifted in for the meal like a conjuring trick. At one moment there would be nobody at the edge of the clearing, at the next half a dozen right inside it—green or sunburned men who had silently appeared out of the bracken or the trees. In the end there were about a hundred of them, eating merrily and laughing. They were not outlaws because they were murderers, or for any reason like that. They were Saxons who had revolted against Uther Pendragon's conquest, and who refused to accept a foreign king. The fens and wild woods of England were alive with them. They were like soldiers of the resistance in later occupations. Their food was dished out from a leafy bower, where Marian and her attendants cooked.

The partisans usually posted a sentry to take the tree messages, and slept during the afternoon, partly because so much of their hunting had to be done in the times when most workmen sleep, and partly because the wild beasts take a nap in the afternoon and so should their hunters. This afternoon, however, Robin called the boys to a council.

"Look," he said, "you had better know what we are going to do. My band of a hundred will march with you toward Queen Morgan's castle, in four parties. You two will be in Marian's party. When we get to an oak which was struck by lightning in the year of the great storm, we shall be within a mile of the griffin guard. We shall meet at a rendezvous there, and afterward we shall have to move like shadows. We must get past the griffin without an alarm. If we do get past it and if all goes well, we shall halt at the castle at a distance of about four hundred yards. We can't come nearer, because of the iron in our arrow-heads, and from that moment you will have to go alone.

"Now, Kay and Wart, I must explain about iron. If our friends have really been captured by—by the Good People —and if Queen Morgan the Fay is really the queen of them, we have one advantage on our side. None of the Good People can bear the closeness of iron. The reason is that the Oldest Ones of All began in the days of flint, before iron was ever invented, and all their troubles have come from the new metal. The people who conquered them had steel swords (which is even better than iron) and that is how they succeeded in driving the Old Ones underground.

"This is the reason why we must keep away tonight, for fear of giving them the uncomfortable feeling. But you two, with an iron knife-blade hidden close in your hands, will be safe from the Queen, so long as you do not let go of it. A couple of small knives will not give them the feeling without being shown. All you will have to do is to walk the last distance, keeping a good grip of your iron: enter the castle in safety: and make your way to the cell where the prisoners are. As soon as the prisoners are protected by your metal they will be able to walk out with you. Do you understand this, Kay and Wart?"

"Yes, please," they said. "We understand this perfectly."

"There is one more thing. The most important is to hold your iron, but the next most important is not to eat. Anybody who eats in you-know-what stronghold has to stay there for ever, so, for all sake's sake, don't eat anything whatever inside the castle, however tempting it may look. Will you remember?"

"We will."

After the staff lecture, Robin went to give his orders to the men. He made them a long speech, explaining about the griffin and the stalk and what the boys were going to do.

When he had finished his speech, which was listened to in perfect silence, an odd thing happened. He began at the beginning and spoke it from start to finish in the same words. On finishing it for the second time, he said, "Now, captains," and the hundred men split into groups of twenty which went to different parts of the clearing and stood round Marian, Little John, Much, Scarlett and Robin. From each of these groups a humming noise rose to the sky.

"What on earth are they doing?"

"Listen," said the Wart.

They were repeating the speech, word for word. Probably none of them could read or write, but they had learned to listen and remember. This was the way in which Robin kept touch with his night raiders, by knowing that each man knew by heart all that the leader himself knew, and why he was able to trust them, when necessary, each man to move by himself.

When the men had repeated their instructions, and everyone was word perfect in the speech, there was an issue of war arrows, a dozen to each. These arrows had bigger heads, ground to razor sharpness, and they were heavily feathered in a square cut. There was a bow inspection, and two or three men were issued with new strings. Then all fell silent.

"Now then," cried Robin cheerfully.

He waved his arm, and the men, smiling, raised their bows in salute. Then there was a sigh, a rustle, a snap of one incautious twig, and the clearing of the giant lime tree was as empty as it had been before the days of man.

"Come with me," said Marian, touching the boys on the shoulder. Behind them the bees hummed in the leaves.

It was a long march. The artificial glades which led to the lime tree in the form of a cross were no longer of use after the first half-hour. After that they had to make their way through the virgin forest as best they might. It would not have been so bad if they had been able to kick and slash their way, but they were supposed to move in silence. Marian showed them how to go sideways, one side after the other; how to stop at once when a bramble caught them, and take it patiently out; how to put their feet down sensitively and roll their weight to that leg as soon as they were certain that no twig was under the foot; how to distinguish at a glance the places which gave most hope of an easy passage; and how a kind of rhythm in their movements would help them in spite of obstacles. Although there were a hundred invisible men on every side of them, moving toward the same goal, they heard no sounds but their own.

The boys had felt disgruntled at first, at being put in a woman's band. They would have preferred to have gone with Robin, and thought that being put under Marian was like being trusted to a governess. They soon found their mistake. She had objected to their coming, but, now that their coming was ordered, she accepted them as companions. It was not easy to be a companion of hers. In the first place, it was impossible to keep up with her unless she waited for them—for she could move on all fours or even wriggle like a snake almost as quickly as they could walk—and in the second place she was an accomplished soldier, which they were not. She was a true Weyve—except for her long hair, which most of the female outlaws of those days used to clip. One of the bits of advice which she gave them before talking had to be stopped was this: Aim high when you shoot in battle, rather than low. A low arrow strikes the ground, a high one may kill in the second rank.

"If I am made to get married," thought the Wart, who had doubts on the subject, "I will marry a girl like this: a kind of golden vixen."

As a matter of fact, though the boys did not know it, Marian could hoot like an owl by blowing into her fists, or whistle a shrill blast between tongue and teeth with the fingers in the corner of the mouth; could bring all the birds to her by imitating their calls, and understand much of their small language—such as when the tits exclaim that a hawk is coming; could hit the popinjay twice for three times of Robin's; and could turn cartwheels. But none of these accomplishments was necessary at the moment.

The twilight fell mistily—it was the first of the autumn mists—and in the dimity the undispersed families of the tawny owl called to each other, the young with keewick and the old with the proper hooroo, hooroo. The noise called Tu-Whit, Tu-Whoo, which is wished by poets on the owl, is really a family noise, made by separate birds. Proportionally as the brambles and obstacles became harder to see, so did they become easier to feel. It was odd, but in the deepening silence the Wart found himself able to move more silently, instead of less. Being reduced to touch and sound, he found himself in better sympathy with these, and could go quietly and quick.

It was about compline, or, as we should call it, at nine o'clock at night—and they had covered at least seven miles of the toilsome forest—when Marian touched Kay on the shoulder and pointed into the blue darkness. They could see in the dark now, as well as human beings can see in it and much better than townspeople will ever manage to, and there in front of them, struck through seven miles of trackless forest by Marian's wood-craft, was the smitten oak. They decided with one accord, without even a whisper, to creep up to it so silently that even the members of their own army, who might already be waiting there, would not know of their arrival.

But a motionless man has the advantage of a man in motion, and they had hardly reached the outskirts of the roots when friendly hands took hold of them, patted their backs with pats as light as thistledown, and guided them to seats. The roots were crowded. It was like being a member of a band of starlings, or of roosting rooks. In the night mystery a hundred men breathed on every side of Wart, like the surge of our own blood which we can hear when we are writing or reading in the late and lonely hours. They were in the dark and stilly womb of night.

Presently the Wart noticed that the grasshoppers were creaking their shrill note, so tiny as to be almost extra-audible, like the creak of the bat. They creaked one after another. They creaked, when Marian had creaked three times to account for Kay and Wart as well as for herself, one hundred times. All the outlaws were present, and it was time to go.

There was a rustle, as if the wind had moved in the last few leaves of the nine-hundred-year-old oak. Then an owl hooted softly, a field mouse screamed, a rabbit thumped, a dog-fox barked his deep, single lion's cough, and a bat twittered above their heads. The leaves rustled again more lengthily while you could count a hundred, and then Maid Marian, who had done the rabbit's thump, was surrounded by her band of twenty plus two. The Wart felt a man on either side of him take his hand, as they stood in a circle, and then he noticed that the stridulation of the grasshoppers had begun again. It was going round in a circle, towards him, and, as the last grasshopper rubbed its legs together, the man on his right squeezed his hand. Wart stridulated. Instantly the man on his left did the same, and pressed his hand also. There were twenty-two grasshoppers before Maid Marian's band was ready for its last stalk through the silence.

The last stalk might have been a nightmare, but to the Wart it was heavenly. Suddenly he found himself filled with an exaltation of night, and felt that he was bodiless, silent, transported. He felt that he could have walked upon a feeding rabbit and caught her up by the ears, furry and kicking, before she knew of his presence. He felt that he could have run between the legs of the men on either side of him, or taken their bright daggers from their sheaths, while they still moved on undreaming. The passion of nocturnal secrecy was a wine in his blood. He really was small and young enough to move as secretly as the warriors. Their age and weight made them lumber, in spite of all their woodcraft, and his youth and lightness made him mobile, in spite of his lack of it.

It was an easy stalk, except for its danger. The bushes thinned and the sounding bracken grew rarely in the the swampy earth, so that they could move three times as fast. They went in a dream, unguided by owl's hoot or bat's squeak, but only kept together by the necessary pace which the sleeping forest imposed upon them. Some of them were fearful, some revengeful for their comrade, some, as it were, disbodied in the sleep-walk of their stealth.

They had hardly crept for twenty minutes when Maid Marian paused in her tracks. She pointed to the left.

Neither of the boys had read the book of Sir John de Mandeville, so they did not know that a griffin was eight times larger than a lion. Now, looking to the left in the silent gloom of night, they saw cut out against the sky and against the stars something which they never would have believed possible. It was a young male griffin in its first plumage.

The front end, and down to the forelegs and shoulders, was like a huge falcon. The Persian beak, the long wings in which the first primary was the longest, and the mighty talons: all were the same, but, as Mandeville observed, the whole eight times bigger than a lion. Behind the shoulders, a change began to take place. Where an ordinary falcon or eagle would content itself with the twelve feathers of its tail, Falco leonis serpentis began to grow the leonine body

and the hind legs of the beast of Africa, and after that a
snake's tail. The boys saw, twenty-four feet high in the
mysterious night-light of the moon, and with its sleeping
head bowed upon its breast so that the wicked beak lay on
the breast feathers, an authentic griffin that was better worth
seeing than a hundred condors. They drew their breath
through their teeth and for the moment hurried secretly on,
storing the majestic vision of terror in the chambers of remembrance.

They were close to the castle at last, and it was time for
the outlaws to halt. Their captain touched hands silently
with Kay and Wart, and the two went forward through the
thinning forest, towards a faint glow which gleamed behind
the trees.

They found themselves in a wide clearing or plain. They
stood stock still with surprise at what they saw. It was a
castle made entirely out of food, except that on the highest
tower of all a carrion crow was sitting, with an arrow in its
beak.

The Oldest Ones of All were gluttons. Probably it was because they seldom had enough to eat. You can read even
nowadays a poem written by one of them, which is known
as the Vision of Mac Conglinne. In this Vision there is a
description of a castle made out of different kinds of food.
The English for part of the poem goes like this:

> A lake of new milk I beheld
> In the midst of a fair plain.
> I saw a well-appointed house
> Thatched with butter.
>
> Its two soft door-posts of custard,
> Its dais of curds and butter,
> Beds of glorious lard,
> Many shields of thin pressed cheese.
>
> Under the straps of those shields
> Were men of soft sweet smooth cheese,
> Men who knew not to wound a Gael,
> Spears of old butter had each of them.
>
> A huge cauldron full of meat
> (Methought I'd try to tackle it),

Boiled, leafy kale, browny-white,
A brimming vessel full of milk.

A bacon house of two-score ribs,
A wattling of tripe—support of clans—
Of every food pleasant to man,
Meseemed the whole was gathered there.

Of chitterlings of pigs were made
Its beautiful rafters,
Splendid the beams and the pillars
Of marvellous pork.

The boys stood there in wonder and nausea, before just such a stronghold. It rose from its lake of milk in a mystic light of its own—in a greasy, buttery glow. It was the fairy aspect of Castle Chariot, which the Oldest Ones—sensing the hidden knife blades after all—had thought would be tempting to the children. It was to tempt them to eat.

The place smelt like a grocer's, a butcher's, a dairy and a fishmonger's, rolled into one. It was horrible beyond belief—sweet, sickly and pungent—so that they did not feel the least wish to swallow a particle of it. The real temptation was, to run away.

However, there were prisoners to rescue.

They plodded over the filthy drawbridge—a butter one, with cow hairs still in it—sinking to their ankles. They shuddered at the tripe and the chitterlings. They pointed their iron knives at the soldiers made of soft, sweet, smooth cheese, and the latter shrank away.

In the end they came to the inner chamber, where Morgan le Fay herself lay stretched upon her bed of glorious lard.

She was a fat, dowdy, middle-aged woman with black hair and a slight moustache, but she was made of human flesh. When she saw the knives, she kept her eyes shut—as if she were in a trance. Perhaps, when she was outside this very strange castle, or when she was not doing that kind of magic to tempt the appetite, she was able to assume more beautiful forms.

The prisoners were tied to pillars of marvellous pork.

"I am sorry if this iron is hurting you," said Kay, "but we have come to rescue our friends."

Queen Morgan shuddered.

"Will you tell your cheesy men to undo them?"

She would not.

"It is magic," said the Wart. "Do you think we ought to go up and kiss her, or something frightful like that?"

"Perhaps if we went and touched her with the iron?"

"You do it."

"No, you."

"We'll go together."

So they joined hands to approach the Queen. She began to writhe in her lard like a slug. She was in agony from the metal.

At last, and just before they reached her, there was a sloshing rumble or mumble—and the whole fairy appearance of Castle Chariot melted together in collapse, leaving the five humans and one dog standing together in the forest clearing—which still smelt faintly of dirty milk.

"Gor-blimey!" said Friar Tuck. "Gor-blimey and cool! Dash my vig if I didn't think we was done for!"

"Master!" said Dog Boy.

Cavall contented himself with barking wildly, biting their toes, lying on his back, trying to wag his tail in that position, and generally behaving like an idiot. Old Wat touched his forelock.

"Now then," said Kay, "this is my adventure, and we must get home quick."

# 12

But Morgan le Fay, although in her fairy shape she could not stand iron, still had the griffin. She had cast it loose from its golden chain, by a spell, the moment her castle disappeared.

The outlaws were pleased with their success, and less careful than they should have been. They decided to take a detour round the place where they had seen the monster tied up, and marched away through the darksome trees without a thought of danger.

There was a noise like a railway train letting off its whistle, and, answering to it—riding on it like the voice of the Arabian Bird—Robin Wood's horn of silver began to blow. "Tone, ton, tavon, tontavon, tantontavon, tontantontavon," went the horn. "Moot, troot, trourourout, troutourourout. Troot, troot. Tran, tran, tran, tran."

Robin was blowing his hunting music and the ambushed archers swung round as the griffin charged. They set forward their left feet in the same movement and let fly such a shower of arrows as it had been snow.

The Wart saw the creature stagger in its tracks, a cloth-yard shaft sprouting from between the shoulder blades. He saw his own arrow fly wide, and eagerly bent to snatch another from his belt. He saw the rank of his companion archers sway as if by a preconcerted signal, when each man stooped for a second shaft. He heard the bowstrings twang again, the purr of the feathers in the air. He saw the phalanx of arrows gleam like an eyeflick in the moonlight. All his life up to then he had been shooting into straw targets which made a noise like Phutt! He had often longed to hear the noise that these clean and deadly missiles would make in solid flesh. He heard it.

But the griffin's plates were as thick as a crocodile's and all but the best placed arrows glanced off. It still came on. It squealed as it came. Men began to fall, swept to the left or right by the lashing tail.

The Wart was fitting an arrow to his bow. The cock feather would not go right. Everything was in slow motion.

He saw the huge body coming blackly through the moon-glare. He felt the claw which took him in the chest. He felt himself turning somersaults slowly, with a cruel weight on top of him. He saw Kay's face somewhere in the cartwheel of the universe, flushed with starlit excitement, and Maid Marian's on the other side with its mouth open, shouting. He thought, before he slid into blackness, that it was shouting at him.

They dragged him from under the dead griffin and found Kay's arrow sticking in its eye. It had died in its leap.

Then there was a time which made him feel sick—while Robin set his collar-bone and made him a sling from the green cloth of his hood—and after that the whole band lay down to sleep, dog-tired, beside the body. It was too late to return to Sir Ector's castle, or even to get back to the outlaws' camp by the big tree. The dangers of the expedition

were over and all that could be done that night was to make
fires, post sentries, and sleep where they were.

Wart did not sleep much. He sat propped against a tree,
watching the red sentries passing to and fro in the firelight,
hearing their quiet passwords and thinking about the excitements of the day. These went round and round in his
head, sometimes losing their proper order and happening
backwards or by bits. He saw the leaping dragon, heard
Marian shouting "Good shot!", listened to the humming of
the bees muddled up with the stridulation of the grasshoppers, and shot and shot, hundreds and thousands of times,
at popinjays which turned into griffins. Kay and the liberated Dog Boy slept twitching beside him, looking alien and
incomprehensible as people do when they are asleep, and
Cavall, lying at his good shoulder, occasionally licked his
hot cheeks. The dawn came slowly, so slowly and pausingly
that it was impossible to determine when it really had
dawned, as it does during the summer months.

"Well," said Robin, when they had wakened and eaten
the breakfast of bread and cold venison which they had
brought with them, "you will have to love us and leave us,
Kay. Otherwise I shall have Sir Ector fitting out an expedition against me, to fetch you back. Thank you for your
help. Can I give you any little present as a reward?"

"It has been lovely," said Kay. "Absolutely lovely. May I
have the griffin I shot?"

"He will be too heavy to carry. Why not take his head?"

"That would do," said Kay, "if somebody would not
mind cutting it off. It was my griffin."

"What are you going to do about old Wat?" asked the
Wart.

"It depends on what he wants to do. Perhaps he will like
to run off by himself and eat acorns, as he used to, or if he
likes to join our band we shall be glad to have him. He ran
away from your village in the first place, so I don't suppose
he will care to go back there. What do you think?"

"If you are going to give me a present," said the Wart,
slowly, "I would like to have him. Do you think that would
be right?"

"As a matter of fact," said Robin, "I don't. I don't think
you can very well give people as presents: they might not
like it. That is what we Saxons feel, at any rate. What did
you intend to do with him?"

"I don't want to keep him or anything like that. You see,

we have a tutor who is a magician and I thought he might be able to restore him to his wits."

"Good boy," said Robin. "Have him by all means. I am sorry I made a mistake. At least, we will ask him if he would like to go."

When somebody had gone off to fetch Wat, Robin said, "You had better talk to him yourself."

They brought the poor old man, smiling, confused, hideous and very dirty, and stood him before Robin.

"Go on," said Robin.

The Wart did not know quite how to put it, but he said, "I say, Wat, would you like to come home with me, please, just for a little?"

"AhnaNanaWarraBaaBaa," said Wat, pulling his forelock, smiling, bowing and gently waving his arms in various directions.

"Come with me?"

"WanaNanaWanawana."

"Dinner?" asked the Wart in desperation.

"R!" cried the poor creature affirmatively, and his eyes glowed with pleasure at the prospect of being given something to eat.

"That way," said the Wart, pointing in the direction which he knew by the sun to be that of his guardian's castle. "Dinner. Come with. I take."

"Measter," said Wat, suddenly remembering one word, the word which he had always been accustomed to offer to the great people who made him a present of food, his only livelihood. It was decided.

"Well," said Robin, "it has been a good adventure and I am sorry you are going. I hope I shall see you again."

"Come any time," said Marian, "if you are feeling bored. You only have to follow the glades. And you, Wart, be careful of that collar-bone for a few days."

"I will send some men with you to the edge of the chase," said Robin. "After that you must go by yourselves. I expect the Dog Boy can carry the griffin's head."

"Good-bye," said Kay.

"Good-bye," said Robin.

"Good-bye," said Wart.

"Good-bye," said Marian, smiling.

"Good-bye," cried all the outlaws, waving their bows.

And Kay and the Wart and the Dog Boy and Wat and Cavall and their escort set off on the long track home.

They had an immense reception. The return on the previous day of all the hounds, except Cavall and the Dog Boy, and in the evening the failure to return of Kay and Wart, had set the household in an uproar. Their nurse had gone into hysterics—Hob had stayed out till midnight scouring the purlieus of the forest—the cooks had burnt the joint for dinner—and the sergeant-at-arms had polished all the armour twice and shapened all the swords and axes to a razor blade in case of an invasion. At last somebody had thought of consulting Merlyn, whom they had found in the middle of his third nap. The magician, for the sake of peace and quietness to go on with his rest, had used his insight to tell Sir Ector exactly what the boys were doing, where they were, and when they might be expected back. He had prophesied their return to the minute.

So, when the small procession of returning warriors came within sight of the drawbridge, they were greeted by the whole household. Sir Ector was standing in the middle with a thick walking-stick with which he proposed to whack them for going out of bounds and causing so much trouble; the nurse had insisted on bringing out a banner which used to be put up when Sir Ector came home for the holidays, as a small boy, and this said Welcome Home; Hob had forgotten about his beloved hawks and was standing on one side, shading his eagle eyes to get the first view; the cooks and all the kitchen staff were banging pots and pans, singing "Will Ye No Come Back Again?" or some such music, out of tune; the kitchen cat was yowling; the hounds had escaped from the kennel because there was nobody to look after them, and were preparing to chase the kitchen cat; the sergeant-at-arms was blowing out his chest with pleasure so far that he looked as if he might burst at any moment, and was commanding everybody in an important voice to get ready to cheer when he said, "One, Two!"

"One, Two!" cried the sergeant.

"Huzza!" cried everybody obediently, including Sir Ector.

"Look what I have got," shouted Kay. "I have shot a griffin and the Wart has been wounded."

"Yow-yow-yow!" barked all the hounds, and poured over the Dog Boy, licking his face, scratching his chest, sniffing him all over to see what he had been up to, and looking hopefully at the griffin's head which the Dog Boy held high in the air so that they could not eat it.

"Bless my soul!" exclaimed Sir Ector.

"Alas, the poor Phillip Sparrow," cried the nurse, dropping her banner. "Pity his poor arm all to-brast in a green sling, God bless us!"

"It is all right," said the Wart. "Ah, don't catch hold of me. It hurts."

"May I have it stuffed?" asked Kay.

"Well, I be dommed," said Hob. "Be'nt thick wold chappie our Wat, that erst run lunatical?"

"My dear, dear boys," said Sir Ector. "I am so glad to see you back."

"Wold chuckle-head," exclaimed the nurse triumphantly. "Where be thy girt cudgel now?"

"Hem!" said Sir Ector. "How dare you go out of bounds and put us all to this anxiety?"

"It is a real griffin," said Kay, who knew there was nothing to be afraid of. "I shot dozens of them. Wart broke his collar-bone. We rescued the Dog Boy and Wat."

"That comes of teaching the young Hidea 'ow to shoot," said the sergeant proudly.

Sir Ector kissed both boys and commanded the griffin to be displayed before him.

"Well!" he exclaimed. "What a monster! We'll have him stuffed in the dinin'-hall. What did you say his measurements were?"

"Eighty-two inches from ear to ear. Robin said it might be a record."

"We shall have to get it chronicled."

"It is rather a good one, isn't it?" remarked Kay with studied calm.

"I shall have it set up by Sir Rowland Ward," Sir Ector went on in high delight, "with a little ivory card with KAY'S FIRST GRIFFIN on it in black letters, and the date."

"Arrah, leave thy childishness," exclaimed the nurse. "Now, Master Art, my innocent, be off with thee to thy bed upon the instant. And thou, Sir Ector, let thee think shame to be playing wi' monsters' heads like a godwit when the poor child stays upon the point of death. Now, sergeant, leave puffing of thy chest. Stir, man, and take horse to Cardoyle for the chirurgeon."

She waved her apron at the sergeant, who collapsed his chest and retreated like a shoo'd chicken.

"It is all right," said the Wart, "I tell you. It is only a broken collar-bone, and Robin set it for me last night. It does not hurt a bit."

"Leave the boy, nurse," commanded Sir Ector, taking sides with the men against the women, anxious to re-establish his superiority after the matter of the cudgel. "Merlyn will see to him if he needs it, no doubt. Who is this Robin?"

"Robin Wood," cried the boys together.

"Never heard of him."

"You call him Robin Hood," explained Kay in a superior tone. "But it is Wood really, like the Wood that he is the spirit of."

"Well, well, well, so you've been foragin' with that rascal! Come in to breakfast, boys, and tell me all about him."

"We have had breakfast," said the Wart, "hours ago. May I please take Wat with me to see Merlyn?"

"Why, it's the old man who went wild and started rootin' in the forest. Wherever did you get hold of him?"

"The Good People had captured him with the Dog Boy and Cavall."

"But we shot the griffin," Kay put in. "I shot it myself."

"So now I want to see if Merlyn can restore him to his wits."

"Master Art," said the nurse sternly. She had been breathless up to now on account of Sir Ector's rebuke. "Master Art, thy room and thy bed is where thou art tending to, and that this instant. Wold fools may be wold fools, whether by yea or by nay, but I ha'nt served the Family for fifty year without a-learning of my duty. A flibberty-gibbeting about wi' a lot of want-wits, when thy own arm may be dropping to the floor!

"Yes, thou wold turkey-cock," she added, turning fiercely upon Sir Ector, "and thou canst keep thy magician away from the poor mite's room till he be rested, that thou canst!"

"A-wantoning wi' monsters and lunaticals," continued the victor as she led her helpless captive from the stricken field. "I never heard the like."

"Please someone to tell Merlyn to look after Wat," cried the victim over his shoulder, in diminishing tones.

He woke up in his cool bed, feeling better. The old fire-eater who looked after him had covered the windows with a curtain, so that the room was dark and comfortable, but he could tell by the one ray of golden sunlight which shot across the floor that it was late afternoon. He not only felt better. He felt very well, so well that it was not possible to stay in bed. He moved quickly to throw back the sheet but stopped with a hiss at the creak or scratch of his shoulder, which he had forgotten in his sleep. Then he got out more carefully by sliding down the bed and pushing himself upright with one hand, shoved his bare feet into a pair of slippers, and managed to wrap a dressing-gown round him more or less. He padded off through the stone passages up the worn circular stairs to find Merlyn.

When he reached the schoolroom, he found that Kay was continuing his First Rate Eddication. He was doing dictation, for as Wart opened the door he heard Merlyn pronouncing in measured tones the famous mediaeval mnemonic: "Barabara Celarent Darii Ferioque Prioris," and Kay saying, "Wait a bit. My pen has gone all squee-gee."

"You will catch it," remarked Kay, when they saw him. "You are supposed to be in bed, dying of gangrene or something."

"Merlyn," said the Wart. "What have you done with Wat?"

"You should try to speak without assonances," said the wizard. "For instance, 'The beer is never clear near here, dear,' is unfortunate, even as an assonance. And then again, your sentence is ambiguous to say the least of it. 'What what?' I might reply, taking it to be a conundrum, or if I were King Pellinore, 'What what, what?' Nobody can be too careful about their habits of speech."

Kay had evidently been doing his dictation well and the old gentleman was in a good humour.

"You know what I mean," said the Wart. "What have you done with the old man with no nose?"

"He has cured him," said Kay.

"Well," said Merlyn, "you might call it that, and then again you might not. Of course, when one has lived in the world as long as I have, and backwards at that, one does learn to know a thing or two about pathology. The wonders of analytical psychology and plastic surgery are, I am afraid, to this generation but a closed book."

"What did you do to him?"

"Oh, I just psycho-analysed him," replied the magician grandly. "That, and of course I sewed on a new nose on both of them."

"What kind of nose?" asked the Wart.

"It is too funny," said Kay. "He wanted to have the griffin's nose for one, but I would not let him. So then he took the noses off the young pigs which we are going to have for supper, and used those. Personally I think they will grunt."

"A ticklish operation," said Merlyn, "but a successful one."

"Well," said the Wart, doubtfully. "I hope it will be all right. What did they do then?"

"They went off to the kennels. Old Wat is very sorry for what he did to the Dog Boy, but he says he can't remember having done it. He says that suddenly everything went black, when they were throwing stones once, and he can't remember anything since. The Dog Boy forgave him and said he did not mind a bit. They are going to work together in the kennels in future, and not think of what is past any more. The Dog Boy says that the old man was good to him while they were prisoners of the Fairy Queen, and that he knows he ought not to have thrown stones at him in the first place. He says he often thought about that when other boys were throwing stones at him."

"Well," said the Wart, "I am glad it has all turned out for the best. Do you think I could go and visit them?"

"For heaven's sake, don't do anything to annoy your nurse," exclaimed Merlyn, looking about him anxiously. "That old woman hit me with a broom when I came to see you this forenoon, and broke my spectacles. Could you not wait until tomorrow?"

On the morrow Wat and the Dog Boy were the firmest of friends. Their common experiences of being stoned by the mob and then tied to columns of pork by Morgan le Fay served as a bond and a topic of reminiscence, as they lay among the dogs at night, for the rest of their lives. Also, by the morning, they had both pulled off the noses which Merlyn had kindly given them. They explained that they had got used to having no noses, now, and anyway they preferred to live with the dogs.

# 13

*In spite of his protests, the unhappy invalid was* confined to his chamber for three mortal days. He was alone except at bedtime, when Kay came, and Merlyn was reduced to shouting his eddication through the key-hole, at times when the nurse was known to be busy with her washing.

The boy's only amusement was the ant-nests—the ones between glass plates which had been brought when he first came from Merlyn's cottage in the forest.

"Can't you," he howled miserably under the door, "turn me into something while I'm locked up like this?"

"I can't get the spells through the key-hole."

"Through the what?"

"The KEY-HOLE."

"Oh!"

"Are you there?"

"Yes."

"What?"

"What?"

"Confusion take this shouting!" exclaimed the magician, stamping on his hat. "May Castor and Pollux. . . . No, not again. God bless my blood pressure. . . ."

"Could you turn me into an ant?"

"A what?"

"An ANT! It would be a small spell for ants, wouldn't it? It would go through the key-hole?"

"I don't think we ought to."

"Why?"

"They are dangerous."

"You could watch with your insight, and turn me back again if it got too bad. Please turn me into something, or I shall go weak in the head."

"The ants are not our Norman ones, dear boy. They come from the Afric shore. They are belligerent."

"I don't know what belligerent is."

There was a long silence behind the door.

"Well," said Merlyn eventually. "It is far too soon in your education. But you would have had to do it sometime. Let me see. Are there two nests in that contraption?"

"There are two pairs of plates."

"Take a rush from the floor and lean it between the two nests, like a bridge. Have you done that?"

"Yes."

The place where he was seemed like a great field of boulders, with a flattened fortress at one end of it—between the glass plates. The fortress was entered by tunnels in the rock, and, over the entrance to each tunnel, there was a notice which said:

EVERYTHING NOT FORBIDDEN IS COMPULSORY

He read the notice with dislike, though he did not understand its meaning. He thought to himself: I will explore a little, before going in. For some reason the notice gave him a reluctance to go, making the rough tunnel look sinister.

He waved his antennae carefully, considering the notice, assuring himself of his new senses, planting his feet squarely in the insect world as if to brace himself in it. He cleaned his antennae with his forefeet, frisking and smoothing them so that he looked like a Victorian villain twirling his moustachios. He yawned—for ants do yawn—and stretch themselves too, like human beings. Then he became conscious of something which had been waiting to be noticed—that there was a noise in his head which was articulate. It was either a noise or a complicated smell, and the easiest way to explain it is to say that it was like a wireless broadcast. It came through his antennae.

The music had a monotonous rhythm like a pulse, and the words which went with it were about June—moon—noon—spoon, or Mammy—mammy—mammy—mammy, or Ever—never, or Blue—true—you. He liked them at first, especially the ones about Love—dove—above, until he found that they did not vary. As soon as they had been finished once, they were begun again. After an hour or two, they began to make him feel sick inside.

There was a voice in his head also, during the pauses of the music, which seemed to be giving directions. "All two-day-olds will be moved to the West Aisle" it would say, or "Number 210397/WD will report to the soup squad, in replacement for 333105/WD who has fallen off the nest." It was a fruity voice, but it seemed to be somehow impersonal —as if its charm were an accomplishment that had been practised, like a circus trick. It was dead.

The boy, or perhaps we ought to say the ant, walked away from the fortress as soon as he was prepared to walk about. He began exploring the desert of boulders uneasily, reluctant to visit the place from which the orders were coming, yet bored with the narrow view. He found small pathways among the boulders, wandering tracks both aimless and purposeful, which led toward the grain store, and also in various other directions which he could not understand. One of these paths ended at a clod with a natural hollow underneath it. In the hollow—again with the strange appearance of aimless purpose—he found two dead ants. They were laid there tidily but yet untidily, as if a very tidy person had taken them to the place, but had forgotten the reason when he got there. They were curled up, and did not seem to be either glad or sorry to be dead. They were there, like a couple of chairs.

While he was looking at the corpses, a live ant came down the pathway carrying a third one.

It said: "Hail, Barbarus!"

The boy said Hail, politely.

In one respect, of which he knew nothing, he was lucky. Merlyn had remembered to give him the proper smell for the nest—for, if he had smelled of any other nest, they would have killed him at once. If Miss Edith Cavell had been an ant, they would have had to write on her statue: SMELL IS NOT ENOUGH.

The new ant put down the cadaver vaguely and began dragging the other two in various directions. It did not seem to know where to put them. Or rather, it knew that a certain arrangement had to be made, but it could not figure how to make it. It was like a man with a tea-cup in one hand and a sandwich in the other, who wants to light a cigarette with a match. But, where the man would invent the idea of putting down the cup and sandwich—before picking up the cigarette and the match—this ant would have put down the sandwich and picked up the match, then it would have been down with the match and up with the cigarette, then down with the cigarette and up with the sandwich, then down with the cup and up with the cigarette, until finally it had put down the sandwich and picked up the match. It was inclined to rely on a series of accidents to achieve its object. It was patient, and did not think. When it had pulled the three dead ants into several positions, they would fall into line under the clod eventually, and that was its duty.

Wart watched the arrangements with a surprise which turned into vexation and then into dislike. He felt like asking why it did not think things out in advance—the annoyed feeling which people have on seeing a job being badly done. Later he began to wish that he could put several other questions, such as "Do you like being a sexton?" or "Are you a slave?" or even "Are you happy?"

The extraordinary thing was that he could not ask these questions. In order to ask them, he would have had to put them into ant language through his antennae—and he now discovered, with a helpless feeling, that there were no words for the things he wanted to say. There were no words for happiness, for freedom, for liking, nor were there any words for their opposites. He felt like a dumb man trying to shout "Fire!" The nearest he could get to Right or Wrong, even, was to say Done or Not Done.

The ant finished fiddling with its corpses and turned back down the pathway, leaving them in the haphazard order. It found that the Wart was in its way, so it stopped, waving its wireless aerials at him as if it were a tank. With its mute, menacing helmet of a face, and its hairiness, and the things like spurs on the front leg-joint, perhaps it was more like a knight-in-armour on an armoured horse: or like a combination of the two, a hairy centaur-in-armour.

It said "Hail, Barbarus!" again.

"Hail!"

"What are you doing?"

The boy answered truthfully: "I am not doing anything."

It was baffled by this for several seconds, as you would be if Einstein had told you his latest ideas about space. Then it extended the twelve joints of its aerial and spoke past him into the blue.

It said: "105978/UDC reporting from square five. There is an insane ant on square five. Over to you."

The word it used for insane was Not-Done. Later on, the Wart discovered that there were only two qualifications in the language, Done and Not-Done—which applied to all questions of value. If the seeds which the collectors found were sweet, they were Done seeds. If somebody had doctored them with corrosive sublimate, they would have been Not-Done seeds, and that was that. Even the moons, mammies, doves, etc., in the broadcasts were completely described when they were stated to be done ones.

The broadcast stopped for a moment, and the fruity voice said: "G.H.Q. replying to 105978/UDC. What is its number? Over."

The ant asked: "What is your number?"

"I don't know."

When this news had been exchanged with headquarters, a message came back to ask whether he could give an account of himself. The ant asked him. It used the same words as the broadcaster had used, and in the same voice. This made him feel uncomfortable and angry, two emotions which he disliked.

"Yes," he said sarcastically, for it was obvious that the creature could not detect sarcasm, "I have fallen on my head and can't remember anything about it."

"105978/UDC reporting. Not-Done ant has a blackout from falling off the nest. Over."

"G.H.Q. replying to 105978/UDC. Not-Done ant is number 42436/WD, who fell off the nest this morning while working with mash squad. If it is competent to continue its duties—" Competent-to-continue-its-duties was easier in the ant speech, for it was simply Done, like everything else that was not Not Done. But enough of the language question. "If it is competent to continue its duties, instruct 42436/WD to rejoin mash squad, relieving 210021/WD, who was sent to replace it. Over."

The creature repeated the message.

It seemed that he could not have made a better explanation than this one about falling on his head, even if he had meant to—for the ants did occasionally tumble off. They were a species of ant called Messor barbarus.

"Very well."

The sexton paid no further attention to him, but crawled off down the path for another body, or for anything else that needed to be scavenged.

The Wart took himself away in the opposite direction, to join the mash squad. He memorized his own number and the number of the unit who had to be relieved.

The mash squad were standing in one of the outer chambers of the fortress like a circle of worshippers. He joined the circle, announcing that 210021/WD was to return to the main nest. Then he began filling himself with the sweet mash like the others. They made it by scraping the seeds which others had collected, chewing up the scrapings till they made a kind of paste or soup, and then swallowing it into their own crops. At first it was delicious to him, so that he ate greedily, but in a few seconds it began to be unsatisfactory. He could not understand why. He chewed and swallowed busily, copying the rest of the squad, but it was like eating a banquet of nothing, or like a dinner-party on the stage. In a way it was like a nightmare, in which you might continue to consume huge masses of putty without being able to stop.

There was a coming and going round the pile of seeds. The ants who had filled their crops to the brim were walking back to the inner fortress, to be replaced by a procession of empty ants who were coming from the same direction. There were never any new ants in the procession, only this same dozen going backward and forward, as they would do during all their lives.

He realized suddenly that what he was eating was not going into his stomach. A small proportion of it had penetrated to his private self at the beginning, and now the main mass was being stored in a kind of upper stomach or crop, from which it could be removed. It dawned on him at the same time that when he joined the westward stream he would have to disgorge the store, into a larder or something of that sort.

The mash squad conversed with each other while they worked. He thought this was a good sign at first, and listened, to pick up what he could.

"Oh Ark!" one of them would say. "Ear comes that Mammy—mammy—mammy—mammy song again. I dew think that Mammy—mammy—mammy—mammy song is loverly (done). It is so high-class (done)."

Another would remark, "I dew think our beloved Leader is wonderful, don't yew? They sigh she was stung three hundred times in the last war, and was awarded the Ant Cross for Valour."

"How lucky we are to be born in the 'A' nest, don't yew think, and wouldn't it be hawful to be one of those orrid 'B's."

"Wasn't it hawful about 310099/WD! Of course e was

hexecuted at once, by special order of ar beloved Leader."

"Oh Ark! Ear comes that Mammy—mammy—mammy —mammy song again. I dew think . . ."

He walked away to the nest with a full gorge, leaving them to do the round again. They had no news, no scandal, nothing to talk about. Novelties did not happen to them. Even the remarks about the executions were in a formula, and only varied as to the registration number of the criminal. When they had finished with the mammy—mammy— mammy—mammy, they had to go on to the beloved Leader, and then to the filthy Barbarus B and to the latest execution. It went round in a circle. Even the beloveds, wonderfuls, luckies and so on were all Dones, and the awfuls were Not-Dones.

The boy found himself in the hall of the fortress, where hundreds and hundreds of ants were licking or feeding in the nurseries, carrying grubs to various aisles to get an even temperature, and opening or closing the ventilation passages. In the middle, the Leader sat complacently, laying eggs, attending to the broadcasts, issuing directions or commanding executions, surrounded by a sea of adulation. (He learned from Merlyn later that the method of succession among these Leaders was variable according to the different kind of ant. In Bothriomyrmex, for instance, the ambitious founder of a New Order would invade a nest of Tapinoma and jump on the back of the older tyrant. There, concealed by the smell of her host, she would slowly saw off the latter's head, until she herself had achieved the right of leadership.)

There was no larder for his store of mash, after all. When anybody wanted a meal, they stopped him, got him to open his mouth, and fed from it. They did not treat him as a person, and indeed, they were impersonal themselves. He was a dumbwaiter from which dumb-diners fed. Even his stomach was not his own.

But we need not go on about the ants in too much detail—they are not a pleasant subject. It is enough to say that the boy went on living among them, conforming to their habits, watching them so as to understand as much as he could, but unable to ask questions It was not only that their language had not got the words in which humans are interested—so that it would have been *impossible* to ask them whether they believed in Life, Liberty and the Pursuit of Happiness—but also that it was dangerous to ask questions at all. A question was a sign of insanity to them. Their life was not questionable: it was dictated. He crawled from nest to seeds and back again, exclaimed that the Mammy song was loverly, opened his jaws to regurgitate, and tried to understand as well as he could.

Later in the afternoon a scouting ant wandered across the rush bridge which Merlyn had commanded him to make. It was an ant of exactly the same species, but it came from the other nest. It was met by one of the scavenging ants and murdered.

The broadcasts changed after this news had been reported —or rather, they changed as soon as it had been discovered by spies that the other nest had a good store of seeds.

*Mammy—mammy—mammy* gave place to *Antland, Antland Over All,* and the stream of orders were discontinued in favour of lectures about war, patriotism or the economic situation. The fruity voice said that their beloved country was being encircled by a horde of filthy Other-nesters—at which the wireless chorus sang:

> When Other blood spurts from the knife,
> Then everything is fine.

It also explained that Ant the Father had ordained in his wisdom that Othernest pismires should always be the slaves of Thisnest ones. Their beloved country had only one feeding tray at present—a disgraceful state of affairs which would have to be remedied if the dear race were not to perish. A third statement was that the national property of Thisnest was being threatened. Their boundaries were to be violated, their domestic animals, the beetles, were to be kidnapped, and their communal stomach would be starved. The Wart listened to two of these broadcasts carefully, so that he would be able to remember them afterwards.

The first one was arranged as follows:

A. We are so numerous that we are starving.
B. Therefore we must encourage still larger families so as to become yet more numerous and starving.
C. When we are so numerous and starving as all that, obviously we shall have a right to take other people's stores of seed. Besides, we shall by then have a numerous and starving army.

It was only after this logical train of thought had been put into practice, and the output of the nurseries trebled—both nests meanwhile getting ample mash for all their needs from Merlyn—for it has to be admitted that starving nations never seem to be quite so starving that they cannot afford to have far more expensive armaments than anybody else—it was only then that the second type of lecture was begun.

This is how the second kind went:

A. We are more numerous than they are, therefore we have a right to their mash.
B. They are more numerous than we are, therefore they are wickedly trying to steal our mash.
C. We are a mighty race and have a natural right to subjugate their puny one.
D. They are a mighty race and are unnaturally trying to subjugate our inoffensive one.
E. We must attack them in self-defence.
F. They are attacking us by defending themselves.
G. If we do not attack them today, they will attack us tomorrow.
H. In any case we are not attacking them at all. We are offering them incalculable benefits.

After the second kind of address, the religious services began. These dated—the Wart discovered later—from a fabulous past so ancient that one could scarcely find a date for it—a past in which the emmets had not yet settled down to communism. They came from a time when ants were still like men, and very impressive some of the services were.

A psalm at one of them—beginning, if we allow for the difference of language, with the well-known words, "The earth is the Sword's and all that therein is, the compass of the bomber and they that bomb therefrom"—ended with the terrific conclusion: "Blow up your heads, O ye Gates, and be ye blown up, ye Everlasting Doors, that the King of Glory may come in. Who is the King of Glory? Even the Lord of Ghosts, He is the King of Glory."

A strange feature was that the ordinary ants were not excited by the songs, nor interested by the lectures. They accepted them as matters of course. They were rituals to them, like the Mammy songs or the conversations about their Beloved Leader. They did not look at these things as good or bad, exciting, rational or terrible. They did not look at them at all, but accepted them as Done.

The time for the war came soon enough. The preparations were in order, the soldiers were drilled to the last ounce, the walls of the nest had patriotic slogans written on them, such as *"Stings or Mash?"* or *"I Vow to Thee, my Smell,"* and the Wart was past hoping. The repeating voices in his head, which he could not shut off—the lack of privacy, under which others ate from his stomach while others again sang in his brain—the dreary blank which replaced feeling—the dearth of all but two values—the total monotony more than the wickedness: these had begun to kill the joy of life which belonged to his boyhood.

The horrible armies were on the point of joining battle, to dispute the imaginary boundary between their glass trays when Merlyn came to his rescue. He magicked the sickened explorer of animals back to bed, and glad enough he was to be there.

# 14

*In the autumn everybody was preparing for the* winter. At night they spent the time rescuing Daddy-long-legs from their candles and rushlights. In the daytime the cows were turned into the high stubble and weeds which had been left by the harvest sickles. The pigs were driven into the purlieus of the forest, where boys beat the trees to supply them with acorns. Everybody was at a different job. From the granary there proceeded an invariable thumping of flails; in the strip fields the slow and enormously heavy wooden ploughs sailed up and down for the rye and the wheat, while the sowers swung rhythmically along, with their hoffers round their necks, casting right hand for left foot and vice versa. Foraging parties came lumbering in with their spike-wheeled carts full of bracken, remarking wisely that they must:

> Get whome with ee breakes ere all summer be gone
> For tethered up cattle to sit down upon,

while others dragged in timber for the castle fires. The forest rang in the sharp air with the sound of beetle and wedge.

Everybody was happy. The Saxons were slaves to their Norman masters if you chose to look at it in one way—but, if you chose to look at it in another, they were the same farm labourers who get along on too few shillings a week today. Only neither the villein nor the farm labourer starved, when the master was a man like Sir Ector. It has never been an economic proposition for an owner of cattle to starve his cows, so why should an owner of slaves starve them? The truth is that even nowadays the farm labourer accepts so little money because he does not have to throw his soul in with the bargain—as he would have to do in a town— and the same freedom of spirit has obtained in the country since the earliest times. The villeins were labourers. They lived in the same one-roomed hut with their families, few chickens, litter of pigs, or with a cow possibly called Crumbocke—most dreadful and insanitary! But they liked it. They were healthy, free of an air with no factory smoke in it, and, which was most of all to them, their heart's interest was bound up with their skill in labour. They knew that Sir Ector was proud of them. They were more valuable to him than his cattle even, and, as he valued his cattle more than anything else except his children, this was saying a good deal. He walked and worked among his villagers, thought of their welfare, and could tell the good workman from the bad. He was the eternal farmer, in fact—one of those people who seem to be employing labour at so many shillings a week, but who are actually paying half as much again in voluntary overtime, providing a cottage free, and possibly making an extra present of milk and eggs and home-brewed beer into the bargain.

In other parts of Gramarye, of course, there did exist wicked and despotic masters—feudal gangsters whom it was to be King Arthur's destiny to chasten—but the evil was in the bad people who abused it, not in the feudal system.

Sir Ector was moving through these activities with a brow of thunder. When an old lady who was sitting in a hedge by one of the strips of wheat, to scare away the rooks and pigeons, suddenly rose up beside him with an unearthly screech, he jumped nearly a foot in the air. He was in a nervous condition.

"Dang it," said Sir Ector. Then, considering the subject more attentively, he added in a loud, indignant voice, "Splendour of God!" He took the letter out of his pocket and read it again.

The Overlord of The Castle of Forest Sauvage was more than a farmer. He was a military captain, who was ready to organize and lead the defence of his estate against the gangsters, and he was a sportsman who sometimes took a day's joustin' when he could spare the time. But he was not only these. Sir Ector was an M.F.H.—or rather a Master of stag and other hounds—and he hunted his own pack himself. Clumsy, Trowneer, Phoebe, Colle, Gerland, Talbot, Luath, Luffra, Apollon, Orthros, Bran, Gelert, Bounce, Boy, Lion, Bungey, Toby, Diamond and Cavall were not pet dogs. They were the Forest Sauvage Hounds, no subscription, two days a week, huntsman the Master.

This is what the letter said, if we translate it from Latin:

The King to Sir Ector, etc.

We send you William Twyti, our huntsman, and his fellows to hunt in the Forest Sauvage with our boarhounds (canibus nostris porkericis) in order that they may capture two or three boars. You are to cause the flesh they capture to be salted and kept in good condition, but the skins you are to cause to be bleached which they give you, as the said William shall tell you. And we command you to provide necessaries for them as long as they shall be with you by our command, and the cost, etc., shall be accounted, etc.

Witnessed at the Tower of London, 20 November, in the twelfth year of our reign.

UTHER PENDRAGON

12 Uther.

Now the forest belonged to the King, and he had every right to send his hounds to hunt in it. Also he maintained a number of hungry mouths—what with his court and his army—so that it was natural that he should want as many dead boars, bucks, roes, etc., to be salted down as possible.

He was in the right. This did not take away the fact that Sir Ector regarded the forest as *his* forest, and resented the intrusion of the royal hounds—as if his own would not do just as well! The King had only to send for a couple of boars and he would have been delighted to supply them himself. He feared that his coverts would be disturbed by a lot of wild royal retainers—never know what these city chaps will be up to next—and that the King's huntsman, this fellow Twyti, would sneer at his humble hunting establishment, unsettle the hunt servants and perhaps even try to interfere with his own kennel management. In fact, Sir Ector was shy. Then there was another thing. Where the devil were the royal hounds to be kept? Was he, Sir Ector, to turn his own hounds into the street, so as to put the King's hounds in his kennels? "Splendour of God!" repeated the unhappy master. It was as bad as paying tithes.

Sir Ector put the accursed letter in his pocket and stumped off the ploughing. The villeins, seeing him go, remarked cheerfully, "Our wold measter be on the gad again seemingly."

It was a confounded piece of tyranny, that was what it was. It happened every year, but it was still that. He always solved the kennel problem in the same way, but it still worried him. He would have to invite his neighbours to the meet specially, to look as impressive as possible under the royal hunstman's eye, and this would mean sendin' messengers through the forest to Sir Grummore, etc. Then he would have to show sport. The King had written early, so that evidently he intended to send the fellow at the very beginnin' of the season. The season did not begin till the 25th of December. Probably the chap would insist on one of these damned Boxin' Day meets—all show-off and no business—with hundreds of foot people all hollerin' and headin' the boar and trampin' down the seeds and spoilin' sport generally. How the devil was he to know in November where the best boars would be on Boxin' Dáy? What with sounders and gorgeaunts and hogsteers, you never knew where you were. And another thing. A hound that was going to be used next summer for the proper Hart huntin' was always entered at Christmas to the boar. It was the very beginnin' of his eddication—which led up through hares and whatnots to its real quarry—and this meant that the fellow Twyti would be bringin' down a lot of raw puppies which would

be nothin' but a plague to everybody. "Dang it!" said Sir
Ector, and stamped upon a piece of mud.

He stood gloomily for a moment, watching his two boys
trying to catch the last leaves in the chase. They had not
gone out with that intention, and did not really, even in
those distant days, believe that every leaf you caught would
mean a happy month next year. Only, as the west wind
tore the golden rags away, they looked fascinating and difficult to catch. For the mere sport of catching them, of shouting and laughing and feeling giddy as they looked up, and
of darting about to trap the creatures, which were certainly
alive in the cunning with which they slipped away, the two
boys were prancing about like young fauns in the ruin of
the year. Wart's shoulder was well again.

The only chap, reflected Sir Ector, who could be really
useful in showin' the King's huntsman proper sport was that
fellow Robin Hood. Robin Wood, they seemed to be callin'
him now—some new-fangled idea, no doubt. But Wood or
Hood, he was the chap to know where a fine tush was to be
found. Been feastin' on the creatures for months now, he
would not be surprised, even if they were out of season.

But you could hardly ask a fellow to hunt up a few beasts
of venery for you, and then not invite him to the meet.
While, if you did invite him to the meet, what would the
King's huntsman and the neighbours say at havin' a parti-
san for a fellow guest? Not that this Robin Wood was not
a good fellow: he was a good chap, and a good neighbour
too. He had often tipped Sir Ector the wink when a raiding
party was on its way from the Marches, and he never mo-
lested the knight or his farming in any way. What did it
matter if he did chase himself a bit of venison now and
then? There was four hundred square miles of forest, so they
said, and enough for all. Leave well alone, that was Sir
Ector's motto. But that did not alter the neighbours.

Another thing was the riot. It was all very well for the
crack hunts in practically artificial forests like those at Wind-
sor, where the King hunted, but it was a different thing in
the Forest Sauvage. Suppose His Majesty's famous hounds
were to go runnin' riot after a unicorn or something? Everybody knew that you could never catch a unicorn without a
young virgin for bait (in which case the unicorn meekly
laid its white head and mother-of-pearl horn in her lap)
and so the puppies would go chargin' off into the forest for
leagues and leagues, and never catch it, and get lost, and

then what would Sir Ector say to his sovereign? It was not only unicorns. There was the Beast Glatisant that everybody had heard so much about. If you had the head of a serpent, the body of a leopard, the haunches of a lion, and were footed like a hart, and especially if you made a noise like thirty couple of hounds questin', it stood to reason that you would account for an excessive number of royal puppies before they pulled you down. Serve them right too. And what would King Pellinore say if Master William Twyti did succeed in killing his beast? Then there were the small dragons which lived under stones and hissed like kettles—dangerous varmints, very. Or suppose they were to come across one of the really big dragons? Suppose they was to run into a griffin?

Sir Ector considered the prospect moodily for some time, then began to feel better. It would be a jolly good thing, he concluded, if Master Twyti and his beastly dogs did meet the Questing Beast, yes, and get eaten up by it too, every one.

Cheered by this vision, he turned round at the edge of the ploughing and stumped off home. At the hedge where the old lady lay waiting to scare rooks he was lucky enough to spot some approaching pigeons before she was aware of him or them, which gave him a chance to let out such a screech that he felt amply repaid for his own jump by seeing hers. It was going to be a good evening after all. "Good night to you," said Sir Ector affably, when the old lady recovered herself enough to drop him a curtsey.

He felt so much restored by this that he called on the parish priest, half-way up the village street, and invited him to dinner. Then he climbed to the solar, which was his special chamber, and sat down heavily to write a submissive message to King Uther in the two or three hours which remained to him before the meal. It would take him quite that time, what with sharpening pens, using too much sand to blot with, going to the top of the stairs to ask the butler how to spell things, and starting again if he had made a mess.

Sir Ector sat in the solar, while the wintering sunlight threw broad orange beams across his bald head. He scratched and pluttered away, and laboriously bit the end of his pen, and the castle room darkened about him. It was a room as big as the main hall over which it stood, and it could afford to have large southern windows because it was on the second story. There were two fireplaces, in which the ashy logs of wood turned from grey to red as the sunlight retreated. Round these, some favourite hounds lay snuffling in their dreams, or scratching themselves for fleas, or gnawing mutton bones which they had scrounged from the kitchens. The peregrine falcon stood hooded on a perch in the corner, a motionless idol dreaming of other skies.

If you were to go now to view the solar of Castle Sauvage, you would find it empty of furniture. But the sun would still stream in at those stone windows two feet thick, and, as it barred the mullions, it would catch a warmth of sandstone from them—the amber light of age. If you went to the nearest curiosity shop you might find some clever copies of the furniture which it was supposed to contain. These would be oak chests and cupboards with Gothic panelling and strange faces of men or angels—or devils—carved darkly upon them, black, bees-waxed, worm-eaten and shiny—gloomy testimonies to the old life in their coffin-like solidity. But the furniture in the solar was not like that. The devil's heads were there and the linen-fold panelling, but the wood was six or seven or eight centuries younger. So, in the warm-looking light of sunset, it was not only the mullions which had an amber glow. All the spare, strong chests in the room (they were converted for sitting by laying bright carpets on them) were the young, the golden oak, and the cheeks of the devils and cherubim shone as if they had been given a good soaping.

# 15

It was Christmas night, the eve of the Boxing Day Meet. You must remember that this was in the old Merry England of Gramarye, when the rosy barons ate with their fingers, and had peacocks served before them with all their tail feathers streaming, or boars' heads with the tusks stuck in again—when there was no unemployment because there were too few people to be unemployed—when the forests rang with knights walloping each other on the helm, and the unicorns in the wintry moonlight stamped with their silver feet and snorted their noble breaths of blue upon the frozen air. Such marvels were great and comfortable ones. But in the Old England there was a greater marvel still. The weather behaved itself.

In the spring, the little flowers came out obediently in the meads, and the dew sparkled, and the birds sang. In the summer it was beautifully hot for no less than four months, and, if it did rain just enough for agricultural purposes, they managed to arrange it so that it rained while you were in bed. In the autumn the leaves flamed and rattled before the west winds, tempering their sad adieu with glory. And in the winter, which was confined by statute to two months, the snow lay evenly, three feet thick, but never turned into slush.

It was Christmas night in the Castle of the Forest Sauvage, and all around the castle the snow lay as it ought to lie. It hung heavily on the battlements, like thick icing on a very good cake, and in a few convenient places it modestly turned itself into the clearest icicles of the greatest possible length. It hung on the boughs of the forest trees in rounded lumps, even better than apple-blossom, and occasionally slid off the roofs of the village when it saw the chance of falling on some amusing character and giving pleasure to all. The boys made snowballs with it, but never put stones in them to hurt each other, and the dogs, when they were taken out to scombre, bit it and rolled in it, and looked surprised but delighted when they vanished into the bigger drifts. There was skating on the moat, which roared with the gliding bones which they used for skates, while hot chestnuts and spiced mead were served on the bank to all and sundry. The owls hooted. The cooks put out plenty of crumbs for the small birds. The villagers brought out their red mufflers. Sir Ector's face shone redder even than these. And reddest of all shone the cottage fires down the main street of an evening, while the winds howled outside and the old English wolves wandered about slavering in an appropriate manner, or sometimes peeping in at the key-holes with their blood-red eyes.

It was Christmas night and the proper things had been done. The whole village had come to dinner in hall. There had been boar's head and venison and pork and beef and mutton and capons—but no turkey, because this bird had not yet been invented. There had been plum pudding and snap-dragon, with blue fire on the tips of one's fingers, and as much mead as anybody could drink. Sir Ector's health had been drunk with "Best respects, Measter," or "Best compliments of the Season, my lords and ladies, and many of them." There had been mummers to play an exciting dramatic presentation of a story in which St. George and a Saracen and a funny Doctor did surprising things, also carol-singers who rendered "Adeste Fideles" and "I Sing of a Maiden," in high, clear, tenor voices. After that, those children who had not been sick from their dinner played Hoodman Blind and other appropriate games, while the young men and maidens danced morris dances in the middle, the tables having been cleared away. The old folks sat round the walls holding glasses of mead in their hands and feeling thankful that they were past such capers, hoppings and skippings, while those children who had not been sick sat with them, and soon went to sleep, the small heads leaning against their shoulders. At the high table Sir Ector sat with his knightly guests, who had come for the morrow's hunting, smiling and nodding and drinking burgundy or sherries sack or malmsey wine.

After a bit, silence was prayed for Sir Grummore. He stood up and sang his old school song, amid great applause —but forgot most of it and had to make a humming noise in his moustache. Then King Pellinore was nudged to his feet and sang bashfully:

"Oh, I was born a Pellinore in famous Lincolnshire.
Full well I chased the Questing Beast for more than
                                        seventeen year.
Till I took up with Sir Grummore here
In the season of the year.
(Since when) 'tis my delight
On a feather-bed night
To sleep at home, my dear.

"You see," explained King Pellinore blushing, as he sat down with everybody whacking him on the back, "old Grummore invited me home, what, after we had been having a pleasant joust together, and since then I've been letting my beastly Beast go and hang itself on the wall, what?"

"Well done," they told him. "You live your own life while you've got it."

William Twyti was called for, who had arrived on the

previous evening, and the famous huntsman stood up with a perfectly straight face, and his crooked eye fixed upon Sir Ector, to sing:

> "D'ye ken William Twyti
> With his jerkin so dagged?
> D'ye ken William Twyti
> Who never yet lagged?
> Yes, I ken William Twyti,
> And he ought to be gagged
> With his hounds and his horn in the morning."

"Bravo!" cried Sir Ector. "Did you hear that, eh? Said he ought to be gagged, my dear feller. Blest if I didn't think he was going to boast when he began. Splendid chaps, these huntsmen, eh? Pass Master Twyti the malmsey, with my compliments."

The boys lay curled up under the benches near the fire, Wart with Cavall in his arms. Cavall did not like the heat and the shouting and the smell of mead, and wanted to go away, but Wart held him tightly because he needed something to hug, and Cavall had to stay with him perforce, panting over a long pink tongue.

"Now Ralph Passelewe." "Good wold Ralph." "Who killed the cow, Ralph?" "Pray silence for Master Passelewe that couldn't help it."

At this the most lovely old man got up at the furthest and humblest end of the hall, as he had got up on all similar occasions for the past half-century. He was no less than eighty-five years of age, almost blind, almost deaf, but still able and willing and happy to quaver out the same song which he had sung for the pleasure of the Forest Sauvage since before Sir Ector was bound up in a kind of tight linen puttee in his cradle. They could not hear him at the high table—he was too far away in Time to be able to reach across the room—but everybody knew what the cracked voice was singing and everybody loved it. This is what he sang:

> "Whe-an/Wold King-Cole/was a /wakkin doon-t'street,
> H-e /saw a-lovely laid-y a /steppin-in-a-puddle. /
> She-a /lifted hup-er-skeat/
> For to /
> Hop acrorst ter middle, /

An ee /saw her. /an-kel.
Wasn't that a fuddle? /
Ee could'ernt elp it, /ee Ad to."


There were about twenty verses of this song, in which
Wold King Cole helplessly saw more and more things that
he ought not to have seen, and everybody cheered at the
end of each verse until, at the conclusion, old Ralph was
overwhelmed with congratulations and sat down smiling
dimly to a replenished mug of mead.

It was now Sir Ector's turn to wind up the proceedings.
He stood up importantly and delivered the following speech:

"Friends, tenants and otherwise. Unaccustomed as I am
to public speakin'—"

There was a faint cheer at this, for everybody recognized
the speech which Sir Ector had made for the last twenty
years, and welcomed it like a brother.

"—unaccustomed as I am to public speakin', it is my
pleasant duty—I might say my *very* pleasant duty—to welcome all and sundry to this our homely feast. It has been a
good year, and I say it without fear of contradiction, in
pasture and plow. We all know how Crumbocke of Forest
Sauvage won the first prize at Cardoyle Cattle Show for
the second time, and one more year will win the cup outright. More power to the Forest Sauvage. As we sit down
tonight, I notice some faces now gone from among us
and some which have added to the family circle. Such matters are in the hands of an almighty Providence, to which
we all feel thankful. We ourselves have been first created
and then spared to enjoy the rejoicin's of this pleasant evening. I think we are all grateful for the blessin's which have
been showered upon us. Tonight we welcome in our midst
the famous King Pellinore, whose labours in riddin' our
forest of the redoubtable Questin' Beast are known to all.
God bless King Pellinore. (Hear, hear!) Also Sir Grummore Grummursum, a sportsman, though I say it with his
face, who will stick to his mount as long as his Quest will
stand up in front of him. (Hooray!) Finally, last but not
least, we are honoured by a visit from His Majesty's most
famous huntsman, Master William Twyti, who will, I feel
sure, show us such sport tomorrow that we will rub our
eyes and wish that a royal pack of hounds could always be
huntin' in the Forest which we all love so well. (Viewhalloo
and several recheats blown in imitation.) Thank you, my

dear friends, for your spontaneous welcome to these gentlemen. They will, I know, accept it in the true and warm-hearted spirit in which it is offered. And now it is time that I should bring my brief remarks to a close. Another year has almost sped and it is time that we should be lookin' forward to the challengin' future. What about the Cattle Show next year? Friends, I can only wish you a very Merry Christmas, and, after Father Sidebottom has said our Grace for us, we shall conclude with a singin' of the National Anthem."

The cheers which broke out at the end of Sir Ector's speech were only just prevented, by several hush-es, from drowning the last part of the vicar's Grace in Latin, and then everybody stood up loyally in the firelight and sang:

> "God save King Pendragon,
>   May his reign long drag on,
>     God save the King.
>   Send him most gorious,
>   Great and uproarious,
>   Horrible and Hoarious,
>     God save our King."

The last notes died away, the hall emptied of its rejoicing humanity. Lanterns flickered outside, in the village street, as everybody went home in bands for fear of the moonlit wolves, and The Castle of the Forest Sauvage slept peacefully and lightless, in the strange silence of the holy snow.

# 16

*The Wart got up early next morning. He made a* determined effort the moment he woke, threw off the great bearskin rug under which he slept, and plunged his body into the biting air. He dressed furiously, trembling, skipping about to keep warm, and hissing blue breaths to himself as if he were grooming a horse. He broke the ice in a basin and dipped his face in it with a grimace like eating something sour, said A-a-ah, and rubbed his stinging cheeks vigorously with a towel. Then he felt quite warm again and scampered off to the emergency kennels, to watch the King's huntsman making his last arrangements.

Master William Twyti turned out in daylight to be a shrivelled, harassed-looking man, with an expression of melancholy on his face. All his life he had been forced to pursue various animals for the royal table, and, when he had caught them, to cut them up into proper joints. He was more than half a butcher. He had to know what parts the hounds should eat, and what parts should be given to his assistants. He had to cut everything up handsomely, leaving two vertebrae on the tail to make the chine look attractive, and almost ever since he could remember he had been either pursuing a hart or cutting it up into helpings.

He was not particularly fond of doing this. The harts and hinds in their herds, the boars in their singulars, the skulks of foxes, the richesses of martens, the bevies of roes, the cetes of badgers and the routs of wolves—all came to him more or less as something which you either skinned or flayed and then took home to cook. You could talk to him about os and argos, suet and grease, croteys, fewmets and fiants, but he only looked polite. He knew that you were showing off your knowledge of these words, which were to him a business. You could talk about a mighty boar which had nearly slashed you last winter, but he only stared at you with his distant eyes. He had been slashed sixteen times by mighty boars, and his legs had white weals of shiny flesh that stretched right up to his ribs. While you talked, he got on with whatever part of his profession he had in hand. There was only one thing which could move Master William Twyti. Summer or winter, snow or shine, he was running or galloping after boars and harts, and all the time his soul was somewhere else. Mention a *hare* to Master Twyti and, although he would still go on galloping after the wretched hart which seemed to be his destiny, he would gallop with one eye over his shoulder yearning for puss. It was the only thing he ever talked about. He was always being sent to one castle or another, all over England, and when he was there the local servants would fête him and keep his glass filled and ask him about his greatest hunts. He would answer distractedly in monosyllables. But if anybody mentioned a huske of hares he was all attention, and then he would thump his glass upon the table and discourse upon the marvels of this astonishing beast, declaring that you could never blow a menee for it, because the same hare could at one time be male and another time female, while it carried grease and croteyed and gnawed, which things no beast in the earth did except it.

Wart watched the great man in silence for some time, then went indoors to see if there was any hope of breakfast. He found that there was, for the whole castle was suffering from the same sort of nervous excitement which had got him out of bed so early, and even Merlyn had dressed himself in a pair of breeches which had been fashionable some centuries later with the University Beagles.

Boar-hunting was fun. It was nothing like badger-digging or covert-shooting or fox-hunting today. Perhaps the nearest thing to it would be ferreting for rabbits—except that you used dogs instead of ferrets, had a boar that easily might kill you, instead of a rabbit, and carried a boar-spear upon which your life depended instead of a gun. They did not usually hunt the boar on horseback. Perhaps the reason for this was that the boar season happened in the two winter months, when the old English snow would be liable to ball in your horse's hoofs and render galloping too dangerous. The result was that you were yourself on foot, armed only with steel, against an adversary who weighed a good deal more than you did and who could unseam you from the nave to the chaps, and set your head upon his battlements. There was only one rule in boar-hunting. It was: Hold on. If the boar charged, you had to drop on one knee and present your boar-spear in his direction. You held the butt of it with your right hand on the ground to take the shock, while you stretched your left arm to its fullest extent and kept the point toward the charging boar. The spear was as sharp as a razor, and it had a cross-piece about eighteen inches away from the point. This cross-piece or horizontal bar prevented the spear from going more than eighteen inches into his chest. Without the cross-piece, a charging boar would have been capable of rushing right up the spear, even if it did go through him, and getting at the hunter like that. But with the cross-piece he was held away from you at a spear's length, with eighteen inches of steel inside him. It was in this situation that you had to hold on.

He weighed between ten and twenty score, and his one

object in life was to heave and weave and sidestep, until he could get at his assailant and champ him into chops, while the assailant's one object was not to let go of the spear, clasped tight under his arm, until somebody had come to finish him off. If he could keep hold of his end of the weapon, while the other end was stuck in the boar, he knew that there was at least a spear's length between them, however much the boar ran him round the forest. You may be able to understand, if you think this over, why all the sportsmen of the castle got up early for the Boxing Day Meet, and ate their breakfast with a certain amount of suppressed feeling.

"Ah," said Sir Grummore, gnawing a pork chop which he held in his fingers, "down in time for breakfast, hey?"

"Yes, I am," said the Wart.

"Fine huntin' mornin'," said Sir Grummore. "Got your spear sharp, hey?"

"Yes, I have, thank you," said the Wart. He went over to the sideboard to get a chop for himself.

"Come on, Pellinore," said Sir Ector. "Have a few of these chickens. You're eatin' nothin' this mornin'."

King Pellinore said, "I don't think I will, thank you all the same. I don't think I feel quite the thing, this morning, what?"

Sir Grummore took his nose out of his chop and inquired sharply, "Nerves?"

"Oh, no," cried King Pellinore. "Oh, no, really not that, what? I think I must have taken something last night that disagreed with me."

"Nonsense, my dear fellah," said Sir Ector, "here you are, just you have a few chickens to keep your strength up."

He helped the unfortunate King to two or three capons, and the latter sat down miserably at the end of the table, trying to swallow a few bits of them.

"Need them," said Sir Grummore meaningly, "by the end of the day, I dare say."

"Do you think so?"

"Know so," said Sir Grummore, and winked at his host.

The Wart noticed that Sir Ector and Sir Grummore were eating with rather exaggerated gusto. He did not feel that he could manage more than one chop himself, and, as for Kay, he had stayed away from the breakfast-room altogether.

When breakfast was over, and Master Twyti had been consulted, the Boxing Day cavalcade moved off to the Meet. Perhaps the hounds would have seemed rather a mixed pack to a master of hounds today. There were half a dozen black and white alaunts, which looked like greyhounds with the heads of bull-terriers or worse. These, which were the proper hounds for boars, wore muzzles because of their ferocity. The gaze-hounds, of which there were two taken just in case, were in reality nothing but greyhounds according to modern language, while the lymers were a sort of mixture between the bloodhound and the red setter of today. The latter had collars on, and were led with straps. The braches were like beagles, and trotted along with the master in the way that beagles always have trotted, and a charming way it is.

With the hounds went the foot-people. Merlyn, in his running breeches, looked rather like Lord Baden-Powell, except, of course, that the latter did not wear a beard. Sir Ector was dressed in "sensible" leather clothes—it was not considered sporting to hunt in armour—and he walked beside Master Twyti with that bothered and important expression which has always been worn by masters of hounds. Sir Grummore, just behind, was puffing and asking everybody whether they had sharpened their spears. King Pellinore had dropped back among the villagers, feeling that there was safety in numbers. All the villagers were there, every male soul on the estate from Hob the austringer down to old Wat with no nose, every man carrying a spear or a pitchfork or a worn scythe blade on a stout pole. Even some of the young women who were courting had come out, with baskets of provisions for the men. It was a regular Boxing Day Meet.

At the edge of the forest the last follower joined up. He was a tall, distinguished-looking person dressed in green, and he carried a seven-foot bow.

"Good morning, Master," he said pleasantly to Sir Ector.

"Ah, yes," said Sir Ector. "Yes, yes, good mornin', eh? Yes, good mornin'."

He led the gentleman in green aside and said in a loud whisper that could be heard by everybody, "For heaven's sake, my dear fellow, do be careful. This is the King's own huntsman, and those two other chaps are King Pellinore and Sir Grummore. Now do be a good chap, my dear fellow, and don't say anything controversial, will you, old boy, there's a good chap?"

"Certainly I won't," said the green man reassuringly, "but I think you had better introduce me to them."

Sir Ector blushed deeply and called out: "Ah, Grummore, come over here a minute, will you? I want to introduce a friend of mine, old chap, a chap called Wood, old chap—Wood with a W, you know, not an H. Yes, and this is King Pellinore. Master Wood—King Pellinore."

"Hail," said King Pellinore, who had not quite got out of the habit when nervous.

"How do?" said Sir Grummore. "No relation to Robin Hood I suppose?"

"Oh, not in the least," interrupted Sir Ector hastily. "Double you, double owe, dee, you know, like the stuff they make furniture out of—furniture, you know, and spears, and—well—spears, you know, and furniture."

"How do you do?" said Robin.

"Hail," said King Pellinore.

"Well," said Sir Grummore, "it is funny you should both wear green."

"Yes, it is funny, isn't it?" said Sir Ector anxiously. "He wears it in mournin' for an aunt of his, who died by fallin' out of a tree."

"Beg pardon, I'm sure," said Sir Grummore, grieved at having touched upon this tender subject—and all was well.

"Now, then, Mr. Wood," said Sir Ector when he had recovered. "Where shall we go for our first draw?"

As soon as this question had been put, Master Twyti was fetched into the conversation, and a brief confabulation followed in which all sorts of technical terms like "lesses" were bandied about. Then there was a long walk in the wintry forest, and the fun began.

Wart had lost the panicky feeling which had taken hold of his stomach when he was breaking his fast. The exercise and the snow-wind had breathed him, so that his eyes sparkled almost as brilliantly as the frost crystals in the white winter sunlight, and his blood raced with the excitement of the chase. He watched the lymerer who held the two bloodhound dogs on their leashes, and saw the dogs straining more and more as the boar's lair was approached. He saw how, one by one and ending with the gaze-hounds—who did not hunt by scent—the various hounds became uneasy and began to whimper with desire. He noticed Robin pause and pick up some lesses, which he handed to Master Twyti, and then the whole cavalcade came to a halt. They had reached the dangerous spot.

Boar-hunting was like cub-hunting to this extent, that the boar was attempted to be held up. The object of the hunt was to kill him as quickly as possible. Wart took up his position in the circle round the monster's lair, and knelt down on one knee in the snow, with the handle of his spear couched on the ground, ready for emergencies. He felt the hush which fell upon the company, and saw Master Twyti wave silently to the lymerer to uncouple his hounds. The two lymers plunged immediately into the covert which the hunters surrounded. They ran mute.

There were five long minutes during which nothing happened. The hearts beat thunderously in the circle, and a small vein on the side of each neck throbbed in harmony with each heart. The heads turned quickly from side to side, as each man assured himself of his neighbours, and the breath of life steamed away on the north wind sweetly, as each realized how beautiful life was, which a reeking tusk might, in a few seconds, rape away from one or another of them if things went wrong.

The boar did not express his fury with his voice. There was no uproar in the covert or yelping from the lymers. Only, about a hundred yards away from the Wart, there was suddenly a black creature standing on the edge of the clearing. It did not seem to be a boar particularly, not in the first seconds that it stood there. It had come too quickly to seem to be anything. It was charging Sir Grummore before the Wart had recognized what it was.

The black thing rushed over the white snow, throwing up little puffs of it. Sir Grummore—also looking black against the snow—turned a quick somersault in a larger puff. A kind of grunt, but no noise of falling, came clearly on the north wind, and then the boar was gone. When it was gone, but not before, the Wart knew certain things about it—things which he had not had time to notice while the boar was there. He remembered the rank mane of bristles standing upright on its razor back, one flash of a sour tush, the staring ribs, the head held low, and the red flame from a piggy eye.

Sir Grummore got up, dusting snow out of himself unhurt, blaming his spear. A few drops of blood were to be seen frothing on the white earth. Master Twyti put his horn to his lips. The alaunts were uncoupled as the exciting notes of the menee began to ring through the forest, and then the whole scene began to move. The lymers which had reared the boar—the proper word for dislodging—were allowed to pursue him to make them keen on their work. The braches gave musical tongue. The alaunts galloped baying through the drifts. Everybody began to shout and run.

"Avoy, avoy!" cried the foot-people. "Shahou, shahou! Avaunt, sire, avaunt!"

"Swef, swef!" cried Master Twyti anxiously. "Now, now, gentlemen, give the hounds room, if you please."

"I say, I say!" cried King Pellinore. "Did anybody see which way he went? What an exciting day, what? Sa sa cy avaunt, cy sa avaunt, sa cy avaunt!"

"Hold hard, Pellinore!" cried Sir Ector. " 'Ware, hounds, man, 'ware hounds. Can't watch him yourself, you know. Il est hault. Il est hault!"

And "Til est ho," echoed the foot-people. "Tilly-ho," sang the trees. "Tally-ho," murmured the distant snow drifts as the heavy branches, disturbed by the vibrations, slid noiseless puffs of sparkling powder to the muffled earth.

The Wart found himself running with Master Twyti.

It was like beagling in a way, except that it was beagling in a forest where it was sometimes difficult even to move. Everything depended on the music of the hounds and the various notes which the huntsman could blow to tell where he was and what he was doing. Without these the whole field would have been lost in two minutes—and even with them about half of it was lost in three.

Wart stuck to Twyti like a burr. He could move as quickly as the huntsman because, although the latter had the experience of a life-time, he himself was smaller to get through obstacles and had, moreover, been taught by Maid Marian. He noticed that Robin kept up too, but soon the grunting of Sir Ector and the baa-ing of King Pellinore were left behind. Sir Grummore had given in early, having had most of the breath knocked out of him by the boar, and stood far in the rear declaring that his spear could no longer be quite sharp. Kay had stayed with him, so that he should not get lost. The foot-people had been early mislaid because they did not understand the notes of the horn. Merlyn had torn his breeches and stopped to mend them up by magic. The sergeant had thrown out his chest so far in crying Tally-ho and telling everybody which way they ought to run that he had lost all sense of place, and was leading a disconsolate party of villagers, in Indian file, at the double, with knees up, in the wrong direction. Hob was still in the running.

"Swef, swef," panted the huntsman, addressing the Wart as if he had been a hound. "Not so fast, master, they are going off the line."

Even as he spoke, Wart noticed that the hound music was weaker and more querulous.

"Stop," said Robin, "or we may tumble over him."

The music died away.

"Swef, swef!" shouted Master Twyti at the top of his voice. "Sto arere, so howe, so howe!" He swung his baldrick in front of him, and, lifting the horn to his lips, began to blow a recheat.

There was a single note from one of the lymers.

"Hoo arere," cried the huntsman.

The lymer's note grew in confidence, faltered, then rose to the full bay.

"Hoo arere! Here how, amy. Hark to Beaumont the valiant! Ho moy, ho moy, hole, hole, hole, hole."

The lymer was taken up by the tenor bells of the braches. The noises grew to a crescendo of excitement as the blood-thirsty thunder of the alaunts pealed through the lesser notes.

"They have him," said Twyti briefly, and the three humans began to run again, while the huntsman blew encouragement with Trou-rou-root.

In a small bushment the grimly boar stood at bay. He had got his hindquarters into the nook of a tree blown down by a gale, in an impregnable position. He stood on the defensive with his upper lip writhed back in a snarl. The blood of Sir Grummore's gash welled fatly among the bristles of his shoulder and down his leg, while the foam of his chops dropped on the blushing snow and melted it. His small eyes darted in every direction. The hounds stood round, yelling at his mask, and Beaumont, with his back broken, writhed at his feet. He paid no further attention to the living hound, which could do him no harm. He was black, flaming and bloody.

"So-ho," said the huntsman.

He advanced with his spear held in front of him, and the hounds, encouraged by their master, stepped forward with him pace by pace.

The scene changed as suddenly as a house of cards falling down. The boar was not at bay any more, but charging Master Twyti. As it charged, the alaunts closed in, seizing it fiercely by the shoulder or throat or leg, so that what surged down on the huntsman was not one boar but a bundle of animals. He dared not use his spear for fear of hurting the dogs. The bundle rolled forward unchecked, as if the hounds did not impede it at all. Twyti began to reverse his spear, to keep the charge off with its butt end, but even as he reversed it the tussle was upon him. He sprang back, tripped over a root, and the battle closed on top. The Wart pranced round the edge, waving his own spear in an agony, but there was nowhere where he dared to thrust it in. Robin dropped his spear, drew his falchion in the same movement, stepped into the huddle of snarls, and calmly picked an alaunt up by the leg. The dog did not let go, but there was space where its body had been. Into this space the falchion went slowly, once, twice, thrice. The whole superstructure stumbled, recovered itself, stumbled again, and sank down ponderously on its left side. The hunt was over.

Master Twyti drew one leg slowly from under the boar, stood up, took hold of his knee with his right hand, moved it inquiringly in various directions, nodded to himself and stretched his back straight. Then he picked up his spear without saying anything and limped over to Beaumont. He knelt down beside him and took his head on his lap. He stroked Beaumont's head and said, "Hark to Beaumont. Softly, Beaumont, mon amy. Oyez à Beaumont the valiant. Swef, le douce Beaumont, swef, swef." Beaumont licked his hand but could not wag his tail. The huntsman nodded to Robin, who was standing behind, and held the hound's eyes with his own. He said, "Good dog, Beaumont the valiant, sleep now, old friend Beaumont, good old dog." Then Robin's falchion let Beaumont out of this world, to run free with Orion and roll among the stars.

The Wart did not like to watch Master Twyti for a moment. The strange, leathery man stood up without saying anything and whipped the hounds off the corpse of the boar as he was accustomed to do. He put his horn to his lips and blew the four long notes of the mort without a quaver. But he was blowing the notes for a different reason, and he startled the Wart because he seemed to be crying.

The mort brought most of the stragglers up in due time. Hob was there already and Sir Ector came next, whacking the brambles aside with his boar-spear, puffing importantly and shouting, "Well done, Twyti. Splendid hunt, very. That's the way to chase a beast of venery, I will say. What does he weigh?" The others dribbled in by batches, King Pellinore bounding along and crying out, "Tally-ho! Tally-ho! Tally-ho!" in ignorance that the hunt was done. When informed of this, he stopped and said "Tally-ho, what?" in a feeble voice, then relapsed into silence. Even the sergeant's Indian file arrived in the end, still doubling with knees up, and were halted in the clearing while the sergeant explained to them with great satisfaction that if it had not been for him, all would have been lost. Merlyn appeared holding up his running shorts, having failed in his magic. Sir Grummore came stumping along with Kay, saying that it had been one of the finest points he had ever seen run, although he had not seen it, and then the butcher's business of the "undoing" was proceeded with apace.

Over this there was a bit of excitement. King Pellinore, who had really been scarcely himself all day, made the fatal mistake of asking when the hounds were going to be given their quarry. Now, as everybody knows, a quarry is a reward of entrails, etc., which is given to the hounds on the hide of the dead beast (sur le quir), and, as everybody else knows, a slain boar is not skinned. It is disembowelled without the hide being taken off, and, since there can be no hide, there can be no quarry. We all know that the hounds are rewarded with a fouail, or mixture of bowels and bread cooked over a fire, and, of course, poor King Pellinore had used the wrong word.

So King Pellinore was bent over the dead beast amid loud huzzas, and the protesting monarch was given a hearty smack with a sword blade by Sir Ector. The King then said, "I think you are all a lot of beastly cads," and wandered off mumbling into the forest.

The boar was undone, the hounds rewarded, and the foot-people, standing about in chattering groups because they would have got wet if they had sat down in the snow, ate the provisions which the young women had brought in baskets. A small barrel of wine which had been thoughtfully provided by Sir Ector was broached, and a good drink was had by all. The boar's feet were tied together, a pole was slipped between his legs, and two men hoisted it upon their shoulders. William Twyti stood back, and courteously blew the prise.

It was at this moment that King Pellinore reappeared. Even before he came into view they could hear him crashing in the undergrowth and calling out, "I say, I say! Come here at once! A most dreadful thing has happened!" He appeared dramatically upon the edge of the clearing, just as a disturbed branch, whose burden was too heavy, emptied a couple of hundredweight of snow on his head. King Pellinore paid no attention. He climbed out of the snow heap as if he had not noticed it, still calling out, "I say. I say!"

"What is it, Pellinore?" shouted Sir Ector.

"Oh, come quick!" cried the King, and, turning round distracted, he vanished again into the forest.

"Is he all right," inquired Sir Ector, "do you suppose?"

"Excitable character," said Sir Grummore. "Very."

"Better follow up and see what he's doin'."

The procession moved off sedately in King Pellinore's direction, following his erratic course by the fresh tracks in the snow.

The spectacle which they came across was one for which they were not prepared. In the middle of a dead gorse bush King Pellinore was sitting, with the tears streaming down his face. In his lap there was an enormous snake's head, which he was patting. At the other end of the snake's head there was a long, lean, yellow body with spots on it. At the end of the body there were some lion's legs which ended in the slots of a hart.

"There, there," the King was saying. "I did not mean to leave you altogether. It was only because I wanted to sleep in a feather bed, just for a bit. I was coming back, honestly I was. Oh, please don't die, Beast, and leave me without any fewmets!"

When he saw Sir Ector, the King took command of the situation. Desperation had given him authority.

"Now, then, Ector," he exclaimed. "Don't stand there like a ninny. Fetch that barrel of wine along at once."

They brought the barrel and poured out a generous tot for the Questing Beast.

"Poor creature," said King Pellinore indignantly. "It has pined away, positively pined away, just because there was nobody to take an interest in it. How I could have stayed all that while with Sir Grummore and never given my old Beast a thought I really don't know. Look at its ribs, I ask you. Like the hoops of a barrel. And lying out in the snow all by itself, almost without the will to live. Come on, Beast, you see if you can't get down another gulp of this. It will do you good.

"Mollocking about in a feather bed," added the remorseful monarch, glaring at Sir Grummore, "like a—like a kidney!"

"But how did you—how did you find it?" faltered Sir Grummore.

"I happened on it. And small thanks to you. Running about like a lot of nincompoops and smacking each other with swords. I happened on it in this gorse bush here, with snow all over its poor back and tears in its eyes and nobody to care for it in the wide world. It's what comes of not leading a regular life. Before, it was all right. We got up at the same time, and quested for regular hours, and went to bed at half past ten. Now look at it. It has gone to pieces altogether, and it will be your fault if it dies. You and your bed."

"But, Pellinore!" said Sir Grummore. . . .

"Shut your mouth," replied the King at once. "Don't stand there bleating like a fool, man. Do something. Fetch another pole so that we can carry old Glatisant home. Now, then, Ector, haven't you got any sense? We must just carry him home and put him in front of the kitchen fire. Send somebody on to make some bread and milk. And you, Twyti, or whatever you choose to call yourself, stop fiddling with that trumpet of yours and run ahead to get some blankets warmed.

"When we get home," concluded King Pellinore, "the first thing will be to give it a nourishing meal, and then, if it is all right in the morning, I will give it a couple of hours' start and then hey-ho for the old life once again. What about that, Glatisant, hey? You'll tak' the high road and I'll tak' the low road, what? Come along, Robin Hood, or whoever you are—you may think I don't know, but I do— stop leaning on your bow with that look of negligent woodcraft. Pull yourself together, man, and get that musclebound sergeant to help you carry her. Now then, lift her easy. Come along, you chuckle-heads, and mind you don't trip. Feather beds and quarry, indeed; a lot of childish non-sense. Go on, advance, proceed, step forward, march! Feather brains, I call it, that's what I do.

"And as for you, Grummore," added the King, even after he had concluded, "you can just roll yourself up in your bed and stifle in it."

## 17

*"I think it must be time,"* said Merlyn, looking at him over the top of his spectacles one afternoon, "that you had another dose of education. That is, as Time goes."

It was an afternoon in early spring and everything outside the window looked beautiful. The winter mantle had gone, taking with it Sir Grummore, Master Twyti, King Pellinore and the Questing Beast—the latter having revived under the influence of kindliness and bread and milk. It had bounded off into the snow with every sign of gratitude, to be followed two hours later by the excited King, and the watchers from the battlements had observed it confusing its snowy footprints most ingeniously, as it reached the edge of the chase. It was running backward, bounding twenty foot sideways, rubbing out its marks with its tail, climbing along horizontal branches, and performing many other tricks with evident enjoyment. They had also seen King Pellinore—who had dutifully kept his eyes shut and counted ten thousand while this was going on—becoming quite confused when he arrived at the difficult spot, and finally galloping off in the wrong direction with his brachet trailing behind him.

It was a lovely afternoon. Outside the schoolroom window the larches of the distant forest had already taken on the fullness of their dazzling green, the earth twinkled and swelled with a million drops, and every bird in the world had come home to court and sing. The village folk were forth in their gardens every evening, planting garden beans, and it seemed that, what with these emergencies and those of the slugs (coincidentally with the beans), the buds, the lambs, and the birds, every living thing had conspired to come out.

"What would you like to be?" asked Merlyn.

Wart looked out of the window, listening to the thrush's twice-done song of dew.

He said, "I have been a bird once, but it was only in the mews at night, and I never got a chance to fly. Even if one ought not to do one's education twice, do you think I could be a bird so as to learn about that?"

He had been bitten with the craze for birds which bites all sensible people in the spring, and which sometimes even leads to excesses like birds' nesting.

"I can see no reason why you should not," said the magician. "Why not try it at night?"

"But they will be asleep at night."

"All the better chance of seeing them, without their flying away. You could go with Archimedes this evening, and he would tell you about them."

"Would you do that, Archimedes?"

"I should love to," said the owl. "I was feeling like a little saunter myself."

"Do you know," asked the Wart, thinking of the thrush, "why birds sing, or how? Is it a language?"

"Of course it is a language. It is not a big language like human speech, but it is large."

"Gilbert White," said Merlyn, "remarks, or will remark, however you like to put it, that 'the language of birds is very ancient, and, like other ancient modes of speech, little is said, but much is intended.' He also says somewhere that 'the rooks, in the breeding season, attempt sometimes, in the gaiety of their hearts, to sing—but with no great success.'"

"I love rooks," said the Wart. "It is funny, but I think they are my favourite bird."

"Why?" asked Archimedes.

"Well, I like them. I like their sauce."

"Neglectful parents," quoted Merlyn, who was in a scholarly mood, "and saucy, perverse children."

"It is true," said Archimedes reflectively, "that all the corvidae have a distorted sense of humour."

Wart explained.

"I love the way they enjoy flying. They don't just fly, like other birds, but they fly for fun. It is lovely when they hoist home to bed in a flock at night, all cheering and making rude remarks and pouncing on each other in a vulgar way. They turn over on their backs sometimes and tumble out of the air, just to be ridiculous, or else because they have forgotten they are flying and have coarsely began to scratch themselves for fleas, without thinking about it."

"They are intelligent birds," said Archimedes, "in spite of their low humour. They are one of the birds that have parliaments, you know, and a social system."

"Do you mean they have laws?"

"Certainly they have laws. They meet in the autumn, in a field, to talk them over."

"What sort of laws?"

"Oh, well, laws about the defence of the rookery, and marriage, and so forth. You are not allowed to marry outside the rookery, and, if you do become quite lost to all sense of decency, and bring back a sable virgin from a neighbouring settlement, then everybody pulls your nest to pieces as fast as you can build it up. They make you go into the suburbs, you know, and that is why every rookery has out-lying nests all round it, several trees away."

"Another thing I like about them," said the Wart, "is their Go. They may be thieves and practical jokers, and they do quarrel and bully each other in a squawky way, but they have got the courage to mob their enemies. I should think it takes some courage to mob a hawk, even if there is a pack of you. And even while they are doing it they clown."

"They are mobs," said Archimedes, loftily. "You have said the word."

"Well, they are larky mobs, anyway," said the Wart, "and I like them."

"What is your favourite bird?" asked Merlyn politely, to keep the peace.

Archimedes thought this over for some time, and then said, "Well, it is a large question. It is rather like asking you what is your favourite book. On the whole, however, I think that I must prefer the pigeon."

"To eat?"

"I was leaving that side of it out," said the owl in civilized tones. "Actually the pigeon is the favourite dish of all raptors, if they are big enough to take her, but I was thinking of nothing but domestic habits."

"Describe them."

"The pigeon," said Archimedes, "is a kind of Quaker. She dresses in grey. A dutiful child, a constant lover, and a wise parent, she knows, like all philosophers, that the hand of every man is against her. She has learned throughout the centuries to specialize in escape. No pigeon has ever committed an act of aggression nor turned upon her persecutors: but no bird, likewise, is so skilful in eluding them. She has learned to drop out of a tree on the opposite side to man, and to fly low so that there is a hedge between them. No other bird can estimate a range so well. Vigilant, powdery, odorous and loose-feathered—so that dogs object to take them in their mouths—armoured against pellets by the padding of these feathers, the pigeons coo to one another with true love, nourish their cunningly hidden children with true solicitude, and flee from the aggressor with true philosophy —a race of peace lovers continually caravaning away from the destructive Indian in covered wagons. They are loving individualists surviving against the forces of massacre only by wisdom in escape.

"Did you know," added Archimedes, "that a pair of pigeons always roost head to tail, so that they can keep a look-out in both directions?"

"I know our tame pigeons do," said the Wart. "I suppose the reason why people are always trying to kill them is because they are so greedy. What I like about wood-pigeons is the clap of their wings, and how they soar up and close their wings and sink, during their courting flights, so that they fly rather like woodpeckers."

"It is not very like woodpeckers," said Merlyn.

"No, it is not," admitted the Wart.

"And what is your favourite bird?" asked Archimedes, feeling that his master ought to be allowed a say.

Merlyn put his fingers together like Sherlock Holmes and replied immediately, "I prefer the chaffinch. My friend Linnaeus calls him coelebs or bachelor bird. The flocks have the sense to separate during the winter, so that all the males are in one flock and all the females in the other. For the winter months, at any rate, there is perfect peace."

"The conversation," observed Archimedes, "arose out of whether birds could talk."

"Another friend of mine," said Merlyn immediately, in his most learned voice, "maintains, or will maintain, that the question of the language of birds arises out of imitation. Aristotle, you know, also attributes tragedy to imitation."

Archimedes sighed heavily, and remarked in prophetic tones, "You had better get it off your chest."

"It is like this," said Merlyn. "The kestrel drops upon a mouse, and the poor mouse, transfixed with those needle talons, cries out in agony his one squeal of K-e-e-e! Next time the kestrel sees a mouse, his own soul cries out Kee in imitation. Another kestrel, perhaps his mate, comes to that cry, and after a few million years all the kestrels are calling each other with their individual note of Kee-kee-kee."

"You can't make the whole story out of one bird," said the Wart.

"I don't want to. The hawks scream like their prey. The mallards croak like the frogs they eat, the shrikes also, like these creatures in distress. The blackbirds and thrushes click like the snail shells they hammer to pieces. The various finches make the noise of cracking seeds, and the woodpecker imitates the tapping on wood which he makes to get the insects that he eats."

"But all birds don't give a single note!"

"No, of course not. The call note arises out of imitation and then the various bird songs are developed by repeating the call note and descanting upon it."

"I see," said Archimedes coldly. "And what about me?"

"Well, you know quite well," said Merlyn, "that the shrew-mouse you pounce upon squeals out Kweek! That is why the young of your species call Kee-wick."

"And the old?" inquired Archimedes sarcastically.

"Hooroo, Hooroo," cried Merlyn, refusing to be damped. "It is obvious, my dear fellow. After their first winter, that is the wind in the hollow trees where they prefer to sleep."

"I see," said Archimedes, more coolly than ever. "This time, we note, it is not a question of prey at all."

"Oh, come along," replied Merlyn. "There are other things besides the things you eat. Even a bird drinks sometimes, for instance, or bathes itself in water. It is the liquid notes of a river that we hear in a robin's song."

"It seems now," said Archimedes, "that it is no longer a question of what we eat, but also what we drink or hear."

"And why not?"

The owl said resignedly, "Oh, well."

"I think it is an interesting idea," said the Wart, to encourage his tutor. "But how does a language come out of these imitations?"

"They repeat them at first," said Merlyn, "and then they vary them. You don't seem to realize what a lot of meaning there resides in the tone and the speed of voice. Suppose I were to say 'What a nice day,' just like that. You would answer, 'Yes, so it is.' But if I were to say, 'What a *nice* day,' in caressing tones, you might think I was a nice person. But then again, if I were to say, 'What a nice day,' quite breathless, you might look about you to see what had put me in a fright. It is like this that the birds have developed their language."

"Would you mind telling us," said Archimedes, "since you know so much about it, how many various things we birds are able to express by altering the tempo and emphasis of the elaborations of our call-notes?"

"But a large number of things. You can cry Kee-wick in tender accents, if you are in love, or Kee-wick angrily in challenge or in hate: you can cry it on a rising scale as a call-note, if you do not know where your partner is, or to attract their attention away if strangers are straying near your nest: if you go near the old nest in the winter-time you may cry Kee-wick lovingly, a conditioned reflex from the pleasures which you once enjoyed within it, and if I come near to you in a startling way you may cry out Keewick-keewick-keewick, in loud alarm."

"When we come to conditioned reflexes," remarked Archimedes sourly, "I prefer to look for a mouse."

"So you may. And when you find it I dare say you will make another sound characteristic of owls, though not often mentioned in books of ornithology. I refer to the sound 'Tock' or 'Tck' which human beings call a smacking of the lips."

"And what sound is that supposed to imitate?"

"Obviously, the breaking of mousy bones."

"You are a cunning master," said Archimedes, "and as far as a poor owl is concerned you will just have to get away with it. All I can tell you from my personal experience is that it is not like that at all. A tit can tell you not only that it is in danger, but what kind of danger it is in. It can say, 'Look out for the cat,' or 'Look out for the hawk,' or 'Look out for the tawny owl,' as plainly as A.B.C."

"I don't deny it," said Merlyn. "I am only telling you the beginnings of the language. Suppose you try to tell me the song of any single bird which I can't attribute originally to imitation?"

"The night-jar," said the Wart.

"The buzzing of the wings of beetles," replied his tutor at once.

"The nightingale," cried Archimedes desperately.

"Ah," said Merlyn, leaning back in his comfortable chair. "Now we are to imitate the soul-song of our beloved Proserpine, as she stirs to wake in all her liquid self."

"Tereu," said the Wart softly.

"Pieu," added the owl quietly.

"Music!" concluded the necromancer in ecstasy, unable to make the smallest beginnings of an imitation.

"Hallo," said Kay, opening the door of the afternoon school room. "I'm sorry I am late for the geography lesson. I was trying to get a few small birds with my cross-bow. Look, I have killed a thrush."

# 18

*The Wart lay awake as he had been told to do. He* was to wait until Kay was asleep, and then Archimedes would come for him with Merlyn's magic. He lay under the great bearskin and stared out of the window at the stars of spring, no longer frosty and metallic, but as if they had been new washed and had swollen with the moisture. It was a lovely evening, without rain or cloud. The sky between the stars was of the deepest and fullest velvet. Framed in the thick western window, Alderbaran and Betelgeuse were racing Sirius over the horizon, the hunting dog-star looking back to his master Orion, who had not yet heaved himself above the rim. In at the window came also the unfolding scent of benighted flowers, for the currants, the wild cherries, the plums and the hawthorn were already in bloom, and no less than five nightingales within earshot were holding a contest of beauty among the bowery, the looming trees.

Wart lay on his back with his bearskin half off him and his hands clasped behind his head. It was too beautiful to sleep, too temperate for the rug. He watched out at the stars in a kind of trance. Soon it would be the summer again, when he could sleep on the battlements and watch these stars hovering as close as moths above his face—and, in the Milky Way at least, with something of the mothy pollen. They would be at the same time so distant that un- utterable thoughts of space and eternity would baffle them- selves in his sighing breast, and he would imagine to him- self how he was falling upward higher and higher among them, never reaching, never ending, leaving and losing everything in the tranquil speed of space.

He was fast asleep when Archimedes came for him.

"Eat this," said the owl, and handed him a dead mouse.

The Wart felt so strange that he took the furry atomy without protest, and popped it into his mouth without any feelings that it was going to be nasty. So he was not sur- prised when it turned out to be excellent, with a fruity taste like eating a peach with the skin on, though naturally the skin was not so nice as the mouse.

"Now, we had better fly," said the owl. "Just flip to the window-sill here, to get accustomed to yourself before we take off."

Wart jumped for the sill and automatically gave himself an extra kick with his wings, just as a high jumper swings his arms. He landed on the sill with a thump, as owls are apt to do, did not stop himself in time, and toppled straight out of the window. "This," he thought to himself, cheer- fully, "is where I break my neck." It was curious, but he was not taking life seriously. He felt the castle walls streaking past him, and the ground and the moat swimming up. He kicked with his wings, and the ground sank again, like water in a leaking well. In a second that kick of his wings had lost its effect, and the ground was welling up. He kicked again. It was strange, going forward with the earth ebbing and flowing beneath him, in the utter silence of his down-fringed feathers.

"For heaven's sake," panted Archimedes, bobbing in the dark air beside him, "stop flying like a woodpecker. Any- body would take you for a Little Owl, if the creatures had been imported. What you are doing is to give yourself fly- ing speed with one flick of your wings. You then rise on that flick until you have lost flying speed and begin to stall. Then you give another just as you are beginning to drop out of the air, and do a switch-back. It is confusing to keep up with you."

"Well," said the Wart recklessly, "if I stop doing this I shall go bump altogether."

"Idiot," said the owl. "Waver your wings all the time, like me, instead of doing these jumps with them."

The Wart did what he was told, and was surprised to find that the earth became stable and moved underneath him without tilting, in a regular pour. He did not feel himself to be moving at all.

"That's better."

"How curious everything looks," observed the boy with some wonder, now that he had time to look about him.

And, indeed, the world did look curious. In some ways the best description of it would be to say that it looked like a photographer's negative, for he was seeing one ray beyond the spectrum which is visible to human beings. An infra-red camera will take photographs in the dark, when we cannot see, and it will also take photographs in daylight. The owls are the same, for it is untrue that they can only see at night. They see in the day just as well, only they happen to possess the advantage of seeing pretty well at night also. So naturally they prefer to do their hunting then, when other creatures are more at their mercy. To the Wart the green trees would have looked whitish in the daytime, as if they were covered with apple blossom, and now, at night, everything had the same kind of different look. It was like flying in a twilight which had reduced everything to shades of the same colour, and, as in the twilight, there was a considerable amount of gloom.

"Do you like it?" asked the owl.

"I like it very much. Do you know, when I was a fish there were parts of the water which were colder or warmer than the other parts, and now it is the same in the air."

"The temperature," said Archimedes, "depends on the vegetation of the bottom. Woods or weeds, they make it warm above them."

"Well," said the Wart, "I can see why the reptiles who had given up being fishes decided to become birds. It certainly is fun."

"You are beginning to fit things together," remarked Archimedes. "Do you mind if we sit down?"

"How does one?"

"You must stall. That means you must drive yourself up until you lose flying speed, and then, just as you feel yourself beginning to tumble—why, you sit down. Have you never noticed how birds fly upward to perch? They don't come straight down on the branch, but dive below it and then rise. At the top of their rise they stall and sit down."

"But birds land on the ground too. And what about mallards on the water? They can't rise to sit on that."

"Well, it is perfectly possible to land on flat things, but more difficult. You have to glide in at stalling speed all the way, and then increase your wind resistance by cupping your wings, dropping your feet, tail, etc. You may have noticed that few birds do it gracefully. Look how a crow thumps down and how the mallard splashes. The spoon-winged birds like heron and plover seem to do it best. As a matter of fact, we owls are not so bad at it ourselves."

"And the long-winged birds like swifts, I suppose they are the worst, for they can't rise from a flat surface at all?"

"The reasons are different," said Archimedes, "yet the fact is true. But need we talk on the wing? I am getting tired."

"So am I."

"Owls usually prefer to sit down every hundred yards."

The Wart copied Archimedes in zooming up toward the branch which they had chosen. He began to fall just as they were above it, clutched it with his furry feet at the last moment, swayed backward and forward twice, and found that he had landed successfully. He folded up his wings.

While the Wart sat still and admired the view, his friend proceeded to give him a lecture about flight in birds. He told how, although the swift was so fine a flyer that he could sleep on the wing all night, and although the Wart himself had claimed to admire the way in which rooks enjoyed their flights, the real aeronaut of the lower strata—which cut out the swift—was the plover. He explained how plovers indulged in aerobatics, and would actually do such stunts as spins, stall turns and even rolls for the mere grace of the thing. They were the only birds which made a practice of slipping off height to land—except occasionally the oldest, gayest and most beautiful of all the conscious aeronauts, the raven. Wart paid little or no attention to the lecture, but got his eyes accustomed to the strange tones of light instead, and watched Archimedes from the corner of one of them. For Archimedes, while he was talking, was absent-mindedly spying for his dinner. This spying was an odd performance.

A spinning top which is beginning to lose its spin slowly

describes circles with its highest point before falling down. The leg of the top remains in the same place, but the apex makes circles which get bigger and bigger toward the end. This is what Archimedes was absent-mindedly doing. His feet remained stationary, but he moved the upper part of his body round and round, like somebody trying to see from behind a fat lady at a cinema, and uncertain which side of her gave the best view. As he could also turn his head almost completely round on his shoulders, you may imagine that his antics were worth watching.

"What are you doing?" asked the Wart.

Even as he asked, Archimedes was gone. First there had been an owl talking about plover, and then there was no owl. Only, far below the Wart, there was a thump and a rattle of leaves, as the aerial torpedo went smack into the middle of a bush, regardless of obstructions.

In a minute the owl was sitting beside him again on the branch, thoughtfully breaking up a dead sparrow.

"May I do that?" asked the Wart, inclined to be bloodthirsty.

"As a matter of fact," said Archimedes, after waiting to crop his mouthful, "you may not. The magic mouse which turned you into an owl will be enough for you—after all, you have been eating as a human all day—and no owl kills for pleasure. Besides, I am supposed to be taking you for education, and, as soon as I have finished my snack here, that is what we shall have to do."

"Where are you going to take me?"

Archimedes finished his sparrow, wiped his beak politely on the bough, and turned his eyes full on the Wart. These great, round eyes had, as a famous writer has expressed it, a bloom of light upon them like the purple bloom of powder on a grape.

"Now that you have learned to fly," he said, "Merlyn wants you to try the Wild Geese."

The place in which he found himself was absolutely flat. In the human world we seldom see flatness, for the trees and houses and hedges give a serrated edge to the landscape. Even the grass sticks up with its myriad blades. But here, in the belly of the night, the illimitable, flat, wet mud was as featureless as a dark junket. If it had been wet sand, even, it would have had those little wave marks, like the palate of your mouth.

In this enormous flatness, there lived one element—the wind. For it was an element. It was a dimension, a power of darkness. In the human world, the wind comes from somewhere, and goes somewhere, and, as it goes, it passes through somewhere—through trees or streets or hedgerows. This wind came from nowhere. It was going through the flatness of nowhere, to no place. Horizontal, soundless except for a peculiar boom, tangible, infinite, the astounding dimensional weight of it streamed across the mud. You could have ruled it with a straight-edge. The titanic grey line of it was unwavering and solid. You could have hooked the crook of your umbrella over it, and it would have hung there.

The Wart, facing into this wind, felt that he was un-created. Except for the wet solidity under his webbed feet, he was living in nothing—a solid nothing, like chaos. His were the feelings of a point in geometry, existing mysteriously on the shortest distance between two points: or of a line, drawn on a plane surface which had length, breadth but no magnitude. No magnitude! It was the very self of magnitude. It was power, current, force, direction, a pulse-less world-stream steady in limbo.

Bounds had been set to this unhallowed purgatory. Far away to the east, perhaps a mile distant, there was an un-broken wall of sound. It surged a little, seeming to expand and contract, but it was solid. It was menacing, being de-sirous for victims—for it was the huge, remorseless sea.

Two miles to the west, there were three spots of light in a triangle. They were the weak wicks from fishermen's cot-tages, who had risen early to catch a tide in the complicated creeks of the salt marsh. Its waters sometimes ran contrary to the ocean. These were the total features of his world—the sea sound and the three small lights: darkness, flatness, vastness, wetness: and, in the gulf of night, the gulf-stream of the wind.

When daylight began to come, by premonition, the boy found that he was standing among a crowd of people like himself. They were seated on the mud, which now began to be disturbed by the angry, thin, returning sea, or else were already riding on the water, wakened by it, outside the an-noyance of the surf. The seated ones were large teapots, their spouts tucked under their wings. The swimming ones sometimes ducked their heads and shook them. Some, waking on the mud, stood up and wagged their wings vigorously. Their profound silence became broken by a conversational gabble. There were about four hundred of them in the grey vicinity—very beautiful creatures, the wild White-fronted Geese, whom, once he has seen them close, no man ever forgets.

Long before the sun came, they were making ready for flight. Family parties of the previous year's breeding were coming together in batches, and these batches were themselves inclined to join with others, possibly under the command of a grandfather, or else of a great-grandfather, or else of some noted leader in the host. When the drafts were complete, there came a faint tone of excitement into their speech. They began moving their heads from side to side in jerks. And then, turning into the wind, suddenly they would all be in the air together, fourteen or forty at a time, with wide wings scooping the blackness and a cry of triumph in their throats. They would wheel round, climbing rapidly, and be gone from sight. Twenty yards up, they were invisible in the dark. The earlier departures were not vocal. They were inclined to be taciturn before the sun came, only making occasional remarks, or crying their single warning-note if danger threatened. Then, at the warning, they would all rise vertically to the sky.

The Wart began to feel an uneasiness in himself. The dim squadrons about him, setting out minute by minute, infected him with a tendency. He became restless to embrace their example, but he was shy. Perhaps their family groups, he thought, would resent his intrusion. Yet he wanted not to be lonely. He wanted to join in, and to enjoy the exercise of morning flight, which was so evidently a pleasure. They had a comradeship, free discipline and *joie de vivre*.

When the goose next to the boy spread her wings and leaped, he did so automatically. Some eight of those nearby had been jerking their bills, which he had imitated as if the act were catching, and now, with these same eight, he found himself on pinion in the horizontal air. The moment he had left the earth, the wind had vanished. Its restlessness and brutality had dropped away as if cut off by a knife. He was in it, and at peace.

The eight geese spread out in line astern, evenly spaced, with him behind. They made for the east, where the poor lights had been, and now, before them, the bold sun began to rise. A crack of orange-vermilion broke the black cloud-bank far beyond the land. The glory spread, the salt marsh growing visible below. He saw it like a featureless moor or bogland, which had become maritime by accident—its heather, still looking like heather, having mated with the seaweed until it was a salt wet heather, with slippery fronds. The burns which should have run through the moorland were of sea-water on blueish mud. There were long nets here and there, erected on poles, into which unwary geese might fly. These, he now guessed, had been the occasions for those warning-notes. Two or three widgeon hung in one of them, and, far away to the eastward, a fly-like man was plodding over the slob in tiny persistence, to collect his bag.

The sun, as it rose, tinged the quick-silver of the creeks and the gleaming slime itself with flame. The curfew, who had been piping their mournful plaints since long before the light, flew now from weed-bank to weed-bank. The widgeon, who had slept on water, came whistling their double notes, like whistles from a Christmas cracker. The mallard toiled from land, against the wind. The redshanks scuttled and prodded like mice. A cloud of tiny dunlin, more compact than starlings, turned in the air with the noise of a train. The black-guard of crows rose from the pine trees on the dunes with merry cheers. Shore birds of every sort populated the tide line, filling it with business and beauty.

The dawn, the sea-dawn and the mastery of ordered flight, were of such intense beauty that the boy was moved to sing. He wanted to cry a chorus to life, and, since a thousand geese were on the wing about him, he had not long to wait. The lines of these creatures, wavering like smoke upon the sky as they breasted the sunrise, were all at once in music and in laughter. Each squadron of them was in different voice, some larking, some triumphant, some in sentiment or glee. The vault of daybreak filled itself with heralds, and this is what they sang:

You turning world, pouring beneath our pinions,
Hoist the hoar sun to welcome morning's minions.

See, on each breast the scarlet and vermilion,
Hear, from each throat the clarion and carillion.

Hark, the wild wandering lines in black battalions,
Heaven's horns and hunters, dawn-bright hounds
    and stallions.

Free, free: far, far: and fair on wavering wings
Comes Anser albifrons, and sounds, and sings.

He was in a coarse field, in daylight. His companions of
the flight were grazing round him, plucking the grass with
sideways wrenches of their soft small bills, bending their
necks into abrupt loops, unlike the graceful curves of the
swan. Always, as they fed, one of their number was on
guard, its head erect and snakelike. They had mated during
the winter months, or else in previous winters, so that they
tended to feed in pairs within the family and squadron. The
young female, his neighbour of the mud-flats, was in her
first year. She kept an intelligent eye upon him.

The boy, watching her cautiously, noted her plump com-
pacted frame and a set of neat furrows on her neck. These
furrows, he saw out of the corner of his eye, were caused
by a difference in the feathering. The feathers were concave,
which separated them from one another, making a texture
of ridges which he considered graceful.

Presently the young goose gave him a shove with her bill.
She had been acting sentry.

"You next," she said.

She lowered her head without waiting for an answer, and
began to graze in the same movement. Her feeding took her
from his side.

He stood sentry. He did not know what he was watching
for, nor could he see any enemy, except the tussocks and
his nibbling mates. But he was not sorry to be a trusted sen-
tinel for them.

"What are you doing?" she asked, passing him after half
an hour.

"I was on guard."

"Go on with you," she said with a giggle, or should it be
a gaggle? "You are a silly!"

"Why?"

"You know."

"Honestly," he said, "I don't. Am I doing it wrong? I
don't understand."

"Peck the next one. You have been on for twice your
time, at least."

He did as she told him, at which the grazer next to them
took over, and then he walked along to feed beside her.
They nibbled, noting one another out of beady eyes.

"You think I am stupid," he said shyly, confessing the

secret of his real species for the first time to an animal, "but it is because I am not a goose. I was born as a human. This is my first flight really."

She was mildly surprised.

"It is unusual," she said. "The humans generally try the swans. The last lot we had were the Children of Lir. However, I suppose we're all anseriformes together."

"I have heard of the Children of Lir."

"They didn't enjoy it. They were hopelessly nationalistic and religious, always hanging about round one of the chapels in Ireland. You could say that they hardly noticed the other swans at all."

"I am enjoying it."

"I thought you were. What were you sent for?"

"To learn my education."

They grazed in silence, until his own words reminded him of something he had wanted to ask.

"The sentries," he asked. "Are we at war?"

She did not understand the word.

"War?"

"Are we fighting people?"

"Fighting?" she asked doubtfully. "The men fight sometimes, about their wives and that. Of course there is no bloodshed—only scuffling, to find the better man. Is that what you mean?"

"No. I meant fighting against armies—against other geese, for instance."

She was amused.

"How ridiculous! You mean a lot of geese all scuffling at the same time. It would be fun to watch."

Her tone surprised him, for his heart was still a kind one, being a boy's.

"Fun to watch them kill each other?"

"To kill each other? An army of geese to kill each other?"

She began to understand this idea slowly and doubtfully, an expression of distaste coming over her face. When it had sunk in, she left him. She went away to another part of the field in silence. He followed, but she turned her back. Moving round to get a glimpse of her eyes, he was startled by their dislike—a look as if he had made some obscene suggestion.

He said lamely: "I am sorry. I don't understand."

"Leave talking about it."

"I am sorry."

Later he added, with annoyance, "A person can ask, I suppose. It seems a natural question, with the sentries."

But she was thoroughly angry.

"Will you stop about it at once! What a horrible mind you must have! You have no right to say such things. And of course there are sentries. There are the jer-falcons and the peregrines, aren't there: the foxes and the ermines and the humans with their nets? These are natural enemies. But what creature could be so low as to go about in bands, to murder others of its own blood?"

"Ants do," he said obstinately. "And I was only trying to learn."

She relented with an effort to be good-natured. She wanted to be broad-minded if she could, for she was rather a blue-stocking.

"My name is Lyo-lyok. You had better call yourself Kee-kwa, and then the rest will think you came from Hungary."

"Do you all come here from different places?"

"Well, in parties, of course. There are some here from Siberia, some from Lapland and I can see one or two from Iceland."

"But don't they fight each other for the pasture?"

"Dear me, you are a silly," she said. "There are no boundaries among the geese."

"What are boundaries, please?"

"Imaginary lines on the earth, I suppose. How can you have boundaries if you fly? Those ants of yours—and the humans too—would have to stop fighting in the end, if they took to the air."

"I like fighting," said the Wart. "It is knightly."

"Because you're a baby."

# 19

There was something magical about the time and space commanded by Merlyn, for the Wart seemed to be passing many days and nights among the grey people, during the one spring night when he had left his body asleep under the bearskin.

He grew to be fond of Lyo-lyok, in spite of her being a girl. He was always asking her questions about the geese. She taught him what she knew with gentle kindness, and the more he learned, the more he came to love her brave, noble, quiet and intelligent relations. She told him how every White-front was an individual—not governed by laws or leaders, except when they came about spontaneously. They had no Kings like Uther, no laws like the bitter Norman ones. They did not own things in common. Any goose who found something nice to eat considered it his own, and would peck any other one who tried to thieve it. At the same time, no goose claimed any exclusive territorial right in any part of the world—except its nest, and that was private property. She told him a great deal about migration.

"The first goose," she said, "I suppose, who made the flight from Siberia to Lincolnshire and back again must have brought up a family in Siberia. Then, when the winter came and it was necessary to find new food, he must have groped his way over the same route, being the only one who knew it. He will have been followed by his growing family, year after year, their pilot and their admiral. When the time came for him to die, obviously the next best pilots would have been his eldest sons, who would have covered the route more often than the others. Naturally the younger sons and fledglings would have been uncertain about it, and therefore would have been glad to follow somebody who knew. Perhaps, among the eldest sons, there would have been some who were famous for being muddle-headed, and the family would hardly care to trust to them.

"This," she said, "is how an admiral is elected. Perhaps Wink-wink will come to our family in the autumn, and he will say: 'Excuse me, but have you by any chance got a re-liable pilot in your lot? Poor old grand-dad died at cloud-berry time, and Uncle Onk is inefficient. We were looking for somebody to follow.' Then we will say: 'Great-uncle will be delighted if you care to hitch up with us; but mind, we cannot take responsibility if things go wrong.' 'Thank you very much,' he will say. 'I am sure your great-uncle can be relied on. Do you mind if I mention this matter to the Honks, who are, I happen to know, in the same difficulty?' 'Not at all.'

"And that," she explained, "is how Great-uncle became an admiral."

"It is a good way."

"Look at his bars," she said respectfully, and they both glanced at the portly patriarch, whose breast was indeed barred with black stripes, like the gold rings on an admiral's sleeve.

There was a growing excitement among the host. The young geese flirted outrageously, or collected in parties to discuss their pilots. They played games, too, like children excited at the prospect of a party. One of these games was to stand in a circle, while the junior ganders, one after another, walked into the middle of it with their heads stretched out, pretending to hiss. When they were half-way across the circle they would run the last part, flapping their wings. This was to show how brave they were, and what excellent admirals they would make, when they grew up. Also the strange habit of shaking their bills sideways, which was usual before flight, began to grow upon them. The elders and sages, who knew the migration routes, became uneasy also. They kept a wise eye on the cloud formations, summing up the wind, and the strength of it, and what airt it was coming from. The admirals, heavy with responsibility, paced their quarter-decks with ponderous tread.

"Why am I restless?" he asked. "Why do I have this feeling in my blood?"

"Wait and see," she said mysteriously. "Tomorrow, perhaps, or the day after. . . ."

When the day came, there was a difference about the salt marsh and the slob. The ant-like man, who had walked out so patiently every sunrise to his long nets, with the tides fixed firmly in his head—because to make a mistake in them was certain death—heard a far bugle in the sky. He saw no thousands on the mud flats, and there were none in the pastures from which he had come. He was a nice man in his way—for he stood still solemnly, and took off his leather hat. He did this every spring religiously, when the wild geese left him, and every autumn, when he saw the first returning gaggle.

In a steamer it takes two or three days to cross the North Sea—so many hours of slobbering through the viscous water. But for the geese, for the sailors of the air, for the angled wedges tearing clouds to tatters, for the singers of the sky with the gale behind them—seventy miles an hour behind another seventy—for those mysterious geographers —three miles up, they say—with cumulus for their floor instead of water—for them it was a different matter.

The songs they sang were full of it. Some were vulgar, some were sagas, some were light-hearted to a degree. One silly one which amused the Wart was as follows:

We wander the sky with many a Cronk
And land in the pasture fields with a Plonk.
 'Hank-hank, Hink-hink, Honk-honk.

Then we bend our necks with a curious kink
Like the bend which the plumber puts under the sink.
 Honk-honk, Hank-hank, Hink-hink.

And we feed away in a sociable rank
Tearing the grass with a sideways yank.
 Hink-hink, Honk-honk, Hank-hank.

But Hink or Honk we relish the Plonk,
And Honk or Hank we relish the Rank,
And Hank or Hink we think it a jink
 To Honk or Hank or Hink!

A sentimental one was:

Wild and free, wild and free,
 Bring back my gander to me, to me.

And once, while they were passing over a rocky island populated by barnacle geese, who looked like spinsters in black leather gloves, grey toques and jet beads, the entire squadron burst out derisively with:

Branta bernicla sits a-slumming in the slob,
Branta bernicla sits a-slumming in the slob,
Branta bernicla sits a-slumming in the slob,
 While we go sauntering along.
Glory, glory, here we go, dear.
Glory, glory, here we go, dear.
Glory, glory, here we go, dear.
 To the North Pole sauntering along.

One of the more Scandinavian songs was called "The Boon of Life":

Ky-yow replied: The boon of life is health.
Paddle-foot, Feather-straight, Supple-neck, Button-eye:
These have the world's wealth.

Aged Ank answered: Honour is our all.
Path-finder, People-feeder, Plan-provider, Sage-commander:
These hear the call.

Lyo-lyok the lightsome said: Love I had liefer.
Douce-down, Tender-tread, Warm-nest and Walk-in-line:
These live for ever.

Aahng-ung was for Appetite. Ah, he said, Eating!
Gander-gobble, Tear-grass, Stubble-stalk, Stuff-crop:
These take some beating.

Wink-wink praised Comrades, the fair free fraternity.
Line-astern, Echelon, Arrow-head, Over-cloud:
These learn Eternity.

But I, Lyow, choose Lay-making, of loud lilts which linger.
Horn-music, Laughter song, Epic-heart, Ape-the-world:
These Lyow, the singer.

Sometimes, when they came down from the cirrus levels to catch a better wind, they would find themselves among the flocks of cumulus—huge towers of modelled vapour, looking as white as Monday's washing and as solid as meringues. Perhaps one of these piled-up blossoms of the sky, these snow-white droppings of a gigantic Pegasus, would lie before them several miles away. They would set their course toward it, seeing it grow bigger silently and imperceptibly, a motionless growth—and then, when they were at it, when they were about to bang their noses with a shock against its seeming solid mass, the sun would dim. Wraiths of mist suddenly moving like serpents of the air would coil about them for a second. Grey damp would be around them, and the sun, a copper penny, would fade away. The wings next to their own wings would shade into vacancy, until each bird was a lonely sound in cold annihilation, a presence after uncreation. And there they would

hang in chartless nothing, seemingly without speed or left
or right or top or bottom, until as suddenly as ever the copper penny glowed and the serpents writhed. Then, in a moment of time, they would be in the jewelled world once
more—a sea under them like turquoise and all the gorgeous
palaces of heaven new created, with the dew of Eden not yet
dry.

One of the peaks of the migration came when they passed
a rock-cliff of the ocean. There were other peaks, when,
for instance, their line of flight was crossed by an Indian
file of Bewick Swans who were off to Abisko, making a
noise as they went like little dogs barking through handkerchiefs, or when they overtook a horned owl plodding manfully along—among the warm feathers of whose back, *so
they said*, a tiny wren was taking her free ride. But the
lonely island was the best.

It was a town of birds. They were all hatching, all quarrelling, all friendly nevertheless. On top of the cliff, where
the short turf was, there were myriads of puffins busy with
their burrows. Below them, in Razorbill Street, the birds
were packed so close, and on such narrow ledges, that they
had to stand with their backs to the sea, holding tight with
long toes. In Guillemot Street, below that, the guillemots
held their sharp, toy-like faces upward, as thrushes do when
hatching. Lowest of all, there were the Kittiwake Slums.
And all the birds—who, like humans, only laid one egg each
—were jammed so tight that their heads were interlaced—
had so little of this famous living-space of ours that, when
a new bird insisted on landing at a ledge which was already
full, one of the other birds had to tumble off. Yet they were
in good humour, so cheerful and cockneyfied and teasing one
another. They were like an innumerable crowd of fish-wives
on the largest grandstand in the world, breaking out into
private disputes, eating out of paper bags, chipping the ref-
eree, singing comic songs, admonishing their children and
complaining of their husbands. "Move over a bit, Auntie,"
they said, or "Shove along, Grandma"; "There's that Flossie
gone and sat on the shrimps"; "Put the toffee in your
pocket, dearie, and blow your nose"; "Lawks, if it isn't Uncle
Albert with the beer"; "Any room for a little 'un?"; "There
goes Aunt Emma, fallen off the ledge"; "Is me hat on
straight?"; "Crikey, this isn't arf a do!"

They kept more or less to their own kind, but they were
not mean about it. Here and there, in Guillemot Street,

there would be an obstinate Kittiwake sitting on a projection and determined to have her rights. Perhaps there were ten thousand of them, and the noise they made was deafening.

Then there were the fiords and islands of Norway. It was about one of these islands, by the way, that the great W. H. Hudson related a true goose-story which ought to make people think. There was a coastal farmer, he tells us, whose islands suffered under a nuisance of foxes—so he set up a fox-trap on one of them. When he visited the trap next day, he found that an old wild goose had been caught in it, obviously a Grand Admiral, because of his toughness and his heavy bars. This farmer took the goose home alive, pinioned it, bound up its leg, and turned it out with his own ducks and poultry in the farmyard. Now one of the effects of the fox plague was that the farmer had to lock his henhouse at night. He used to go round in the evening to drive them in, and then he would lock the door. After a time, he began to notice a curious circumstance, which was that the hens, instead of having to be collected, would be found waiting for him in the hut. He watched the process one evening, and discovered that the captive potentate had taken on himself the responsibility, which he had with his own intelligence observed. Every night at locking-up time, the sagacious old admiral would round up his domestic comrades, whose leadership he had assumed, and would prudently assemble them in the proper place by his own efforts, as if he had fully understood the situation. Nor did the free wild geese, his sometime followers, ever again settle on the other island—previously a haunt of theirs—from which their captain had been spirited away.

Last of all, beyond the islands, there was the landing at their first day's destination. Oh, the whiffling of delight and self-congratulation! They tumbled out of the sky, side-slipping, stunting, even doing spinning nose-dives. They were proud of themselves and of their pilot, agog for the family pleasures which were in store.

They planed for the last part on down-curved wings. At the last moment they scooped the wind with them, flapping them vigorously. Next—bump—they were on the ground. They held their wings above their heads for a moment, then folded them with a quick and pretty neatness. They had crossed the North Sea.

"Well, Wart," said Kay in an exasperated voice, "do you want all the rug? And why do you heave and mutter so? You were snoring, too."

"I don't snore," replied the Wart indignantly.

"You do."

"I don't."

"You do. You honk like a goose."

"I don't."

"You do."

"I don't. And you snore worse."

"No, I don't."

"Yes, you do."

"How can I snore worse if you don't snore at all?"

By the time they had thrashed this out, they were late for breakfast. They dressed hurriedly and ran out into the spring.

# 20

*It was hay-making again, and Merlyn had been with* them a year. The wind had visited them, and the snow, and the rain, and the sun once more. The boys looked longer in the leg, but otherwise everything was the same.

Six other years passed by.

Sometimes Sir Grummore came on a visit. Sometimes King Pellinore could be descried galloping over the purlieus after the Beast, or with the Beast after him if they happened to have got muddled up. Cully lost the vertical stripes of his first year's plumage and became greyer, grimmer, madder, and distinguished by smart horizontal bars where the long stripes had been. The merlins were released every winter and new ones caught again next year. Hob's hair went white. The sergeant-at-arms developed a pot-belly and nearly died of shame, but continued to cry out One-Two, in a huskier voice, on every possible occasion. Nobody else seemed to change at all, except the boys.

These grew longer. They ran like wild colts as before, and went to see Robin when they had a mind to, and had innumerable adventures too lengthy to be recorded.

Merlyn's extra tuition went on just the same—for in those days even the grown-up people were so childish that they saw nothing uninteresting in being turned into owls. The Wart was changed into countless different animals. The only difference was that now, in their fencing lessons, Kay and his companion were an easy match for the pot-bellied sergeant, and paid him back accidentally for many of the buffets which he had once given them. They had more and more proper weapons as presents, when they had reached their 'teens, until in the end they had full suits of armour and bows nearly six feet long, which would shoot the cloth-yard shaft. You were not supposed to use a bow longer than your own height, for it was considered that by doing so you were expending unnecessary energy, rather like using an elephant-gun to shoot an *ovis ammon* with. At any rate, modest men were careful not to over-bow themselves. It was a form of boasting.

As the years went by, Kay became more difficult. He always used a bow too big for him, and did not shoot very accurately with it either. He lost his temper and challenged nearly everybody to have a fight, and in those few cases where he did actually have the fight he was invariable beaten. Also he became sarcastic. He made the sergeant miserable by nagging about his stomach, and went on at the Wart about his father and mother when Sir Ector was not about. He did not seem to want to do this. It was as if he disliked it, but could not help it.

The Wart continued to be stupid, fond of Kay, and interested in birds.

Merlyn looked younger every year—which was only natural, because he was.

Archimedes was married, and brought up several handsome families of quilly youngsters in the tower room.

Sir Ector got sciatica. Three trees were struck by lightning. Master Twyti came every Christmas without altering a hair. Master Passelewe remembered a new verse about King Cole.

The years passed regularly and the Old English snow lay as it was expected to lie—sometimes with a Robin Red-breast in one corner of the picture, a church bell or lighted window in the other—and in the end it was nearly time for Kay's initiation as a fullblown knight. Proportionately as the day became nearer, the two boys drifted apart—for Kay did not care to associate with the Wart any longer on the same terms, because he would need to be more dignified as a knight, and could not afford to have his squire on intimate terms with him. The Wart, who would have to be the squire, followed him about disconsolately as long as he was allowed to do so, and then went off full miserably to amuse himself alone, as best he might.

He went to the kitchen.

"Well, I am a Cinderella now," he said to himself. "Even if I have had the best of it for some mysterious reason, up to the present time—in our education—now I must pay for my past pleasures and for seeing all those delightful dragons, witches, fishes, cameleopards, pismires, wild geese and such like, by being a second-rate squire and holding Kay's extra spears for him, while he hoves by some well or other and jousts with all comers. Never mind, I have had a good time while it lasted, and it is not such bad fun being a Cinderella, when you can do it in a kitchen which has a fireplace big enough to roast an ox."

And the Wart looked round the busy kitchen, which was coloured by the flames till it looked like hell, with sorrowful affection.

The education of any civilized gentleman in those days used to go through three stages, page, squire, knight, and at any rate the Wart had been through the first two of these. It was rather like being the son of a modern gentleman who has made his money out of trade, for your father started you on the bottom rung even then, in your education of manners. As a page, Wart had learned to lay the tables with three cloths and a carpet, and to bring meat from the kitchen, and to serve Sir Ector or his guests on bended knee, with one clean towel over his shoulder, one for each visitor, and one to wipe the basins. He had been taught all the noble arts of servility, and, from the earliest time that he could remember, there had lain pleasantly in the end of his nose the various scents of mint—used to freshen the water in the ewers—or of basil, camomile, fennel, hysop and lavender—which he had been taught to strew on the rushy floors—or of the angelica, saffron, aniseed, and tarragon, which were used to spice the savouries which he had to carry. So he was accustomed to the kitchen, quite apart from the fact that everybody who lived in the castle was a friend of his who might be visited on any occasion.

Wart sat in the enormous firelight and looked about him with pleasure. He looked upon the long spits which he had often turned when he was smaller, sitting behind an old straw target soaked in water, so that he would not be roasted himself, and upon the ladles and spoons whose handles could be measured in yards, with which he had been accustomed to baste the meat. He watched with water in his mouth the arrangements for the evening meal—a boar's head with a lemon in its jaws and split almond whiskers, which would be served with a fanfare of trumpets—a kind of pork pie with sour apple juice, peppered custard, and several birds' legs, or spiced leaves sticking out of the top to show what was in it—and a most luscious-looking frumenty. He said to himself with a sigh, "It is not so bad being a servant after all."

"Still sighing?" asked Merlyn, who had turned up from somewhere. "As you were that day when we went to watch King Pellinore's joust?"

"Oh, no," said the Wart. "Or rather, oh yes, and for the same reason. But I don't really mind. I am sure I shall make a better squire than old Kay would. Look at the saffron going into that frumenty. It just matches the fire-light on the hams in the chimney."

"It is lovely," said the magician. "Only fools want to be great."

"Kay won't tell me," said the Wart, "what happens when you are made a knight. He says it is too sacred. What does happen?"

"Only a lot of fuss. You will have to undress him and put him into a bath hung with rich hangings, and then two experienced knights will turn up—probably Sir Ector will get hold of old Grummore and King Pellinore—and they will both sit on the edge of the bath and give him a long lecture about the ideals of chivalry such as they are. When they have done, they will pour some of the bath water over him and sign him with the cross, and then you will have to conduct him into a clean bed to get dry. Then you dress him up as a hermit and take him off to the chapel, and there he stays awake all night, watching his armour and saying prayers. People say it is lonely and terrible for him in this vigil, but it is not at all lonely really, because the vicar and the man who sees to the candles and an armed guard, and prob- ably you as well, as his esquire, will have to sit up with him at the same time. In the morning you lead him off to bed to have a good sleep—as soon as he has confessed and heard mass and offered a candle with a piece of money stuck into it as near the lighted end as possible—and then, when all are rested, you dress him up again in his very best clothes for dinner. Before dinner you lead him into the hall, with his spurs and sword all ready, and King Pellinore puts on the first spur, and Sir Grummore puts on the second, and then Sir Ector girds on the sword and kisses him and smacks him on the shoulder and says, 'Be thou a good knight.' "

"Is that all?"

"No. You go to the chapel again then, and Kay offers his sword to the vicar, and the vicar gives it back to him, and after that our good cook over there meets him at the door and claims his spurs as a reward, and says, 'I shall keep these spurs for you, and if at any time you don't behave as a true knight should do, why, I shall pop them in the soup.' "

"That is the end?"

"Yes, except for the dinner."

"If I were to be made a knight," said the Wart, staring dreamily into the fire, "I should insist on doing my vigil by myself, as Hob does with his hawks, and I should pray to God to let me encounter all the evil in the world in my own person, so that if I conquered there would be none left, and, if I were defeated, I would be the one to suffer for it."

"That would be extremely presumptuous of you," said Merlyn, "and you would be conquered, and you would suffer for it."

"I shouldn't mind."

"Wouldn't you? Wait till it happens and see."

"Why do people not think, when they are grown up, as I do when I am young?"

"Oh dear," said Merlyn. "You are making me feel con- fused. Suppose you wait till you are grown up and know the reason?"

"I don't think that is an answer at all," replied the Wart, justly.

Merlyn wrung his hands.

"Well, anyway," he said, "suppose they did not let you stand against all the evil in the world?"

"I could ask," said the Wart.

"You could ask," repeated Merlyn.

He thrust the end of his beard into his mouth, stared tragically at the fire, and began to munch it fiercely.

# 21

*The day for the ceremony drew near, the invitations* to King Pellinore and Sir Grummore were sent out, and the Wart withdrew himself more and more into the kitchen.

"Come on, Wart, old boy," said Sir Ector ruefully. "I didn't think you would take it so bad. It doesn't become you to do this sulkin'."

"I am not sulking," said the Wart. "I don't mind a bit and I am very glad that Kay is going to be a knight. Please don't think I am sulking."

"You are a good boy," said Sir Ector. "I know you're not sulkin' really, but do cheer up. Kay isn't such a bad stick, you know, in his way."

"Kay is a splendid chap," said the Wart. "Only I was not happy because he did not seem to want to go hawking or anything, with me, any more."

"It is his youthfulness," said Sir Ector. "It will all clear up."

"I am sure it will," said the Wart. "It is only that he does not want me to go with him, just at the moment. And so, of course, I don't go.

"But I will go," added the Wart. "As soon as he commands me, I will do exactly what he says. Honestly, I think Kay is a good person, and I was not sulking a bit."

"You have a glass of this canary," said Sir Ector, "and go and see if old Merlyn can't cheer you up."

"Sir Ector has given me a glass of canary," said the Wart, "and sent me to see if you can't cheer me up."

"Sir Ector," said Merlyn, "is a wise man."

"Well," said the Wart, "what about it?"

"The best thing for being sad," replied Merlyn, beginning to puff and blow, "is to learn something. That is the only thing that never fails. You may grow old and trembling in your anatomies, you may lie awake at night listening to the disorder of your veins, you may miss your only love, you may see the world about you devastated by evil lunatics, or know your honour trampled in the sewers of baser minds. There is only one thing for it then—to learn. Learn why the world wags and what wags it. That is the only thing which the mind can never exhaust, never alienate, never be tortured by, never fear or distrust, and never dream of regretting. Learning is the thing for you. Look at what a lot of things there are to learn—pure science, the only purity there is. You can learn astronomy in a lifetime, natural history in three, literature in six. And then, after you have exhausted a milliard lifetimes in biology and medicine and theocriticism and geography and history and economics —why, you can start to make a cartwheel out of the appropriate wood, or spend fifty years learning to begin to learn to beat your adversary at fencing. After that you can start again on mathematics, until it is time to learn to plough."

"Apart from all these things," said the Wart, "what do you suggest for me just now?"

"Let me see," said the magician, considering. "We have had a short six years of this, and in that time I think I am right in saying that you have been many kinds of animal, vegetable, mineral, etc.—many things in earth, air, fire and water?"

"I don't know much," said the Wart, "about the animals and earth."

"Then you had better meet my friend the badger."

"I have never met a badger."

"Good," said Merlyn. "Except for Archimedes, he is the most learned creature I know. You will like him.

"By the way," added the magician, stopping in the middle of his spell, "there is one thing I ought to tell you. This is the last time I shall be able to turn you into anything. All the magic for that sort of thing has been used up, and this will be the end of your education. When Kay has been knighted my labours will be over. You will have to go away then, to be his squire in the wide world, and I shall go elsewhere. Do you think you have learned anything?"

"I have learned, and been happy."

"That's right, then," said Merlyn. "Try to remember what you learned."

He proceeded with the spell, pointed his wand of lignum vitae at the Little Bear, which had just begun to glow in the dimity as it hung by its tail from the North Star, and called out cheerfully, "Have a good time for the last visit. Give love to Badger."

The call sounded from far away, and Wart found himself standing by the side of an ancient tumulus, like an enormous mole hill, with a black hole in front of him.

"Badger lives in there," he said to himself, "and I am supposed to go and talk to him. But I won't. It was bad enough never to be a knight, but now my own dear tutor that I found on the only Quest I shall ever have is to be taken from me also, and there will be no more natural history. Very well, I will have one more night of joy before I am condemned, and, as I am a wild beast now, I will be a wild beast, and there it is."

So he trundled off fiercely over the twilight snow, for it was winter.

If you are feeling desperate, a badger is a good thing to be. A relation of the bears, otters and weasels, you are the nearest thing to a bear now left in England, and your skin is so thick that it makes no difference who bites you. So far as your own bite is concerned, there is something about the formation of your jaw which makes it almost impossible to be dislocated—and so, however much the thing you are biting twists about, there is no reason why you should ever let go. Badgers are one of the few creatures which can munch up hedgehogs unconcernedly, just as they can munch up everything else from wasps' nests and roots to baby rabbits.

It so happened that a sleeping hedgehog was the first thing which came in the Wart's way.

"Hedge-pig," said the Wart, peering at his victim with blurred, short-sighted eyes, "I am going to munch you up."

The hedgehog, which had hidden its bright little eye-buttons and long sensitive nose inside its curl, and which had ornamented its spikes with a not very tasteful arrangement of dead leaves before going to bed for the winter in its grassy nest, woke up at this and squealed most lamentably.

"The more you squeal," said the Wart, "the more I shall gnash. It makes my blood boil within me."

"Ah, Measter Brock," cried the hedgehog, holding himself tight shut. "Good Measter Brock, show mercy to a poor urchin and don't 'ee be tyrannical. Us be'nt no common tiggy, measter, for to be munched and mumbled. Have mercy, kind sir, on a harmless, flea-bitten crofter which can't tell his left hand nor his right."

"Hedge-pig," said the Wart remorselessly, "forbear to whine, neither thrice nor once."

"Alas, my poor wife and childer!"

"I bet you have not got any. Come out of that, thou tramp. Prepare to meet thy doom."

"Measter Brock," implored the unfortunate pig, "come now, doan't 'ee be okkerd, sweet Measter Brock, my duck. Hearken to an urchin's prayer! Grant the dear boon of life to this most uncommon tiggy, lordly measter, and he shall sing to thee in numbers sweet or teach 'ee how to suck cow's milk in the pearly dew."

"Sing?" asked the Wart, quite taken aback.

"Aye, sing," cried the hedgehog. And it began hurriedly to sing in a very placating way, but rather muffled because it dared not uncurl.

"Oh, Genevieve," it sang most mournfully into its stomach, "Sweet Genevieve,

> Ther days may come,
> Ther days may go,
> But still the light of Mem'ry weaves
> Those gentle dreams
> Of long ago."

It also sang, without pausing for a moment between the songs, *Home Sweet Home* and *The Old Rustic Bridge by the Mill*. Then, because it had finished its repertoire, it drew a hurried but quavering breath, and began again on *Genevieve*. After that, it sang *Home Sweet Home* and *The Old Rustic Bridge by the Mill*.

"Come," said the Wart, "you can stop that. I won't bite you."

"Clementious measter," whispered the hedge-pig humbly. "Us shall bless the saints and board of governors for thee and for thy most kindly chops, so long as fleas skip nor urchins climb up chimbleys."

Then, for fear that its brief relapse into prose might have hardened the tyrant's heart, it launched out breathlessly into *Genevieve*, for the third time.

"Stop singing," said the Wart, "for heaven's sake. Uncurl. I won't do you any harm. Come, you silly little urchin, and tell me where you learned these songs."

"Uncurl is one word," answered the porpentine tremblingly—it did not feel in the least fretful at the moment—"but curling up is still another. If 'ee was to see my liddle naked nose, measter, at this dispicuous moment, 'ee might feel a twitching in thy white toothsomes; and all's fear in love and war, that we do know. Let us sing to 'ee again, sweet Measter Brock, concerning thic there rustic mill?"

"I don't want to hear it any more. You sing it very well, but I don't want it again. Uncurl, you idiot, and tell me where you learned to sing."

"Us be'nt no common urchin," quavered the poor creature, staying curled up as tight as ever. "Us wor a-teuk when liddle by one of them there gentry, like, as it might be from the mother's breast. Ah, doan' 'ee nip our tender vitals, lovely Measter Brock, for ee wor a proper gennelman, ee wor, and brought us up full comely on cow's milk an' that, all supped out from a lordly dish. Ah, there be'nt many urchins what a drunken water outer porcelain, that there be'nt."

"I don't know what you are talking about," said the Wart.

"Ee wor a gennelman," cried the hedgehog desperately, "like I tell 'ee. Ee teuk un when us wor liddle, and fed un when us ha'nt no more. Ee wor a proper gennelman what fed un in ter parlour, like what no urchins ha'nt been afore nor since; fed out from gennelman's porcelain, aye, and a dreary day it wor whenever us left un for nought but wilfulness, that thou may'st be sure."

"What was the name of this gentleman?"

"Ee wor a gennelman, ee wor. Ee hadden no proper neame like, not like you may remember, but ee wor a gennelman, that ee wor, and fed un out a porcelain."

"Was he called Merlyn?" asked the Wart curiously.

"Ah, that wor is neame. A proper fine neame it wor, but us never lay tongue to it by nary means. Ah, Mearn ee called to iself, and fed un out a porcelain, like a proper fine gennelman."

"Oh, do uncurl," exclaimed the Wart. "I know the man who kept you, and I think I saw you, yourself, when you were a baby in cotton wool at his cottage. Come on, urchin, I am sorry I frightened you. We are friends here, and I want to see your little grey wet twitching nose, just for old time's sake."

"Twitching noase be one neame," answered the hedgehog obstinately, "and a-twitching of that noase be another, measter. Now you move along, kind Measter Brock, and leave a poor crofter to teak 'is winter drowse. Let you think of beetles or honey, sweet baron, and flights of angels sing thee to thy rest."

"Nonsense," exclaimed the Wart. "I won't do you any harm, because I knew you when you were little."

"Ah, them badgers," said the poor thing to its stomach, "they go a-barrowing about with no harm in their hearts, Lor bless 'em, but doan't they fair give you a nip without a-noticing of it, and Lor bless 'ee what is a retired mun to do? It's that there skin of theirs, that's what it be, which from earliest childer they've been a-nipping of among each other, and also of their ma's, without a-feeling of anything among theirselves, so natural they nips elsewhere like the seame. Now my poor gennelman, Measter Mearn, they was allars a-rushing arter his ankels, with their yik-yik-yik, when they wanted to be fed like, those what ee kept from liddles—and, holy church, how ee would scream! Aye, 'tis a mollocky thing to deal with they badgers, that us may be sure.

"Doan't see nothing," added the hedgehog, before the Wart could protest. "Blunder along like one of they ambling hearth rugs, on the outsides of their girt feet. Get in their way for a moment, just out of fortune like, without nary wicked intention and 'tis snip-snap, just like that, out of self-defence for the hungry blind, and then where are you?

"On'y pleace us can do for un," continued the urchin, "is to hit un on ter noase. A killee's heel they neame un on ter scriptures. Hit one of they girt trollops on ter noase, bim-bam, like that 'ere, and the sharp life is fair outer him ere ee can snuffle. 'Tis a fair knock-out, that it is.

"But how can a pore urchin dump un on ter noase? When ee ha'nt got nothing to dump with, nor way to hold 'un? And then they comes about 'ee and asks 'ee for to uncurl!"

"You need not uncurl," said the Wart resignedly. "I am sorry I woke you up, chap, and I am sorry I frightened you. I think you are a charming hedgehog, and meeting you has made me feel more cheerful again. You just go off to sleep like you were when I met you, and I shall go to look for my fiiend badger, as I was told to do. Good night, urchin, and good luck in the snow."

"Good night it may be," muttered the pig grumpily. "And then again it mayern't. First it's uncurl and then it's curl. One thing one moment, and another thing ter next. Hey-ho, 'tis a turvey world. But Good night, Ladies, is my motter, come hail, come snow, and so us shall be continued in our next."

With these words the humble animal curled himself up still more snugly than before, gave several squeaky grunts, and was far away in a dream-world so much deeper than our human dreams as a whole winter's sleep is longer than the quiet of a single night.

"Well," thought the Wart, "he certainly gets over his troubles pretty quickly. Fancy going to sleep again as quick as that. I dare say he was never more than half-awake all the time, and will think it was only a dream when he gets up properly in the spring."

He watched the dirty little ball of leaves and grass and fleas for a moment, curled up tightly inside its hole, then grunted and moved off toward the badger's sett, following his own oblong footmarks backward in the snow.


"So Merlyn sent you to me," said the badger, "to finish your education. Well, I can only teach you two things—to dig, and love your home. These are the true end of philosophy."

"Would you show me your home?"

"Certainly," said the badger, "though, of course, I don't use it all. It is a rambling old place, much too big for a single man. I suppose some parts of it may be a thousand years old. There are about four families of us in it, here and there, take it by and large from cellar to attics, and sometimes we don't meet for months. A crazy old place, I suppose it must seem to you modern people—but there, it's cosy."

He went ambling down the corridors of the enchanted sett, rolling from leg to leg with the queer badger paddle, his white mask with its black stripes looking ghostly in the gloom.

"It's along that passage," he said, "if you want to wash your hands."

Badgers are not like foxes. They have a special midden

where they put out their used bones and rubbish, proper earth closets, and bedrooms whose bedding they turn out frequently, to keep it clean. The Wart was charmed with what he saw. He admired the Great Hall most, for this was the central room of the tumulus—it was difficult to know whether to think of it as a college or as a castle—and the various suites and bolt holes radiated outward from it. It was a bit cobwebby, owing to being a sort of common-room instead of being looked after by one particular family, but it was decidedly solemn. Badger called it the Combination Room. All round the panelled walls there were ancient paintings of departed badgers, famous in their day for scholarship or godliness, lit from above by shaded glow-worms. There were stately chairs with the badger arms stamped in gold on their Spanish leather seats—the leather was coming off—and a portrait of the Founder over the fireplace. The chairs were arranged in a semi-circle round the fire, and there were mahogany fans with which everybody could shield their faces from the flames, and a kind of tilting board by means of which the decanters could be slid back from the bottom of the semi-circle to the top. Some black gowns hung in the passage outside, and all was extremely ancient.

"I am a bachelor at the moment," said the badger apologetically, when they got back to his own snug room with the flowered wallpaper, "so I am afraid there is only one chair. You will have to sit on the bed. Make yourself at home, my dear, while I brew some punch, and tell me how things are going in the wide world."

"Oh, they go on much the same. Merlyn is well, and Kay is to be made a knight next week."

"An interesting ceremony."

"What enormous arms you have," remarked the Wart, watching him stir the spirits with a spoon. "So have I, for that matter." And he looked down at his own bandy-legged muscles. He was mainly a tight chest holding together a pair of forearms, mighty as thighs.

"It is to dig with," said the learned creature complacently. "Mole and I, I suppose you would have to dig pretty quick to match with us."

"I met a hedgehog outside."

"Did you now? They say nowadays that hedgehogs can carry swine fever and foot-and-mouth disease."

"I thought he was rather nice."

"They do have a sort of pathetic appeal," said the badger sadly, "but I'm afraid I generally just munch them up. There is something irresistible about pork crackling.

"The Egyptians," he added. and by this he meant the gypsies, "are fond of them for eating, too."

"Mine would not uncurl."

"You should have pushed him into some water, and then he'd have shown you his poor legs quick enough. Come, the punch is ready. Sit down by the fire and take your ease."

"It is nice to sit here with the snow and wind outside."

"It is nice. Let us drink good luck to Kay in his knighthood."

"Good luck to Kay, then."

"Good luck."

"Well," said the badger, setting down his glass again with a sigh. "Now what could have possessed Merlyn to send you to me?"

"He was talking about learning," said the Wart.

"Ah, well, if it is learning you are after, you have come to the right shop. But don't you find it rather dull?"

"Sometimes I do," said the Wart, "and sometimes I don't. On the whole I can bear a good deal of learning if it is about natural history."

"I am writing a treatise just now," said the badger, coughing diffidently to show that he was absolutely set on explaining it, "which is to point out why Man has become the master of the animals. Perhaps you would like to hear it?

"It's for my doctor's degree, you know," he added hastily, before the Wart could protest. He got few chances of reading his treatises to anybody, so he could not bear to let the opportunity slip by.

"Thank you very much," said the Wart.

"It will be good for you, dear boy. It is just the thing to top off an education. Study birds and fish and animals: then finish off with Man. How fortunate that you came! Now where the devil did I put that manuscript?"

The old gentleman scratched about with his great claws until he had turned up a dirty bundle of papers, one corner of which had been used for lighting something. Then he sat down in his leather armchair, which had a deep depression in the middle of it; put on his velvet smoking-cap with the tassel; and produced a pair of tarantula spectacles, which he balanced on the end of his nose.

"Hem," said the badger.

He immediately became paralysed with shyness, and sat blushing at his papers, unable to begin.

"Go on," said the Wart.

"It is not very good," he explained coyly. "It is just a rough draft, you know. I shall alter a lot before I send it in."

"I am sure it must be interesting."

"Oh no, it is not a bit interesting. It is just an odd thing I threw off in an odd half-hour, just to pass the time. But still, this is how it begins.

"Hem!" said the badger. Then he put on an impossibly high falsetto voice and began to read as fast as possible.

"People often ask, as an idle question, whether the process of evolution began with the chicken or the egg. Was there an egg out of which the first chicken came, or did a chicken lay the first egg? I am in a position to say that the first thing created was the egg.

"When God had manufactured all the eggs out of which the fishes and the serpents and the birds and the mammals and even the duck-billed platypus would eventually emerge, he called the embryos before Him, and saw that they were good.

"Perhaps I ought to explain," added the badger, lowering his papers nervously and looking at the Wart over the top of them, *"that all embryos look very much the same*. They are what you are before you are born—and, whether you are going to be a tadpole or a peacock or a cameleopard or a man, when you are an embryo you just look like a peculiarly repulsive and helpless human being. I continue as follows:

"The embryos stood in front of God, with their feeble hands clasped politely over their stomachs and their heavy heads hanging down respectfully, and God addressed them.

"He said: 'Now, you embryos, here you are, all looking exactly the same, and We are going to give you the choice of what you want to be. When you grow up you will get bigger anyway, but We are pleased to grant you another gift as well. You may alter any parts of yourselves into anything which you think would be useful to you in later life. For instance, at the moment you cannot dig. Anybody who would like to turn his hands into a pair of spades or garden forks is allowed to do so. Or, to put it another way, at present you can only use your mouths for eating. Anybody who would like to use his mouth as an offensive weapon, can change it by asking, and be a corkindrill or a sabre-toothed tiger. Now then, step up and choose your tools, but remember that what you choose you will grow into, and will have to stick to.'

"All the embryos thought the matter over politely, and then, one by one, they stepped up before the eternal throne. They were allowed two or three specializations, so that some chose to use their arms as flying machines and their mouths as weapons, or crackers, or drillers, or spoons, while others selected to use their bodies as boats and their hands as oars. We badgers thought very hard and decided to ask three boons. We wanted to change our skins for shields, our mouths for weapons, and our arms for garden forks. These boons were granted. Everybody specialized in one way or another, and some of us in very queer ones. For instance, one of the desert lizards decided to swap his whole body for blotting-paper, and one of the toads who lived in the drouthy antipodes decided simply to be a water-bottle.

"The asking and granting took up two long days—they were the fifth and sixth, so far as I remember—and at the very end of the sixth day, just before it was time to knock off for Sunday, they had got through all the little embryos except one. This embryo was Man.

" 'Well, Our little man,' said God. 'You have waited till the last, and slept on your decision, and We are sure you have been thinking hard all the time. What can We do for you?'

" 'Please God,' said the embryo, 'I think that You made me in the shape which I now have for reasons best known to Yourselves, and that it would be rude to change. If I am to have my choice I will stay as I am. I will not alter any of the parts which You gave me, for other and doubtless inferior tools, and I will stay a defenceless embryo all my life, doing my best to make myself a few feeble implements out of the wood, iron and the other materials which You have seen fit to put before me. If I want a boat I will try to construct it out of trees, and if I want to fly, I will put together a chariot to do it for me. Probably I have been very silly in refusing to take advantage of Your kind offer, but I have done my very best to think it over carefully, and now hope that the feeble decision of this small innocent will find favour with Yourselves.'

" 'Well done,' exclaimed the Creator in delighted tones.

'Here, all you embryos, come here with your beaks and whatnots to look upon Our first Man. He is the only one who has guessed Our riddle, out of all of you, and We have great pleasure in conferring upon him the Order of Dominion over the Fowls of the Air, and the Beasts of the Earth, and the Fishes of the Sea. Now let the rest of you get along, and love and multiply, for it is time to knock off for the week-end. As for you, Man, you will be a naked tool all your life, though a user of tools. You will look like an embryo till they bury you, but all the others will be embryos before your might. Eternally undeveloped, you will always remain potential in Our image, able to see some of Our sorrows and to feel some of Our joys. We are partly sorry for you, Man, but partly hopeful. Run along then, and do your best. And listen, Man, before you go . . .'

" 'Well?' asked Adam, turning back from his dismissal.

" 'We were only going to say,' said God shyly, twisting Their hands together. 'Well, We were just going to say, God bless you.' "

"It's a good story," said the Wart doubtfully. "I like it better than Merlyn's one about the Rabbi. And it is interesting, too."

The badger was covered with confusion.

"No, no, dear boy. You exaggerate. A minor parable at most. Besides, I fear it is a trifle optimistic."

"How?"

"Well, it is true that man has the Order of Dominion and is the mightiest of the animals—if you mean the most terrible one—but I have sometimes doubted lately whether he is the most blessed."

"I don't think Sir Ector is very terrible."

"All the same, if even Sir Ector was to go for a walk beside a river, not only would the birds fly from him and the beasts run away from him, but the very fish would dart to the other side. They don't do this for each other."

"Man is the king of the animals."

"Perhaps. Or ought one to say the tyrant? And then again we do have to admit that he has a quantity of vices."

"King Pellinore has not got many."

"He would go to war, if King Uther declared one. Do you know that Homo sapiens is almost the only animal which wages war?"

"Ants do."

"Don't say 'Ants do' in that sweeping way, dear boy. There are more than four thousand different sorts of them, and from all those kinds I can only think of five which are belligerent. There are the five ants, one termite that I know of, and Man."

"But the packs of wolves from the Forest Sauvage attack our flocks of sheep every winter."

"Wolves and sheep belong to different species, my friend. True warfare is what happens between bands of the same species. Out of the hundreds of thousands of species, I can only think of seven which are belligerent. Even Man has a few varieties like the Esquimaux and the Gypsies and the Lapps and certain Nomads in Arabia, who do not do it, because they do not claim boundaries. True warfare is rarer in Nature than cannibalism. Don't you think that is a little unfortunate?"

"Personally," said the Wart, "I should have liked to go to war, if I could have been made a knight. I should have liked the banners and the trumpets, the flashing armour and the glorious charges. And oh, I should have liked to do great deeds, and be brave, and conquer my own fears. Don't you have courage in warfare, Badger, and endurance, and comrades whom you love?"

The learned animal thought for a long time, gazing into the fire.

In the end, he seemed to change the subject.

"Which did you like best," he asked, "the ants or the wild geese?"

# 22

*King Pellinore arrived for the important week-end in* a high state of flurry.

"I say," he exclaimed, "do you know? Have you heard? Is it a secret, what?"

"Is what a secret, what?" they asked him.

"Why, the King," cried his majesty. "You know, about the King?"

"What's the matter with the King?" inquired Sir Ector. "You don't say he's comin' down to hunt with those demned hounds of his or anythin' like that?"

"He's dead," cried King Pellinore tragically. "He's dead, poor fellah, and can't hunt any more."

Sir Grummore stood up respectfully and took off his cap of maintenance.

"The King is dead," he said. "Long live the King."

Everybody else felt they ought to stand up too, and the boys' nurse burst into tears.

"There, there," she sobbed. "His loyal highness dead and gone, and him such a respectful gentleman. Many's the illuminated picture I've cut out of him, from the Illustrated Missals, aye, and stuck up over the mantel. From the time when he was in swaddling bands, right through them world towers till he was a-visiting the dispersed areas as the world's Prince Charming, there wasn't a picture of 'im but I had it out, aye, and give 'im a last thought o' nights."

"Compose yourself, Nannie," said Sir Ector.

"It is solemn, isn't it?" said King Pellinore, "what? Uther the Conqueror, 1066 to 1216."

"A solemn moment," said Sir Grummore. "The King is dead. Long live the King."

"We ought to pull down the curtains," said Kay, who was always a stickler for good form, "or half-mast the banners."

"That's right," said Sir Ector. "Somebody go and tell the sergeant-at-arms."

It was obviously the Wart's duty to execute this command, for he was now the junior nobleman present, so he ran out cheerfully to find the sergeant. Soon those who were left in the solar could hear a voice crying out, "Nah then, one-two, special mourning fer 'is lite majesty, lower awai on the command Two!" and then the flapping of all the standards, banners, pennons, pennoncells, banderolls, guidons, streamers and cognizances which made gay the snowy turrets of the Forest Sauvage.

"How did you hear?" asked Sir Ector.

"I was pricking through the purlieus of the forest after that Beast, you know, when I met with a solemn friar of orders grey, and he told me. It's the very latest news."

"Poor old Pendragon," said Sir Ector.

"The King is dead," said Sir Grummore solemnly. "Long live the King."

"It is all very well for you to keep on mentioning that, my dear Grummore," exclaimed King Pellinore petulantly, "but who is this King, what, that is to live so long, what, accordin' to you?"

"Well, his heir," said Sir Grummore, rather taken aback.

"Our blessed monarch," said the Nurse tearfully, "never had no hair. Anybody that studied the loyal family knowed that."

"Good gracious!" exclaimed Sir Ector. "But he must have had a next-of-kin?"

"That's just it," cried King Pellinore in high excitement. "That's the excitin' part of it, what? No hair and no next of skin, and who's to succeed to the throne? That's what my friar was so excited about, what, and why he was asking who could succeed to what, what? What?"

"Do you mean to tell me," exclaimed Sir Grummore indignantly, "that there ain't no King of Gramarye?"

"Not a scrap of one," cried King Pellinore, feeling important. "And there have been signs and wonders of no mean might."

"I think it's a scandal," said Sir Grummore. "God knows what the dear old country is comin' to. Due to these lollards and communists, no doubt."

"What sort of signs and wonders?" asked Sir Ector.

"Well, there has appeared a sort of sword in a stone, what, in a sort of a church. Not in the church, if you see what I mean, and not in the stone, but that sort of thing, what, like you might say."

"I don't know what the Church is coming to," said Sir Grummore.

"It's in an anvil," explained the King.

"The Church?"

"No, the sword."

"But I thought you said the sword was in the stone?"

"No," said King Pellinore. "The stone is outside the church."

"Look here, Pellinore," said Sir Ector. "You have a bit of a rest, old boy, and start again. Here, drink up this horn of mead and take it easy."

"The sword," said King Pellinore, "is stuck through an anvil which stands on a stone. It goes right through the anvil and into the stone. The anvil is stuck to the stone. The stone stands outside a church. Give me some more mead."

"I don't think that's much of a wonder," remarked Sir Grummore. "What I wonder at is that they should allow such things to happen. But you can't tell nowadays, what with all these Saxon agitators."

"My dear fellah," cried Pellinore, getting excited again, "it's not where the stone is, what, that I'm trying to tell you, but what is written on it, what, where it is."

"What?"

"Why, on its pommel."

"Come on, Pellinore," said Sir Ector. "You just sit quite still with your face to the wall for a minute, and then tell us what you are talkin' about. Take it easy, old boy. No need for hurryin'. You sit still and look at the wall, there's a good chap, and talk as slow as you can."

"There are words written on this sword in this stone outside this church," cried King Pellinore piteously, "and these words are as follows. Oh, do try to listen to me, you two, instead of interruptin' all the time about nothin', for it makes a man's head go ever so."

"What are these words?" asked Kay.

"These words say this," said King Pellinore, "so far as I can understand from that old friar of orders grey."

"Go on, do," said Kay, for the King had come to a halt.

"Go on," said Sir Ector, "what do these words on this sword in this anvil in this stone outside this church, say?"

"Some red propaganda, no doubt," remarked Sir Grummore.

King Pellinore closed his eyes tight, extended his arms in both directions, and announced in capital letters, "Whoso Pulleth Out This Sword of this Stone and Anvil, is Rightwise King Born of All England."

"Who said that?" asked Sir Grummore.

"But the sword said it, like I tell you."

"Talkative weapon," remarked Sir Grummore sceptically.

"It was written on it," cried the King angrily. "Written on it in letters of gold."

"Why didn't you pull it out then?" asked Sir Grummore.

"But I tell you that I wasn't there. All this that I am telling you was told to me by that friar I was telling you of, like I tell you."

"Has this sword with this inscription been pulled out?" inquired Sir Ector.

"No," whispered King Pellinore dramatically. "That's

where the whole excitement comes in. They can't pull this sword out at all, although they have all been tryin' like fun, and so they have had to proclaim a tournament all over England, for New Year's Day, so that the man who comes to the tournament and pulls out the sword can be King of all England for ever, what, I say?"

"Oh, father," cried Kay. "The man who pulls that sword out of the stone will be the King of England. Can't we go to the tournament, father, and have a shot?"

"Couldn't think of it," said Sir Ector.

"Long way to London," said Sir Grummore, shaking his head.

"My father went there once," said King Pellinore.

Kay said, "Oh, surely we could go? When I am knighted I shall have to go to a tournament somewhere, and this one happens at just the right date. All the best people will be there, and we should see the famous knights and great kings. It does not matter about the sword, of course, but think of the tournament, probably the greatest there has ever been in Gramarye, and all the things we should see and do. Dear father, let me go to this tourney, if you love me, so that I may bear away the prize of all, in my maiden fight."

"But, Kay," said Sir Ector, "I have never been to London."

"All the more reason to go. I believe that anybody who does not go for a tournament like this will be proving that he has no noble blood in his veins. Think what people will say about us, if we do not go and have a shot at that sword. They will say that Sir Ector's family was too vulgar and knew it had no chance."

"We all know the family has no chance," said Sir Ector, "that is, for the sword."

"Lot of people in London," remarked Sir Grummore, with a wild surmise. "So they say."

He took a deep breath and goggled at his host with eyes like marbles.

"And shops," added King Pellinore suddenly, also beginning to breathe heavily.

"Dang it!" cried Sir Ector, bumping his horn mug on the table so that it spilled. "Let's all go to London, then, and see the new King!"

They rose up as one man.

"Why shouldn't I be as good a man as my father?" exclaimed King Pellinore.

"Dash it all," cried Sir Grummore. "After all, damn it all, it is the capital!"

"Hurray!" shouted Kay.

"Lord have mercy," said the nurse.

At this moment the Wart came in with Merlyn, and everybody was too excited to notice that, if he had not been grown up now, he would have been on the verge of tears.

"Oh, Wart," cried Kay, forgetting for the moment that he was only addressing his squire, and slipping back into the familiarity of their boyhood. "What do you think? We are all going to London for a great tournament on New Year's Day!"

"Are we?"

"Yes, and you will carry my shield and spears for the jousts, and I shall win the palm of everybody and be a great knight!"

"Well, I am glad we are going," said the Wart, "for Merlyn is leaving us too."

"Oh, we shan't need Merlyn."

"He is leaving us," repeated the Wart.

"Leavin' us?" asked Sir Ector. "I thought it was we that were leavin'?"

"He is going away from the Forest Sauvage."

Sir Ector said, "Come now, Merlyn, what's all this about? I don't understand all this a bit."

"I have come to say Good-bye, Sir Ector," said the old magician. "Tomorrow my pupil Kay will be knighted, and the next week my other pupil will go away as his squire. I have outlived my usefulness here, and it is time to go."

"Now, now, don't say that," said Sir Ector. "I think you're a jolly useful chap whatever happens. You just stay and teach me, or be the librarian or something. Don't you leave an old man alone, after the children have flown."

"We shall all meet again," said Merlyn. "There is no cause to be sad."

"Don't go," said Kay.

"I must go," replied their tutor. "We have had a good time while we were young, but it is in the nature of Time to fly. There are many things in other parts of the kingdom which I ought to be attending to just now, and it is a specially busy time for me. Come, Archimedes, say Good-bye to the company."

"Good-bye," said Archimedes tenderly to the Wart.

"Good-bye," said the Wart without looking up at all.

"But you can't go," cried Sir Ector, "not without a month's notice."

"Can't I?" replied Merlyn, taking up the position always used by philosophers who propose to dematerialize. He stood on his toes, while Archimedes held tight to his shoulder—began to spin on them slowly like a top—spun faster and faster till he was only a blur of greyish light—and in a few seconds there was no one there at all.

"Good-bye, Wart," cried two faint voices outside the solar window.

"Good-bye," said the Wart for the last time—and the poor fellow went quickly out of the room.


# 23


*The knighting took place in a whirl of preparations.* Kay's sumptuous bath had to be set up in the box-room, between two towel-horses and an old box of selected games which contained a worn-out straw dart-board—it was called fléchette in those days—because all the other rooms were full of packing. The nurse spent the whole time constructing new warm pants for everybody, on the principle that the climate of any place outside the Forest Sauvage must be treacherous to the extreme, and, as for the sergeant, he polished all the armour till it was quite brittle and sharpened the swords till they were almost worn away.

At last it was time to set out.

Perhaps, if you happen not to have lived in the Old England of the twelfth century, or whenever it was, and in a remote castle on the borders of the Marches at that, you will find it difficult to imagine the wonders of their journey.

The road, or track, ran most of the time along the high ridges of the hills or downs, and they could look down on either side of them upon the desolate marshes where the snowy reeds sighed, and the ice crackled, and the duck in the red sunsets quacked loud on the winter air. The whole country was like that. Perhaps there would be a moory marsh on one side of the ridge, and a forest of a hundred thousand acres on the other, with all the great branches weighted in white. They could sometimes see a wisp of smoke among the trees, or a huddle of buildings far out among the impassable reeds, and twice they came to quite respectable towns which had several inns to boast of, but on the whole it was an England without civilization. The better roads were cleared of cover for a bow-shot on either side of them, lest the traveller should be slain by hidden thieves.

They slept where they could, sometimes in the hut of some cottager who was prepared to welcome them, sometimes in the castle of a brother knight who invited them to refresh themselves, sometimes in the firelight and fleas of a dirty little hovel with a bush tied to a pole outside it— this was the sign-board used at that time by inns—and once or twice on the open ground, all huddled together for warmth between their grazing chargers. Wherever they went and wherever they slept, the east wind whistled in the reeds, and the geese went over high in the starlight, honking at the stars.

London was full to the brim. If Sir Ector had not been lucky enough to own a little land in Pie Street, on which there stood a respectable inn, they would have been hard put to it to find a lodging. But he did own it, and as a matter of fact drew most of his dividends from that source, so they were able to get three beds between the five of them. They thought themselves fortunate.

On the first day of the tournament, Sir Kay managed to get them on the way to the lists at least an hour before the jousts could possibly begin. He had lain awake all night, imagining how he was going to beat the best barons in England, and he had not been able to eat his breakfast. Now he rode at the front of the cavalcade, with pale cheeks, and Wart wished there was something he could do to calm him down.

For country people, who only knew the dismantled tilting ground of Sir Ector's castle, the scene which met their eyes was ravishing. It was a huge green pit in the earth, about as big as the arena at a football match. It lay ten feet lower than the surrounding country, with sloping banks, and the snow had been swept off it. It had been kept warm with straw, which had been cleared off that morning, and now the close-worn grass sparkled green in the white landscape. Round the arena there was a world of colour so dazzling and moving and twinkling as to make one blink one's eyes. The wooden grandstands were painted in scarlet and white. The silk pavilions of famous people, pitched on every side, were azure and green and saffron and chequered. The pennons and pennoncells which floated everywhere in the sharp wind were flapping with every colour of the rainbow, as they strained and slapped at their flag-poles, and the barrier down the middle of the arena itself was done in chessboard squares of black and white. Most of the combatants and their friends had not yet arrived, but one could see from those few who had come how the very people would turn the scene into a bank of flowers, and how the armour would flash, and the scalloped sleeves of the heralds jig in the wind, as they raised their brazen trumpets to their lips to shake the fleecy clouds of winter with joyances and fanfares.

"Good heavens!" cried Sir Kay. "I have left my sword at home."

"Can't joust without a sword," said Sir Grummore. "Quite irregular."

"Better go and fetch it," said Sir Ector. "You have time."

"My squire will do," said Sir Kay. "What a damned mistake to make! Here, squire, ride hard back to the inn and fetch my sword. You shall have a shilling if you fetch it in time."

The Wart went as pale as Sir Kay was, and looked as if he were going to strike him. Then he said, "It shall be done, master," and turned his ambling palfrey against the stream of newcomers. He began to push his way toward their hostelry as best he might.

"To offer me money!" cried the Wart to himself. "To look down at this beastly little donkey-affair off his great charger and to call me Squire! Oh, Merlyn, give me patience with the brute, and stop me from throwing his filthy shilling in his face."

When he got to the inn it was closed. Everybody had thronged to see the famous tournament, and the entire household had followed after the mob. Those were lawless days and it was not safe to leave your house—or even to go to sleep in it—unless you were certain that it was impregnable. The wooden shutters bolted over the downstairs windows were two inches thick, and the doors were double-barred.

"Now what do I do," asked the Wart, "to earn my shilling?"

He looked ruefully at the blind little inn, and began to laugh.

"Poor Kay," he said. "All that shilling stuff was only because he was scared and miserable, and now he has good cause to be. Well, he shall have a sword of some sort if I have to break into the Tower of London.

"How does one get hold of a sword?" he continued. "Where can I steal one? Could I waylay some knight even if I am mounted on an ambling pad, and take his weapons by force? There must be some swordsmith or armourer in a great town like this, whose shop would be still open."

He turned his mount and cantered off along the street. There was a quiet churchyard at the end of it, with a kind of square in front of the church door. In the middle of the square there was a heavy stone with an anvil on it, and a fine new sword was stuck through the anvil.

"Well," said the Wart, "I suppose it is some sort of war memorial, but it will have to do. I am sure nobody would grudge Kay a war memorial, if they knew his desperate straits."

He tied his reins round a post of the lych-gate, strode up the gravel path, and took hold of the sword.

"Come, sword," he said. "I must cry your mercy and take you for a better cause.

"This is extraordinary," said the Wart. "I feel strange when I have hold of this sword, and I notice everything much more clearly. Look at the beautiful gargoyles of the church, and of the monastery which it belongs to. See how splendidly all the famous banners in the aisle are waving. How nobly that yew holds up the red flakes of its timbers to worship God. How clean the snow is. I can smell something like fetherfew and sweet briar—and is it music that I hear?"

It was music, whether of pan-pipes or of recorders, and the light in the churchyard was so clear, without being dazzling, that one could have picked a pin out twenty yards away.

"There is something in this place," said the Wart. "There are people. Oh, people, what do you want?"

Nobody answered him, but the music was loud and the light beautiful.

"People," cried the Wart, "I must take this sword. It is not for me, but for Kay. I will bring it back."

There was still no answer, and Wart turned back to the anvil. He saw the golden letters, which he did not read, and the jewels on the pommel, flashing in the lovely light.

"Come, sword," said the Wart.

He took hold of the handles with both hands, and strained against the stone. There was a melodious consort on the recorders, but nothing moved.

The Wart let go of the handles, when they were beginning to bite into the palms of his hands, and stepped back, seeing stars.

"It is well fixed," he said.

He took hold of it again and pulled with all his might. The music played more strongly, and the light all about the churchyard glowed like amethysts; but the sword still stuck.

"Oh, Merlyn," cried the Wart, "help me to get this weapon."

There was a kind of rushing noise, and a long chord played along with it. All round the churchyard there were hundreds of old friends. They rose over the church wall all together, like the Punch and Judy ghosts of remembered days, and there were badgers and nightingales and vulgar crows and hares and wild geese and falcons and fishes and dogs and dainty unicorns and solitary wasps and corkin-drills and hedgehogs and griffins and the thousand other animals he had met. They loomed round the church wall, the lovers and helpers of the Wart, and they all spoke solemnly in turn. Some of them had come from the banners in the church, where they were painted in heraldry, some from the waters and the sky and the fields about—but all, down to the smallest shrew mouse, had come to help on account of love. Wart felt his power grow.

"Put your back into it," said a Luce (or pike) off one of the heraldic banners, "as you once did when I was going to snap you up. Remember that power springs from the nape of the neck."

"What about those forearms," asked a Badger gravely, "that are held together by a chest? Come along, my dear embryo, and find your tool."

A Merlin sitting at the top of the yew tree cried out,

"Now then, Captain Wart, what is the first law of the foot? I thought I once heard something about never letting go?"

"Don't work like a stalling woodpecker," urged a Tawny Owl affectionately. "Keep up a steady effort, my duck, and you will have it yet."

A white-front said, "Now, Wart, if you were once able to fly the great North Sea, surely you can co-ordinate a few little wing-muscles here and there? Fold your powers together, with the spirit of your mind, and it will come out like butter. Come along, Homo sapiens, for all we humble friends of yours are waiting here to cheer."

The Wart walked up to the great sword for the third time. He put out his right hand softly and drew it out as gently as from a scabbard.


There was a lot of cheering, a noise like a hurdy-gurdy which went on and on. In the middle of this noise, after a long time, he saw Kay and gave him the sword. The people at the tournament were making a frightful row.

"But this is not my sword," said Sir Kay.

"It was the only one I could get," said the Wart. "The inn was locked."

"It is a nice-looking sword. Where did you get it?"

"I found it stuck in a stone, outside a church."

Sir Kay had been watching the tilting nervously, waiting for his turn. He had not paid much attention to his squire.

"That is a funny place to find one," he said.

"Yes, it was stuck through an anvil."

"What?" cried Sir Kay, suddenly rounding upon him. "Did you just say this sword was stuck in a stone?"

"It was," said the Wart. "It was a sort of war memorial."

Sir Kay stared at him for several seconds in amazement, opened his mouth, shut it again, licked his lips, then turned his back and plunged through the crowd. He was looking for Sir Ector, and the Wart followed after him.

"Father," cried Sir Kay, "come here a moment."

"Yes, my boy," said Sir Ector. "Splendid falls these professional chaps do manage. Why, what's the matter, Kay? You look as white as a sheet."

"Do you remember that sword which the King of England would pull out?"

"Yes."

"Well, here it is. I have it. It is in my hand. I pulled it out."

Sir Ector did not say anything silly. He looked at Kay and he looked at the Wart. Then he stared at Kay again, long and lovingly, and said, "We will go back to the church."

"Now then, Kay," he said, when they were at the church door. He looked at his first-born kindly, but straight between the eyes. "Here is the stone, and you have the sword. It will make you the King of England. You are my son that I am proud of, and always will be, whatever you do. Will you promise me that you took it out by your own might?"

Kay looked at his father. He also looked at the Wart and at the sword.

Then he handed the sword to the Wart quite quietly.

He said, "I am a liar. Wart pulled it out."

As far as the Wart was concerned, there was a time after this in which Sir Ector kept telling him to put the sword back into the stone—which he did—and in which Sir Ector and Kay then vainly tried to take it out. The Wart took it out for them, and stuck it back again once or twice. After this, there was another time which was more painful.

He saw that his dear guardian was looking quite old and powerless, and that he was kneeling down with difficulty on a gouty knee.

"Sir," said Sir Ector, without looking up, although he was speaking to his own boy.

"Please do not do this, father," said the Wart, kneeling down also. "Let me help you up, Sir Ector, because you are making me unhappy."

"Nay, nay, my lord," said Sir Ector, with some very feeble old tears. "I was never your father nor of your blood, but I wote well ye are of an higher blood than I wend ye were."

"Plenty of people have told me you are not my father," said the Wart, "but it does not matter a bit."

"Sir," said Sir Ector humbly, "will ye be my good and gracious lord when ye are King?"

"Don't!" said the Wart.

"Sir," said Sir Ector, "I will ask no more of you but that you will make my son, your foster-brother, Sir Kay, seneschal of all your lands?"

Kay was kneeling down too, and it was more than the Wart could bear.

"Oh, do stop," he cried. "Of course he can be seneschal,

if I have got to be this King, and, oh, father, don't kneel down like that, because it breaks my heart. Please get up, Sir Ector, and don't make everything so horrible. Oh, dear, oh, dear, I wish I had never seen that filthy sword at all."

And the Wart also burst into tears.

# 24

*Perhaps there ought to be a chapter about the coronation.* The barons naturally kicked up a fuss, but, as the Wart was prepared to go on putting the sword into the stone and pulling it out again till Doomsday, and as there was nobody else who could do the thing at all, in the end they had to give in. A few of the Gaelic ones revolted, who were quelled later, but in the main the people of England and the partizans like Robin were glad to settle down. They were sick of the anarchy which had been their portion under Uther Pendragon: sick of overlords and feudal giants, of knights who did what they pleased, of racial discrimination, and of the rule of Might as Right.

The coronation was a splendid ceremony. What was still more splendid, it was like a birthday or Christmas Day. Everybody sent presents to the Wart, for his prowess in having learned to pull swords out of stones, and several burghers of the City of London asked him to help them in taking stoppers out of unruly bottles, unscrewing taps which had got stuck, and in other household emergencies which had got beyond their control. The Dog Boy and Wat clubbed together and sent him a mixture for the distemper, which contained quinine and was absolutely priceless. Lyo-lyok sent him some arrows made with her own feathers. Cavall came simply, and gave him his heart and soul. The Nurse of the Forest Sauvage sent a cough mixture, thirty dozen handkerchiefs all marked, and a pair of combinations with a double chest. The sergeant sent him his crusading medals, to be preserved by the nation. Hob lay awake in agony all night, and sent off Cully with brand-new white leather jesses, silver varvels and silver bell. Robin and Marian went on an expedition which took them six weeks, and sent a whole gown made out of the skins of pine martens. Little John added a yew bow, seven feet long, which he was quite unable to draw. An anonymous hedgehog sent four or five dirty leaves with fleas on them. The Questing Beast and King Pellinore put their heads together and sent some of their most perfect fewmets, wrapped up in the green leaves of spring, in a golden horn with a red velvet baldrick. Sir Grummore sent a gross of spears, with the old school crest on all of them. The cooks, tenants, villeins and retainers of The Castle of the Forest Sauvage, who were given an angel each and sent up for the ceremony in an ox-drawn char-à-banc at Sir Ector's charge, brought an enormous silver model of cow Crumbrocke, who had won the championship for the third time, and Ralph Passelewe to sing at the coronation banquet. Archimedes sent his own great-great-grandson, so that he could sit on the back of the King's throne at dinner, and make messes on the floor. The Lord Mayor and Aldermen of the City of London subscribed for a spacious aquarium-mews-cum-menagerie at the Tower in which all the creatures were starved one day a week for the good of their stomachs—and here, for the fresh food, good bedding, constant attention, and every modern convenience, the Wart's friends resorted in their old age, on wing and foot and fin, for the sunset of their happy lives. The citizens of London sent fifty million pounds, to keep the menagerie up, and the Ladies of Britain constructed a pair of black velvet carpet slippers with the Wart's initials embroidered in gold. Kay sent his own record griffin, with honest love. There were many other tasteful presents, from various barons, archbishops, princes, landgraves, tributary kings, corporations, popes, sultans, royal commissions, urban district councils, czars, beys, mahatmas, and so forth, but the nicest present of all was sent most affectionately by his own guardian, old Sir Ector. This present was a dunce's cap, rather like a pharaoh's serpent, which you lit at the top end. The Wart lit it, and watched it grow. When the flame had quite gone out, Merlyn was standing before him in his magic hat.

"Well, Wart," said Merlyn, "here we are—or were—again. How nice you look in your crown. I was not allowed to tell you before, or since, but your father was, or will be, King Uther Pendragon, and it was I myself, disguised as a beggar, who first carried you to Sir Ector's castle, in your golden swaddling bands. I know all about your birth and parentage, and who gave you your real name. I know the sorrows before you, and the joys, and how there will never again be anybody who dares to call you by the friendly name of Wart. In future it will be your glorious doom to take up the burden and to enjoy the nobility of your proper title: so now I shall crave the privilege of being the very first of your subjects to address you with it—as my dear liege lord, King Arthur."

"Will you stay with me for a long time?" asked the Wart, not understanding much of this.

"Yes, Wart," said Merlyn. "Or rather, as I should say (or is it have said?), Yes, King Arthur."

EXPLICIT LIBER PRIMUS

*Incipit Liber*
*Secundus*

# THE
# QUEEN
# OF
# AIR AND
# DARKNESS

*When shall I be dead and rid*
*Of the wrong my father did?*
*How long, how long, till spade and hearse*
*Put to sleep my mother's curse?*

# 1

*There was a round tower with a weather-cock on it.*
The weather-cock was a carrion crow, with an arrow in its
beak to point to the wind.

There was a circular room at the top of the tower, curiously uncomfortable. It was draughty. There was a closet
on the east side which had a hole in the floor. This hole
commanded the outer doors of the tower, of which there
were two, and people could drop stones through it when
they were besieged. Unfortunately the wind used to come
up through the hole and go pouring out of the unglazed shot-
windows or up the chimney—unless it happened to be blowing the other way, in which case it went downward. It was
like a wind tunnel. A second nuisance was that the room
was full of peat-smoke, not from its own fire but from the
fire in the room below. The complicated system of draughts
sucked the smoke down the chimney. The stone walls
sweated in damp weather. The furniture itself was uncomfortable. It consisted solely of heaps of stones—which were
handy for throwing down the hole—together with a few
rusty Genoese cross-bows with their bolts and a pile of
turfs for the unlit fire. The four children had no bed. If it
had been a square room, they might have had a cupboard
bed, but, as it was, they had to sleep on the floor—where
they covered themselves with straw and plaids as best they
could.

The children had erected an amateur tent over their
heads, out of the plaids, and under this they were lying close
together, telling a story. They could hear their mother stok-
ing the fire in the room below, which made them whisper
for fear that she could hear. It was not exactly that they
were afraid of being beaten if she came up. They adored
her dumbly and uncritically, because her character was
stronger than theirs. Nor had they been forbidden to talk
after bedtime. It was more as if she had brought them up—

perhaps through indifference or through laziness or even through some kind of possessive cruelty—with an imperfect sense of right and wrong. It was as if they could never know when they were being good or when they were being bad.

They were whispering in Gaelic. Or rather, they were whispering in a strange mixture of Gaelic and of the Old Language of chivalry—which had been taught to them because they would need it when they were grown. They had little English. In later years, when they became famous knights at the court of the great king, they were to speak English perfectly—all of them except Gawaine, who, as the head of the clan, was to cling to a Scots accent on purpose, to show that he was not ashamed of his birth.

Gawaine was telling the story, because he was the eldest. They lay together, like thin, strange, secret frogs, their bodies well-boned and ready to fill out into toughness as soon as they might be given decent nourishment. They were fair-haired. Gawaine's was bright red and Gareth's whiter than hay. They ranged from ten years old to fourteen, and Gareth was the youngest of the four. Gaheris was a stolid child. Agravaine, the next after Gawaine, was the bully of the family—he was shifty, inclined to cry, and frightened of pain. It was because he had a good imagination and used his head more than the others.

"Long time past, my heroes," Gawaine was saying, "before ourselves were born or thought of, there was a beautiful grandmother at us, called Igraine."

"She is the Countess of Cornwall," said Agravaine.

"Our grandmother is the Countess of Cornwall," agreed Gawaine, "and the bloody King of England fell in love with her."

"His name was Uther Pendragon," said Agravaine.

"Who is at telling this story?" asked Gareth angrily. "Close your mouth."

"King Uther Pendragon," continued Gawaine, "let send for the Earl and Countess of Cornwall——"

"Our Grandfather and Granny," said Gaheris.

"——and he proclaimed to them that they must stay with him at his house in the Tower of London. Then, when they were at staying with him therein, he asked our Granny that she would become the wife of himself, instead of being with our Grandfather at all. But the chaste and beautiful Countess of Cornwall——"

"Granny," said Gaheris.

Gareth exclaimed: "Sorrow take it, will you give us peace?" There was a muffled argument, punctuated by squeaks, bumps and complaining remarks.

"The chaste and beautiful Countess of Cornwall," resumed Gawaine, "spurned the advances of King Uther Pendragon, and she told our Grandfather about it. She said: 'I suppose we were sent for that I should be dishonoured. Wherefore, husband, I counsel you that we depart from hence suddenly, that we may ride all night to our own castle.' So they went out of the King's rath in the middle night——"

"At dead of night," Gareth corrected.

"——when all the people of the house had gone on sleep, and there they saddled their prancing, fire-eyed, swift-footed, symmetrical, large-lipped, small-headed, vehement steeds, by the light of a dark lantern, and they rode away into Cornwall, as fast as they could go."

"It was a terrible ride," said Gaheris.

"They killed the horses underneath them," said Agravaine.

"So they did not, then," said Gareth. "Our Grandfather and Granny would not have ridden any horses to kill them."

"Did they?" asked Gaheris.

"No, they did not," said Gawaine, after considering. "But they nearly did so."

He went on with the story.

"When King Uther Pendragon learned what had happened in the morning, he was wonderly wroth."

"Wood wroth," suggested Gareth.

"Wonderly wroth," said Gawaine. "King Uther Pendragon was wonderly wroth. He said, 'I will have that Earl of Cornwall's head in a pie-dish, by my halidome!' So he sent our Grandfather a letter which bid him to stuff him and garnish him, for within forty days he would fetch him out of the strongest castle that he had!"

"There were two castles at him," said Agravaine haughtily. "They were the Castle Tintagil and the Castle Terrabil."

"So the Earl of Cornwall put our Granny in Tintagil, and he himself went into Terrabil, and King Uther Pendragon came to lay them siege."

"And there," cried Gareth, unable to contain himself, "the king pight many pavilions, and there was great war made on both parties, and much people slain!"

"A thousand?" suggested Gaheris.

"Two thousand at least," said Agravaine. "We of the Gael would not have slain less than two thousand. In truth, it was a million probably."

"So when our Grandfather and Granny were winning the sieges, and it looked as if King Uther would be utterly defeated, there came along a wicked magician called Merlyn——"

"A nigromancer," said Gareth.

"And this nigromancer, would you believe it, by means of his infernal arts, succeeded in putting the treacherous Uther Pendragon inside our Granny's Castle. Granda immediately made a sortie out of Terrabil, but he was slain in the battle——"

"Treacherously."

"And the poor Countess of Cornwall——"

"The chaste and beautiful Igraine——"

"Our Granny——"

"——was captured prisoner by the blackhearted, southron, faithless King of the Dragon, and then, in spite of it that she had three beautiful daughters already whatever——"

"The lovely Cornwall Sisters."

"Aunt Elaine."

"Aunt Morgan."

"And Mammy."

"And if she had these lovely daughters, she was forced into marrying the King of England—the man who had slain her husband!"

They considered the enormous English wickedness in silence, overwhelmed by its *dénouement*. It was their mother's favourite story, on the rare occasions when she troubled to tell them one, and they had learned it by heart. Finally Agravaine quoted a Gaelic proverb, which she had also taught them.

"Four things," he whispered, "that a Lothian cannot trust —a cow's horn, a horse's hoof, a dog's snarl, and an Englishman's laugh."

They moved in the straw uneasily, listening to some secret movements in the room below.

The room underneath the story-tellers was lit by a single candle and by the saffron light of its peat fire. It was a poor room for a royal one, but at least it had a bed in it—

the great four-poster which was used as a throne during the daytime. An iron cauldron with three legs was boiling over the fire. The candle stood in front of a sheet of polished brass, which served as a mirror. There were two living beings in the chamber, a Queen and a cat. Both of them had black hair and blue eyes.

The black cat lay on its side in the firelight as if it were dead. This was because its legs were tied together, like the legs of a roe deer which is to be carried home from the hunt. It had given up struggling and now lay gazing into the fire with slit eyes and heaving sides, curiously resigned. Or else it was exhausted—for animals know when they have come to the end. Most of them have a dignity about dying, denied to human beings. This cat, with the small flames dancing in its oblique eyes, was perhaps seeing the pageant of its past eight lives, reviewing them with an animal's stoicism, beyond hope or fear.

The Queen picked up the cat. She was trying a well-known piseog to amuse herself, or at any rate to pass the time while the men were away at the war. It was a method of becoming invisible. She was not a serious witch like her sister Morgan le Fay—for her head was too empty to take any great art seriously, even if it were the black one. She was doing it because the little magics ran in her blood— as they did with all the women of her race.

In the boiling water, the cat gave some horrible convulsions and a dreadful cry. Its wet fur bobbed in the steam, gleaming like the side of a speared whale, as it tried to leap or to swim with its bound feet. Its mouth opened hideously, showing the whole of its pink gullet, and the sharp, white cat-teeth, like thorns. After the first shriek it was not able to articulate, but only to stretch its jaws. Later it was dead.

Queen Morgause of Lothian and Orkney sat beside the cauldron and waited. Occasionally she stirred the cat with a wooden spoon. The stench of boiling fur began to fill the room. A watcher would have seen, in the flattering peat light, what an exquisite creature she was tonight: her deep, big eyes, her hair glinting with dark lustre, her full body, and her faint air of watchfulness as she listened for the whispering in the room above.

Gawaine said: "Revenge!"
"They had done no harm to King Pendragon."
"They had only asked to be left in peace."

It was the unfairness of the rape of their Cornish grandmother which was hurting Gareth—the picture of weak
and innocent people victimized by a resistless tyranny—the
old tyranny of the Gall—which was felt like a personal
wrong by every crofter of the Islands. Gareth was a generous boy. He hated the idea of strength against weakness.
It made his heart swell, as if he were going to suffocate.
Gawaine, on the other hand, was angry because it had
been against his family. He did not think it was wrong for
strength to have its way, but only that it was intensely wrong
for anything to succeed against his own clan. He was
neither clever nor sensitive, but he was loyal—stubbornly
sometimes, and even annoyingly and stupidly so in later
life. For him it was then as it was always to be: Up Orkney, Right or Wrong. The third brother, Agravaine, was
moved because it was a matter which concerned his mother.
He had curious feelings about her, which he kept to himself. As for Gaheris, he did and felt what the others did.

The cat had come to pieces. The long boiling had shred-
ded its meat away until there was nothing in the cauldron
except a deep scum of hair and grease and gobbets. Underneath, the white bones revolved in the eddies of the water,
the heavy ones lying still and the airy membranes lifting
gracefully, like leaves in an autumn wind. The Queen,
wrinkling her nose slightly in the thick stench of unsalted
broth, strained the liquid into a second pot. On top of the
flannel strainer there was left a sediment of cat, a sodden
mass of matted hair and meat shreds and the delicate bone.
She blew on the sediment and began turning it over with
the handle of the spoon, prodding it to let the heat out.
Later, she was able to sort it with her fingers.

The Queen knew that every pure black cat had a certain
bone in it, which, if it were held in the mouth after boiling
the cat alive, was able to make you invisible. But nobody
knew precisely, even in those days, which the bone was. This
was why the magic had to be done in front of a mirror, so
that the right one could be found by practice.

It was not that Morgause courted invisibility—indeed, she
would have detested it, because she was beautiful. But the
men were away. It was something to do, an easy and well-
known charm. Besides, it was an excuse for lingering with
the mirror.

The Queen scraped the remains of her cat into two heaps,

one of them a neat pile of warm bones, the other a miscellaneous lump which softly steamed. Then she chose one of the bones and lifted it to her red lips, cocking the little finger. She held it between her teeth and stood in front of the polished brass, looking at herself with sleepy pleasure. She threw the bone into the fire and fetched another.

There was nobody to see her. It was strange, in these circumstances, the way in which she turned and turned, from mirror to bone-pile, always putting a bone in her mouth, and looking at herself to see if she had vanished, and throwing the bone away. She moved so gracefully, as if she were dancing, as if there really was somebody to see her, or as if it were enough that she should see herself.

Finally, but before she had tested all the bones, she lost interest. She threw the last ones down impatiently and tipped the mess out of the window, not caring where it fell. Then she smoored the fire, stretched herself on the big bed with a strange motion, and lay there in the darkness for a long time without sleeping—her body moving discontentedly.

"And this, my heroes," concluded Gawaine, "is the reason why we of Cornwall and Orkney must be against the Kings of England ever more, and most of all against the clan Mac Pendragon."

"It is why our Da has gone away to fight against King Arthur whatever, for Arthur is a Pendragon. Our Mammy said so."

"And we must keep the feud living forever," said Agravaine, "because Mammy is a Cornwall. Dame Igraine is our Granny."

"We must avenge our family."

"Because our Mammy is the most beautiful woman in the high-ridged, extensive, ponderous, pleasantly-turning world."

"And because we love her."

Indeed, they did love her. Perhaps we all give the best of our hearts uncritically—to those who hardly think about us in return.

# 2

*On the battlements of their castle at Camelot, dur-*
ing an interval of peace between the two Gaelic Wars, the
young king of England was standing with his tutor, looking
across the purple wastes of evening. A soft light flooded
the land below them, and the slow river wound between ven-
erable abbey and stately castle, while the flaming water of
sunset reflected spires and turrets and pennoncells hanging
motionless in the calm air.

The world was laid out before the two watchers like a
toy, for they were on a high keep which dominated the
town. At their feet they could see the grass of the outer
bailey—it was horrible looking down on it—and a small
foreshortened man, with two buckets on a yoke, making his
way across to the menagerie. They could see, further off at
the gatehouse, which was not so horrible to look at because
it was not vertically below, the night guard taking over
from the sergeant. They were clicking their heels and salut-
ing and presenting pikes and exchanging passwords as merrily as a marriage bell—but it was done in silence for the
two, because it was so far below. They looked like lead
soldiers, the little gallow-glasses, and their footsteps could
not sound upon the luscious sheep-nibbled green. Then, outside the curtain wall, there was the distant noise of old wives
bargaining, and brats bawling, and corporals quaffing, and
a few goats mixed with it, and two or three lepers in white
hoods ringing bells as they walked, and the swishing robes
of nuns who were kindly visiting the poor, two by two, and
a fight going on between some gentlemen who were interested in horses. On the other side of the river, which ran
directly beneath the castle wall, there was a man ploughing
in the fields, with his plough tied to the horse's tail. The
wooden plough squeaked. There was a silent person near
him, fishing for salmon with worms—the rivers were not
polluted in those days—and further off, there was a donkey
giving his musical concert to the coming night. All these

noises came up to the two on the tower smally, as though they were listening through the wrong end of a megaphone.

Arthur was a young man, just on the threshold of life. He had fair hair and a stupid face, or at any rate there was a lack of cunning in it. It was an open face, with kind eyes and a reliable or faithful expression, as though he were a good learner who enjoyed being alive and did not believe in original sin. He had never been unjustly treated, for one thing, so he was kind to other people.

The King was dressed in a robe of velvet which had belonged to Uther the Conqueror, his father, trimmed with the beards of fourteen kings who had been vanquished in the olden days. Unfortunately some of these kings had had red hair, some black, some pepper-and-salt, while their growth of beard had been uneven. The trimming looked like a feather boa. The moustaches were stuck on round the buttons.

Merlyn had a white beard which reached to his middle, horn-rimmed spectacles, and a conical hat. He wore it in compliment to the Saxon serfs of the country, whose national headgear was either a kind of diving-cap, or the Phrygian cap, or else this cone of straw.

The two of them were speaking sometimes, as the words came to them, between spells of listening to the evening.

"Well," said Arthur, "I must say it is nice to be a king. It was a splendid battle."

"Do you think so?"

"Of course it was splendid. Look at the way Lot of Orkney ran, after I had begun to use Excalibur."

"He got you down first."

"That was nothing. It was because I was not using Excalibur. As soon as I drew my trusty sword they ran like rabbits."

"They will come again," said the magician, "all six. The Kings of Orkney, Garloth, Gore, Scotland, The Tower, and the Hundred Knights have started already—in fact, the Gaelic Confederation. You must remember that your claim to the throne is hardly a conventional one."

"Let them come," replied the King. "I don't mind. I will beat them properly this time, and then we will see who is master."

The old man crammed his beard in his mouth and began to chew it, as he generally did when he was put about. He bit through one of the hairs, which stuck between two teeth. He tried to lick it off, then took it out with his fingers. Finally he began curling it into two points.

"I suppose you will learn some day," he said, "but God knows it is heartbreaking, uphill work."

"Oh?"

"Yes," cried Merlyn passionately. "Oh? oh? oh? That is all you can say. Oh? oh? oh? Like a schoolboy."

"I shall cut off your head if you are not careful."

"Cut it off. It would be a good thing if you did. I should not have to keep on tutoring, at any rate."

Arthur shifted his elbow on the battlement and looked at his ancient friend.

"What is the matter, Merlyn?" he asked. "Have I been doing something wrong? I am sorry if I have."

The magician uncurled his beard and blew his nose.

"It is not so much what you are doing," he said. "It is how you are thinking. If there is one thing I can't stand, it is stupidity. I always say that stupidity is the Sin against the Holy Ghost."

"I know you do."

"Now you are being sarcastic."

The King took him by the shoulder and turned him round. "Look," he said, "what is wrong? Are you in a bad temper? If I have done something stupid, tell me. Don't be in a bad temper."

It had the effect of making the aged nigromant angrier than before.

"Tell you!" he exclaimed. "And what is going to happen when there is nobody to tell you? Are you never going to think for yourself? What is going to happen when I am locked up in this wretched tumulus of mine, I should like to know?"

"I didn't know there was a tumulus in it."

"Oh, hang the tumulus! What tumulus? What am I supposed to be talking about?"

"Stupidity," said Arthur. "It was stupidity when we started."

"Exactly."

"Well, it's no good saying Exactly. You were going to say something about it."

"I don't know what I was going to say about it. You put one in such a passion with all your this and that, that I am sure nobody would know what they were talking about for two minutes together. How did it begin?"

"It began about the battle."

"Now I remember," said Merlyn. "That is exactly where it did begin."

"I said it was a good battle."

"So I recollect."

"Well, it was a good battle," he repeated defensively. "It was a jolly battle, and I won it myself, and it was fun."

The magician's eyes veiled themselves like a vulture's, as he vanished inside his mind. There was silence on the battlements for several minutes, while a pair of peregrines that were being hacked in a nearby field flew over their heads in a playful chase, crying out Kik-kik-kik, their bells ringing. Merlyn looked out of his eyes once more.

"It was clever of you," he said slowly, "to win the battle."

Arthur had been taught that he ought to be modest, and he was too simple to notice that the vulture was going to pounce.

"Oh, well. It was luck."

"Very clever," repeated Merlyn. "How many of your kerns were killed?"

"I don't remember."

"No."

"Kay said——"

The King stopped in the middle of the sentence, and looked at him.

"Well," he said. "It was not fun, then. I had not thought."

"The tally was more than seven hundred. They were all kerns, of course. None of the knights were injured, except the one who broke his leg falling off the horse."

When he saw that Arthur was not going to answer, the old fellow went on in a bitter voice.

"I was forgetting," he added, "that you had some really nasty bruises."

Arthur glared at his finger-nails.

"I hate you when you are a prig."

Merlyn was charmed.

"That's the spirit," he said, putting his arm through the King's and smiling cheerfully. "That's more like it. Stand up for yourself, that's the ticket. Asking advice is the fatal thing. Besides, I won't be here to advise you, fairly soon."

"What is this you keep talking about, about not being here, and the tumulus and so on?"

"It is nothing. I am due to fall in love with a girl called Nimue in a short time, and then she learns my spells and locks me up in a cave for several centuries. It is one of those things which are going to happen."

"But, Merlyn, how horrible! To be stuck in a cave for centuries like a toad in a hole! We must do something about it."

"Nonsense," said the magician. "What was I talking about?"

"About this maiden. . . ."

"I was talking about advice, and how you must never take it. Well, I am going to give you some now. I advise you to think about battles, and about your realm of Gramarye, and about the sort of things a king has to do. Will you do that?"

"I will. Of course I will. But about this girl who learns your spells. . . ."

"You see, it is a question of the people, as well as of the kings. When you said about the battle being a lovely one, you were thinking like your father. I want you to think like yourself, so that you will be a credit to all this education I have been giving you—afterwards, when I am only an old man locked up in a hole."

"Merlyn!"

"There, there! I was playing for sympathy. Never mind. I said it for effect. As a matter of fact, it will be charming to have a rest for a few hundred years, and, as for Nimue, I am looking backward to her a good deal. No, no, the important thing is this thinking-for-yourself business and the matter of battles. Have you ever thought seriously about the state of your country, for instance, or are you going to go on all your life being like Uther Pendragon? After all, you are the King of the place."

"I have not thought very much."

"No. Then let me do some thinking for you. Suppose we think about your Gaelic friend, Sir Bruce Sans Pitié."

"That fellow!"

"Exactly. And why do you say it like that?"

"He is a swine. He goes murdering maidens—and, as soon as a real knight turns up to rescue them, he gallops off for all he is worth. He breeds special fast horses so that nobody can catch him, and he stabs people in the back. He's a marauder. I would kill him at once if I could catch him."

"Well," said Merlyn, "I don't think he is very different from the others. What is all this chivalry, anyway? It simply means being rich enough to have a castle and a suit of armour, and then, when you have them, you make the Saxon people do what you like. The only risk you run is of getting a few bruises if you happen to come across another knight. Look at that tilt you saw between Pellinore and Grummore, when you were small. It is this armour that does it. All the barons can slice the poor people about as much as they want, and it is a day's work to hurt each other, and the result is that the country is devastated. Might is Right, that's the motto. Bruce Sans Pitié is only an example of the general situation. Look at Lot and Nentres and Uriens and all that Gaelic crew, fighting against you for the Kingdom. Pulling swords out of stones is not a legal proof of paternity, I admit, but the kings of the Old Ones are not fighting you about that. They have rebelled, although you are their feudal sovereign, simply because the throne is insecure. England's difficulty, we used to say, is Ireland's opportunity. This is their chance to pay off racial scores, and to have some blood-letting as sport, and to make a bit of money in ransoms. Their turbulence does not cost them anything themselves because they are dressed in armour—and you seem to enjoy it too. But look at the country. Look at the barns burnt, and dead men's legs sticking out of ponds, and horses with swelled bellies by the roadside, and mills falling down, and money buried, and nobody daring to walk abroad with gold or ornaments on their clothes. That is chivalry nowadays. That is the Uther Pendragon touch. And then you talk about a battle being fun!"

"I was thinking of myself."

"I know."

"I ought to have thought of the people who had no armour."

"Quite."

"Might isn't Right, is it, Merlyn?"

"Aha!" replied the magician, beaming. "Aha! You are a cunning lad, Arthur, but you won't catch your old tutor like that. You are trying to put me in a passion by making me do the thinking. But I am not to be caught. I am too old a fox for that. You will have to think the rest yourself. Is might right—and if not, why not, give reasons and draw a plan. Besides, what are you going to do about it?"

"What . . ." began the King, but he saw the gathering frown.

"Very well," he said. "I will think about it."

And he began thinking, stroking his upper lip, where the moustache was going to be.

There was a small incident before they left the keep. The man who had been carrying the two buckets to the menagerie came back with his buckets empty. He passed directly under them, looking small, on his way to the kitchen door. Arthur, who had been playing with a loose stone which he had dislodged from one of the machicolations, got tired of thinking and leaned over with the stone in his hand.

"How small Curselaine looks."

"He is tiny."

"I wonder what would happen if I dropped this stone on his head?"

Merlyn measured the distance.

"At thirty-two feet per second," he said, "I think it would kill him dead. Four hundred $g$ is enough to shatter the skull."

"I have never killed anybody like that," said the boy, in an inquisitive tone.

Merlyn was watching.

"You are the King," he said.

Then he added, "Nobody can say anything to you if you try."

Arthur stayed motionless, leaning out with the stone in his hand. Then, without his body moving, his eyes slid sideways to meet his tutor's.

The stone knocked Merlyn's hat off as clean as a whistle, and the old gentleman chased him featly down the stairs, waving his wand of lignum vitae.

Arthur was happy. Like the man in Eden before the fall, he was enjoying his innocence and fortune. Instead of being a poor squire, he was a king. Instead of being an orphan, he was loved by nearly everybody except the Gaels, and he loved everybody in return.

So far as he was concerned, as yet, there might never have been such a thing as a single particle of sorrow on the gay, sweet surface of the dew-glittering world.

# 3

*Sir Kay had heard stories about the Queen of Orkney,* and he was inquisitive about her.

"Who is Queen Morgause?" he asked one day. "I was told that she is beautiful. What did these Old Ones want to fight us about? And what is her husband like, King Lot? What is his proper name? I heard somebody calling him the King of the Out Isles, and then there are others who call him the King of Lothian and Orkney. Where is Lothian? Is it near Hy Brazil? I can't understand what the revolt was about. Everybody knows that the King of England is their feudal overlord. I heard that she has four sons. Is it true that she doesn't get on with her husband?"

They were riding back from a day on the mountain, where they had been hunting grouse with the peregrines, and Merlyn had gone with them for the sake of the ride. He had become a vegetarian lately—an opponent of blood-sports on principle—although he had gone through most of them during his thoughtless youth—and even now he secretly adored to watch the falcons for themselves. Their masterly circles, as they waited on—mere specks in the sky—and the bur-r-r with which they scythed on the grouse, and the way in which the wretched quarry, killed instantaneously, went end-over-tip into the heather—these were a temptation to which he yielded in the uncomfortable knowledge that it was sin. He consoled himself by saying that the grouse were for the pot. But it was a shallow excuse, for he did not believe in eating meat either.

Arthur, who was riding watchfully like a sensible young monarch, withdrew his eye from a clump of whins which might have held an ambush in those early days of anarchy, and cocked one eyebrow at his tutor. He was wondering with half his mind which of Kay's questions the magician would choose to answer, but the other half was still upon the martial possibilities of the landscape. He knew how far the falconers were behind them—the cadger carrying the hooded hawks on a square framework slung from his shoulders, with a man-at-arms on either side—and how far in front was the next likely place for a William Rufus arrow.

Merlyn chose the second question.

"Wars are never fought for one reason," he said. "They are fought for dozens of reasons, in a muddle. It is the same with revolts."

"But there must have been a main reason," said Kay.

"Not necessarily."

Arthur observed: "We might have a trot now. It is clear going for two miles since those whins, and we can have a canter back again, to keep with the men. It would breathe the horses."

Merlyn's hat blew off. They had to stop to pick it up. Afterwards they walked their horses sedately in a row.

"One reason," said the magician, "is the immortal feud of Gael and Gall. The Gaelic Confederation are representatives of an ancient race which has been harried out of England by several races which are represented by you. Naturally they want to be as nasty as possible to you when they can."

"Racial history is beyond me," said Kay. "Nobody knows which race is which. They are all serfs, in any case."

The old man looked at him with something like amusement.

"One of the startling things about the Norman," he said, "is that he really does not know a single thing about anybody except himself. And you, Kay, as a Norman gentleman, carry the peculiarity to its limit. I wonder if you even know what a Gael is? Some people call them Celts."

"A celt is a kind of battle-axe," said Arthur, surprising the magician with this piece of information more than he had been surprised for several generations. For it was true, in one of the meanings of the word, although Arthur ought not to have known it.

"Not that kind of celt. I am talking about the people. Let's stick to calling them Gaels. I mean the Old Ones who live in Brittany and Cornwall and Wales and Ireland and Scotland. Picts and that."

"Picts?" asked Kay. "I think I have heard about Picts. Pictures. They were painted blue."

"And I am supposed to have managed your education!"

The King said thoughtfully: "Would you mind telling me about the races, Merlyn? I suppose I ought to understand the situation, if there has to be a second war."

This time it was Kay who looked surprised.

"Is there to be a war?" he asked. "This is the first I've heard of it. I thought the revolt was crushed last year?"

"They have made a new confederation since they went home, with five new kings, which makes them eleven altogether. The new ones belong to the old blood too. They are Clariance of North Humberland, Idres of Cornwall, Cradelmas of North Wales, Brandegoris of Stranggore and Anguish of Ireland. It will be a proper war, I'm afraid."

"And all about races," said his foster-brother in disgust. "Still, it may be fun."

The King ignored him.

"Go on," he said to Merlyn. "I want you to explain."

"Only," he added quickly, as the magician opened his mouth, "not too many details."

Merlyn opened his mouth and shut it twice, before he was able to comply with this restriction.

"About three thousand years ago," he said, "the country you are riding through belonged to a Gaelic race who fought with copper hatchets. Two thousand years ago they were hunted west by another Gaelic race with bronze swords. A thousand years ago there was a Teuton invasion by people who had iron weapons, but it didn't reach the whole of the Pictish Isles because the Romans arrived in the middle and got mixed up with it. The Romans went away about eight hundred years ago, and then another Teuton invasion—of people mainly called Saxons—drove the whole ragbag west as usual. The Saxons were just beginning to settle down when your father the Conqueror arrived with his pack of Normans, and that is where we are today. Robin Wood was a Saxon partizan."

"I thought we were called the British Isles."

"So we are. People have got the B's and P's muddled up. Nothing like the Teuton race for confusing its consonants. In Ireland they are still chattering away about some people called Fomorians, who were really Pomeranians, while . . ."

Arthur interrupted him at the critical moment.

"So it comes to this," he said, "that we Normans have the Saxons for serfs, while the Saxons once had a sort of under-serfs, who were called the Gaels—the Old Ones. In that case I don't see why the Gaelic Confederation should want to fight against me—as a Norman king—when it was really the Saxons who hunted them, and when it was hundreds of years ago in any case."

"You are under-rating the Gaelic memory, dear boy. They don't distinguish between you. The Normans are a Teuton race, like the Saxons whom your father conquered. So far as the ancient Gaels are concerned, they just regard both your races as branches of the same alien people, who have driven them north and west."

Kay said definitely: "I can't stand any more history. After all, we are supposed to be grown up. If we go on, we shall be doing dictation."

Arthur grinned and began in the well-remembered singsong voice: Barbara Celarent Darii Ferioque Prioris, while Kay sang the next four lines with him antiphonically.

Merlyn said: "You asked for it."

"And now we have it."

"The main thing is that the war is going to happen because the Teutons or the Galls or whatever you call them upset the Gaels long ago."

"Certainly not," exclaimed the magician. "I never said anything of the sort."

They gaped.

"I said the war will happen for dozens of reasons, not for one. Another of the reasons for this particular war is because Queen Morgause wears the trousers. Perhaps I ought to say the trews."

Arthur asked painstakingly: "Let me get this clear. First I was given to understand that Lot and the rest had rebelled because they were Gaels and we were Galls, but now I am told that it deals with the Queen of Orkney's trousers. Could you be more definite?"

"There is the feud of Gael and Gall which we have been talking about, but there are other feuds too. Surely you have not forgotten that your father killed the Earl of Cornwall before you were born? Queen Morgause was one of the daughters of that Earl."

"The Lovely Cornwall Sisters," observed Kay.

"Exactly. You met one of them yourselves—Queen Morgan le Fay. That was when you were friends with Robin Wood, and you found her on a bed of lard. The third sister was Elaine. All three of them are witches of one sort or another, though Morgan is the only one who takes it seriously."

"If my father," said the King, "killed the Queen of Orkney's father, then I think she has a good reason for wanting her husband to rebel against me."

"It is only a personal reason. Personal reasons are no excuse for war."

"And furthermore," the King continued, "if my race has driven out the Gaelic race, then I think the Queen of Orkney's subjects have a good reason too."

Merlyn scratched his chin in the middle of the beard, with the hand which held the reins, and pondered.

"Uther," he said at length, "your lamented father, was an aggressor. So were his predecessors the Saxons, who drove the Old Ones away. But if we go on living backward like that, we shall never come to the end of it. The Old Ones themselves were aggressors, against the earlier race of the copper hatchets, and even the hatchet fellows were aggressors, against some earlier crew of esquimaux who lived on shells. You simply go on and on, until you get to Cain and Abel. But the point is that the Saxon Conquest did succeed, and so did the Norman Conquest of the Saxons. Your father settled the unfortunate Saxons long ago, however brutally he did it, and when a great many years have passed one ought to be ready to accept a *status quo*. Also I would like to point out that the Norman Conquest was a process of welding small units into bigger ones—while the present revolt of the Gaelic Confederation is a process of disintegration. They want to smash up what we may call the United Kingdom into a lot of piffling little kingdoms of their own. That is why their reason is not what you might call a good one."

He scratched his chin again, and became wrathful.

"I never could stomach these nationalists," he exclaimed. "The destiny of Man is to unite, not to divide. If you keep on dividing you end up as a collection of monkeys throwing nuts at each other out of separate trees."

"All the same," said the King, "there seems to have been a good deal of provocation. Perhaps I ought not to fight?"

"And give in?" asked Kay, more in amusement than dismay.

"I could abdicate."

They looked at Merlyn, who refused to meet their eyes. He rode on, staring straight in front of him, munching his beard.

"Ought I to give in?"

"You are the King," said the old man stubbornly. "Nobody can say anything if you do."

Later on, he began to speak in a gentler tone.

"Did you know," he asked rather wistfully, "that I was

one of the Old Ones myself? My father was a demon, they say, but my mother was a Gael. The only human blood I have comes from the Old Ones. Yet here I am denouncing their ideas of nationalism, being what their politicians would call a traitor—because, by calling names, they can score the cheap debating points. And do you know another thing, Arthur? Life is too bitter already, without territories and wars and noble feuds."

# 4

*The hay was safe and the corn would be ripe in a week.* They sat in the shade at the edge of a cornfield, watching the dark brown people with their white teeth who were aimlessly busy in the sunlight, rehanging their scythes, sharpening their sickles and generally getting ready for the end of farm year. It was peaceful in the fields which were close to the castle, and no arrows needed to be apprehended. While they watched the harvesters, they stripped the half-ripe heads of corn with their fingers and bit the grain daintily, tasting the furry milkiness of the wheat, and the husky, less generous flesh of the oats. The pearly taste of barley would have been strange to them, for it had not yet come to Gramarye.

Merlyn was still explaining.

"When I was a young man," he said, "there was a general idea that it was wrong to fight in wars of any sort. Quite a lot of people in those days declared that they would never fight for anything whatever."

"Perhaps they were right," said the King.

"No. There is one fairly good reason for fighting—and that is, if the other man starts it. You see, wars are a wickedness, perhaps the greatest wickedness of a wicked species. They are so wicked that they must not be allowed. When you can be perfectly certain that the other man started them, then is the time when you might have a sort of duty to stop him."

"But both sides always say that the other side started them."

"Of course they do, and it is a good thing that it should be so. At least, it shows that both sides are conscious, inside themselves, that the wicked thing about a war is its beginning."

"But the reasons," protested Arthur. "If one side was starving the other by some means or other—some peaceful, economic means which were not actually warlike—then the starving side might have to fight its way out—if you see what I mean?"

"I see what you think you mean," said the magician, "but you are wrong. There is no excuse for war, none whatever, and whatever the wrong which your nation might be doing to mine—short of war—my nation would be in the wrong if it *started* a war so as to redress it. A murderer, for instance, is not allowed to plead that his victim was rich and oppressing him—so why should a nation be allowed to? Wrongs have to be redressed by reason, not by force."

Kay said: "Suppose King Lot of Orkney was to draw up his army all along the northern border, what could our King here do except send his own army to stand on the same line? Then supposing all Lot's men drew their swords, what could we do except draw ours? The situation could be more complicated than that. It seems to me that aggression is a difficult thing to be sure about."

Merlyn was annoyed.

"Only because you want it to seem so," he said. "Obviously Lot would be the aggressor, for making the threat of force. You can always spot the villain, if you keep a fair mind. In the last resort, it is ultimately the man who strikes the first blow."

Kay persisted with his argument.

"Let it be two men," he said, "instead of two armies. They stand opposite each other—they draw their swords, pretending it is for some other reason—they move about, so as to get the weak side of one another—they even make feints with their swords, pretending to strike, but not doing so. Do you mean to tell me that the aggressor is the one who actually hits first?"

"Yes, if there is nothing else to decide by. But in your case it is obviously the man who first took his army to the frontier."

"This first blow business brings it down to a matter of

nothing. Suppose they both struck at once, or suppose you could not see which one gave the first blow, because there were so many facing each other?"

"But there nearly always is something else to decide by," exclaimed the old man. "Use your common sense. Look at this Gaelic revolt, for example. What reason has the King here for being an aggressor? He is their feudal overlord already. It isn't sensible to pretend that he is making the attack. People don't attack their own possessions."

"I certainly don't feel, " said Arthur, "as if I had started it. Indeed, I didn't know it was going to start, until it had. I suppose that was due to my having been brought up in the country."

"Any reasoning man," continued his tutor, ignoring the interruption, "who keeps a steady mind, can tell which side is the aggressor in ninety wars out of a hundred. He can see which side is likely to benefit by going to war in the first place, and that is a strong reason for suspicion. He can see which side began to make the threat of force or was the first to arm itself. And finally he can often put his finger on the one who struck the first blow."

"But supposing," said Kay, "that one side was the one to make the threat, while the other side was the one to strike the first blow?"

"Oh, go and put your head in a bucket. I'm not suggesting that all of them can be decided. I was saying, from the start of the argument, that there are many wars in which the aggression is as plain as a pike-staff, and that in those wars at any rate it might be the duty of decent men to fight the criminal. If you aren't sure that he is the criminal—and you must sum it up for yourself with every ounce of fairness you can muster—then go and be a pacifist by all means. I recollect that I was a fervent pacifist myself once, in the Boer War, when my own country was the aggressor, and a young woman blew a squeaker at me on Mafeking Night."

"Tell us about Mafeking Night," said Kay. "One gets sick of these discussions about right and wrong."

"Mafeking Night . . ." began the magician, who was prepared to tell anybody about anything. But the King prevented him.

"Tell us about Lot," he said. "I want to know about him, if I have to fight him. Personally I am beginning to be interested in right and wrong."

"King Lot . . ." began Merlyn in the same tone of voice, only to be interrupted by Kay.

"No," said Kay. "Talk about the Queen. She sounds more interesting."

"Queen Morgause. . . ."

Arthur assumed the right of veto for the first time in his life. Merlyn, catching the lifted eyebrow, reverted to the King of Orkney with unexpected humility.

"King Lot," said he, "is simply a member of your peerage and landed royalty. He's a cipher. You don't have to think about him at all."

"Why not?"

"In the first place, he is what we used to call in my young days a Gentleman of the Ascendancy. His subjects are Gaels and so is his wife, but he himself is an import from Norway. He is a Gall like yourself, a member of the ruling class who conquered the Islands long ago. This means that his attitude to the war is the same as your father's would have been. He doesn't care a fig about Gaels or Galls, but he goes in for wars in the same way as my Victorian friends used to go in for foxhunting or else for profit in ransoms. Besides, his wife makes him."

"Sometimes," said the King, "I wish you had been born forwards like other people. What with Victorians and Mafeking Night. . . ."

Merlyn was indignant.

"The link between Norman warfare and Victorian foxhunting is perfect. Leave your father and King Lot outside the question for the moment, and look at literature. Look at the Norman myths about legendary figures like the Angevin kings. From William the Conqueror to Henry the Third, they indulged in warfare seasonally. The season came round, and off they went to the meet in splendid armour which reduced the risk of injury to a foxhunter's minimum. Look at the decisive battle of Brenneville in which a field of nine hundred knights took part, and only three were killed. Look at Henry the Second borrowing money from Stephen, to pay his own troops in fighting Stephen. Look at the sporting etiquette, according to which Henry had to withdraw from a siege as soon as his enemy Louis joined the defenders inside the town, because Louis was his feudal overlord. Look at the siege of Mont St. Michel, at which it was considered unsporting to win through the defenders' lack of water. Look at the battle of Malmesbury, which was

given up on account of bad weather. That is the inheritance
to which you have succeeded, Arthur. You have become the
king of a domain in which the popular agitators hate each
other for racial reasons, while the nobility fight each other
for fun, and neither the racial maniac nor the overlord
stops to consider the lot of the common soldier, who is the
one person that gets hurt. Unless you can make the world
wag better than it does at present, King, your reign will be
an endless series of petty battles, in which the aggressions
will either be from spiteful reasons or from sporting ones,
and in which the poor man will be the only one who dies.
That is why I have been asking you to think. That is
why. . . ."

"I think," said Kay, "that Dinadan is waving to us, to say
that dinner is ready."

# 5

*Mother Morlan's house in the Out Isles was hardly*
bigger than a large dog kennel—but it was comfortable and
full of interesting things. There were two horseshoes nailed
on the door—five statues bought from pilgrims, with the
used-up rosaries wound round them—for beads break, if one
is a good prayer—several bunches of fairy-flax laid on top of
the salt-box—some scapulars wound round the poker—
twenty bottles of mountain dew, all empty but one—about
a bushel of withered palm, relic of Palm Sundays for the
past seventy years—and plenty of woollen thread for tying
round the cow's tail when she was calving. There was also a
large scythe blade which the old lady hoped to use on a
burglar—if ever one was foolish enough to come that way
—and, in the chimney, there were hung some ash-rungs
which her deceased husband had been intending to use for
flails, together with eel skins and strips of horse leather as
hangings to them. Under the eel skins was an enormous
bottle of holy water, and in front of the turf fire sat one of
the Irish Saints who lived in the beehive cells of the outer
islands, with a glass of water-of-life in his hand. He was a re-

lapsed saint, who had fallen into the Pelagian heresy of Celestius, and he believed that the soul was capable of its own salvation. He was busy saving it with Mother Morlan and the usquebaugh.

"God and Mary to you, Mother Morlan," said Gawaine. "We have come for a story, ma'am, about the shee."

"God and Mary and Andrew to you," exclaimed the beldame. "And you asking me for a story, whateffer, with his reverence here among the ashes!"

"Good evening, St. Toirdealbhach, we did not notice you because of the dark."

"The blessing of God to you."

"The same blessing to you yourself."

"It must be about murders," said Agravaine. "About murders and some corbies which peck out your eyes."

"No, no," cried Gareth. "It must be about a mysterious girl who marries a man because he has stolen the giant's magic horse."

"Glory be to God," remarked St. Toirdealbhach. "It does be a strange story yer after wanting entirely."

"Come now, St. Toirdealbhach, tell us one yourself."

"Tell us about Ireland."

"Tell us about Queen Maeve, who desired the bull."

"Or dance us one of the jigs."

"Maircy on the puir bairns, to think of his holiness dancing a jig!"

The four representatives of the upper classes sat down wherever they could—there were only two stools—and stared at the holy man in receptive silence.

"Is it a moral tale yer after?"

"No, no. No morals. We like a story about fighting. Come, St. Toirdealbhach, what about the time you broke the Bishop's head?"

The saint drank a big gulp of his white whisky and spat in the fire.

"There was a king in it one time," said he, and the whole audience made a rustling noise with their rumps, as they settled down.

"There was a king in it, one time," said St. Toirdealbhach, "and this king, what do you think, was called King Conor Mac Nessa. He was a whale of a man who lived with his relations at a place called Tara of the Kings. It was not long before this king had to go out to battle against thim bloody O'Haras, and he got shot in the conflict with a magic ball.

You are to understand that the ancient heroes were after
making themselves bullets out of the brains of their adver-
saries—which they would roll between the palms of their
hands in little pieces, and leave them to dry in the sun. I
suppose they must have shot them out of the arquebus, you
know, as if they were sling-shot or bolts. Well, and if they
did, this old King was shot in the temples with one of thim
same bullets, and it lodging against the bone of the skull,
at the critical point whatever. 'I'm a fine man now,' says
the King, and he sends for the brehons and those to advise
with them about the obstetrics. The first brehon says,
'You're a dead man, King Conor. This ball is at the lobe of
the brain.' So said all the medical gintlemen, widout respect
of person nor creed. 'Oh, what'll I do at all,' cries the King
of Ireland. 'It's a hard fortune evidently, when a man can't
be fighting a little bit unless he comes to the end of his
days.' 'None of yer prate, now,' say the surgeons, 'there's
wan thing which can be done, and that same thing is to keep
from all unnatural excitement from this time forward.' 'For
that matter,' says they, 'ye must keep from all natural excitement also, or otherwise the bullet will cause a rupture, and
the rupture rising to a flux, and the flux to a conflammation,
will occasion an absolute abruption in the vital functions
at all. It's yer only hope, King Conor, or otherwise ye will lie
compunctually as the worms made ye.' Well, begor, it was a
fine state of business, as you may imagine. There was that
poor Conor in his castle, and he not able to laugh nor fight
nor take any small sup of spirited water nor to look upon
a white colleen anyhow, for fear that his brains would burst.
The ball stood in his temples, half in, half out, and that was
the sorrow with him, from that day forward."

"Wurra the doctors," said Mother Morlan. "Hoots, but
they're na canny."

"What happened him?" asked Gawaine. "Did he live long
in this dark room?"

"What happened him? I was now coming to that. Wan
day there was a slashing thunderstorm in it, and the castle
walls shook like a long-net, and great part of the bailey
fell upon them. It was the worst storm that was known in
those parts for whiles, and King Conor rushed out into the
element to seek advice. He found wan of his brehons standing there whatever, and axed him what could it be. This
brehon was a learned man, and he told King Conor. He said
how our Saviour had been hanged on a tree in Jewry that

day, and how the storm was broken on account of it, and he spoke to King Conor about the gospel of God. Then, what do you think, King Conor of Ireland ran back into his palace for to seek his sword in righteous passion, and he ran out with it throughout the tempest to defend his Saviour—and that was how he died."

"He was dead?"

"Yes."

"Well!"

"What a nice way to do it," said Gareth. "It was no good to him, but it was grand!"

Agravaine said, "If I was told by my doctors to be careful, I would not lose my temper over nothing. I should think what was happening, whatever."

"But it was chivalrous?"

Gawaine began to fidget with his toes.

"It was silly," he said eventually. "It did no good."

"But he was trying to do the good."

"It was not for his family," said Gawaine. "I do not know why he was so excited at all."

"Of course it was for his family. It was for God, who is the family of every person. King Conor went out on the side of right, and gave his life to help it."

Agravaine moved his stern in the soft, rusty ashes of the turf impatiently. He considered that Gareth was a fool.

"Tell us the story," he said, to change the subject, "about how pigs were made."

"Or the one," said Gawaine, "about the great Conan who was enchanted to a chair. He was stuck on it, whatever, and they could not get him off. So they pulled him from it by force, and then there was a necessity on them to graft a piece of skin on his bottom—but it was sheepskin, and from thenceforth the stockings worn by the Fianna were made from the wool which grew on Conan!"

"No, do not," said Gareth. "Let there be no stories. Let us sit and talk wisely, my heroes, on deep matters. Let us talk about our father, who is away to the wars."

St. Toirdealbhach took a deep draught of his mountain dew, and spat in the fire.

"Isn't war the grand thing," he observed reminiscently. "I did be going to wars a great deal wan time, before I was sainted. Only I got tired on them."

Gawaine said: "I cannot see how people ever get tired of wars. I am sure I will not. After all, it is a gentleman's occupation. I mean, it would be like getting tired of hunting, or of hawks."

"War," said Toirdealbhach, "be's a good thing if there doesn't be too many in it. When there's too many fighting, how would you know what you are fighting about at all? There did be fine wars in Old Ireland, but it would be about a bull or something, and every man had his heart in it from the start."

"Why did you get tired of wars?"

" 'Twas thim same numbers had thim destroyed altogether. Who would want to be killing a mortal for what he didn't understand, or for nothing? I took up with the single combats instead."

"That must have been a long time ago."

"Aye," said the saint regretfully. "Thim bullets I was telling ye about, now: the brains didn't be much good widout they were taken in single combat. It was the virtue of them."

"I incline my agreement with Toirdealbhach," said Gareth. "After all, what is the good of killing poor kerns who do not know anything? It would be much better for the people who are angry to fight each other themselves, knight against knight."

"But you could not have any wars at all, like that," exclaimed Gaheris.

"It would be absurd," said Gawaine. "You must have people, galore of people, in a war."

"Otherwise you could not kill them," explained Agravaine.

The saint helped himself to a fresh dose of whisky, hummed a few bars of *Poteen, Good Luck to Ye, Dear,* and glanced at Mother Morlan. He was feeling a new heresy coming over him, possibly as a result of the spirits, and it had something to do with the celibacy of the clergy. He had one already about the shape of his tonsure, and the usual one about the date of Easter, as well as his own Pelagian business—but the latest was beginning to make him feel as if the presence of children was unnecessary.

"Wars," he said with disgust. "And how would kids like you be talking about them, will ye tell me, and you no bigger than sitting hens? Be off now, before I beget an ill wish toward ye."

Saints, as the Old Ones knew very well, were a bad class of people to cross, so the children stood up hastily.

"Och, now," they said. "Your Holiness, no offence, we are sure. We were only at wishing to make an exchange of ideas."

"Ideas!" he exclaimed, reaching for the poker—and they were outside the low door in the twinkling of an eye, standing in the level rays of sunset on the sandy street, while his anathemas or whatever they may have been rumbled behind them from the dark interior.

In the street, there were two moth-eaten donkeys searching for weeds in the cracks of a stone wall. Their legs were tied together so that they could hardly hobble, and their hoofs were cruelly overgrown, so that they looked like rams' horns or curly skates. The boys commandeered them at once, a new idea springing fully armed from their heads as soon as they had seen the animals. They would stop hearing stories or discussing warfare, and they would take the donkeys to the little harbour beyond the sand-dunes, in case the men who had been out in their currachs should have made a catch. The donkeys would be useful for carrying the fish.

Gawaine and Gareth took turns with the fat ass, one of them whacking it while the other rode bareback. The ass gave a hop occasionally, but refused to trot. Agravaine and Gaheris both sat on the thin one, the former being mounted back to front so that he faced the creature's behind—which he thrashed furiously with a thick root of sea-weed. He beat it round the vent, to hurt it more.

It was a strange scene which they presented when they reached the sea—the thin children whose sharp noses had a drop on the end of each, and their bony wrists which had outgrown their coats—the donkeys scampering round in small circles, with an occasional frisk as the tangle bit into their grey quarters. It was strange because it was circumscribed, because it was concentrated on a single intention. They might have been a solar system of their own, with nothing else in space, as they went round and round among the dunes and coarse grass of the estuary. Probably the planets have few ideas in their heads, either.

The idea which the children had was to hurt the donkeys. Nobody had told them that it was cruel to hurt them, but then, nobody had told the donkeys either. On the rim of the world they knew too much about cruelty to be surprised by it. So the small circus was a unity—the beasts reluctant to move and the children vigorous to move them, the two parties bound together by the link of pain to which they both agreed without question. The pain itself was so much a matter of course that it had vanished out of the picture, as if by a process of cancellation. The animals did not seem to be suffering, and the children did not seem to be enjoying the suffering. The only difference was that the boys were violently animated while the donkeys were as static as possible.

Into this Eden-like scene, and almost before the memory of Mother Morlan's interior had faded from their minds, there came a magic barge from over the water, a barge draped with white samite, mystic, wonderful, and it made a music of its own accord as its keel passed through the waves. Inside it there were three knights and a seasick brachet. Anything less suitable than these to the tradition of the Gaelic world, it would have been impossible to imagine.

"I say," said the voice of one of the knights in the barge, while they were still far out, "there is a castle, isn't it, what? I say, isn't it a pretty one!"

"Stop joggin' the boat, my dear fellow," said the second, "or you will have us in the sea."

King Pellinore's enthusiasm evaporated at the rebuke, and he startled the petrified children by bursting into tears. They could hear his sobs, mingling with the lapping of the waves and with the music of the boat, as it drew near.

"Oh, sea!" he said. "I wish I was in you, what? I wish I was full of five fathoms, that I do. Woe, woe, oh, woe!"

"It is no good saying Whoa, old boy. The thing will whoa when it wants to. It is a magic 'un."

"I was not saying Whoa," retorted the King. "I was saying Woe."

"Well, it won't whoa."

"I don't care if it does or if it don't. I said Woe!"

"Well, whoa, then."

And the magic barge whoaed, just where the currachs were usually drawn up. The three knights got out, and it could be seen that the third was a black man. He was a learned paynim or saracen, called Sir Palomides.

"Happy landing," said Sir Palomides, "by golly!"

The people came from everywhere, silently, vaguely. When they were near the knights, they walked slowly, but in the remoter distance they were running. Men, women and children were scuttling over the dunes or down from the castle cliff, only to break into the crawling pace as soon as they were near. At a distance of twenty yards, they halted altogether. They made a ring, staring at the newcomers mutely, like people staring at pictures in the Uffizzi. They studied them. There was no hurry now, no need to dash off to the next picture. Indeed, there were no other pictures—had been no others, except for the accustomed scenes of Lothian, since they were born. Their stare was not exactly an offensive one, nor was it friendly. Pictures exist to be absorbed. It began at the feet, especially as the strangers were dressed in outlandish clothes like knights-in-armour, and it mastered the texture, the construction, the articulation and the probable price of their sabathons. Then it went on to the greaves, the cuisses, and so up. It might take half an hour to reach the face, which was to be examined last of all.

The Gaels stood round the Galls with their mouths open, while the village children shouted the news in the distance and Mother Morlan came jogging with her skirts tucked up and the currachs at sea came rowing madly home. The young princelings of Lothian got off their donkeys as if in a trance, and joined the circle. The circle itself began to press inward on its focus, moving as slowly and as silently as the minute hand of a clock, except for the suppressed shouts from the late arrivals who fell silent themselves as soon as they were within the influence. The circle was contracting because it wanted to touch the knights—not now, not for half an hour or so, not until the examination was over, perhaps never. But it would have liked to touch them in the end, partly to be sure that they were real, partly to sum up the price of their clothes. And, as the pricing was continued, three things began to happen. Mother Morlan and the auld wives started to say the rosary, while the young women pinched each other and giggled—the men, having doffed their caps in deference to the praying, began to exchange in Gaelic such remarks as "Look at the black man, God between us and harm," or "Do they be naked at bedtime, or how do they get the iron pots off them whatever?" —and, in the minds of both women and men, irrespective of age or circumstance, there began to grow, almost visibly, almost tangibly, the enormous, the incalculable miasma which is the leading feature of the Gaelic brain.

These were Knights of the Sassenach, they were thinking—for they could tell by the armour—and, if so, knights of that very King Arthur against whom their own king had for the second time revolted. Had they come, with typical Sassenach cunning, so as to take King Lot in the rear? Had they come, as representatives of the feudal overlord—the Landlord—so as to make an assessment for the next scutage? Were they Fifth Columnists? More complicated even than this—for surely no Sassenach could be so simple as to come in the garb of the Sassenach—were they perhaps not representatives of King Arthur at all? Were they, for some purpose almost too cunning for belief, only disguised as themselves? Where was the catch? There always was one in everything.

The people of the circle closed in, their jaws dropping even further, their crooked bodies hunching into the shapes of sacks and scarecrows, their small eyes glinting in every direction with unfathomable subtlety, their faces assuming an expression of dogged stupidity even more vacant than they actually were.

The knights drew closer for protection. In point of fact, they did not know that England was at war with Orkney. They had been involved in a Quest, which had kept them away from the latest news. Nobody in Orkney was likely to tell them.

"Don't look just now," said King Pellinore, "but there are some people. Do you think they are all right?"

# 6

*In Carlion everything was at sixes and sevens in prep*-aration for the second campaign. Merlyn had made suggestions about the way to win it, but, as these involved an ambush with secret aid from abroad, they had had to be kept dark. Lot's slowly approaching army was so much more numerous than the King's forces that it had been necessary to resort to stratagems. The way in which the battle was to be fought was a secret only known to four people.

The common citizens, who were in ignorance of the

higher policy, had a great deal to do. There were pikes to
be ground to a fine edge, so that the grindstones in the town
were roaring day and night—there were thousands of arrows
to be dressed, so that there were lights in the fletchers'
houses at all hours—and the unfortunate geese on the commons were continually being chased by excited yeomen who
wanted feathers. The royal peacocks were as bare as an old
broom—most of the crack shots liked to have what Chaucer
calls pecock arwes, because they were more classy—and
the smell of boiling glue rose to high heaven. The armourers, accomplishing the knights, hammered away with
musical clinks, working double shifts at it, and the black-
smiths shod the chargers, and the nuns never stopped knitting comforters for the soldiers or making the kind of bandages which were called tents. King Lot had already named a
rendezvous for the battle, at Bedegraine.

The King of England painfully climbed the two hundred
and eight steps which led to Merlyn's tower room, and
knocked on the door. The magician was inside, with Archimedes sitting on the back of his chair, busily trying to find
the square root of minus one. He had forgotten how to do it.

"Merlyn," said the King, panting, "I want to talk to you."

He closed his book with a bang, leaped to his feet, seized
his wand of lignum vitae, and rushed at Arthur as if he were
trying to shoo away a stray chicken.

"Go away!" he shouted. "What are you doing here?
What do you mean by it? Aren't you the King of England?
Go away and send for me! Get out of my room! I never
heard of such a thing! Go away at once and send for me!"

"But I am here."

"No, you're not," retorted the old man resourcefully.
And he pushed the King out of the door, slamming it in his
face.

"Well!" said Arthur, and he went off sadly down the two
hundred and eight stairs.

An hour later, Merlyn presented himself in the Royal
Chamber, in answer to a summons which had been delivered by a page.

"That's better," he said, and sat down comfortably on a
carpet chest.

"Stand up," said Arthur, and he clapped his hands for a
page to take away the seat.

Merlyn stood up, boiling with indignation. The whites of
his knuckles blanched as he clenched them.

"About our conversation on the subject of chivalry," began the King in an airy tone. . . .

"I don't recollect such a conversation."

"No?"

"I have never been so insulted in my life!"

"But I am the King," said Arthur. "You can't sit down in front of the King."

"Rubbish!"

Arthur began to laugh more than was seemly, and his foster-brother, Sir Kay, and his old guardian, Sir Ector, came out from behind the throne, where they had been hiding. Kay took off Merlyn's hat and put it on Sir Ector, and Sir Ector said, "Well, bless my soul, now I am a nigromancer. Hocus-Pocus." Then everybody began laughing, including Merlyn eventually, and seats were sent for so that they could sit down, and bottles of wine were opened so that it should not be a dry meeting.

"You see," he said proudly, "I have summoned a council."

There was a pause, for it was the first time that Arthur had made a speech, and he wanted to collect his wits for it.

"Well," said the King. "It is about chivalry. I want to talk about that."

Merlyn was immediately watching him with a sharp eye. His knobbed fingers fluttered among the stars and secret signs of his gown, but he would not help the speaker. You might say that this moment was the critical one in his career—the moment towards which he had been living backward for heaven knows how many centuries, and now he was to see for certain whether he had lived in vain.

"I have been thinking," said Arthur, "about Might and Right. I don't think things ought to be done because you are *able* to do them. I think they should be done because you *ought* to do them. After all, a penny is a penny in any case, however much Might is exerted on either side, to prove that it is or is not. Is that plain?"

Nobody answered.

"Well, I was talking to Merlyn on the battlements one day, and he mentioned that the last battle we had—in which seven hundred kerns were killed—was not so much fun as I had thought it was. Of course, battles are not fun when you come to think about them. I mean, people ought not to be killed, ought they? It is better to be alive.

"Very well. But the funny thing is that Merlyn was helping me to win battles. He is still helping me, for that matter, and we hope to win the battle of Bedegraine together, when it comes off."

"We will," said Sir Ector, who was in the secret.

"That seems to me to be inconsistent. Why does he help me to fight wars, if they are bad things?"

There was no answer from anybody, and the King began to speak with agitation.

"I could only think," said he, beginning to blush, "I could only think that I—that we—that he—that he wanted me to win them for a reason."

He paused and looked at Merlyn, who turned his head away.

"The reason was—was it?—the reason was that if I could be the master of my kingdom by winning these two battles, I could stop them afterwards and then do something about the business of Might. Have I guessed? Was I right?"

The magician did not turn his head, and his hands lay still in his lap.

"I was!" exclaimed Arthur.

And he began talking so quickly that he could hardly keep up with himself.

"You see," he said, "Might is not Right. But there is a lot of Might knocking about in this world, and something has to be done about it. It is as if People were half horrible and half nice. Perhaps they are even more than half horrible, and when they are left to themselves they run wild. You get the average baron that we see nowadays, people like Sir Bruce Sans Pitié, who simply go clod-hopping round the country dressed in steel, and doing exactly what they please, for sport. It is our Norman idea about the upper classes having a monopoly of power, without reference to justice. Then the horrible side gets uppermost, and there is thieving and rape and plunder and torture. The people become beasts.

"But, you see, Merlyn is helping me to win my two battles so that I can stop this. He wants me to put things right.

"Lot and Uriens and Anguish and those—they are the old world, the old-fashioned order who want to have their private will. I have got to vanquish them with their own weapons—they force it upon me, because they live by force —and then the real work will begin. This battle at Bedegraine is the preliminary, you see. It is *after* the battle that Merlyn is wanting me to think about."

Arthur paused again for comment or encouragement, but the magician's face was turned away. It was only Sir Ector, sitting next to him, who could see his eyes.

"Now what I have thought," said Arthur, "is this. Why can't you harness Might so that it works for Right? I know it sounds nonsense, but, I mean, you can't just say there is no such thing. The Might is there, in the bad half of people, and you can't neglect it. You can't cut it out, but you might be able to direct it, if you see what I mean, so that it was useful instead of bad."

The audience was interested. They leaned forward to listen, except Merlyn.

"My idea is that if we can win this battle in front of us, and get a firm hold of the country, then I will institute a sort of order of chivalry. I will not punish the bad knights, or hang Lot, but I will try to get them into our Order. We shall have to make it a great honour, you see, and make it fashionable and all that. Everybody must want to be in. And then I shall make the oath of the order that Might is only to be used for Right. Do you follow? The knights in my order will ride all over the world, still dressed in steel and whacking away with their swords—that will give an outlet for wanting to whack, you understand, an outlet for what Merlyn calls the foxhunting spirit—but they will be bound to strike only on behalf of what is good, to defend virgins against Sir Bruce and to restore what has been done wrong in the past and to help the oppressed and so forth. Do you see the idea? It will be using the Might instead of fighting against it, and turning a bad thing into a good. There, Merlyn, that is all I can think of. I have thought as hard as I could, and I suppose I am wrong, as usual. But I did think. I can't do any better. Please say something!"

The magician stood up as straight as a pillar, stretched out his arms in both directions, looked at the ceiling and said the first few words of the Nunc Dimittis.

# 7

*The situation at Dunlothian was complicated. Nearly* every situation tended to be when it was connected with King Pellinore, even in the wildest North. In the first place, he was in love—that was why he had been weeping in the boat. He explained it to Queen Morgause on the first opportunity —because he was lovesick, not seasick.

What had happened was this. The King had been hunting the Questing Beast a few months earlier, on the south coast of Gramarye, when the animal had taken to the sea. She had swam away, her serpentine head undulating on the surface like a swimming grass-snake, and the King had hailed a passing ship which looked· as if it were off to the Crusades. Sir Grummore and Sir Palomides had been in the ship, and they had kindly turned it round to pursue the Beast. The three of them had arrived on the coast of Flanders, where the Beast had disappeared in a forest, and there, while they were staying at a hospitable castle, Pellinore had fallen in love with the Queen of Flanders' daughter. This was fine so far as it went—for the lady of his choice was a managing, middle-aged, stout-hearted creature, who could cook, ride a straight line, and make beds—but the hopes of all parties had been dashed at the start by the arrival of the magic barge. The three knights had got into it, and sat down to see what would happen, because knights were never supposed to refuse an adventure. But the barge had promptly sailed away of its own accord, leaving the Queen of Flanders' daughter anxiously waving her pocket handkerchief. The Questing Beast had thrust her head out of the forest before they lost sight of land, looking, so far as they could see at the distance, even more surprised than the lady. After that, they had gone on sailing till they arrived in the Out Isles, and the further they went the more lovesick the King had become, which made his company intolerable. He spent the time writing poems and letters, which could never be posted, or telling his companions about the princess, whose nickname in her family circle was Piggy.

A state of affairs like this might have been bearable in England, where people like the Pellinores did sometimes turn up, and even won a sort of tolerance from their fellow men. But in Lothian and Orkney, where Englishmen were tyrants, it achieved an almost supernatural impossibility. None of the islanders could understand what King Pellinore was trying to cheat them out of—by pretending to be himself—and it was thought wiser and safer not to acquaint any of the visiting knights with the facts about the war against Arthur. It was better to wait until their plots had been penetrated.

On top of this, there was a trouble which distressed the children in particular. Queen Morgause had set her cap at the visitors.

"What was our mother at doing," asked Gawaine, as they made their way toward St. Toirdealbhach's cell one morning, "with the knights on the mountain?"

Gaheris answered with some difficulty, after a long pause: "They were at hunting a unicorn."

"How do you do that?"

"There must be a virgin to attract it."

"Our mother," said Agravaine, who also knew the details, "went on a unicorn hunt, and she was the virgin for them."

His voice sounded strange as he made this announcement.

Gareth protested: "I did not know she was wanting a unicorn. She has never said so."

Agravaine looked at him sideways, cleared his throat and quoted: "Half a word is sufficient to the wise man."

"How do you know this?" asked Gawaine.

"We listened."

They had a way of listening on the spiral stairs, during the times when they were excluded from their mother's interest.

Gaheris explained, with unusual freedom since he was a taciturn boy:

"She told Sir Grummore that this King's lovesick melancholy could be dispelled by interesting him in his old pursuits. They were at saying that this King is in the habit of hunting a Beast which has become lost. So she said that they were to hunt a unicorn instead, and she would be the virgin for them. They were surprised, I think."

They walked in silence, until Gawaine suggested, almost

as if it were a question: "I was hearing it told that the King is in love with a woman out of Flanders, and that Sir Grummore is married already? Also the Saracen is black in his skin?"

No answer.

"It was a long hunt," said Gareth. "I heard they did not catch one."

"Do these knights enjoy to be playing this game with our mother?"

Gaheris explained for the second time. Even if he were silent, he was not unobservant.

"I do not think they would be understanding at all."

They plodded on, reluctant to disclose their thoughts.


St. Toirdealbhach's cell was like an old-fashioned straw beehive, except that it was bigger and made of stone. It had no windows and only one door, through which you had to crawl.

"Your Holiness," they shouted when they got there, kicking the heavy unmortared stones. "Your Holiness, we have come to hear a story."

He was a source of mental nourishment to them—a sort of guru, as Merlyn had been to Arthur, who gave them what little culture they were ever to get. They resorted to him like hungry puppies anxious for any kind of eatable, when their mother had cast them out. He had taught them to read and write.

"Ah, now," said the saint, sticking his head out of the door. "The prosperity of God on you this morning."

"The selfsame prosperity on you."

"Is there any news at you?"

"There is not," said Gawaine, suppressing the unicorn.

St. Toirdealbhach heaved a deep sigh.

"There is none at me either," he said.

"Could you tell us a story?"

"Thim stories, now. There doesn't be any good in them. What would I be wanting to tell you a story for, and me in my heresies? 'Tis forty years since I fought a natural battle, and not a one of me looking upon a white colleen all that time—so how would I be telling stories?"

"You could tell us a story without any colleens or battles in it."

"And what would be the good of that, now?" he exclaimed indignantly, coming out into the sunlight.

"If you were to fight a battle," said Gawaine, but he left out about the colleens, "you might feel better."

"My sorrow!" cried Toirdealbhach. "What do I want to be a saint for at all, is my puzzle! If I could fetch one crack at somebody with me ould shillelagh"—here he produced a frightful-looking weapon from under his gown—"wouldn't it be better than all the saints in Ireland?"

"Tell us about the shillelagh."

They examined the club carefully, while his holiness told them how a good one should be made. He told them that only a root growth was any good, as common branches were apt to break, especially if they were of crab-tree, and how to smear the club with lard, and wrap it up, and bury it in a dunghill while it was being straightened, and polish it with black-lead and grease. He showed the hole where the lead was poured in, and the nails through the end, and the notches near the handle which stood for ancient scalps. Then he kissed it reverently and replaced it under his gown with a heartfelt sigh. He was play-acting, and putting on the accent.

"Tell us the story about the black arm which came down the chimney."

"Ah, the heart isn't in me," said the saint. "I haven't the heart of a hare. It's bewitched I am entirely."

"I think we are bewitched too," said Gareth. "Everything seems to go wrong."

"There was this one in it," began Toirdealbhach, "and she was a woman. There was a husband living in Malainn Vig with this woman. There was only one little girl that they had between them. One day the man went out to cut in the bog, and when it was the time for his dinner, this woman sent the little girl out with his bit of dinner. When the father was sitting to his dinner, the little girl suddenly made a cry, 'Look now, father, do you see the large ship out yonder under the horizon? I could make it come in to the shore beneath the coast.' 'You could not do that,' said the father. 'I am bigger than you are, and I could not do it myself.' 'Well, look at me now,' said the little girl. And she went to the well that was near there, and made a stirring in the water. The ship came in at the coast."

"She was a witch," explained Gaheris.

"It was the mother was the witch," said the saint, and continued with his story.

" 'Now,' says she, 'I could make the ship be struck against

the coast.' 'You could not do that,' says the father. 'Well, look at me now,' says the little girl, and she jumped into the well. The ship was dashed against the coast and broken into a thousand pieces. 'Who has taught you to do these things?' asked the father. 'My mother. And when you do be at working she teaches me to do things with the Tub at home.' "

"Why did she jump into the well?" asked Agravaine. "Was she wet?"

"Hush."

"When this man got home to his wife, he set down his turf-cutter and put himself in his sitting. Then he said, 'What have you been teaching to the little girl? I do not like to have this piseog in my house, and I will not stay with you any longer.' So he went away, and they never saw a one of him again. I do not know how they went on after that."

"It must be dreadful to have a witch for a mother," said Gareth when he had finished.

"Or for a wife," said Gawaine.

"It's worse not to be having a wife at all," said the saint, and he vanished into his beehive with startling suddenness, like the man in the Swiss weather clock who retires into a hole when it is going to be fine.

The boys sat round the door without surprise, waiting for something else to happen. They considered in their minds the questions of wells, witches, unicorns and the practices of mothers.

"I make this proposition," said Gareth unexpectedly, "my heroes, that we have a unicorn hunt of our own!"

They looked at him.

"It would be better than not having anything. We have not seen our Mammy for one week."

"She has forgotten us," said Agravaine bitterly.

"She has not so. You are not to speak in that way of our mother."

"It is true. We have not been to serve at dinner even."

"It is because she has a necessity to be hospitable to these knights."

"No, it is not."

"What is it, then?"

"I will not say."

"If we could do a unicorn hunt," said Gareth, "and bring this unicorn which she requires, perhaps we would be allowed to serve?"

They considered the idea with a beginning of hope.

"St. Toirdealbhach," they shouted, "come out again! We want to catch a unicorn."

The saint put his head out of the hole and examined them suspiciously.

"What is a unicorn? What are they like? How do you catch them?"

He nodded the head solemnly and vanished for the second time, to return on all fours in a few moments with a learned volume, the only secular work in his possession. Like most saints, he made his living by copying manuscripts and drawing pictures for them.

"You need a maid for bait," they told him.

"We have goleor of maids," said Gareth. "We could take any of the maids, or cook."

"They would not come."

"We could take the kitchenmaid. We could make her to come."

"And then, when we have caught the unicorn which is wanted, we will bring it home in triumph and give it to our mother! We will serve at supper every night!"

"She will be pleased."

"Perhaps after supper, whatever the event."

"And Sir Grummore will knight us. He will say, 'Never has such a doughty deed been done, by my halidome!'"

St. Toirdealbhach laid the precious book on the grass outside his hole. The grass was sandy and had empty snail shells scattered over it, small yellowish shells with a purple spiral. He opened the book, which was a Bestiary called *Liber de Natura Quorundam Animalium,* and showed that it had pictures on every page.

They made him turn the vellum quickly, with its lovely Gothic manuscript, skipping the enchanting Griffins, Bonnacons, Cocodrills, Manticores, Chaladrii, Cinomulgi, Sirens, Peridexions, Dragons, and Aspidochelones. In vain for their eager glances did the Antalop rub its complicated horns against the tamarisk tree—thus, entangled, becoming a prey to its hunters—in vain did the Bonnacon emit its flatulence in order to baffle the pursuers. The Peridexions, sitting on trees which made them immune to dragons, sat unnoticed. The Panther blew out his fragrant breath, which attracted his prey, without interest for them. The Tigris, who could be deceived by throwing down a glass ball at its feet, in which, seeing itself reflected, it thought to see its own cubs—the Lion, who spared prostrate men or captives, was afraid of white cocks, and brushed out his own tracks with a foliated tail—the Ibex, who could bound down from mountains unharmed because he bounced upon his curly horns—the Yale, who could move his horns like ears—the She-Bear who was accustomed to bear her young as lumps of matter and lick them into whatever shape she fancied afterwards—the Chaladrius bird who, if facing you when it sat on your bedrail, showed that you were going to die—the Hedgehogs who collected grapes for their progeny by rolling on them, and brought them back on the end of their prickles—even the Aspidochelone, who was a large whale-like creature with seven fins and a sheepish expression, to whom you were liable to moor your boat in mistake for an island if you were not careful: even the Aspidochelone scarcely detained them. At last he found them the place at the Unicorn, called by the Greeks, Rhinoceros.

It seemed that the Unicorn was as swift and timid as the Antalop, and could only be captured in one way. You had to have a maid for bait, and, when the Unicorn perceived her alone, he would immediately come to lay his horn in her lap. There was a picture of an unreliable-looking virgin, holding the poor creature's horn in one hand, while she beckoned to some spearmen with the other. Her expression of duplicity was balanced by the fatuous confidence with which the Unicorn regarded her.

Gawaine hurried off, as soon as the instructions had been read and the picture digested, to fetch the kitchenmaid without delay.

"Now then," he said, "you have to come with us on the mountain, to catch a unicorn."

"Oh, Master Gawaine," cried the maid he had caught hold of, whose name was Meg.

"Yes, you have. You are to be the bait whatever. It will come and put its head in your lap."

Meg began to weep.

"Now then, do not be silly."

"Oh, Master Gawaine, I do not want a unicorn. I have been a decent girl, I have, and there is all the washing up to do, and if Mistress Truelove do catch me playing at truant I shall get stick, Master Gawaine, that I will."

He took her firmly by the plaits and led her out.

In the clean bog-wind of the high tops, they discussed the hunt. Meg, who cried incessantly, was held by the hair to prevent her from running away, and occasionally passed from one boy to the other, if the one who was holding her happened to want both hands for gestures.

"Now then," said Gawaine. "I am the captain. I am the oldest, so I am the captain."

"I thought of it," said Gareth.

"The question is, it says in the book that the bait must be left alone."

"She will run away."

"Will you run away, Meg?"

"Yes, please, Master Gawaine."

"There."

"Then she must be tied."

"Oh, Master Gaheris, if it is your will, need I be tied?"

"Close your mouth. You are only a girl."

"There is nothing to tie her with."

"I am the captain, my heroes, and I command that Gareth runs back home to fetch some rope."

"That I will not."

"But you will destroy everything, if you do not do so."

"I do not see why I should have to go. I thought of it."

"Then I command our Agravaine to go."

"Not I."

"Let Gaheris go."

"I will not."

"Meg, you wicked girl, you are not to run away, do you hear?"

"Yes, Master Gawaine. But, oh, Master Gawaine . . ."

"If we could find a strong heather root," said Agravaine, "we could tie her pigtails together, round the other side of it."

"We will do that."

"Oh, oh!"

After they had secured the virgin, the four boys stood round her, discussing the next stage. They had abstracted real boar-spears from the armoury, so they were properly armed.

"This girl," said Agravaine, "is my mother. This is what our Mammy was at doing yesterday. And I am going to be Sir Grummore."

"I will be Pellinore."

"Agravaine can be Grummore if he wants to be, but the bait has got to be left alone. It says so in the book."

"Oh, Master Gawaine, oh, Master Agravaine!"

"Stop howling. You will frighten the unicorn."

"And then we must go away and hide. That is why our mother did not catch it, because the knights stayed with her."

"I am going to be Finn MacCoul."

"I shall be Sir Palomides."

"Oh, Master Gawaine, pray do not leave me alone."

"Hold in your noise," said Gawaine. "You are silly. You ought to be proud to be the bait. Our mother was, yesterday."

Gareth said, "Never mind, Meg, do not cry. We will not let it hurt you."

"After all, it can only kill you," said Agravaine brutally.

At this the unfortunate girl began to weep more than ever.

"Why did you say that?" asked Gawaine angrily. "You always try to frighten people. Now she is at howling more than before."

"Look," said Gareth. "Look, Meg. Poor Meg, do not cry. It will be with me to let you have some shots with my catapult, when we go home."

"Oh, Master Gareth!"

"Ach, come your ways. We cannot bother with her."

"There, there!"

"Oh, oh!"

"Meg," said Gawaine, making a frightful face, "if you do not stop squealing, I will look at you like this."

She dried her tears at once.

"Now," he said, "when the unicorn comes, we must all rush out and stick it. Do you understand?"

"Must it be killed?"

"Yes, it must be killed dead."

"I see."

"I hope it will not hurt it," said Gareth.

"That is the sort of foolish hope you would have," said Agravaine.

"But I do not see why it should be killed."

"So that we may take it home to our mother, you amadan."

"Could we catch it," asked Gareth, "and lead it to our mother, do you think? I mean, we could get Meg to lead it, if it was tame."

Gawaine and Gaheris agreed to this.

"If it is tame," they said, "it would be better to bring it back alive. That is the best kind of Big Game Hunting."

"We could drive it," said Agravaine. "We could hit it along with sticks.

"We could hit Meg, too," he added, as an afterthought.

Then they hid themselves in their ambush, and decided to keep silence. There was nothing to be heard except the gentle wind, the heather bees, the skylarks very high, and a few distant snuffles from Meg.

When the unicorn came, things were different from what had been expected. He was such a noble animal, to begin with, that he carried a beauty with him. It held all spellbound who were within sight.

The unicorn was white, with hoofs of silver and a graceful horn of pearl. He stepped daintily over the heather, scarcely seeming to press it with his airy trot, and the wind made waves in his long mane, which had been freshly combed. The glorious thing about him was his eyes. There was a faint bluish furrow down each side of his nose, and this led up to the eye-sockets, and surrounded them in a pensive shade. The eyes, circled by this sad and beautiful darkness, were so sorrowful, lonely, gentle and nobly tragic, that they killed all other emotion except love.

The unicorn went up to Meg the kitchenmaid, and bowed his head in front of her. He arched his neck beautifully to do this, and the pearl horn pointed to the ground at her feet, and he scratched in the heather with his silver hoof to make a salute. Meg had forgotten her tears. She made a royal gesture of acknowledgment, and held her hand out to the animal.

"Come, unicorn," she said. "Lay your head in my lap, if you like."

The unicorn made a whinny, and pawed again with his hoof. Then, very carefully, he went down first on one knee and then on the other, till he was bowing in front of her. He looked up at her from this position, with his melting eyes, and at last laid his head upon her knee. He stroked his flat, white cheek against the smoothness of her dress, looking at her beseechingly. The whites of his eyes rolled with an upward flash. He settled his hind quarters coyly, and lay still, looking up. His eyes brimmed with trustfulness, and he lifted his near fore in a gesture of pawing. It was a movement in the air only, which said, "Now attend to me. Give me some love. Stroke my mane, will you, please?"

There was a choking noise from Agravaine in the ambush,

and at once he was rushing toward the unicorn, with the sharp boar-spear in his hands. The other boys squatted upright on their heels, watching him.

Agravaine came to the unicorn, and began jabbing his spear into its quarters, into its slim belly, into its ribs. He squealed as he jabbed, and the unicorn looked to Meg in anguish. It leaped and moved suddenly, still looking at her reproachfully, and Meg took its horn in one hand. She seemed entranced, unable to help it. The unicorn did not seem able to move from the soft grip of her hand on its horn. The blood, caused by Agravaine's spear, spurted out upon the blue-white coat of hair.

Gareth began running, with Gawaine close after him. Gaheris came last, stupid and not knowing what to do.

"Don't!" cried Gareth. "Leave him alone. Don't! Don't!"

Gawaine came up, just as Agravaine's spear went in under the fifth rib. The unicorn shuddered. He trembled in all his body, and stretched his hind legs out behind. They went out almost straight, as if he were doing his greatest leap—and then quivered, trembling in the agony of death. All the time his eyes were fixed on Meg's eyes, and she still looked down at his.

"What are you doing?" shouted Gawaine. "Leave him alone. No harm at him."

"Oh, Unicorn," whispered Meg.

The unicorn's legs stretched out horizontally behind him, and stopped trembling. His head dropped in Meg's lap. After a last kick they became rigid, and the blue lids rose half over the eye. The creature lay still.

"What have you done?" cried Gareth. "You have killed him. He was beautiful."

Agravaine bawled, "This girl is my mother. He put his head in her lap. He had to die."

"We said we would keep him," yelled Gawaine. "We said we would take him home, and be allowed to supper."

"Poor unicorn," said Meg.

"Look," said Gaheris, "I am afraid he is dead."

Gareth stood square in front of Agravaine, who was three years older than he was and could have knocked him down quite easily. "Why did you do it?" he demanded. "You are a murderer. It was a lovely unicorn. Why did you kill it?"

"His head was in our mother's lap."

"It did not mean any harm. Its hoofs were silver."

"It was a unicorn, and it had to be killed. I ought to have killed Meg too."

"You are a traitor," said Gawaine. "We could have taken it home, and been allowed to serve at supper."

"Anyway," said Gaheris, "now it is dead."

Meg bowed her head over the unicorn's forelock of white, and once again began to sob.

Gareth began stroking the head. He had to turn away to hide his tears. By stroking it, he had found out how smooth and soft its coat was. He had seen a near view of its eye, now quickly fading, and this had brought the tragedy home to him.

"Well, it is dead now, whatever," said Gaheris for the third time. "We had better take it home."

"We managed to catch one," said Gawaine, the wonder of their achievement beginning to dawn on him.

"It was a brute," said Agravaine.

"We caught it! We of ourselves!"

"Sir Grummore did not catch one."

"But we did."

Gawaine had forgotten about his sorrow for the unicorn. He began to dance round the body, waving his boar-spear and uttering horrible shrieks.

"We must have a gralloch," said Gaheris. "We must do the matter properly, and cut its insides out, and sling it over a pony, and take it home to the castle, like proper hunters."

"And then she will be pleased!"

"She will say, God's Feet, but my sons are of mickle might!"

"We shall be allowed to be like Sir Grummore and King Pellinore. Everything will go well with us from now."

"How must we set about the gralloch?"

"We cut out its guts," said Agravaine.

Gareth got up and began to go away into the heather. He said, "I do not want to help cut him. Do you, Meg?"

Meg, who was feeling ill inside herself, made no answer. Gareth untied her hair—and suddenly she was off, running for all she was worth away from the tragedy, toward the castle. Gareth ran after her.

"Meg, Meg!" he called. "Wait for me. Do not run."

But Meg continued to run, as swiftly as an antalop, with her bare feet twinkling behind her, and Gareth gave it up. He flung himself down in the heather and began to cry in earnest—he did not know why.

At the gralloch, the three remaining huntsmen were in trouble. They had begun to slit at the skin of the belly, but they did not know how to do it properly and so they had perforated the intestines. Everything had begun to be horrible, and the once beautiful animal was spoiled and repulsive. All three of them loved the unicorn in their various ways, Agravaine in the most twisted one, and, in proportion as they became responsible for spoiling its beauty, so they began to hate it for their guilt. Gawaine particularly began to hate the body. He hated it for being dead, for having been beautiful, for making him feel a beast. He had loved it and helped to trap it, so now there was nothing to be done except to vent his shame and hatred of himself upon the corpse. He hacked and cut and felt like crying too.

"We shall not ever get it done," they panted. "How can we ever carry it down, even if we manage the gralloch?"

"But we must," said Gaheris. "We must. If we do not, what will be the good? We must take it home."

"We cannot carry it."

"We have not a pony."

"At a gralloch, they sling the beast over a pony."

"We must cut his head off," said Agravaine. "We must cut its head off somehow, and carry that. It would be enough if we took the head. We could carry it between us."

So they set to work, hating their work, at the horrid business of hacking through its neck.


Gareth stopped crying in the heather. He rolled over on his back, and immediately he was looking straight into the sky. The clouds which were sailing majestically across its endless depth made him feel giddy. He thought: How far is it to that cloud? A mile? And the one above it? Two miles? And beyond that a mile and a mile, and a million million miles, all in the empty blue. Perhaps I will fall off the earth now, supposing the earth is upside down, and then I shall go sailing and sailing away. I shall try to catch hold of the clouds as I pass them, but they will not stop me. Where shall I go?

This thought made Gareth feel sick, and, as he was also feeling ashamed of himself for running away from the gralloch, he became uncomfortable all over. In these circumstances, the only thing to do was to abandon the place in which he was feeling uncomfortable, in the hope of leaving his discomfort behind him. He got up and went back to the others.

"Hallo," said Gawaine, "did you catch her?"

"No, she escaped away to the castle."

"I hope she will not tell anybody," said Gaheris. "It has to be a surprise, or it is no good for us."

The three butchers were daubed with sweat and blood, and they were absolutely miserable. Agravaine had been sick twice. Yet they continued in their labour and Gareth helped them.

"It is no good stopping now," said Gawaine. "Think how good it will be, if we can take it to our mother."

"She will probably come upstairs to say good night to us, if we can take her what she needs."

"She will laugh, and say we are mighty hunters."

When the grisly spine was severed, the head was too heavy to carry. They got themselves in a mess, trying to lift it. Then Gawaine suggested that it had better be dragged with rope. There was none.

"We could drag it by the horn," said Gareth. "At any rate we could drag and push it like that, so long as it was downhill."

Only one of them at a time could get a good hold of the horn, so they took it in turns to do the hauling, while the others pushed behind when the head got snagged in a heather root or a drain. It was heavy for them, even in this way, so that they had to stop every twenty yards or so, to change over.

"When we get to the castle," panted Gawaine, "we will prop it up in the seat in the garden. Our mother is bound to walk past there, when she goes for her walk before supper. Then we will stand in front of it until she is ready, and all will suddenly step back at once, and there it will be."

"She will be surprised," said Gaheris.

When they had at last got it down from the sloping ground, there was another hitch. They found that it was no longer possible to drag it on the flat land, because the horn did not give enough purchase.

In this emergency, for it was getting near to suppertime, Gareth voluntarily ran ahead to fetch a rope. The rope was tied round what remained of the head, and thus at last, with eyes ruined, flesh bruised and separating from the bones, the muddy, bloody, heather-mangled exhibit was conveyed on its last stage to the herb garden. They heaved it to the seat, and arranged its mane as well as they could. Gareth particularly tried to prop it up so that it would give a little idea of the beauty which he remembered.

The magic queen came punctually on her walk, conversing with Sir Grummore and followed by her lap dogs: Tray, Blanche and Sweetheart. She did not notice her four sons, lined up in front of the seat. They stood respectfully in a row, dirty, excited, their breasts beating with hope.

"Now!" cried Gawaine, and they stood aside.

Queen Morgause did not see the unicorn. Her mind was busy with other things. With Sir Grummore she passed by.

"Mother!" cried Gareth in a strange voice, and he ran after her, plucking at her skirt.

"Yes, my white one? What do you want?"

"Oh, Mother. We have got you a unicorn."

"How amusing they are, Sir Grummore," she said. "Well, my doves, you must run along and ask for your milk."

"But, Mammy. . . ."

"Yes, yes," she said in a low voice. "Another time."

And the Queen passed on with the puzzled knight of the Forest Sauvage, electrical and quiet. She had not noticed that her children's clothes were ruined: had not even scolded them about that. When she found out about the unicorn later in the evening she had them whipped for it, for she had spent an unsuccessful day with the English knights.

# 8

*The plain of Bedegraine was a forest of pavilions.* They looked like old-fashioned bathing tents, and were every colour of the rainbow. Some of them were even striped like bathing tents, but the most part were in plain colours, yellow and green and so on. There were heraldic devices worked or stamped on the sides—enormous black eagles with two heads perhaps, or wyverns, or lances, or oak trees, or punning signs which referred to the names of the owners. For instance, Sir Kay had a black key on his tent, and Sir Ulbawes, in the opposing camp, had a couple of elbows in flowing sleeves. The proper name for them would be manchets. Then there were pennons floating from the tops of the tents, and sheaves of spears leaning against them. The more sporting barons had shields or huge copper basins outside their front doors, and all you had to do was to give a thump on one of these with the butt-end of your spear for the baron to come out like an angry bee and have a fight with you, almost before the resounding boom had died away. Sir Dinadan, who was a cheerful man, had hung a chamber-pot outside his. Then there were the people themselves. All round and about among the tents there were cooks quarrelling with dogs who had eaten the mutton, and small pages writing insults on each other's backs when they were not looking, and elegant minstrels with lutes singing tunes similar to "Greensleeves," with soulful expressions, and squires with a world of innocence in their eyes, trying to sell each other spavined horses, and hurdy-gurdy men trying to earn a groat by playing on the vielle, and gipsies telling your fortune for the battle, and enormous knights with their heads wrapped in untidy turbans playing chess, and vivandières sitting on the knees of some of them, and—as for entertainment—there were joculators, gleemen, tumblers, harpers, troubadours, jesters, minstrels, tregetours, bear-dancers, egg-dancers, ladder-dancers, ballette-dancers, mountebanks, fire-eaters and balancers. In a way, it was like Derby Day. The tremendous forest of Sherwood stretched round the tent-forest further than the eye could see—and this was full of wild boars, warrantable stags, outlaws, dragons, and Purple Emperors. There was also an ambush in the forest but nobody was supposed to know about that.

King Arthur paid no attention to the coming battle. He sat invisible in his pavilion, at the hub of the excitement, and talked to Sir Ector or Kay or Merlyn day after day. The smaller captains were delighted to think that their King was having so many councils of war, for they could see the lamp burning inside the silk tent until all hours, and they felt sure that he was inventing a splendid plan of campaign. Actually the conversation was about different things.

"There will be a lot of jealousy," said Kay. "You will

have all these knights in this order of yours saying that they are the best one, and wanting to sit at the top of the table."

"Then we must have a round table, with no top."

"But, Arthur, you could never sit a hundred and fifty knights at a round table. Let me see. . . ."

Merlyn, who hardly ever interfered in the arguments now, but sat with his hands folded on his stomach and beamed, helped Kay out of the difficulty.

"It would need to be about fifty yards across," he said. "You do it by $2\pi r$."

"Well, then. Say it was fifty yards across. Think of all the space in the middle. It would be an ocean of wood with a thin rim of humanity. You couldn't keep the food in the middle even, because nobody would be able to reach it."

"Then we can have a circular table," said Arthur, "not a round one. I don't know what the proper word is. I mean we could have a table shaped like the rim of a cart-wheel, and the servants could walk about in the empty space, where the spokes would be. We could call them the Knights of the Round Table."

"What a good name!"

"And the important thing," continued the King, who was getting wiser the more he thought, "the most important thing, will be to catch them young. The old knights, the ones we are fighting against, will be mostly too old to learn. I think we shall be able to get them in, and keep them fighting the right way, but they will be inclined to stick to the old habits, like Sir Bruce. Grummore and Pellinore—we must have them of course—I wonder where they are now? Grummore and Pellinore will be all right, because they were always kindly in themselves. But I don't think Lot's people will ever really be at home with it. That is why I say we must catch them young. We must breed up a new generation of chivalry for the future. That child Lancelot who came over with You-know-who, for instance: we must get hold of kids like him. They will be the real Table."

"Apropos of this Table," said Merlyn, "I don't see why I should not tell you that King Leodegrance has one which would do very well. As you are going to marry his daughter, he might be persuaded to give you the table as a wedding present."

"Am I going to marry his daughter?"

"Certainly. She is called Guenever."

"Look, Merlyn, I don't like knowing about the future, and I am not sure whether I believe in it. . . ."

"There are some things," said the magician, "which I have to tell you, whether you believe them or not. The trouble is, I can't help feeling there is one thing which I have forgotten to tell. Remind me to warn you about Guenever another time."

"It confuses everybody," said Arthur complainingly. "I get muddled up with half the questions I want to ask you myself. For instance, who was my . . ."

"You will have to have special Feasts," interrupted Kay, "at Pentecost and so on, when all the knights come to dinner and say what they have done. It will make them want to fight in this new way of yours, if they are going to recite about it afterwards. And Merlyn could write their names in their places by magic, and their coat armour could be engraved over their sieges. It would be grand!"

This exciting idea made the King forget his question, and the two young men sat down immediately to draw their own blazons for the magician, so that there should be no mistake about the tinctures. While they were in the middle of the drawing Kay looked up, with his tongue between his teeth, and remarked:

"By the way. You remember that argument we were having about aggression? Well, I have thought of a good reason for starting a war."

Merlyn froze.

"I would like to hear it."

"A good reason for starting a war is simply to have a good reason! For instance, there might be a king who had discovered a new way of life for human beings—you know, something which would be good for them. It might even be the only way of saving them from destruction. Well, if the human beings were too wicked or too stupid to accept his way, he might have to force it on them, in their own interests, by the sword."

The magician clenched his fists, twisted his gown into screws, and began to shake all over.

"Very interesting," he said in a trembling voice. "Very interesting. There was just such a man when I was young —an Austrian who invented a new way of life and convinced himself that he was the chap to make it work. He tried to impose his reformation by the sword, and plunged the civilized world into misery and chaos. But the thing which this fellow had overlooked, my friend, was that he had had a predecessor in the reformation business, called Jesus Christ. Perhaps we may assume that Jesus knew as much as the Austrian did about saving people. But the odd thing is that Jesus did not turn the disciples into storm troopers, burn down the Temple at Jerusalem, and fix the blame on Pontius Pilate. On the contrary, he made it clear that the business of the philosopher was to make ideas *available,* and *not* to impose them on people."

Kay looked pale but obstinate.

"Arthur is fighting the present war," he said, "to impose his ideas on King Lot."

# 9

*The Queen's suggestion about hunting unicorns had* a curious result. The more lovelorn King Pellinore became, the more obvious it was that something would have to be done. Sir Palomides had an inspiration.

"The royal melancholy," said he, "can only be dispelled by Questing Beast. This is the subject to which the maharajah sahib has been accustomed by lifelong habit. Yours truly has said so all along."

"Personally," said Sir Grummore, "I believe the Questin' Beast is dead. Anyway, it is in Flanders."

"Then we must dress up," said Sir Palomides. "We must assume the rôle of Questing Beast and be hunted ourselves."

"We could scarcely dress as the Beast."

But the Saracen had run away with the idea.

"Why not?" he asked. "Why not, by Jingo? Joculators assume garb of animals—as stags, goats and so forth— and dance to bells and tabor with many gyrings and circumflexions."

"But really, Palomides, we are not joculators."

"Then we must learn to be so!"

"Joculators!"

A joculator was a juggler, a low kind of minstrel, and Sir Grummore did not relish the idea at all.

"However could we dress as the Questin' Beast?" he asked weakly. "She is a frightfully complicated animal."

"Describe this animal."

"Well, dash it all. She has a snake's head and the body of a leopard and haunches like a lion and feet like a hart. And, hang it, man, how could we make this noise in her belly, like thirty couple of hounds questin'?"

"Yours truly will be the belly," replied Sir Palomides, "and will give tongue as follows."

He began yodelling.

"Hush!" cried Sir Grummore. "You will wake the Castle."

"Then it is agreed?"

"No, it is not agreed. Never heard such nonsense in me life. Besides, she don't make a noise like that. She makes a noise like this."

And Sir Grummore began cackling in a tuneless alto, like thousands of wild geese on the Wash.

"Hush! Hush!" cried Sir Palomides.

"I won't hush. The noise you was makin' was like pigs."

The two naturalists began hooting, grunting, squawking, squealing, crowing, mooing, growling, snuffling, quacking, snarling and mewing at one another, until they were red in the face.

"The head," said Sir Grummore, stopping suddenly, "will have to be of cardboard."

"Or canvas," said Sir Palomides. "The fishing populace will be in possession of canvas."

"We can make leather boots for hoofs."

"Spots can be painted on the body."

"It will have to button round the middle—"

"—where we join."

"And you," added Sir Palomides generously, "can be the back end, and do hounds. The noise is plainly stated to come from the belly."

Sir Grummore blushed with pleasure and said gruffly, in his Norman way, "Well, thanks, Palomides. I must say, I think that's demned decent of you."

"Not at all."

For a week King Pellinore saw hardly anything of his friends. "You write poems, Pellinore," they told him, "or go and sigh on the cliffs, there's a good fellow." He wandered about, occasionally crying out, "Flanders—Glanders" or "Daughter—ought to," whenever the ideas occurred to him, while the dark Queen hung in the background.

Meanwhile, in Sir Palomides' room, where the door was kept locked, there was such a stitching and snipping and painting and arguing as had seldom been known before.

"My dear chap, I tell you a libbard has black spots."

"Puce," Sir Palomides said obstinately.

"What is puce? And anyway we have not got any."

They glared at each other with the fury of creators.

"Try on the head."

"There, you've torn it. I said you would."

"Construction was of feeble nature."

"We must construct the thing again."

When the reconstruction was finished, the paynim stood back to admire it.

"Look out for the spots, Palomides. There, you've smudged them."

"A thousand pardons!"

"You ought to look where you are goin'."

"Well, who put his foot through the ribs?"

On the second day there was trouble with the back end.

"These haunches are too tight."

"Don't bend over."

"I have to bend over, if I am the back end."

"They won't split."

"Yes, they will."

"No, they won't."

"Well, they have."

"Look out for my tail," said Sir Grummore on the third day. "You are treadin' on it."

"Don't hold so tight, Grummore. My neck is twisted."

"Can't you see?"

"No, I can't. My neck is twisted."

"There goes my tail."

There was a pause while they sorted themselves out.

"Now, carefully this time. We must walk in step."

"You give the step."

"Left! Right! Left! Right!"

"I think my haunches are comin' down."

"If you let go of yours truly's waist, we shall come in half."

"Well, I can't hold up my haunches unless I do."

"There go the buttons."

"Damn the buttons."

"Yours truly told you so."

So they sewed on buttons during the fourth day, and started again.

"Can I practise my bayin' now?"

"Yes, indeed."

"How does my bayin' sound from inside?"

"It sounds splendid, Grummore, splendid. Only it is strange, in a way, coming from behind, if you follow my argument."

"I thought it sounded muffled."

"It did, a bit."

"Perhaps it will be all right from outside."

On the fifth day they were far advanced.

"We ought to practise a gallop. After all, we can't walk all the time, not when he is hunting us."

"Very good."

"When I say Go, then Go. Ready, steady, Go!"

"Look out, Grummore, you are butting me."

"Buttin'?"

"Be careful of the bed."

"What did you say?"

"Oh, dear!"

"Confound the bed to blazes. Oh, my shins!"

"You have burst the buttons again."

"Damn the buttons. I have stubbed my toe."

"Well, yours truly's head has come off also."

"We shall have to stick to walkin'."

"It would be easier to gallop," said Sir Grummore on the sixth day, "if we had some music. Somethin' like Tantivvy, you know."

"Well, we have not got any music."

"No."

"Could you sing out Tantivvy, Palomides, while I am bayin'?"

"Yours truly could try."

"Very well, then, off we go!"

"Tantivvy, tantivvy, tantivvy!"

"Damn!"

"We shall have to make the whole thing again," said Sir Palomides over the week-end. "We can still use the hoofs."

"I don't suppose it will hurt so much fallin' down out of doors—not on the moss, you know."

"And probably it won't tear the canvas so badly."

"We will make it double strength."

"Yes."

"I am glad the hoofs will still do."


"By jove, Palomides, don't he look a monster!"

"A splendid effort, this time."

"Pity you can't make fire come out of his mouth, or somethin'."

"A danger of combustion there."

"Shall we try another gallop, Palomides?"

"By all means."

"Push the bed in the corner, then."

"Look out for the buttons."

"If you see anythin' we are runnin' into, just stop, see?"

"Yes."

"Keep a sharp look-out, Palomides."

"Right ho, Grummore."

"Ready, then?"

"Ready."

"Off we go."

"That was a splendid burst, Palomides," exclaimed the Knight of the Forest Sauvage.

"A noble gallop."

"Did you notice how I was bayin' all the time?"

"I could not fail to notice it, Sir Grummore."

"Well, well, I don't know when I have enjoyed myself so much."

They panted with triumph, standing amid their monster.

"I say, Palomides, look at me swishin' my tail!"

"Charming, Sir Grummore. Look at me winking one of my eyes."

"No, no, Palomides. You look at my tail. You ought not to miss it, really."

"Well, if I look at you swishing, you ought to look at me winking. That is only fair."

"But I can't see anythin' from inside."

"As for that, Sir Grummore, yours truly can't see so far round as the anal appanage."

"Now, then, we will have one last go. I shall swish my tail round and round all the time, and bay like mad. It will be a frightful spectacle."

"And yours truly will continuously wink one optic or the other."

"Could we put a bit of a bound into the gallop, Palomides, every now and then, do you think? You know, a kind of prance?"

"The prance could more naturally be effected by the back end, solo."

"You mean I could do it alone?"

"Effectually."

"Well, I must say that is uncommonly decent of you, Palomides, to let me do the prancin'."

"Yours truly trusts that a modicum of caution will be exercised in the prance, to prevent delivery of uncomfortable blows to the posterior of the forequarters?"

"Just as you say, Palomides."

"Boot and saddle, Sir Grummore."

"Tally-ho, Sir Palomides."

"Tantivvy, tantivvy, tantivvy, a-questing we will go!"

The Queen had recognized the impossible. Even in the miasma of her Gaelic mind, she had come to see that asses do not mate with pythons. It was useless to go on dramatizing her charms and talents for the benefit of these ridiculous knights—useless to go on hunting them with the tyrannous baits of what she thought was love. With a sudden turn of feeling she discovered that she hated them. They were imbeciles, as well as being the Sassenach, and she herself was a saint. She was, she discovered with a change of posture, interested in nothing but her darling boys. She was the best mother to them in the world! Her heart ached for them, her maternal bosom swelled. When Gareth nervously brought white heather to her bedroom as an apology for being whipped, she covered him with kisses, glancing in the mirror.

He escaped from the embrace and dried his tears—partly uncomfortable, partly in rapture. The heather which he had brought was set up dramatically in a cup with no water—she was every inch the homebody—and he was free to go. He scampered from the royal chamber with the news of forgiveness, went spinning down the circular stairs like a tee-to-tum.

It was a different castle to the one in which King Arthur used to scamper. A Norman would hardly have recognized it as a castle, except for the pele tower. It was a thousand years more ancient than anything the Normans knew.

This castle, through which the child was running to

bring the good news of their mother's love to his brothers, had begun, in the mists of the past, as that strange symbol of the Old Ones—a promontory fort. Driven to the sea by the volcano of history, they had turned at bay on the last peninsula. With the sea literally at their backs, on a cliffy tongue of land, they had built their single wall across the root of the tongue. The sea which was their doom had also been their last defender on every other side. There, on the promontory, the blue-painted cannibals had piled up their cyclopean wall of unmortared stones, fourteen feet high and equally thick, with terraces on the inside from which they could hurl their flints. All along the outside of the wall they had embedded thousands of sharp stones in the scraw, each stone pointing outward in a *chevaux de frise* which was like a petrified hedgehog. Behind it, and behind the enormous wall, they had huddled at night in wooden shacks, together with their domestic animals. There had been heads of enemies erected on poles for decoration, and their king had built himself an underground treasure chamber which was also a subterranean passage for escape. It had led under the wall, so that even if the fort were stormed he could creep out behind the attackers. It had been a passage along which only one man could crawl at a time, and it had been constructed with a special kink in it, at which he could wait to knock a pursuer on the head, as the latter negotiated the obstacle. The diggers of the souterrain had been executed by their own priest-king, to keep the secret of it.

All that was in an earlier millennium.

Dunlothian had grown with the slow conservancy of the Old Ones. Here, with a Scandinavian conquest, had sprung up a wooden long-house—there, the original stones of the curtain wall had been pulled down to build a round tower for priests. The pele tower, with a cow-byre under the two living chambers, had come the last of all.

So it was among the untidy wreckage of centuries that Gareth scampered, looking for his brothers. It was among lean-to's and adaptations—past ogham stones commemorating some long-dead Deag the son of No, built into a later bastion upside down. It was on the top of a wind-swept cliff purged to the bone by the airs of the Atlantic, under which the little fishing village nestled among the dunes. It was as the inheritor of a view which covered a dozen miles of rollers, and hundreds of miles of cumulus. All along the coast-

line the saints and scholars of Eriu inhabited their stone
igloos in holy horribleness—reciting fifty psalms in their
beehives and fifty in the open air and fifty with their bodies
plunged in cold water, in their loathing for the twinkling
world. St. Toirdealbhach was far from typical of their
species.

Gareth found his brothers in the store-room.

It smelt of oatmeal, ham, smoked salmon, dried cod,
onions, shark oil, pickled herrings in tubs, hemp, maize,
hen's fluff, sailcloth, milk—the butter was churned there on
Thursdays—seasoning pine wood, apples, herbs drying, fish
glue and varnish used by the fletcher, spices from overseas,
dead rat in trap, venison, seaweed, wood shavings, litter of
kittens, fleeces from the mountain sheep not yet sold, and
the pungent smell of tar.

Gawaine, Agravaine and Gaheris were sitting on the
fleeces, eating apples. They were in the middle of an argument.

"It is not our business," said Gawaine stubbornly.

Agravaine whined: "But it is our business. It is at us
more than anybody, and it is not right."

"How dare you to say that our mother is not right?"

"She is not."

"She is."

"If you can but contradict. . . ."

"They are decent for the Sassenach," said Gawaine. "Sir
Grummore let me try his helm last night."

"That has nothing to do with it."

Gawaine said: "I am not wishing to talk about it. It is
base to be talking."

"Pure Gawaine!"

As Gareth came in, he could see Gawaine's face flaming
at Agravaine, under its red hair. It was obvious that he
was going to have one of his rages—but Agravaine was one
of those luckless intellectuals who are too proud to give
in to brute force. He was the kind who gets knocked down
in an argument because he cannot defend himself, but
continues the argument on the floor, sneering, "Go on, then,
hit me again to show how clever you are."

Gawaine glared at him.

"Silence your mouth!"

"I will not."

"I will make you."

"If you will make me or not, it will be the same."

Gareth said: "Be quiet, Agravaine. Gawaine, leave him alone; Agravaine, if you do not be quiet he will kill you."

"I do not care if he does kill me. What I say is true."

"Hold your noise."

"I will not. I say we ought to indite a letter to our father about these knights. We ought to tell him about our mother. We—"

Gawaine was upon him before he could finish the sentence.

"Your soul to the devil!" he shouted. "Traitor! Ach, so you would!"

For Agravaine had done something unprecedented in the family troubles. He was the weaker of the two and he was afraid of pain. As he went down, he had drawn his dirk upon his brother.

"Look to his arm," cried Gareth.

The two were going over and over among the rolled fleeces.

"Gaheris, catch his hand! Gawaine, leave him alone! Agravaine, drop it! Agravaine, if you do not drop it, he will kill you. Ah, you brute!"

The boy's face was blue and the dirk nowhere to be seen. Gawaine, with his hands round Agravaine's throat, was ferociously beating his head on the floor. Gareth took hold of Gawaine's shirt at the neck and twisted it to choke him. Gaheris, hovering round the edge, ferreted for the dirk.

"Leave me," panted Gawaine. "Let me be." He gave a coughing or husky noise in his chest, like a young lion making its roar.

Agravaine, whose Adam's apple had been hurt, relaxed his muscles and lay hiccoughing with his eyes shut. He looked as if he were going to die. They dragged Gawaine off and held him down, still struggling to get at his victim and finish the work.

It was curious that when he was in one of these black passions he seemed to pass out of human life. In later days he even killed women, when he had been worked into such a state—though he regretted it bitterly afterwards.

When the counterfeit Beast was perfected, the knights took it away and hid it in a cave at the foot of the cliffs, above high-water mark. Then they had some whisky to celebrate, and set off in search of the King, as darkness fell.

They found him in his chamber, with a quill pen and a

sheet of parchment. There was no poetry on the parchment
—only a picture which was intended to be a heart transfixed by an arrow, with two P's drawn inside it, interlaced.
The King was blowing his nose.

"Excuse me, Pellinore," said Sir Grummore, "but we
have seen something on the cliffs."

"Something nasty?"

"Well, not exactly. . . ."

"I hoped it would be."

Sir Grummore thought the situation over, and drew the
Saracen aside. They decided that tact was needed.

"Oh, Pellinore," said Sir Grummore nonchalantly, "what
is this that you are drawin'?"

"What do you think it is?"

"It looks like a sort of drawin'."

"That is what it is," said the King. "I wish you two would
go away. I mean, if you could take a hint."

"It would be better if you were to make a line here,"
pursued Sir Grummore.

"Where?"

"Here, where the pig is."

"My dear fellow, I don't know what you are talking
about."

"I am sorry, Pellinore, I thought you was drawin' a pig
with your eyes shut."

Sir Palomides thought it was time to interfere.

"Sir Grummore," he said coyly, "has observed a phenomenon, by Jove!"

"A phenomenon?"

"A thing," explained Sir Grummore.

"What sort of thing?" asked the King suspiciously.

"Something you will like."

"It has four legs," added the Saracen.

"Is it animal?" asked the King, "vegetable or mineral?"

"Animal."

"A pig?" inquired the King, who was beginning to feel
they must be driving at something.

"No, no, Pellinore. Not a pig. Get pigs out of your head
right away. This thing makes a noise like hounds."

"Like sixty hounds," explained Sir Palomides.

"It is a whale!" cried the King.

"No, no, Pellinore. A whale has no legs."

"But it makes such a noise."

"Does a whale?"

"My dear fellow, how am I to know? You must try to keep the issue clear."

"I see, but what is the issue, what? It seems to be a menagerie game."

"No, no, Pellinore. It is something we have seen which bays."

"Oh, I say," he wailed. "I do wish you two would either shut up or go away. What with whales and pigs, and now this thing which bays, a fellow does not know where he is half the time. Can't you leave a fellow alone, to draw his little things and hang himself quietly, for once? I mean to say, it is not much to ask, is it, what, don't you know?"

"Pellinore," said Sir Grummore, "you must pull yourself together. We have seen the Questing Beast!"

"Why?"

"Why?"

"Yes, why?"

"Why do you say why?"

"I mean," explained Sir Grummore, "you could say Where? or When? But why Why?"

"Why not?"

"Pellinore, have you lost all sense of decency? We have seen the *Questing Beast*, I tell you—seen it on the cliffs here, quite close."

"It is not an it. It is a She."

"My dear chap, it doesn't matter what she is. We have seen her."

"Then why don't you go and catch her?"

"It is not for us to catch her, Pellinore. It is for you. After all, she is your life's work, isn't she?"

"She's stupid," said the King.

"She may be stupid, or she may not," said Sir Grummore in an offended tone. "The point is, she is your *magnum opus*. Only a Pellinore can catch her. You have told us so often."

"What is the point of catching her?" asked the monarch. "What? After all, she is probably quite happy on the cliffs. I don't see what you are fussing about.

"It seems dreadfully sad," he added at a tangent, "that people can't be married when they want to. I mean, what is the good of this animal to me? I have not married it, have I? So why am I chasing it all the time? It doesn't seem logical."

"What you want, Pellinore, is a good hunt. Shake up your liver."

They took away his pen and poured him several bumpers of usquebaugh, not forgetting to take a nip or two themselves.

"It seems the only thing to do," he said suddenly. "After all, only a Pellinore can catch it."

"That's the brave fellow."

"Only I do feel sad sometimes," he added, before they could stop him, "about the Queen of Flanders' daughter. She was not beautiful, Grummore, but she understood me. We seemed to get on together, if you see what I mean. I amn't clever, perhaps, and I may get into trouble when I am by myself, but when I was with Piggy she always knew what to do. It was company too. It is not bad to have a bit of company when you are getting on in life, especially when you have been chasing the Questing Beast all the time, what? It gets a bit lonely in the Forest. Not that the Questing Beast wasn't company in her way—so far as she went. Only you couldn't talk things over with her, not like with Piggy. And she couldn't cook. I don't know why I am boring you fellows with all this talk, but really sometimes one feels as if one could hardly carry on. It is not as if Piggy were a flapper, you see. I really did love her, Grummore, really, and if only she would have answered my letters it would have been ever so nice."

"Poor old Pellinore," they said.

"I saw seven maggot pies today, Palomides. They were flying along like frying pans."

"One for sorrow," explained the King. "Two for joy, three for a marriage, and four for a boy. So seven ought to be four boys, ought it, what?"

"Bound to be," said Sir Grummore.

"They were going to be called Aglovale, Percivale, and Lamorak, and then there was one with a funny name which I can't remember. That's all off now. Still, I must say I would have liked to have had a son called Dornar."

"Look here, Pellinore, you must learn to let bygones be bygones. You will only wear yourself out. Why don't you be a brave chap and catch your Beast for instance?"

"I suppose I must."

"That's it. Take your mind off things."

"It is eighteen years since I have been after it," said the

King pensively. "It would be a change to catch it. I wonder where the brachet is?"

"Ah, Pellinore! Now you're talking!"

"Suppose our honoured monarch were to start at once?"

"What? This evening, Palomides? In the dark?"

Sir Palomides nudged Sir Grummore secretly. "Administer blows to iron," he whispered, "while at high temperature."

"I see what you mean."

"I don't suppose it matters," said the King. "Nothing does, really."

"Very well, then," cried Sir Grummore, taking control of the situation. "That is what we will do. We will put old Pellinore at one end of the cliffs this very night, in an ambush, and then we two will drive the place methodically toward him. The Beast is bound to be there, as it was seen only this afternoon."

"Don't you think," he inquired, as they were dressing up in the darkness, "that it was clever, the way I explained about our bein' here, I mean to drive the animal?"

"An inspiration," said Sir Palomides. "Is my head on straight?"

"My dear chap, I can't see an inch."

The Saracen's voice sounded uneasy.

"This darkness," he said, "seems jolly palpable."

"Never mind," said Sir Grummore. "It will hide any little faults in our make-up. Perhaps the moon will come out later."

"Thank goodness his sword is generally blunt."

"Oh, come now, Palomides, you mustn't get cold feet. I can't think why it is, but I feel perfectly splendid. Perhaps it was those bumpers. I am goin' to prance and bay tonight, I can tell you."

"You are buttoning yourself to me, Sir Grummore. Those are the wrong buttons."

"Beg pardon, Palomides."

"Would it be enough if you were to wave your tail in the air, instead of prancing? There is a certain discomfort for the forequarters during the prance."

"I shall wave my tail as well as prance," said Sir Grummore firmly.

"Just as you say."

"Take your hoof off my tail for a moment, Palomides."

"Could you carry your tail over your arm for the first part of the journey?"

"It would hardly be natural."

"No."

"And now," added Sir Palomides bitterly, "it is going to rain. Come to think of it, it nearly always does rain in these parts."

He thrust his brown hand out of the serpent's mouth and felt the drops on the back of it. They drummed on the canvas like hail.

"Dear old forequarters," said Sir Grummore cheerfully, for he had plenty of whisky, "it was you who thought of this expedition in the first place. Cheer up, old blackamoor. It will be much worse for Pellinore, waitin' for us to come. After all, he has not got a canvas hide with spots on it, to shelter under."

"Perhaps it will stop."

"Of course it will stop. That's the ticket, old pagan. Now then, are we ready?"

"Yes."

"Give the step then."

"Left! Right!"

"Don't forget the Tantivvy."

"Left! Right! Tantivvy! Tantivvy! I beg your pardon?"

"I was only bayin'."

"Tantivvy! Tantivvy!"

"Now for the prance!"

"Oh, dear, Sir Grummore!"

"Sorry, Palomides."

"Yours truly will hardly be able to sit down."

Under the dripping cliffs King Pellinore stood stock still, looking vaguely in front of him. His brachet, on a long string, was wound round him several times. He was in full armour, which was getting rusty, and the rain came in at five places. It ran down both shins and both forearms, but the worst place was his vizor. This was constructed on the snout principle, since it was found that if one had an ugly helmet it frightened the enemy. King Pellinore's looked like an inquisitive pig. It let the rain in through the nostrils, however, and the water ran down in front in a steady trickle which tickled his chest. The King was thinking.

Well, he thought, he supposed this would keep them quiet. It was not very nice in all this rain and everything, but the dear fellows seemed keen on it. It would be difficult to find anybody kinder than old Grum, and Palomides seemed a friendly chap, though he was a paynim. If they wanted to have a lark like this, it was only decent to humour them. Besides, it was nice for the brachet to have an outing. It was a pity that it could never keep unwound, but there, you could not interfere with nature. He would have to spend all tomorrow scrubbing his armour.

It would give him something to do, reflected the King miserably, which was better than wandering about all the time, with his eternal sorrow gnawing at his heart. And he fell to thinking about Piggy.

The nice thing about the Queen of Flanders' daughter, had been that she did not laugh at him. A lot of people laughed at you when you went after the Questing Beast— and never caught it—but Piggy never laughed. She seemed to understand at once how interesting it was, and made several sensible suggestions about the way to trap it. Naturally one did not pretend to be clever or anything, but it was nice not to be laughed at. One was doing one's best.

And then the dreadful day had come when that cursed boat had floated to the shore. They had got into it, because knights must always accept an adventure, and it had sailed away at once. They had waved to Piggy ever so, and the Beast had put its head out of the wood and waded out to sea after them, looking most upset. But the boat had gone on and on, and the small figures on the shore had dwindled till they could hardly see the kerchief which Piggy was waving, and then the brachet had been sick.

From every port he had written to her. He had given letters to the innkeepers everywhere, and they had promised to send them on. But she had never sent a syllable in reply.

It was because he was unworthy, decided the King. He was vague and not clever and always getting in a muddle. Why should the daughter of the Queen of Flanders write to a person like that, especially when he had gone and got into a magic boat and sailed away? It was like deserting her, and of course she was right to be angry. Meanwhile it would keep raining, and the water did trickle so, and now that brachet was sneezing. The armour would be rusty, and there was a sort of draught down the back of his neck where the helmet screwed on. It was dark and horrible. Some sticky stuff was dripping off the cliffs.

"Excuse me, Sir Grummore, but is that you snuffling in my ear?"

"No, no, my dear fellow. Go on, go on. I am only doin' my bayin' as well as I can."

"It is not the baying I refer to, Sir Grummore, but a kind of breathing noise of a husky nature."

"My dear chap, it is no good askin' me. All you can hear in here is a kind of creakin', like a bellows."

"Yours truly thinks the rain is going to stop. Do you mind if we stop, too?"

"Well, Palomides, if you must stop, you must. But if we don't get this over quickly, I shall get my stitch again. What do you want to stop for?"

"I wish it was not so dark."

"But you can't stop just because it is dark."

"No. One appreciates that."

"Go on, then, old boy. Left! Right! That's the ticket."

"I say, Grummore," said Sir Palomides later. "There it is again."

"What is?"

"The puffing, Sir Grummore."

"Are you sure it is not me?" inquired Sir Grummore.

"Positive. It is a menacing or amorous puff, similar to the grampus. This paynim sincerely wishes that it were not so dark."

"Ah, well, we can't have everythin'. Now march on, Palomides, there's a good fellow, do."

After a bit, Sir Grummore said sepulchrally:

"Dear old boy, can't you stop bumpin' all the time?"

"But I am not bumping, Sir Grummore."

"Well, what is, then?"

"Yours faithfully can feel no bumps."

"Somethin' keeps bumpin' me behind."

"Is it your tail, perhaps?"

"No. I have that wound round me."

"In any case it would be impossible to bump you from the back, because the forelegs are in front."

"There it is again!"

"What?"

"The bump! It was a definite assault. Palomides, we are bein' attacked!"

"No, no, Sir Grummore. You are imagining things."

"Palomides, we must turn round!"

"What for, Sir Grummore?"

"To see what is bumping me behind."

"Yours truly can see nothing, Sir Grummore. It is too dark."

"Put your hand out of your mouth, and see what you can feel."

"I can feel a sort of round thing."

"That is me, Sir Palomides. That is me, from the back."

"Sincere apologies, Sir Grummore."

"Not at all, my dear chap, not at all. What else can you feel?"

The kindly Saracen's voice began to falter.

"Something cold," he said, "and—slippery."

"Does it move, Palomides?"

"It moves, and—it snuffles!"

"Snuffles?"

"Snuffles!"

At this moment the moon came out.

"Merciful powers!" cried Sir Palomides, in a high squealing voice, as he peered out of his mouth. "Run, Grummore, run! Left, right! Quick march! Double march! Faster, faster! Keep in step! Oh, my poor heels! Oh, my God! Oh, my hat!"

It was no good, decided the King. Probably they had got lost, or wandered off somewhere to amuse themselves. It was beastly wet, as it nearly always was in Lothian, and really he had done his best to fall in with their plans. Now they had wandered off—one might almost say inconsiderately— and left him with his wretched brachet to get rusty. It was too bad.

With a determined motion he marched away to bed, heaving the brachet along behind him.

Half-way up a fissure in one of the steepest cliffs, with most of its buttons burst, the counterfeit Beast was arguing with its stomach.

"But, my dear knight, how could yours truly foresee a calamity of this nature?"

"You thought of it," replied the stomach furiously. "You made us dress up. It is your fault."

At the foot of the cliff the Questing Beast herself, in a

sentimental attitude, waited in the romantic moonlight for her better half. Behind her was a background of the silver sea. In various parts of the landscape several dozens of bent and distorted Old Ones were intently examining the situation from the concealment of rocks, sandhills, shell-mounds, igloos and so forth—still vainly trying to fathom the subtle secrets of the English.

# 10

*In Bedegraine it was the night before the battle. A* number of bishops were blessing the armies on both sides, hearing confessions and saying Mass. Arthur's men were reverent about this, but King Lot's men were not—for such was the custom in all armies that were going to be defeated. The bishops assured both sides that they were certain to win, because God was with them, but King Arthur's men knew that they were outnumbered by three to one, so they thought it was best to get shriven. King Lot's men, who also knew the odds, spent the night dancing, drinking, dicing and telling each other dirty stories. This is what the chronicles say, at any rate.

In the King of England's tent, the last staff talk had been held, and Merlyn had stayed behind to have a chat. He was looking worried.

"What are you worried about, Merlyn? Are we going to lose this battle, after all?"

"No. You will win the battle all right. There is no harm in telling you so. You will do your best, and fight hard, and call in You-know-whom at the right moment. It will be in your nature to win the battle, so it doesn't matter telling you. No. It is something else which I ought to have told you that is worrying me just now."

"What was it about?"

"Gracious heavens! Why should I be worrying if I could remember what it was about?"

"Was it about the maiden called Nimue?"

"No. No. No. No. That's quite a different business. It was something—it was something I can't remember."

After a bit, Merlyn took his beard out of his mouth and began counting on his fingers.

"I have told you about Guenever, haven't I?"

"I don't believe it."

"No matter. And I have warned you about her and Lancelot."

"That warning," said the King, "would be a base one anyway, whether it was true or false."

"Then I have said the bit about Excalibur, and how you must be careful of the sheath?"

"Yes."

"I have told you about your father, so it can't be him, and I have given the hint about the person.

"What is confounding me," exclaimed the magician, pulling out his hair in tufts, "is that I can't remember whether it is in the future or in the past."

"Never mind about it," said Arthur. "I don't like knowing the future anyway. I had much rather you didn't worry about it, because it only worries me."

"But it is something I must say. It is vital."

"Stop thinking about it," suggested the King, "and then perhaps it will come back. You ought to take a holiday. You have been bothering your head too much lately, what with all these warnings and arranging about the battle."

"I *will* take a holiday," exclaimed Merlyn. "As soon as this battle is over, I will go on a walking tour into North Humberland. I have a Master called Bleise who lives in North Humberland, and perhaps he will be able to tell me what it is I am trying to remember. Then we could have some wild fowl watching. He is a great man for wild fowl."

"Good," said Arthur. "You take a long holiday. Then, when you come back, we can think of something to prevent Nimue."

The old man stopped fiddling with his fingers, and looked sharply at the King.

"You are an innocent fellow, Arthur," he said. "And a good thing too, really."

"Why?"

"Do you remember anything about the magic you had when you were small?"

"No. Did I have some magic? I can remember that I was interested in birds and beasts. Indeed, that is why I still keep my menagerie at the Tower. But I don't remember about magic."

"People don't remember," said Merlyn. "I suppose you wouldn't remember about the parables I used to tell you, when I was trying to explain things?"

"Of course I do. There was one about some Rabbi or other which you told me when I wanted to take Kay somewhere. I never could understand why the cow died."

"Well, I want to tell you another parable now."

"I shall love it."

"In the East, perhaps in the same place which that Rabbi Jachanan came from, there was a certain man who was walking in the market of Damascus when he came face to face with Death. He noticed an expression of surprise on the spectre's horrid countenance, but they passed one another without speaking. The fellow was frightened, and went to a wise man to ask what should be done. The wise man told him that Death had probably come to Damascus to fetch him away next morning. The poor man was terrified at this, and asked however he could escape. The only way they could think of between them was that the victim should ride all night to Aleppo, thus eluding the skull and bloody bones.

"So this man did ride to Aleppo—it was a terrible ride which had never been done in one night before—and when he was there he walked in the market place, congratulating himself on having eluded Death.

"Just then, Death came up to him and tapped him on the shoulder. 'Excuse me,' he said, 'but I have come for you.' 'Why,' exclaimed the terrified man, 'I thought I met you in Damascus yesterday!' 'Exactly,' said Death. 'That was why I looked surprised—for I had been told to meet you today, in Aleppo.' "

Arthur reflected on this gruesome chestnut for some time, then he said:

"So it is no good trying to escape Nimue?"

"Even if I wanted to," said Merlyn, "it would be no good. There is a thing about Time and Space which the philosopher Einstein is going to find out. Some people call it Destiny."

"But what I can't get over is this toad-in-the-hole business."

"Ah, well," said Merlyn, "people will do a lot for love. And then the toad is not necessarily unhappy in its hole, not more than when you are asleep, for instance. I shall do some considering, until they let me out again."

"So they will let you out?"

"I will tell you something else, King, which may be a surprise for you. It will not happen for hundreds of years, but both of us are to come back. Do you know what is going to be written on your tombstone? *Hic jacet Arthurus Rex quandam Rexque futurus.* Do you remember your Latin? It means, the once and future king."

"I am to come back as well as you?"

"Some say from the vale of Avilion."

The King thought about it in silence. It was full night outside, and there was stillness in the bright pavilion. The sentries, moving on the grass, could not be heard.

"I wonder," he said at last, "whether they will remember about our Table?"

Merlyn did not answer. His head was bowed on the white beard and his hands clasped between his knees.

"What sort of people will they be, Merlyn?" cried the young man's voice, unhappily.

# 11

The Queen of Lothian had taken to her chamber, cutting off communication with her guests, and Pellinore broke his fast alone. Afterwards he went for a walk along the beach, admiring the gulls who flew above him like white quill pens whose heads had been neatly dipped in ink. The old cormorants stood like crucifixes on the rocks, drying their wings. He was feeling sad as usual, but he was also feeling uncomfortable, because he was missing something. He did not know what it was. He was missing Palomides and Grummore, if he had been able to remember.

Presently he was attracted by shouting, and went to investigate.

"Here, Pellinore! Hi! We are over here!"

"Why, Grummore," he asked with interest, "whatever are you doing up that cliff?"

"Look at the Beast, man, look at the Beast!"

"Oh, hallo, you have got old Glatisant."

"My dear chap, for heaven's sake do something. We have been here all night."

"But why are you dressed up like that, Grummore? You have got spots, or something. And what has Palomides got on his head?"

"Don't stand there arguin', man."

"But you have a sort of tail, Grummore. I can see it hanging down behind."

"Of course I have a tail. Can't you stop talkin' and do somethin'? We have been in this damned crevice all night, and we are droppin' with fatigue. Go on, Pellinore, kill that Beast of yours at once."

"Oh, I say, whatever should I want to kill her for?"

"Good gracious heavens, haven't you been tryin' to kill her for the last eighteen years? Now, come along, Pellinore, be a good chap and do somethin'. If you don't do somethin' quick, we shall both tumble out."

"What I can't understand," said the King plaintively, "is why you should be in this cliff at all. And why are you dressed up like that? You look as if you were dressed as a sort of Beast yourselves. And where did the Beast come from, anyway, what? I mean, the whole thing is so sudden."

"Pellinore, once and for all, will you kill that Beast?"

"Why?"

"Because it has chased us up this cliff."

"It is unusual for the Beast," remarked the King. "She does not generally take an interest in people like this."

"Palomides," said Sir Grummore hoarsely, "says he believes she has fallen in love with us."

"Fallen in love?"

"Well, you see, we were dressed up as a Beast."

"Like likes Like," explained Sir Palomides faintly.

King Pellinore slowly began to laugh for the first time since he had arrived in Lothian.

"Well!" he said. "Bless my soul! Did you ever hear of anything to match it? Why does Palomides think she has fallen for him?"

"The Beast," said Sir Grummore with dignity, "has been walkin' round and round the cliff all night. She has been rubbin' herself against it, and purrin'. And she sometimes curls her neck round the rocks, and gazes up at us in a sort of way."

"What sort of way, Grummore?"

"My dear fellow, look at her now."

The Questing Beast, who had not paid the least attention to the arrival of her master, was staring up at Sir Palomides with her soul in her eyes. Her chin was pressed to the foot of the cliffs in a passion of devotion, and occasionally she gave her tail a wag. She moved it laterally on the surface of pebbles, where its numerous heraldic tufts and foliations made a rustling noise, and sometimes she scratched the bluff with a small whimper. Then, feeling that she had been too forward, she would arch her graceful serpent neck and hide her head beneath her belly, peeping upwards from the corner of one eye.

"Well, Grummore, what do you want me to do?"

"We want to come down," said Sir Grummore.

"I can see that," said the King. "It seems a sensible idea. Mind you, I don't understand exactly how the whole thing started, what, but I can see that, absolutely."

"Then kill it, Pellinore. Kill the wretched creature."

"Oh, really," said the King. "I don't know about that! After all, what harm has she done? All the world loves a lover. I don't see why the poor beastie should be killed, just because she has got the gentle passion. I mean to say, I am in love myself, amn't I, what? It gives you a sort of fellow feeling."

"King Pellinore," said Sir Palomides definitely, "unless some steps are taken pretty dam' quick, yours affectionately will be instantaneously martyred, R.I.P."

"But, my dear Palomides, I can't possibly kill the old Beast, don't you see, because my sword is blunt."

"Then stun her with it, Pellinore. Give her a good bang on the head with it, man, and perhaps she will get concussion."

"That is all very well for you, Grummore, old fellow. But suppose it doesn't stun her? It might make her lose her temper, Grummore, and then where should I be? Personally I can't see why you should want to have the creature assaulted at all. After all, she is in love with you, isn't she, what?"

"Whatever the reasons for the animal's behaviour, the point is we are on this ledge."

"Then all you need to do is to come off it."

"My good man, how can we come down to be attacked?"

"It will only be a loving sort of attack," the King pointed

out reassuringly. "Sort of making advances. I don't suppose she will do you any harm. All you would have to do would be to walk along in front of her until you reached the castle, what? As a matter of fact you could perhaps encourage her a bit. After all, everybody likes to have their affection returned."

"Are you suggesting," asked Sir Grummore coldly, "that we should flirt with this reptile of yours?"

"It would certainly make it easier. I mean, the walk back."

"And how are we to do this, pray?"

"Well, Palomides could twine his neck round hers occasionally, you know, and you could wag your tail. I suppose you could not lick her nose?"

"Yours truly," said Sir Palomides feebly, finally and with aversion, "can neither twine nor lick. Also he is now about to fall. Adieu."

With this the unfortunate paynim let go of the cliff with both hands and appeared to be sinking into the monster's jaws—but that Sir Grummore caught him, and the remaining buttons held him in position.

"There!" said Sir Grummore. "Now look what you have done."

"But, my dear fellow . . ."

"I am not your dear fellow. You are simply abandonin' us to destruction."

"Oh, I say!"

"Yes, you are. Heartlessly."

The King scratched his head.

"I suppose," he said doubtfully, "I could hold her by the tail, while you made a dash for it."

"Then do so. If you don't do somethin' immediately, Palomides will fall, and then we shall come in half."

"I still don't see," said the King sadly, "why you had to dress up like this to begin with. It is all a mystery to me.

"However," he added, taking the Beast by the tail, "come on, old girl. Heave-ho! We shall have to do the best we can in the circumstances. Now then, you two, run for your lives. Hurry up, Grummore, I don't think the Beast is pleased, by the feel of her. Ah, you naughty thing, leave it! Run, Grummore! Naughty Beast! Pah! Nasty, nasty! Leave it! Quick, man, quick! Come away then! Don't touch! Trust! She'll be off in a minute! Come to heel, will you? Heel! Come behind! Oh, you horrid Beast! Faster, Grummore!

Sit, sit! Lie down, Beast! How dare you? Look out, man, she's coming! Oh, you would, would you? There! Now she's bitten me!"

They won the drawbridge by a short head, and it was drawn up after them in the nick of time.

"Phew!" said Sir Grummore, unbuttoning the back end and standing up to mop his brow.

"Hoots!" cried various auld wives who were in the castle delivering eggs. Some of the castle circle could speak English after a fashion, including St. Toirdealbhach and Mother Morlan.

"Wee sleekit, cow'ring, timorous Beastie," said the drawbridge man. "Oh, what a panic's in thy breastie!"

"Aroint us!" said the bystanders.

"Bonnie Sir Palomides," said a number of Old Ones who had known of their plight on the cliff ledge all night —without saying anything about it, as was their custom, for fear of being caught out, "is going to lay him doon and dee."

They turned round to examine the paynim, and found that it was as they said. Sir Palomides had collapsed on a stone mounting block, without troubling to take his head off, and was breathing heavily. They took it off for him and threw a bucket of water in his face. Then they fanned him with their aprons.

"Ah, the puir churl," they said compassionately. "The sassenagh! The sable savage! Will he no' come back again? Gie him anither drappie there. Ah, the braw splash!"

Sir Palomides revived slowly, blowing bubbles out of his nose.

"Where is yours truly?" he asked.

"Here we are, old boy. We got back safe. The Beast is outside."

Through the portcullis there came a sorrowful howling to bear out Sir Grummore's statement, as it had been thirty couple of hounds baying the moon. Sir Palomides shuddered.

"We ought to look out, to see if King Pellinore is comin'."

"Yes, Sir Grummore. Allow one sec. for recuperation."

"The Beast may have done him a mischief."

"Poor fellow!"

"How do you feel yourself?"

"The indisposition is passing," said Sir Palomides bravely.

"Not much time to waste. It may be eatin' him at this moment."

"Lead on," said the paynim, heaving himself to his feet. "Forward to the battlements."

So the whole party set off to climb the narrow stairs of the Pele Tower.

Below them, looking small and upside down from this height, the Questing Beast could be seen sitting in the ravine which bounded the castle on that side. She was sitting on a boulder in it, with her tail in the burn, and looking up at the drawbridge with her head on one side. Her tongue was hanging out. Nothing could be seen of Pellinore.

"Evidently she is not eatin' him," said Sir Grummore.

"Unless she has eaten him."

"I hardly think she would have had time to do that, old boy, not in the time."

"You would think she would have left some bones or something. Or at any rate the armour."

"Quite."

"What do you think we ought to do?"

"It seems bafflin'."

"Do you think we ought to make a sortie?"

"We could wait to see what happens, Palomides, don't you think?"

"No leaps," assented Sir Palomides, "without previous looks."

After they had been watching for half an hour or so, the faction of the Old Ones grew bored with the lack of entertainment. They clattered off down the stairs, to throw stones at the Questing Beast off the top of the wall. The two knights stayed on the lookout.

"This is a pretty state of affairs."

"Indeed, it is."

"I mean, when you work it out."

"Exactly."

"Here is the Queen of Orkney angry about something on one side—I could not help noticing that she seemed a little queer about that unicorn—and Pellinore moping on the other. And you are supposed to be in love with La Beale Isoud, isn't it? And now this Beast is after both of us."

"A confusing situation."

"Love," said Sir Grummore uneasily, "is a pretty strong passion, when you come to think of it."

At this moment, as if to confirm Sir Grummore's opinion,

a pair of enlaced figures sauntered along the cliff road.

"Good gracious," exclaimed Sir Grummore. "What are these?"

As they drew nearer, their identity became clear. One of them was King Pellinore, and he had his arm round the waist of a stout, middle-aged lady in a side-saddle skirt. She had a red, horsey face, and carried a hunting crop in her free hand. Her hair was in a bun.

"It must be the Queen of Flanders' daughter!"

"I say, you two!" cried King Pellinore, as soon as he had observed them. "I say, look here, what do you think, can you guess? Whoever would have thought it, what? What do you think I have found?"

"Aha!" cried the stout lady in a booming voice, archly tapping his cheek with her hunting crop. "But who did the findin', eh?"

"Yes, yes, I know! It was not me that found her at all; it was she that found me! What do you think of that?

"And do you know what?" went on the King, in high delight. "None of my letters could possibly be answered! I never put our address on them! We hadn't got one! I always knew there was something wrong. So Piggy got on her horse, you know, and came huntin' after me by moor and fell! The Questing Beast helped her a great deal—it has an excellent nose—and that magic barge of ours, can you imagine it, must have had an idea or two in its head, for it went back to fetch them when it saw that I was upset! How nice of it! They found it in a creek somewhere, and here they are!

"But why are we standing about?" shouted the King. He was so excited that nobody else had time to talk. "I mean to say, why are we shouting so? Is it polite, do you think? Ought you two to come down and let us in? What is wrong with this drawbridge anyway?"

"It is the Beast, Pellinore, the Beast! She is in the ravine!"

"What is wrong with the Beast?"

"She is besiegin' the castle."

"Oh, yes," said the King. "Now I remember. She bit me.

"And what do you think?" he went on, waving one hand in the air to show that it was bandaged. "Piggy tied it up for me like one o'clock. She tied it up with a bit of—well, you know."

"Petticoats," boomed the Queen of Flanders' daughter.

"Yes, yes, her petticoats!"

The King was convulsed with giggles.

"That is all very well, Pellinore, that is all very well. But what are you goin' to do about the Beast?"

His Majesty was intoxicated with gaiety. "Ho, the Beast!" he cried. "Is that the trouble? I'll soon settle her!

"Now then!" he exclaimed, marching to the edge of the ravine and waving his sword. "Now then! Off you go! Shoo! Shoo!"

The Questing Beast looked at him absently. She moved her tail in a vague gesture of recognition, then returned her attention to the gatehouse. The occasional stones which were being thrown at her by the Old Ones she dexterously caught and swallowed, in the maddening way which chickens have when you are trying to drive them off.

"Let down the drawbridge!" commanded the King. "I will attend to her! Shoo, now shoo!"

The drawbridge was lowered with hesitation. The Beast immediately drew closer to it, with a hopeful expression.

"Now then," cried the King. "You rush in, while I defend the rear."

The drawbridge reached the ground and Piggy was speeding across before it touched. King Pellinore, less agile or more bemused by the gentle passion, collided with her in the gateway. The Questing Beast ran into them behind, knocking the King flat.

"Beware! Beware!" cried all the retainers, fishwives, falconers, farriers, fletchers, and other well-wishers who were assembled within.

The Queen of Flanders' daughter turned like a tigress to defend her young.

"Be off, you shameless hussy," she cried, bringing her hunting crop down on the creature's nose. The Questing Beast recoiled with the tears springing to its eyes, and the portcullis crashed between them.

In the evening a new crisis began to develop. It became obvious that Glatisant intended to besiege the castle until her mate had been produced, and, in these circumstances, the Old Ones who had brought their eggs to market refused to leave the gate without an escort. Eventually the three southern knights had to convoy them to the foot of the cliff, with drawn swords in their hands.

In the village street St. Toirdealbhach was waiting to receive the convoy, a raffish Silenus supported by four small boys. His breath smelt strongly of whisky and he was in tearing spirits, waving his shillelagh.

"Not a one more stories," he was shouting. "Am not I going to be married wid ould Mother Morlan. and after having a fight wid Duncan this minute, and never more to be a saint?"

"Congratulations!" the children told him for the hundredth time.

"We are all right also," added Gareth. "We are allowed to serve at dinner every day."

"Glory be to God! Is it every day, begor?"

"Yes, and our mother takes us for walks."

"Well, there now. Praise youth and it will come!"

The saint caught sight of the convoy and began to howl like an Iroquois.

"Up the ribels!"

"Be easy now," they told him. "Be easy, your Holiness. The swords are not for fighting with at all."

"Why wouldn't they be?" he inquired indignantly, and he proceeded to kiss King Pellinore and breathe on him.

The King said: "I say, are you really going to be married? So am I. Are you excited?"

For answer, the holy man twined his arms round the King's neck and drew him into Mother Morlan's shebeen— not entirely to Pellinore's satisfaction, for he would have liked to hurry back to Piggy—but it was obvious that a bachelor party would have to be held in celebration. The whole Gaelic miasma had faded like the mist it was— whether under the influence of love or of whisky or of its own nature as mist—and the three southerners found themselves accepted at last as individuals and guests, irrespective of the racial trauma, into the warm heart of the North.

# 12

*The battle of Bedegraine was fought near Sorhaute* in the forest of Sherwood, during the Whitsun holiday. It was a decisive battle, because it was in some ways the twelfth century equivalent of what later came to be called a Total War.

The Eleven Kings were ready to fight their sovereign in the Norman way—in the foxhunting way of Henry the Second and of his sons—for sport and acquisition and without the real intention of doing each other a personal injury. They—the kings with the tank-like knights of their nobility—were prepared to take a sporting risk. It was the kind of risk which Jorrocks talked about. King Lot might have said with justice that the rebellion which he led against Arthur was the image of foxhunting without its guilt, and only twenty-five per cent of its danger.

But the Eleven Kings needed a background for their exploits. Even if the knights had little wish to kill each other on the grand scale, there was no reason why they should not kill the serfs. It would have been a poor day's sport indeed, according to their estimation, without a bag to count at the end of it.

So the war, as the rebel lords had wished to fight it, was a kind of double battle, or a war within a war. On the outer circle there were sixty thousand kerns and gallowglasses marching with the Eleven, and these ill-armed levies of the Old Ones were inflamed against the twenty thousand foot-soldiers of Arthur's Sassenach army by the tragedy of the Gael. Between the armies there was a serious racial enmity. But it was an enmity controlled from above—by nobles who were not sincerely anxious for each other's blood. The armies were packs of hounds, as it were, whose struggle with each other was to be commanded by Masters of Hounds, who took the matter as an exciting gamble. If the hounds had turned mutinous, for instance, Lot and his allies would have been ready to ride with Arthur's knights, in quelling what they would have considered a real rebellion.

The nobles of the inner circle on both sides were in a way traditionally more friendly with each other than with their own men. For them the numbers were necessary for the sake of the bag, and for scenic purposes. For them a good war had to be full of "arms, shoulders and heads flying about the field and blows ringing by the water and the wood." But the arms, shoulders and heads would be those of villeins, and the blows which rang, without removing many limbs, would be exchanged by the iron nobility. Such, at any rate, was the idea of battle in Lot's command. When sufficient kerns had been decapitated and sufficient rough handling had been dealt out to the English captains, Arthur would recognize the impossibility of further resistance. He would capitulate. Financial terms of peace would be agreed on—which would yield an excellent profit in ransoms—and all would be more or less as it had been before—except that the fiction of feudal overlordship would be abolished, which was a fiction in any case.

Naturally a war of this sort was likely to be hedged with etiquette, just as foxhunting is hedged with it. It would begin at the advertised meet, weather permitting, and it would be conducted according to precedent.

But Arthur had a different idea in his head. It did not seem to him to be sporting, after all, that eighty thousand humble men should be leu'd against each other while a fraction of their number, in carapaces like the skins of tanks, manœuvred for the sake of ransom. He had begun to set a value on heads, shoulders and arms—their owners' value, even if the owner was a serf. Merlyn had taught him to distrust the logic by which countrysides could be pillaged for forage, husbandmen ruined, soldiers slaughtered, so that he himself should pay a scathless ransom, like the Cœur de Lion of the legends.

The King of England had ordered that there were to be no ransoms in his sort of battle. His knights were to fight, not against gallowglasses, but against the knights of the Gaelic Confederation. Let the gallowglasses fight among themselves if they must—indeed, since there was a real aggression for them to settle, apart from the question of ransoms, let them fight to the best of their ability. But, as for his nobles, they were to attack the nobles of the rebels as if they were gallowglasses and nothing more. They were to accept no composition, observe no ballet-dancer's rules. They were to press the war home to its real lords—until they themselves were ready to refrain from warfare, being confronted with its reality.

Afterwards, he knew for certain now, it was to be the destiny of his life to deal with every way of twisting decency by threats of Power.

So we may well believe that the King's men were shriven on the night before they fought. Something of the young man's vision had penetrated to his captains and his soldiers. Something of the new ideal of the Round Table which was to be born in pain, something about doing a hateful and dangerous action for the sake of decency—for they knew that the fight was to be fought in blood and death without reward. They would get nothing but the unmarketable conscience of having done what they ought to do in spite of fear—something which wicked people have often debased by calling it glory with too much sentiment, but which is glory all the same. This idea was in the hearts of the young men who knelt before the God-distributing bishops—knowing that the odds were three to one, and that their own warm bodies might be cold at sunset.

Arthur began with an atrocity and continued with other atrocities. The first one was that he did not wait the fashionable hour. He ought to have marshalled his Battle opposite Lot's, as soon as their breakfast was over, and then, at about midday, when the lines were properly in order, he should have given the signal to begin. The signal having been given, he should have charged Lot's footmen with his knights, while Lot's knights charged his footmen, and there would have been a splendid slaughter.

Instead, he attacked by night. In the darkness, with a war-whoop—deplorable and ungentlemanly tactics—he fell on the insurgent camp with the blood pounding in the veins of his neck, and Excalibur dancing in his hand. He had taken the odds three to one. In knights he was wildly outmatched. A single King of the rebels—the King of the Hundred Knights—had with his own forces two-thirds of the total number to which the Round Table was ever to grow. And Arthur had not started the war. He was fighting in his own country, hundreds of miles within his own borders, against an aggression which he had not provoked.

Down came the tents, up flared the torches, out flew the

blades, and the yell of battle mingled with the lamentation
of surprise. The noise, the slaughtering and slaughtered demons black against the flames—what scenes there have
been in Sherwood, where now the oak trees crowd into a
shade!

It was a masterful start, and it was rewarded by success.
The Eleven Kings and their baronage were in armour already—it took so long to arm a nobleman that he was often
accomplished overnight. If they had not been, it might have
been an almost bloodless victory. Instead, it was an initiative
and the initiative held. The chivalry of the Old Ones fought
their way from the ruined encampment, hand to hand. They
managed to unite into an armoured regiment—which was
still several times larger than anything in armour which the
King could bring against them—but they were deprived of
their accustomed screen of footmen. There had been no
time to organize the gallowglasses, and such of these as did
remain with the nobility were demoralized, or leaderless.
Arthur detached his own footmen, under Merlyn, to deal
with the infantry battle which was centred round the
camp, and he himself pressed on with his cavalry against
the kings themselves. He had them on the run, and saw that
he must keep them on it. They were indignantly surprised
by what they considered an unchivalrous personal outrage
—outrageous to be attacked with positive manslaughter, as
if a baron could be killed like a Saxon kern.

The King's second atrocity was that he neglected the
kerns themselves. That part of the battle, the racial struggle
which had a certain reality even if it was a wicked one, he
left to the races themselves—to the infantry and to Merlyn's
direction, at the struggling camp from which the cavalry
was already sweeping away. There were three Gaels to every
Gall among the tents, but they were surprised and taken at
a disadvantage. He wished them no particular harm—con-
centrating his indignation upon the leaders who had seduced their addled pates—but he knew that they would have
to be allowed their fight. He hoped that it would be a victorious one so far as his own troops were concerned. In the
meantime, his business was with the leaders—and, as the
day dawned, the atrociousness of his conduct became apparent.

For the Eleven Kings had assembled some apology for an
infantry screen, behind which to wait his charges. He
ought to have charged this screen of terrified men, dealing

them an enormous execution. Instead, he neglected them. He galloped through the infantry as if they were not his enemies at all—not even troubling to strike at them—pressing his charge against the armoured core itself. The infantry, for their part, accepted the mercy only too thankfully. They behaved as if it was not an honour to be allowed to die for Lothian. The discipline, as the rebel generals said afterwards, was not Pictish.

The charges began with the growing day.

At a military tattoo perhaps, or at some old piece of show-ground pageantry, you may have seen a cavalry charge. If so, you know that "seen" is not the word. It is heard—the thunder, earthshake, drum-fire, of the bright and battering sandals! Yes, and even then it is only a cavalry charge you are thinking of, not a chivalry one. Imagine it now, with the horses twice as heavy as the soft-mouthed hunters of our own midnight pageants, with the men themselves twice heavier on account of arms and shield. Add the cymbal-music of the clashing armour to the jingle of the harness. Turn the uniforms into mirrors, blazing with the sun, the lances into spears of steel. Now the spears dip, and now they are coming. The earth quakes under feet. Behind, among the flying clods, there are hoof-prints stricken in the ground. It is not the men that are to be feared, not their swords nor even their spears, but the hoofs of the horses. It is the impetus of that shattering phalanx of iron—spread across the battlefront, inescapable, pulverizing, louder than drums, beating the earth.

The knights of the confederation met the outrage as they could. They stood to it, and fought back. But the novelty of their situation as objects of ferocity in spite of their rank, and also as a large body being charged with arrogance by a body numbering less than a quarter of their own—and being charged again and again into the bargain—this had an effect on their morale. They gave ground before the charges, still orderly but giving, and were shepherded along a glade of Sherwood forest—a wide glade like an estuary of grass with trees on either side.

During this phase of the battle there was a display of bravery by various individuals. King Lot had personal success against Sir Meliot de la Roche and against Sir Clariance. He was unhorsed by Kay, and horsed again, only to be wounded in the shoulder by Arthur himself—who was everywhere, youthful, triumphant, over-excited.

As a general, Lot seems to have been a martinet and something of a coward. But he was a tactician in spite of his formality. He seems to have recognized by noon that he was faced by a new kind of warfare, which required a new defence. The demons of Arthur's cavalry were not concerned with ransoms, it was now seen, and they were prepared to go on smashing their heads against the wall of his cavalry until it broke. He decided to wear them out. At a hurried council of war behind the line, it was arranged that he himself, with four other kings and half the defenders, should retire along the glade to prepare a position. The remaining six kings were sufficient to hold the English, while Lot's men rested and re-formed. Then, when the position was prepared, the six kings of the advance guard were to retire through it, leaving Lot in the front line while they re-formed.

The army split accordingly.

Arthur accepted this moment of division as the opportunity for which he had been waiting. He sent an equerry to gallop for the trees. He had made a pact of mutual aid with two French kings, called Ban and Bors—and these two allies had come from France with about ten thousand men, to lend him aid. The Frenchmen had been hidden in the forest on either side of the clearing, as reserves. It had been in their direction that the King had tried to drive the enemy. The equerry galloped, there was a twinkle of armour among the leafy oaks, and Lot's mind jumped to the trap. He looked only to the one side of the glade, where Bors was issuing already upon his flank, being unaware at present that Ban was on the other wing.

Lot's nerve began to collapse at this stage. He was wounded in the shoulder, faced by an enemy who seemed to accept the death of gentlemen as a part of warfare, and now he was in an ambush. "Oh, defend us from death and horrible maims," he is reported to have said, "for I see well we be in great peril of death."

He detached King Carados with a strong squadron to meet King Bors, only to find that a second equerry had sprung King Ban from the opposite side of him. He was still in numerical superiority, but his nerve was now gone for good. "Ha," he said to the Duke of Cambenet, "we must be discomfited." He is even supposed to have wept "for pity and dole."

Carados was personally unhorsed, and his squadron

broken by King Bors. The advance guard of six kings was driven in by Arthur's charges. Lot, with King Morganore's division, faced about in order to hold King Ban upon his wing.

The rebellion would have been ended on that day, with one more hour of daylight. But the sun set, coming to the rescue of the Old Ones, and there was no moon for that quarter. Arthur called off the hunt, judged accurately that the insurgents were demoralized, and allowed his men to sleep in comfort on their arms, with few but careful sentries.

The exhausted army of his enemies, who had diced the night before, now spent the hours of darkness sleepless again, standing to arms or in their councils. Like all the highland armies that have ever marched against Gramarye, they were distrustful of each other. They expected another night attack. They were dismayed by what they had suffered. They were divided on the subject of capitulation or resistance. It was the brink of daylight before King Lot could have his way.

The remaining infantry, by his orders, were to be turned off like so many cattle, to stray and save their naked legs however they could. The knights were to band themselves into a single phalanx to resist the charges, and any man who ran away thereafter was to be shot at once for cowardice.

In the morning, almost before they were formed, Arthur was on them. In conformity with his own tactics, he sent only a small troop of forty spears to start the work. These men, a picked striking force of gallants, resumed the onslaughts of the previous afternoon. They came down at a hand gallop, smashed through the rank or broke it, reformed, and came again. The dogged regiment withdrew before them, sullen, dispirited, the fight knocked out of it.

At noon the three kings of the allies struck with their full force, in a final blow. There was the moment of intermingling with a noise like thunder, the spectacle of broken lances sailing in the air while horses pawed that element before they went down backward. There was a yell that shook the forest. After it, on the trodden turf with its hoof marks and kicked sods and a debris of offensive weapons, there was an unnatural silence. There were people riding about aimlessly at a walk. But there were no longer any organized traces of the chivalry of the Gael.

Merlyn met the King as he rode back from Sorhaute—a magician rather tired, and still unmounted. He was dressed in the infantry habergeon in which he had insisted on fighting. He brought the news that the clans on foot had offered their capitulation.

# 13

*In the September moonlight, several weeks later,* King Pellinore was sitting on the cliff top with his fiancée, staring out to sea. Soon they were setting off for England, to be married. His arm was about her waist and his ear was pressed to the top of her head. They were unconscious of the world.

"But Dornar is such a funny name," the King was saying. "I can't think how you thought of it."

"But you thought of it, Pellinore."

"Did I?"

"Yes. Aglovale, Percivale, Lamorak and Dornar."

"They will be like cherubs," said the King fervently. "Like cherubim! What are cherubim?"

Behind them the ancient castle loomed against the stars. There was a faint noise of shouting from the top of the Round Tower, where Grummore and Palomides were arguing with the Questing Beast. She was still in love with her counterfeit, and still kept the castle in a state of siege—which had only been broken for a few hours on the day of Lot's return with his defeated army. It had been a surprise for the English knights to learn that they had been at war with Orkney all the time, but it was too late to do anything about it, since the war was over. Now everybody was inside, the drawbridge was permanently up, and Glatisant lay in the moonlight at the foot of the tower, her head gleaming like silver. Pellinore had refused to have her killed.

Merlyn arrived one afternoon in the course of his northern walking tour, wearing a haversack and a pair of monstrous boots. He was sleek and snowy and shining, like an eel preparing for its nuptial journey to the Sargasso Sea, for the time of Nimue was at hand. But he was absent-minded, unable to remember the one thing which he ought to have told his pupil, and he listened to their difficulties with an impatient ear.

"Excuse me," they shouted from the top of the wall, as the magician stood outside, "but it's about the Questin' Beast. The Queen of Lothian and Orkney is in a frightful temper about her."

"Are you sure it is about the Beast?"

"Certain, my dear fellow. You see, she has us besieged."

"We dressed up," bawled Sir Palomides miserably, "as a sort of Beast ourselves, respected sir, and she saw us coming into the castle. There are signs, ahem, of ardent affection. Now this creature will not go away, because she believes her mate to be inside, and it is of a great unsafety to lower the drawbridge."

"You had better explain to her. Stand on the battlements and explain the mistake."

"Do you think she will understand?"

"After all," the magician said, "she is a magic beast. It seems possible."

But the explanation was a failure—she looked at them as if she thought they were lying.

"I say, Merlyn! Don't go yet."

"I have to go," he said absently. "I have to do something somewhere, but I can't remember what it is. Meanwhile I shall have to carry on with my walking tour. I am to meet my master Bleise in North Humberland, so that he can write down the chronicles of the battle, and then we are to have a little wild-goose watching, and after that—well, I can't remember."

"But Merlyn, the Beast would not believe!"

"Never mind." His voice was vague and troubled. "Can't stop. Sorry. Apologize to Queen Morgause for me, will you, and say I was asking after her health?"

He began to revolve on his toes, preparatory to vanishing. Not much of his walking tour was done on foot.

"Merlyn, Merlyn! Wait a bit!"

He reappeared for a moment, saying in a cross voice: "Well, what is it?"

"The Beast will not believe us. What are we to do?"

He frowned.

"Psycho-analyse her," he said eventually, beginning to spin.

"But, Merlyn, wait! How are we to do this thing?"

"The usual method."

"But what is it?" they cried in despair.

He disappeared completely, his voice remaining in the air.

"Just find out what her dreams are and so on. Explain the facts of life. But not too much of Freud."

After that, as a background to the felicity of King Pellinore—who refused to bother with trivial problems—Grummore and Palomides had to do their best.

"Well, you see," Sir Grummore was shouting, "when a hen lays an egg..."

Sir Palomides interrupted with an explanation about pollen and stamens.

Inside the castle, in the royal chamber of the Pele Tower, King Lot and his consort were laid in the double bed. The king was asleep, exhausted by the effort of writing his memoirs about the war. He had no particular reason for staying awake. Morgause was sleepless.

Tomorrow she was going to Carlion for Pellinore's wedding. She was going, as she had explained to her husband, in manner of a messenger, to plead for his pardon. She was taking the children with her.

Lot was angry about the journey and wished to forbid it, but she knew how to deal with that.

The Queen drew herself silently out of bed, and went to her coffer. She had been told about Arthur since the army returned—about his strength, charm, innocence and generosity. His splendour had been obvious, even through the envy and suspicion of those he had conquered. Also there had been talk about a girl called Lionore, the daughter of the Earl of Sanam, with whom the young man was supposed to be having an affair. The Queen opened the coffer in the darkness and stood near the moonlit patch from the window, holding a strip of something in her hands. It was like a tape.

The strip was a less cruel piece of magic than the black cat had been, but more gruesome. It was called the Spancel

—after the rope with which domestic animals were hobbled —and there were several of them in the secret coffers of the Old Ones. They were a piseog rather than a great magic. Morgause had got it from the body of a soldier which had been brought home by her husband, for burial in the Out Isles.

It was a tape of human skin, cut from the silhouette of the dead man. That is to say, the cut had been begun at the right shoulder, and the knife—going carefully in a double slit so as to make a tape—had gone down the outside of the right arm, round the outer edge of each finger as if along the seams of a glove, and up on the inside of the arm to the arm-pit. Then it had gone down the side of the body, down the leg and up it to the crotch, and so on until it had completed the circuit of the corpse's outline, at the shoulder from which it had started. It made a long ribbon.

The way to use a Spancel was this. You had to find the man you loved while he was asleep. Then you had to throw it over his head without waking him, and tie it in a bow. If he woke while you were doing this, he would be dead within the year. If he did not wake until the operation was over, he would be bound to fall in love with you.

Queen Morgause stood in the moonlight, drawing the Spancel through her fingers.

The four children were awake too, but they were not in their bedroom. They had listened on the stairs during the royal dinner, so they knew that they were off to England with their mother.

They were in the tiny Church of the Men—a chapel as ancient as Christianity in the islands, though it was scarcely twenty feet square. It was built of unmortared stones, like the great wall of the keep, and the moonlight came through its single unglazed window to fall on the stone altar. The basin for holy water, on which the moonlight fell, was scooped out of the living stone, and it had a stone lid cut from a flake, to match it.

The Orkney children were kneeling in the home of their ancestors. They were praying that they might be true to their loving mother—that they might be worthy of the Cornwall feud which she had taught them—and that they might never forget the misty land of Lothian where their fathers reigned.

Outside the window the thin moon stood upright in a

deep sky, like the paring of a finger nail for magic, and against the sky the weather vane of the carrion crow with arrow in mouth pointed its arrow to the south.

# 14

*Fortunately for Sir Palomides and Sir Grummore,* the Questing Beast saw reason at the last moment, before the cavalcade set out—otherwise they would have had to stay in Orkney and miss the marriage altogether. Even as it was, they had to stay up all night. She recovered quite suddenly.

The drawback was that she transferred her affection to the successful analyst—to Palomides—as so often happens in psycho-analysis—and now she refused to take any further interest in her early master. King Pellinore, not without a few sighs for the good old days, was forced to resign his rights in her to the Saracen. This is why, although Malory clearly tells us that only a Pellinore could catch her, we always find her being pursued by Sir Palomides in the later parts of the Morte d'Arthur. In any case, it makes very little difference who could catch her, because nobody ever did.

The long march southward toward Carlion, with litters swaying and the mounted escort jogging under flapping pennoncells, was exciting for everybody. The litters themselves were interesting. They consisted of ordinary carts with a kind of flag-staff at each end. Between the staffs a hammock was slung, in which the jolts were hardly felt. The two knights rode behind the royal conveyances, delighted at being able to get out of the castle and see the marriage after all. St. Toirdealbhach followed with Mother Morlan, so that it would be a double wedding. The Questing Beast brought up the rear, keeping a tight eye on Palomides, for fear of being let down once again.

All the saints came out of their beehives to see them off. All the Fomorians, Fir Bolg, Tuatha de Danaan, Old People and others waved to them without the least suspicion from cliffs, currachs, mountains, bogs and shell-mounds. All the red deer and unicorns lined the high tops to bid good-bye. The terns came with their forked tails from the estuary, squeaking away as if intent upon imitating an embarkation scene on the wireless—the white-bottomed wheatears and pipits flitted along beside them from whin to whin—the eagles, peregrines, ravens and chuffs made circles over them in the air—the peat smoke followed them as if anxious to make one last curl in the tips of their nostrils—the ogham stones and souterrains and promontory forts exhibited their prehistoric masonry in a blaze of sunlight—the sea-trout and salmon put their gleaming heads out of the water—the glens, mountains and heather-shoulders of the most beautiful country in the world joined the general chorus—and the soul of the Gaelic world said to the boys in the loudest of fairy voices: Remember Us!

If the march was exciting for the children, the metropolitan glories of Carlion were enough to take their breath away. Here, round the King's castle, there were streets—not just one street—and castles of dependent barons, and monasteries, chapels, churches, cathedrals, markets, merchants' houses. There were hundreds of people in the streets, all dressed in blue or red or green or any bright colour, with shopping baskets over their arms, or driving hissing geese before them, or hurrying hither and thither in the livery of some great lord. There were bells ringing, clocks smiting in belfries, standards floating—until the whole air above them seemed to be alive. There were dogs and donkeys and palfreys in caparison and priests and farm wagons—whose wheels creaked like the day of judgment—and booths which sold gilt gingerbread, and shops where the finest bits of armour in the very latest fashions were displayed. There were silk merchants and spice merchants and jewellers. The shops had painted trade signs hung over them, like the inn signs which we have today. There were servitors carousing outside wine shops, and old ladies haggling over eggs, and itinerant cads carrying cadges of hawks for sale, and portly aldermen with gold chains, and brown ploughmen with hardly any clothes on except a few bits of leather, and leashes of greyhounds, and strange Eastern men selling parrots, and pretty ladies mincing along in high dunces' caps with veils floating from the top of them, and perhaps a page in front of the lady, carrying a prayer book, if she was going to church.

Carlion was a walled town, so that this excitement was surrounded by a battlement which seemed to go on for ever and ever. The wall had towers every two hundred yards, and four great gates as well. When you were approaching the town from across the plain, you could see the castle keeps and church spires springing out of the wall in a clump —like flowers growing in a pot.

King Arthur was delighted to see his old friends again, and to hear of Pellinore's engagement. He was the first knight he had taken a fancy to, when he was a small boy in the Forest Sauvage, and he decided to give the dear fellow a marriage of unexampled splendour. The cathedral of Carlion was booked for it, and no trouble was spared that a good time should be had by all. The pontifical nuptial high mass was celebrated by such a galaxy of cardinals and bishops and nuncios that there seemed to be no part of the immense church which was not teeming with violet and scarlet and incense and little boys ringing silver bells. Sometimes a boy would rush at a bishop and ring a bell at him. Sometimes a nuncio would pounce on a cardinal and cense him all over. It was like a battle of flowers. Thousands of candles blazed before the gorgeous altars. In every direction the blunt, accustomed, holy fingers were spreading little tablecloths, or holding up books, or blessing each other thoroughly, or soaking each other with Holy Water, or reverently displaying God to the people. The music was heavenly, both Gregorian and Ambrosian, and the church was packed. There were monks and friars and abbots of every description, standing about in sandals among the knights, whose armour flashed by candlelight. There was even a Franciscan bishop, wearing grey, with a red hat. The copes and mitres were almost all of solid gold cloth crusted with diamonds, and there was such a putting of them on and taking of them off that the whole cathedral rustled. As for the Latin, it was talked at such a speed that the rafters rang with genitive plurals—and there was such a prelatical issuing of admonitions, exhortations and benedictions that it was a wonder the whole congregation did not go to heaven on the spot. Even the Pope, who was as keen as anybody that the thing should go with a swing, had kindly sent a number of indulgences for everybody he could think of.

After the marriage came the wedding feast. King Pellinore and his Queen—who had stood hand in hand throughout the previous ceremony, with St. Toirdealbhach and Mother Morlan behind them, quite dazzled with candle-light and incense and aspersion—were propped up in the place of honour and served by Arthur himself on bended knee. You can imagine how charmed Mother Morlan was. There was peacock pie, jellied eels, Devonshire cream, cur-ried porpoise, iced fruit salad, and two thousand side dishes. There were speeches, songs, healths, and bumpers. A special courier arrived at full speed from North Humberland, and delivered a message to the bridegroom. He said, "Best Wishes from Merlyn stop. The present is under the throne Stop. Love to Aglovale, Percivale, Lamorak, Dornar."

When the excitement over the message had died down, and the wedding present had been found, some round games were immediately arranged for the younger members of the party. In these a small page of the King's household excelled. He was a son of Arthur's ally at Bedegraine—King Ban of Benwick—and his name was Lancelot. There was bobbing for apples, shovelboard, titter-totter, and a puppet or motion play called *Mac and the Shepherds,* which made everybody laugh. St. Toirdealbhach disgraced himself by stunning one of the fatter bishops with his shillelagh, during an argument about the Bull called Laudabiliter. Finally, at a late hour, the party broke up after a feeling rendering of *Auld Lang Syne.* King Pellinore was sick, and the new Queen Pellinore put him to bed, explaining that he was over-excited.


Far away in North Humberland, Merlyn jumped out of bed. They had been out at dawn and sunset to watch the geese, and he had gone to his rest very tired. But suddenly he had remembered it in his sleep—the simplest thing! It was Arthur's *mother's* name which he had forgotten to men-tion in the confusion! There he had been, chattering away about Uther Pendragon and Round Tables and battles and Guenever and sword sheaths and things past and things to come—but he had forgotten the most important thing of all.

Arthur's mother was Igraine—that very Igraine who had been captured at Tintagil, the one that the Orkney children had been talking about in the Round Tower at the beginning of this book. Arthur had been begotten on the night when Uther Pendragon burst into her castle. Since Uther naturally could not marry her until she was out of mourning for the earl, the boy had been born too soon. That was why Arthur had been sent away to be brought up by Sir Ector. Not a soul had known where he was sent, except for Merlyn and Uther —and now Uther was dead. Even Igraine had not known.

Merlyn stood swaying in his bare feet on the cold floor. If only he had spun himself to Carlion at once, before it was too late! But the old man was tired and muddled with his backsight, and dreams were in his noddle. He thought it would do in the morning—could not remember whether he was in the future or the past. He put the veined hand blindly toward the bedclothes, the image of Nimue already weaving itself in his sleepy brain. He tumbled in. The beard went under the covering, the nose into the pillow. Merlyn was asleep.

King Arthur sat back in the Great Hall, which was empty. A few of his favourite knights had been taking their night-cap with him, but now he was alone. It had been a tiring day, although he had reached the full strength of his youth, and he leaned his head against the back of his throne, thinking about the events of the marriage. He had been fighting, on and off, ever since he had come to be King by drawing the sword out of the stone, and the anxiety of these campaigns had grown him into a splendid fellow. At last it looked as if he might have peace. He thought of the joys of peace, of being married himself one day as Merlyn had prophesied, and of having a home. He thought of Nimue at this, and then of any beautiful woman. He fell asleep.

He woke with a start, to find a black-haired, blue-eyed beauty in front of him, who was wearing a crown. The four wild children from the north were standing behind their mother, shy and defiant, and she was folding up a tape.

Queen Morgause of the Out Isles had stayed away from the feasting on purpose—had chosen her moment with the utmost care. This was the first time that the young King had seen her, and she knew that she was looking her best.

It is impossible to explain how these things happen. Perhaps the Spancel had a strength in it. Perhaps it was because she was twice his age, so that she had twice the power of his weapons. Perhaps it was because Arthur was always a simple fellow, who took people at their own valuation easily. Perhaps it was because he had never known a mother of his own, so that the rôle of mother love, as she stood with her children behind her, took him between wind and water.

Whatever the explanation may have been, the Queen of Air and Darkness had a baby by her half-brother nine months later. It was called Mordred. And this, as Merlyn drew it later, was what the magician called its pied-de-grue:

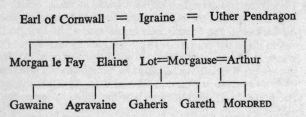

Even if you have to read it twice, like something in a history lesson, this pedigree is a vital part of the tragedy of King Arthur. It is why Sir Thomas Malory called his very long book the *Death* of Arthur. Although nine tenths of the story seems to be about knights jousting and quests for the holy grail and things of that sort, the narrative is a whole, and it deals with the reasons why the young man came to grief at the end. It is the tragedy, the Aristotelian and comprehensive tragedy, of sin coming home to roost. That is why we have to take note of the parentage of Arthur's son Mordred, and to remember, when the time comes, that the king had slept with his own sister. He did not know he was doing so, and perhaps it may have been due to her, but it seems, in tragedy, that innocence is not enough.

**EXPLICIT LIBER SECUNDUS**

*Incipit Liber*
*Tertius*

# THE
# ILL-MADE
# KNIGHT

*"Nay," said Sir Lancelot
". . . for once shamed may never
be recovered."*

# 1

*In the castle of Benwick, the French boy was look-*ing at his face in the polished surface of a kettle-hat. It flashed in the sunlight with the stubborn gleam of metal. It was practically the same as the steel helmet which soldiers still wear, and it did not make a good mirror, but it was the best he could get. He turned the hat in various directions, hoping to get an average idea of his face from the different distortions which the bulges made. He was trying to find out what he was, and he was afraid of what he would find.

The boy thought that there was something wrong with him. All through his life—even when he was a great man with the world at his feet—he was to feel this gap: something at the bottom of his heart of which he was aware, and ashamed, but which he did not understand. There is no need for us to try to understand it. We do not have to dabble in a place which he preferred to keep secret.

The Armoury, where the boy stood, was lined with weapons of war. For the last two hours he had been whirling a pair of dumb-bells in the air—he called them "poises"—and singing to himself a song with no words and no tune. He was fifteen. He had just come back from England, where his father King Ban of Benwick had been helping the English King to quell a rebellion. You remember that Arthur wanted to catch his knights young, to train them for the Round Table, and that he had noticed Lancelot at the feast, because he was winning most of the games.

Lancelot, swinging his dumb-bells fiercely and making his wordless noise, had been thinking of King Arthur with all his might. He was in love with him. That was why he had been swinging the poises. He had been remembering all the words of the only conversation which he had held with his hero.

The King had called him over when they were embark-

ing for France—after he had kissed King Ban good-bye—
and they had gone alone into a corner of the ship. The heraldic sails of Ban's fleet, and the sailors in the rigging, and
the armed turrets and archers and seagulls, like flake-white,
had been a background to their conversation.

"Lance," the King had said, "come here a moment, will
you?"

"Sir."

"I was watching you playing games at the feast."

"Sir."

"You seemed to win most of them."

Lancelot squinted down his nose.

"I want to get hold of a lot of people who are good at
games, to help with an idea I have. It is for the time when
I am a real King, and have got this kingdom settled. I was
wondering whether you would care to help, when you are
old enough?"

The boy had made a sort of wriggle, and had suddenly
flashed his eyes at the speaker.

"It is about knights," Arthur had continued. "I want to
have an Order of Chivalry, like the Order of the Garter,
which goes about fighting against Might. Would you like to
be one of those?"

"Yes."

The King had looked at him closely, unable to see
whether he was pleased or frightened or merely being polite.

"Do you understand what I am talking about?"

Lancelot had taken the wind out of his sails.

"We call it Fort Mayne in France," he had explained.
"The man with the strongest arm in a clan gets made the
head of it, and does what he pleases. That is why we call
it Fort Mayne. You want to put an end to the Strong Arm,
by having a band of knights who believe in justice rather
than strength. Yes, I would like to be one of those very
much. I must grow up first. Thank you. Now I must say
good-bye."

So they had sailed away from England—the boy standing in the front of the ship and refusing to look back, because he did not want to show his feelings. He had already
fallen in love with Arthur on the night of the wedding feast,
and he carried with him in his heart to France the picture of
that bright northern king, at supper, flushed and glorious
from his wars.

Behind the black eyes which were searching intently in the kettle-hat there was a dream which had come to him the previous night. Seven hundred years ago—or it may have been fifteen hundred according to Malory's notation—people took dreams as seriously as the psychiatrists do today, and Lancelot's had been a disturbing one. It was not disturbing because of anything it might mean—for he had not the least idea of its meaning—but because it had left him with a sense of loss. This was what it was.

Lancelot and his young brother, Ector Demaris, had been sitting in two chairs. They got out of these chairs and were mounted on two horses. Lancelot said: "Go we, and seek that which we shall not find." So they did. But a Man or a Power set upon Lancelot, and beat him and despoiled him, and clothed him in another array which was full of knots, and made him ride on an ass instead of on the horse. Then there was a beautiful well, with the fairest waters he had ever seen, and he got off his ass to drink out of it. It seemed to him that there could be nothing in the world more beautiful than to drink of this well. But as soon as he stooped his lips toward it, the water sank away. It went right down into the barrel of the well, sinking and sinking from him so that he could not get it. It made him feel desolate, to be abandoned by the water of the well.

Arthur and the well, and the dumb-bells which were to make him worthy of Arthur, and the ache in his tired arms from swinging them—all these were at the back of the boy's mind as he tilted the tin hat backward and forward between his fingers, but there was a more insistent thought in his head also. It was a thought about the face in the metal, and about the thing which must have gone wrong in the depths of his spirit to make a face like that. He was not a self-deceiver. He knew that whichever way he turned the morion, it would tell him the same story. He had already decided that when he was a grown knight he would give himself a melancholy title. He was the eldest son, so he was bound to be knighted, but he would not call himself Sir Lancelot. He would call himself the Chevalier Mal Fet—the Ill-Made Knight.

So far as he could see—and he felt that there must be some reason for it somewhere—the boy's face was as ugly as a monster's in the King's menagerie. He looked like an African ape.

# 2

*Lancelot ended by being the greatest knight King Arthur had.* He was a sort of Bradman, top of the battling averages. Tristram and Lamorak were second and third.

But you have to remember that people can't be good at cricket unless they teach themselves to be so, and that jousting was an art, just as cricket is. It was like cricket in many ways. There was a scorer's pavilion at a tournament, with a real scorer inside it, who made marks on the parchment just like the mark for one run which is made by the cricket scorer today. The people, walking round the ground in their best frocks, from Grand Stand to Refreshment Tent, must have found the fighting very like the game. It took a frightfully long time—Sir Lancelot's innings frequently lasted all day, if he were battling against a good knight—and the movements had a feeling of slow-motion, because of the weight of armour. When the sword-play had begun, the combatants stood opposite each other in the green acre like batsman and bowler—except that they stood closer together—and perhaps Sir Gawaine would start with an in-swinger, which Sir Lancelot would put away to leg with a beautiful leg-glide, and then Lancelot would reply with a yorker under Gawaine's guard—it was called "foining"—and all the people round the field would clap. King Arthur might turn to Guenever in the Pavilion, and remark that the great man's footwork was as lovely as ever. The knights had little curtains on the back of their helms, to keep the hot sun off the metal, like the handkerchief which cricketers will sometimes arrange behind their caps today.

Knightly exercise was as much an art as cricket is, and perhaps the only way in which Lancelot did not resemble Bradman was that he was more graceful. He did not have that crouching on the bat and hopping out to the pitch of the ball. He was more like Woolley. But you can't be like Woolley by simply sitting still and wanting to be so.

The Armoury, where the small boy who was later to be

Sir Lancelot was standing with his morion, was the largest single room in the castle of Benwick. It was to be the room in which this boy was to spend most of his waking hours for the next three years.

The rooms of the main castle—which he could see from the windows—were mostly small, because people can't afford to build for luxury when they are making a fortification. Round the inner fort with its small rooms there was a wide byre, or shell-keep, into which the castle herds were driven during a siege. This was surrounded by a high wall with towers, and, on the inner side of this wall, the big rooms which were needed for stores, barns, barracks, and stables were built. The Armoury was one of these rooms. It stood between the stables, for fifty horses, and the cowsheds. The best family armour—the bits which were actually in use—was kept in a little room in the castle itself, and it was only the arms of the troops, and the spare parts of the family stuff, and the things which were needed for gymnastics, practice, or physical training, which reposed in the Armoury.

Under the raftered ceiling, and the nearest to it, there hung or leaned a collection of bannerettes and pennoncels, blazoned with the Ban charges—France Ancient, as they are now called—which would be needed on various occasions. Along the wall there were tilting lances, resting horizontally on nails so that they should not warp. These looked like bars for exercises in a gymnasium. In one corner a collection of old lances which had already warped or got injured in some way, but which might still be useful for something, were standing upright. A rack, running the whole length of the second main wall, held the infantry issue of mail habergeons with mittens, spears, morions, and Bordeaux swords. King Ban was fortunate in living at Benwick, for the Bordeaux swords were local and particularly good. Then there were harness-barrels, in which the armour was packed in hay for expeditions overseas—some of it was still packed from the last expedition, and a curious mixture it was. Uncle Dap, who looked after the Armoury, had been unpacking one of the barrels to make an inventory of its contents—and had gone away in despair on discovering ten pounds of dates and five loaves of sugar in it. It must have been some sort of honey sugar, unless it was loaf sugar brought back from the Crusades. He had left his list beside the barrel, and this recorded, among other articles: a salade garnessed with golde, iij peire gantelez, a vestment, a mesbooke, an auter cloth, a peir of brigandines, a pyssying basin of silver, x schertes for my Lord, a jakete of leather, and a bagge of chessmen. Then, in an alcove formed by the harness-barrels, there was a set of shelves which formed the dispensary for sick armour. On the shelves there were huge bottles of olive oil—nowadays they prefer a mineral oil for armour, but they did not understand such niceties in Lancelot's time—together with boxes of fine sand for polishing, bags of brigandine nails at eleven shillings and eightpence the twenty thousand, rivets, spare rings for chain mail, leather skins for cutting new straps and bases for the knee harness, together with a thousand other details then fascinating, but now lost to us. There were gambesons like the pads which the goalkeeper wears in hockey, or like the quilted protections which Americans have at football. In various corners there were pushed, so as to leave a free space in the middle of the room, a collection of gymnastic apparatus such as quintains and so on, while Uncle Dap's desk stood near the door. On the desk there were splattering quill pens, blotting sand, sticks for beating Lancelot when he was stupid, and notes, in unutterable confusion, as to which jupons had lately been pawned—pawning was a great institution for valuable armour—and which helms had been brought up to date with a glancing surface, and whose vambrace stood in need of repair, and what had been paid to whom for fforbeshynge which when. Most of the accounts were wrongly added up.

Three years may seem a long time for a boy to spend in one room, if he only goes out of it to eat and sleep and to practise tilting in the field. It is even difficult to imagine a boy who would do it, unless you realize from the start that Lancelot was not romantic and debonair. Tennyson and the Pre-Raphaelites would have found it difficult to recognize this rather sullen and unsatisfactory child, with the ugly face, who did not disclose to anybody that he was living on dreams and prayers. They might have wondered what store of ferocity he had against himself, that could set him to break his own body so young. They might have wondered why he was so strange.

To begin with, he had to spend the weary months charging against Uncle Dap, with a blunt spear under his arm. Uncle Dap, armed cap-à-pie, would sit on a stool—and Lancelot, with the morne-headed spear, would charge and charge against him, learning the best lodges on armour for a point. Then there were lonely hours with poises, with many other hours out of doors—before he was even allowed to touch real arms—in which he learned various kinds of throwing, casting with the sling-stick or the casting spear, and tossing the bar. After that, after a year of toil, there was his promotion to the pel-quintain. It was a stake driven upright in the ground, and he had to fight against it with sword and shield—rather like shadow-boxing, or using a punch-ball. He had to use arms for this exercise which weighed twice as much as the ordinary sword and shield. Sixty pounds was considered a good weight for the arms used on the pel-quintain—so that, when he did come at length to the usual weapons, he would wield them featly. They would seem light by comparison. The final stage of breaking to the cricket standard was by mock combats. In these at last, and after all the bitter setbacks of discipline, he was allowed to fight battles which were nearly real ones, against his brother and cousins. The combats were held under strict rules. They might begin with a cast of the spear blunted, followed by seven strokes with the sword, point and edge rebated, "without close, or griping one another with the handes, upon paine of punishment as the judges for the time being shall thinke requisite." It was not lawful in these matches to foin—that is, to make a thrust of the point. Finally there was swashbuckling. The now vigorous boy might go at his companions harum-scarum, with sword and buckler.

If you have been down in one of the old-fashioned diving suits which used to be standard in the Royal Navy before frogmen and free diving came along, you will know why divers move slowly. A diver has forty pounds of lead on each foot and two plaques of lead—each weighing fifty pounds—one on his back and one on his chest. These are apart from the weight of the suit and the helmet. Except when he is in the sea, he weighs twice as much as a man. When he has to step over a rope or an air-tube on deck, it is hard work—like climbing a wall. If you push him from in front, the weight behind him tends to take over, so that he might fall backwards. The same thing happens vice versa. Practised divers become adept at dealing with these handicaps, and can hoist those forty pound feet up and down the ship's ladder fairly nimbly—but an amateur half kills himself with the mere toil of movement. Lancelot, like the diver, had to learn to be nimble against the force of gravity.

Knights-in-armour were like divers in more ways than one.

Apart from their helmets and encumbrances and the difficulty of breathing, they had to be dressed in their suits by kind and careful assistants. They had to rely on these assistants to do it properly. A diver puts his life in the hands of the ratings who are dressing him. These young men, like pages or squires, mother him with great tenderness and concentration and with a sort of protective respect. They always address him by his title, not by his name. They say, "Sit down, diver," or "Now the left foot, diver," or "Diver Two, can you hear me on the inter-com?"

It is good to put your life in other people's hands.

Three years of it. The other boys did not worry, for they had other things to think about—but for the ugly one it was the whole of an obscure and mystic life. He had to perfect himself for Arthur as somebody who was good at games, and he had to think about the theories of chivalry even when he was in bed at night. He had to teach himself to possess a sound opinion on hundreds of disputed points —on the proper length of weapons, or the cut of a mantling, or the articulation of a pauldron, or whether cedarwood was better than ash for spears, as Chaucer seems to have believed.

Here is a short example of the problems of chivalry, which he thought about in his early times. There was a knight once called Reynaud de Roy, who had a tilting match with another one called John de Holland. Reynaud purposely fastened his tilting helm—the huge straw-padded drum which sometimes fitted over the helmet proper—so that it was loose. When John of Holland's spear point struck it, it simply fell off. This meant that the helm came off Reynaud, instead of Reynaud coming off his horse. An effective trick, but a dangerous one—the whole of chivalry argued about it for a long time, some saying that it was unsporting, some that it was fair but too risky, and some that it was a good idea.

Three years of discipline made Lancelot, not a merry heart and a capacity for singing tirra-lirra. Out of a lifetime which at his age must have seemed to stretch little more than a week ahead, he gave thirty-six months to another man's idea because he was in love with it. He supported himself meanwhile on daydreams. He wanted to be the best knight in the world, so that Arthur would love him in return, and he wanted one other thing which was still possible in those days. He wanted, through his purity and excellence, to be able to perform some ordinary miracle—to heal a blind man or something like that, for instance.

# 3

*There was a feature about the great families which* centred round the doom of Arthur. All three had a resident genius of the family, half-way between a tutor and a confidant, who affected the characters of the children in each. At Sir Ector's castle there had been Merlyn, who was the main influence in Arthur's life. In lonely and distant Lothian there had been St. Toirdealbhach, whose warlike philosophy must have had something to do with the clannishness of Gawaine and his brothers. In King Ban's castle there was an uncle of Lancelot's, whose name was Gwenbors. Actually he was the old man we have met, known to everybody as Uncle Dap, but his given name was Gwenbors. In those days you generally named your children in the same way as we name foxhounds and foals today. If you happened to be Queen Morgause and had four children, you put a G in all their names (Gawaine, Agravaine, Gaheris, and Gareth)— and, naturally if your brothers happened to be called Ban and Bors, you were doomed to be called Gwenbors yourself. It made it easier to remember who you were.

Uncle Dap was the only one in the family who took Lancelot seriously, and Lancelot was the one who was serious about Uncle Dap. It was easy not to be serious about the old fellow, for he was that peculiar creation which ignorant people laugh at—a genuine maestro. His branch of learning was chivalry. There was not a piece of armour proofed in Europe but what Uncle Dap had a theory about it. He was furious with the new Gothic style, with its ridges and scallop-patterns and fluting. He considered it ridicu-

lous to wear armour like the ropework on a Nelson sideboard, for it was obvious that every groove would be liable
to hold a point. The whole object of good armour, he said,
was to throw the point off—and, when he thought of the
people in Germany making their horrible furrows, he nearly
went frantic. There was nothing in Heraldry which he did
not know. If anybody committed any of the grosser errors
—such as putting metal on metal or colour on colour—he
became electrified with passion. His long white moustaches
quivered at their tips like antennae, the ends of his fingers
came together in gestures of the wildest passion, and he
waved his arms and jumped up and down and wagged his
eyebrows and almost fizzed. Nobody can be a maestro without being subject to these excitements, so Lancelot seldom
minded when he got his face slapped in a mêlée about
shields cut *à bouche* or about whether it was a good idea to
have a guige on your shield or not. Sometimes Uncle Dap
was tantalized into beating him, but he bore that also. In
those days they did.

One reason for not minding Uncle Dap's transports was
that everything the boy wanted could be learned from him.
He was not only a distinguished clerk and authority on his
own subjects—he was also one of the finest swordsmen in
France. It was for this, really, that the boy had attached himself. It was in order to rase and trace and foin under the
brutal tuition of genius—in order to hold out a heavy sword
at arm's length in a lunge until he felt he would split in half
only to have Uncle Dap catch hold of his point and pull
him into a crueler stretch.

Ever since he could remember, there had been the excited man with the eyes of blue steel, jumping up and
down, and snapping his fingers, and shouting out as if life
itself depended on it: "Doublez! Dédoublez! Dégagez! Un!
Deux!"

One fine day in late summer, Lancelot was sitting in the
Armoury with his uncle. In the big room there was a lot
of dust dancing in the sunbeams, dust which they had themselves been stirring up a moment before, and round the
walls there were the ranks of polished armour, and the
rack of spears, and helms and morions hanging on pegs.
There were misericordes and harness and the various banners and pennoncels, blazoned with the Ban chargers. The
two fencers had sat down to rest after an exciting bout, and

Uncle Dap was blown. Lancelot was eighteen now. He was a better fencer than his maestro—though Uncle Dap would not admit it, and his pupil tactfully pretended that he was not.

A page came in while they were still panting, and told him that he was wanted by his mother.

"Why?"

The page said that a gentleman had arrived who wanted to see him, and the Queen had said that he was to come at once.

Queen Elaine was sitting in the solar, where she had been doing tapestry work, and her two guests were sitting on either side of her. She was not the Elaine who had been one of the Cornwall sisters. It was a popular name in those days and several women in the Morte d'Arthur had it, particularly as some of its manuscript sources have got mixed up. The three grown-ups at the long table looked like a row of examiners in the dim room. One of the guests was an elderly gentleman with a white beard and pointed hat, and the other was a handsome minx with an olive complexion and plucked eyebrows. They all three looked at Lancelot, and the old gentleman spoke first.

"Hum!"

They waited.

"You called him Galahad," said the old gentleman.

"His first name was Galahad," he added, "and now he is Lancelot, since he was confirmed."

"However did you know?"

"It can't be helped," said Merlyn. "It is one of the things one does know, and there's an end on't. Now, let me see, what are the other things I was supposed to tell you?"

The young lady with the plucked eyebrows put her hand before her mouth and yawned gracefully, like a cat.

"He will get the hope of his heart thirty years from now, and he will be the best knight in the world."

"Shall I live to see it?" asked Queen Elaine.

Merlyn scratched his head, gave it a bump on the top with his knuckles, and replied:

"Yes."

"Well, " said the Queen, "it is all very wonderful, I must say. Do you hear that, Lance? You are to be the best knight in the world!"

The boy asked: "Have you come from the court of King Arthur?"

"Yes."

"Is everything well?"

"Yes. He sent you his love."

"Is the King happy?"

"Very happy. Guenever sent her love too."

"Who is Guenever?"

"Good gracious!" exclaimed the magician. "Didn't you know about that? No, of course not. I have been getting bejingled in my brains."

Here he glanced at the beautiful lady, as if she might be responsible for the jingling—which she was. She was Nimue, and he had fallen in love with her at last.

"Guenever," said Nimue, "is Arthur's new queen. They have been married for some time."

"Her father is King Leodegrance," explained Merlyn. "He gave Arthur a present of a round table when they were married, and a hundred knights to go with it. There is room at the table for a hundred and fifty."

Lancelot said: "Oh!"

"The King meant to tell you," said Merlyn. "Perhaps the messenger got drowned on the way over. There may have been a storm. He really did mean to tell you."

"Oh," said the boy, for the second time.

Merlyn began to talk quickly, because he saw that it was a difficult situation. From Lancelot's face he could not tell whether he was hurt or whether it was like that always.

"He has only managed to fill in twenty-nine of the seats so far," he said. "There is room for twenty-one more. Plenty of room. All the knights' names are written on them in gold."

There was a pause, during which nobody knew what to say. Then Lancelot cleared his throat.

"There was a boy," he said, "when I was in England. His name was Gawaine. Has he been made one of the knights of the table?"

Merlyn looked guilty, and nodded his head.

"He was created on the day Arthur was married."

"I see."

There was another long pause.

"This lady," said Merlyn, feeling that he had better fill in the silence, "is called Nimue. I am in love with her. We are having a sort of honeymoon together—only it is a magical one—and now we shall have to be off to Cornwall. I am sorry we could not visit you for longer."

"My dear Merlyn," exclaimed the Queen, "but surely you will stay the night?"

"No, no. Thank you. Thank you very much. We are in a hurry just now."

"You will have a glass of something before you leave?"

"No, thank you. It is very kind of you, but really, we must be off. We have some magic to attend to in Cornwall."

"Such a short visit——" began the Queen.

Merlyn cut her short by standing up and taking Nimue's hand in his.

"Good-bye now," he said with determination—and in a couple of spins they were both gone.

Their bodies were gone, but the magician's voice remained in the air.

"That's that," they could hear him saying in a relieved tone. "Now then, my angel, what about that place I was telling you of in Cornwall, the one with the magical cave in it?"

Lancelot went back to Uncle Dap in the Armoury, with slow steps. He stood in front of his uncle, and bit his lip.

"I am going to England," he said.

Uncle Dap looked at him in amazement, but said nothing.

"I shall start this evening."

"It seems sudden," said Uncle Dap. "Your mother does not usually make up her mind so quickly."

"My mother does not know."

"Do you mean that you are going to run away?"

"If I told my mother and father, there would only be a fuss," he said. "It is not that I am running away. I shall come back again. But I must go to England as quick as I can."

"Do you expect me not to tell your mother?"

"Yes, I do."

Uncle Dap gnawed the ends of his moustache, and wrung his hands.

"If they get to know that I could have prevented it," he said, "Ban will cut off my head."

"They will not know," said the boy indifferently, and he went away to arrange about his packing.

A week later, Lancelot and Uncle Dap were sitting in a peculiar boat in the middle of the English Channel. The boat had a sort of castle at each end. There was another castle

half-way up the single mast, which gave it the appearance
of a dovecote. It had flags fore and aft. The one gay sail had
a Cross Potent on it, while an enormous streamer floated
from the top of the mast. There were eight oars, and the two
passengers were seasick.

# 4

    *The hero-worshipper rode towards Camelot with a*
bitter heart. It was hard for him at eighteen to have given
his life to a king, only to be forgotten—hard to have spent
those sorrowful hours with the heavy arms in the dust of
the Armoury, only to see Sir Gawaine knighted first—hard-
est of all to have broken his body for the older man's
ideal, only to find this mincing wife stepping in at the end
of it to snatch away his love at no cost at all. Lancelot was
jealous of Guenever, and he was ashamed of himself for
being so.

Uncle Dap rode behind the grieving boy in silence. He
knew a thing which the other was still too green to know—
that he had taught the finest knight in Europe. Like an excited tit which had nursed a cuckoo, Uncle Dap fluttered
along behind his prodigy. He was carrying the fighting
harness, which was strapped up in apple-pie order according to his own dodges and wrinkles—for, from now on, he
was Lancelot's squire.

They came to a clearing in the wood, and a little stream
ran through the middle. There was a ford here and the
stream ran tinkling over the clean stones, only a few inches
deep. The sun shone down into the clearing. Some wood-
pigeons sang drowsily their Take Two Cows Taffy, and, on
the other side of the musical water, there was an enormous
knight in black armour with his tilting helm in position. He
sat motionless on a black charger, and his shield was still
in its canvas case. It was impossible to read his blazon.
Being so still, so portly in his iron sheath, and having the
great blind helm over his head so that he had no proper
face, he had a look of danger about him. You did not know

what he was thinking, nor what action he might be going to take. He was a menace.

Lancelot halted, and so did Uncle Dap. The black knight walked his horse into the shallow water, and drew rein in front of them. He raised his lance in a gesture of salute, then pointed with it to a place behind Lancelot's back. Either he was telling him to go home again, or else he was pointing out a good position from which they could start their charges. Whichever the case might be, Lancelot saluted with his gauntlet and turned round to go to the place. He took one of his spears from Uncle Dap, pulled his tilting helm round in front of him—it had been hanging behind on a chain—and lifted the steel turret into position on his head. He laced it on. Now he too had become a man without an expression.

The two knights faced each other from opposite ends of the little glade. Then, although neither of them had so far spoken a word, they fewtered their spears, put spurs to their horses, and began to charge. Uncle Dap, drawn up safely behind a near-by tree, could hardly contain his delight. He knew what was going to happen to the black knight, although Lancelot did not know, and he began to snap his fingers.

The first time you do a thing, it is often exciting. To go alone in an airplane for the first time used to be so exciting that it nearly choked you. Lancelot had never ridden a serious joust before—and, although he had charged at hundreds of quintains and thousands of rings, he had never taken his life in his hands in earnest. In the first moment of the charge, he felt to himself: "Well, now I am off. Nothing can help me now." In the second moment he settled down to behave automatically, in the same way as he had always behaved with the quintain and the rings.

The point of his spear took the black knight under the rim of his shoulder-harness at exactly the right place. His mount was in full gallop, and the black knight's was still in a canter. The black knight and his horse revolved rapidly toward their sinister side, left the ground together in a handsome parabola, and came down again with a clash. As Lancelot rode by, he could see them sprawling on the ground together, with the knight's broken lance between the horse's legs and one flashing horse-shoe tearing the canvas from the fallen shield. The man and the horse were mixed together. Each was afraid of the other, and each was kicking against the other in the effort to be parted. Then the horse got up on its forelegs, its haunches heaved upright, and the knight sat up, lifting one steel gauntlet, as if to rub his head. Lancelot reined in and rode back to him.

Generally, when one knight had given another a fall with the lance, the fallen one used to lose his temper, blame the fall on his horse, and insist upon fighting it out with swords on foot. The usual excuse was to say: "The son of a mare hath failed me, but I wote well my father's sword never shall."

The black knight, however, did not do the usual thing. He was evidently a more cheerful kind of person than the colour of his armour would suggest, for he sat up and blew through the split of his helm, making a note of surprise and admiration. Then he took off the helm and mopped his brow. The shield, whose cover the horse's hoof had torn, bore, *or, a dragon rampant gules.*

Lancelot threw his spear into a bush, got off his horse very quickly, and knelt down beside the knight. All his love was back again inside him. It was typical of Arthur not to lose his temper, typical of him to sit on the ground making noises of admiration when he had just been given a great fall.

"Sir," said Lancelot, taking off his own helm with a humble gesture; and he bowed his head in the French fashion.

The King began scrambling to his feet in great excitement.

"Lancelot!" he exclaimed. "Why, it's the boy Lancelot! You are the king's son of Benwick. I remember seeing you when he came over for the Battle of Bedegraine. What a fall! I never saw anything like it. Where did you learn to do this? It was terrific! Were you coming to my Court? How is King Ban? How is your charming mother? Really, my dear chap, this is magnificent!"

Lancelot looked up at the breathless King, who held out both hands to help him to his feet, and his jealousy and grief were over.

They caught their horses and jogged off toward the palace side by side, forgetting Uncle Dap. They had so much to say to each other that they both talked all the time. Lancelot gave imaginary messages from King Ban or from Queen Elaine, and Arthur talked about how Gawaine had killed a lady. He told how King Pellinore had got so courageous since his marriage that he had killed King Lot of Orkney by mistake in a tournament, and how the Round Table was going as well as could be expected, but very slowly, and how, now that Lancelot had arrived, everything would come right before they knew where they were.

He was knighted the first day—he might have been knighted at any time during the past two years, but he had refused to be done by anybody except Arthur—and he was introduced to Guenever the same evening. There is a story that her hair was yellow, but it was not. It was so black that it was startling, and her blue eyes, deep and clear, had a sort of fearlessness which was startling too. She was surprised by the young man's twisted face, but not frightened.

"Now," said the King, putting their hands together. "This is Lancelot, the one I told you about. He is going to be the best knight I have. I never saw such a fall as he gave me. I want you to be kind to him, Gwen. His father is one of my oldest friends."

He kissed the Queen's hand coldly.

He did not notice anything particular about her, because his mind was filled with previous pictures which he had made for himself. There was no room for pictures of what she was really like. He thought of her only as the person who had robbed him, and, since robbers are deceitful, designing, and heartless people, he thought of her as these.

"How do you do?" asked the Queen.

Arthur said: "We shall have to tell him what has been happening since he went away. What a lot of things to tell! Where can we begin?"

"Begin with the Table," said Lancelot.

"Oh dear!"

The Queen laughed and smiled at the new knight.

"Arthur thinks about it all the time," she said. "He even dreams about it at night. He won't be able to tell you unless he talks for a week."

"It is not going badly," said the King. "You can't expect a thing like that to go smoothly the whole time. The idea is there, and people are beginning to understand it, and that is the great thing. I am sure it will work."

"What about the Orkney faction?"

"They will come round in time."

"Is that Gawaine?" inquired Lancelot. "What is the matter with the Orkney faction?"

The King looked uncomfortable. He said: "The real matter with them is Morgause, their mother. She brought them up with so little love or security that they find it difficult to understand warm-hearted people themselves. They are suspicious and frightened. They don't get hold of the idea as I wanted them to do. We have three of them here—Gawaine, Gaheris and Agravaine. It is not their fault."

"Arthur had his first Pentecost feast the year we were married," explained Guenever, "and sent everybody out looking for good adventures, to see how the idea would work. When they came back, Gawaine had cut a lady's head off, and even dear old Pellinore had failed to rescue a damsel in distress. Arthur was furious about it."

"It is not Gawaine's fault," said the King. "He is a nice fellow. I like him. It is the fault of that woman."

"I hope things have got better since then?"

"Yes. It is slow work, of course, but I am sure we could say that things have got better."

"Did Pellinore repent?"

Arthur said: "Pellinore repented, yes. There was not much to repent. It was one of his muddles. But the trouble is that he has got so valiant since he married the Queen's daughter of Flanders that he has taken to jousting in earnest, and quite often wins. I was telling you how he killed King Lot one day, when they were having a practice. It has created a great deal of ill-feeling. The Orkney children have sworn to revenge their father's death, and they are out on the warpath for poor old Pellinore's blood. I am having difficulty in making them behave."

"Lancelot will help you," said the Queen. "It will be nice to have an old friend to help."

"Yes, it will be nice. Now, Lance, I expect you will want to see your room."

It was the second half of summer, and the amateur falconers in Camelot were bringing their peregrines to the last stages of their training. If you are a clever falconer, you get your hawk on the wing quickly. If you are not, you are apt to make mistakes, and the result is that the hawk does not finish her training for some time. So all the falconers in Camelot were trying to show that they were clever ones— by getting their hawks entered as quickly as possible—and, in all directions, if you went for a walk in the fields, there were atrabilious hawk-masters stretching out their creances and quarrelling with their assistants. Hawking, as James the First pointed out, is an extreme stirrer up of passions. It is because the hawks themselves are furious creatures, and the people who associate with them catch it.

Arthur presented Sir Lancelot with an inter-mewed jerfalcon, with which to keep himself amused. This was a great compliment, for jerfalcons were only supposed to be used by kings. At any rate that is what the Abbess Juliana Berners tell us—perhaps incorrectly. An emperor was allowed an eagle, a king could have a jerfalcon, and after that there was the peregrine for an earl, the merlin for a lady, the goshawk for a yeoman, the sparrow hawk for a priest, and the musket for a holy-water clerk. Lancelot was pleased with his present, and settled down busily in competition with the other angry falconers, who were hard at work criticizing each other's methods and sending each other messages of sugary venom and getting yellow about the eyeballs.

The jerfalcon which had been given to Lancelot was not properly through her moult. Like Hamlet, she was fat and scant of breath. Her long confinement in the mews, while she moulted, had got her into a sulky and temperamental state. So Lancelot had to fly her on the creance for several days before he could be sure that she was safe to the lure.

If you have ever flown a hawk on a creance, which is a long line tied to the hawk's jesses so that she cannot fly away, you know what a nuisance the thing can be. Nowadays people use a fishing reel, which makes it easier to stretch it out and to wind it up—but in Lancelot's day there were no good reels, and you simply had to wind your creance into a ball, like string. There were two main horrors to which it was subject, the first of which was the horror peculiar to all balls of string—that they invariably became tangles instead of balls. The second was that if you flew the hawk in any field which had not been carefully mowed, the string became wound round thistles or tufts of grass, thus checking the hawk and doing damage to its training. So Lancelot, and all the other angry men, went circling round Camelot in a bitter atmosphere of knots and competition and bating hawks.

King Arthur had asked his wife to be kind to the young man. She was fond of her husband, and she realized that she had come between him and his friend. She was not such a fool as to try to atone to Lancelot for this, but she had taken a fancy for him as himself. She liked his broken face, however hideous it was, and Arthur had asked her to be kind. There was a shortage of assistants in Camelot for the hawking, because there were so many people at it. So Guenever began going with Lancelot to help him with the balls of string.

He did not take much notice of the woman. "Here comes that woman," he would remark to himself, or "There goes that woman." He was already deep in the hawking atmosphere, which was only partly an affair for females, and he seldom thought of her more than that. He had grown into a beautifully polite youth, in spite of his ugliness, and he was too self-conscious to allow himself to have petty thoughts for long. His jealousy had turned into unconsciousness of her existence. He went on with his hawk-mastery, thanking her politely for her help and accepting it with courtesy.

One day there was particular trouble with a thistle, and he had miscalculated the amount of food which ought to have been given the day before. The jerfalcon was in a foul temper, and Lancelot caught its mood. Guenever, who was not particularly good with hawks and had no special interest in them, was frightened by his frowning brow, and, because she was frightened, she became clumsy. She was sweetly trying her best to help, but she knew that she was not clever at falconry, and there was confusion in her mind. Very carefully and kindly, and with the best intentions, she wound the creance up quite wrong. He took the wretched ball away from her with a gesture which was almost rough.

"That's no good," he said, and he began to unwind her hopeful work with angry fingers. His eyebrows made a horrible scowl.

There was a moment in which everything stood still. Guenever stood, hurt in her heart. Lancelot, sensing her stillness, stood also. The hawk stopped bating and the leaves did not rustle.

The young man knew, in this moment, that he had hurt a real person, of his own age. He saw in her eyes that she thought he was hateful, and that he had surprised her badly. She had been giving kindness, and he had returned it with unkindness. But the main thing was that she was a real person. She was not a minx, not deceitful, not designing and heartless. She was pretty Jenny, who could think and feel.

# 5

*The first two people to notice that Lancelot and* Guenever were falling in love with each other were Uncle Dap and King Arthur himself. Arthur had been warned about this by Merlyn—who was now safely locked up in his cave by the fickle Nimue—and he had been fearing it subconsciously. But he always hated knowing the future and had managed to dismiss it from his mind. Uncle Dap's reaction was to give his pupil a lecture, as they stood in the mews with the chastened jer.

"God's Feet!" said Uncle Dap, with other exclamations of the same kind. "What is this? What are you doing? Is the finest knight in Europe to throw away everything I have taught him for the sake of a lady's beautiful eyes? And a married lady too!"

"I don't know what you are talking about."

"Don't know! Won't know! Holy Mother!" shouted Uncle Dap. "Is it Guenever I am talking about, or is it not? Glory be to God for evermore!"

Lancelot took the old gentleman by the shoulders and sat him down on a chest.

"Look, Uncle," he said with determination. "I have been wanting to talk to you. Isn't it time you went back to Benwick?"

"Benwick!" cried his uncle, as if he had been stabbed to the heart.

"Yes, Benwick. You can't go on pretending to be my squire for ever. For one thing, you are the brother of two kings, and for another thing, you are three times as old as I am. It would be against the laws of arms."

"Laws of arms!" shouted the old man. "Pouf!"

"Well, it is no good saying Pouf."

"And me that has taught you everything you know! Me to go back to Benwick without having seen you prove yourself at all! Why, you have not even used your sword in front of me, not used Joyeux! It is ingratitude, perfidy, treachery! Sorrow to the grave! My faith! By the Blue!"

And the agitated old fellow went off into a long string of Gallic remarks, including the so-called William the Conqueror's oath of *Per Splendorem Dei*, and the *Pasque Dieu* which was the imaginary King Louis the Eleventh's idea of a joke. Inspired by the royal train of thought he added the exclamations of Rufus, Henry the First, John, and Henry the Third, which were, in that order, By the Holy Face of Lucca, By God's Death, By God's Teeth, and By God's Head. The jerfalcon, seeming to appreciate the display, roused his feathers heartily, like a housemaid shaking a mop out of the window.

"Well, if you won't go, you won't," said Lancelot. "But please don't talk to me about the Queen. I can't help it if we are fond of each other, and there is nothing wrong in being fond of people, is there? It is not as if the Queen and I were villains. When you begin lecturing me about her, you are making it seem as if there was something wrong between us. It is as if you thought ill of me, or did not believe in my honour. Please do not mention the subject again."

Uncle Dap rolled his eyes, disarranged his hair, cracked his knuckles, kissed his finger-tips, and made other gestures calculated to express his point of view. But he did not refer to the love affair afterwards.


Arthur's reaction to the problem was complicated. Merlyn's warning about his lady and his best friend had contained within itself the seeds of its own contradiction, for your friend can hardly be your friend if he is also going to be your betrayer. Arthur adored his rose-petalled Guenever for her dash, and had an instinctive respect for Lancelot, which was soon to become affection. This made it difficult either to suspect them or not to suspect.

The conclusion which he came to was that it would be best to solve the problem by taking Lancelot with him to the Roman war. That, at any rate, would separate the boy from Guenever, and it would be pleasant to have his disciple with him—a fine soldier—whether Merlyn's warning were true or not.


The Roman war was a complicated business which had been brewing for years. It need not concern us long. It was in its way the logical consequence of Bedegraine—the continuation of that battle on a European scale. The feudal idea of war for ransom had been squashed in Britain, but not abroad, and now the foreign ransom-hunters were after the newly settled King. A gentleman called Lucius, who was the Dictator of Rome—and it is strange to reflect that Dictator is the very word which Malory uses—had sent an embassy asking for tribute from Arthur—it was called a tribute before a battle and a ransom afterward—to which the King, after consulting his parliament, had returned a message that no tribute was due. So the Dictator Lucius had declared war. He had also sent his messengers, like Lars Porsena in Macaulay, to all the points of the compass to gather allies. He had no less than sixteen kings marching with him from Rome into High Germany, on their way to do battle with the English. He had allies from Ambage, Arrage, Alisandrie, Inde, Hermonie, Euphrates, Affrike, Europe the Large, Ertaine, Elamie, Arabie, Egypt, Damaske, Damiete, Cayer, Capadoce, Tarce, Turkey, Pounce, Pampoille, Surrie and Galacie, beside others from Greece, Cyprus, Macedone, Calabre, Cateland, Portingale, and many thousands of Spaniards.

During the first weeks of Lancelot's infatuation for Guenever, it became time for Arthur to cross the Channel to meet his enemy in France—and it was on this war that he decided to carry the young man with him. Lancelot, of course, was not at that time recognized as the chief knight of the Round Table, or he would have been taken in any case. At the present period of his life he had only fought one joust with Arthur himself, and the accepted captain of the knights was Gawaine.

Lancelot was angry at being taken from Guenever, because he felt that it implied a lack of trust. Besides, he knew that Sir Tristram had been left with King Mark's wife of Cornwall on a similar occasion. He did not see why he should not be left with Guenever in the same way.

There is no need to go into the whole story of the Roman campaign, although it lasted several years. It was the usual sort of war, with a great deal of shoving and shouting on both sides, great strokes smitten, many men overthrown, and great valiances, prowesses, and feats of arms shown every day. It was Bedegraine enlarged—with the same refusal on Arthur's part to regard it as a sporting or commercial enterprise—although it did have its characteristic touches. Redheaded Gawaine lost his temper when sent on an embassy and killed a man in the middle of the negotiations. Sir Lancelot led a terrific battle in which his men were outnumbered by three to one. He slew the King Lyly and three great lords called Alakuke, Herawd, and Heringdale. During the campaign three notorious giants were accounted for—two of them by Arthur himself. Finally, in the last engagement, Arthur gave the Emperor Lucius such a blow on the head that Excalibur stinted not till it came to his breast, and it was discovered that the Sowdan of Surrie and the King of Egypt and the King of Ethiope—an ancestor of Haile Selassie—together with seventeen other kings of diverse regions and sixty senators of Rome, were among the slain. Arthur put their bodies into sumptuous coffins—not sarcastically—and sent them to the Lord Mayor of Rome, instead of the tribute which had been demanded. This induced the Lord Mayor and nearly the whole of Europe to accept him as overlord. The lands of Pleasance, Pavia, Petersaint, and the Port of Tremble yielded him homage. The feudal convention of battle was broken for good, on the Continent as well as in England.

During this warfare Arthur became genuinely fond of Lancelot, and, by the time they came home, he no longer believed in Merlyn's prophecy at all. He had put it at the back of his mind. Lancelot was acknowledged to be the greatest fighter in the army. Both of them were determined that Guenever could not come between them, and the first few years were safely past.

# 6

*What sort of picture do people have of Sir Lancelot* from this end of time? Perhaps they only think of him as an ugly young man who was good at games. But he was more than this. He was a knight with a medieval respect for honour.

There is a phrase which you sometimes come across in country districts even nowadays, which sums up a good deal of what he might have tried to say. Farmers use it in Ireland, as praise or compliment, saying, "So-and-so has a Word. He will do what he promised."

Lancelot tried to have a Word. He considered it, as the ignorant country people still consider it, to be the most valuable of possessions.

But the curious thing was that under the king-post of keeping faith with himself and with others, he had a contradictory nature which was far from holy. His Word was valuable to him not only because he was good, but also because he was bad. It is the bad people who need to have principles to restrain them. For one thing, he liked to hurt people. It was for the strange reason that he was cruel, that the poor fellow never killed a man who asked for mercy, or committed a cruel action which he could have prevented. One reason why he fell in love with Guenever was because the first thing he had done was to hurt her. He might never have noticed her as a person, if he had not seen the pain in her eyes.

People have odd reasons for ending up as saints. A man who was not afflicted by ambitions of decency in his mind might simply have run away with his hero's wife, and then perhaps the tragedy of Arthur would never have happened. An ordinary fellow, who did not spend half his life torturing himself by trying to discover what was right so as to conquer his inclination towards what was wrong, might have cut the knot which brought their ruin.

When the two friends arrived in England from the Roman war, the fleet landed at Sandwich. It was a grey September day, with the blue and copper butterflies flitting in the after-grass, the partridges calling like crickets, the blackberries colouring, and the hazel nuts still nursing their tasteless little kernels in cradles of cotton wool. Queen Guenever was on the beach to meet them, and the first thing Lancelot knew after she had kissed the King, was that she was able to come between them after all. He made a movement as if his entrails were tying themselves in knots, saluted the Queen, went off to bed in the nearest inn at once, and lay awake all night. In the morning, he asked leave of absence from the court.

"But you have hardly been at court at all," said Arthur. "Why do you want to go away so soon?"

"I ought to go away."

"Ought to go away?" asked the King. "What do you mean, you ought to go away?"

Lancelot clenched his fist until the knuckles stood out, and said, "I want to go on a quest. I want to find an adventure."

"But, Lance—"

"It is what the Round Table is for, isn't it?" shouted the young man. "The knights are to go on quests, aren't they, to fight against Might? What are you trying to stop me for? It's the whole point of the idea."

"Oh, come," said the King. "You needn't get excited about it. If you want to go, of course you can do whatever you like. I only thought it would be nice to have you with us for a little. Don't be cross, Lance. I don't know what has come over you."

"Come back soon," said the Queen.


# 7


*This was the beginning of the famous quests. They* were not made to win him fame or recreation. They were an attempt to escape from Guenever. They were his struggles to save his honour, not to establish it.

We shall have to describe one of the quests in detail—so as to show the way in which he tried to distract himself, and the way in which this famous honour of his worked. Also it will give a picture of the state of England, which forced King Arthur to work for his theory of justice. It was not that Arthur was a prig—it was that his country of Gramarye lay in such a toil of anarchy in the early days that some idea like the Round Table was needed to make the place survive. The warfare of people like Lot had been suppressed, but not the unbiddable baronage who lived like gangsters on their own estates. Barons were pulling teeth out of Jews to get their money, or roasting bishops who contradicted them. The villeins who belonged to bad masters were being basted over slow fires, or sprinkled with molten lead, or impaled, or left to die with their eyes gouged out, or else they were crawling along the roads on hands and knees, because they had been hamstrung. Petty feuds were raging to the destruction of the poor and helpless, and, if a knight did happen to be dragged from his horse in a battle, he was so well screwed up that only an expert could do him harm. Philip Augustus of France, for instance, was dismounted and surrounded at the legendary battle of Bouvines: yet, as the unfortunate infantry were quite unable to puncture him, he was rescued soon after, and continued to fight all the better because he had lost his temper. But the story of Lancelot's first quest must speak for their troubled age of Might in its own way.

There were two knights on the borders of Wales called Sir Carados and Sir Turquine. They were of Celtic stock. These two conservative barons had never yielded to Arthur, and they did not believe in any form of government except the rule of force. They had strong castles and wicked retainers, who found more opportunity for wickedness under their leadership than they would have found in a settled state of society. They existed like eagles, to prey on weaker brethren. It is unfair to compare them with eagles, for many of these birds are noble creatures, while Sir Turquine at any rate was not noble. If he had lived now he would even have been locked in a lunatic hospital, and his friends would certainly have urged him to be psycho-analysed.

One day, when Sir Lancelot had been riding on his adventure for about a month—and all the time going away from where he wanted to be, so that every pace of his horse was a torment—there appeared a knight in armour riding a great mare, with another bound knight thrown across the saddlebow. The bound knight had fainted. He was bloody and bedraggled, and his head, which hung by the mare's shoulders, had red hair. The riding knight who had captured him was a man of enormous stature, and Lancelot recognized him by his blazon as Sir Carados.

"Who is your prisoner?"

The big knight lifted the prisoner's shield, which was hanging behind him, and showed *or, a chevron gules, between three thistles vert.*

"What are you doing with Sir Gawaine?"

"Mind your own business," said Sir Carados.

Gawaine must have come to his senses when the mare halted, for his voice now said, coming from upside down: "Is that you, man, Sir Lancelot?"

"What cheer, Gawaine. How stands it with you?"

"Never so hard," said Sir Gawaine, "unless that ye help me, for without ye rescue me, I know nae knight that may."

He was speaking formally in the High Language of Chivalry—for in those days there were two kinds of speech like High and Low Dutch or Norman French and Saxon English.

Lancelot looked at Sir Carados, and said in the vernacular: "Will you put that fellow down, and fight with me instead?"

"You are a fool," said Sir Carados. "I shall only serve you in the same way."

Then they put Gawaine on the ground, tied up so that he could not get away, and prepared for battle. Sir Carados had a squire to give him his spear, but Lancelot had insisted on leaving Uncle Dap at home. He had to serve himself alone.

The fight was different from the one with Arthur. For one thing, the knights were more evenly matched, and, in the tilt with which it began, neither of them was unhorsed. They broke their ashwood spears to splinters, but both stayed in the saddle, and the horses stood the shock. In the sword-play which followed, Lancelot proved to be the better of the two. After little more than an hour's fighting he managed to give Sir Carados such a buffet on the helm that it pierced his brain-pan—and then, while the dead man was still swaying in the saddle, he caught him by the collar, pulled him under his horse's feet, dismounted in the same instant, and struck off his head. He liberated Sir Gawaine, who thanked him heartily, and rode on again into the wild ways of England, without giving Carados another thought. He fell in with a young cousin of his own, Sir Lionel, and they rode together in search of wrongs to redress. But it was unwise of them to have forgotten Sir Carados.

One day, when they had been riding for some time, they came to a forest during a sultry noon, and Lancelot was so worn out by the struggle inside him about the Queen, and by the weather as well, that he felt he could not go further. Lionel felt sleepy also, so they decided to lie down under an apple tree in a hedge, after tying their horses to sundry branches. Lancelot went to sleep at once—but the buzzing of the flies kept Sir Lionel awake, and while he was awake a curious sight came by.

The sight was of three knights fully armed, galloping for their lives, with a single knight in pursuit of them. The horses' hoofs thundered on the ground and shook it—so that it was peculiar that Lancelot did not wake up—until, one by one, the huge pursuer ran his quarries down, unhorsed them, and bound them prisoners.

Lionel was an ambitious boy. He thought that he would steal a march on his famous cousin. He got up quietly, put his armour to rights, and rode off to challenge the victor. In less than a minute he too was lying on the ground, trussed so that he could not move, and before Lancelot woke the whole pageant had disappeared. The mysterious conqueror in these four battles was Sir Turquine, a brother to the Carados whom Lancelot had lately killed. His habit was to take his captives into his grimly castle, where he took off all their clothes and whacked them to his heart's content, as a hobby.

Lancelot was still asleep when a new pageant came prancing by. In the middle of it there was a green silk canopy borne on four spears by four knights gorgeously apparelled. Under the canopy there rode four middle-aged queens on white mules, looking picturesque. They were passing the apple tree, when Lancelot's charger gave a brassy neigh.

Queen Morgan le Fay, who was the senior queen of the four—all witches—halted the procession and rode over to Sir Lancelot. He looked dangerous as he lay there in full armour of war, among the long grasses.

"It is Sir Lancelot!"

Nothing travels quicker than scandal, especially among supernatural people, so the four queens knew that he was in love with Guenever. They also knew that he was now recognized as the strongest knight in the world. They were jealous of Guenever on this account. They were delighted by the opportunity which they saw before them. They began to quarrel among themselves, about which of them should have him for her magic.

"We need not quarrel," said Morgan le Fay. "I will put an enchantment on him so that he does not wake for six hours. When we have got him safely into my castle, he can choose which of us he will have, himself."

This was done. The sleeping champion was carried on his shield, between two knights, into the Castle Chariot. The castle no longer had its fairy appearance as a castle of food, but its everyday aspect of an ordinary fortress. There he was put into a cold, bare chamber, fast asleep, and left until the enchantment wore off.

When Lancelot woke, he did not know where he was. The room was dark, and seemed to be made of stone like a dungeon. He lay in the dark wondering what would happen next. Later he began to think about Queen Guenever.

The thing which did happen, was that a young damsel came in with his dinner and asked him what cheer?

"How are you, Sir Lancelot?"

"I don't know, fair damsel. I don't know how I got here, so I don't rightly know how I am."

"No need to be frightened," she said. "If you are as great a man as you are supposed to be, I may be able to help you tomorrow morning."

"Thank you. Whether you can help me or not, I should like you to think kindly of me."

So the fair maid went away.

In the morning there was banging of bolts and creaking of rusty locks and several retainers in chain mail came into the dungeon. They lined up on either side of the door, and the magic queens came in behind them, all dressed in their best clothes. Each of the queens made a stately curtsey to Sir Lancelot. He stood up politely and bowed gravely to each of the queens. Morgan le Fay introduced them as the queens of Gore, Northgalis, Eastland, and the Out Isles.

"Now," said Morgan le Fay, "we know about you, so you need not think we don't. You are Sir Lancelot Dulac, and you are having a love affair with Queen Guenever. You are supposed to be the best knight in the world, and that is why the woman is fond of you. Well, that is all over now. We four queens have you in our power, and you have to choose which of us you will have for your mistress. It would be no good unless you choose for yourself, obviously —but one of us you must have. Which is it to be?"

Lancelot said: "How can I possibly answer a thing like that?"

"You have to answer."

"In the first place," he said, "what you say about me and the King's wife of Britain is untrue. Guenever is the truest lady unto her lord living. If I were free, or had my armour, I would fight any champion you liked to put forward, to prove that. And in the second place, I certainly will not have any of you for my mistress. I am sorry if this is discourteous, but it is all I can say."

"Oh!" said Morgan le Fay.

"Yes," said Lancelot.

"That is all?"

"Yes."

The four queens curtsied with frigid dignity, and marched out of the room. The sentries made smart about-turns, their mail ringing on the stone floor. The light went out of the door. The door slammed, and the key creaked, and the bolts rumbled into their sockets.

When the fair damsel came in with the next meal, she showed signs of wanting to talk to him. Lancelot noticed that she was a bold creature, who was probably fond of getting her own way.

"You said you might be able to help me?"

The girl looked suspiciously at him and said: "I can help you if you are who you are supposed to be. Are you really Sir Lancelot?"

"I am afraid I am."

"I will help you," she said, "if you will help me."

Then she burst into tears.

While the damsel is weeping, which she did in a charming and determined way, we had better explain about the tournaments which used to take place in Gramarye in the early days. A real tournament was distinct from a joust. In a joust the knights tilted or fenced with each other singly, for a prize. But a tournament was more like a free fight. A body of knights would pick sides, so that there were twenty or thirty on either side, and then they would rush together harum-scarum. These mass battles were considered to be important—for instance, once you had paid your green fee for the tournament, you were admitted on the same ticket to fight in the jousts—but if you had only paid the jousting fee, you were not allowed to fight in the tourney. People were liable to be dangerously injured in the mêlées. They were not bad things altogether, provided they were properly controlled. Unfortunately, in the early days, they were seldom controlled at all.

Merry England in Pendragon's time was a little like Poor Ould Ireland in O'Connell's. There were factions. The knights of one county, or the inhabitants of one district, or the retainers of one nobleman, might get themselves into a state in which they felt a hatred for the faction which lived next door. This hatred would become a feud, and then the king or leader of the one place would challenge the leader of the other one to a tourney—and both factions would go to the meeting with full intent to do each other mischief. It was the same in the days of Papist and Protestant, or Stuart and Orangeman, who would meet together with shillelaghs in their hands and murder in their hearts.

"Why are you crying?" asked Sir Lancelot.

"Oh, dear," sobbed the damsel. "That horrid King of Northgalis has challenged my father to a tournament next Tuesday, and he has got three knights of King Arthur's on his side, and my poor father is bound to lose. I am afraid he will get hurt."

"I see. And what is your father's name?"

"He is King Bagdemagus."

Sir Lancelot got up and kissed her politely on the forehead. He saw at once what he was expected to do.

"Very well," he said. "If you can rescue me out of this prison, I will fight in the faction of King Bagdemagus next Tuesday."

"Oh, thank you," said the maiden, wringing out her handkerchief. "Now I must go, I am afraid, or they will miss me downstairs."

Naturally she was not going to help the magic Queen of Northgalis to keep Lancelot in prison—when it was the King of Northgalis himself who was going to fight her father.

In the morning, before the people of the castle had got up, Lancelot heard the heavy door opening quietly. A soft hand was put in his, and he was led out in the darkness. They went through twelve magic doors, until they reached the armoury, and there was all his armour bright and ready. When he had put it on, they went to the stables, and there was his charger scratching on the cobbles with a sparkling shoe.

"Remember."

"Of course," he said. And he rode out over the drawbridge into the morning light.

While they had crept through the corridors of Castle Chariot, they had made a plan about meeting King Bagdemagus. Lancelot was to ride to an abbey of white friars which was situated near by, and there he was to meet the damsel—who would, of course, be forced to flee from Queen Morgan because of her treachery in letting him escape. At this abbey they were to wait until King Bagdemagus could be brought over, and then the arrangements for the tournament were to be made. Unfortunately, the Castle Chariot was in the Forest Sauvage, and Lancelot now lost his way to the abbey. He and his horse wandered about all day, bumping against branches, getting tangled in blackberry bushes, and rapidly losing their tempers. In the evening they stumbled on a pavilion of red sendal, with nobody inside.

He got off his horse and looked at the pavilion. There was something queer about it—luxurious as it was in the rooky wood, and without anybody in sight.

"This is a strange pavilion," he thought sadly, for his mind was full of Guenever, "but I suppose I may as well stay in it for the night. Either it is here for some adventure or other, in which case I ought to try the adventure, or else the owners have gone away on holiday, and in that case they will not mind my taking shelter for one evening. Anyway, I am lost, and there is nothing else I can do."

He unharnessed the horse and spancelled him. Then he took off his own armour and hung it neatly on a nearby tree with the shield on top. After this he ate some bread which the girl had given him, drinking water from a stream which ran beside the pavilion, stretched his arms out until the elbows went click, yawned, hit his front teeth with his fist three times, and went to bed. The bed was a sumptuous one with a coverlet of red sendal, to match the tent. Lancelot rolled himself in it, pressed his nose into the silk pillow, kissed it for Guenever, and was fast asleep.

It was moonlight when he woke, and a naked man was sitting on his left foot, trimming his finger-nails.

Lancelot, who had been woken from his love sleep with a start, moved suddenly in the bed when he felt the man. The man, equally surprised at feeling a movement, jumped up and snatched his sword. Lancelot jumped out on the other side of the bed and ran for his own arms, where they were hanging in the tree. The man came after him, waving his blade and trying to get a cut at him from behind. Lancelot reached the tree in safety and swung round with his weapon in his hand. They looked strange and terrible in the moonlight, both stark naked, with their silver steel glancing under the harvest moon.

"Now," cried the man, and he aimed a furious swipe at Lancelot's legs. The next minute he had dropped his sword and was holding his stomach with both hands, doubled up and whistling. The cut which Lancelot had given welled over with blood which looked black in the moonlight, and you could see some of the insides of the stomach with their secret life laid open.

"Don't hit me," cried the man. "Mercy. Don't hit me again. You have killed me."

"I am sorry," said Lancelot. "You did not even wait till I had a sword."

The man went on wailing: "Mercy! Mercy!"

Lancelot stuck his blade in the ground and went over to examine the wound.

"I am not going to hurt you," he said. "It's all right. Let me see."

"You have cut open my liver," said the man accusingly.

"Well, I can't do more than say I am sorry, even if I have. I don't know what we were fighting about anyway. Lean on my shoulder and we will get you into bed."

When he had got the man to bed, and stopped his bleeding, and discovered that the wound was not a mortal one, a beautiful lady appeared in the opening of the tent. They had lit a rush light, so that she saw what had happened in a flash, and immediately she began screaming at the top of her voice. She rushed over to comfort the wounded man, and accused Lancelot of being a murderer, and carried on a great deal.

"Do stop howling," said the man. "He is not a murderer. We just made a mistake."

"I was in bed," said Lancelot, "when he came and sat on me, and we were both so startled that we had a fight. I am sorry that I hurt him."

"But it was our bed," cried the lady, like one of the Three Bears. "What were you doing in our bed?"

"Really," he said, "I am sorry. There was nobody in the pavilion when I found it, and I was lost and tired, so I thought it would not matter if I took a night's lodging."

"Nor did it matter," said the man. "You are welcome to a night's lodging, and I don't think the wound is going to be a bad one after all. May I inquire your name?"

"Lancelot."

"Well!" exclaimed the man. "There now, my dear, look who I have been fighting. No wonder I got a bit of a chip. I was wondering why my life was spared so easily."

So they insisted that Lancelot should stay the night, and

in the morning they put him on the correct road for the abbey of white friars.

Nothing much came of this encounter in the main story, except that the knight, whose name was Belleus, was introduced to the Round Table by Lancelot as soon as he was well again. He was the kind of generous fellow that Arthur needed, and Lancelot tried to make up for the trouble which he had caused by getting him a seat at the Table.

At the abbey of white friars the fair damsel was waiting in a state of excitement. She was afraid that he might have let her down. His horse's hoofs, however, had no sooner clattered on the cobbles than she came flying from her tower room to welcome him with delight.

"Father will be here this evening," she cried. "Oh, I am so glad you came! I was afraid you might have forgotten."

Lancelot's twisted mouth grinned at the word she had chosen to use. Then he changed into civilian dress, had a bath, and waited for King Bagdemagus.

"It is a puzzling life in Gramarye," he said to himself, trying to keep his mind off the young Queen. "Things happen so quickly. One hardly knows where one is half the time, and there is that cousin of mine who vanished under the apple tree, who has still to be accounted for. What with magic queens and faction tournaments and people getting into bed with you at night, and half the family vanishing without trace, it is difficult to keep in line."

Then he brushed his hair, smoothed his gown, and went down to meet King Bagdemagus.

There is no need to give a long description of the tourney. Malory gives it. Lancelot picked three knights who were recommended by the young damsel to go with him, and he arranged that all four of them should bear the vergescu. This was the white shield carried by unfledged knights, and Lancelot insisted on this arrangement because he knew that three of his own brethren of the Round Table were going to fight on the other side. He did not want them to recognize him, because it might cause ill-feeling at court. On the other hand, he felt that it was his duty to fight against them because of the promise which he had given to the damsel. The King of Northgalis, who was the leader of the opposite side, had one hundred and sixty knights in his faction, and King Bagdemagus only had eighty. Lancelot went for the first knight of the Round Table, and put his shoulder out of joint. He went for the second one so hard that the unlucky fellow was carried over his horse's tail and buried his helm several inches in the ground. He hit the third knight on the head so hard that his nose bled, and his horse ran away with him. By the time he had broken the thigh of the King of Northgalis, everybody could see that to all intents and purposes the tournament was over.

The next thing that happened was that our hero set out to discover what had become of Lionel. He was free to do so, for the first time—for, since the disappearance of his cousin, he had either been imprisoned by the malignant queens or else he had been discharging his obligations to the girl who had rescued him from them. King Bagdemagus got the prize at the tournament before he left, and the damsel was almost tearfully grateful. Everybody said that they would be friends for ever, and that they had only to send each other word if there was anything that anybody could do for anybody in return. Then Lancelot mounted his horse, got his bearings by asking several peasants where he was, and rode off toward the forest of the apple tree where he had lost his cousin. He thought that by making an all-round-the-hat cast at the place where he had last seen his cousin, he might be able to pick up the scent once more, although it was cold.

In the forest of the apple tree, indeed at the very foot of the tree itself, he came across a lady riding a white palfrey. The tree was thought to be a magic one, which was the reason why such a lot of traffic went on round it.

"Lady," said he, "do you know of any adventures in this forest?"

"Plenty," she said, "if you are man enough to take them on."

"I could try."

"You look a strong man," said the lady. "You have a bold look, too, in spite of your ears which stick out so frightfully. If you like, I will take you where the fiercest baron in the world lives, but he is sure to kill you."

"Never mind."

"I will only take you if you tell me your name. It would be murder to take you unless you are a famous knight."

"My name is Lancelot."

"I thought it was," said the lady. "Well, it is lucky it is.

According to the things which people are saying about you, you are probably the only knight in the world who can beat the man I am taking you to. His name is Sir Turquine."

"Good."

"Some say he is a madman. He has sixty-four knights in prison, whom he has captured in single combat, and he spends the time beating them with thorns. If he captures you, he will beat you too, all naked."

"He sounds an exciting man to fight."

"It is a sort of concentration camp."

"That is what I have been getting ready for," said Sir Lancelot. "It is what Arthur invented the Round Table to prevent."

"If I take you to him, you must promise to do something for me afterwards—that is, if you win."

"What sort of thing?" he asked cautiously.

"You need not be afraid," said the lady. "It is only to vanquish another knight I know of, who is distressing some damsels."

"I will promise that gladly."

"Well," said the lady, "God, He knows how you will get on. Anyway, I will say a prayer for you while you are fighting."

When they had been riding for some time, they came to a ford like the one at which he had fought the first fight with King Arthur. On the trees round the ford there were hanging rusty helms and melancholy shields—sixty-four of them, with their bends and chevrons and luces hauriant and merles and eagles displayed and lions passant guardant looking desolate and abandoned. The leather of their guiges was green and mildewy. It looked like a gamekeeper's gallows.

In the middle of the glade, on the chief tree, there hung an enormous copper basin, triumphing over the beaten shields. The latest shield under it was Lionel's—argent, a bend gules distinguished with some sort of label of cadency.

Lancelot knew what he had to do with this basin, and he did it. He put his helm in position, rode through the dripping leaves to the basin, and beat on it with the butt of his spear until the bottom fell out. Then he and the lady stood still in the forest, which was as if it had been shocked silent by the hideous noise.

Nobody came.

"His castle is beyond," said the lady.

They went to the castle gates in silence, and rode up and down in front of them for half an hour. He took off his helm and gauntlets, and frowned, and bit his finger-nails from anxiety.

After the half-hour was over, a gigantic knight came riding through the forest. He looked so like Sir Carados—the knight who had been slain at the rescue of Gawaine—that Lancelot was startled. Not only was he of the same build, but he also had a bound knight thrown across the saddlebow of his mare. Most peculiar of all, the bound knight's shield carried the three thistles and the chevron, with a red canton. In fact, the second of the big knights had captured Gaheris—Gawaine's brother. Lancelot watched him with a critical eye.

It may not be amiss to mention that a good judge of style could often recognize a knight in armour, even if he was disguised and bearing the vergescu. In later life Lancelot sometimes had to fight disguised, because otherwise nobody would fight him. Yet Arthur and others generally guessed him by his riding. People nowadays can recognize cricketers, even when their faces are too far away to be seen, and so it was then.

Lancelot was a good judge of style, because of his long practice. As soon as he had watched Sir Turquine for a moment or two, he noticed that there was a slight weakness in his seat. He remarked to the lady that unless Turquine sat better, he thought he would be able to rescue the prisoners. As it turned out, Turquine did sit better when it came to the tilt, so that this particular criticism came to nothing—but it throws a sidelight on jousting and may have been worth mentioning.

The riding was the whole thing. If a man had the courage to throw himself into the fullest gallop at the moment of impact, he generally won. Most men faltered a little, so that they were not at their best momentum. This was why Lancelot constantly gained his tilts. He had what Uncle Dap called the *élan*. Sometimes, when he was in disguise, he would ride clumsily on purpose, showing daylight at his seat. But at the last moment there was always the true dash—so that the onlookers, and frequently his wretched opponent, could exclaim, "Ah, Lancelot!" even before the lance drove home.

"Fair knight," he said, "put down that wounded man and

let him rest a little. Then we two can prove our strengths."

Sir Turquine rode up to him, and said through his teeth: "If you are a knight of the Round Table, it will give me great pleasure to knock you down first and whack you afterwards. I could do that to you, and your whole table with you."

"It seems a tall order."

Then they retreated in the usual way, fewtered their spears, and charged together like thunder. Lancelot, at the last moment, noticed that he was wrong about Turquine's seat. In the last flash he realized that Turquine was the finest tilter he had met, that he was coming with a hurl as great as his own, and that his aim was sure.

The knights ducked and drew themselves together; the spears struck at the same moment; the horses, checked in mid-career, reared up and fell over backward; the spears burst and went sailing high in the air, turning over and over gracefully like the results of high explosive; and the lady on the palfrey looked away. When she looked again, both horses were down with their backs broken, and the knights lay still.

Two hours later, Lancelot and Turquine were still fighting with their swords.

"Stop," said Turquine. "I want to speak to you."

Lancelot stopped.

"Who are you?" asked Sir Turquine. "You are the finest knight I ever fought with. I never saw a man with such good wind. Listen, I have sixty-four prisoners in my castle, and I have killed or maimed hundreds of others, but none were as good as you. If you will have peace, and be my friend, I will loose my prisoners."

"It is kind of you."

"I will do this for you, if you are anybody except one person. If you are he, I must fight you to the death."

"Who is this person?"

"Lancelot," said Sir Turquine. "If you are Lancelot, I must never yield or make friends. He killed my brother Carados."

"I am that man."

Sir Turquine made a hissing through his helm and struck craftily, before his enemy was ready.

"Ah, would you?" said Lancelot. "I only had to pretend I was not myself, and I could have had the prisoners safe. But you try to kill me without warning."

Sir Turquine continued to hiss.

"I am sorry about Carados," said Lancelot. "He was killed in fair fight and never offered to yield. I never had him at mercy. He was killed in the middle of the fight."

They fought for two more hours. The blade was not the only weapon used by knights in armour. Sometimes they struck each other with the edges of their shields, sometimes they clubbed each other with the pommels of their swords. The grass all round was speckled with their blood—little spots like those on trout, but with a kind of tail on each spot, like a tadpole. Sometimes, because of their weight, they fell over each other. The heavy, straw-stuffed helms of chivalry had such small holes to breathe through that they felt like suffocating. Their shields hung wearily, not covering them properly.

It was over in a second. Neither of them spoke. Lancelot dropped his sword at a moment of opportunity and caught Turquine by the snout of his helm. They fell over, and the helm came off. They drew their misericordes for the close work. Turquine bounced and shuddered and was dead.

Later, while Gaheris and the lady were giving him some water, Lancelot said: "Whatever was wrong with him, he was game. I am sorry he would not yield."

"But think of the maimed knights and the beating."

"He was the old school," he said. "It is what we have to stop. But he was a credit to the old school as a fighter, all the same."

"He was a brute," said the lady.

"Whatever he was, he was fond of his brother. Look Gaheris, will you lend me your horse? I want to go on, and my own is dead, poor creature. If you could lend me yours, you could go forward and let Lionel and the others out of the castle. Tell Lionel to go back to court and not to be a silly fellow. I have to ride with this lady. Will you do that?"

"You can have my horse, certainly," said Gaheris. "You have saved him and me as well. How you keep on saving the Orkneys! Last time it was Gawaine. And Agravaine is in that castle at this minute. Of course you can have my horse, Lancelot, of course you can."

# 8

*Lancelot had several other adventures during his* first quest—it lasted a year—but perhaps only two are worth repeating in detail. They were both mixed up with the conservative ethics of Force Majeur against which the King had started his crusade. It was the old school, the Norman baronial attitude, which provided the adventures at this period—for few people can hate so bitterly and so self-righteously as the members of a ruling caste which is being dispossessed. The knights of the Round Table were sent out as a measure against Fort Mayne, and the choleric barons who lived by Fort Mayne took up the cudgels with the ferocity of despair. They would have written to *The Times* about it, if there had been such a paper. The best of them convinced themselves that Arthur was newfangled, and that his knights were degenerate from the standards of their fathers. The worst of them made up uglier names than Bolshevist even, and allowed the brutal side of their natures to dwell on imaginary enormities which they attributed to the knights. The situation became divorced from common sense, so that atrocity stories were accepted by the atrocious people. Many of the barons whom Lancelot had to put down had worked themselves into such a state about him, through fear of losing their ancient powers, that they believed him to be a sort of poison-gas man. They fought him with as much unscrupulousness and hatred as if he had been an antichrist, and they truly believed themselves to be defending the right. It became a civil war of ideologies.

One day in the fine summer, he was riding through the park land of a castle which was strange to him. The trees grew dispersedly about the sward—great elms and oaks and beeches—and Lancelot was thinking about Guenever with a heavy heart. Before he had parted from the lady who led him to Sir Turquine—and he had done the thing for her which he had promised—they had started a conversation about marriage, which had upset him. The lady had said that he ought either to have a wife or a mistress, and Lancelot had been angry. "I can't stop people from saying things if they want to," he had said, "but circumstances make it impossible for me to marry, while I consider that having a mistress is no good." They argued about it for some time, and then parted. Now, although he had passed several adventures in between, he was still thinking of the lady's advice and feeling wretched.

There was the sound of bells in the air—and he looked up immediately.

A fine peregrine falcon, with her music jingling in the whistling wind als clear, and her creance trailing behind her, was beating along above his head toward the top of one of the elms. She was in a temper. As soon as she reached the top of the elm she sat down in it, looking about her with raging eye and panting beak. The creance wrapped itself three times round the nearest bough. When she noticed Sir Lancelot riding toward her, she tried to fly away again in fury. The creance caught her. She hung upside down, bating with her wings. His heart came into his mouth for fear that she would break some feathers. In a few moments she ceased to flap, and hung upside down, revolving slowly, looking ignoble and indignant and ridiculous, holding her head the right way up like a snake's.

"Oh, Sir Lancelot, Sir Lancelot!" cried an unknown gentlewoman, riding toward him at full speed and evidently trying to wring her hands in spite of the reins. "Oh, Sir Lancelot! I have lost my falcon."

"There she is," he said, "in that tree."

"Oh, dear! Oh, dear!" cried the lady. "I was only trying to call her in cranes and the string broke! My husband will kill me if I do not catch her again. He is so hasty and such a keen falconer."

"But surely he will not kill you?"

"Oh, he will! He will not mean it, but he will do it! He is such a hasty man."

"Perhaps I could stop him?"

"Oh, no," said the gentlewoman. "That would not do at all. You might hurt him. I would not like you to hurt my dear husband. Don't you think you could climb up the tree and catch the hawk instead?"

Lancelot looked at the gentlewoman and at the tree. Then he heaved a deep sigh and remarked, as Malory reports him: "Well, fair lady, since that ye know my name, and require me of my knighthood to help you, I will do what I may to get your hawk; and yet truly I am an ill climber, and the tree is passing high, and few boughs to help me withal."

He had spent his childhood learning to be a fighter. It had left him no time for birds'-nesting like other boys. The lady's request, which would have given no trouble to people brought up like Arthur or Gawaine, really was an upset for him.

Lancelot took off his armour sadly, with an occasional crooked glance at the horrible tree, until he was dressed in his shirt and breeches. Then he assaulted the first boughs manfully, while the gentlewoman ran about underneath, talking about hawks and husbands and the nice weather they were having.

"All right," he said, with his eyes full of bark and a hideous scowl on his face. "All right. All right."

At the top of the tree, the falcon was in such a tangle with her creance—she had wound it round her neck and wings, as usual, and was under the impression that it was assaulting her—that Lancelot had to let her stand on the bare hand. This she gripped with the fury of hysteria, but he patiently disentangled her without minding the stabs. Falconers seldom fuss when their hawks hurt them. They are too interested.

When the hawk was safely rescued from the branches, he realized that he would not be able to climb down again with one hand. He shouted to the lady, who seemed small at the foot of the tree: "Look out, I am going to tie her jesses to a heavy branch, if I can break one off, and then throw her down. I will get one that is not too heavy, so that she comes gently. I shall have to throw her out a bit, so that she is clear of the boughs."

"Oh, do be careful!" cried the lady.

When Lancelot had done what he said, he began to make his way down again with care. There were some bad bits on the way, where he had to rely on balance alone. He was about twenty feet from the ground when a fat knight in full armour came galloping up.

"Ha, Sir Lancelot!" shouted the fat knight. "Now I have you where I want you."

The lady picked up the falcon and began to go away.

"Lady!" said Lancelot, wondering how everybody came to know his name.

The fat man screamed out: "You leave her alone, you assassin. That is my wife, that is. She has only been doing what I told her. It was a trick. Ha! Ha! Now I have got you without any of your famous armour on, and I am going to kill you, like drowning a kitten."

"It is not very knightly," said Lancelot, with a grimace. "You might at least let me arm and fight fair."

"Let you arm, you puppy! Whatever do you take me for? I don't want any of this newfangled nonsense. When I catch a man who eats human children roasted, I kill him like the vermin he is."

"But really——"

"Come down, come down! I can't wait about all day. Come down and take your medicine like a man, if you are a man."

"I assure you that I do not roast children."

The fat knight grew quite purple in the face and shouted: "Liar! Liar! Devil! Come down at once."

Lancelot sat on a branch and dangled his feet and bit his fingernails.

"Do you mean to say," he asked, "that you loosed that falcon on purpose, with her cranes on, so as to be able to murder me when I was naked?"

"Come down!"

"If I come down, I shall do my best to kill you."

"Buffoon!" cried the fat knight.

"Well," said Lancleot, "it is your own fault. You should not play dirty tricks. For the last time, will you let me arm like a gentleman?"

"Certainly not."

Lancelot broke off a bough of rotten wood, and jumped down on the other side of his horse, so that the horse was between them. The fat knight rode at him, and tried to swipe off his head, leaning across the horse between. Lancelot parried the stroke with his bough, and the knight's sword stuck in the wood. Then he took the sword away from its owner and slit his throat.

"Go away," said Lancelot to the gentlewoman. "Stop howling. Your husband was a fool and you are a bore. I am not sorry I killed him."

But he was sorry.

The last adventure was also concerned with treachery and a lady. The young man was riding mournfully through the fen country—which had not been drained in those days and was probably the wildest part of England. It was all secret ways through the marshes, which were known only to the Saxon marsh men who had been conquered by Uther Pendragon, and the whole sea-smelling plain was one vast quack under the low sky. The bitterns boomed and the marsh harriers skimmed over the reeds and millions of widgeon and mallard and tufted ducks flew about in various wedges, looking like champagne bottles balanced on a nimbus of wings. On the salt marshes the geese from Spitzbergen walked and nibbled, with their necks bent into their peculiar loop, and the fen men stalked them with nets and engines. The fen people had spotted bellies and their toes were webbed—at any rate that was the belief in the rest of England. They generally killed foreigners.

While Lancelot was riding along a straight road which seemed to lead nowhere, he saw two people galloping towards him from the other end. They turned out to be a knight and his lady. The lady was in front, going like mad, and the knight was after her. His sword flashed against the dull sky.

"Here! Here!" cried Lancelot, riding at them.

"Help!" screamed the lady. "Oh, save me! He is trying to cut my head off."

"Leave her alone! Get out!" shouted the knight. "She is my wife, and she has been committing adultery!"

"I never did," wailed the lady. "Oh, sir, save me from him. He is a cruel, beastly brute. Just because I am fond of my cousin german, he is jealous. Why should I not be fond of my cousin german?"

"Scarlet woman!" exclaimed the knight, and he tried to get at her.

Lancelot rode between them and said: "Really, you must not go for a woman like that. I don't care whose fault it is, but you can't kill women."

"Since when?"

"Since King Arthur was king."

"She is my wife," said the knight. "She is nothing to do with you. Get out! And she is an adulteress, whatever she says."

"Oh no, I am not," said the lady. "But you are a bully. And you drink."

"Who made me drink, then? And, besides, it is no worse to drink than be an adulteress."

"Be quiet," said Lancelot, "both of you. This is a nuisance. I shall have to ride between you until you cool off. I suppose you would not care to have a fight with me, sir, instead of killing this lady?"

"Certainly not," said the knight. "I know by your argent, a bend gules, that you are Lancelot; and I would not be such a fool as to fight you, especially for a bitch like this. What the devil has it got to do with you?"

"I will go," said Lancelot, "as soon as you promise on your knighthood not to kill women."

"Well, I won't promise."

"You wouldn't," said the lady. "Anyway, you would not keep your promise, if you did."

"There are some marsh soldiers," said the knight, "cantering after us. Look behind. They are armed cap-à-pie."

Lancelot reined his horse and looked over his shoulder. At the same moment the knight leaned over to his near side and swapped off the lady's head. When Lancelot looked back again, without seeing any soldiers, he found the lady sitting beside him with no head on. She slowly began to sag to the left, throbbing horribly, and fell in the dust. There was blood all over his horse.

Lancelot grew white about the nostrils.

He said, "I shall kill you for that."

The knight immediately jumped off his horse and lay on the ground.

"Don't kill me!" he said. "Mercy! She was an adulteress."

Lancelot dismounted also and drew his sword.

"Get up," he said. "Get up and fight, you, you——"

The knight scrambled along the ground toward him, and threw his arms round his thighs. By being close to the avenger, he made it difficult for him to swing the sword. "Mercy!" His abjection made Lancelot feel horrible.

"Get up," he said. "Get up and fight. Look, I will take my armour off and fight you with my sword only."

But "Mercy, mercy!" was all the knight would say.

Lancelot began to shudder, not at the knight but at the cruelty in himself. He held his sword loathingly, and pushed the knight away.

"Look at all the blood," he said.

"Don't kill me," said the knight. "I yield. I yield. You can't kill a man at mercy."

Lancelot put up his sword and went back from the knight, as if he were going back from his own soul. He felt in his heart cruelty and cowardice, the things which made him brave and kind.

"Get up," he said. "I won't hurt you. Get up, go."

The knight looked at him, on all fours like a dog, and stood up, crouching uncertainly.

Lancelot went away and was sick.

At the feast of Pentecost it was customary for the knights who had been on Table quests to gather again at Carlion so as to relate their adventures. Arthur had found that this made people keener on fighting in the new way of Right, if they had to tell about it afterwards. Most of them preferred to bring their prisoners with them, as witnesses to their stories. It was as if some Inspector General of Police in a very distant part of Africa were to send out his superintendents into the jungle, asking them to come back next Christmas with all the savage chiefs whom they had brought to righteousness. For one thing, it impressed the savage chiefs to see the great court, and they often went home reformed.

The Pentecost next after Lancelot's first quest was almost a fiasco. A few seedy giants of the Strong Arm, who had been captured by the Orkney faction, turned up and said their homage, but the Lancelot contingent was a spate. "Whose man are you?" "Lancelot's." "And whose are you, my good fellow?" "Lancelot's." After a bit the whole Table began shouting the answers. Arthur would say: "You are welcome to Carlion, Sir Belleus, and may I ask which of my knights you have yielded to?" "Lancelot," the Table would shout in chorus. And Sir Belleus, blushing rather and wondering whether the laughter was at him, would say in a small voice: "Yes, I yielded to Sir Lancelot."

Sir Bedivere came and admitted how he had swapped off his adulterous wife's head. He had brought it with him, and was told to take it to the Pope as a penance—he became very holy after that. Gawaine came gruffly and told in Scottish English how he had been rescued from Sir Carados. Gaheris, at the head of a deputation of sixty-four knights with rusty shields, related his rescue from Sir Turquine. The daughter of King Bagdemagus arrived in an enthusiastic state and told about the tournament with the King of Northgalis. Besides these, there were many people from adventures which we have left out—mainly knights who had yielded to Sir Lancelot when he was disguised as Sir Kay.

You may remember from the first book that Kay was inclined to throw his tongue a bit too much, and he had got himself unpopular on account of this. Lancelot had been compelled during the quest to rescue him from three knights who were pursuing him. Then, so that Kay could get home to court unmolested, Lancelot had changed armour with him one night while he was asleep—and thereafter the knights who went for Lancelot under the impression that he was Kay had gotten the surprise of their lives, while the knights who met Kay in Lancelot's armour had given him a wide berth. Knights yielded under this category included Gawaine, Uwaine, Sagramour, Ector de Maris, and three others. Also there came a knight called Sir Meliot de Logres, who had been rescued under supernatural circumstances.

All these people gave themselves up, not to King Arthur, but to Guenever. Lancelot had kept himself away for a whole year, but there was a limit to his endurance. Thinking of her all the time and longing to be back with her, he had allowed himself this one indulgence. He had sent his captives to kneel at her feet. It was a fatal course of action.

# 9

*It is difficult to explain about Guenever, unless it* it is possible to love two people at the same time. Probably it is not possible to love two people in the same way, but there are different kinds of love. Women love their children and their husbands at the same time—and men often feel a lusty thought for one woman while they are feeling a love of the heart for another. In some way such as this Guenever did come to love the Frenchman without losing her affection for Arthur. She and Lancelot were hardly more than children when it began, and the King was about eight years their senior. At twenty-two, the age of thirty seems to be the verge of senility. The marriage between her and Arthur had been what they call a "made" marriage. That is to say, it had been fixed by treaty with King Leodegrance, without consulting her. It had been a successful union, as "made" marriages generally are, and before Lancelot came on the scene the young girl had adored her famous husband, even if he was so old. She had felt respect for him, with gratitude, kindness, love, and a sense of protection. She had felt more than this—you might say that she had felt everything except the passion of romance.

And then the captives arrived. A blushing queen of little more than twenty summers on her throne, and the whole flame-lit hall filling with noble knights on bended knee. "Whose prisoner are you?" "I am the Queen's prisoner, to live or die, sent by Sir Lancelot." "Whose you?" "The Queen's, by Lancelot's arm." Sir Lancelot—the name on everybody's lips: the best knight in the world, top of the averages, even above Tristram: the courtly, the merciful, the ugly, the invincible: and he had sent them all to her. It was like a birthday party, so many presents. It was like the story books.

Guenever sat straight and bowed royally to her prisoners. She pardoned them all. Her eyes were brighter than her crown.

Lancelot came last. There was a stir among the torch-bearers near the door, and a sound went round the hall. The clatter of knives and plates and tankards, the noise of friendly shouting which had sounded a moment before like a meeting of seabirds on St. Kilda, the yells for more mutton or a pint of mead were stilled—and the blurs of white faces turned toward the door. There was Lancelot, no longer in armour but dressed in a magnificent velvet robe, scalloped and diapered. He hesitated in the dark frame, hideous and friendly, wondering why the silence was—and the lights showed him up. Then the faces turned back again, the seabird meeting started once more, and Lancelot came forward to kiss the King's hand.

It was the moment. Perhaps it is better than trying to explain.

"Well, Lance," said Arthur cheerfully, "these are some high jinks, and no mistake about it. Jenny can hardly sit still, with all her captives."

"They were for her," said Lancelot. The Queen and he did not look at each other. They had done so with the click of two magnets coming together, the moment that he crossed the threshold.

"I can't help thinking they were for me too," said the

King. "The result ought to be that you have made me a present of about three counties."

Lancelot felt a need to prevent silence. He began talking too quickly.

"Three counties is not much," he said, "for the Emperor of all Europe. You speak as if you had never conquered the Dictator of Rome. How are your dominions getting on?"

"They are getting on as you make them, Lance. It was no good conquering the Dictator, unless you and the others do the civilizing part. What is the use of being the Emperor of Europe, if the whole place is fighting mad?"

Guenever supported her hero in the effort against silence. It was their first partnership.

"You are a strange man," she said, "Arthur dear. You fight all the time, and conquer countries and win battles, and then you say that fighting is a bad thing."

"So it is a bad thing. It is the worst thing in the world. Oh, God, we needn't explain it again."

"No."

"How is the Orkney faction?" asked the younger man hastily. "How is your famous civilization going? Might for Right? You mustn't forget I have been away a year."

The King put his head in his hands and looked miserably at the table between his elbows. He was a kind, conscientious, peace-loving fellow, who had been afflicted in his youth by a tutor of genius. Between the two of them they had worked out their theory that killing people, and being a tyrant over them, was wrong. To stop this sort of thing, they had invented the idea of the Table—a vague idea like democracy, or sportsmanship, or morals—and now, in the effort to impose a world of peace, he found himself up to the elbows in blood. When he was feeling healthy he did not grieve much, because he knew the dilemma was inevitable—but in weak moments he was persecuted by shame and indecision. He was one of the first Nordic men who had invented civilization, or who had desired to do otherwise than Attila the Hun had done, and the battle against chaos sometimes did not seem to be worth fighting. He often thought that it might have been better for all his dead soldiers to be alive—even if they had lived under tyranny and madness—rather than be quite dead.

"The Orkney faction is bad," he said. "So is civilization, except for the bit which you have just brought in. Before you came, I was thinking that I was the Emperor of nothing—now I feel as if I were the Emperor of three counties."

"What is wrong with the Orkney faction?"

"Oh, God, must we talk about it when we were feeling happy because you had come back? I suppose we must."

"It is Morgause," said the Queen.

"Partly. Morgause is having love affairs with anybody she can get hold of, now that Lot is dead. How I wish King Pellinore had not had that unfortunate accident when he killed him! It is having a bad effect on her children."

"How do you mean?"

The King scratched on the table and stated: "I wish you had not conquered Gawaine, that time when you were disguised as Kay. I almost wish you had not made such brilliant successes in rescuing him and his brothers from Carados and Turquine."

"Why not?"

"This Round Table," said the older man slowly, "was a good thing when we thought of it. It was necessary to invent a way for the fighting men to express themselves without doing harm. I can't see how we could have done it otherwise than by starting a fashion, like children. To get them in, we had to have a gang, as kids have in schools. Then the gang had to swear a darksome oath that they would only fight for our ideas. You could call it for civilization. What I meant by civilization when I invented it, was simply that people ought not to take advantage of weakness—not violate maidens, and rob widows, and kill a man when he was down. People ought to be civil. But it has turned into sportsmanship. Merlin always said that sportsmanship was the curse of the world, and so it is. My scheme is going wrong. All these knights now are making a fetish of it. They are turning it into a competitive thing. Merlin used to call it Games-Mania. Everybody gossips and nags and hints and speculates about who unseated whom last, and who has rescued most virgins, and who is the best knight of the Table. I made it a round table to prevent that very thing, but it has not prevented it. The Orkney faction have got the craze worst. I suppose their sense of insecurity over their mother makes it necessary for them to be sure of a safe place at the top of the list. They have to excel, to make up for her. That is why I wish you had not beaten Gawaine. He is a decent chap, but he will hold it against you inside himself. You have hurt him in his tilting average—it is a part of their make-up which has now become more important to my knights than their souls. If you are not careful, you will have the Orkney faction after your blood, as well as after poor Pellinore's. It's a foul position. People will do the basest things on account of their so-called honour. I wish I had never invented honour, or sportsmanship, or civilization."

"What a speech!" said Lancelot. "Cheer up. The faction won't hurt me, even if it does come after my blood. As for your scheme going wrong, that is nonsense. The Round Table is the best thing that ever happened."

Arthur, whose head was still in his hands, raised his eyes. He saw that his friend and his wife were looking at each other with the wide pupils of madness, so he quickly attended to his plate.

# 10

Uncle Dap said, turning the helm round in his hands: "Your mantling is cut and torn. We shall have to get another. It is honourable to have the mantling slashed, but dishonourable to keep it so when there is an opportunity to replace it. Such a course of action would be boastful."

They were talking in a little closet with a north window, cold and grey, and the blue light lay like frozen oil upon the steel.

"Yes."

"How did Joyeux go? Is he sharp still? Did you like his balance?"

Joyeux had been made by Galand, the greatest swordsmith of the Middle Ages.

"Yes."

"Yes! Yes!" cried Uncle Dap. "Can you say nothing but Yes? Death of my soul, Lancelot, but one asks if you are dumb! What in the world is this that has come over you, in the end?"

Lancelot had been smoothing the panache of feathers which was used as a distinguishing mark on the helm in

Uncle Dap's hands. It was detachable. People have got it into their heads, through the cinema and the comic advertisements, that knights in armour generally wore ostrich plumes, nodding like stalks of pampas grass. This was not the case. Kay's panache, for instance, was shaped like a rigid, flat fan, with its edges pointing fore and aft. It was carefully arranged out of the eyes of peacock feathers, exactly as if a stiff peacock fan had been erected endwise on his head. It was not a tuft of plumes, and it did not nod. It was rather like the adipose fin of a fish, but gaudy. Lancelot, who did not care for gaudy things, wore a few heron's hackles bound with silver thread, which suited the argent of his shield. He had been stroking them. Now he threw them violently into a corner and stood up. He began walking the narrow room in a jerky way.

"Uncle Dap," he said, "do you remember how I asked you not to talk about something?"

"I do."

"Is Guenever in love with me?"

"You should ask her," replied his uncle, with French logic.

"What must I do?" he cried. "What must I do?"

If it is difficult to explain about Guenever's love for two men at the same time, it is almost impossible to explain about Lancelot. At least it would be impossible nowadays, when everybody is so free from superstitions and prejudice that it is only necessary for all of us to do as we please. Why did not Lancelot make love to Guenever, or run away with his hero's wife altogether, as any enlightened man would do today?

One reason for his dilemma was that he was a Christian. The modern world is apt to forget that several people were Christians in the remote past, and in Lancelot's time there were no Protestants—except John Scotus Erigena. His Church, in which he had been brought up—and it is difficult to escape from your upbringing—directly forbade him to seduce his best friend's wife. Another stumbling block to doing as he pleased was the very idea of chivalry or of civilization which Arthur had first invented and then introduced into his own young mind. Perhaps a bad baron who believed in the Strong Arm might have gone off with Guenever, even in the face of his Church's councils, because taking your neighbour's wife was really a form of Fort Mayne. It was a matter of the stronger bull winning.

But Lancelot had spent his childhood between knightly exercises and thinking out King Arthur's theory for himself. He believed as firmly as Arthur did, as firmly as the benighted Christian, that there was such a thing as Right. Finally, there was the impediment of his nature. In the secret parts of his peculiar brain, those unhappy and inextricable tangles which he felt at the roots, the boy was disabled by something which we cannot explain. He could not have explained either, and for us it is all too long ago. He loved Arthur and he loved Guenever and he hated himself. The best knight of the world: everybody envied the self-esteem which must surely be his. But Lancelot never believed he was good or nice. Under the grotesque, magnificent shell with a face like Quasimodo's, there was shame and self-loathing which had been planted there when he was tiny, by something which it is now too late to trace. It is so fatally easy to make young children believe that they are horrible.

"It seems to me," said Uncle Dap, "that it depends very largely on what the Queen wants to do."

# 11

*Lancelot stayed at the court for several weeks this* time, and each week made it more difficult to go away. On top of the more or less social tangle in which he found himself, there was a personal puzzle—for he put a higher value on chastity than is fashionable in our century. He believed, like the man in Lord Tennyson, that people could only have the strength of ten on account of their hearts being pure. It so happened that his strength was as the strength of ten, and such was the medieval explanation which had been discovered for it. As a corollary to this belief, he supposed that if he gave in to the Queen he would lose his tenfold might. So, for this reason, as well as for the other ones, he fought against her with the courage of despair. It was not pleasant for Guenever either.

One day Uncle Dap said: "You had better go away. You have lost nearly two stone in weight. If you go away something will either snap or not snap. It is better to get it over quickly."

Lancelot said: "I cannot go."

Arthur said: "Please stay."

Guenever said: "Go."

The second quest which he embarked upon was the turning-point of his life. There had been a good deal of talk in Camelot about a certain King Pelles, who was lame and lived in the haunted castle of Corbin. He was supposed to be slightly mad, because he believed himself to be a relation of Joseph of Arimathea. He was the sort of man who would become a British Israelite nowadays, and spend the rest of his life prophesying the end of the world by measuring the passages in the Great Pyramid. However, King Pelles was only slightly mad, and his castle was certainly haunted. It had a haunted room in it, with innumerable doors out of which things came and fought you in the night. Arthur thought it was worth sending Lancelot to investigate the place.

On the way to Corbin Lancelot had a strange adventure, which he remembered for many years with awful grief. He was to look back on it as the last adventure of his virginity, and to believe, day by day for the next twenty years, that before it had happened he had been God's man, while, after it, he had become a lie.

There was a village under the castle of Corbin, which seemed a prosperous one. It had cobbled streets and stone houses and old bridges. The castle stood on a hill to one side of the valley, and there was a handsome pele tower on the hill of the other side. All the people of the village were in the street, as if they were waiting for him, and there was a dreamlike quality in the air, as if a shower of gold dust had come from the sun. Lancelot felt peculiar. His blood might have had too much oxygen in it, from the way he was conscious of every stone in every wall, and all the colours in the valley, and the joyful stepping of his horse. The people of the enchanted village knew his name.

"Welcome, Sir Lancelot Dulac," they cried, "the flower of all knighthood! By thee we shall be holpen out of danger."

He reined his horse and spoke to them.

"Why do you call out to me?" he asked, thinking of other things. "How do you know my name? What is the matter?"

They answered in chorus, speaking together solemnly and without difficulty.

"Ah, fair knight," they said. "Do you see that tower on the hill? There is a dolorous lady in it, who has been kept boiling in scalding water for many winters by magic, and nobody can get her out except the best knight in the world. Sir Gawaine was here last week, but he could not do it."

"If Sir Gawaine could not do it," he said, "I am sure that I can't."

He did not like this sort of competition. The danger about being the best knight in the world was that if you were always being tested about it, the day was bound to come when you would fail to retain the title.

"I think I had better ride on," he said, and he gave his reins a shake.

"No, no," said the people gravely. "You are Sir Lancelot and we know it. You will get our lady out of the boiling water."

"I must go."

"She is in pain."

Lancelot leaned on the withers of his horse, lifted his right leg over the crupper, and found himself on the ground. "Tell me what I must do," he said.

The people formed in a procession round him, and the mayor of the village took him by the hand. They walked together silently up the hill to the pele tower, except that the major explained the situation as they went.

"Our lady of the manor," said the mayor, "used to be the most beautiful girl in the country. So Queen Morgan le Fay and the Queen of Northgalis grew jealous of her, and they have put her in this magic for revenge. It is terrible how it hurts her, and she has been boiling for five years. Only the best knight in the world can get her out."

When they came to the tower gate, another strange thing happened. It was heavily bolted and barred in the old-fashioned way. The masonry of the doorway was constructed with deep slots in it, in which heavy beams ran to and fro— heavy enough to withstand a battering ram. Now these beams withdrew into the wall of their own accord, and the iron locks turned their own wards with a grinding noise. The door quietly opened.

"Go in," said the mayor, and the people stood still outside, waiting for what was to happen.

On the first floor of the tower there was the furnace

which kept the magic water hot. Lancelot could not enter
there. On the second floor there was a room full of steam,
so that he could not see across it. He went into this room,
holding his hands joined together in front of him, as blind
people do, until he heard a squeak. A clearing in the
steam, caused by the draught from the door so long un-
opened, showed him the lady who had given the squeak.
She was sitting shyly in the bath looking at him, a charming little lady, who was—as Malory puts it—as naked as
a needle.

"Well!" said he.

The girl blushed, so far as she could blush when she was
boiled, and said in a small voice: "Please give me your
hand." She knew how the magic had to be undone.

Lancelot gave her his hand, and she stood up, and got
out of the bath, and all the people outside began cheering,
as though they knew exactly what was happening. They had
brought a dress with them, and the proper underwear, and
the ladies of the village formed a circle in the gateway while
the pink girl was dressed.

"Oh, it does feel lovely to be dressed!" she said.

"My popsy!" cried a fat old woman who had evidently
been her nurse when she was small, weeping tears of joy.

"Sir Lancelot done it," shouted the villagers. "Three
cheers for Sir Lancelot!"

When the cheering had died away, the boiled girl came
to him and put her hand in his.

"Thank you," she said. "Ought we to go to church now,
and thank God as well as you?"

"Certainly we must."

So they went to the clean little chapel in the village
and thanked God for His mercies. They kneeled between
the frescoed walls, where some important-looking saints with
blue haloes were standing on tiptoe to avoid foreshortening,
and the gay paints of the stained-glass window poured
upon their heads. They were cobalt blue, purple from
manganese, yellow from copper, red, and a green which
was also got from copper. The whole inside of the place
was a tankful of colour. It was half-way through the service
before he realized that he had been allowed to do a miracle,
just as he had always wanted.

King Pelles limped down from his castle on the other
side of the valley, to find out what the excitement was

about. He looked at Lancelot's shield, kissed the boiled child absent-mindedly, leaning over like an obedient stork to have his cheek pecked, and remarked: "Dear me, you are Sir Lancelot! And I see you have fetched my daughter out of that kettle arrangement. How kind of you! It was prophesied long ago. I am King Pelles, near cousin to Joseph of Arimathea—and you, of course, are but the eighth degree from Our Lord Jesus Christ."

"Good gracious!"

"Indeed, indeed," said King Pelles. "It is all written down arithmetically in the stones at Stonehenge, and I have some sort of holy dish in my castle at Carbonek, together with a dove which flies about in various directions holding a censer of gold in its beak. Still, it was extremely kind of you to fetch my daughter out of the kettle."

"Daddy," said the girl. "We ought to be introduced."

King Pelles waved his hand as if he were trying to scare away the midges.

"Elaine," he said. It was another one with the same name. "This is my daughter, Elaine. How do you do? And this is Sir Lancelot Dulac. How do you do? All written in the stones."

Lancelot, perhaps slightly biased by having first met her with no clothes on, thought that Elaine was the most beautiful girl he had seen, except Guenever. He felt shy too.

"You must come and stay with me," said the King. "That is in the stones also. Show you the holy dish some day, and all that. Teach you arithmetic. Nice weather. Don't have daughters unboiled every day. I think dinner will be ready."

# 12

*Lancelot stayed at the castle of Corbin for days.* Its haunted rooms were up to expectation, and there was nothing else to do. He felt such feelings in his breast because of Guenever—the frightful pang of hopeless love—that he was drained of effort. He could not summon the energy to go elsewhere. At the beginning of his love for her there had been restlessness, so that he had felt that if only he kept moving and doing new things every moment there might be a hope of escape. Now his power to be busy was gone. He felt that he might as well be in one place as another, if he was only waiting to see whether his heart would break or not. He was too simple to see that if the finest knight in the world rescued you out of a kettle of boiling water, with no clothes on, you would be likely to fall in love with him— if you were only eighteen.

One evening, when Pelles had been particularly tiresome about religious family trees, and when the gnawing in the boy's heart had made it impossible for him to eat properly or even to sit still at dinner, the butler took the situation in hand. He had served the Pelles family for forty years, was married to the nurse who had greeted Elaine with tears of joy, and he approved of love. He also understood about young men like Lancelot—young men who might still be undergraduates or jet-pilots if they were in England today. He would have made an excellent college butler.

"More wine, sir?" asked the butler.

"No, thank you."

The butler bowed politely and poured another horn, which Lancelot drained without looking at it.

"A nice vintage, sir," said the butler. "His Majesty takes great trouble with his cellar."

King Pelles had gone to the library to work out some prognostications, and his guest was left gloomily in the hall.

"Yes."

There was a rustling outside the buttery door, and the butler went over to it while Lancelot was drinking another measure.

"Now this is a fine wine, sir," said the butler. "His Majesty sets great store by this wine, and my wife has just fetched up a fresh bottle from the cellar. Observe the crust, sir. It is a wine which I am sure you will appreciate."

"All wines are the same to me."

"You modest young gentleman," said the butler, substituting a large horn. "If I may say so, sir, you will have your little joke. But it is easy to recognize a judge of wine when you come across him."

He was bothering Lancelot, who wanted to be alone with his misery, and Lancelot realized that he was being bothered. For this reason he automatically wondered whether he had not perhaps been discourteous to the butler in his distraction. Perhaps the butler was really keen on the wine, and had troubles of his own. He politely drank it up.

"Very nice," he said encouragingly. "A splendid vintage."

"I am glad to hear you praise it, sir."

"Have you ever," asked Lancelot, putting the question which all young men are always asking, and without noticing that it had anything to do with the drink, "have you ever been in love?"

The butler smiled discreetly and poured another bumper.

By midnight Lancelot and the butler were sitting on opposite sides of the table, both looking red in the face. They had a brew of piment between them—a mixture of red wine, honey, spices, and whatever else the butler's wife had added.

"So I tell you," said Lancelot, glaring like an ape. "Wouldn't tell everybody, but you are a nice chap. Understanding chap. Pleasure to tell anything. Have another drink."

"Good health," said the butler.

"What am I to do?" he cried. "What am I to do?"

He put his horrible head between his arms on the table, and began to weep.

"Courage!" said the butler. "Do or die!"

He made a rapping on the table with one hand, looking at the buttery door, and with the other poured out another bumper.

"Drink," he said. "Drink hearty. Be a man, sir, if I may make so bold. You will have good news in a minute, that you will, and you want to seize the unforgiving minute, as the bard says."

"Good chap," said Lancelot. "Damned if I wouldn't, if I could."

"Jack is as good as his master."

"Certainly is," said the young man, winking in a way which he was afraid must look most beastly. "Better, in fact, eh, butler?"

He began to grin like an ass.

"Ah," said the butler, "and there is my wife Brisen at the buttery door, holding a message. I dare say it might be for you.

"What does it say?" asked the butler, watching the boy who sat staring at the paper.

"Nothing," he said, throwing the paper on the table and walking unsteadily to the door.

The butler read the paper.

"It says that Queen Guenever is at the castle of Case, five miles from here, and she wants you. It says the King is not with her. There are some kisses on it."

"Well?"

"You dare not go," said the butler.

"Dare not?" shouted Sir Lancelot, and he went into the darkness staggering, laughing like a caricature, and calling for his horse.

In the morning he woke suddenly in a strange room. It was quite dark, with tapestry over the windows, and he had no headache because his constitution was good. He jumped out of bed and went to the window, to draw the curtain. He was fully aware, in the suddenness of a second, of all that had happened on the previous night—aware of the butler and of the drink and of the love-potion which had perhaps been put in it, of the message from Guenever, and of the dark, solid, cool-fired body in the bed which he had just got out of. He drew the curtain and leaned his forehead against the cold stone of the mullion. He was miserable.

"Jenny," he said, after minutes which seemed to be hours. There was no answer from the bed.

He turned round and found himself looking at the boiled girl, Elaine. She lay in the bed, her small bare arms holding the bedclothes to her sides, with her violet eyes fixed on his.

Lancelot was always a martyr to his feelings, never any good at disguising them. When he saw Elaine his head went back. Then his ugly face took on a look of profound and outraged sorrow, so simple and truthful that his nakedness in the window-light was dignity. He began to tremble.

Elaine did not move, but only looked upon him with her quick eyes, like a mouse.

Lancelot went over to the chest where his sword was lying.

"I shall kill you."

She only looked. She was eighteen, pitifully small in the big bed, and she was frightened.

"Why did you do it?" he cried. "What have you done? Why have you betrayed me?"

"I had to."

"But it was treachery!"

He could not believe it of her.

"It was treachery! You have betrayed me."

"Why?"

"You have made me—taken from me—stolen——"

He threw his sword into a corner and sat down on the chest. When he began to cry, the gross lines of his face screwed themselves up fantastically. The thing which Elaine had stolen from him was his might. She had stolen his strength of ten. Children believe such things to this day, and think that they will only be able to bowl well in the cricket match tomorrow, provided that they are good today.

Lancelot stopped crying, and spoke with his eyes on the floor.

"When I was little," he said, "I prayed to God that he would let me work a miracle. Only virgins can work miracles. I wanted to be the best knight in the world. I was ugly and lonely. The people of your village said that I was the best knight of the world, and I did work my Miracle when I got you out of the water. I did not know it would be my last as well as my first."

Elaine said: "Oh, Lancelot, you will work plenty more."

"Never. You have stolen my miracles. You have stolen my being the best knight. Elaine, why did you do it?"

She began to cry.

He got up, wrapped himself in a towel, and went over to the bed.

"Never mind," he said. "It was my fault for getting drunk. I was miserable, and I got drunk. I wonder if that butler tried to make me? It was not very fair if he did. Don't cry, Elaine. It was not your fault."

"It was. It was."

"Probably your father made you do it, so as to have the eighth degree from Our Lord in the family. Or else it was that enchantress Brisen, the butler's wife. Don't be sorry about it, Elaine. It is over now. Look, I will give you a kiss."

"Lancelot!" cried Elaine. "It was because I loved you. Haven't I given something too? I was a maiden, Lancelot. I didn't rob you. Oh, Lancelot—it was my fault. I ought to be killed. Why didn't you kill me with your sword? But it was because I loved you, and I couldn't help it."

"There, there."

"Lancelot, suppose I have a baby?"

He stopped comforting her and went to the window again, as if he were going mad.

"I want to have your baby," said Elaine. "I shall call him Galahad, like your first name."

She still held the coverlet to her sides with the small, bare arms. Lancelot turned upon her in fury.

"Elaine," he said, "if you have a baby, it is your baby. It is unfair to bind me with pity. I am going straight away now, and I hope I shall never see you again."

# 13

*Guenever was doing some petit point in the gloomy* room, which she hated doing. It was for a shield-cover for Arthur, and had the dragon rampant gules. Elaine was only eighteen, and it is fairly easy to explain the feelings of a child—but Guenever was twenty-two. She had grown to have some of the nature of an individual, stamped on the simple feelings of the child-queen who had once received her present of captives.

There is a thing called knowledge of the world, which people do not have until they are middle-aged. It is something which cannot be taught to younger people, because it is not logical and does not obey laws which are constant. It has no rules. Only, in the long years which bring women to the middle of life, a sense of balance develops. You can't teach a baby to walk by explaining the matter to her logically—she has to learn the strange poise of walking by experience. In some way like that, you cannot teach a young woman to have knowledge of the world. She has to be left to the experience of the years. And then, when she is beginning to hate her used body, she suddenly finds that she can do it. She can go on living—not by principle, not by deduction, not by knowledge of good and evil, but simply by a peculiar and shifting sense of balance which defies each of these things often. She no longer hopes to live by seeking the truth—if women ever do hope this—but continues henceforth under the guidance of a seventh sense. Balance was the sixth sense, which she won when she first learned to walk, and now she has the seventh one—knowledge of the world.

The slow discovery of the seventh sense, by which both men and women contrive to ride the waves of a world in which there is war, adultery, compromise, fear, stultification and hypocrisy—this discovery is not a matter for triumph. The baby, perhaps, cries out triumphantly: I have balance! But the seventh sense is recognized without a cry. We only carry on with our famous knowledge of the world, riding the queer waves in a habitual, petrifying way, because we have reached a stage of deadlock in which we can think of nothing else to do.

And at this stage we begin to forget that there ever was a time when we lacked the seventh sense. We begin to forget, as we go stolidly balancing along, that there could have been a time when we were young bodies flaming with the impetus of life. It is hardly consoling to remember such a feeling, and so it deadens in our minds.

But there was a time when each of us stood naked before the world, confronting life as a serious problem with which we were intimately and passionately concerned. There was a time when it was of vital interest to us to find out whether there was a God or not. Obviously the existence or otherwise of a future life must be of the very first importance to somebody who is going to live her present one, because her manner of living it must hinge on the problem. There was a time when Free Love versus Catholic Morality was a question of as much importance to our hot bodies as if a pistol had been clapped to our heads.

Further back, there were times when we wondered with all our souls what the world was, what love was, what we were ourselves.

All these problems and feelings fade away when we get the seventh sense. Middle-aged people can balance between believing in God and breaking all the commandments, without difficulty. The seventh sense, indeed, slowly kills all the other ones, so that at last there is no trouble about the commandments. We cannot see any more, or feel, or hear about them. The bodies which we loved, the truths which we sought, the Gods whom we questioned: we are deaf and blind to them now, safely and automatically balancing along toward the inevitable grave, under the protection of our last sense. "Thank God for the aged," sings the poet:

Thank God for the aged
And for age itself, and illness and the grave.

When we are old and ill, and particularly in the coffin,
It is no trouble to behave.


Guenever was twenty-two as she sat at her petit point
and thought of Lancelot. She was not half-way to her coffin,
not ill even, and she only had six senses. It is difficult to
imagine her.

A chaos of the mind and body—a time for weeping at
sunsets and at the glamour of moonlight—a confusion and
profusion of beliefs and hopes, in God, in Truth, in Love,
and in Eternity—an ability to be transported by the beauty
of physical objects—a heart to ache or swell—a joy so
joyful and a sorrow so sorrowful that oceans could lie between them: then, as a counterpoise to these attractive
features, outcrops of selfishness indecently exposed—restlessness or inability to settle down and stop bothering the
middle-aged—pert argument on abstract subjects like
Beauty, as if they were of any interest to the middle-aged—
lack of experience as to when truth should be suppressed
in deference to the middle-aged—general effervescence and
nuisance and unfittingness to the set patterns of the seventh
sense—these must have been some of Guenever's charac-
teristics at twenty-two, because they are everybody's. But
on top of them there were the broad and yet uncertain
lines of her personal character—lines which made her different from the innocent Elaine, lines of less pathos perhaps but more reality, lines of power which made her into
the individual Jenny that Lancelot loved.

"Oh, Lancelot," she sang as she stitched at the shield-
crown. "Oh, Lance, come back soon. Come back with your
crooked smile, or with your own way of walking which
shows whether you are angry or puzzled—come back to
tell me that it does not matter whether love is a sin or not.
Come back to say that it is enough that I should be Jenny
and you should be Lance, whatever may happen to anybody."

The startling thing was that he came. Straight from
Elaine, straight from her robbery, Lancelot came like an
arrow to the heart of love. He had slept with Guenever already in deceit, already had been cheated of his tenfold
might. He was a lie now, in God's eyes as he saw them, so
he felt that he might as well be a lie in earnest. No more to
be the best knight in the world, no more to work miracles
against magic, no more to have compensation for ugliness

and emptiness in his soul, the young man sped to his sweetheart for consolation. There was the clatter of his iron-shod horse on the cobbles, which made the Queen drop her needlework to see whether it was Arthur back from his hunting—the ring of his chain-mail feet upon the stairs, going chink-chink like spurs against the stone—and then, before she was quite certain of what had happened, Guenever was laughing or weeping, unfaithful to her husband, as she had always known she would be.

# 14

Arthur said: "Here is a letter from your father, Lance. He says he is being atttacked by King Claudas. I promised to help him against Claudas, if it was necessary, in exchange for his help at Bedegraine. I shall have to go."

"I see."

"What do you want to do?"

"How do you mean, what do I want to do?"

"Well, do you want to come with me or to stay here?"

Lancelot cleared his throat and said: "I want to do whatever you think best."

"It will be difficult for you," said Arthur. "I hate to ask you. But would you mind if I asked you to stay?"

Lancelot could not think of the safe words, so the King mistook his silence for disappointment.

"Of course, you have a right to see your father and mother," he said. "I don't want you to stay, if it hurts too much. Probably we can manage it another way."

"Why did you want to leave me in England?"

"There ought to be somebody here to look after the factions. I should feel safer in France if I knew there was a strong man left behind. There is going to be trouble in Cornwall soon, between Tristram and Mark, and there is the Orkney feud. You know the difficulties. And it would be nice to think there was somebody looking after Gwen."

"Perhaps," said Lancelot, choosing the words with pain, "it would be better to trust somebody else."

"Don't be absurd. How could I trust anybody more? You would only have to show that mug of yours outside the dog kennel and all the thieves would run away at once."

"It is not a very handsome one."

"Cut-throat!" exclaimed the King affectionately, and he thumped his friend on the back. He went off to arrange about the expedition.

They had a year of joy, twelve months of the strange heaven which the salmon know on beds of river shingle, under the gin-clear water. For twenty-four years they were guilty, but this first year was the only one which seemed like happiness. Looking back on it, when they were old, they did not remember that in this year it had ever rained or frozen. The four seasons were coloured like the edge of a rose petal for them.

"I don't understand," said Lancelot, "why you should love me. Are you sure you do? Is there some mistake about it?"

"My Lance."

"But my face," he said. "I am so horrible. Now I can believe that God might love the world, whatever it was like, because of himself."

At other times, they were in a terror which came from him. Guenever did not feel remorse on her own account, but she caught it from her lover.

"I dare not think. Don't think. Kiss me, Jenny."

"Why think?"

"I can't help thinking."

"Dear Lance!"

Then there were different times when they quarrelled about nothing—but even the quarrels were those of lovers, which seemed sweet when they remembered them afterwards.

"Your toes are like the little pigs which went to market."

"I wish you would not say things like that. It is not respectful."

"Respectful!"

"Yes, respectful. Why shouldn't you be respectful? I am the Queen, after all."

"Do you seriously mean to tell me that I am supposed to treat you with respect? I suppose I am to kneel on one knee all the time and kiss your hand?"

"Why not?"

"I wish you wouldn't be so selfish. If there is one thing I can't stand, it is being treated like a possession."

"Selfish, indeed!"

· And the Queen would stamp her foot, or perhaps sulk for a day. But she forgave him when he had made a proper act of contrition.

One day, when they were at the stage of telling each other their private feelings, with a sort of innocent amazement when they corresponded, Lancelot gave the Queen his secret.

"Jenny, when I was little I hated myself. I don't know why. I was ashamed. I was a very holy little boy."

"You are not very holy now," she said, laughing. She did not understand what she was being told.

"One day my brother asked me to lend him an arrow. I had two or three specially straight ones, which I was very careful of, and his were a bit warped. I pretended that I had lost my straight arrows, and said I couldn't lend them to him."

"Little liar!"

"I know I was. Afterwards I had the most dreadful remorse for having told him the lie, and I thought I had been untrue to God. So I went out to a bed of stinging nettles that was on the moat, and put my arrow arm into them, as a punishment. I rolled up my sleeve and put it right in."

"Poor Lance! What an innocent you must have been."

"But, Jenny, they didn't sting me! I am sure I am right in remembering that they didn't sting me."

"Do you mean there was a miracle?"

"I don't know. It is difficult to be sure. I was such a dreamy boy, always living in a make-up world where I was Arthur's greatest knight. I may have made it up about the nettles. But I think I can remember the shock when they didn't sting."

"I am sure it was a miracle," said the Queen decidedly.

"Jenny, all my life I have wanted to do miracles. I have wanted to be holy. I suppose it was ambition or pride or some other unworthy thing. It was not enough for me to conquer the world—I wanted to conquer heaven too. I was so grasping that it was not enough to be the strongest knight—I had to be the best as well. That is the worst of making day-dreams. It is why I tried to keep away from you. I knew that if I was not pure, I could never do miracles.

And I did do a miracle, too: a splendid one. I got a girl out of some boiling water, who was enchanted into it. She was called Elaine. Then I lost my power. Now that we are together, I shall never be able to do my miracles any more."

He did not like to tell her the full truth about Elaine, for he thought that it would hurt her feelings to know that he had come to her as the second.

"Why not?"

"Because we are wicked."

"Personally I have never done a miracle," said the Queen, rather coldly. "So I have less to regret."

"But, Jenny, I am not regretting anything. You are my miracle, and I would throw them overboard all over again for the sake of you. I was only trying to tell you about the things I felt when I was small."

"Well, I can't say I understand."

"Can't you understand wanting to be good at things? No, I can see that you would not have to. It is only people who are lacking, or bad, or inferior, who have to be good at things. You have always been full and perfect, so you had nothing to make up for. But I have always been making up. I feel dreadful sometimes, even now, with you, when I know that I can't be the best knight any longer."

"Then we had better stop, and you can make a good confession, and do some more miracles."

"You know we can't stop."

"The whole thing seems fanciful to me," said the Queen. "I don't understand it. It seems unpractical and selfish."

"I know I am selfish. I can't help it. I try not to be. But how can I help being what I was made? Oh, can't you understand what I am telling you? I was lonely when I was small, and I worked hard at my exercises. I used to tell myself that I would be a great explorer, and cross the Chorasmian Waste: or I would be a great king, like Alexander or St. Louis: or a great healer: I would find out a balsam which cured wounds and give it away free: perhaps I would be a saint, and salve wounds just by touching them, or I would find something important—a relic of the True Cross, or the Holy Grail, or something like that. These were my dreams, Jenny. I am only telling you what I used to day-dream about. They are what I mean by my miracles, which are lost now. I have given you my hopes, Jenny, as a present from my love."

# 15

*The year of their happiness ended with Arthur's re-*
turn—and almost immediately collapsed in ruin, but not on
account of the King. The evening after his home-coming,
while he was still giving them details of the defeat of Claudas as they happened to come into his memory, there was a
disturbance at the Porter's Lodge, and Sir Bors was ushered into the Great Hall at dinner. He was Lancelot's
cousin, and had been spending a holiday at the castle of
Corbin, investigating the hauntings. He had some news for
Lancelot, which he told him in a whisper after dinner—but
unfortunately he was a misogynist, and, like most people of
that sort, he had the female failing of indiscretion. He told
the news to some of his bosom friends as well. Soon it was
all over the court. The news was that Elaine of Corbin had
given birth to a fine son, whom she had christened Galahad
—which was Lancelot's first name, as you remember.

"So this," said Guenever, when she next saw her lover
alone, "so this is why you lost your miracles. It was all lies
about your giving them to me."

"What do you mean?"

Guenever began to breathe through her nose. She was
feeling as if there were two red thumbs behind her eyeballs,
trying to push them out, and she did not want to look at
him. She was trying not to make a scene, and she dreaded
her heart. She had shame and hatred of what she might
say, but she could not help saying it. She was like a person
swimming in a rough sea.

"You know what I mean," she said bitterly, looking away.

"Jenny, I wanted to tell you, but it was too difficult to explain."

"I can understand the difficulty."

"It is not what you think."

"What I think!" she cried. "How do you know what I

think? I think what everybody would think—that you are a mean seducer, just a liar, you and your miracles. And I was fool enough to believe you."

Lancelot turned his head at each of her stabs, as if he were trying to let them glance off him. He looked on the ground, to hide his eyes. He had wide eyes, which generally gave him an expression of fear or surprise.

"Elaine means nothing to me," he said.

"Then she ought to do. How can you say that she means nothing to you when she is the mother of your child? When you tried to keep her secret? No, don't touch me, go away."

"I can't go away, when it is like this."

"If you touch me I shall go to the King."

"Guenever, I was made drunk at Corbin. Then they told me that you were waiting for me at Case, and they took me to a dark room with Elaine in it. I came away next morning."

"A clumsy lie."

"It is true."

"A baby wouldn't believe it."

"I can't make you believe it, if you don't want to. I drew my sword to kill Elaine, when I found out."

"I will have her killed."

"It was not her fault."

The Queen began plucking at the neck of her dress, as if it were too tight for her.

"You are standing up for her," she said. "You are in love with her, and deceiving me. I thought so all along."

"I swear I am telling the truth."

She suddenly gave up and began to cry.

"Why didn't you tell me before?" she asked. "Why didn't you tell me you had a baby? Why have you lied to me all the time? I suppose she was your famous miracle, which you were so proud of."

Lancelot, who also suffered from violent emotions, began to cry in turn. He put his arms around her.

"I didn't know I had one," he said. "I didn't want one. It was not my seeking."

"If you had told me the truth, I could have believed you."

"I wanted to tell you, but I couldn't. I was afraid you would be hurt."

"It has hurt me worse like this."

"I know it has."

The Queen dried her tears and looked at him, smiling like a spring shower. In a minute they were kissing, feeling like the green earth refreshed by rain. They thought that they understood each other once more—but their doubt had been planted. Now, in their love, which was stronger, there were the seeds of hatred and fear and confusion growing at the same time: for love can exist with hatred, each preying on the other, and this is what gives it its greatest fury.

# 16

*In the castle of Corbin, the child Elaine was making* ready for her journey. She was coming to capture Lancelot from Guenever, an expedition of which everybody except herself could feel the pathos. She had no weapons to fight with, and did not know how to fight. She was quite without character. Lancelot did not love her. And she was in the yet more hopeless position of loving him. She had nothing to oppose against the Queen's maturity except her own immaturity and humble love, nothing except the fat baby which she was carrying to its father—a baby which was to him only the symbol of a cruel trick. It was an expedition like that of an army without weapons against an impregnable fortress, an army which at the same time had its hands tied behind its back. Elaine, with an artlessness which could only be explained by the fact that she had spent most of her life in the seclusion of her magic cauldron, had decided to meet Guenever on her own ground. She had ordered gowns of the utmost magnificence and sophistication—and in these, which would only make her look all the more stupid and provincial, she was going to Camelot to fight her battle with the English Queen.

If Elaine had not been Elaine, she might have taken Galahad as her weapon. Pathos and proprietorship, rightly applied to a nature like Lancelot's, might have been successful in binding him. But Elaine was not clever, did not understand the attempt to bind her hero. She took Galahad because she adored him. She took him only because she did not want to be parted from her baby, and because she wanted to show him off to his father, and partly because she wanted to compare the faces. It was a year since she had set eyes on the man for whom her child-mind lived.

Lancelot, while Elaine was planning his capture, remained with the Queen at court. But he now remained without the temporary peace of heart which he had been able to invent for himself while the King was away. In the King's absence he had been able to drown himself in the passing minute—but Arthur was perpetually at his elbow now, as a comment on his treachery. He had not buried his love for Arthur in his passion for Guenever, but still felt for him. To a medieval nature like Lancelot's, with its fatal weakness for loving the highest when he saw it, this was a position of pain. He could not bear to be made to feel that his sentiment for Guenever was an ignoble sentiment, for it was the profound feeling of his life—yet every circumstance now conspired to make it seem ignoble. The hasty moments together, the locked doors and base contrivances, the guilty manœuvres which the husband's presence forced on the lovers—these had the effect of soiling what had no excuse unless it was beautiful. On top of this stain there was the torture of knowing that Arthur was kind, simple and upright—of knowing that he was always on the edge of hurting Arthur dreadfully, although he loved him. Then there was pain about Guenever herself, the tiny plant of bitterness which they had sown, or seen sown, in each other's eyes, on the occasion of their first quarrel of suspicion. It was a pain to him to be in love with a jealous and suspicious woman. She had given him a mortal blow by not believing his explanation about Elaine instantly. Yet he was unable not to love her. Finally there were the revolted elements of his own character—his strange desire for purity and honour and spiritual excellence. All these things, working together with the unconscious dread of Elaine's arrival with his son, broke his happiness without allowing him to escape. He seldom sat down, but strayed about with nervous movements, picking things up and setting them down without looking at them, walking to windows and looking out but seeing nothing.

For Guenever the dread of Elaine's arrival was not unconscious. She had known from the first moment that Elaine was bound to come. For her, however, as for all women, the dreads were in advance of the male horizon. Men often accuse women of driving them to unfaithfulness by senseless jealousy, before there has been any thought of unfaithfulness on their own part. Yet the thought was probably there, unconscious and undetectable except to women. The great Anna Karenina, for instance, forced Vronsky into a certain position by the causeless jealousy of a maniac—yet that position was the only real solution to their problem, and it was the inevitable solution. Seeing so much further into the future than he did, she pressed towards it with passionate tread, wrecking the present because the future was bound to be a wreck.

So with Guenever. Probably she was not over-strained by Elaine's immediate problem. Probably she had no real suspicion against that side of Lancelot. Yet, with her prescience, she was aware of dooms and sorrows outside her lover's purview. It would not be accurate to say that she was aware of them in a logical sense, but they were present in her deeper mind. It is a pity that language is such a clumsy weapon that we cannot say that a mother was "unconscious" of her baby crying in the next room—with the meaning that the mother somehow, unconsciously, knew that it *was* crying. Facts of which Guenever was subconscious, in this sense, included the whole of the Arthur-Lancelot situation, most of the future tragedy at court, and the grievous fact of her own childlessness—which was never to be remedied.

She said to herself that Lancelot had betrayed her, that she was the victim of Elaine's cunning, that her lover was sure to betray her again. She tormented herself with a thousand words of the same sort. But what she felt to herself, in the uncharted regions of her heart, was a different matter. Perhaps she was actually jealous, not of Elaine, but of the baby. Perhaps it was Lancelot's love for Arthur that she feared. Or it may have been a fear of the whole position, of its instability and the nemesis inherent in it. Women know, far better than men, that God's laws are not mocked. They have more cause to know it.

Whatever the explanation of Guenever's attitude, the fruits of it were pain for her lover. She became as restless as he was, more unreasonable, and much more cruel.

Arthur's feelings completed the misery of the court. He, unfortunately for himself, had been beautifully brought up. His teacher had educated him as the child is educated in the womb, where it lives the history of man from fish to mammal—and, like the child in the womb, he had been protected with love meanwhile. The effect of such an education was that he had grown up without any of the useful accomplishments for living—without malice, vanity, suspicion, cruelty, and the commoner forms of selfishness. Jealousy seemed to him the most ignoble of vices. He was sadly unfitted for hating his best friend or for torturing his wife. He had been given too much love and trust to be good at these things.

Arthur was not one of those interesting characters whose subtle motives can be dissected. He was only a simple and affectionate man, because Merlyn had believed that love and simplicity were worth having.

Now, with a situation developing before his eyes which has always been notoriously difficult of solution—so difficult that it has been given a label and called the Eternal Triangle, as if it were a geometrical problem like the Pons Asinorum in Euclid—Arthur was only able to retreat. It is generally the trustful and optimistic people who can afford to retreat. The loveless and faithless ones are compelled by their pessimism to attack. Arthur was strong and gentle enough to hope that, if he trusted Lancelot and Guenever, things would come right in the end. It seemed to him that this was better than trying to bring them right at once by such courses as, for instance, by cutting off the lovers' heads for treason.

Arthur did not know that Lancelot and Guenever were lovers. He had never actually found them together or unearthed proofs of their guilt. It was in the nature of his bold mind to hope, in these circumstances, that he would not find them together—rather than to lay a trap by which to wreck the situation. This is not to say that he was a conniving husband. It is simply that he was hoping to weather the trouble by refusing to become conscious of it. Unconsciously, of course, he knew perfectly well that they were sleeping together—knew too, unconsciously, that if he were to ask his wife, she would admit it. Her three great virtues were courage, generosity and honesty. So he could not ask her.

Such an attitude to the position did not make it easier for the King to be happy. He became, not excitable like Guenever nor restless like Lancelot, but reserved. He moved about his own palace like a mouse. Yet he made one effort to grasp the nettle.

"Lancelot," said the King, finding him one afternoon in the rose garden, "you have been looking wretched lately. Is there anything the matter?"

Lancelot had snapped off one of the roses, and was pinching the sepals. These ancient roses, it has lately been asserted, were so constructed that the five sepals did actually stick out beyond the petals—just as they are represented to do in the heraldic rose.

"Is it anything," asked the King, hoping against hope, "about this girl who is said to have had your baby?"

If Arthur had left him alone with the first question, and a silence to answer it in, perhaps they would have had the matter out. But Arthur was afraid of what might come in the silence, and, once he had given the lead of the second question, the chance was gone.

"Yes," said Lancelot.

"You could not bring yourself to marry her, I suppose?"

"I don't love her."

"Well, you know your own business best."

Lancelot, with an uncontrollable desire to get some of his misery off his chest by telling about it—and yet unable to tell the true story to this particular listener—began a long rigmarole about Elaine. He began telling Arthur half the truth: how he was ashamed and had lost his miracles. But he was forced to make Elaine the central figure of this confession, and, after half an hour, he had unwittingly presented the King with a story to believe in—a story with which Arthur could content himself if he did not want to be conscious of the true tale. This half-truth was of great use to the poor fellow, who learned to substitute it for the real trouble in later years. We civilized people, who would immediately fly to divorce courts and alimony and other forms of attrition in such circumstances, can afford to look with proper contempt upon the spineless cuckold. But Arthur was only a medieval savage. He did not understand our civilization, and knew no better than to try to be too decent for the degradation of jealousy.

Guenever was the next person to find Lancelot in the rose garden. She was all sweetness and reason.

"Lance, have you heard the news? A messenger has just arrived to say that this girl who is persecuting you is on her way to court, bringing the baby. She will be here this evening."

"I knew she would come."

"We shall have to do our best for her, of course. Poor child, I expect she is unhappy."

"It is not my fault if she is unhappy."

"No, of course it isn't. But people get made unhappy by the world, and we must help them when we can."

"Jenny, it is sweet of you to be kind about it."

He turned towards her, and made a movement to catch her hand. Her words had made him hope that all would be well. But Jenny took her hand away.

"No, dear," she said. "I don't want you to make love to me until she has gone. I want you to be quite free."

"Free?"

"She is the mother of your baby, and she is unmarried. We two can't ever be married. I want you to be able to marry her if you would like it, because that is the only thing which can be done."

"But, Jenny——"

"No, Lance. We must be sensible. I want you to keep away from me while she is here, and to find out whether you could love her after all. It is the least that I can do for you."

# 17

Elaine arrived at the yawning barbican, and Guenever kissed her coolly. "You are welcome to Camelot," she said. "Five thousand welcomes."

"Thank you," said Elaine.

They looked at each other with hostile, smiling faces.

"Lancelot will be delighted to see you."

"Oh!"

"Everybody knows about the baby, dear. There is nothing to be shy about. The King and I are quite excited to see whether he will be like his father."

"It is kind of you," said Elaine uncomfortably.

"You must let me be the first to see him. You have called him Galahad, have you not? Is he strong? Does he notice things?"

"He weighs fifteen pounds," the girl announced with pride. "You can see him now, if you like."

Guenever took hold of herself with an effort which was hardly noticeable, and began fussing with Elaine's wraps.

"No, dear," she said. "I must not be so selfish as that. You must rest after your long journey, and probably Baby will have to be settled down. I can come to see him this evening, when he has had a sleep. There will be plenty of time."

But she had to see the baby in the end.

When Lancelot next met the Queen, her sweetness and reason were gone. She was cold and proud, and spoke as if she were addressing a meeting.

"Lancelot," she said, "I think you ought to go to your son. Elaine is grieving because you have not been to see him."

"Have you seen him?"

"Yes."

"Is he ugly?"

"He takes after Elaine."

"Thank God. I will go at once."

The Queen called him back.

"Lancelot," she said, taking a breath through her nose, "I am trusting you not to make love to Elaine under my roof. If you and I are to keep apart until it is settled, it is only fair that you should keep away from her."

"I don't want to make love to Elaine."

"You must say that, of course. And I will believe you. But if you break your word this time, it will be finished between us. Absolutely finished."

"I have said all I can say."

"Lancelot, you have deceived me once, so how can I be sure? I have put Elaine in the next room to mine, and I shall see if you go to it. I want you to keep in your own room."

"If you like."

"I shall send for you some time tonight, if I can get away from Arthur. I will not tell you when. If you are not in your room when I send for you, I shall know that you are with Elaine."

The girl was weeping in her chamber, while Dame Brisen arranged the cradle for the little boy.

"I saw him in the archery butts, and he saw me too. But he looked away. He made an excuse and went out. He has not even seen our baby."

"There, there," said Dame Brisen. "Lawks a mussy."

"I ought not to have come. It has only made me more miserable, and him too."

" 'Tis that there Queen."

"She is beautiful, isn't she?"

The Dame said darkly: "Handsome is as handsome does."

Elaine began to sob helplessly. She looked repulsive, with her red nose, as people do when they abdicate their dignity.

"I wanted him to be pleased."

There was a knock on the door, and Lancelot came in—which made her quickly dry the eyes. They greeted each other with constraint.

"I am glad you have come to Camelot," he said. "I hope you are well?"

"Yes, thank you."

"How is—the baby?"

"Your lordship's son," said Dame Brisen with emphasis.

She turned the cradle towards him, and moved back so that he could see.

"My son."

They stood looking down at the fresh thing, helpless and only half alive. They were strong, as the poet sings, and it was weak—one day they would be weak, and it strong.

"Galahad," said Elaine, and she leaned over the wrappings, making the foolish gestures and meaningless sounds which mothers delight to use when their babies are beginning to pay attention. Galahad clenched his fist and hit himself in the eye with it, an achievement which seemed to give pleasure to the women. Lancelot watched them in amazement "My son," he thought. "It is a part of me, yet it is fair. It does not seem to be ugly. How can you tell with babies?" He held out his right finger to Galahad, putting it inside the fat palm of his hand, which clutched it. The hand looked as if it had been fitted to the arm by a cunning doll maker. There was a deep crease round the wrist.

"Oh, Lancelot!" cried Elaine.

She tried to throw herself into his arms, but he pushed her off. He looked at Brisen over her shoulder with fear and exasperation. He made a wild, senseless sound—and rushed out of the room. Elaine, unsupported, sank down beside the bed and began to sob more than ever. Brisen, standing rigid, as she had stood to bear Sir Lancelot's glare, looked at the closed door with an inscrutable expression.

# 18

*In the morning he and Elaine were summoned to* the Queen's chamber. He, for his part, went with a kind of happiness. He was remembering how Guenever must have pleaded illness on the previous evening, so as to leave the King's room. Her lover had been sent for in the darkness. The usual conniving hand had led him by the finger on tiptoe to the chosen bed. In the silence forced on them by being next to Arthur's chamber, but in passionate tenderness, they had done their best to make it up. Lancelot was happier today than he had been since the story of Elaine started. He felt that if he could only persuade his Guenever to make a clean break with the King, so that everything was in the open, there might still be a possibility of honour.

Guenever was stiff, as if she were in a rigor, and her face was drained white—except that there was a red spot on either side of her nostrils. She looked as if she had been seasick. She was alone.

"So," said the Queen.

Elaine looked straight in her blue eyes, but Lancelot stopped as if he had been shot.

"So."

They stood, waiting for Guenever to speak or die.

"Where did you go last night?"

"I——"

"Don't tell me," shouted the Queen, moving her hand so that they could see a ball of handkerchief in it, which she had torn to pieces. "Traitor! Traitor! Get out of my castle with your strumpet."

"Last night——" said Lancelot. His head was whirling

with a desperation which neither of the women noticed.

"Don't speak to me. Don't lie to me. Go!"

Elaine said calmly: "Sir Lancelot was in my room last night. My woman Brisen brought him in the dark."

The Queen began pointing at the door. She made stabbing movements at it with her finger, and, in her trembling, her hair began to come down. She looked hideous.

"Get out! Get out! And you go too, you animal! How dare you speak so in my castle? How dare you admit it to me? Take your fancy man and go!"

Lancelot was breathing heavily and looking upon the Queen with a fixed stare. He might have been unconscious.

"He thought he was coming to you," said Elaine. She had her hands folded together, and watched the Queen passively.

"The old lie!"

"It is not a lie," said Elaine. "I could not live without him. Brisen helped me to pretend."

Guenever ran up to her with tottering steps. She wanted to hit Elaine in the mouth, but the girl did not move. It was as if she was hoping that Guenever would hit her.

"Liar!" screamed the Queen.

She ran back to Lancelot, where he had sat down on a chest and was staring blankly at the floor, with his head between his hands. She caught hold of his mantle and began pushing or heaving him toward the door, but he would not move.

"So you taught her the story! Why couldn't you think of a new one? You might have given me something interesting. I suppose you thought the old, stale stuff would do?"

"Jenny——" he said, without looking up.

The Queen tried to spit on him, but she had never practised spitting.

"How dare you call me Jenny? You are reeking of her still. I am the Queen, the Queen of England! I am not your trull!"

"Jenny——"

"Get out of my castle," screamed the Queen at the top of her voice. "Never show your face in it again. Your evil, ugly, beastlike face."

Lancelot suddenly said to the floor, in a loud voice· "Galahad!"

Then he took down his hands from his head and looked

up, so that they could see the face she spoke of. It had a surprised look, and one of the eyes had begun to squint.

He said, more quietly: "Jenny." But he looked like a blind man.

The Queen opened her mouth to say something, though nothing came out.

"Arthur," he said. Then he gave a loud shriek, and jumped straight out of the window, which was on the first floor. They could hear him crash into some bushes, with a crump and crackle of boughs, and then he was running off through the trees and shrubbery with a loud sort of warbling cry, like hounds hunting. The hullabaloo faded into the distance, and there was silence in the chamber with the women.

Elaine, who was now as white as the Queen had been but still held herself proud and upright, said: "You have driven him mad. His wits must have been weak."

Guenever said nothing.

"Why have you driven him mad?" asked Elaine. "You have a fine husband of your own, the greatest in the land. You are a Queen, with honour and happiness and a home. I had no home, and no husband, and my honour was gone too. Why would you not let me have him?"

The Queen was silent.

"I loved him," said Elaine. "I bore a fine son for him, who will be the best knight of the world."

"Elaine," said Guenever, "go away from my court."

"I am going."

Guenever suddenly caught her by the skirt.

"Don't tell anybody," she said quickly. "Don't say anything about what happened. It will be his death if you do."

Elaine freed the skirt.

"Did you expect I would?"

"But what are we to do?" cried the Queen. "Is he mad? Will he get better? What will happen? Ought we to do something? What are we to say?"

Elaine would not stay to talk with her. At the door, however, she turned with a trembling lip.

"Yes, he is mad," she said. "You have won him, and you have broken him. What will you do with him next?"

When the door was closed, Guenever sat down. She dropped her tattered handkerchief. Then—slowly, deeply,

primitively—she began to cry. She put her face in her hands
and throbbed with sorrow. (Sir Bors, who did not care for
the Queen, once said to her: "Fie on your weeping, for ye
weep never but when there is no boot.")

# 19

*King Pelles was sitting in the solar with Sir Bliant*
two years later. It was a fine winter morning with the fields
frosted, no wind, and a light fog which was not enough to
confuse the pigeons. Sir Bliant, who had been staying the
night, was dressed in scarlet furred with miniver. His horse
and squire were in the courtyard, ready to take him back to
Castle Bliant, but the two men were having their elevenses
before he started. Sitting with their hands spread to the
splendid log fire, they sipped their mulled wine, nibbled
pastry, and talked about the Wild Man.

"I am sure he must have been a gentleman," said Sir
Bliant. "He kept doing things which nobody but a gentleman would do. He had a natural leaning to arms."

"Where is he now?" asked King Pelles.

"God He knows. He vanished one morning when the
hounds were at Castle Bliant. But I am sure he was a gentleman."

They sipped and gazed into the flames.

"If you want to have my opinion," added Sir Bliant, lowering his voice, "I believe he was Sir Lancelot."

"Nonsense," said the King.

"He was tall and strong."

"Sir Lancelot is dead," said the King. "God be good to
him. Everybody knows that."

"It was not proved."

"If he had been Sir Lancelot, you could not have mis-
taken him. He was the ugliest man I have ever seen."

"I never met him," said Sir Bliant.

"It was proved that Lancelot ran mad in his shirt and

breeches, until he got gored by a wild boar and died in a hermitage."

"When was that?"

"Last Christmas."

"It was about the same time that my Wild Man ran away with the hunt. Ours was a boar hunt too."

"Well," said King Pelles, "they *may* have been the same person. If they were, it is interesting. How did your fellow arrive?"

"It was during the summer questing, the year before last. I had my pavilion pitched in a fair meadow, in the usual way, and I was inside it, waiting for something to turn up. I was playing chess, I remember. Then there was a frightful row outside, and I went out, and there was this naked lunatic lashing on my shield. My dwarf was sitting on the ground, rubbing his neck—the maniac had half broken it —and he was calling out for help. I went to the fellow and said: 'Look here, my good man, you don't want to be fighting me. Come now, you lay down that sword and be a good chap.' He had got hold of one of my own swords, you know, and I could see that he was mad straightway. I said: 'You ought not to be fighting, old boy. I can see that what you need is a good sleep and something to eat.' And, really, he did look dreadful. He was like a man who had been watching a passager for three nights. His eyeballs were bright red."

"What did he say?"

"He just said: 'As for that, come not too nigh: for, an thou do, wit thou well I will slay thee.'"

"Strange."

"Yes, it was strange, wasn't it? That he should have known the high language, I mean."

"What did he do?"

"Well, I was only in my gown, and the man looked dangerous. I went back into the pavilion and did on my armour."

King Pelles handed him another pasty, which Sir Bliant accepted with a nod.

"When I was armed," he went on, with his mouth full, "I went out with a spare sword to disarm the chap. I did not intend to strike him, or anything like that, but he was a homicidal maniac and there was no other way of getting the sword from him. I went up to him like you do to a dog, holding out my hand and saying: 'There's a poor fellow: come now, there's a good chap.' I thought it would be easy."

"Was it?"

"The moment he saw me in armour, and with a sword, he came straight at me like a tiger. I never saw such an attack. I tried to parry a bit, and I dare say I would have killed him in self-defence, if he had given me a chance. But the next thing I knew was that I was sitting on the ground, and my nose and ears were bleeding. He had given me a buffet, you know, which troubled my brains."

"Goodness," said King Pelles.

"The next thing he did was to throw away his sword and rush straight into the pavilion. My poor wife was there, in bed, with no clothes on. But he just jumped straight into bed with her, snatched the coverlet, rolled himself up in it, and went fast asleep."

"Must have been a married man," said King Pelles.

"The wife gave some frightful shrieks, hopped out of bed on the other side, jumped into her smock, and came running out to me. I was still a bit astonied, lying on the ground, so she thought I was dead. I can tell you we had a fine to-do."

"Did he sleep right through it?"

"He slept like a log. We managed to pull ourselves together eventually, and the wife put one of my gauntlets down my neck to stop the nosebleed, and then we talked it over. My dwarf, who is a splendid little chap, said we ought not to do him any harm, because he was touched by God. As a matter of fact, it was the dwarf who suggested that he might be Sir Lancelot. There was a good deal of talk about the Lancelot mystery that year."

Sir Bliant paused to take another bite.

"In the end," he said, "we took him to Castle Bliant in a horse litter, bed and all. He never stirred. When we got him there, we tied his hands and feet against the hour when he would wake up. I am sorry about it now, but we could not chance it according to what we knew at the time. We kept him in a comfortable room, with clean clothes, and the wife gave him a lot of nourishing food, to build up his strength, but we thought it best to keep him handcuffed all the same. We kept him for a year and a half."

"How did he get away?"

"I was coming to that. It is the plum of the story. One

afternoon I was out in the forest for half an hour's questing, when I was set upon by two knights from behind."

"Two knights?" asked the King. "From behind?"

"Yes. Two of them, and from behind. It was Sir Bruce Saunce Pité and a friend of his."

King Pelles thumped his knee.

"That man," he exclaimed, "is a public menace. I can't think why somebody doesn't do away with him."

"The trouble is to catch the fellow. However, I was telling you about the Wild Man. Sir Bruce and the other one had me at a considerable disadvantage, as you will admit, and I regret to say that I was compelled to run away."

Sir Bliant stopped and gazed into the fire. Then he cheered up.

"Ah, well," he said, "we can't all be heroes, can we?"

"Not all," said King Pelles.

"I was sore wounded," said Sir Bliant, discovering a formula, "and I felt myself faint."

"Quite."

"These two came galloping with me all the way to the Castle, one on either side, and they kept hitting me all the time. I don't know to this day how I got away with my life."

"It was written in the Stones," said the King.

"We rode past the barbican loopholes, hell-for-leather, and it was there that the Wild Man must have seen us. We kept him in the barbican chamber, you know. Well, he saw us at all events, and we found out afterwards that he broke his fetters with his bare hands. They were iron fetters, and he had them on his ankles also. He wounded himself dreadfully doing it. Then he came hurling out of the postern, with his hands all bloody and the chains flying about him, and he pulled Bruce's ally out of the saddle, and took his sword from him, and walloped Bruce on the head so that he knocked him noseling, clean off his horse. The second knight tried to stab the Wild Man from behind—he was absolutely unarmed—but I cut off the fellow's hand at the wrist, just as he stabbed. Then the both of them caught their horses, and rode away for all they were fit. They rode more than a pace, I can tell you."

"That was Bruce all over."

"My brother was staying with me that year. I said to him: 'Why ever have we kept this dear fellow chained up?' I was ashamed when I saw his wounded hands. 'He is happy and gracious,' I said, 'and now he has saved my life. We must never chain him up again, but give him his freedom and do everything we can for him.' You know, Pelles, I liked that Wild Man. He was gentle and grateful, and he used to call me Lord. It is a dreadful thing to think that he might have been the great Dulac, and us keeping him tied up and letting him call me Lord so humbly."

"What happened in the end?"

"He stayed quietly for several months. Then the boar hounds came to the castle, and one of the followers left his horse and spear by a tree. The Wild Man took them and rode away. It was as if he were excited by gentlemanly pursuits, you know—as if a suit of armour, or a fight, or a hunt, stirred something in his poor head. They made him want to join in."

"Poor boy," said the King. "Poor, poor boy! It might well have been Sir Lancelot. He is known to have been killed by a boar last Christmas."

"I should like to know that story."

"If your man was Lancelot, he rode straightaway after the boar they were hunting. It was a famous boar which had troubled the hounds for several years, and that was why the field was not on foot. Lancelot was the only man up at the kill, and the boar slew his horse. It gave him a dreadful wound in the thigh, riving him to the hough bone, before he cut off its head. He killed it near a hermitage, with one blow. The hermit came out, but Lancelot was so mad with his pain and everything that he threw his sword at the man. I heard this from a knight who was actually there. He said there was no doubt about its being Sir Lancelot—he was ugly and all that—and he said that he and the hermit carried him into the hermitage after he had fainted. He said that nobody could possibly have recovered from the wound, and that, in any case, he saw him die. What made him most certain, he said, about the Wild Man being a great knight, was that when he was standing in his death agony beside the dead boar, he spoke to the hermit as 'Fellow'. So you see, there may have been a touch of sanity at the end."

"Poor Lancelot," said Sir Bliant.

"God be good to him," said King Pelles.

"Amen."

"Amen," repeated Sir Bliant, looking into the fire. Then he stood up and shook his shoulders.

"I shall have to be going," he said. "How is your daughter? I forgot to ask."

King Pelles sighed, and stood up also.

"She spends her time at the convent," he said. "I believe she is going to be received next year. However, we are to be allowed to see her next Saturday, when she comes home on a short visit."

# 20

*After Sir Bliant had ridden away, King Pelles* stumped upstairs to do some biblical genealogy. He was puzzled about the Lancelot affair, and interested in it on account of his grandson Galahad. All of us have been driven nearly mad by our wives and sweethearts, but King Pelles was aware that there is a tough streak in human nature which generally prevents us from being quite driven. He thought it eccentric of Lancelot, to say the least, to lose his reason over a lover's tiff—and he wanted to find out, by looking up the Ban genealogy, whether there had been a streak of lunacy in the family which could account for it. If there were, it might descend on Galahad. The child might have to be sent to the hospital of Bethlehem, which later ages were to call Bedlam. There had been enough trouble without that.

"Ban's father," said King Pelles to himself, polishing his spectacles and blowing dust off numerous works of Heraldry, Genealogy, Nigromancy, and Mystical Mathematics, "was King Lancelot of Benwick, who married the King of Ireland's daughter. King Lancelot's father, in his turn, was Jonas, who married the daughter of Manuel of Gaul. Now who was the father of Jonas?"

When one comes to think of it, there may have been a weak link in Lancelot's mind. This may have been the cupboard skeleton we noticed, ten years ago, at the back of the small boy's head as he turned the kettle-hat to and fro, in the Armoury of Benwick Castle.

"Nacien," said King Pelles. "Drat this Nacien. There seem to be two of him."

He had got back, through Lisais, Hellias le Grose, Nacien the Hermit—from whom Lancelot probably inherited his visionary tendency—and Nappus, to a second Nacien, who, if he existed, would quite upset the King's theory that Lancelot was but the eighth degree from Our Lord. As a matter of fact, nearly all hermits seemed to be called Nacien in those days.

"Drat him," repeated the King, and he glanced out of the window to see what the noise was about in the street outside the castle.

A Wild Man—there seemed to be a lot of them about this morning—was being run through Corbin by the villagers who had once gone out to welcome Lancelot. He was naked, as thin as a ghost, and he ran along with his hands over his head, to protect it. The small boys running all round him were throwing turfs at him. He stopped every now and then, and caught one of the boys and threw him over the hedge. This only made the boys throw stones. King Pelles could clearly see the blood running over his high cheek-bones, and the sunken cheeks, and the hunted eyes, and the blue shadows between his ribs. He could also see that the man was making for the castle.

In the castle yard, when King Pelles had gone dot-and-carry downstairs, there was quite a crowd of castle folk standing round the Wild Man in admiration. They had lowered the portcullis, to keep the village boys out, and they were disposed to treat the fugitive with kindness.

"Look at his wounds," said one of the squires. "Look at that great scar there. Perhaps he was a knight errant before he went mad, and so we ought to give him courtesy."

The Wild Man stood in the middle of the ring, while the ladies giggled and the pages pointed. He hung his head and stood motionless, without speaking, waiting for what was to be done to him next.

"Perhaps he is Sir Lancelot."

There was a great laugh at this.

"No, but seriously. It was never exactly proved that Lancelot is dead."

King Pelles went right up to the Wild Man and looked into his face. He had to stoop sideways to do this.

"Are you Sir Lancelot?" he asked.

The emaciated, dirty, bearded face: its eyes never even blinked.

"Are you?" repeated the King.

But there was no answer from the dummy.

"He is deaf and dumb," said the King. "We will keep him as a jester. He looks funny enough, I must say. Somebody get the man some clothes—you know, comic clothes—and put him to sleep in the pigeon house. Give him some clean straw."

The dummy suddenly lifted both its hands and let out a roar, which made everybody start back. The King dropped his spectacles. Then it lowered its hands again and stood sheepishly, so that the people gave a nervous giggle.

"Better lock him in," said the King wisely. "Safety first. And do not hand him his food—throw it to him. Can't be too careful."

So Sir Lancelot was led away to the pigeon house, to be King Pelles' fool—and there he was locked in, and fed by throwing, and lodged on clean straw.

When the King's nephew, a boy called Castor, came to be knighted on the following Saturday—this was the ceremony which Elaine was coming home to attend—there was gaiety in the castle. The King, who was addicted to festivals and ceremonials of all sorts, celebrated the occasion royally, by presenting a new gown to every man on the estate. He also celebrated it, regrettably, by making too generous a use of the cellars over which Dame Brisen's husband presided.

"Wossle," cried the King.

"Drink hail," replied Sir Castor, who was on his best behaviour.

"Everybody gotter gown?" shouted the King.

"Yes, thank you, Your Majesty," replied the attendants.

"Sure?"

"Quite sure, Your Majesty."

"Thas alri, then. Goo' ole gown!"

And the King wrapped himself in his own gown with great affection. He was a different man on occasions like this.

"Everybody wants to thank Your Majesty very much for his generous present."

"Notter tall."

"Three cheers for King Pelles."

"Hurrah, hurrah, hurrah!"

"Warrabout the fool?" inquired the King suddenly. "Fool gotter gown? Where's the pore fool?"

There was a silence at this, for nobody had remembered to put a gown aside for Sir Lancelot.

"Notter gown? Nottergotter gown?" cried the King. "Fesha fool at once."

Sir Lancelot was fetched from the pigeon house, for the royal favour. He stood still in the torchlight with some straws in his beard, a pitiful figure in his jester's patch-work.

"Pore fool," said the King sadly. "Pore fool. Here, have mine."

And, in spite of all remonstrances and advices to the contrary, King Pelles struggled out of his costly robe, which he popped over Lancelot's head.

"Lettim loose," cried the King. "Givim holly-holly day. Karnkeepamanlocktupforever."

Sir Lancelot, standing upright in the grand dress, looked strangely stately in the Great Hall. If only his beard had been trimmed—our clean-shaven generation has forgotten what a difference the trimming of a beard can make—if only he had not starved away to a skeleton in the cell of the poor hermit after the boar hunt—if only he had not been rumoured to be dead—but, even as it was, a sort of awe came into the Hall. The King did not notice it. With measured tread Sir Lancelot walked back to his pigeon loft, and the house carls made an avenue for him as he went.

# 21

*Elaine had done the ungraceful thing as usual.* Guenever, in similar circumstances, would have been sure to grow pale and interesting—but Elaine had only grown plump. She walked in the castle garden with her companions, dressed in the white clothes of a novice, and there was a clumsy action in her walk. Galahad, now three years old, walked with her, holding hands.

It was not that Elaine was going to be a nun because she was desperate. She was not going to spend the rest of her life acting the cinema nun. A woman can forget a lot of love in two years—or at any rate she can pack it away, and grow accustomed to it, and hardly remember it more than a business-man might remember an occasion when, by ill-luck, he failed to make an investment which would have made him a millionaire.

Elaine was going to leave her son and become the bride of Christ, because she saw that this was the only thing to do. It was not a dramatic thing, and perhaps it was not very reverent—but she knew that she would never again love any human person as she had loved her dead knight. So she was giving in. She could not tack against the wind any longer.

She was not moping for Lancelot, nor did she weep for him on her pillow. She hardly ever thought of him. He had worn a place for himself in some corner of her heart, as a sea shell, always boring against the rock, might do. The making of the place had been her pain. But now the shell was safely in the rock. It was lodged, and ground no longer. Elaine, walking in the garden with her girls, thought only about the ceremony at which Sir Castor had been knighted, and whether there would be enough cakes for the feast, and that Galahad's stockings needed mending.

One of the girls who had been playing a kind of ball game to keep warm—the same game as Nausicaa was playing when Ulysses arrived—came running back to Elaine from the shrubbery by the well. Her ball had taken her in that direction.

"There is a Man," she whispered, much as if it had been a rattlesnake. "There is a Man, sleeping by the well!"

Elaine was interested—not because it was a man, nor because the girl was frightened, but because it was unusual to sleep out of doors in January.

"Hush, then," said Elaine. "We will go and see."

The plump novice in the white clothes who tiptoed over to Lancelot, the homely girl going composedly towards him with a round face which had stubbornly refused to accept the noble traces of grief, the young matron who had been thinking about Galahad's mending—this person was not conscious of vulnerability or needs. She went over calmly and innocently, busy about quite different concerns, like the thoughtless rabbit who goes hop-and-nibble along the accustomed path. But the wire loop tightens suddenly.

Elaine recognized Lancelot in two heartbeats. The first beat was a rising one which faltered at the top. The second one caught up with it, picked its momentum from the crest of the wave, and both came down together like a rearing horse that falls.

Lancelot was stretched out in his knightly gown. Sir Bliant, in remarking that gentlemanly things seemed to stir something in his head, had noticed truly. Moved by the gown, by some strange memory of miniver and colour, the poor Wild Man had gone from the King's table to the well. There, alone in the darkness, without a mirror, he had washed his face. He had swilled out his eye sockets with bony knuckles. With a currycomb and a pair of shears from the stables he had tried to arrange his hair.

Elaine sent her women away. She gave Galahad's hand to one of them, and he went without protest. He was a mysterious child.

Elaine knelt down beside Sir Lancelot and looked at him. She did not touch him or cry. She lifted her hand to stroke his thin one, but thought better of it. She squatted on her hams. Then, after a long time, she did begin to cry—but it was for Lancelot, for his tired eyes smoothed in sleep, and for the white scars on his hands.

"Father," said Elaine, "if you don't help me now, nobody ever can."

"What is it, my dear?" asked the King. "I have a headache."

Elaine paid no attention.

"Father, I have found Sir Lancelot."

"Who?"

"Sir Lancelot."

"Nonsense," said the King. "Lancelot was killed by a boar."

"He is asleep in the garden."

The King suddenly pulled himself out of his chair of state.

"I knew it all along," he said. "Only I was too stupid to know. It is the Wild Man. Obviously."

He reeled a little and put his hand to his head.

"Leave this to me," said the King. "You let me deal. I

know exactly what to do. Butler! Brisen! Where the devil
has everybody gone to? Hi! Hi! Oh, there you are. Now,
butler, you go and fetch your wife, Dame Brisen, and get
two other men that we can trust. Let me see. Get Humbert
and Gurth. Where did you say he was?"

"Asleep by the well," said Elaine quickly.

"Quite. So everybody must be told to keep out of the rose
garden. Do you hear, butler? All people are to avoid, that
none may be in the way where the King will come. And get
a sheet. A strong sheet. We shall have to carry him in it,
by the four corners. And get the tower room ready. Tell
Brisen to air the bedclothes. Better have a feather bed. Light
a fire, and fetch the doctor. Tell him to look up Madness in
*Bartholomeus Anglicus*. Oh, and you had better get some
jellies made, and things like that. In the heaviness of his
sleep we shall have to put fresh garments on him."

The next time he woke they could see that his eyes were
clear. But he was evidently in a pitiful state of mind. He was
relying on them to save him.

The third time he woke, he said: "O Lord Jesus, how did
I get here?"

They said the usual things about resting now, and not
talking till he was stronger, and so forth. The doctor waved
his hand to the Royal Orchestra, who immediately struck up
with *Jesu Christes Milde Moder*—since Dr. Bartholomew's
book had recommended that madmen should be gladded
with instruments. Everybody watched hopefully, to see the
effect, but Lancelot grabbed the King's hand and cried in
anguish: "For God's sake, my lord, tell me how I came
here?"

Elaine put her hand on his forehead and made him lie
down.

"You came like a madman," she said, "and nobody knew
who you were. You have been having a breakdown."

Lancelot turned his puzzled eyes on her, and smiled
nervously.

"I have been making a fool of myself," he said.

Later he asked: "Did many people see me while I was
mad?"

# 22

*Lancelot's body revenged itself on his mind. He lay* in bed for a fortnight in the airy bedroom with an ache in every bone, while Elaine kept herself outside the room. She had him at her mercy, and could have nursed him day and night. But there was something in her heart—either decency, or pride, or generosity, or humility, or the determination not to be a cannibal—which spared him. She visited him not more than once a day, and thrust nothing on him.

One day he stopped her as she was going out. He was sitting up in a day-gown, and his hands lay still in his lap.

"Elaine," he said, "I suppose I ought to be making plans."

She waited for her sentence.

"I cannot stay here for ever," he said.

"You know you will be welcome as long as you like."

"I cannot go back to court."

Elaine remarked, with hesitation: "My father would give you a castle, if you like, and we—could live there together."

He looked at her, and looked away.

"Or you could have the castle."

Lancelot took her hand and said: "Elaine, I don't know what to say. I can't very well say anything."

"I know you don't love me."

"Do you think we should be happy, then?"

"I only know when I shall be unhappy."

"I don't want you to be unhappy. But there are different ways of being that. Don't you think it might turn out that you would be more unhappy if we lived together?"

"I should be the happiest woman in the world."

"Look, Elaine, our only hope is to speak plainly, even if it sounds horrible. You know that I don't love you, and that I do love the Queen. It is an accident which has happened and it can't be changed. Things do happen like that: I can't alter it. And you have trapped me twice. If it had not been for you, I should still be at court. Do you think we could ever be happy, living together, like that?"

"You were my man," said Elaine proudly, "before you were ever the Queen's."

He passed a hand over his eyes.

"Do you want to have a husband on those terms?"

"There is Galahad," said Elaine.

They sat side by side, looking into the fire. She did not cry or bid for pity—and he knew she was sparing him these things.

He said, with difficulty: "I will stay with you, Elaine, if you want me to. I don't understand why you should want it. I am fond of you, very fond of you. I don't know why, after what has happened. I don't want you to be hurt. But, Elaine—I can't marry you."

"I don't mind."

"It is because—it is because marriage is a contract. I—I have always been proud of my Word. And if I do not—and if I have not that feeling for you—hang it, Elaine, I am under no obligation to marry you, when it was you who tricked me."

"No obligation."

"Obligation!" exclaimed Lancelot, with a wry face. He threw the word into the fire as if it had a bad taste. "I must be sure that you understand, and that I am not cheating you. I will not marry you, because I do not love you. I did not start this, and I can't give you my freedom: I can't promise to stay with you for ever. I don't want you to accept these terms, Elaine: they are humiliating ones. They are dictated by the circumstances. If I were to say anything else it would be lies, and things would be worse——"

He broke off and hid his head in his hands.

"I don't understand," he said. "I am trying to do my best."

Elaine said: "Under any terms, you are my good and gracious lord."

King Pelles gave them a castle which was already known to Sir Lancelot. The King's tenant, Sir Bliant, had to move out to make room for them—which he did the more readily when he knew that he was obliging the Wild Man who had saved his life.

"Is he Sir Lancelot?" asked Bliant.

"No," said King Pelles. "He is a French knight who calls himself the Chevalier Mal Fet. I told you I was right about Sir Lancelot being dead."

It had been arranged that Lancelot was to live incognito —because, if it were allowed to get about that he was still living and lodged at Bliant Castle, there would only be a hue-and-cry for him from the court.

Bliant Castle had such a fine moat that it was practically an island. The only way to get to it was by boat, from a barbican on the land side, and the castle itself was surrounded by a magic fence of iron, probably a sort of cheval de frise. Ten knights were appointed to serve Lancelot there, and twenty ladies to serve Elaine.

She was wild with joy.

"We will call it the Joyous Island," she said. "We shall be so happy there. And, Lance"—he flinched when she called him by the pet name—"I want you to have your hobbies. We must have tournaments, and hawking, and plenty of things to do. You must invite people to stay, so that we can have company. I promise I won't be jealous of you, Lance, and I won't try to live in your pocket. Don't you think we might have a happy time if we are careful? Don't you think the Joyous Isle would be a lovely name?"

Lancelot cleared his throat and said: "Yes, it would be an excellent one."

"You must have a new shield made for you, so that you can go on with your tournaments without being recognized. What sort of blazon will you have?"

"Anything," said Lancelot. "We can arrange that later."

"The Chevalier Mal Fet. What a romantic name! What does it mean?"

"You could make it mean several things. The Ugly Knight would be one meaning, or the Knight Who Has Done Wrong."

He did not tell her that it could also mean the Ill-Starred Knight—the Knight with a Curse on Him.

"I don't think you are ugly—or wrong."

Lancelot pulled himself together. He knew that it would be most unfair to stay with Elaine if he were going to mope about it, or to do the Grand Renunciation—but, on the other hand, it was empty work to pretend.

"That is because you are a darling," he said. He kissed

her quickly and clumsily, to cover the crack in the word. But Elaine noticed it.

"You will be able to attend to Galahad's education personally," she said. "You will be able to teach him all your tricks, so that he grows up to be the greatest knight in the world."

He kissed her again. She had said, "If we are careful," and she was trying to be careful. He felt pity for her trying, and gratitude for the decency of her mind. He was like a distracted man doing two things at once, one of them important and the other unimportant. He felt a duty to the unimportant one. But it is always embarrassing to be loved. And he did not like to accept Elaine's humility because of his opinion of himself.

The morning when they were to set out for Bliant arrived, and the newly-made knight, Sir Castor, stopped Lancelot in the Hall. He was only seventeen.

"I know you are calling yourself the Ill-Made Knight," said Sir Castor, "but I think you are Sir Lancelot. Are you?"

Lancelot took the boy by the arm.

"Sir Castor," he said, "do you think that is a knightly question? Suppose I were Sir Lancelot, and was only calling myself the Chevalier Mal Fet—don't you think I might have some reasons for doing that, reasons which a gentleman of lineage ought to respect?"

Sir Castor blushed very much and knelt on one knee.

"I won't tell anybody," he said. Nor did he.

# 23

*The spring came slowly, the new menage settled* down, and Elaine arranged a tournament for her cavalier. There was to be a prize of a fair maid and a jerfalcon.

Five hundred knights came from all parts of the kingdom to compete in the tournament—but the Chevalier Mal Fet knocked down anybody who would stand up to him, with a kind of absent-minded ferocity, and the thing was a failure. The knights went away puzzled and frightened. Not a single person had been killed—he spared everybody indifferently as soon as he had knocked them down—and, by the Chevalier at any rate, not a single word had been spoken. The defeated knights, jogging home with their bruises, missed the conviviality which usually happened on tournament evenings, wondered who the taciturn champion could be, and talked superstitiously among themselves. Elaine, smiling bravely until the last of them had gone, went up to her room and cried. Then she dried her eyes and set out to find her lord. He had vanished as soon as the fighting was over, for he had got into the habit of going away by himself at sunset every evening—she did not know where.

She found him on the battlements, in a blaze of gold. Their shadows, and the shadow of the tower on which they stood, and all the spectres of the burning trees, stretched over the parkland in broad strips of indigo. He was looking towards Camelot with desperate eyes. His new shield, with the blazon of his incognito, was propped in front of him. The cognizance was of a silver woman on a sable field, with a knight kneeling at her feet.

In her simplicity, Elaine had been delighted by the compliment on the shield. She had never been clever. Now she realized, for the first time, that the silver woman was crowned. She stood helplessly, wondering what she could do—but there was nothing she could do. Her weapons were blunt ones, of soft metal. She could only use patience and self-restraint, poor tools when matched against the heartfelt mania of love to which the ancient race was martyred.

One morning they were sitting on a green bank at the edge of the lake. Elaine was doing embroidery, while Lancelot watched his son. Galahad, a priggish, mute little boy, was playing some private game with his dolls—to which he remained attached long after most boys would have taken to soldiers. Lancelot had carved two knights in armour for him out of wood. They were mounted on wheeled horses, from which they were detachable, and they held their spears in fewter. By pulling the horses towards each other, with strings tied to the platform on which they stood, the knights could be made to tilt. They could be made to knock each other out of the saddle. Galahad did not care for them at all, but played with a rag doll which he called the Holy Holy.

"Gwyneth will ruin that sparrow hawk," remarked Lancelot.

They could see one of the castle gentlewomen coming towards them at a great pace, with the sparrow hawk on her fist. Her haste had excited the hawk, which was bating continuously—but Gwyneth paid no attention to it, beyond giving it an occasional angry shake.

"What is the matter, Gwyneth?"

"Oh, my lady, there are two knights waiting beyond the water, and they say they have come to tilt with the Chevalier."

"Tell them to go away," said Lancelot. "Say I am not at home."

"But, sir, the porter has told them the way to the boat, and they are coming over one at a time. They say they won't both come, but the second will come if you beat the first. He is in the boat already."

He got up and dusted his knees.

"Tell him to wait in the tilt yard," he said. "I will be twenty minutes."

The tilt yard was a long, sanded passage between the walls, with a tower at each end. It had galleries looking down on it from the walls, like a racquets court, and was open to the sky. Elaine and the domestics sat in these galleries to watch, and the two knights fought beneath them for a long time. The tilting was even—each of them had a fall—and the sword-play lasted for two hours. At the end of this time, the strange knight cried: "Stop!"

Lancelot stopped at once, as if he were a farm labourer who had been given permission to knock off for his dinner. He stuck his sword in the ground, as if it were a pitchfork, and stood patiently. He had, indeed, only been working with the quiet patience of a farm hand. He had not been trying to hurt his opponent.

"Who are you?" asked the stranger. "Please tell me your name? I have never met a man like you."

Lancelot suddenly lifted both gauntlets to his helm, as if he were trying to bury in them the face which was already hidden, and said miserably: "I am Sir Lancelot Dulac."

"What!"

"I am Lancelot, Degalis."

Degalis threw his sword against the stone wall with a clang, and began running back towards the tower by the moat. His iron feet threw echoes down the yard. He unlaced and tossed away his helm as he ran. When he had reached the portcullis of the gate-house, he put his hands to his mouth and shouted with all his might:

"Ector! Ector! It *is* Lancelot! Come over!"

Immediately he was running back towards his friend.

"Lancelot! My dear, dear fellow! I was sure it was you, I was sure it was you!"

He began fumbling with the laces, trying to get the helm off with clumsy fingers. He snatched off his own gauntlets and hurled them, too, with a clash against the wall. He could hardly wait to see Sir Lancelot's face. Lancelot stood still, like a tired child being undressed.

"But what have you been doing? Why are you here? It was feared that you were dead."

The helm came off, and went to join the rest of the discards.

"Lancelot!"

"Did you say that Ector was with you?"

"Yes, it is your brother Ector. We have been looking for you for two years. Oh, Lancelot, I am glad to see you!"

"You must come in," he said, "and refresh yourselves."

"But what have you been doing all this time? Where have you been hidden? The Queen sent out three knights to search for you at the beginning. In the end there were twenty-three of us. It must have cost her twenty thousand pounds."

"I have been here and there."

"Even the Orkney faction helped. Sir Gawaine is one of the searchers."

By this time Sir Ector had arrived in the boat—Sir Ector Demaris, not King Arthur's guardian—and the portcullis had been raised for him. He ran for the Chevalier, as if he were to tackle him at football.

"Brother!"

Elaine had come down from her gallery and was waiting at the end of the tilt yard. She was now to welcome, as she knew well, the people who were to break her heart. She did not interfere with their greetings, but watched them like a child who had been left out of a game. She stood still, gathering her forces. All her powers, all the frontier guards

of her spirit, were being called in and concentrated at the
citadel of her heart.

"This is Elaine."

They turned to her and began to bow.

"You are welcome to Bliant Castle."

# 24

*"I can't leave Elaine," he said.*

Ector Demaris said: "Why not? You don't love her. You
are under no obligation to her. You are only making yourselves miserable by staying together."

"I am under an obligation to her. I can't explain it, but
I am."

"The Queen," said Degalis, "is desperate. She has spent
a fortune looking for you."

"I can't help that."

"It is no good sulking," said Ector. "It seems to me that
you are sulking. If the Queen is sorry for what she has
done, whatever it was, you ought to behave generously and
forgive her."

"I have nothing to forgive the Queen."

"That is just what I say. You ought to go back to court
and follow your career. For one thing, you owe it to
Arthur: don't forget that you are one of his sworn knights.
He has been needing you badly."

"Needing me?"

"There is the usual trouble with the Orkneys."

"What have the Orkneys been doing? Oh, Degalis, you
don't know how it does my heart good to hear the old
names. Tell me all the gossip. Has Kay been making a fool
of himself lately? Is Dinadan still laughing? What is the
news about Tristram and King Mark?"

"If you are so keen about the news, you ought to come
back to court."

"I have told you I can't."

"Lancelot, you are not looking at this realistically. Do you seriously think you can stay here incognito with this wench, and still be yourself? Do you think you can beat five hundred knights in a tournament without being recognized?"

"The moment we heard about the tournament," said Ector, "we came at once. Degalis said: 'That is Lancelot, or I'm a Dutchman.'"

"It would mean," said Degalis, "if you insist on staying here, that you would have to give up arms altogether. One more fight, and you would be known all over the country. For that matter, I think you are known already."

"Staying with Elaine would mean giving up everything. It would mean absolute retirement—no quests, no tournaments, no honour, no love: and you might even have to stay indoors all day. Yours is not an easy face to forget, you know."

"Whatever it means, Elaine is kind and good. Ector, when people trust you and depend on you, you can't hurt them. You could not treat a dog so."

"People don't marry dogs, however."

"Damn it, this girl loves me."

"So does the Queen." ·

Lancelot turned the cap round in his hands.

"The last time I saw the Queen," he said, "she told me never to come near her again."

"But she has spent twenty thousand pounds looking for you."

He waited for some time and then asked, in a voice which sounded rough: "Is she well?"

"She is absolutely wretched."

Ector said: "She knows it was her fault. She cried a great deal, and Bors told her she was a fool, but she didn't argue with him. Arthur is wretched too, because the whole Table is upside down."

Lancelot threw his cap on the ground and stood up.

"I told Elaine," he said, "that I would not promise to stay with her: so I must."

"Do you love her?" asked Degalis, cutting to the root.

"Yes, I do. She has been good to me. I am fond of her."

At their looks, he changed the word.

"I love her," he said defiantly.

The knights had been staying for a week, and Lancelot, listening hungrily to their Table news, was weakening every day. Elaine, sitting at the high table beside her lord at dinner, lived in a flow of conversation about people whose names she had never heard and about events which she could not understand. There was nothing to do except to offer second helpings, which Ector would accept without interrupting the anecdote of the moment. They leaned across her and talked and laughed, and Elaine busily laughed too. Every day Lancelot went to his turret at sunset—she had tiptoed away when she first found him there, and he did not know it was a discovered rendezvous.

"Lancelot," she said one morning, "there is a man waiting on the other side of the moat, with a horse and armour."

"A knight?"

"No. He looks like a squire."

"I wonder who it can be this time. Tell the porter to fetch him across."

"The porter says he won't come across. He says he will wait there for Sir Lancelot."

"I will go and see."

Elaine detained him as he went down to the boat.

"Lancelot," she said, "what do you want me to do with Galahad, if you should go away?"

"Go away? Who says I am going away?"

"Nobody has said so, but I want to know."

"I don't understand what you are talking about."

"I want to know how Galahad is to be brought up."

"Well, I suppose in the usual way. He will learn to be a good knight, I hope. But the whole question is imaginary."

"That is what I wanted to know."

She detained him once more, however.

"Lancelot, will you tell me one other thing? If you should go away, if you should have to leave me—would you be coming back?"

"I have told you that I am not going away."

She was trying the meaning of her words, as she made them, like a man walking slowly over a bog and feeling in front of him as he went.

"It would help me to go on with Galahad—it would help me to go on living—if I knew that it was for something—if I knew that one day—if I knew that you would be coming back."

"Elaine, I don't know why you are talking like this."

"I am not trying to stop you, Lance. Perhaps it will be best for you to go. Perhaps it is a thing which has to happen. Only, I wanted to know if I should see you again—because it is important to me."

He took her hands.

"If I go," he said, "I will come back."

The man on the other side of the moat was Uncle Dap. He was standing with Lancelot's old charger, now two years older, and all his accustomed armour neatly stowed on the saddle, as if for a kit inspection. Everything was correctly folded and strapped in the proper military place. The habergeon was rolled in a tight bundle. The helm, pauldrons, and vambraces were polished, literally by weeks of polishing, to that veneer or patina of light which is to be found only on things bought newly from the shop before they have been dulled by household cleaning. There was a smell of saddle soap, mixed with the unmistakable, personal smell of armour—as individual a smell as that which you get in the professional's shop on a golf course, and, to a knight, as exciting.

All Lancelot's muscles made an empathic sortie towards the feeling of his own armour, which he had not seen since he left Camelot. His forefinger felt where the handle of his sword would use it for a fulcrum. His thumb knew the exact weight in ounces which it would have to exert on the near side of the fulcrum. The pad on the inside of his palm lusted for the gripe of the hilt. His whole arm remembered the balance of Joyeux and wanted to wag him in the air.

Uncle Dap looked older, and would not speak. He only held the bridle and displayed the gear, waiting for the knight to mount and ride. His stern eye, as fierce as a goshawk's, waited on his charge. He held out the great tilting helm silently, with its familiar panache of heron hackles and the silver thread.

Lancelot took the helm from Uncle Dap, with both hands, and turned it round. His hands knew the weight to expect —exactly twenty-two and a half pounds. He saw the superb polish, the fresh padding, and the new mantling set behind. It was of azure sarsenet, hand-embroidered in gold thread with the numerous small fleur-de-lis of ancient France. He knew at once whose fingers had done the embroidery. He lifted the helm to his nose and sniffed the mantling.

Immediately she was there—not the Guenever whom he had remembered on the battlements, but the real Jenny, in a different posture, with every lash of her eyelids and every pore of her skin and every note of her voice and every articulation of her smile.

He did not look back as he rode away from Bliant Castle—and Elaine, standing on the barbican tower, did not wave. She watched him going with a still-struck concentration, like somebody who, shipwrecked, gets as much fresh water into the little boat as possible. She had a few seconds left, to make her store of Lancelot that must last her through the years. There would be only this store, and their son, and a lot of gold. He had left her all his money, enough to bring a thousand pounds a year for life—in those days a huge sum.

# 25

*Fifteen years after leaving Elaine, Lancelot was still* at court. The King's relations with Guenever and her lover were much as they had always been. The great difference was that everybody was older. Lancelot's hair, which had already turned badger-grey when he first came back from his madness as a fellow of twenty-six, was quite white. Arthur's also was prematurely snowed—both men's lips were red in their silky nests of beard. Guenever alone had contrived to keep the raven on her head. She looked a splendid figure when she was forty.

Another difference was that a new generation had come to court. In their own hearts the chief characters of the Round Table felt the ardent feelings which they had always felt—but now they were figures instead of people. They were surrounded by younger clients for whom Arthur was not the crusader of a future day, but the accepted conqueror of a past one—for whom Lancelot was the hero of a hundred victories, and Guenever the romantic mistress of a nation.

To these young people, a sight of Arthur as he hunted in the greenwood was like seeing the idea of Royalty. They saw no man at all, but England. When Lancelot rode by, laughing at some private joke with the Queen, the commonalty were amazed that he could laugh. "Look," they would say to each other, "he is laughing, as if he were a vulgar person like ourselves. How condescending, how splendidly democratic of Sir Lancelot, to laugh, as if he were an ordinary man! Perhaps he eats and drinks as well, or even sleeps at night." But in their hearts the new generation was quite sure that the great Dulac did no such things.

Indeed, a lot of water had flowed under the bridges of Camelot in twenty-one years. They had been the years of building. When they began, they had been years of perrières and mangonels trundling along the rutty highways from one siege to another, to hurl destruction over castle walls—of movable wooden towers on wheels, going lumbering against recreant keeps, so that the archers, shooting down from the top of them, could throw death into treacherous strongholds—of companies of engineers marching along in clouds of summer dust, their picks and shovels on their shoulders, to undermine revolted bartizans so that the great stones caved and fell tottering. When Arthur had been unable to take a strong-arm castle by assault, he had caused tunnels to be dug under selected parts of the wall. These tunnels, being supported on beams of wood which could be burned away with fire at the proper moment, had collapsed, bringing the rubble-filled baileys down on top of them.

The early years had been times of battle, in which those who insisted on living by the sword had been made to die by it. They had been years lit by whole towersful of combatants roasting like so many Guy Fawkes—for the great objection to a pele tower as a stronghold was that it made a first-class chimney—years ringing with the sound of battle-axes thudding on battle-axe-proof doors—which were constructed by nailing the first ply of boards horizontally, and the second ply vertically, so that the wood could not be split along the grain—years illustrated by the shambling tumble of Norman giants—who were most conveniently dealt with by cutting off their legs first, so that you could get a fair reach at their heads—and by the flicker of swords round helmets or elbow-cops, a flickering which, in extreme cases, was attended by such a shower of sparks as to make the struggling knights seem perfectly incandescent.

Wherever you went, during the first years, every vista had been terminated by a marching column of mercenaries, robbing and piling from the Marches—or by a knight of the new order exchanging buffets with a conservative baron whom he was trying to restrain from murdering serfs—or by a golden-haired maiden being rescued out of some lofty keep by means of leather ladders—or by Sir Bruce Saunce Pité riding a full wallop with Sir Lancelot coming deliverly after him—or by a few surgeons carefully ransacking the wounds of an unfortunate combatant, and making him eat onions or garlic, so that, by smelling at the wound, they could discover whether the intestines had been perforated or not. When they had examined the wounds they dressed them with the oily wool from the udders of sheep, which made a natural lanolin dressing. Here would be Sir Gawaine sitting on his antagonist's chest, and finishing him off, through the ventails of his helm, with the long sharp poinard called the Mercy of God. There would be a couple of knights who had suffocated themselves in their own helms during the course of a battle, a misfortune which frequently happened in those days of violent exercise and small vents. On one side would be a commodious gibbet set up by some old-fashioned princeling to hang King Arthur's knights and the common Saxons who trusted them—a gibbet perhaps nearly as sumptuous as that constructed at Montfaucon, which could support sixty bodies depending like drab fuchsias between its sixteen stone pillars. The humbler gallows had rungs on them, like the footholds on telegraph poles, so that the executioners could scramble up and down. On another side would be a demesne so hedged about with mantraps in its shrubberies that none dared walk within a mile of it. In front of you, there might be a daffish knight who had been caught in a buck-trap, which, swinging him into the air on the end of a stout branch released by the action of the trap, had left him dangling helplessly between heaven and earth. Behind you, there might be a savage tournament or faction fight going on, with all the heralds crying out, *"Laissez les aller"* to ranks of chivalry who were about to charge—a cry which was exactly equivalent to the shout, "They're off!" which is still to be heard at the Grand National today.

The World had been expected to end in the year one thousand, and, in the reaction which followed its reprieve, there had been a burst of lawlessness and brutality which had sickened Europe for centuries. It had been responsible for the doctrine of Might which was the Table's enemy. The fierce lords of the Strong Arm had hunted the wild woodlands—only, of course, there had always been exceptions like the good Sir Ector of Forest Sauvage—till John of Salisbury had been forced to advise his readers: "If one of these great and merciless hunters shall pass by your habitation, bring forth hastily all the refreshment you have in your house, or that you can readily buy, or borrow from your neighbour: that you may not be involved in ruin, or even accused of treason." Children, Duruy tells us, had been seen hanging in trees, by the sinews of their thighs. It had been no uncommon sight to see a man-at-arms whistling like a lobster, and looking like porridge, because they had emptied a bucket of boiling bran over his armour during a siege. Other spectacles even more dramatic have been mentioned by Chaucer: the smyler with the knyf under the cloke, the careyne in the bush with throte y-corve, or the colde deeth with mouth gaping upright. Everywhere it had been blood on steel, and smoke on sky, and power unbridled —and, in the general confusion of the times, Gawaine had at last contrived to murder our dear old friend King Pellinore, in revenge for the death of his own father, King Lot.

Such had been the England which Arthur had inherited, such the birthpangs of the civilization which he had sought to invent. Now, after twenty-one years of patient success, the land presented a different picture.

Where the black knights had hoved, all brim and furious by some ford, to take toll of anybody rash enough to pass that way, now any virgin could circumambulate the whole country, even with gold and ornaments upon her person, without the least fear of harm. Where once the horrible lepers—they called them Measles—had been accustomed to ramble through the woods in white cowls, ringing their doleful clappers if they wanted to give warning, or just pouncing on you without ringing them if they did not, now there were proper hospitals, governed by religious orders of knighthood, to look after those who had come back sick with leprosy from the Crusades. All the tyrannous giants were dead, all the dangerous dragons—some of which used to come down with a burrr like the peregrine's stoop—had been put out of action. Where the raiding parties had once streamed along the highways with fluttering pennoncels, now there were merry bands of pilgrims telling each other dirty stories on the way to Canterbury. Demure clerics, taking a day's outing to Our Lady of Walsingham, were singing *Alleluia Dulce Carmen,* while the less demure ones were warbling the great medieval drinking-song of their own composition: *Meum est propositum in taberna mori.* There were urbane abbots, titupping along on ambling palfreys, in furred hoods which were against the rules of their orders, and yeomen in smart tackle with hawks on their fists, and sturdy peasants quarrelling with their wives about new cloaks, and jolly parties going out to hunt without armour of any sort. Some were riding to fairs as great as that of Troyes, others to universities which rivalled Paris, where there were twenty thousand scholars whose ranks eventually provided seven popes. In the abbeys all the monks were illuminating the initial letters of their manuscripts with such a riot of invention that it was impossible to read the first page at all. Those who were not doing the chi-ro page were carefully copying out the Historia Francorum of Gregory of Tours, or the Legenda Aurea, or the Jeu d'Echecs Moralisé, or a Treatise of Hawkynge—that is, if they were not engaged upon the Ars Magna of the magician Lully or the Speculum Majus by the greatest of all magicians. In the kitchens the famous cooks were preparing menus which included, for one course alone: ballock broth, caudle ferry, lampreys en galentine, oysters in civey, eels in sorré, baked trout, brawn in mustard, numbles of a hart, pigs farsed, cockintryce, goose in hoggepotte, venison in frumenty, hens in brewet, roast squirrels, haggis, capon-neck pudding, garbage, tripe, blaundesorye, caboges, buttered worts, apple mousse, gingerbread, fruit tart, blancmange, quinces in comfit, stilton cheese, and causs boby. In the dining halls the older gentlemen, who had spoiled their palates with drinking, were relishing those strange delicacies of the Middle Ages—the strong flavours of whale and porpoise. Their dainty ladies were putting roses and violets in their dishes—baked marigolds still make an excellent flavouring for bread-and-butter puddings—while the squires were showing their weakness for sheep's-milk cheese. In the nurseries all the little boys were moving heaven and earth to persuade their mothers to have hard pears for dinner, which were stewed in honey-syrup and vinegar, and eaten with whipped cream.

The manners of the table, too, had reached a pitch of civilization far beyond our own. Now, instead of the plates made of bread, there were covered dishes, scented finger bowls, sumptuous table cloths, a plethora of napkins. The diners themselves were wearing chaplets of flowers and graceful draperies. The pages were serving the food with the formal movements of a ballet. Wine bottles were being placed on the tables, but ale, being less respectable, was being put beneath. The musicians, with strange orchestras of bells, large horns, harps, viols, zithers and organs, were playing as the people ate. Where once, before King Arthur had made his chivalry, the Knight of the Tower Landry had been compelled to warn his daughter against entering her own dining hall in the evening unaccompanied—for fear of what might happen in the dark corners—now there was music and light. In the smoky vaults, where once the grubby barons had gnawed their bones with bloody fingers, now there were people eating with clean fingers, which they had washed with herb-scented toilet soap out of wooden bowls. In the cellars of the monasteries the butlers were tapping new and old ale, mead, port, clarée, dry sherry, hock, beer, metheglyn, perry, hippocras, and the best white whisky. In the law courts the judges were dispensing the King's new law, instead of the fierce law of Fort Mayne. In the cottages the good wives were making hot griddle bread enough to make your mouth water, and putting fine turf on their fires regardless of expense, and herding fat geese on the commons enough to support twenty families for twenty years. The Saxons and Normans of Arthur's accession had begun to think of themselves as Englishmen.

No wonder that the young, ambitious knights of Europe flocked to the great court. No wonder that they saw a king when they looked on Arthur, a conqueror when they looked on Lancelot.

One of the young men who came to court in those days was Gareth. Another was Mordred.

# 26

*"We don't see many arrows thrilling in people's* hearts nowadays," remarked Lancelot one afternoon at the archery butts.

"Thrilling!" exclaimed Arthur. "What a splendid word to describe an arrow vibrating, just after it has hit!"

Lancelot said: "I heard it in a ballad."

They went away and sat in an arbour, from which they could watch the young people practising their shots.

"It is true," said the King gloomily. "We don't get much of the old fighting in these decadent days.".

"Decadent!" protested his commander-in-chief. "What are you so gloomy about? I thought this was what you wanted?"

Arthur changed the subject.

"Gareth is shaping well," he said, watching the boy. "It's funny. He can't be many years younger than you are, yet one thinks of him as a child."

"Gareth is a dear."

The King put his hand on Lancelot's knee and squeezed it affectionately.

"Some people might say that you are the dear," he said, "so far as Gareth is concerned. It has come to be quite a legend how the boy arrived at court anonymously, so that his own brothers didn't recognize him, and how he worked in the kitchen, and got nicknamed Beaumains when Kay wanted to be nasty, and how you were the only person who was decent to him until he did his great adventure and became a knight."

"Well," said Lancelot defensively, "his brothers hadn't seen him for fifteen years. You can't blame Gawaine for that."

"I am not blaming anybody. I was just saying that it was

nice of you to take notice of a kitchen page, and help him along, and knight him in the end. But then, you always were nice to people."

"It is strange how they come here," said his friend. "I suppose they can't keep away. Any boy with a bit of go in him feels that he has to come to Arthur's court, even if it is to work in the kitchen, because it is the centre of the new world. That is why Gareth ran away from his mother. She wouldn't let him come, so he ran away and came incognito."

"Nonsense. Morgause is a bad old woman—that's all you can say about her. She forbade him to come to court because she hated you, but he came for all that."

"Morgause is my half-sister, and I have hurt her badly. It can't be nice for a woman to have all her sons going away to serve the man she hates. Even Mordred, her last."

Lancelot looked uncomfortable. He had an instinctive dislike for Mordred, and did not like having it. He did not know about Arthur being Mordred's father—for that was a story which had been hushed up in the earliest days, before either he or Guenever came to court, just as Arthur's own birth had been. But he did feel that there was something strange between the young man and the King. He disliked Mordred irrationally, as a dog dislikes a cat—and he felt ashamed of the dislike, because it was a confused principle of his to help the younger Knights.

"It must have hurt her worst of all when Mordred came," pursued the King. "Women are always fondest of their last babies."

"So far as I can learn, she was never particularly fond of any of them. If she was hurt by their coming to court, it was only because she hated you. Why does she?"

"It's a bad story. I would rather not talk about it.

"Morgause," added the King, "is a woman—is a woman of pronounced character."

Lancelot laughed rather sourly.

"She must be," he said, "from the way she is carrying on. I hear she is making a dead set at Pellinore's son Lamorak now, although she is a grandmother."

"Who told you?"

"It's all over the court."

Arthur got up and walked three steps in agitation.

"Good God!" he exclaimed. "And Lamorak's father killed

her husband! And her son killed Lamorak's father! And Lamorak is hardly of age!"

He sat down and looked at Lancelot, as if he were afraid of what he might say next.

"All the same, that is what she is doing."

The King suddenly and vehemently asked: "Where is Gawaine? Where is Agravaine? Where is Mordred?"

"They are supposed to be on some quest or other."

"Not—not in the North?"

"I don't know."

"Where is Lamorak?"

"I think he is staying in Orkney."

"Lancelot, if you had only known my sister—if you had only known the Orkney clan at home. They are mad on their family. If Gawaine—if Lamorak—O my God, have mercy on my sins, and on the sins of other people, and on the tangle in this world!"

Lancelot looked at him in consternation.

"What are you afraid of?"

Arthur stood up for the second time, and began talking fast.

"I am afraid for my Table. I am afraid of what is going to happen. I am afraid it was all wrong."

"Nonsense."

"When I started the Table, it was to stop anarchy. It was a channel for brute force, so that the people who had to use force could be made to do it in a useful way. But the whole thing was a mistake. No, don't interrupt me. It was a mistake because the Table itself was founded on force. Right must be established by right: it can't be established by Force Majeur. But that is what I have been trying to do. Now my sins are coming home to roost. Lancelot, I am afraid I have sown the whirlwind, and I shall reap the storm."

"I don't understand what you are talking about."

"Here comes Gareth," said the King calmly, suddenly, and as if everything were over. "I think you will understand in a minute."

While they had been talking, a messenger in leather leggings had arrived at the butts. The King had seen him out of the corner of his eye as he hastily sought Sir Gareth and handed him a letter. He had watched the boy reading the letter, once, twice, three times, and later as he spoke confusedly with the man. Now, after handing his bow to the messenger without noticing that he was doing so, Gareth was coming to them slowly.

"Gareth," said the King.

The young man knelt down and took the King's hand. He held it as if it were a banister or a life-line. He looked at Arthur with dull eyes, and did not cry.

"My mother is dead," said Gareth.

"Who killed her?" asked the King, as if it were the natural question.

"My brother Agravaine."

"What!"

The exclamation was from Lancelot.

"My brother has killed our mother, because he found her sleeping with a man."

"Keep quiet, Lancelot, please," said the King. Then to Gareth: "What did they do to Sir Lamorak?"

But Gareth had not finished the first part of his story.

"Agravaine cut off her head," he said. "Like the unicorn."

"The unicorn?"

"Please, Lancelot."

"He killed our mother in her blood."

"I am sorry."

"I always knew he would," said Gareth.

"Are you sure the news is true?"

"It is true. It is true. It was Agravaine who killed the unicorn."

"Was Lamorak the unicorn?" asked the King gently. He did not know what his nephew was talking about, but he was anxious to help. "Is Lamorak dead?"

"Oh, Uncle! It says that Agravaine found her naked in a bed with Sir Lamorak, and he cut off her head. Now they have hunted Lamorak down as well."

Lancelot was less patient than the King, because he knew fewer of the sorrows which had happened in the early days.

"Who were they?" he asked.

"Mordred, Agravaine, and Gawaine."

"So it comes to this," said Sir Lancelot, "that your three brothers have first murdered King Pellinore—who would not willingly have hurt a fly—murdered him because he killed their father by accident in a tournament—then murdered their own mother in bed—and finally butchered Pellinore's young son Lamorak, for being seduced by their mother who was three times as old as he was. I suppose they set upon him all against one?"

Gareth held the King's hand tighter, and began to droop his head.

"They surrounded him," he said numbly, "and Mordred stabbed him in the back."

# 27

*Gawaine and Mordred came straight to Camelot* from their foray among the Old Ones, but Agravaine did not come with them. They had quarrelled as soon as Lamorak was dead, or rather, as soon as they had found time to realize what had happened. The murder of Queen Morgause had not been done on purpose. Agravaine had done it on the spur of the moment—in his outraged passion, he said —but they knew by instinct that it was from jealousy. So they had raised the old charge against him, that he was only a fat bully whose noblest employment was the killing of defenceless people or women, and they had left him, weeping, after a furious scene. Gawaine, who now remembered all his adoration for their peculiar mother—an adoration which the queen-witch had wished on each of her sons —rode to the King's court in gloomy penitence. He knew that Arthur would be furious about the way in which young Lamorak had been killed, for the boy had been the third best knight of the Table, and yet he was not ashamed of having killed him. To his mind Lamorak deserved death, like a felon, because he and his father had injured the Orkney clan. He knew that the whole court would look at him sideways on account of his mother's murder, and how the old talk would be revived about that woman whom he had slain himself in temper, when he was young. Even this did not dismay him much. But he was penitent and miserable because his own dear Orkney mother was gone— he was only beginning to realize how it had happened—

because he had hurt Arthur's ideal, and because he was generous in his own heart. He hoped that the King would hang him, or send him into exile, or punish him severely. He went into the royal chamber with a sulky shame.

Mordred walked into the room behind Gawaine, as if nothing had happened. He was a thin wisp of a fellow, so fair-haired that he was almost an albino: and his bright eyes were so blue, so palely azure in their faded depths, that you could not see into them. He was clean-shaven. It seemed that there was no part of him which you could catch hold of, neither his hair, nor his eyes, nor his whiskers. Even the colour had been washed out of him, it seemed, so as to leave no handle. Only, in the skeletal, pink face, the brilliant eyes had crow's-feet round them—a twinkle which you could assume to be of humour, if you liked, or else of irony, or merely of screwing up those sky-blue pupils so as to look far and deep. He walked with an upright carriage, both ingratiating and defiant—but one shoulder was higher than the other. He had been born slightly crooked—a clumsy delivery by the midwife—like Richard III.

Arthur was waiting for them, with Guenever and Lancelot on either hand.

The burly, red-haired Gàwaine knelt down clumsily on one knee. He did not look at the King, but spoke to the floor.

"Pardon."

"Pardon," said Mordred also—but he, kneeling beside his half-brother, looked the King between the eyes. He had a non-committal voice, beautifully modulated—its words might have meant the opposite of what they said.

"You are pardoned," said Arthur. "Go away."

"Go?" asked Gawaine. He was not sure whether he was being banished.

"Yes, go. We can meet at dinner. But go, now. Leave me, please."

Gawaine said roughly: "The half of yon was done by sore ill fortune."

This time Arthur's voice was neither tired nor miserable. "Go!"

He stamped his foot like a war-horse, pointing to the door as if he would throw them out of it. His eyes flashed from his face, like a sudden flame of green ash, so that even

Mordred got up quickly. Gawaine was startled and stumbled out of the door in confusion, but the crooked man recollected himself before he left. He made a play-actor's bow, a low, luxurious simulacrum of humility—then, straightening himself up, he looked the King in the eye, and smiled, and went.

Arthur sat down, trembling. Lancelot and Guenever looked at each other over his head. They would have liked to ask why he was going to forgive his nephews, or to protest that it was impossible to pardon matricides without damaging the Round Table. But they had never seen Arthur in his royal rage before. They felt that there was something in it which they did not understand, so they held their peace.

Presently the King said: "I was trying to tell you something, Lance, before this happened."

"Yes."

"You two have always listened to me about my Table. I want you to understand."

"We will do our best."

"Long ago, when I had my Merlyn to help, he tried to teach me to think. He knew he would have to leave in the end, so he forced me to think for myself. Don't ever let anybody teach you to think, Lance: it is the curse of the world."

The King sat looking at his fingers, and they waited while the old thoughts ran sideways across his hands like crabs.

"Merlyn," he said, "approved of the Round Table. Evidently it was a good thing at the time. It must have been a step. Now we must think of making the next one."

Guenever said: "I don't see what is wrong with the Round Table, just because the Orkney faction chooses to get murderous."

"I was explaining to Lance. The idea of our Table was that Right was to be the important thing, not Might. Unfortunately we have tried to establish Right by Might, and you can't do that."

"I don't see why you can't do it."

"I tried to dig a channel for Might, so that it would flow usefully. The idea was that all the people who enjoyed fighting should be headed off, so that they fought for justice, and I hoped that this would solve the problem. It has not."

"Why not?"

"Simply because we have got justice. We have achieved what we were fighting for, and now we still have the fighters on our hands. Don't you see what has happened? We have run out of things to fight for, so all the fighters of the Table are going to rot. Look at Gawaine and his brothers. While there were still giants and dragons and wicked knights of the old brigade, we could keep them occupied: we could keep them in order. But now that the ends have been achieved, there is nothing for them to use their might on. So they use it on Pellinore and Lamorak and my sister—God be good to them. The first sign of the fester was when our chivalry turned into Games-Mania—all that nonsense about who had the best tilting average and so forth. This is the second sign, when murder begins again. That is why I say that dear Merlyn would want me to start another thinking, now, if only he were here to help."

"It is something like idleness and luxury unmanning us —the strings have gone slack and out of tune."

"No: it is not that at all. It is simply that I have kept a rod in pickle for my own back. I ought to have rooted Might out altogether, instead of trying to adapt it. Though I don't know how the rooting could have been done. Now the Might is left, with nothing to use it on, so it is working wicked channels for itself."

"You ought to punish it," said Lancelot. "When Sir Bedivere killed his wife you made him carry her head to the Pope. You ought to send Gawaine to the Pope now."

The King opened his hands and looked up for the first time.

"I am going to send you all to the Pope," he said.

"What!"

"Not exactly to the Pope. You see, the trouble is—as I see it—that we have used up the worldly objects for our Might—so there is nothing left but the spiritual ones. I was thinking about this all night. If I can't keep my fighters from wickedness by matching them against the world—because they have used up the world—then I must match them against the spirit."

Lancelot's eye caught fire, and he began to watch the other man attentively. At the same moment Guenever withdrew into herself. She glanced quickly at her lover, a covert glance, then gave a new, reserved attention to her husband.

"If something is not done," went on the King, "the whole Table will go to ruin. It is not only that feud and open manslaughter have started: there is the bold bawdry as well. Look at the Tristram business with King Mark's wife. People seem to be siding with Tristram. Morals are difficult things to talk about, but what has happened is that we have invented a moral sense, which is rotting now that we can't give it employment. And when a moral sense begins to rot it is worse than when you had none. I suppose that all endeavours which are directed to a purely worldly end, as my famous Civilization was, contain within themselves the germs of their own corruption."

"What is this about sending us to the Pope?"

"I was speaking metaphorically. What I mean is, that the ideal of my Round Table was a temporal ideal. If we are to save it, it must be made into a spiritual one. I forgot about God."

"Lancelot," said the Queen in a peculiar voice, "has never forgotten."

But her lover was too interested to notice her tone.

"What do you intend to do?" he asked.

"I thought we could start by trying to achieve something which would be helpful to the spirit, if you see what I mean. We have achieved the bodily things: peace and prosperity: now we lack work. If we invent another bodily employment, a temporal employment—mere empire building or something like that—we shall be faced by the same problem again, probably worse, as soon as it has been achieved. But why can't we pull our Table together by turning its energies to the spirit? You know what I mean by the spirit. If our Might was given a channel so that it worked for God, instead of for the rights of man, surely that would stop the rot, and be worth doing?"

"A Crusade!" exclaimed Lancelot. "You are going to send us to the rescue of the Holy Sepulchre!"

"We could try that," said the King. "I hadn't exactly thought of it, but it might be a good thing to try."

"Or we could look for relics," cried his commander, who was quite on fire. "If all the knights were looking for a piece of the True Cross, they might not even need to fight.

I mean, if we were to go on a Crusade, we should still be using force: we should be putting the Might into a channel against the infidels. But if we really and truly banded the whole Table together to search for something which belonged to God himself, why, that would be infinitely worth doing—and, although we should be busy, there might be no need for fighting at all. If it comes to that, we needn't necessarily look for one thing alone. Why, if all our knights —one hundred and fifty men, all specialists in questing, like detectives—if all our knights were to turn their energies to the quest for things which belonged to God—why, we might find hundreds and hundreds of things which would be of huge value. The Round Table might have been positively invented and trained just for that object. We might find some new gospels, even. The whole of Christianity might be helped by what we did. Think of a hundred and fifty men all trained for the search! And it is not too late to try. The True Cross was found in 326, but the Holy Shroud was not discovered at Lirey until 1360! We might find the spear which killed Our Lord!"

"I was thinking of that."

"We must look for manuscripts particularly."

"Yes."

"We must fare forth everywhere, to the Holy Land, to every place! We shall be like my dear de Joinville!"

"Yes."

"I think," said Sir Launcelot, "this is the most splendid idea you have ever had!"

"I am afraid of it," said the King, and this time it was his voice which sounded strange. "I thought, in the night time, that perhaps it was aiming too high. If people reach perfection they vanish, you know. It may mean the end of the Table. Supposing somebody were to find God?"

But Lancelot's mind was not made for metaphysics. He did not notice the change in Arthur's voice. He began to hum to himself the great Crusader's hymn:

> Lignum crucis,
> Signum ducis,
> Sequitur exercitus . . .

"We could search for the Holy Grail!" he cried triumphantly.

It was at this moment that a messenger arrived from King Pelles. Sir Lancelot was wanted, he said, to knight a young man at an abbey. He was a fine young fellow, seemly and demure as a dove. He had been educated in a convent. His name, said the messenger, was thought to be Galahad.

Queen Guenever stood up, and sat down. She opened her hands, and closed them again. She knew that Sir Lancelot was going to his son by another woman—but she hardly minded that.

# 28

*If you want to read about the beginning of the Quest* for the Grail, about the wonders of Galahad's arrival— Guenever, in a strange mixture of curiosity, envy and horror, made a half-hearted attempt to vamp him—and of the last supper at court, when the thunder came and the sunbeam and the covered vessel and the sweet smell through the Great Hall—if you want to read about these, you must seek them in Malory. That way of telling the story can only be done once. The material facts were that the knights of the Round Table set out in a body, soon after Pentecost, with the immediate object of finding the Holy Grail.

It was two years before Lancelot came back to court— and it was a lonely time for those at home. Slowly those knights who had survived began to trickle back in twos and threes, tired men bearing news of loss or rumours of success. They came limping on crutches, or leading spent horses which could carry them no longer, or, as one did who had lost a hand in battle, carrying the one hand in the other. All these men looked worn and confused. Their faces were fanatical, and they babbled of dreams. Ships which moved of their own power, silver tables on which strange Masses had been said, spears which flew through the air, visions of bulls and of thorn trees, demons in old tombs, kings and hermits who had been living for four hundred years—these figured in the rumours which filled the palace. A count taken by Sir Bedivere showed that half the knights were missing. They were presumed dead. But all the time Sir Lancelot did not come back.

The first reliable witness to return was Gawaine, who reached the court in a black temper, with his head bandaged. He was the only one of the Orkney clan who had refused to learn English correctly and spoke in a Northern accent—almost an assumed one. He still thought half in Gaelic. He was defiant of the Southerners, proud of his race.

"Blindness and Darkness on the Quest," said Gawaine. "If I was e'er upon a sleeveless errand, it was yon."

"What happened?"

Arthur and Guenever, like good children, sat with their hands in their laps to listen to the stories. Like children, they were alert and eager, sifting the truth as best they could.

"What happened, is it? Why, what happened was that I wasted eighteen months and mair forbye in seeking footless for adventure—and ended up half deid with what ye name concussion. May God presairve me from the Holy Grail, whatever."

"Tell us from the beginning."

"From the beginning?"

He was surprised at his uncle's interest.

"Tuts, there is thing-a-bit to tell."

"Tell it all the same."

"Fetch some drink for Sir Gawaine," said the Queen. "Sit down, my lord. You are welcome home. Make yourself easy and tell the story—if you are not too tired?"

"I am nae tired—but only for the ache within my heid. I can relate the tale. Thanks to you, I will take whisky, Ma'am. Let see, where did yon stour begin?"

The laird of the Orkneys sat down and tried to remember.

"When we left the castle of Vagon ... Ye mind we rode to Vagon in a body, the first day, and aye dispairsed next morn? When we left thence, I raid north-west. It didna signify which way. Lancelot gave all men the hint, the day before we scattered, that auld King Pelles mentioned him a sacred dish one time, in yin of his great castles. He didna cleave importance tae it, but told the people for its worth.

The best half went in that deerection, but I didna fash masel'. North-west, I raid."

He took a good swallow.

"The first tracks e'er I happened on," he said, "were Galahad's. For a conceited, kindless carl, commend me to yon mannie.

"Yon laddie," continued Sir Gawaine, taking another gulp and warming to his work, "yon lily laddie is, without discussion, the utmost catamite which it had been my woe to smell the stink of through the world—he is."

"Did he knock you down?" asked the King.

"Na, na. 'Twas later. I crossed his tracks at the outsetting.

"Bred in a nunnery," he went on furiously, "amidst a paircel of auld hens! I have news at me about his pairsonal quest from various who have fronted him—the holy milksop with his hairt of a cold puttock. . . . But there, the chiel's an Englishman. He wad be cut, if he dared cross the Border.

"Unless he will have been cut already," he concluded, struck by the idea.

"What has Sir Galahad been doing wrong?"

"Thing a bit. The man's a vegetarian and teetotaller, and he makes believe he is a vairgin. But I encountered with Sir Melias—ye ken Sir Melias is sairely maimed? He telt me how yon Galahad behaved. By some cause Melias had taken to the carl, and asked permissions of the boy to go the one way with him. I canna fathom why he would be doing sic a thing, for the first one that had sought to go with Galahad was Uwaine. Sir Galahad refused it! Sir Uwaine wasna guid enough for him! Well, well, he condescended to let Melias go, however, and he knighted him to boot! My soul to the devil—to be knighted by a gomeril of eighteen! When he had knighted Melias, he quoth these verra words: 'Now, fair sir,' says he, 'sith ye be come of kings and queens, now look that knighthood be well set in you, for ye ought to be a mirror unto all chivalry!' What like do ye name it? Aye, a Southron snob. The next act was that they twa came their ways to an adventure by the crossroads, where Melias had a wish to ride toward the left. Galahad said: 'It were better ye rode not that way, for I deem I should better escape in that way than ye.' There was nae fause modesty abune the bonnie Galahad, ye see? Well, Melias went left for a' that—and he came by ill-luck stricken through the hauberk at the hands of some mysterious knight wha rode upon him, as Galahad foretold. He was like to die—the broken truncheon in his side. When the great Galahad found him wounded, what does my mannie say, but: 'Therefore it had been better to have ridden that other way!' A handsome chiel to say I-told-ye-so to one half deid! Nor did he give him aid."

"What happened to Sir Melias?"

"He said to Galahad: 'Sir, let death come when it pleaseth him.' He drew the truncheon forth himself. Melias is a bonnie knight, and there is gladness on me that I may tell you he is still on life."

Arthur said: "After all, Galahad is only a child! He has growing pains, perhaps. I don't think we ought to judge him unkindly for little faults of social intercourse."

"Did ye ken that he has aye attacked his father, and unhorsed him too? Do ye ken that he has let his father kneel before him, for to ask his blessing? Do ye ken that peoples have been asking for to die in Galahad's arms, and that he has been granting them to do so, as a favour?"

"Well, perhaps it was a favour."

"Diabhal!" exclaimed Gawaine, and he buried his nose in the beaker.

"You are not telling us about yourself."

"The first adventure which I suffered—indeed it wasna far from being the single one—fell at the Castle of Maidens. It were best not tell of yon, before the Queen."

Arthur said rather coldly: "My wife is not a baby or an imbecile, Sir Gawaine. Everybody knows about the custom of that Castle."

Guenever said politely: "They call it *droit de seigneur* in French."

"Well then, indeed, I came to the Castle of Maidens with Uwaine and Sir Gareth. It was kept by seven knights, whatever, who insisted on the custom. We found those seven outside the castle fully armed, and had braw fight with them, and slew them all. When all was done, 'twas manifest that Galahad had been before us. 'Twas he had driven them forth at first, without his killing e'er a one of them, and he himself was ben the castle at the very time. All we had done was play the butcher's part, in finishing what wasna rightly ours."

"Bad luck."

"Galahad rode his gait and wouldna speak with us. The meaning was that we were sinful—he was blessed. I dinna mind what happened after that."

"Did you ride on with Uwaine and Gareth?"

"Nay, we parted after Maiden Castle. I rode all airts until I found a hermitage, with its releegious man. Ye ken the sort, e wheen salvationist. The first demand he made was: 'I would wit how it standeth betwixt your God and you?' I asked that he should gie me lodging for the nicht. Well, he was host and priest as well, so when he pressed me to confession, I couldna well refuse. He clattered waeful havers of the seven knights—they being the seven deadly sins, said he—and told me, calm as daylight, that I was but a murdering man masel'."

"Did he tell you," asked the King with interest, "that it was wrong to kill people for any reason, and especially when you were looking for the Grail?"

"My soul to the devil he did so. He preached that Galahad had aye expelled the seven knights without a slaughter, and mentioned that the Holy Grail was nae for bloodshed."

"What else did he say?"

"I canna mind. When he had complimented me as I was telling ye, he counselled I should make a penance. Unless a body made his guid confession—and was absolvit fair —it would be bootless seeking for the Grail, says he. The chiel was daffish. An errant knight stands in a posture which should make the penance needless—as I shewed him—the like that manual labourers dinna fast in Lent. I gave the man the lie and took my way forthwith. I met with Aglovale and Griflet after that . . . What then, what then? I rode with them four days, I mind . . . Aye then we parted once again, and darkness on me if I didna ride till Michaelmas without adventure!

"Troth is," added Gawaine, "there are nae ventures to be found in England, these late days. The place is failed."

"Fetch Sir Gawaine another drink."

"When Michaelmas was gone and past, I met with Ector Demaris. He had been luckless like masel'! We rode to a wee chapel in the forest, and slept there with a dram inside us—and each man had the one same dream that night. It concairned a hand and arm, in samite, with a bridle and a candle in its gripe. A voice made known that we twa were in need of them. I encountered with a second priest thereafter, wha said the bridle was for continence and the candle was for faith—it seems that Ector and masel' were lacking these. Ye mind how any man may twist a dream. The next thing after was a piece of dour misfortune, the like of that which has been on me all the while. We came, the twa of us, upon my cousin Uwaine with his shield in cover—and didna recognize his blazon. Ector conceded me the first fall with my cousin, my ain kin. The spear went fair through Uwaine's chest. There will have been a weakness in his brigandine."

"Is Uwaine dead?"

"Aye, dead, man. It is the black ill-happening that was on me."

Arthur cleared his throat.

"I should have thought it was worse happening for Uwaine," he said, "God rest him. Perhaps it might not have been a bad thing if you had listened to that priest of yours at the beginning."

"I had nae wish to kill! He was own cousin to the Orkneys! And think ye that the southron prig, him of the white shield, had before refused to ride with him!"

"Do you mean Galahad? Was he bearing the vergescu?"

"Aye, Galahad. It wasna the vergescu. He had laid hold upon a shield in some place, which was to have belonged to Joseph Arimathea, so he said. The cognizance was argent, a tau cross gules. The argent was to signify the white of virgins, we were let to know, and the red cross was for the Grail . . . I am from my tale."

"You had just killed Uwaine," said Arthur patiently.

"Ector and I rode on to one more hermitage, and it was there the priest made known about the bridle in our dream. This priest was vegetarian, may I tell ye! He gave the auld tale about murder, hot and hot, and was for pressing our repentance. We made excuses, and we rode out gait."

"Did he tell you that the reason why neither of you had any luck was because you were only looking for slaughter?"

"Aye, did he. He said that Lancelot was better man than us because he rarely killed his adversary—and in parteecular by cause he didna in this quest. Also he said that many other knights—Ector himself met twenty—were in the same case with us from their sins. He said manslaughter was contrary to the quest. We juist made speech with him, and slipped away while he was talking yet."

"And then?"

"We came upon a castle then, Ector and I, a bonnie tournament was forward. We joined the attacking men—and had fine battle—and were at point to force our way inside —the tempers were a wee bit risen—when Galahad came up. God the Almighty knows what ill wind brought yon mannie. It seems he wasna for approving of such knights as fight for sport. He joined the ither side, and drove us forth the castle, and he gave me this."

Gawaine touched his bandage.

"Ector was not for fighting him," he explained. "They were related. But I fought none the less for that, and small thanks with it. He gave a blow which split my helm whatever, and broke the iron coif—aye, and it glanced off too, killing my horse. Yon was the end for me, by Christ. I was for bed during one month and more."

"And then you came home?"

"Aye, home."

"You certainly seem to have been unlucky," said the Queen.

"Unlucky!"

Gawaine looked into his empty beaker for a moment or two. Then he cheered up.

"I slew King Bagdemagus," he said. "Nae doot ye heard of yon. I missed to tell ye in my tale."

Arthur had been listening closely and turning over his own thoughts. Now he made a movement of impatience.

"Go to bed, Gawaine," he said. "You must be tired. Go to bed and think about it."

# 29

The next person to get home was Sir Lionel, one of Lancelot's cousins. Lancelot had one brother called Ector, and two cousins called Lionel and Bors. Lionel was in a temper, rather like Gawaine, but the object of his annoyance was not Galahad. It was his own brother, Bors.

"Morals," said Lionel, "are a form of insanity. Give me a moral man who insists on doing the right thing all the time, and I will show you a tangle which an angel couldn't get out of."

The King and Queen were sitting side by side as usual, to hear the traveller's story. They had formed a habit of carrying the refreshments into the Great Hall with their own hands, as soon as any knight got back, so that they could hear the news while he ate. The light fell on the table between them—from a high stained window—so that their hands moved among plates and glasses which were rubies, emeralds or pools of flame. They were in a magic world of gems, a glade under trees whose leaves were jewels.

"Has Bors been going in for morals?"

"Bors always did," said Lionel, "curse him. Morals seem to run in my family. Lancelot is bad enough to begin with, but Bors beats him to a frazzle. Did you know that Bors has only once committed the sexual act?"

"Really."

"Yes, really. And, so far as this Quest for the Holy Grail is concerned, he seems to have been doing a sort of advanced course in Catholic dogma."

"Do you mean he is studying?"

Lionel relented a little. He was fond of his brother in his heart, but he had been through an experience which had embittered their relations. Now that he could talk about it, and had had time to think it over, he was beginning to see the other side of the quarrel.

"No," he said. "You musn't take me seriously. Bors is a dear fellow and, if ever there is to be a saint in our family, it will be him. He isn't bright in the head, and he is a bit of a prig, but his guesses are sometimes pure gold. I believed God has been testing him, during this quest, and I'm not sure that he has not come out trumps. I tried to kill him."

"You had better begin your story at the beginning," said Arthur, "or we shan't understand how it goes along."

"My story is nothing. I have been footling about like Gawaine, being called a murderer by a few hermits. I'll tell you the story of Bors, because I come into it.

"God," began Lionel, "has been making a trial of Bors, I suppose. It is as if he was going to be priested, and they wanted to be sure if he was orthodox. Do you know, I think that where Gawaine and myself and Ector and all the rest of us went off the right line, was when we didn't go to confession at the beginning? Bors went, the first day, and he took a penance too. He promised to eat nothing but bread and water, and to wear a Garment, and to sleep on the floor. Of course he was not going to have anything to do with the ladies—but then, he only once had. That's his trouble. Well, the first thing that happened after putting his life in order was that he began having visions. He saw the pelican in her piety, and a swan and a raven and some rotten wood and some flowers. It all had to do with his theology, and he did explain it to me, but I can't remember. The next thing which happened was that a lady begged him to rescue her from a knight called Sir Pridam. He rescued the lady easily enough and had an opportunity to kill Sir Pridam. Mark this. He told me the story after our battle, and he insisted that it was his first trial. He said that he felt like a show jumper, being put over bigger leaps each time, and he was afraid that if he ever bungled a leap he would be sent back to the stable. If he had killed Sir Pridam he would have been finished. They would have put him out to grass again, just as they did with Gawaine and the rest of us. He said that nobody told him these things—the leaps suddenly appeared in front of him, and it was as if there were somebody watching—somebody who would not help or hint, but who just watched to see if he would get over. Well, he didn't kill Pridam. He only squealed at him to give in and hit his face with the flat of the sword until he yielded. And that jump was safely done. Do you think there can have been something against killing people in this quest, King? You know, some sort of supernatural No?"

"I think you are a wise man, Lionel," said the King, "even if you did try to kill your brother. Go on with the story."

"Well, the next trial was directly about me. It was the reason why I tried to kill him. I'm sorry about it now I have only just realized I'm sorry. At the time I didn't understand."

"What was the second trial?"

"Bors and I have always been fond of each other, as you know. This tiff is nothing. We have always loved each other in our way, and Bors was riding through the forest, when he came face to face with two things. One was me, bound naked on a hackney, with two knights riding on either side, and flogging me with thorns. The other was a virgin, riding more than a pace, with a knight galloping after her, to have her maidenhead. The two convoys were going in opposite directions, and Bors was alone.

"Come to think of it," remarked Sir Lionel ruefully, "I am unlucky about getting flogged with thorns. I got it from Sir Turquine once before."

"Which party did Bors choose?"

"Bors decided to rescue the maiden. When I eventually asked him what the devil he meant by deserting his own brother, at the time of our battle later on, he explained that he had thought I was inclined to be a dirty dog—though fond of me—while the maiden was a maiden after all. So he thought his duty was toward the better party. That was why I tried to kill him.

"But now," added Lionel, "I can see his point. I can see it was his second trial, and a difficult decision it must have been to make."

"Poor Bors. I hope he was not too much of a prig about it?"

"He was humble. These trials just used to loom up in front of the old gossip, and he would make a wild guess, generally thinking that he had guessed wrong—and in the end he would come out bewildered, and find that he had guessed right. He sweated along, doing the best he could."

"What was the third trial?"

"They got worse as they went. In the third trial a man came to him dressed as a priest, and told him that there was a lady in a castle nearby who was doomed to death unless Bors made love to her. This supposed priest pointed out that he had already sacrificed the life of his own brother— that was me—by wrongly choosing to help the maiden, and that if he did not sin with the new lady now, he would have a second life on his conscience. I ought to have mentioned that the two knights left me for dead, and Bors found me apparently dead, and he had taken my body to an abbey for burial. Of course, I recovered later.

"Well, the lady appeared in the castle—as stated by the feigned priest—and she confirmed the story. She said that there was a magic which would make her die for love, unless my brother was good to her. Bors now realized that he must either commit mortal sin and save the lady, or refuse to commit it and let her die. He told me afterwards that he remembered some bits out of the penny catechism, and a sermon which was once given when there was a mission at Camelot. He decided that he was not responsible for the lady's actions, while he was responsible for his own. So he refused the lady."

Guenever giggled.

"That was not the end of it. The lady was dazzlingly beautiful, and she climbed to the highest keep of her castle, with twelve lovely gentlewomen, and she said that if Bors would not stop being so pure, they would all jump off together. She said she would force them to do so. She said that he only had to have one night with her—and why need it not be fun?—for the gentlewomen to be saved. All twelve of them shouted out to Bors, and begged him for mercy, and wept for dole.

"I can tell you my brother was in a quandary. The poor things were so frightened and so pretty, and he only had to stop being obstinate to save their lives."

"What did he do?"

"He let them jump."

"Shame!" cried the Queen.

"Oh, they were only a collection of fiends, of course. The whole tower turned up-so-down and vanished immediately, and it turned out that they had been fiends all the time, including the priest."

"I suppose the moral is," said Arthur, "that you must not commit mortal sin, even if twelve lives depend upon it. Dogmatically speaking, I believe that is sound."

"I don't know what the dogma is, but I know it nearly turned my brother's hair grey."

"And a good right it had to. What was the fourth trial, if there was one?"

"The fourth one was me, and it was the last hurdle. I revived at the abbey where he had left me to be buried, and, when I was well enough, I rode to seek him out. I am sorry about it now—by the way, I shall have to ask your pardon for some of the things I did—but, when you come to think of it, it does seem a bit steep to be left by your own brother to be beaten to death. What with taking one's meals off the mantelpiece, and not understanding at the time about the things which were happening to Bors, and knowing that, just before I lost consciousness, I had seen him leave me to my fate—well, I admit that I was in a bitter frame of mind. In fact, I was murderous.

"I found Bors at a chapel in the forest, and I told him at once that I was going to kill him. I said: 'I shall do to thee as a felon or a traitor, for ye be the untruest knight that ever came out of so worthy an house.' Bors refused to fight. I said: 'If you don't fight, I shall kill you as you stand.' Bors said that he couldn't fight his own brother, of all people. He said that he was not even allowed to kill ordinary chaps on the Grail Quest, so how could he kill his brother? I said: 'I do not care what you are allowed to do, or not allowed to do. If you like to defend yourself, I shall fight you: if not, I shall kill you anyway.' I was furious. Bors just knelt down and asked for mercy.

"I can see now," he went on, "that it was right enough for Bors to do as he did. He was after the Grail, he was in the anti-homicide squadron, and I was his brother. Also it was brave of him. But I couldn't see it at the time. I simply thought he was being obstinate, and I knocked him feet-upwards as he knelt. Then I drew my sword to cut off his head."

Lionel sat in silence for a minute, looking at the plate in front of him, where there was a bright pool of ruby from the stained glass, shaped like an egg.

"You know," he said, "it's all very well to take up with morals and dogmas, so long as there is only yourself in it: but what are you to do when other people join the muddle? I suppose it was clear enough for Bors to kneel down and let me kill him, but the next thing was that a hermit came rushing out of the chapel and threw himself across my brother's body. He said he was going to prevent me at all costs from becoming a fratricide. I killed the hermit."

"Killed a defenceless man?"

"I am desperately sorry, King, but it is true. Don't forget that I was in a frightful rage, and the fellow prevented me from getting at Bors, and I am a plain man of my hands. They were baffling me with a sort of moral weapon, and I used my own weapon against it. I felt that Bors was standing up to me in an unfair way, and that this hermit was helping him. I felt he was setting his will against mine. If he wanted to save the hermit, let him stop being obstinate and get up and fight. If you see what I mean, I felt that the hermit was his business, not mine.

"I'm afraid that I was simply in a passion," admitted Lionel after a bit. "You know how you get. I wanted to fight and I was going to have it. I had said I would kill him if not, and I was going to kill him. You know how it is. It is like the sulks."

There was an uncomfortable silence.

"I had better finish my story," he said awkwardly.

"Go on."

"Well, Bors let me kill the hermit. He just lay on the ground and asked for love. I was more maddened than ever, by this time, partly by shame, and I raised my sword to cut off my brother's head there and then—when Sir Colgrevance of Gore turned up. He put himself between us and said fie on me for trying to shed my father's blood. That was the last straw, with all the hermit's blood round my feet, so I just went for Colgrevance instead. And in a few minutes I had him on the run."

"What did Bors do?"

"Poor Bors. What his feelings were at that moment, I don't like to think. There he was at his fence again, you see, and he only had to refuse it to save another life. He had wasted the hermit's, apparently through obstinacy, and now I was going to kill the innocent Colgrevance, who had tried to help him. Colgrevance kept sobbing out to him, too, saying: 'Get up and help, man. Why are you letting me be killed for you?' "

"Passive resistance," said Arthur with intense interest. "It is a new weapon. But it seems difficult to use. Go on, please."

"Well, I killed Colgrevance in fair fight. I am sorry, but I did. Then I came back to Bors, to finish the matter. He held his shield over his head, but would not struggle."

"What happened?"

"God came," said the boy solemnly. "He came between us, and dazzled us, and made our shields burn."

There was a long pause while Arthur digested the first tidings of certain things which he had hoped or feared.

"You see," said Lionel, "Bors prayed."

"And God came?"

"I don't know exactly what happened, but the sun was flaming on our shields. Something happened. We suddenly stopped fighting and began to laugh. I saw that Bors was an idiot, and he kissed me and we made it up. Then he told me his story, as I have told you, and sailed away in a magic ship, covered in white samite. Bors will find the Grail, if anybody does find it, and that is the end of my story."

They sat silent, finding it difficult to talk about spiritual matters, until finally Sir Lionel spoke for the last time.

"It is all very well for Bors," he said complainingly, "but what about the hermit? What about Sir Colgrevance? Why didn't God save them?"

"Dogmas are difficult things," said Arthur.

Guenever said: "We don't know what their past history was. The killing didn't do any harm to their souls. Perhaps it even helped their souls, to die like that. Perhaps God gave them this good death because it was the best thing for them."

# 30

*The third important arrival was Sir Aglovale, who* came rather late in the afternoon, when the rubies had left the table and climbed the wall. He was a lad of less than twenty summers, with a fine noble face and a sense of humour. He was still in mourning for his Father, King Pellinore—and he signified this by wearing a black sash on his shield arm. At least, they thought it was for King Pellinore. As a matter of fact, his mother had died as well since they last saw him. He was also bringing news of the death of a sister—for nearly all of Pellinore's family had been unfortunate.

"Is Gawaine here?" asked Aglovale. "Where are Mordred and Agravaine?"

He glanced about him, as if he might actually find them in the Hall. Above his head, the coloured beam of light fell upon a small and primitive piece of tapestry—a picture of some knights in chain mail, with nose guards on their painted helmets, chasing a boar.

Arthur said: "Aglovale, they are here. My happiness is in your hands."

"I see."

"Are you going to kill them?"

"I came to kill Gawaine first. It seems queer, after looking for the Holy Grail."

"Aglovale, you have every right to try for revenge against the Orkneys, and I will not stop you if you do try. But I want you to know what you are doing. Your father killed their father and your brother slept with their mother. No, don't explain about it—let me remind you of the facts. Then the Orkneys killed your father and brother. Now you are going to kill some of the Orkneys, and Gawaine's sons will kill your sons, and so we shall go on. That is the law of the North.

"But, Aglovale, I am trying to make a new law in Britain, by which people don't have to go on shedding young blood for ever. Have you thought that it may be uphill work for me? There is a saying that two wrongs don't make a right, and I am fond of this saying. Don't apply it to yourself— apply it to me. I could have punished the Orkneys for murdering your brother. I could have cut their heads off. Would you have liked me to do that?"

"Yes."

"Perhaps I ought to have."

Arthur looked at his hands, as he often did when he was in trouble.

Then he said: "It is a pity you never had the opportunity of seeing the Orkneys at home. They didn't have a happy family life like yours."

Aglovale said: "Do you think my family life is very happy now? Do you know that my mother died a few months ago? Father used to call her Piggy."

"Aglovale, I am sorry. We had not heard."

"People used to laugh at my father, King. I know he was not a formidable character. But he must have made a fairly good husband, mustn't he, for my mother to die of loneliness because he had gone? Mother was not an introspective person, King, but she faded away after the Orkneys had killed father and Lamorak. Now she is in the same grave."

"You must do what you think right, Aglovale. I know you are a true Pellinore, and will do that. I won't ask any favours for myself. But will you let me mention three things? The first is that your father was the first knight I ever fell in love with: yet I didn't punish Gawaine. The second is that all the Orkneys adored their mother. She made them love her too much, but she only loved herself. And the third thing—oh, Aglovale, listen to this one—is that a king can only work with his best tools."

"I'm afraid I don't follow the third point."

"Do you think," asked Arthur, "that feuds are good things? Are they making for happiness in your two families?"

"Not exactly."

"If I want to stop the feud law, do you think it would be any good my appealing to Gawaine, and to people like him?"

"I see."

"What good would it have done if I had executed all the Orkney family? We should only have had three knights less to work with. And their lives have been unhappy, Aglovale. So, you see, my hope is with you."

"I must think it over."

"Do. Don't decide anything quickly. Don't consider me. Just do what you think right, because you are a Pellinore—and then I know all will turn out for the best. Now tell me about your Grail adventures, and forget about the Orkneys for one evening."

Aglovale heaved a sigh, and said: "So far as I am concerned, there have not been any Grail adventures. But it has cost me a sister. Perhaps a brother as well."

"Is your sister dead? My poor boy, I thought she was safe in a convent."

"They have found her dead in a sort of boat."

"Dead in a boat!"

"Yes, a magic boat. She had a long letter in her hands, all about the Grail Quest and about my brother Percy."

"Are we hurting you by asking questions?"

"No. I like to talk about it. I still have Dornar left, and it seems that Percy has been distinguishing himself."

"What has Sir Percivale been doing?"

"Perhaps I had better tell you what the letter said, from the start.

"As you know," began Sir Aglovale, "Percy was the one in our family who took after Daddy most. He was gentle and humble, and a bit vague. He was shy too. When he met Bors in this magic boat of theirs, he was abashed of him, it says in the letter. He was a maiden knight, like Galahad, you see. I used often to think, when I saw them together, that he and Daddy made a good pair. They were both fond of animals, for one thing, and they knew how to get on with them. There was Daddy's Questing Beast, and now Percy seems to have been befriending lions mainly, since he went away. Also Percy was benevolent and simple. One day, when they were trying to pull a blessed sword out of a scabbard—I mean the three of them in the holy boat—Percy was given the first pull. He did not succeed, of course—all that sort of thing was reserved for Galahad—but when he had failed he just looked round proudly and said: 'By my faith, now I have failed!' However, I am getting ahead of my story.

"It says in the letter that the first adventure Percy had, after leaving Vagon, was to ride off with Sir Lancelot until they met Sir Galahad. They jousted with him, and Galahad gave them both a fall. Then Percy left Lancelot, and went to a hermitage, where he was confessed. The hermit advised him to follow Galahad to Goothe or Carbonek, and never to fight him. As a matter of fact, Percy had been seized by a sort of enthusiastic hero worship for Galahad, so the advice suited him. He rode on to Carbonek, where he heard the abbey clock smite as he was pricking through the forest—and it was there that he came across King Evelake, who was about four hundred years old. I had better leave out about Evelake, for I don't quite understand it. I think the old man couldn't die until the Holy Grail had been found, or something like that. But King Pelles is mixed up with it too, and all that part of the letter is a bit difficult to follow. Anyway, Percy had a fight with eight knights and twenty men-at-arms, who set on him at Carbonek, and he was rescued in the nick of time by Galahad himself. Unfortunately his horse was killed, and Galahad rode away again without even passing the time of day.

"You know," said Lionel, pausing, "it may be all very well to be holy and invincible, and I don't hold it against Galahad for being a virgin, but don't you think that people might be a little human? I don't want to be catty, but that young man makes my hair go the wrong way. Why couldn't he say Good-morning or something, instead of rescuing a fellow and then riding away in silence with that white nose of his in the air?"

Arthur made no comment, and the young man resumed his story.

"Percy was trying to join up with Galahad, according to instructions, and Galahad had ridden off, so the poor old fellow just went running after him shouting out, 'I say!' He had some dreadful troubles trying to borrow horses from people, and finally ended up on a groom's hackney, cantering after Galahad as fast as it could go. But a knight turned up and knocked him off his hackney—I'm afraid our family was never exactly in the heroic style—and there he was on foot again, with Galahad no nearer. Well, a lady appeared at this point—they found out afterwards that she was a fairy, and not a very nice one at that—and asked him fiercely what he was trying to do. Percy said: 'I do neither good nor great ill, what?' So the lady lent him a black horse which turned out to be a fiend, and it vanished in dramatic circumstances when Percy luckily crossed himself that evening. He was in a sort of desert by that time, where he proceeded to make friends with a lion by rescuing it from a serpent. Percy was always keen on our Dumb Friends, as I said.

"The next thing that happened was that a perfectly delicious gentlewoman turned up, with full camping equipment, and invited Percy to dinner. He was hungry—what with the desert and so forth—and he had never been accustomed to drinking wine, so he had a terrific party. I'm afraid he got a bit huffed, and the upshot was that he laughed too much and got excited, and asked the lady—well, you know. The lady was agreeable, and it was just going to come off nicely, when Percy luckily noticed the cross on the pommel of his sword, which was lying on the ground. He blessed himself again, and the lady's pavilion turned up-so-down, and off she went in a ship, roaring and yelling, and the water burned after her.

"Percy was so ashamed of himself, and had such a headache next morning, that he stuck his sword into his own thigh as a punishment. After that, the holy boat turned up, with Bors inside it, and the two of them sailed away together, wherever it would take them."

Guenever said: "If that holy boat was intended to convey people to the Grail, I can perfectly well understand how Bors was in it. We know that he had been through some dreadful tests. But why Sir Percivale? I don't mean to be rude, Sir Aglovale, but your brother does not seem to have *done* much."

"He had preserved his integrity," said Arthur. "He was as clean as Bors—indeed, he was cleaner. He was perfectly innocent. God says something about suffering little children to come unto Him."

"But such a muddle!"

Arthur was annoyed.

"If God is supposed to be merciful," he retorted, "I don't see why He shouldn't allow people to stumble into heaven, just as well as climb there. Go on with your letter, Sir Aglovale."

"It is at this point that my sister comes into it. She was a nun, you know, and when they first cut off her hair, there was a vision to say that it ought to be kept in a box. My sister was a learned woman, who had a vocation to pursue religious studies. Just about the time when Percy and Bors entered the boat, a new vision came to the convent which told her to do certain things. The first was to look for Sir Galahad.

"Galahad was spending a night in a hermitage near Carbonek, after knocking out Sir Gawaine, when my sister found him. She made him get up and arm himself, and together they rode off to the Collibe Sea, where, beyond a strong castle, they found the blessed barge with Bors and Percy waiting. They all sailed away together, until they came to a swallow of the sea, between two high rocks—and there a second barge was waiting. There was some reticence about entering the new boat, because it had a scroll on it which warned people off unless they were in perfect faith—but Galahad stepped aboard as usual, with his insufferable self-confidence. They followed him and found a rich bed with a crown of silk on it and a part-drawn sword. It was King David's sword. There were also three magic spindles, made out of the Eden tree, and two inferior swords for Percy and Bors. Naturally the main sword was for Galahad. The pommel was of marvellous stone, the scales of the haft were of the ribs of two beasts called Calidone and Ertanax, the scabbard was of serpent's skin, and one side of the sword was as red as blood. But the girdle was only plain hemp.

"My sister set to work with the spindles, and made a new girdle out of her own hair, which she had brought in the box according to instructions. She explained to them about the history of the sword, which she knew from her studies, and how the spindles had come to be made of wood which was coloured all through the grain, and finally the sword was put on Galahad. She was a virgin, and she fixed it on a virgin, with her own hair. Then they returned to their first vessel and sailed away toward Carlisle.

"On the way to Carlisle they rescued an old gentleman who was being kept prisoner by some wicked men in his castle. They killed a lot of these men in the fight, and Bors and Percy were upset about it, but Galahad said it was perfectly all right killing people who had not been christened—and it turned out that these had not been. So the old man of the castle asked permission to die in Galahad's arms, and Galahad condescendingly granted it.

"When they got to Carlisle, there was another castle which belonged to a lady who had the measle. The doctors told her that the only cure was to bathe in a dish filled with blood from a clean virgin of royal lineage. Everybody who went that way was forced to be bled by the people of the castle, and the description fitted my sister. The three knights fought all day to save her, but in the evening the reason for the custom was explained to them, and my siser said: 'Better is one harm than two.' She consented to be bled, stopped the fighting, and the next morning they did it. She blessed the surgeons, arranged for her body to be floated off in the holy boat with this letter in her hand, and then she died under the operation."

Sir Aglovale came back to the King, as he was going up to bed after the usual condolences and exclamations had been made. The Hall was dark, and the jewels of light had gone.

"By the way," he said shyly. "Will you ask the Orkney faction to have dinner with me tomorrow?"

Arthur looked at him closely through the looming twilight —then began an enormous smile. He kissed Aglovale, with a tear which ran into one corner of his smile. He said: "Now I have got a new Pellinore to love."

# 3

*Still there was no news of the great Dulac. He had* become a magical name which gave warmth to all hearts, particularly women's, in whatever place he was. He had become a *maestro* himself—was regarded as he had once regarded Uncle Dap. If you have learned to fly, or been

taught by a great musician or fencer, you have only to remember that teacher, to know how the people of Camelot
had come to think of Lancelot. They would have died for
him—for his mastery. And he was lost.

The survivors trickled in—Palomides, now christened
and bored to death with the Questing Beast and aged by
his long poetic rivalry with Sir Tristram for the love of La
Beale Isoud—Sir Grummore Grummursum, as bald as an
egg now, nearly eighty, afflicted by gout, but still bravely
questin'—Kay, keen-eyed and sarcastic—Sir Dinadan making jokes about his own defeats, although he was so tired
he could barely keep his lids apart—even old Sir Ector of
the Forest Sauvage, eighty-five years old and tottering.

They brought with them broken arms and rumours. One
said that Galahad, Bors, the other Ector and a nun had
been present at a miraculous Mass. It had been celebrated
by a lamb, served by a man, a lion, an eagle, and an ox.
After the Mass, the celebrant had passed out through a
stained-glass lamb in one of the church windows, without
breaking the glass, thus signifying the immaculate concep-
tion. Another told how pitilessly Galahad had dealt with
a fiend in a tomb, how he had cooled the well of lust, and
how the castle of the leprous lady had finally been tumbled down.

These people, with their rusty armour and hewn shields,
had seen Lancelot here and there. They spoke of a harnessed
ugly man, praying at a wayside cross—of a worn face
asleep in the moonlight on its shield. They spoke also of
unbelievable things—of Lancelot unhorsed, defeated, kneeling after he had been knocked down.

Arthur asked questions, sent messengers, remembered his
captain in his prayers. Guenever, in a dangerous frame of
mind, began walking on the edge of a verbal precipice. At
any moment she might say or do something which would
be a compromise upon herself and upon her lover. Mordred
and Agravaine, who had been among the first to retire from
the Quest, watched and waited with bright eyes. They were
as motionless as Lord Burleigh is said to have been at Queen
Elizabeth's councils, or as a sleek cat who faces the mousehole secretly—a presence, a concentration.

The rumours began to be of Lancelot's death. He had
been killed by a black knight at a ford—he had jousted with
his own son, who had broken his neck—he had gone mad
again, after being beaten by his son, and was riding over-

thwart and endlong—his armour had been stolen by a mysterious knight, and he had been eaten by a beast—he had fought against two hundred and fifty knights, been taken captive, and hanged like a dog. A strong faction believed and hinted that he had been murdered, sleeping, by the Orkneys, and had been buried under a pile of leaves.

The faint tail of knighthood straggled in by twos and threes, then one at a time, then with intervals of days between the solitary riders. The list of dead and missing, kept by Sir Bedivere, began to settle down into a list of dead, as the missing either returned exhausted or were confirmed dead by reliable report. An obituary tinge began to be present in the whispers about Lancelot. He was loved by nearly everybody, so that the speakers did not like to do more than whisper of his death, for fear that if they spoke of it aloud they would make it true. But they whispered about his goodness and remarkable visage: about such-and-such a blow which he had once given to so-and-so: about the grace of his leg-glides. A few obscure pages and kitchenmaids, who remembered vividly a smile or a tip at Christmas, went to sleep with damp pillows, although they knew that the great captain could not have been expected even to remember their names. Kay startled everybody by declaring with a sniff that he himself had always been a mean blackguard, and then went quickly out of the room blowing his nose. In all the court a tension grew, and a feeling of doom.

Lancelot came back out of a rainstorm, wet and small. He was leading an old barrel of a white mare, without a trot left in her. The black autumn clouds were behind them, and her hollow ribs stood out like flake-white against their indigo. A magic, a mind-reading, an intuition must have taken place—for all the palace battlements and turrets, and the drawbridge of the Great Gate, were thronged with people waiting, and watching, and pointing in silence, before ever he appeared. When the tiny figure could be seen, threading wearily through the far trees of the chase, a murmuration went up among the people. It was Lancelot in a scarlet gown beside the white. He was safe. Everything was known about all his adventures, before anything had been spoken. Arthur ran about like a madman, telling everybody to go in, to leave the battlements, to give the man a chance. By the time the figure arrived, there was nobody to hurt him. Only, the Great Gate stood open and Uncle Dap was there, bent and white-headed, to receive his horse.

Hundreds of eyes, glancing from behind curtains, saw the
spent man hand the reins to his squire—saw him standing
with bowed head, which he had never raised—saw him turn
and pace toward his own apartment, and vanish in the darkness of the turret stair.

Two hours later Uncle Dap presented himself in the
King's chamber. He had been undressing Lancelot and putting him to bed. Under the scarlet gown, he said, there had
been a fair white garment—under that, a horrible shirt of
hair. Sir Lancelot had sent him with a message. He was
very tired, and begged the King's pardon. He would wait
on him tomorrow. Meanwhile, so that there should be no
delay about the important news, Uncle Dap was to tell the
King that the Holy Grail had been found. Galahad, Percivale and Bors had found it, and with it, and with the body
of Percivale's sister, they had arrived at Sarras in Babylon.
The Grail could not be brought to Camelot. Bors would be
coming home eventually, but the others were never to
return.

# 32

*Guenever had overdressed for the occasion. She had*
put on a make-up which she did not need, and put it on
badly. She was forty-two.

When Lancelot saw her waiting for him at the table, with
Arthur beside her, the heart-sack broke in his wame, and
the love inside it ran about his veins. It was his old love
for a girl of twenty, standing proudly by her throne with
the present of captives about her—but now the same girl
was standing in other surroundings, the surroundings of
bad make-up and loud silks, by which she was trying to defy
the invincible doom of human destiny. He saw her as the
passionate spirit of innocent youth, now beleaguered by
the trick which is played on youth—the trick of treachery
in the body, which turns flesh into green bones. Her stupid
finery was not vulgar to him, but touching. The girl was
still there, still appealing from behind the breaking barri-

cade of rouge. She had made the brave protest: I will not be vanquished. Under the clumsy coquetry, the undignified clothes, there was the human cry for help. The young eyes were puzzled, saying: It is I, inside here—what have they done to me? I will not submit. Some part of her spirit knew that the powder was making a guy of her, and hated it, and tried to hold her lover with the eyes alone. They said: Don't look at all this. Look at me. I am still here, in the eyes. Look at me, here in the prison, and help me out. Another part said: I am not old, it is illusion. I am beautifully made-up. See, I will perform the movements of youth. I will defy the enormous army of age.

Lancelot saw one soul alone, a condemned and innocent child, holding her indefensible position with the contemptible arms of hair dye and orange silk, with which she had—with what fears?—hoped to please him. He saw

> The impassioned, pigmy fist
> Clenched cloudward and defiant,
> The pride that would prevail, the doomed protagonist
> Grappling the ghostly giant.

Arthur said: "Are you rested now? How are you feeling?"

"We are so glad to see you," said Guenever, "so glad to have you back."

They, on their side, saw a man of serenity—the kind of sage that Kipling described in Kim. They saw their new Lancelot as a silence and perception. He had come from the height of his spirit.

Lancelot said: "I'm quite rested now, thank you. I expect you want to know about the Grail."

The King said: "It has been selfish of me, I'm afraid. I have kept everybody out. We will have it written down and put in almeries at Salisbury. But we did want to hear it from you first, Lance, without interruptions."

"Are you sure you won't be too tired to tell?"

Lancelot smiled and took their hands.

"There isn't much to tell," he said. "After all, I didn't find the Grail myself."

"Sit down and break your fast. You can talk when you have eaten. You are much thinner."

"Would you like a glass of hippocras, or some perry?"

"I am not drinking at present," he said, "thank you."

While he was eating, the King and Queen sat on either

side and watched. Before he knew that he wanted the salt—just as his fingers were beginning to reach for it—they handed it to him. He laughed at their serious faces, which made him feel uncomfortable, and pretended to asperge Arthur with his cup of water to make them smile.

"Do you want a relic?" he asked. "You could have my boots if you like. They are quite worn out."

"Lancelot, it is not a thing to joke about. I believe you have seen the Holy Grail yourself."

"Even if I have seen it, I don't need to be handed the salt."

But they still looked at him.

Lancelot said: "Please understand. It is Galahad and the others who were allowed the Grail. I was not allowed it. So it will be wrong and you will hurt me, if you make a fuss about it. How many of the knights got back?"

"Half," said Arthur. "We have heard their stories."

"I expect you know more about it than I do."

"We only know that the homicides and those who didn't confess were turned back; and you say that Galahad, Bors, and Percivale were allowed. I am told that Galahad and Percivale were virgins; and Bors, although he was not quite a virgin, turned out to be a first-class theologian. I suppose Bors passed for his dogma, and Percivale for his innocence. I know hardly anything about Galahad, except that everybody dislikes him."

"Dislikes him?"

"They complain about his being inhuman."

Lancelot considered his cup.

"He is inhuman," he said at last. "But why should he be human? Are angels supposed to be human?"

"I don't quite follow."

"Do you think that if the Archangel Michael were to come here this minute, he would say: 'What charming weather we are having today! Won't you have a glass of whisky?' "

"I suppose not."

"Arthur, you mustn't feel that I am rude when I say this. You must remember that I have been away in strange and desert places, sometimes quite alone, sometimes in a boat with nobody but God and the whistling sea. Do you know, since I have been back with people, I have felt I was going mad? Not from the sea, but from the people. All my gains are slipping away, with the people round me. A lot of the things which you and Jenny say, even, seem to me to be needless: strange noises: empty. You know what I mean. 'How are you?'—'Do sit down.'—'What nice weather we are having!' What does it matter? People talk far too much. Where I have been, and where Galahad is, it is a waste of time to have 'manners.' Manners are only needed between people, to keep their empty affairs in working order. Manners makyth man, you know, not God. So you can understand how Galahad may have seemed inhuman, and mannerless, and so on, to the people who were buzzing and clacking about him. He was far away in his spirit, living on desert islands, in silence, with eternity."

"I see."

"Please don't think me rude to say these things. I am trying to explain a feeling. If you had ever been to Patrick's Purgatory, you would know what I mean. People seem ridiculous when you come out."

"I see exactly. I understand about Galahad too."

"He was a lovely person really. I spent a long time in a boat with him, and I know. But this did not mean that we always had to be offering each other the best seat in the boat."

"It was my worldly knights who disliked him most. I see. However, we are waiting to hear your story, Lance, not Galahad's."

"Yes, Lance; tell us how you got on, and leave out about the angels."

"As I was never allowed to meet any angels," said Sir Lancelot with a smile, "it's the best thing I can do."

"Go on."

"When I left Vagon," began the commander-in-chief, "I had a shrewd idea that the best place to search would be the castle of King Pelles——"

He stopped, for Guenever had made a sudden move.

"I didn't go to the castle," he said gently, "because I had an accident. Something happened to me which was outside my own plans, and after that I went where I was taken."

"What was the accident?"

"It was not an accident really. It was the first stroke of a correction which I have had, and for which I am thankful. Do you know, I shall be talking about God a great deal, and this is a word which offends unholy people just as badly as words like 'damn' and so on offend the holy ones. What shall we have to do about it?"

"Just assume that we are the holy ones," said the King, "and go on about your accident."

"I was riding with Sir Percivale, when we came across my son. He unhorsed me at the first tilt—my son did."

"A surprise attack," said Arthur quickly.

"It was a fair tilt."

"Naturally you would not want to beat your son."

"I did want to beat him."

Guenever said: "Everybody has to be unlucky sometimes."

"I rode at Galahad with all the skill I could manage, and he gave me the finest fall I ever had.

"Indeed," added Lancelot, with one of his gaping grins, "I might say that he gave me one of the only falls I ever had. The first thing I can remember feeling, when I was lying on the ground, was pure astonishment. It was only later that it turned to something else."

"What did you do?"

"I was lying on the ground, and Galahad was standing his horse beside me without saying a word, when a woman came up who was a recluse in a hermitage where we had been fighting. She made a curtsy and said: 'God be with thee, best knight of the world'."

Lancelot looked on the table, and moved his hand in a gesture to stroke the cloth. Then he cleared his throat and said: "I looked up, to see who was talking to me."

The King and Queen waited.

Lancelot cleared his throat again: "I am trying to tell you about my spirit, if you see what I mean, not about my adventures. So I can't be modest about it. I am a bad man, I know, but I was always good with arms. It was a consolation to me in my badness, sometimes, to think—to know that I was the best knight of the world."

"And so?"

"Well, the lady was not talking to me."

They digested the position in silence, watching a flutter which had developed on the right side of his mouth.

"Galahad?"

"Yes," said Sir Lancelot. "The lady was looking past me at my son Galahad, and he cantered away as soon as she had spoken. Soon afterwards the lady went away as well."

"What a disgusting thing to say!" exclaimed the King. "What a dirty, deliberate outrage! She ought to have been whipped."

"It was true."

"But to come and say it in front of you on purpose!" cried Guenever. "Besides, after a single fall——"

"She said what God told her to say. You see, she was a holy woman. But I couldn't understand it at the time——

"I am much holier now," he added apologetically, "but at the time I couldn't bear it. I felt as if my prop had been taken from me, and I knew that she only said the simple truth. I felt as if she had broken the last piece of my heart. So I rode away from Percivale to be by myself, like an animal, with my hurt. Percivale suggested something to do, but I only said: 'Do as ye list.' I rode away with heavy cheer, overthwart and endlong, to find a place where I could split my heart alone. I rode to a chapel eventually, feeling as if I might be going mad again. You see, Arthur, I had a lot of troubles on my mind which being a famous fighter seemed to make up for, a little, and when that was gone it felt as if there was nothing left to me."

"There was everything left. You are still the finest fighter in the world."

"The funny thing was that the chapel had no door. I don't know whether it was my sins, or my resentment at being broken, but I couldn't get in. I slept on my shield outside, and there was a dream of a knight who came and took away my helm and my sword and my horse. I tried to wake up, but I couldn't. All my knightly things were being taken away from me, but I could not wake, because my heart was full of bitter thoughts. A voice said that I was never more to have worship—but I only rebelled against the voice, and so, when I woke, the things were gone.

"Arthur, if I don't make you understand about that night, you will never understand the rest. I had spent all my childhood, when I might have been chasing butterflies, learning to be your best knight. Afterwards I was wicked, but I had one thing. I used to feel so proud, inside myself, because I knew that I was supposed to be top of the averages. It was a base feeling, I know. But I had nothing else to be proud of. First my Word and my miracles had gone, and now, on the night I am telling you about, this was gone too. When I woke up and found that my arms were taken, I walked about in agony. It was disgusting, but I cried and cursed. That was the time when they began to break me."

"My poor Lance."

"It was the best thing that ever happened. In the morning, do you know, I heard the little fowls singing—and that cheered me up. Funny to be comforted by a lot of birds. I never had time for bird's-nesting when I was small. You would have known what kind of birds they were, Arthur—but I couldn't tell. There was one very small one, which cocked its tail in the air and looked at me. It was about as big as the rowel of a spur."

"Perhaps it was a wren."

"Well, then, it was a wren. Will you show me one to-morrow? The thing which these birds made me see, because my black heart could not see it alone, was that if I was to be punished, it was because of my own nature. What happened to the birds was according to the nature of birds. They made me see that the world was beautiful if you were beautiful, and that you couldn't get unless you gave. And you had to give without wanting to get. So I accepted that beating from Galahad, and the taking away of my armour; and in a blessed moment, I went to find a confessor so that I would not be wicked any more."

"All the knights," said Arthur, "who got to the Grail had the sense to be confessed first."

"I had always made bad confessions before that. I have lived nearly all my life in mortal sin. But this time I confessed everything."

"Everything?" asked the Queen.

"Everything. You see, Arthur, I have had a sin on my conscience all my life, which I thought I could not tell to people, because——"

"There is no need to tell it to us," said the Queen, "if it hurts you. After all, we are not your confessors. It was enough to tell the priest."

"Leave her in peace," agreed the King. "At any rate she bore a fine son, who seems to have achieved the Grail."

He was alluding to Elaine.

Lancelot looked with sudden misery from one to the other, and clenched his fists. All three stopped breathing.

"I confessed, then," he said eventually, and they breathed again—but his voice was leaden. "I was given a penance." He paused, still doubtful, half recognizing the moment as a cross-road of his life. Now was the time, they all knew, if there ever was to be a time, when he ought to have it out with his friend and king—yet Guenever was thwarting him. It was her secret too.

"The penance was to wear the hair shirt of a certain dead

religious that we knew of," he went on at last, defeated. "I was to take no meat or wine, and to hear Mass daily. So I left the priest's house after three days, and rode back to a cross near the place where I had lost my arms. The priest had loaned me some to go on with. Well, I slept at the cross that night, and had another dream—and in the morning, the knight who had stolen my armour came back. I jousted with him and retrieved the armour. Wasn't that strange?"

"I suppose you were in a state of grace now, after your good confession, so you could be trusted with your might."

"That was what I thought, but you will see about it presently. I thought, now that I had got my sin off my chest, I would be allowed to be the best knight in the world once more. I rode away very happy, trying to sing a bit, until I came to a fair plain with a castle and pavilions and everything—and there was a tournament of five hundred knights in black and white. The white knights were winning, so I thought I would join with the black. I thought I would do a great exploit of rescue for the weaker party, now that I was forgiven." He stopped, and closed his eyes. "But the white knights," he added, opening them, "took me prisoner quite soon."

"You mean you were beaten again?"

"I was beaten and disgraced. I thought I was more sinful than ever. When they had set me loose, I rode and cursed just as I had done on the first evening, and, when the night came, I lay down under an apple tree and actually cried myself to sleep."

"But this is heresy," exclaimed the Queen, who was a good theologian, like most women. "If you were clean confessed, and had done penance and been absolved——"

"I had done penance for one sin," said Lancelot. "But I had forgotten about another one. In the night I had a new dream, of an old man who came to me and said: 'Ah, Lancelot of evil faith and poor belief, why is thy will turned so lightly toward thy deadly sin?' Jenny, I have all my life been in another sin, the worst of all. It was pride that made me try to be the best knight in the world. Pride made me show off and help the weaker party of the tournament. You could call it vainglory. Just because I had confessed about—about the woman, that did not make me into a good man."

"So you were beaten."

"Yes, I was beaten. And next morning I went to another hermit to be confessed again. This time I made a thorough job of it. I was told that it was not enough, in the Quest for the Grail, to be continent and to refrain from killing people. All boasting and pride of the world had to be left behind, for God did not like such deeds in his Quest. I had to renounce all earthly glory. And I did renounce it, and was absolved."

"What happened next?"

"I rode to the water of Mortoise, where a black knight came to joust with me. He knocked me down as well."

"A third defeat!"

Guenever cried: "But if you really were absolved this time!"

Lancelot put his hand over hers, and smiled.

"If a boy steals sweets," he said, "and his parents punish him, he may be very sorry and good afterwards. But that doesn't entitle him to steal more sweets, does it? Nor does it mean that he must be given sweets. God was not punishing me by letting the black knight knock me down—he was only withholding the special gift of victory which it had always been within his power to bestow."

"But, my poor Lance, to have given up your glory and not to get anything back! When you were a sinful man you were always victorious, so why should you always be beaten when you were heavenly? And why are you always hurt by the things you love? What did you do?"

"I knelt down in the water of Mortoise, Jenny, where he had knocked me—and I thanked God for the adventure."

# 33

*Arthur could not stand much more of this.*

"It is disgusting," he exclaimed indignantly. "I don't like to listen to it. Why should a good, kind, dear person be tortured like that? It makes me feel ashamed inside, even to hear of it. What——"

"Hush," said Sir Lancelot. "I am very glad that I gave up

love and glory. And, what is more, I was practically forced to do it. God did not take such pains for Gawaine or Lionel, did he?"

"Bah!" said King Arthur, in the tone which Gawaine had used before him.

Lancelot laughed.

"Well," he said, "that's a convincing remark. But perhaps you had better hear the end of the story.

"I lay down by the water of Mortoise that evening, and a dream came which told me to go in a ship. The ship was there when I woke up, sure enough; and when I went inside it there was the most lovely smell and feeling and food to eat and—well, whatever you can think of. I was 'fulfilled with all things that I thought on or desired.' I know I can't explain to you about the ship at this hour, because, for one thing, it is fading from me now that I am with people. But you mustn't think just of incense in the ship, or precious cloths on it. There were these, but they were not the loveliness. You must think of a tar smell too, and the colours of the sea. Sometimes it was quite green, like thick glass, and you could see the bottom. Sometimes it was all in big, slow terraces, and the water fowl who were flying along the top vanished in the hollows. When it was stormy, the huge fangs of the breakers gnawed at the rocky islands. They made white fangs on the cliffs, not as they burst up, but as the water streamed down. At night, when it was calm, you could see the stars reflected on the wet sands. There were two stars quite close together. The sands were all ribbed, like the roof of your mouth. And there was the smell of seaweed, the noise of the lonely wind. There were islands with little birds on them like rabbits, but their noses were rainbows. The winter was the best thing, because then there were the geese on the islands—long smoke lines of them singing like hounds in the cold streak of morning.

"It is no good being indignant about what God did to me at the beginning, Arthur, for he gave me far more in return. I said: 'Fair Sweet Father Jesu Christ, I wot not in what joy I am, for this joy passeth all earthly joys that ever I was in.'

"A strange feature about the ship was that there was a dead woman in it. She had a letter in her hand which told me how the others had been getting on. It was stranger still that I was not frightened of her for being dead. She had such a calm face that she was company for me. We felt a sort of communion together in the ship and in the sea. I don't know what I was fed on.

"When I had been in this ship with the dead lady for a month, Galahad was brought to us. He gave me his blessing, and let me kiss his sword."

Arthur was as red as a turkey cock.

"Did you ask for his blessing?" he demanded.

"Of course."

"Well!" said Arthur.

"We sailed in the holy ship for six months together. I got to know my son very well in that time, and he seemed to care for me. Quite often, he said the most courteous things. We had adventures with animals on the out islands all that time. There were sea weasels which whistled beautifully, and Galahad showed me cranes flying along the water, with their shadows flying under them, upside down. He told me that the fishing people call a cormorant the Old Black Hag, and that ravens live as long as men. They went cronk, cronk, high in the air, and came tumbling down for fun. One day we saw a pair of choughs: they were beautiful! And the seals! They came along beside the music of the ship, and talked like men.

"One Monday we came to a forest land. A white knight rode down on the shore and told Galahad to come out of the boat. I knew that he was being taken away to find the Holy Grail, so I was sad that I couldn't go too. Do you remember, when you were little, how children used to pick up sides for a game and perhaps you wouldn't be picked at all? It felt like that, but worse. I asked Galahad to pray for me. I asked him to pray God to hold me in his service. Then we kissed each other and said good-bye."

Guenever complained: "If you were in a state of grace, I can't understand why you should have been left."

"It is difficult," said Lancelot.

He opened his hands and looked between them on the table.

"Perhaps my intentions were bad," he said at length. "Perhaps, inside myself, unconsciously, you could say, I had not a proper purpose of amendment. . . ."

The Queen was subtly radiant as she listened.

"Nonsense," she whispered, meaning the opposite. She pressed his hand warmly, and Lancelot took it away.

"When I prayed to be *held*," he said, "perhaps it was because . . ."

"It seems to me," said Arthur, "that you are allowing yourself the luxury of a needlessly tender conscience."

"Perhaps. At all events, I was not picked."

He sat, watching the sea heaving between his hands, and hearing the wooden clatter of gannets on an island cliff.

"The ship took me out to sea again," he said at length, "on a big wind. I did not sleep very much, and I prayed a great deal. I asked that, in spite of not being picked, I might be allowed to get *some* tidings of the Sangreal."

In the silence which fell on the room, they pursued their separate thoughts. Arthur's were of the pitiful spectacle—the show of an earthly, sinful man, but the best of them, plodding along behind these three supernatural virgins; his doomed, courageous, vain toil.

"Funny," said Lancelot, "how the people who can't pray say that prayers are not answered, however much the people who can pray say they are. My ship took me at midnight, in a great gale, to the back side of Carbonek Castle. Strange, also, that it should have been the very place I was heading for when I started.

"The moment the ship came alongside, I knew that I was to be granted a part of my desire. I couldn't see it all, of course, because I was not a Galahad or Bors. But they were very kind to me. They went out of their way to be kind.

"It was black as death behind the castle. I put on my armour and went up. There were two lions at the entry of the stairs, who tried to bar my way. I drew my sword to fight them, but a hand struck me on the arm. It was silly of me, of course, to trust in my sword, when I could have trusted in God. So I blessed myself with my numb arm and went in, and the lions didn't hurt me. All the doors were open except the last one, and there I kneeled down. When I prayed, it opened.

"Arthur, this must seem untrue as I tell it. I don't know a way of putting it in words. Behind the last door there was a chapel. They were at Mass.

"Oh, Jenny, the beautiful chapel with all its lights and everything! You would say: 'The flowers and the candles.' But it was not these. Perhaps there were none.

"It was, oh, the shout of it—the power and the glory. It seized on all my senses to drag me in.

"But I couldn't go in, Arthur and Jenny—there was a sword to stop me. Galahad was inside, and Bors, and Percivale. There were nine other knights, from France and Danemark and Ireland: and the lady from my ship was there as well. The Grail was there, Arthur, on a silver table, and other things! But I was forbidden to go in, for all my yearning at the door. I don't know who the priest was. It may have been Joseph of Arimathea, it may have been—oh, well. I did go in to help him—in spite of the sword—because he was carrying what was too heavy to be carried. I only wanted to help, Arthur, as God was my witness. But a breath smote my face at the last door like a blast from a furnace, and there I fell down dumb."

# 34

*In the dark chamber there was a coming and going* of maids. The cans and pails rattled on the stairway, and there was much steam. When the maids trod in the puddles on the floor, they made a slashing noise, and from the next room there was whispering mixed with the secret noise of silk.

The Queen had climbed the six steps of the wooden ladder which led to her bath, and now she was sitting on the plank inside it, with her head showing over the top. The bath was like a large beer barrel, and her head was wrapped in a white turban. She was naked, except for a pearl necklace. There was a mirror—it had been very expensive—in one corner, and a little table in another one held the scents and oils. Instead of a powder puff, there was a chamois leather bag with powdered chalk in it, scented with attar of roses from the crusades. All over the floor between the puddles, there was a confusion of linen towels for drying her, and of jewellery boxes, brocades, garments, garters, shifts, which had been brought from the other room for her to choose. There were some condemned head-dresses lying in disgrace—strange shapes of starch like candle extinguishers, and meringues, and the double horns of cows. The hair nets which kept them together were strung with pearls, and the kerchiefs were of Eastern silk. One of the ladies-in-waiting was standing in front of the Queen's tub, holding an embroidered mantle for inspection. It was charged with the impaled arms of her husband and of her father: the dragon rampant of England and the six charming lioncels passant regardant of King Leodegrance, who bore lions on account of his name. This mantle had a heavy silk tassel, like a curtain cord, to join it across her breast. The silk bordure was furred with countervair, silver and blue.

Guenever had lost her raddled look, and sat accepting the clothes which were recommended for her, without fuss. The ladies-in-waiting had a happy air. For more than a year they had waited on a Queen who was petulant, cruel, contradictory, miserable. Now she was pleased with anything, and did not hurt them. They were all quite sure that Lancelot must have become her lover again. This was not the case.

Guenever looked upon the six lioncels passant regardant —they were marching along with red tongues and claws, winking pertly over their backsides and waving their flame-tipped tails. She nodded her head with a contented, sleepy look, and the lady-in-waiting carried it to the dressing-room with a curtsy. The Queen watched her go.

You could pretend that Guenever was a sort of man-eating lioncelle herself, or that she was one of those selfish women who insist on ruling everywhere. In fact, this is what she did seem to be, to a superficial inspection. She was beautiful, sanguine, hot-tempered, demanding, impulsive, acquisitive, charming—she had all the proper qualities for a man-eater. But the rock on which these easy explanations founder, is that she was not promiscuous. There was never anybody in her life except Lancelot and Arthur. She never ate anybody except these. And even these she did not eat in the full sense of the word. People who have been digested by a man-eating lioncelle tend to become nonentities—to live no life except within the vitals of the devourer. Yet both Arthur and Lancelot, the people whom she apparently devoured, lived full lives, and accomplished things of their own.

One explanation of Guenever, for what it is worth, is that she was what they used to call a "real" person. She was not the kind who can be fitted away safely under some label or other, as "loyal" or "disloyal" or "self-sacrificing" or "jealous". Sometimes she was loyal and sometimes she was disloyal. She behaved like herself. And there must have been something in this self, some sincerity of heart, or she would not have held two people like Arthur and Lancelot. Like likes like, they say—and at least they are certain that her men were generous. She must have been generous too. It is difficult to write about a real person.

She lived in warlike times, when the lives of young people were as short as those of airmen in the twentieth century. In such times, the elderly moralists are content to relax their moral laws a little, in return for being defended. The condemned pilots, with their lust for the life and love which is probably to be lost so soon, touch the hearts of young women, or possibly call up an answering bravado. Generosity, courage, honesty, pity, the faculty to look short life in the face—certainly comradeship and tenderness —these qualities may explain why Guenever took Lancelot as well as Arthur. It was courage more than anything else —the courage to take and give from the heart, while there was time. Poets are always urging women to have this kind of courage. She gathered her rose-buds while she might, and the striking thing was that she only gathered two of them, which she kept always, and that those two were the best.

Guenever's central tragedy was that she was childless. Arthur had two illegitimate children, and Lancelot had Galahad. But Guenever—and she was the one of the three who most ought to have had children, and who would have been best with children, and whom God had seemingly made for breeding lovely children—she was the one who was left an empty vessel, a shore without a sea. This was what broke her when she came to the age at which her sea must finally dry. It is what turned her for a little time into a raving woman, though that time was still in the future. It may be one of the explanations of her double love—perhaps she loved Arthur as a father, and Lancelot because of the son she could not have.

People are easily dazzled by Round Tables and feats of arms. You read of Lancelot in some noble achievement, and, when he comes home to his mistress, you feel resentment at her because she cuts across the achievement, or spoils it. Yet Guenever could not search for the Grail. She could not vanish into the English forest for a year's adventure with the spear. It was her part to sit at home, though passionate, though real and hungry in her fierce and tender heart. For her there were no recognized diversions except what is comparable to the ladies' bridge party of today. She could hawk with a merlin, or play blind man's buff, or pince-merille. These were the amusements of grown-up women in her time. But the great hawks, the hounds, her-aldry, tournaments—these were for Lancelot. For her, un-less she felt like a little spinning or embroidery, there was no occupation—except Lancelot.

So we must imagine the Queen as a woman who had been robbed of her central attribute. As she grew to her difficult age, she did strange things. She was even to be suspected of poisoning a knight. She even became unpopular. But unpopularity is often a compliment—and Guenever, though she lived tempestuously and finally died in an unreconciled sort of way—she was not cut out for religion, as Lancelot was—was never insignificant. She did what women do, on the whole right royally, and at the moment, in the tub with the lioncels before her, she was busy doing it.

When a man had practically seen God, however human he might be, you could not immediately expect him as a lover. When the man was Lancelot, who was mad on God in any case, you had to be both sanguine and cruel to ex-pect him like that at all. But women are cruel in this way. They do not accept excuses.

Guenever knew that Lancelot would come back to her. She had known it from the moment when he had prayed to be "held." The knowledge had revived her like a watered flower too long left unwatered. It had swept away the rouge and bedizening silks which had moved his pity when he first came back. Now it only remained for her to accomplish the reunion smoothly and fully. There was no hurry.

Lancelot, who did not know that he was to betray his much-loved God again for the sake of the Queen, was made happy by her attitude—though it surprised him. He had feared some terrible scene of jealousy or recrimination. He had wondered how he would be able to explain to the tor-tured child, imprisoned in the painted eyes, that he could not come to her—that he had a sweeter necessity, however much her pain. He had been afraid that she would attack him, would lay her poor snares before him—snares which would be all the more pitifully beguiling because of their poverty. He had really not known how he was to face the pity.

Instead, Guenever had bloomed and lost her paints. She had made no assault, no recrimination. She had smiled with real joy. Women, he had told himself wisely, were unpredictable. He had even been able to discuss the matter with her, in complete frankness, and she had agreed with what he said.

Guenever, sitting in the bath and looking sightlessly upon the lioncels, had a sleepy look of secret happiness when she remembered their conversation. She saw the charming, ugly face, talking so seriously about the interests of its honest heart. She loved these interests—loved the old soldier to follow so faithfully his innocent love of God. She knew it was doomed to failure.

Lancelot had said, apologizing and begging her not to think him offensive, (1) that they could not very well go back to the old way, after the Grail; (2) that, had it not been for their guilty love, he might have been allowed to achieve the Grail; (3) that it would be dangerous in any case, because the Orkney faction was beginning to watch them unpleasantly, particularly Agravaine and Mordred; and (4) that it would be a great shame to themselves and also to Arthur. He numbered the points carefully.

At other times he tried to explain to her, in confused words and at great length, about his discovery of God. He thought that if he could convert Guenever to God, this would solve the moral problem. If they could go to God together, he would not be deserting his mistress or sacrificing her happiness to his own.

The Queen smiled outright. He was a darling. She had agreed with every word he said—was a regular convert already!

Then she lifted one white arm out of the bath, and reached for a scrubbing brush on an ivory handle.

# 35

*It was all very well at the first flush of his return.*
Queens may see further ahead than common men, but there
seems to be a limit to their vision. It was fine to wait with a
warm feeling while Lancelot kept faith with his divinity for
a week or for a month. But, when the months began to grow
to a year, then it was a different matter. Perhaps he would
relapse in the end—perhaps. But a woman could wait too
long for victory—she could be too old to enjoy it. It could
be senseless to go on waiting for a joy, when joy was on the
doorstep, and Time hurried by.

Guenever grew slowly, not less blooming, but angrier. A
storm gathered in her deep breasts, as the months of holiness
added together. Holiness? Selfishness, she cried to herself—
selfish to abandon another soul so as to save your own. The
story of Bors, allowing the twelve supposed gentlewomen to
be hurled from the castle turret rather than save them by
committing a mortal sin, had shocked her to the heart. Now
Lancelot was doing the same thing. It was well for him,
with his chivalry and mysticism and all the compensations
of the male world, to make the grand renunciation. But it
took two to make a renunciation, just as it took two to make
love, or to make a quarrel. She was not an insensate piece
of property, to be taken up or laid down at his convenience.
You could not give up a human heart as you could give up
drinking. The drink was yours, and you could give it up:
but your lover's soul was not your own: it was not at your
disposal; you had a duty towards it.

Lancelot saw these things as clearly as the bold Guenever
—and, as their relations gradually worsened, he was hard
put to it to keep his mind. It was for him the same as it had
been for Bors, when the unarmed hermit interfered. So far
as he himself was concerned, he had every right to insist
on yielding to the God he loved, as Bors had yielded to
Lionel. But when Guenever threw herself across him, as

the hermit had thrown himself across Bors, had he the right to sacrifice his old love as the hermit had been sacrificed? Lancelot, like the Queen, was shocked by the solutions of Bors. The hearts of these two lovers were instinctively too generous to fit with dogma. Generosity is the eighth deadly sin.

It came to a head one morning, while they were singing together, alone in the solar. A musical instrument called a regal stood on the table between them. It looked like two large bibles. Guenever had sung a little piece by French Mary, and Lancelot was plodding his way through another by the hunchback of Arras, when the Queen put her right hand on all the notes which she could cover, and pressed both bibles with her left. The regal gave a dreadful sneer, and died.

"Why did you do that?"

"You had better go," she said. "Go away. Start a quest. Can't you see that you are wearing me out?"

Lancelot took a deep breath and said: "Yes, I do see it, every day."

"Then you had better go. No, I am not making a scene. I don't want to quarrel about it, and I don't want to alter your mind. But I think it would be kinder if you went."

"It sounds as if I were hurting you on purpose."

"No. It is not your fault. But I would just like you to go, Lance, so as to give me a rest. For a little while. We needn't fight about it."

"If you want me to go, I will, of course."

"I do want you to."

"Perhaps it would be better."

"Lance, I want you to realize that I am not trying to trick you into anything, or to force you. It is only that I think it would be good for us to be parted for a month or two, as friends. It is only that."

"I know you would never try to trick me, Jenny. And I feel muddled too. I was hoping that you would understand about it. About what has happened to me. It would have been easy if you had been on that boat as well, or felt it yourself. But I can't make you feel it, because you were not there, and so it is difficult for me. I feel as if I were sacrificing you, or us if you like, to a new sort of love . . .

"And besides," he said, turning away, "it is not as if—as if I didn't want my old love too."

After he had stood in silence for a minute, looking out

of the window with his hands unnaturally still at his sides, he added in a harsh voice, without turning round: "If you like, we will start again."

When he swung round from the window, the room was empty. After dinner he asked for the Queen at her door, but received only a verbal message begging him to do as she had asked. He packed his scanty traps, not understanding what had happened, but feeling that he had escaped calamity by a hairbreadth. He said good-bye to his bent old squire, who was now far too ancient to go with him in any case, and rode from Camelot next morning.

# 36

*If the maids-in-waiting were pleased by the Queen's* supposed renewal of intrigue, there were others at court who were not. Or, if they were pleased, it was a cruel and waiting pleasure. The tone of the court had changed for the fourth time.

There had been the first feeling, a companionship of youth under which Arthur had launched his grand crusade—the second, of chivalrous rivalry growing staler every year in the greatest court of Europe, until it had nearly turned to feud and empty competition. Then the enthusiasm of the Grail had burned the bad gasses of the air into a short-lived beauty. Now the maturest or the saddest phase had come, in which enthusiasms had been used up for good, and only our famous seventh sense was left to be practised. The court had "knowledge of the world" now: it had the fruits of achievement, civilization, savoir-vivre, gossip, fashion, malice, and the broad mind of scandal.

Half the knights had been killed—the best half. What Arthur had feared from the start of the Grail Quest had come to pass. If you achieve perfection, you die. There had been nothing left for Galahad to ask of God, except death. The best knights had gone to perfection, leaving the worst to hold their sieges. A leaven of love was left, it is true—Lancelot, Gareth, Aglovale and a few old dodderers like Sir Grummore and Sir Palomides: but the tone was set elsewhere. It came from the surly angers of Gawaine, the fripperies of Mordred, and the sarcasms of Agravaine. Tristram had done no good to it in Cornwall. A magic cloak had gone the rounds, which only a faithful wife could wear—or perhaps it was a magic horn which only a faithful wife could drink from. A canting shield had been presented with a voiceless snigger, a shield whose blazon was a hint to cuckolds. Marital fidelity had become "news." Clothes had become fantastic. The long toes of Agravaine's slippers were secured by gold chains to garters below his knee, and, as for Mordred's toes, their chains were secured to a belt round his waist. The surcoats, which had originally served as covering to armour, were long behind and high in front. You could hardly walk for fear of tripping over your sleeves. Ladies were compelled to shave their foreheads and to show no hair, if they wanted to be in the mode, while, so far as their sleeves were concerned, they had to tie knots in them to keep them off the floor. Gentlemen showed their legs to an equally startling extent. Their clothes were parti-coloured. Sometimes one leg was red and the other was green. And they did not wear their slittered mantle, their gaycoat graceless, from a sense of exuberance. Mordred wore his ridiculous shoes contemptuously: they were a satire on himself. The court was modern.

So there were eyes on Guenever now—not the eyes of strong suspicion or of warm connivance, but the bored looks of calculation and the cold ones of society. At the mousehole the sleek cats were still.

Mordred and Agravaine thought Arthur hypocritical—as all decent men must be, if you assume that decency can't exist. They found Guenever barbarous.

La Beale Isoud, they said, had made a cuckold of King Mark in a civilized way. She had done it with an air, publicly, fashionably, in the best taste. Everybody had been able to rub it into the King, and to enjoy the fun. She had shown a perfect flair for dress, for comic hats which made her look like a tipsy heifer. She had spent millions of Mark's money on peacock tongues for dinner.

Guenever, on the other hand, dressed like a gipsy, entertained like a lodging-house keeper, and kept her lover a secret. On top of this, she was a nuisance. She had no sense of style. She was growing old ungracefully, and she cried or made scenes like a fishwife. It was said that she had sent Lancelot away after a terrible quarrel, during which she had accused him of loving other women. She was supposed to have cried out: "I see and feel daily that thy love beginneth to slake." Mordred said, in his equivocal musical voice, that he could understand a fishwife, but not a fish mistress. The epigram was widely reported.

Arthur, reserved and unhappy in the new atmosphere which had begun to pull away from him instead of with him, moved about the palace in his plain dress, trying to be polite. The Queen, more aggressive—she had been a bold girl as he first remembered her, with dark hair and red lips, tossing her head—went out to meet the situation, and tried to deal with it by entertaining and by pretending to be fashionable herself. She fell back on the paints and finery which she had left when Lancelot returned. She began to behave as if she were a little mad. All glorious reigns have these blank patches, during which the Crown is unpopular.

Trouble came suddenly, while Lancelot was away. The feeling of danger, which had hung in the air since the Grail, suddenly crystallized upon a dinner party given by the Queen.

It seems that Gawaine was fond of fruit. He liked apples and pears best—and the poor Queen, anxious to be successful in her new line as a fashionable entertainer, took particular care to have nice apples when she gave a dinner for twenty-four knights, at which Gawaine was to be present. She knew that the Cornwall and Orkney faction had always been the menace to her husband's hopes—and Gawaine was now the head of the clan. She hoped that the dinner would be a success, that it would help in the new atmosphere, that it would be a sophisticated dinner. She was trying to placate her critics by being a courteous hostess like La Beale Isoud.

Unfortunately there were other people who knew of Gawaine's weakness for apples, and bad blood over the Pellinore murders still existed. Arthur had managed to wean Sir Aglovale from his revenge, it is true, and the old feud seemed to have healed over. But there was a knight called Sir Pinel, who was a distant relative of the Pellinores, and he considered that revenge was necessary. Sir Pinel poisoned the apples.

Poison is a bad weapon. It went astray in this case, as it often does, and an Irish knight called Patrick ate the apple which was intended for Gawaine.

You can imagine the situation: the pale knights starting to their feet in the candlelight, the ineffectual attempts at aid, and their supposing eyes turning upon one another with ashamed suspicion. Everybody knew of Gawaine's foible. His family had never been favourites with the now unpopular Queen. She herself had given the dinner. And Pinel was not in a position to explain. Somebody in that room had murdered Sir Patrick in mistake for Gawaine, and until the murderer was discovered they would all be under the same suspicion. Sir Mador de la Porte—more pompous than the rest, or more malevolent, or more of a stickler—ended by voicing the thought which was in every mind. He accused the Queen of treason.

Nowadays, when a point of justice is obscure and difficult, each side hires lawyers to argue it out. In those days the upper classes hired champions to fight it out—which came to the same thing. Sir Mador decided to save himself the expense of a champion by fighting his own case, and he insisted that Guenever must brief a champion for her defence. Arthur, whose whole philosophy of royalty hinged on justice instead of power, could do nothing to save his wife. If Mador demanded the Court of Honour, he must have it. And Arthur could not fight in his wife's quarrel, just as married people are not allowed to give evidence against each other today.

Here was a pretty state of affairs. Suspicion and rumour and counter-recrimination had obscured the issue almost before it started. The Pellinore feud, the old Pendragon-Cornwall feud, the Lancelot entanglement, and then the sudden death of a person not apparently concerned with any of them—all these mixed themselves together into a fume of venom which coiled about the Queen. If Lancelot had been there, he would have fought as her champion. But she had sent him away—nobody knew where, some thought to his parents in France. Perhaps, if he had been known to be on hand, Sir Mador might have swallowed his accusation.

It seems kinder not to dwell on the days before the trial by battle—not to describe the distracted woman kneeling to Sir Bors, who had never liked her before, and who now, just back from his virginal achievement of the Grail, liked her still less. She begged him to fight for her if Lancelot could not be found. She had to beg for it, poor creature, because the feeling at court had come to such a pitch that nobody would accept her brief. The Queen of England was unable to command a champion.

The night before the battle was the worst. All night, neither she nor Arthur slept. He firmly believed her innocence, but he could not interfere with justice. She, pathetically and repeatedly asserting this innocence, although she was in the entanglement which the other trouble had brought her to, knew that the next night might see her burned to death. Together they saw the tragedy and humiliation of their Table, from which no man was willing to save them—knew that the Queen of it was called, by common breath, a destroyer of good knights. In the bitter darkness Arthur suddenly cried despairingly: "What aileth you, that ye cannot keep Sir Lancelot on your side?" And so it went on until the morning.

# 37

*Sir Bors the misogynist had reluctantly consented to* fight for the Queen, if nobody else could be found. He had explained that it was irregular to do so, because he himself had been present at the dinner—but, when discovered by Arthur with the Queen kneeling at his feet, he had blushed, raised her, and consented. Then he had vanished for a day or two, because the trial was not to take place for a fortnight.

A meadow at Westminster had been prepared for the combat. A barricade of strong logs, like a corral for horses, had been erected round the wide square—which had no barrier down the middle. For an ordinary joust there would have been a barrier: but in this case the fight was to a outrance, which meant that it might end with swords on foot, and so the barrier was left out. A pavilion had been erected for the King on one side, and another one for the Constable on the other. The barricades and the pavilions were decorated with cloth. There was a curtained gateway at each end, like the dramatic hole through which the circus people ride into their arena. In one corner of the corral, visible for all to see, was a great bundle of faggots with an iron stake in the middle, which would not burn or melt. This was for the Queen, if the law went against her. Before Arthur had started his life's work, a man accusing the Queen of anything would have been executed out of hand. Now, because of his own work, he must be ready to burn his wife.

For a new idea had begun to form in the King's mind. The efforts to dig a channel for Might had failed, even when it was turned to the spirit, and now he was feeling his way towards abolishing it. He had decided not to truckle with Might any more—to cut it out, root and branch, by establishing another standard altogether. He was groping towards Right as a criterion of its own—towards Justice as an abstract thing which did not lean upon power. In a few years he would be inventing Civil Law.

It was a cold day. The cloths strained against the scaffolding of barricade and pavilion, and the pennons lay taut on the wind. In the corner the executioner blew on his nails, standing close to the brazier from which he would take the fire for his bigger blaze. The heralds in the Constable's pavilion moistened their lips, which the breeze was cracking, before lifting their trumpets for a fanfare. Guenever, sitting between guards under the Constable's ward, had to ask for a shawl. The people noticed that she was thinner. It was the bleak face of middle age, waiting intent and stoical between the beefy faces of the soldiers.

Naturally it was Lancelot who rescued her. Bors had managed to find him at an abbey, during his two days' absence, and now he came back in the nick of time to fight Sir Mador for the Queen. Nobody who knew him would have expected him to do anything else, whether he had been sent away in disgrace or not—but, as it was thought that he had left the country, his return did have a dramatic quality.

Sir Mador came from his recess at the south end of the lists, and proclaimed the accusation while his herald blew. Sir Bors came from the northern hole to parley with the King and with the Constable—a long, indistinct argument or explanation which the people could not catch on account of the wind. The spectators became restive, wondering what the hitch was, and why the trial by battle did not proceed in the usual way. Then, after several journeys from King's pavilion to Constable's, and vice versa, Sir Bors returned to his own hole. There was an uncomfortable pause, during which a black lap dog with a pug nose escaped into the lists and scampered about on some errand best known to itself. One of the kings-of-arms caught it and tied it with his guige, for which the people gave him an ironic cheer. Then there was silence, except for the vendors who were crying nuts and gingerbread.

Lancelot rode out from the north exit, marked with the Bors escutcheon—and immediately everybody in the amphitheatre knew that it was he, although he was disguised. The silence was as if everybody had caught their breath simultaneously.

He had not come back out of condescension to the Queen. The cruel explanation that he had "given her up" so as to save his soul, and that he had now returned from a sense of dramatic magnanimity, was not the true one. It was more complicated.

This knight's trouble from his childhood—which he never completely grew out of—was that for him God was a real person. He was not an abstraction who punished you if you were wicked or rewarded you if you were good, but a real person like Guenever, or like Arthur, or like anybody else. Of course he felt that God was better than Guenever or Arthur, but the point was that he was personal. Lancelot had a definite idea of what he looked like, and how he felt —and he was somehow in love with this Person.

The Ill-Made Knight was not involved in an Eternal Triangle. It was an Eternal Quadrangle, which was eternal as well as quadrangular. He had not given up his mistress because he was afraid of being punished by some sort of Holy Bogy, but he had been confronted by two people whom he loved. The one was Arthur's Queen, the other a wordless presence who had celebrated Mass at Castle Carbonek. Unfortunately, as so often happens in love affairs, the two objects of his affection were contradictory. It was almost as if he had been confronted with a choice between Jane and Janet—and as if he had gone to Janet, not because he was afraid that she would punish him if he stayed with Jane, but because he felt, with warmth and pity, that he loved her best. He may even have felt that God needed him more than Guenever did. This was the problem, an emotional rather than a moral one, which had taken him into retreat at his abbey, where he had hoped to feel things out.

Still, it would not be quite true to say that he had not come back from some motives of magnanimity. He was a magnanimous man. He was a maestro. Even if God's need for him was the greater in normal times, now it was obvious that his first love's need was pressing. Perhaps a man who had left Jane for Janet might have had enough warmth inside him to return for Jane, when she was in desperate need, and this warmth might be compared to pity or to magnanimity or to generosity—if it were not unfashionable and even a little disgusting to believe in these emotions nowadays. Lancelot, in any case, who was wrestling with his love for Guenever as well as with his love for God, came back to her side as soon as he knew that she was in trouble, and, when he saw her radiant face waiting for him under shameful durance, his heart did turn over inside its habergeon with some piercing emotion—call it love or pity, whatever you please.

Sir Mador de la Porte's heart turned over at the same time—but it was too late to draw back. His face went crimson inside its helm, where nobody could see it, and he felt a warm glow under the straw fillet which padded his skull. Then he went back to his own corner and spurred his horse.

There is something beautiful about the way in which a broken lance sails into the air. Down below it, on the ground, there is much bustle going on. The lazy motion with which the lance goes up, turning over silently and languidly as it goes, contrasts with this. It seems superior to earthly considerations and does not seem to be moving fast. The fast movement—which was, in this case, Sir Mador dismounting backwards and upside down—is going on underneath the lance, which performs its own independent pirouette in graceful detachment, and comes down elsewhere, when everybody has forgotten it. Sir Mador's lance came down on its point, by some ballistic freak, just behind the king-of-arms who was holding the black pug. When the latter turned round later on, and found it upright behind him, looking over his shoulder as it were, he gave a start.

Sir Lancelot dismounted, so as not to have the advantage of a horse. Sir Mador got up and began doing some wild swipes at the enemy with his sword. He was over-excited.

It took two knockouts to finish Sir Mador. The first time he was down, when Lancelot was coming towards him to accept his surrender, he became flustered and thrust at the towering man from below. It was a foul blow, for it went into

the groin from underneath, just at the point where armour
must necessarily be weakest. When Lancelot had withdrawn,
to let Mador get up if he wanted to go on fighting, it was
seen that the blood was streaming down his cuisses and
greaves. There was something terrible about the patient way
in which he withdrew, although he had been badly stabbed
in the thigh. If he had lost his temper it would have been
easier to bear.

The Queen's champion knocked Sir Mador down harder
the second time. Then he jerked off his helm.

"All right," said Sir Mador. "I give in. I was wrong. Spare
my life."

Lancelot did a nice thing. Most knights would have been
satisfied with winning the Queen's case, and would have
left it at that. But Lancelot had a sort of methodical consid-
eration for people—he was sensitive to things which they
might be feeling, or might be likely to feel.

"I will spare your life," he said, "only if you promise that
nothing is to be written about this on Sir Patrick's grave.
Nothing about the Queen."

"I promise," said Mador.

Then, while the defeated advocate was being carried
away by some leeches, Lancelot went to the royal box. The
Queen had been released immediately, and was there with
Arthur.

Arthur said: "Take off your helm, stranger."

They felt a swelling of love when he took it off, and com-
passion to see the hideous, well-known face again, while he
stood in front of them, bleeding hard.

Arthur came down from the box. He made Guenever get
up, and took her hand, and led her down into the arena. He
made a regular bow to Sir Lancelot, and pulled Guenever's
hand so that she curtsied too. He did this in front of his
people. He spoke in the old-fashioned talk, and said with
a full voice: "Sir, grant mercy of your great travail that ye
have had this day for me and for my Queen." Guenever,
behind his smiling loving face, was sobbing as if her heart
would burst.

# 38

*It so happened that the Patrick accusation was* cleared up next day, when Nimue arrived with a second-sighted explanation. Merlyn, before letting her lock him up in the cave, had given the Matter of Britain into her hands. He had made her promise—it was all that he could do—that she would watch over Arthur herself, now that she knew his own magic. Then he had gone meekly to his imprisonment, casting a last long, doting look upon her. Nimue, though scatterbrained and unpunctual, was a good girl in her way. She turned up a day late, told how the apple had come to be poisoned, and went back to her own concerns. Sir Pinel confirmed the statement by running away the same morning, leaving a written confession, and everybody had to admit that it was a lucky thing Sir Lancelot had been about.

It was not so lucky for the Queen. She was alive and saved, it was true—but the unbelievable happened. In spite of the tears, in spite of the fountain of feeling which had sprung between them once again, Lancelot persisted in remaining loyal to his Grail.

Well for him, she exclaimed—she was growing madder every day, and it hurt people to watch it—well for him to wrap himself in his new delight. He had a grand feeling, no doubt, a compensation of vigour and clarity and uplifting of the heart. Perhaps his famous God did give him something which she could not give. Perhaps he was happier with God, and would soon begin doing miracles left and right. But what about her? He was not considering what she got out of God. The position was exactly the same, she railed at him, as if he had left her for another woman. He had taken the best of her, and now that she was old and worthless he had gone elsewhere. He was behaving with the beastly selfishness of Man, taking all he could get from one quarter, and then, when that was used, going to another. He was a sneak-thief. And to think that she had believed in him! She did not love him any more now, would not let him come near her if he were to pray for it on bended knees. As a matter of fact, she had despised him even before the search for the Grail began—yes, despised him, and had determined to throw him over. He was not to think that he was deserting her: it was quite the contrary. She was tossing him away, like a dirty clout, because she felt nothing but contempt for him. For his poses and swelled head and meanness and childishness and conceit. For his futile little God, and his goody-goody lies. To tell him the truth, and really she felt no further interest in concealing it, there was a young knight at court who was already her lover: had been her lover long before the Grail! He was a much finer young man than Lancelot. What would she want with a sour husk when she had a rosy boy at her feet who worshipped her, yes, worshipped the ground she trod on? Lancelot had better return to Elaine, to the mother of his famous son. Perhaps they would be able to say their prayers together, one frump with the other frump, all night. They could talk about their baby, their Galahad, who had found the loathsome Grail, and they could laugh at her if they liked, yes, they were welcome to laugh at her, laughing because she had never managed to bear a son.

Then Guenever would begin the laughing—while always one part of her looked out from the eye windows, and hated the noise which she was making—and the tears would come after the laughter, and she would weep with all her heart.

A strange feature was that Arthur, who wanted to arrange a tournament in celebration of the Queen's acquittal, fixed upon a place near Corbin as the spot where the tournament was to be held. The place may have been Winchester or Brackley, where one of the four surviving English tilting grounds is to be found. It does not matter where it was— what does matter is that Corbin was the castle where the now childless Elaine lived out her lonely middle age.

"I suppose you will go to this tournament?" asked the Queen fiercely. "I suppose you will go to be near your trull?"

Lancelot said: "Jenny, couldn't you forgive her? She is probably ugly as well as miserable now. She never had much to fall back on."

"The generous Lancelot!"

"If you don't want me to go," he said, "I won't. You know I have never loved any human being except you."

"Only Arthur," said the Queen. "Only Elaine. Only God. Unless there are some others I haven't heard about."

Lancelot shrugged his shoulders—one of the stupidest things to do, when the other party wants to have a fight.

"Are you going?" he asked.

"I going? Am I to watch you flirting with that turnip? Certainly I shan't go, and I forbid you to go either."

"Very well," he said. "I will tell Arthur that I am ill. I could say that my wound has not healed yet."

He went to find the King.

Everybody had started for the tournament, and the court was empty, when Guenever changed her mind. Perhaps she had kept Lancelot behind so as to be alone with him, and, finding that it was no good being alone with him, had reversed her decision—but we do not know the reason.

"You had better go," she said. "If I keep you here you will say it was because I was jealous, and you will cast it in my teeth. Besides, there may be a scandal if you stay with me. And I don't want you. I don't want to see your face. Take it away. Go!"

"Jenny," he said reasonably, "I can't go now. There will be much more of a scandal if I do go after all, when I have said that my wound prevents me. They will think that we have had a quarrel."

"Let them think what they please. The only thing I tell you is that you are to go, before you drive me mad."

"Jenny," he said.

He felt that his heart was breaking in two pieces, and that the madness which she had given him once before might well be coming again. Perhaps she noticed this too. At all events, she suddenly relented in her manner. She saw him off to Corbin with a loving kiss.

"I promise I will come back," he had said, and now he was keeping his promise. It was unthinkable that he should go to the tournament without visiting Elaine. He had not only promised to return to her, but he was the repository of all the last messages of their only son, now dead or at least translated. The cruellest man could hardly have refused to visit her with such messages.

He would lodge at Corbin, tell her about Galahad, and

fight in the tournament disguised. He would explain to
Arthur that he had pleaded the wound so as to come unexpectedly, in disguise, because that was one of the new-fashioned things to do. This subterfuge would be assisted by the
fact of his staying at Corbin castle, instead of at the actual
place of the tournament. It would prevent any scandal about
a last-minute quarrel with the Queen.

He was surprised to find, as he rode up the avenue to the
moat, through the cheval de frise, that Elaine was waiting
for him on the battlements, in the same attitude as that in
which he had left her twenty years before. She met him at
the Great Gate.

"I was waiting for you."

She was plump and dumpy now, rather like Queen Vic-
toria, and she received him faithfully. He had said that he
would come back and here he was. She had expected nothing
else.

With her next words she stabbed him to the heart.

"You will be staying for good now," said she, hardly as a
question. It was in this way that she had construed his answer when they parted all that time ago.

# 39

*If people want to read about the Corbin tournament,*
Malory has it. He was a passionate follower of tournaments
—like one of those old gentlemen who nowadays frequent
the cricket pavilion at Lord's—and he may have had access
to some ancient Wisden, or even to the score-books themselves. He reports the celebrated tournaments in full, with
the score of each knight, and the name of the man who
bowled him over, or how knocked out. But the accounts of
old cricket matches are inclined to be boring for those who
did not actually play in them, so we must leave it unre-
ported. The only things which are apt to be dull in Malory
are the detailed score-sheets, which he gives two or three
times—and even they are not dull for anybody who knows

the form of the various smaller knights. It is sufficient for our purposes to say that Lancelot hit the other side all round the field—his skill had come back to him since the Grail—and that he would have carried his sword after the innings of a lifetime, if the wound which he got from Sir Mador had not broken out afresh. It is strange that he should have played well on this occasion—for he was distracted by the triple misery of Guenever and God and Elaine—but great performances have been given by others in similiar circumstances. Finally, when he had made thirty or forty in spite of the old wound (and, incidentally, he had knocked out Mordred and Agravaine), three knights set upon him at the same time, and the spear of one of them penetrated his defence. It broke, leaving the head of the spear in his side.

Lancelot withdrew from the field while he could still sit his horse, and galloped away, lolling in the saddle, to find a place where he could be alone. When he was badly hurt he had this instinct for solitude. To him, there was something private about death—so that, if he had to die, he tried to get a chance of doing it by himself. Only one knight went with him—he was too weak to shake him off—and it was this knight who helped him to draw the spearhead from his ribs, and who eased him when he finally fainted by "turning him into the wind." It was also this knight who brought the distracted Elaine to his bedside, after he had been put to bed.

The importance of the Winchester tournament did not lie in any particular feat of arms, nor even in Lancelot's grievous hurt—for he eventually recovered from it. Where it did touch the lives of our four friends was in a circumstance which remains to be told. For Lancelot, suddenly faced with the unlucky Elaine's unfounded conviction that he was going to stay with her for ever, had faltered in telling her the truth. Perhaps he was a weak man in most ways—weak to have taken Guenever from his best friend in the first place, weak to have tried to exchange his mistress for his God, and weakest of all to have helped Elaine by telling her he would come back. Now, in the face of the poor lady's simple hope, he had lacked the courage to break her illusion with an immediate blow.

One of the troubles in dealing with Elaine, in spite of her simplicity or ignorance, was that her nature was a sensitive one—more sensitive than Guenever's, in fact, although she lacked the power of that bold and extraverted queen. She h?ᴗ been sensitive enough not to overwhelm him with welcomes when he came home from his long absence: not to reproach him—she had never felt that she had reason to reproach him: and, above all, not to suffocate him with pity for herself. She had held her heart with a firm hand while they waited at Corbin for the tournament, carefully hiding the long years during which she had hoped for her lord, and her absolute loneliness now that their son was gone. Lancelot had known quite well what she was hiding. Uncertain and sensitive himself, he had forgotten about the way in which their peculiar relationship had started. He had begun to blame himself exclusively for Elaine's sorrows.

So, when she did make her small request, after having spared him so many tears and welcomes, what could he do but seek her pleasure? He had still to tell her that her unflinching hope was baseless. He was putting it off. Feeling like an executioner who knows that he must kill tomorrow, he had tried to give a little joy today.

"Lance," she had said before the tournament, asking her strange favour humbly and childishly, "now that we are together, you will wear my token at the fight?"

Now that we are together! And in her tone of voice he had read a picture of twenty years' desertion, realizing for the first time that during all that period she had been following his career of chivalry like a schoolchild doting on the batsman Hobbs. The poor bird had been picturing all the fights —almost certainly picturing them quite wrong: nourishing a starved heart on second-hand accounts in secret: wondering whose token was in the place of honour today. Perhaps she had been telling herself for twenty years that some day the great champion would fight under a favour of her own —one of those ridiculous ambitions with which the wretched soul consoles itself, for lack of decent fare.

"I never wear favours," he haid said, truthfully.

She had not pleaded or complained, and she had truly tried to hide her disappointment.

"I will wear yours," he had said immediately. "I shall be proud to wear it. And, besides, it will help my disguise very much. Just because everybody knows that I don't wear favours, it will be a splendid disguise to wear one. How clever of you to think of it! And it will make me fight better. What is it to be?"

It was a scarlet sleeve embroidered with large pearls. You can do good embroidery in twenty years.

A fortnight after the Winchester tournament, while Elaine nursed her hero back to life, Guenever was having a scene with Sir Bors at court. Being a woman-hater, Bors always had instructive scenes with women. He said what he thought, and they said what they thought, and neither of them understood the other a bit.

"Ah, Sir Bors," said the Queen, having sent for him in great haste as soon as she heard about the red sleeve—Bors being one of Lancelot's closest relations. "Ah, Sir Bors, have ye heard say how falsely Sir Lancelot hath betrayed me?"

Bors noted that the Queen was "nigh out of her mind for wrath," blushed deeply, and said with exaggerated patience: "If anybody has been betrayed, it is Lancelot himself. He has been mortally wounded by three knights at once."

"And I am glad," cried the Queen, "glad to hear it! A good thing if he dies. He is a false traitor knight!"

Bors shrugged his shoulders and turned his back, as much as to say that he was not going to listen to talk like that. The whole of his back, as he went to the door, showed what he thought about women. The Queen rushed after him, to retain him by force if necessary. She was not going to be cheated of her scene as easily as that.

"Why should I not call him a traitor," she shouted, "when he bare the red sleeve upon his head at Winchester, at the great jousts?"

Bors, afraid that he was going to be physically assaulted, said: "I am sorry about the sleeve. If he had not worn it as a disguise, perhaps people would not have set upon him three to one."

"Fie on him," exclaimed the Queen. "He got a good thrashing anyway, in spite of all his pride and boasting. He was beaten in fair fight."

"No, he was not. It was three to one, and his old wound broke out too."

"Fie on him," repeated the Queen. "I heard Sir Gawaine say in front of the King that it was wonderful how much he loved Elaine."

"I can't stop Gawaine saying things," retorted Sir Bors hotly, desperately, pathetically, furiously, and with terror. Then he went out and slammed the door, leaving the honours about even.

At Corbin, Elaine and Lancelot were holding hands. He smiled feebly at her, and said in a pale voice: "Poor Elaine.

You always seem to be nursing me back from something. You never seem to have me, except when I am only half alive."

"I have you for good now," she said radiantly.

"Elaine," he said, "I want to talk to you."

# 40

*When the Ill-Made Knight came back from Corbin,* Guenever was still in a rage. For some reason she was determined to believe that Elaine had become his mistress again, possibly because this seemed to be the best way of hurting her lover. She claimed that he had only been pretending about his religious feelings—as was shown by his immediately going off with Elaine when he had the chance. This, she said, had been at the back of his mind all along. He was a sham, and a weak sham at that. They had hysterical scenes together, about his weakness and shamness, alternating with other scenes of a more affectionate kind, which were necessary to counter-balance the idea that she had been in love with a sham man all her life. She began to look healthier, even beautiful again, as the result of these quarrels. But two lines came between her eyebrows, and she had a frightening eye sometimes, which glittered like a diamond. Lancelot began to have a dogged look. They were drifting.

Elaine had been explained to, and it was Elaine who now struck the only strong blow of her life. She struck it unintentionally, by committing suicide.

A death-barge came down the river to the capital, since rivers were the highways of the day, and it was moored beneath the palace wall. She was in it—the plump partridge who had always been helpless. Probably people commit suicide through weakness, not through strength. Her gentle efforts to guide the hand of destiny, by decoying her master with feeble tricks or by reticent considerations—these had not been strong enough to be recognized in the despotism of life. Her son had gone, and her lover, and there was nothing left. Even the promise to return had failed her futile grasp. It had once been something to live for, a handrail—not a particularly sumptuous handrail, but sufficiently serviceable to keep her upright. She had been able to make do. Never having been a high-handed or demanding girl, she had been able to make a little go a long way. But now even the little was gone.

Everybody went down to see the barge. It was not a lily maid of Astolat they saw, but a middle-aged woman whose hands, in stiff-looking gloves, grasped a pair of beads obediently. Death had made her look older and different. The stern, grey face in the barge was evidently not Elaine—who had gone elsewhere, or vanished.

Even if Lancelot was a weak man, or a games-maniac, or that infuriating creation, a person who consistently tries to be decent, he does not seem to have had an easy time of it. With his inherited tendency to madness, and his fantastic face, the confusion of his loyalties and moral standards, it must have been difficult enough to keep the balance of life without the various blows which were given to him above the bargain. He could have supported even the extra blows if he had been blessed with a callous heart. But his heart had been made as a match for Elaine's, and now it was unable to bear the burden which hers had been forced to lay down. All the things which he might have done for the poor creature, but which it was now too late to do, and all the shameful questions about responsibility which go with the irrevocable, united in his mind.

"Why were you not kinder to her?" cried the Queen. "Why could you not have given her something to live for? You might have showed her some bounty and gentleness, which would have preserved her life."

Guenever, who did not yet realize that Elaine had come between them more effectively than ever, said this quite spontaneously, and she meant it. She was overwhelmed with pity for her rival in the barge.

# 41

*The new kind of life went on at Camelot in spite of*
the suicide. Nobody could have called it a specially happy
kind—but people are tenacious of life, and will go on living.
It was not all of it a plot-like life: most of it was just story—
one thing after the other—a chain of unnecessary accidents.
One ridiculous accident which happened about this time is
worth mentioning, not because it had any consequences or
antecedents, but because it was somehow the sort of thing
which happened to Lancelot. He behaved about it in his own
way.

He was lying on his stomach in a wood one day, with what
sad thoughts nobody knows, when a lady archer came by,
who was hunting. It does not say whether she was a masculine sort of lady with a moustache and gentlemen's neck-
wear, or whether she was one of those scatterbrains from
the film world who do archery because it is so cute. Anyway, she saw Lancelot, and she thought he was a rabbit. On
the whole she must have been one of the masculine ladies,
for, although it is a pretty trait to shoot at men in mistake
for rabbits, it would have been unusual for a film star to hit
the mark. Lancelot, bounding to his feet with about six
inches of arrow embedded in his rump, behaved exactly
like Colonel Bogey—driven into on the second tee at golf.
He said passionately: "Lady or damsel, what that thou be, in
an evil time bare ye a bow; the devil made you a shooter!"

In spite of the wound in his backside, Lancelot fought in
the next tournament—an important one, because of several
things which happened at it. The true tension at court—
which was apparent to everybody except Lancelot, who was
too innocent to be conscious of such things—began to show
itself clearly at the Westminster jousts. For one thing,
Arthur began to assert his position in their wretched triangle.
He did this, poor fellow, by suddenly taking the opposite
side to Lancelot in the *grand mêlée*. He set upon his best

friend, and tried to hurt him, and lost his temper. He did nothing unknightly, and, as it happened, did no harm to Lancelot. But the strange turn of feeling was there all the same. Before and afterward they were friends. But just for that one moment of anger Arthur was the cuckold and Lancelot his betrayer. Such is the apparent explanation—an unconscious recognition of their relationship—but there may have been another thought behind it. It was a long time since Arthur had been the happy Wart, long since his home and his kingdom had been at their fortunate peak. Perhaps he was tired of the struggle, tired of the Orkney clique and the strange new fashions and the difficulties of love and modern justice. He may have fought against Lancelot in the hope of being killed by him—not a hope exactly, not a conscious attempt. This just and generous and kind-hearted man may have guessed unconsciously that the only solution for him and for his loved ones must lie in his own death—after which Lancelot could marry the Queen and be at peace with God—and he may have given Lancelot the chance of killing him in fair fight, because he himself was worn out. It may have been. At all events, nothing came of it. There was the blaze of temper, and then their love was fresh again.

Another important feature of the tournament was that Lancelot, with innocent idiocy, alienated the Orkneys finally and for good. He unhorsed the whole clan except Gareth, one after the other, and Mordred and Agravaine he unhorsed twice. Only a saint could have been fool enough to have saved their lives so often in rescues from Dolorous Towers and so on—but to cap it by knocking them down at will, at such a time, was the policy of a natural. Gawaine, it is true, was decent enough to refuse to have a hand in plots against Lancelot's life, and Gaheris was dull. But from this day on it was only a question of time, as between the fashionable party of Mordred and Agravaine and the safety of the commander-in-chief.

A third straw in the wind was that Gareth fought on Lancelot's side at Westminster. The peculiar cross-plays of sentiment were noticed by everybody—the King against his second self, and Gareth against his own brothers. With such an undertow there was evidently a storm to come. It came characteristically, from a quarter which nobody had suspected.

There was a cockney knight called Sir Meliagrance, who had never been happy at court. If he had lived in the earlier days, when a man was judged as a man, he might have got along well enough. Unfortunately he belonged to the later generation, of Mordred's fashions, and he was judged by the new standards. Everybody knew that Sir Meliagrance was not quite out of the top drawer. He knew it himself—the top drawer had been invented by Mordred—and the knowledge did not make him happy. Beside all this, Sir Meliagrance had a special cause for misery which had poisoned society for him. He was desperately, hopelessly—and had been ever since he could remember—in love with Guenever.

The news came while Arthur and Lancelot were at the nine-pin alley. They had got into the habit of going off to this unfashionable spot every day to cheer themselves with a little conversation.

Arthur was saying: "No, no, Lance. You never understood poor Tristram at all."

"He was a cad," said Lancelot obstinately.

They were talking in the past tense because Tristram had finally been murdered, while playing the harp to La Beale Isoud, by the exasperated King Mark.

"Even if he is dead," added the knight.

But the King shook his head vehemently.

"Not a cad," he said. "He was a buffoon, one of the great comic characters. He was always getting himself into extraordinary situations."

"A buffoon?"

"Absent-minded," said the King. "That is the great comic affliction. Look at his love-affairs."

"You mean Isoud White-Hands?"

"I firmly believe that Tristram got those two girls completely mixed up. He goes mad on La Beale Isoud, and then forgets all about her. One day he is getting into bed with the other Isoud when something about the action reminds him of something. It dawns on him that there are two Isouds, not one—and he is terribly upset about it. Here am I getting into bed with Isoud White-Hands, he says, when all the time I was in love with La Beale Isoud! Naturally he was upset. And then being nearly murdered in his bath by the Queen of Ireland. There was a light of high comedy about that young man, and you ought to forgive him for being a cad."

"I——" began Lancelot, but at that moment the messenger arrived.

He was a small, breathless boy with an arrow-slit in his jupon, under the right armpit. He held the rent together with his fingers and talked fast.

It was about the Queen, who had gone a-Maying—for it was the first of May. She had started early, as the custom was, intending to be back by ten o'clock, with all the dewy primroses and violets and hawthorn blooms and green-budding branches which it was proper to gather on such a morning. She had left her bodyguard behind—the Queen's knights, who all bore the vergescu as their badge of office—and had taken with her only ten knights in civilian clothes. They had been dressed in green, to celebrate the festival of spring. Agravaine was among them—he had attached himself to Guenever lately, to spy on her—and Lancelot had been left out on purpose.

Well, they had been riding home cheerfully, all chattering and bloomy and branchy, when Sir Meliagrance had leaped up at their feet, in an ambush. The top-drawer business had preyed on his mind till he had determined to be ungentlemanly in earnest, if everybody accused him of being so. He had known that the Queen's party was unarmed, and that Lancelot was not with them. He had brought a strong force of archers and men-at-arms to take her captive.

There had been a fight. The Queen's knights had defended her as best they could with swords and falchions, until they were all wounded, six of them seriously. Then Guenever had surrendered, to save their lives. She had made a bargain with Sir Meliagrance—whose heart was not really in the business of being a blackguard—that, if she called her defenders off, he must promise to take the wounded knights with her to his castle, and he must let them sleep in the anteroom of her chamber. Meliagrance, loving Guenever, flinching at his own half-hearted wickedness, and knowing the hopelessness of forcing his beloved against her will, had agreed to terms. The poor fellow had never been cut out to be a villain.

In the confusion of getting the sorry procession of hurt men slung across their horses, the Queen had kept her head. She had beckoned the little page, who had a fresh and fast pony, and she had secretly slipped him her ring, with a message for Lancelot. When he saw his opportunity, he was to gallop for his life—and he had done so, with the archers after him. Here was the ring.

Lancelot, half-way through the story, was already shouting for his armour. By the time it was told Arthur was kneeling at his feet, strapping on the greaves.

# 42

*When the mounted archers rode back crestfallen,* saying that they had been unable to shoot the boy, Sir Meliagrance knew what was going to happen. He was distracted with misery, not only because he knew that he had been acting unwisely and wickedly, but also because he was genuinely in love with the Queen. He still had a kick in him, however, and he saw that after having gone so far it was too late to retreat. Lancelot would be bound to come in answer to the message, and it was necessary to gain time. The castle was not ready for a siege—but, if it could be got ready, there would be a fair prospect of making terms with the besiegers, considering that the Queen would be inside. So Lancelot must be stopped at all costs, until the castle had been put in posture of defence. He guessed correctly that Lancelot would come riding helter-skelter to the Queen's aid, as soon as he could get himself armed. The best way of stopping him would be with a second ambush, at a narrow glade in the wood which he would have to ride through—a glade so narrow that archers would certainly be able to kill his horse, if not to pierce his armour. Since the Troubled Times, all roads had been cleared of undergrowth for the distance of a bowshot on either side—but this glade, on account of peculiarities in the terrain, had been overlooked. And a well-shot arrow at fair range could penetrate the best armour, as Meliagrance knew.

So the ambush was sent out post-haste, and everything within the castle was at sixes and sevens. Herdsmen were driving beasts into the keep—and all the beasts strayed, or got muddled with each other, or would not go through gates. Pump boys were feverishly bringing water to the great tubs —it was one of those futile castles, which appear to have originated in Ireland, whose bailey was without a well. Maids were running about on the verge of hysterics—for Sir Meliagrance, like many people out of the wrong drawer, was determined to receive his captive Queen in a way which would be above criticism. They were making boudoirs for her, and taking the tapestries out of his bachelor bedroom to go in hers, and polishing the silver, and sending to the nearest neighbours for the loan of gold plate. Guenever herself, ushered into a small waiting-room while the state apartments were made ready for her reception, added to the confusion by insisting on bandages and hot water and stretchers for her wounded men. Sir Meliagrance, running up and down stairs with cries of "Yes, Ma'am, in 'arf a minute" or "Marian, Marian, where the 'ell have you put the candles?" or "Murdoch, take them sheep out of the solar this instant," found time to lean his forehead against the cold stone of an embrasure, to clutch his bewildered heart, to curse his folly, and further to disarrange his already disordered plots.

The Queen was the first to get her affairs in order. She only had the bandaging to arrange, and naturally her wants were the earliest to be attended. She was sitting with her waiting-women at one of the windows of the castle, a sort of calm-centre in the middle of the whirlwind, when one of the girls called out that something was coming down the road.

"It is a cart," said the Queen. "It will be something to do with the provisions of the castle."

"There is a knight in the cart," said the girl, "a knight in armour. I suppose somebody is taking him away to be hanged."

In those days it was considered disgraceful to ride in a cart.

Later, they saw that there was a horse trotting behind the cart—which was coming at a great gallop—with its reins dangling in the dust. Later still they were horrified to see that all the entrails of the horse were dangling in the dust also. It was stuck full of arrows like a porcupine, and trotted along with a strange look of unconcernedness. Perhaps it was numbed by shock. It was Lancelot's horse, and Lancelot was in the cart, beating the cart-horse with his scabbard. He had fallen into the ambush as expected, had spent some time trying to get at his assailants—who had escaped the heavy dismounted iron man easily, by jumping over hedges and ditches—and then he had set out to walk the rest of the way, in spite of his armour. Meliagrance had counted on the impossibility of such a walk, for a man dressed in an equipment which may have weighed as much as himself—but he had not counted on the cart which Lancelot commandeered. A measure of the great man's anxiety about the Queen on this occasion is that he is said to have swum his horse across the Thames at the beginning of the ride, from Westminster Bridge to Lambeth, in spite of the fact that, if anything had gone wrong, his armour would certainly have drowned him.

"How dare you say it was a knight going to be hanged?" exclaimed the Queen. "You are a hussy. How dare you compare Sir Lancelot to a felon?"

The wretched girl blushed and held her tongue, while Lancelot could be seen throwing his reins to the terrified carter, and storming up the drawbridge, shouting at the top of his voice.

Sir Meliagrance heard of the arrival just as Lancelot was bursting in at the Great Gate. A flustered porter, taken by surprise, tried to shut it in his face, but received a blow on the ear from the iron fist, which knocked him flat. The gate swung open, undefended. Lancelot was in one of his rare passions, possibly on account of the sufferings of his horse.

Meliagrance, who had been overseeing some men-at-arms while they broke up the wooden sheds on the Great Court as a precaution against Greek Fire, lost his nerve. He sprinted for the back stairs and was already kneeling at the Queen's feet, while Lancelot was raging round the Porter's lodge, demanding the Queen.

"What is the matter now?" asked Guenever, looking at the extraordinary, vulgar man who sprawled before her— a look, curiously enough, not without affection. After all, it is a compliment to be kidnapped for love, especially when all ends happily.

"I yield, I yield!" cried Sir Meliagrance. "Ow, I yield to you, dear Queen. Save me from that Sir Lancelot!"

Guenever was looking radiantly beautiful. It may have been the Maying, or the compliment which the cockney Knight had paid her, or some premonition such as comes to women before their joy. At any rate she was feeling happy, and she bore no grudge against her captor.

"Very well," she said, cheerfully and wisely. "The less noise there is about this, the better for my reputation. I will try to calm Sir Lancelot."

Sir Meliagrance positively whistled with relief, he sighed so hard.

"That's right," he said. "That's the old cock sparrer—ahem! ahem! Beg pardon, I'm sure. Will it please your gracious Majesty to stye the night at Meliagrance Castle, when you 'ave been and calmed Sir Lancelot, for the sike of your wounded knights?"

"I don't know," said the Queen.

"You could all go awai in the morning," urged Sir Meliagrance, "and we could sye no more abaht it. It would be more regular like. You could sye you was here on a visit."

"Very well," said the Queen, and she went down to Lancelot while Sir Meliagrance mopped his brow.

He was standing in the Inner Court, shouting for his enemy. When Guenever saw him, and he saw her, the old electric message went between their eyes before they spoke a word. It was as if Elaine and the whole Quest for the Grail had never been. So far as we can make it out, she had accepted her defeat. He must have seen in her eyes that she had given in to him, that she was prepared to leave him to be himself—to love his God, and to do whatever he pleased —so long as he was only Lancelot. She was serene and sane again. She had renounced her possessive madness and was joyful to see him living, whatever he did. They were young creatures—the same creatures whose eyes had met with the almost forgotten click of magnets in the smoky Hall of Camelot so long ago. And, in truly yielding, she had won the battle by mistake.

"What is all the fuss about?" asked the Queen.

They had a light, bantering tone. They were in love again.

"You may well ask."

Then he added in an angrier voice, and flushing: "He has shot my horse."

"Thank you for coming," said the Queen. Her voice was gentle. It was the first voice he remembered. "Thank you for coming so fast and so bravely. But he has given in, and we must forgive him."

"It was shameful to murder my poor horse."

"We have made it up."

"If I had known you were going to make it up," said
Lancelot rather jealously, "I would not have nearly killed
myself in coming."

The Queen took his bare hand. The gauntlet was off.

"Are you sorry," she asked, "because you have done so
well?"

He was silent.

"I don't care about him," said the Queen, blushing. "I
only thought it would be better not to have a scandal."

"I don't want a scandal any more than you do."

"You must do as you please," said the Queen. "Fight him
if you like. You are the one to choose."

Lancelot looked at her.

"Madam," he said, "so ye be pleased, I care not. As for
my part, ye shall soon please."

He always fell into the grandeur of the High Language,
when he was moved.

# 43

*The wounded knights were laid on stretchers in the*
outer room. The inner room, where Guenever slept, had a
window with iron bars. There was no glass.

Lancelot had noticed a ladder in the garden, which was
long enough for his purpose—and, although they had made
no assignation, the Queen was waiting. When she saw his
crumpled face at the window, with the inquisitive nose
against the stars, she did not think it was a gargoyle or a
demon. She stood for a few heartbeats, feeling the wild
blood surge in her neck, then went silently to the window—
the silence of an accomplice.

Nobody knows what they said to each other. Malory says
that "they made either to other their complaints of many
divers things." Probably they agreed that it was impossible
to love Arthur and also to deceive him. Probably Lancelot
made her understand about his God at last, and she made

him understand about her missing children. Probably they fully agreed to accept their guilty love as ended.

Later, Sir Lancelot whispered: "I wish I might come in."

"I would as fain."

"Would you, madam, with all your heart that I were with you?"

"Truly."

The last iron bar, as he broke it out, cut the brawn of his hand to the bone.

Later still, the whispers faltered, and there was silence in the darkness of the room.

Queen Guenever lay long in bed next morning. Sir Meliagrance, anxious to get the whole affair safely ended as soon as possible, fussed in the antechamber, wishing she were gone. For one thing, he was not anxious to prolong his own torture, by keeping the Queen under his roof, whom he loved and could not have.

At last, partly to hurry her off and partly out of a lover's uncontrollable curiosity, he went into the bedroom to wake her up—a proceeding which was possible in the days of the levee.

"Mercy," said Sir Meliagrance, "what ails you, Ma'am, to sleep so long?"

He was looking at his lost beauty in the bed and pretending not to do so. The blood of Lancelot's cut hand was all over the sheets.

"Traitress!" cried Sir Meliagrance suddenly. "Traitress! You are a traitor to King Arthur!"

He was beside himself with rage and jealousy, believing himself deceived. He had been assuming, since his own enterprise had gone agley, that the Queen was a pure woman; and that he, in seeking to enjoy her, was in the wrong. Now he saw that all the time she had been cheating him, only pretending to be too virtuous to love him, and meanwhile sporting with her wounded knights under his very nose. He had jumped to the conclusion that the blood had come from a wounded knight—otherwise why should she have insisted on having them in the antechamber? The wildest envy was mixed with his rage. He never saw the bars of the window, which had been replaced as carefully as possible.

"Traitress! Traitress! I accuse you of high treason!"

The yells of Sir Meliagrance brought the hurt knights hobbling to the door—the commotion spread—tire-women and serving maids, pages, turf boys, a couple of grooms, all came with excitement to the scene.

"They are all false," cried Sir Meliagrance, "all or some. A wounded knight hath been here."

Guenever said, "That is untrue. They can prove it."

"It is a lie," the knights shouted. "Choose which of us you will fight. We will fight you."

"No, you won't," yelled Sir Meliagrance. "Away with your proud language. A wounded knight 'as been sleeping with 'er Majesty!"

And he kept on pointing to the blood, which was certainly good evidence, until Sir Lancelot arrived among the now sheepish bodyguard. Nobody noticed that his hand was in a glove.

"What is the matter?" asked Lancelot.

Meliagrance began telling him, wildly, gesticulating, seizing with excitement upon a fresh person to tell. He was like a man crazy with grief.

Lancelot said coldly: "May I remind you about your own conduct towards the Queen?"

"I don't know what you mean. I don't care. I know a knight was in this room last evening."

"Be careful what you say."

Lancelot looked at him hard, trying to warn him and to bring him to his senses. They both knew that this accusation must end in trial by combat, and Lancelot wanted to make him realize with whom he would have to fight. Sir Meliagrance did realize this eventually. He looked at Lancelot with unexpected dignity.

"And you be careful too, Sir Lancelot," he said quietly. "I know you are the best knight in the world, but be careful 'ow you fight in a wrong quarrel. God might strike a stroke for justice, Sir Lancelot, after all."

The Queen's true lover set his teeth.

"That must be left to God," he said.

Then he added, very meanly: "So far as I am concerned, I say plainly that none of these wounded knights was in the Queen's room. And if you want to fight about it, I will fight you."

Lancelot was, in the end, to fight for the Queen at the stake three times: first in the good quarrel of Sir Mador, second in this very doubtful quibble of words with Sir Meliagrance, and third in a quarrel which was wrong altogether—and each fight brought them nearer to destruction.

Sir Meliagrance threw down his glove. He was so certain of the truth of his assertion that he had become obstinate, as people do in violent arguments. He was prepared to die rather than withdraw. Lancelot took the glove—what else could he do? Everybody began attending to the paraphernalia of a challenge, the usual sealing of the gages with signets and so on, and the fixing of the date. Sir Meliagrance grew quieter. Now that he was caught in the machinery of justice, he had time to reflect, and, as usual, his reflections went the opposite way. He was an inconsistent man.

"Sir Lancelot," he said, "now that we are fixed to have a fight, you won't do nothing treacherous to me meanwhile?"

"Of course not."

Lancelot looked at him in genuine amazement. His heart was like Arthur's. He was always getting himself into trouble—as, for instance, by unhorsing the Orkneys at Westminster—through underestimating the wickedness of the world.

"We will be friends till the battle?"

The old warrior felt his long-accustomed pang of shame. He was to fight this man for saying what was practically true.

"Yes," he said enthusiastically, "friends!"

He moved towards Meliagrance with an uprush of remorse.

"Then we will have peace for now," said Meliagrance in a pleased voice. "Everything above-board. Would you like to see my castle?"

"Indeed I should."

Meliagrance led him all over the castle, from room to room, until they came to a chamber with a trap-door. The board rolled and the trap opened. Lancelot fell sixty feet, landing on deep straw in a dungeon. Then Meliagrance ordered one of the horses to be hidden, and went back to the Queen to tell her that her champion had ridden ahead. Lancelot's well-known habit of abrupt departures lent colour to the story. It seemed to Meliagrance the best way of ensuring that God should not choose the wrong side of this quarrel—for Meliagrance was muddled with his standards too.

# 44

*The second trial by combat was as sensational as*
the Mador one had been. For one thing, Lancelot arrived,
at the last moment, by a still narrower margin. They had
waited for him, and given him up, and persuaded Sir Lavine to fight in his place. Sir Lavine was actually riding into
the lists when the great man came at full gallop, on a white
horse which belonged to Meliagrance. He had been held
captive in the dungeon until that morning—when the girl
who brought him his food had finally liberated him in the
absence of her master, in exchange for a kiss. He had suffered some complicated scruples about this kiss: but had decided in the end that it was permissable.

Meliagrance went down at the first charge, and refused
to get up.

"I yield," he said. "I'm a gonner."

"Get up, get up. You have not fought at all."

"I shan't," said Sir Meliagrance.

Lancelot stood over him in perplexity. He owed him a
thrashing for the business of the horse, and for the treachery
of the trap-door. But he knew that the man's accusation was
essentially right, and he did not like the idea of killing him.

"Mercy," said Sir Meliagrance.

Lancelot turned his eyes sideways to the Queen's pavilion,
where she sat under the Constable's ward. Nobody could see
this look of inquiry because of the great helm.

Guenever saw it, however, or felt it in her heart. She
turned her thumb down, over the edge of the box, and secretly jabbed it downward several times. Meliagrance, she
thought, was a dangerous man to keep alive.

There was great silence in the arena, while everybody
waited without breath, leaning forward and looking upon
the combatants like a circle of vultures whose prey is not
yet dead. Everybody was waiting for the *coup de grâce*,
like the people at a Roman amphitheatre or at a Spanish
bull-fight, and everybody was sure that Lancelot would give

it. The accusation of Meliagrance had been, in their opinion, much more serious than the accusation of Mador—and they thought, like Guenever, that he deserved to perish. For in those days love was ruled by a different convention to ours. In those days it was chivalrous, adult, long, religious, almost platonic. It was not a matter about which you could make accusations lightly. It was not, as we take it to be nowadays, begun and ended in a long week-end.

The spectators saw Lancelot hesitating over the man, then heard his voice coming muffled by the helm. He was making proposals.

"I will give you odds," he was saying, "if you will get up and fight me properly, to the death. I will take off my helm and all the armour on the left side of my body, and I will fight without a shield, with my left hand tied behind my back. That will be fair, surely? Will you get up and fight me like that?"

A sort of high, hysterical squeal came from Sir Meliagrance, who could be seen crawling towards the King's box and making violent gestures.

"Don't forget what 'e said," he was shouting. "Everybody 'eard 'im. I accept 'is terms. Don't let 'im go back on 'em. No harmour for the left side, no shield or 'elm, and 'is left hand tied behind 'is back. Everybody 'eard! Everybody 'eard!"

The King cried, "Ho and abide!" The heralds and kings-at-arms came down the lists, and Meliagrance was silenced. Everybody felt shame on his behalf. In the distasteful still-ness, while he muttered and insisted that the terms should be observed, reluctant hands disarmed Sir Lancelot and tied him. They felt they were helping at the execution of somebody whom they loved very much, for the odds were too heavy. When they had bound him and given him his sword, they patted him—pushing him forward towards Meliagrance with these rough pats, and turning away their faces.

There was a flash in the sandy lists, like a salmon jumping a weir. It was Lancelot showing his naked side to draw the blow. And, as the blow came, there was the click of chang-ing forms—the same click as comes in the kaleidoscope when the image alters. The blow which Meliagrance was giving had changed to a blow which Lancelot was giving.

Sir Meliagrance was dragged out of the field by horses. His helm and head were in two pieces.

# 45

*Well, that is the long story of how the foreigner*
from Benwick stole Queen Guenever's love, of how he left
her for his God and finally returned in spite of the taboo.
It is a story of love in the old days, when adults loved
faithfully—not a story of the present, in which adolescents
pursue the ignoble spasms of the cinematograph. These people had struggled for a quarter of a century to reach their
understanding, and now their Indian Summer was before
them. Lancelot had given his God to Guenever, and she had
given him his freedom in exchange. Elaine, who had never
been more than an incidental part of the muddle, had
achieved a peace of her own. Arthur, whose corner of the
triangle was the least fortunate from a personal point of
view, was not entirely wretched. Merlyn had not intended
him for private happiness. He had been made for royal joys,
for the fortunes of a nation. These, for the time of their
sunset, Lancelot's two sensational victories had restored.
Fashion and modernity and the rot at the Table's heart were
in hiding, and his great idea was on the move once more.
He was inventing Law as Power. Nor had Arthur cause for
private reproach. He had kept himself aloof from the pains
of Guenever and Lancelot, unconsciously trusting them not
to bring the matter to his consciousness, not from motives
of fear or of weak connivance, but from the noblest of motives. The power had been in the King's hands. He had been
in the position of a husband who could, by a single command, solve the problem of eternal triangles by reference to
the headsman's block or to the stake. His wife and her
lover had been at his mercy—and that was the reason, not
any reason of cowardice, why his generous heart had been
determined to remain unconscious.

The Indian Summer was within their grasp, gossip was
silenced, discourtesy put down. The Orkney faction could
only grumble, a distant and almost subterranean complaint.
In the scriptoria of the abbeys, and in the castles of the

great nobles, the harmless writers scribbled away at Missals and Treatises of Knighthood, while the limners illuminated the capital letters and carefully drew blazons of arms. The goldsmiths and silversmiths hammered away, with small hammers, at gold leaf. They twisted gold wire and inlaid interlacements of the wildest complexity on the crosiers of the bishops. Pretty ladies kept robins and sparrows for pets, or tried very hard to teach their magpies to talk. Housewives of a provident turn of mind filled their cupboards with treacle as a medicine for bad air, and with home-made plasters called Flos Unguentorum for the rheumatics and muskballs to smell. They provided against Lent by purchasing dates, and green ginger of almonds, and herrings at 4s. 6d. the horse-load. Falconers and austringers abused each other's hawks to their hearts' content. In the new law courts—for Fort Mayne was over—the lawyers were as busy as bees, issuing writs for attainder, chancery, chevisance, disseisin, distraint, distress, embracery, exigent, fieri facias, maintenance, replevin, right of way, oyer and terminer, scot and lot, Quorum bonorum, Sic et non, Pro et contra, Jus primae noctis, and Questio quid juris? Thieves—it is true—could be hanged for stealing goods to the value of one shilling—for the codification of Justice was still weak and muddled—but that was not so bad as it sounds, when you remember that for a shilling you could buy two geese, or four gallons of wine, or forty-eight loaves of bread—a troublesome load for a thief in any case. In the country lanes the mere lovers, who were not gentles, walked in the sunsets with their arms round each other's waists, so that they gave the impression of a capital X when seen from behind.

Arthur's Gramarye was at peace, and the joys of peace stretched before Lancelot and Guenever. But there was a fourth corner in the puzzle.

God was Lancelot's totem. He was the other person of their battle, and now He chose the final moment to step across the path. The small boy who looked in the kettle-hat, and who dreamed of well-water which always slipped away from his lips, had cherished an ambition to do some ordinary miracle. He had managed a sort of miracle, when he rescued Elaine from her tub by being the best knight in the world—before he was trapped by Elaine on that terrible evening so that he broke his taboo. For a quarter of a century he had remembered the night with grief, and it had been with him through all the searches for the Grail. Before it, he had thought himself a man of God. Since then, he had been a swindle. Now the time had finally come to a head, when he was to be forced to face his doom.

There was a knight from Hungary called Sir Urre, who had received wounds in a tournament seven years before. He had been fighting with a man called Sir Alphagus, whom he had killed after getting these wounds—three of them on the head, four on the body and on the left hand. The mother of the dead Alphagus had been a Spanish witch, and she had put an enchantment on Sir Urre of Hungary, so that none of the wounds could ever heal up. All the time they were to go on bleeding, turn about, until the best knight in the world had tended them and salved them with his hands.

Sir Urre of Hungary had long been carried from country to country—perhaps it was a sort of hemophilia—searching for the best knight who would be able to help him. At last he had braved the channel to reach this foreign, northern land. Everybody had told him, everywhere, that his only chance was Lancelot, and in the end he had come to seek.

Arthur, who always felt the best of everybody, was sure that Lance would be able to do it—but he thought it fair that every knight of the Table should have a try. There might be a hidden excellence lurking somewhere, as had happened before.

The court was at Carlisle at the time, for the feast of Pentecost, and it was arranged that everybody should meet in the town meadow. Sir Urre was carried there in a litter and laid on a cushion of gold cloth, for the attempt at healing to begin. A hundred and ten knights—forty were away on quests—stood round him in ordered ranks, in their best clothes, and there were carpets laid down, and pavilions set up for the great ladies to watch. Arthur loved his Lancelot so much that he wanted him to have a splendid setting, in which his crowning achievement could be done.

This is the end of the book of Sir Lancelot, and now we are to see him for the last time in it. He was hiding in the harness-room of the castle, whence he could spy the field. There were plenty of leather reins in the room, hanging orderly among the saddles and the bright bits. He had noticed that they were strong enough to bear his weight. He was waiting there, hidden, praying that somebody—Gareth perhaps?—would be able to do the miracle quickly: or, if not, that they would overlook him, that his absence would not be noticed.

Do you think it would be fine to be the best knight in the world? Think, then, also, how you would have to defend the title. Think of the tests, such repeated, remorseless, scandal-breathing tests, which day after day would be applied to you—until the last and certain day, when you would fail. Think also that you know of a good reason for your failure, which you have tried to hide, tried pathetically to hide and overlook, for five and twenty years. Think that you are now to go out, before the largest and most honourable gallery that can be assembled, to make a public demonstration of your sin. They are expecting you to succeed, and you are to fail: you are to publish the deceit which you have prac-tised for a quarter of a century, and they will all immedi-ately know the reason for it—that reason of shame which you have sought to conceal from your own mind, and which, when it has remembered itself in the silence of your empty chamber, has pricked you into a physical motion of your head to throw it off. Miracles, which you wanted to do so long ago, can only be done by the pure in heart. The peo-ple outside are waiting for you to do this miracle because you have traded on their belief that your heart was pure—and now, with treachery and adultery and murder wringing the heart like a cloth, you are to go out into the sunlight for the test of honour.

Lancelot stood in the harness-room as white as a sheet. Guenever was out there, he knew, and she was also pale. He twisted his fingers and looked at the strong reins, and prayed as best he could.


"Sir Servause le Breuse!" cried the heralds, and Sir Ser-vause stepped forward—a knight far down the list of com-petitors. He was a shy man, interested only in natural his-tory, who had never fought with anybody in his life. He went over to Sir Urre, who was groaning from all the handling, and he knelt down and did his best.

"Sir Ozanna le Cure Hardy!"

It went on like that down the full list of a hundred and ten, whose gorgeous names are given by Malory in their proper order, so that you almost see the fine cut of their heavy brigandines, the tinctures of their blazons, and the gay colour in each panache. Their feathered heads made them look like Indian braves. The plates of their sabatons clinked as they walked, giving the firm, exciting ring of spurs. They knelt down, and Sir Urre winced, and it was no good.

Lancelot did not hang himself with the reins. He had broken his taboo, deceived his friend, returned to Guenever, and murdered Sir Meliagrance in a wrong quarrel. Now he was ready to take his punishment. He went to the long avenue of knights who waited in the sun. By the very attempt to evade notice, he had brought on himself the conspicuous place of last. He walked down the curious ranks, ugly as ever, self-conscious, ashamed, a veteran going to be broken. Mordred and Agravaine moved forward.

When Lancelot was kneeling in front of Urre, he said to King Arthur: "Need I do this, after everybody has failed?"

"Of course you must do it. I command you."

"If you command me, I must. But it would be presumptuous to try—after everybody. Could I be let off?"

"You are taking it the wrong way," said the King. "Of course it is not presumptuous for you to try. If you can't do it, nobody can."

Sir Urre, who was weak by now, raised himself on an elbow.

"Please," he said. "I came for you to do it."

Lancelot had tears in his eyes.

"Oh, Sir Urre," he said, "if only I could help you, how willingly I would. But you don't understand, you don't understand."

"For God's sake," said Sir Urre.

Lancelot looked into the East, where he thought God lived, and said something in his mind. It was more or less like this: "I don't want glory, but please can you save our honesty? And if you will heal this knight for the knight's sake, please do." Then he asked Sir Urre to show him his head.

Guenever, who was watching from her pavilion like a hawk, saw the two men fumbling together. Then she saw a movement in the people near, and a mutter came, and yells. Gentlemen began throwing their caps about, and shouting, and shaking hands. Arthur was crying the same words again and again, holding gruff Gawaine by the elbow and putting them into his ear. "It shut like a box! It shut like a box!" Some elderly knights were dancing around, banging their shields together as if they were playing Pease Pudding Hot, and poking each other in the ribs. Many of the squires were laughing like madmen and slapping each other on the back. Sir Bors was kissing King Anguish of Ireland, who resented it. Sir Galahalt, the hault prince, had fallen over his scabbard. Generous Sir Belleus, who had borne no grudge for having his liver cut open on that distant evening beside the pavilion of red sendal, was making a horrible noise by blowing on a grass blade held edgewise between his thumbs. Sir Bedivere, frightfully repentant ever since his visit to the Pope, was rattling some holy bones which he had brought home as a souvenir of his pilgrimage: they had written on them in curly letters, "A Present from Rome." Sir Bliant, remembering his gentle Wild Man, was embracing Sir Castor, who had never forgotten the Chevalier's knightly rebuke. Kind and sensitive Aglovale, the forgiver of the Pellinore feud, was exchanging hearty thumps with the beautiful Gareth. Mordred and Agravaine scowled. Sir Mador, as red as a turkey cock, was making it up with Sir Pinel the poisoner, who had come back incognito. King Pelles was promising a new cloak all round, on him. The snow-haired Uncle Dap, so old as to be absolutely fabulous, was trying to jump over his walking-stick. The tents were being let down, the banners waved. The cheers which now began, round after round, were like drumfire or thunder, rolling round the turrets of Carlisle. All the field, and all the people in the field, and all the towers of the castle, seemed to be jumping up and down like the surface of a lake under rain.

In the middle, quite forgotten, her lover was kneeling by himself. This lonely and motionless figure knew a secret which was hidden from the others. The miracle was that he had been allowed to do a miracle. "And ever," says Malory, "Sir Lancelot wept, as he had been a child that had been beaten."

**EXPLICIT LIBER TERTIUS**

# THE
# CANDLE
# IN
# THE
# WIND

*"He thought a little and said:*
*'I have found the Zoological Gardens of*
*service to many of my patients. I should prescribe*
*for Mr. Pontifex a course of the larger*
*mammals. Don't let him think he is*
*taking them medicinally....'"*

# 1

*The addition of years had not been kind to Agra-*vaine. Even when he was forty he had looked his present age, which was fifty-five. He was seldom sober.

Mordred, the cold wisp of a man, did not seem to have any age. His years, like the depths of his blue eyes and the inflexions of his musical voice, were non-committal.

The two were standing in the cloisters of the Orkney palace at Camelot, looking out at the hawks who sat beneath the sun, on their blocks in the green courtyard. The cloisters had the new-fashioned flamboyant arches, in whose graceful frames the hawks stood out with noble indifference—a jerfalcon, a goshawk, a falcon and her tiercel, and four little merlins who had been kept all winter, yet had survived. The blocks were clean—for the sportsmen of those days considered that, if you went in for blood sports, it was your duty to conceal the beastliness with scrupulous care. All were lovingly ornamented with spanish leather in scarlet, and with gold tooling. The leashes of the hawks were plaited out of white horse leather. The jer had a snow-white leash and jesses cut from guaranteed unicorn skin, as a tribute to her station in life. She had been brought all the way from Iceland, and that was the least they could do for her.

Mordred said pleasantly: "For God his sake let's get out of this. The place stinks."

When he spoke the hawks moved slightly, so that their bells gave a whisper of sound. The bells had been brought from the Indies, regardless of expense, and the pair worn by the jer were made of silver. An enormous eagle-owl who was sometimes used as a decoy, but who was at present standing on a perch in the shade of the cloister, opened his eyes when the bells rang. Before he had opened them, he might have been a stuffed owl, a dowdy bundle of feathers. The moment they had dawned, he was a creature from Edgar Allan Poe. You hardly liked to look at him. They were red eyes, homicidal, terrific, seeming actually to give out light. They were like rubies filled with flame. He was called the Grand Duke.

"I don't smell anything," said Agravaine. He sniffed suspiciously, trying to smell. But his palate was gone, both for smell and taste, and he had a headache.

"It stinks of Sport," said Mordred in inverted commas, "and the Done Thing and the Best People. Let's go to the garden."

Agravaine returned tenaciously to the subject which they had been discussing.

"It is no good making a fuss about it," he said. "We know the rights and wrongs, but nobody else knows. Nobody would listen."

"But they must listen." Small flecks in the iris of Mordred's eyes burned with a turquoise light, as bright as the owl's. Instead of being a foppish man with a crooked shoulder, dressed in extravagant clothes, he became a Cause. He became, on this matter, everything which Arthur was not—the irreconcilable opposite of the Englishman. He became the invincible Gael, the scion of desperate races more ancient than Arthur's, and more subtle. Now, when he was on fire with his Cause, Arthur's justice seemed *bourgeois* and obtuse beside him. It seemed merely to be dull complacency, beside the savagery and feral wit of the Pict. His maternal ancestors crowded into his face when he was spurning at Arthur—ancestors whose civilization, like Mordred's, had been matriarchal: who had ridden bare-back, charged in chariots, fought by stratagem, and ornamented their grisly strongholds with the heads of enemies. They had marched, long-haired and ferocious, an ancient writer tells us, "sword in hand, against rivers in flood or against the storm-tossed ocean." They were the race, now represented by the Irish Republican Army rather than by the Scots Nationalists, who had always murdered landlords and blamed them for being murdered—the race which could make a national hero of a man like Lynchahaun, because he bit off a woman's nose and she a Gall—the race which had been expelled by the volcano of history into the far quarters of the globe, where, with a venomous sense of grievance and inferiority, they even nowadays proclaim their ancient megalomania. They were the Catholics who could fly directly in the face of any pope or saint—Adrian, Alexander or St. Jerome—if the saint's policies did not suit their own convenience: the hysterically touchy, sorrowful, flayed defenders of a broken heritage. They were the race whose barbarous, cunning, valiant defiance had been enslaved, long centuries before, by the foreign people whom Arthur represented. This was one of the barriers between the father and his son.

Agravaine said: "Mordred, I want to talk. There doesn't seem to be anywhere to sit. Sit on that thing, and I will sit here. Nobody can hear us."

"I don't mind if they do hear. That is what we want. It should be said out loud, not whispered in cloisters."

"The whispers will get there in the end."

"No, they won't. That is what they won't do. He doesn't want to hear, and, so long as we whisper, he can always pretend that he can't. You are not the King of England for all these years, without knowing how to use hypocrisy."

Agravaine was uncomfortable. His hatred for the King was not a reality like Mordred's—indeed, he had little personal feeling against anybody except Lancelot. His attitude was more of malice at random.

"I don't think it is any good complaining about what happened in the past," he said gloomily. "We can't expect other people to side with us when everything is complicated, and happened so long ago."

"It may have happened long ago, but that doesn't alter the fact that Arthur is my father, and that he turned me adrift in a boat as a baby."

"It may not alter it for you," said Agravaine, "but it alters it for other people. It is such a muddle that nobody cares. You can't expect ordinary people to remember about grandfathers and half-sisters and things of that sort. In any case human beings don't go to war for private quarrels nowadays. You need a national grievance—something to do with politics which is waiting to burst out. You need to use the tools which are ready to hand. This man John Ball, for instance, who believes in communism: he has thousands of followers who would be ready to help in a disturbance, for their own purposes. Or there are the Saxons. We could say we were in favour of a national movement. For that matter, we could join them together and call it national communism. But it has to be something broad and popular, which everybody can feel. It must be against large numbers of people, like the Jews or the Normans or the Saxons, so that everybody can be angry. Either we must be the leaders of the Old Ones, who seek for justice against the Saxon: or of the Saxon against the Norman; or of the serf against society. We want a banner, yes, and a badge too. You could use the Fylfot. Communism, Nationalism, something like that. But as for a private grudge against the old man, it's useless. Anyway it would take you half an hour to explain it, even if you did begin to shout it from the roof tops."

"I could shout that my mother was his sister, and that he tried to drown me because of that."

"If you wanted to," said Agravaine.

They had been talking, before the eagle-owl woke up, about the earlier wrongs of their family—about their grandmother, Igraine, who had been wronged by Arthur's father —about all the long-gone feud of Gael and Gall, which had been taught them by their dam in old Dunlothian. It was these wrongs which Agravaine's colder blood could recognize as far too distant and confused to serve as weapons against the King. Now they had reached the more recent grievance—the sin of Arthur with his half-sister which had ended in an attempt to murder the bastard who resulted. These might certainly be stronger weapons, but the trouble was that Mordred was himself the bastard. The elder brother's cowardice told him, in his craftier head, that a son could hardly raise his illegitimacy as a banner under which to overthrow his father. Besides, the business had been hushed up long before, by Arthur. It seemed bad policy that Mordred should be the one to bring it up.

They sat in silence, looking at the floor. Agravaine was out of condition, with pouches under his eyes. Mordred was as slim as ever, a neat figure in the height of fashion. The exaggeration of his dress made a good camouflage for him, under which you hardly noticed his crooked shoulder.

He said: "I am not proud."

He looked bitterly at his half-brother, putting more meaning into the look than the other could be expected to catch. He was saying with his eyes: "Look at my hump, then. I have no reason to be proud of my birth."

Agravaine got up impatiently.

"I must have a drink in any case," he said, clapping his hands for the page. Then he passed his trembling fingers over his eyelids and stood wearily, looking at the owl with distaste. Mordred, while they were waiting for the drink, watched him with contempt.

"If you rake the old muck," said Agravaine, revived by the hippocras, "you will get yourself in the muck. We are not in Lothian, you must remember. We are in Arthur's England, and his English love him. Either they will refuse to believe you, or, if they do believe you, they will blame you, and not him, because it was you who brought the matter up. It is certain that not a single man would follow a rebellion of that sort."

Mordred looked at him. He was hating him, like the owl—condemning him as a coward. He could not bear to be thwarted in his day-dream of revenge, so he was wreaking his spite on Agravaine in his thoughts, saying to himself that the latter was a drunken traitor to the family.

Agravaine saw this, and, already consoled by half the bottle, laughed in his face. He patted the good shoulder, forcing the younger man to fill his glass.

"Drink," he said, chuckling. Mordred drank like a cat being dosed.

"Have you heard," asked Agravaine waggishly, "of a mighty saint called Lancelot?"

He winked one of the pouchy eyes, looking down his nose with benevolence.

"Go on."

"I gather you have heard about our *preux chevalier.*"

"I know Sir Lancelot, of course."

"I think I am not wrong in saying that this pure gentleman has given both of us a fall or two?"

"The first time Lancelot unhorsed me," said Mordred, "is so long ago that I can't remember. But it means nothing. Because a man can push you off a horse with a stick, it doesn't mean that he is a better man than you are."

It was a strange feature—now that Lancelot was in the conversation—that Mordred's vivid feeling was exchanged for indifference. But Agravaine, who had been reluctant before this, became fluent.

"Precisely," he said. "And our noble knight has been the Queen of England's lover all the time."

"Everybody knows that Gwen has been Lancelot's mistress since before the deluge, but what good is that? The King knows it himself. He has been told so three times, to my certain knowledge. I don't see that we can do anything."

Agravaine put his finger by the side of his nose like a drunken piper, then shook it at his brother.

"He has been told so," he announced, "but in roundabout ways. People have sent him hints, such as shields with cognizances on them that had double meanings, or horns which only faithful wives could drink from. But nobody has told him about it in open court, face to face. Meliagrance only made a general accusation, and even that was in the days of trial by battle. Think what would happen if we were to denounce Sir Lancelot personally, under these new-fashioned Laws, so that the King was forced to investigate."

Mordred's eyes dawned, as the owl's had done.

"Well?"

"I can't see that anything could happen, except a split. Arthur depends on Lancelot as his commander, and the chief of his troops. That is where his power comes from, because everybody knows that nobody can stand against brute force. But if we could make a little merry mischief between Arthur and Lancelot, because of the Queen, their power would be split. Then would be the time for policy. Then would be the time for discontented people, Lollards and Communists and Nationalists and all the riff-raff. Then would be the time to take your famous revenge."

"We could break them up, because they were broken among themselves."

"But it means more than that."

"It means that the Cornwalls would be even for grandfather and I for mother ..."

"... not by using force against force, but by using our brains."

"It means that I could revenge myself on the man who tried to drown me as a baby ..."

"... by getting behind the bully first, and then by being a little careful."

"Behind our famous Double Blue ..."

"... Sir Lancelot!"

The position was, and perhaps it may as well be laboured for the last time, that Arthur's father had killed the Earl of Cornwall. He had killed the man because he wanted to enjoy the wife. On the night of the Earl's killing, Arthur had been conceived upon the unfortunate Countess. Being born too soon for the various conventions of mourning, marriage, and so forth, he had been secretly put to nurse with Sir Ector of the Forest Sauvage. He had grown up in ignorance of his parentage until, when he was a young boy of nineteen summers, he had fallen in with Morgause, without knowing that she was one of his half-sisters by the Countess and the slaughtered Earl. This half-sister, already the mother of Gawaine, Agravaine, Gaheris, and Gareth, had been twice the age of the young King—and she had successfully seduced him. The offspring of their union had been Mordred, who had been brought up alone with his mother, in the barbarous remoteness of the outer Isles. He had been brought up alone with Morgause, because he was so much younger than the rest of the family. The others had already flown to the King's court—forced there by ambition because it was the greatest court in the world, or else to escape their mother. Mordred had been left to be dominated by her, with her ancestral grudge against the King and her personal spite. For, although she had contrived to seduce young Arthur in his nonage, he had escaped her—to settle down with Guenever as his wife. Morgause, brooding in the North with the one child who remained to her, had concentrated her maternal powers on the crooked boy. She had loved and forgotten him by turns, an insatiable carnivore who lived on the affections of her dogs, her children and her lovers. Eventually one of the other sons had cut her head off in a storm of jealousy, on discovering her in bed at the age of seventy with a young man called Sir Lamorak. Mordred—confused between the loves and hatreds of his frightful home—had at the time been a party to her assassination. Now, in the court of a father who had been considerate enough to hide the story of his birth, the wretched son found himself the acknowledged brother of Gawaine, Agravaine, Gaheris and Gareth—found himself lovingly treated by the King-father whom his mother had taught him to hate with all his heart—found himself misshapen, intelligent, critical, in a civilization which was too straightforward for purely intellectual criticism—found himself, finally, the heir to a northern culture which has always been antagonistic to the blunt morals of the south.

# 2

*The page who had brought Sir Agravaine's hippocras* came in from the cloister door. He bowed double, with the exaggerated courtesy which was expected of pages before they became esquires on their way to knighthood, and announced: "Sir Gawaine, Sir Gaheris, Sir Gareth."

The three brothers followed him, boisterous from the open air and their recent doings, so that now the clan was complete. All of them, except Mordred, had wives of their own tucked away somewhere—but nobody ever saw them. Few saw the men themselves separate for long. There was something childish about them when they were together, which was attractive rather than the reverse. Perhaps there was something childish about all the paladins of Arthur's story—if being simple is the same as childishness.

Gawaine, who was the head of the family, walked first, with a falcon in juvenile plumage on his fist. The burly fellow had pale hairs in his red head now. Over the ears it was yellowish, the colour of a ferret's, and would soon be white. Gaheris looked like him, or at least he was more like him than the others. But his was a milder copy; not so red, nor so strong, nor so big, nor so obstinate. Indeed, he was a bit of a fool. Gareth, the youngest of the full brothers, had retained the traces of his youth. He walked with a spring in his step, as though he enjoyed being alive.

"Tuts!" exclaimed Gawaine's hoarse voice in the doorway, "drinking already?" He still kept his outland accent in defiance of the mere English, but he had ceased to think in Gaelic. His English had improved against his will. He was getting old.

"Well, Gawaine, well."

Agravaine, who knew that his nips before noon were disapproved of, asked politely: "Did you have a good day?"

"It wasna bad."

"It was a splendid day," exclaimed Gareth. "We entered her on the *haut vollay* with Lancelot's *passager*, and she was genuinely grey-minded. I never thought she would take to it without a bagman! Gawaine had managed her perfectly. She dropped into it without a second's hesitation, as if she had never been flying to anything but the heron, took a fine circle right round the new ricks by Castle Blanc, and got above him just to the Ganis side of the pilgrim's way. She . . ."

Gawaine, who had noticed that Mordred was yawning on purpose, said, "Ye may spare yer breath."

"It was a fine flight," he concluded lamely. "As she had handled her quarry, we thought we could give her a name."

"What did you call her?" they asked him condescendingly.

"Since she comes from Lundy, and begins with an L, we thought it might be a good idea to call her after Lancelot. We could call her Lancelotta, or something like that. She will be a first-class falcon."

Agravaine looked at Gareth under the lids of his eyes. He said with a slow tone: "Then you had better call her Gwen."

Gawaine came back from the courtyard, where he had been putting the peregrine on her block.

"Leave that," he said.

"I'm sorry if I am not suggesting the truth."

"I care nought about the truth or not. All I say is, Haud yer tongue."

"Gawaine," said Mordred to the air, "is such a *preux chevalier* that nobody must say anything wicked, or there will be trouble. You see, he is strong—and he apes the great Sir Lancelot."

The red fellow turned on him with dignity.

"I am'na muckle strong, brother, and I dinna trade upon it. I only seek to keep my people decent."

"And, of course," said Agravaine, "it is decent to sleep with the King's wife, even if the King's family has smashed our family, and got a son by our mother, and tried to drown him."

Gaheris protested: "Arthur has always been good to us. Do stop this whining for once."

"Because he is afraid of us."

"I don't see," said Gareth, "why Arthur should be afraid, when he has Lancelot. We all know that he is the best knight in the world, and can master anybody. Don't we, Gawaine?"

"For masel', I dinna wish to speak of it."

Suddenly Mordred was flaming at them, fired by Gawaine's lordly tone.

"Very well, and I do. I may be a weak knight at jousting, but I have the courage to stand for my family and rights. I am not a hypocrite. Everybody in this court knows that the Queen and the commander-in-chief are lovers, and yet we are supposed to be pure knights, and protectors of ladies, and nobody talks about anything except this so-called Holy Grail. Agravaine and I have decided to go to Arthur now, in full court, and ask about the Queen and Lancelot to his face."

"Mordred," exclaimed the head of the clan, "ye will do naething of the like! It would be sinful."

"He will," said Agravaine, "and I shall go there with him."

Gareth remained between pain and amazement.

"But they mean it," he protested.

Out of the moment of astonishment, Gawaine took the lead and forged into action.

"Agravaine, I am the head of the clan, and I forbid ye."

"You forbid me."

"Yes, I do forbid ye; for ye will be a sair fule if ye do."

"The honest Gawaine," remarked Mordred, "thinks you are a sair fule."

This time the towering fellow swung on him like a shying horse.

"Nane o' that!" he shouted. "Ye think I winna hit ye because ye are crookit, and ye take advantage. But I wull hit ye, mannie, if ye sneer."

Mordred heard his own voice speaking coldly, seeming to come from behind his ears.

"Gawaine, you surprise me. You have produced a sequence of thought."

Then, as the giant came towards him, the same voice said: "Go on. Strike me. It will show your courage."

"Ah, do stop, Mordred," pleaded Gareth. "Can't you stop this nagging for a minute?"

"Mordred wouldn't nag, as you call it," interjected Agravaine, "if you didn't bully."

Gawaine exploded like one of the new-fashioned cannons. He swung away from Mordred, a baited bull, and shouted at them both.

"My soul to the devil, will ye be quiet or will ye clear

out? Can we have no peace in the family ever? Shut yer trap, in the name of God, and leave this daft clatter about Sir Lancelot."

"It is not daft," said Mordred, "nor shall we leave it."

He stood up.

"Well, Agravaine," he asked. "Do we go to the King? Is any other coming?"

Gawaine planted himself in their path.

"Mordred, ye shallna go."

"Who is to stop me?"

"I am."

"Brave fellow," remarked the icy voice, still from somewhere in the air, and the humpback moved to pass.

Gawaine put out his red hand, with golden hairs on the back of the fingers, and pushed him back. At the same time Agravaine put out his own white hand, with fat fingers, to the hilt of his sword.

"Don't move, Gawaine. I have a sword."

"You would have a sword," cried Gareth, "you devil!"

The younger brother's life had suddenly fitted into a pattern and recognized itself. Their murdered mother, and the unicorn, and the man now drawing, and a child in a store-room flashing a dirk: these things had made him cry out.

"All right, Gareth," snarled Agravaine, as white as a sheet, "I know what you mean, and now I draw."

The situation passed out of control: they began acting like puppets, as if it had happened before—which it had. Gawaine, at the sight of steel, went into one of his blind rages. He swung away from Mordred, burst into a torrent of words, drew the hunting knife which was all he carried, and advanced on Agravaine—these things simultaneously. The fat man, as if thrown back on the defensive by the impact of his brother's fury, retreated before him, holding the sword in front with shaking hand.

"Aye," roared Gawaine, "ye ken fine what he means, my bonny butcher. We maun draw on yer ain brother, for ye ever speired to murder folk unarmed. The curse of the grave-cloth on ye! Put up yon sword, man! Put it up! What d'ye mean? Is it nae enough that ye should slay our mother? Damn ye, lay down yon sword, or hae the spunk to fight with it. Agravaine . . ."

Mordred was slipping behind his back, with a hand on his own dagger. In a second the glint of steel flashed in the shadows, lit by the owl's eyes, and at the same moment Gareth jumped to the defence. He caught Mordred by the wrist, crying: "Now enough! Gaheris, look to the others."

"Agravaine, put the sword up! Gawaine, leave him alone."

"Away, man! I can teach the hound masel'."

"Agravaine, put the sword down quickly, or he will kill you. Be quick, man. Don't be a fool. Gawaine, leave him alone. He didn't mean it. Gawaine! Agravaine!"

But Agravaine had made a feeble thrust at the head of the family, which Gawaine turned contemptuously with his knife. Now the towering old fellow, with the ferret-coloured temples, had rushed in and pinned him round the waist. The sword clattered to the floor as Agravaine went backward over the hippocras table, with Gawaine on top of him. The dagger rose in venom to complete the work—but Gaheris caught it from behind. There was a tableau of perfect silence, all motionless. Gareth held Mordred. Agravaine, hiding his eyes with the free hand, flinched from the knife. And Gaheris held the avenging arm suspended.

At this complicated moment the cloister door was opened for the second time, and the courteous page announced as impassively as ever: "His Majesty the King!"

Everybody relaxed. They let go of whatever they were holding, and began to move. Agravaine sat up panting. Gawaine turned away from him, drawing a hand across his face.

"Ach God!" he muttered. "If but I hadna siclike waeful passions!"

The King was on the threshold.

He came in, the quiet old man who had done his best so long. He looked older than his age, which was considerable. His royal eye took in the situation without a flicker. He moved across the cloister to kiss Mordred gently, smiling upon them all.

# 3

*Lancelot and Guenever were sitting at the solar window.* An observer of the present day, who knew the Arthurian legend only from Tennyson and people of that sort, would have been startled to see that the famous lovers were past their prime. We, who have learned to base our interpretation of love on the conventional boy-and-girl romance of Romeo and Juliet, would be amazed if we could step back into the Middle Ages—when the poet of chivalry could write about Man that he had *"en ciel un dieu, par terre une déesse."* Lovers were not recruited then among the juveniles and adolescents: they were seasoned people, who knew what they were about. In those days people loved each other for their lives, without the conveniences of the divorce court and the psychiatrist. They had a God in heaven and a goddess on earth—and, since people who devote themselves to goddesses must exercise some caution about the ones to whom they are devoted, they neither chose them by the passing standards of the flesh alone, nor abandoned it lightly when the bruckle thing began to fail.

Lancelot and Guenever were sitting by the window in the high keep, and Arthur's England stretched below them, under the level rays of sunset.

It was the Gramarye of the Middle Ages, which some people are accustomed to think of as the Dark Ages, and Arthur had made it what it was. When the old King came to his throne it had been an England of armoured barons, and of famine, and of war. It had been the country of trial by ordeal with red-hot irons, of the Law of Englishry, and of the sad, wordless song of Morfa-Rhuddlan. Then, on the sea-coast, within a foreign vessel's reach, not an animal, not a fruit tree, had been left. Then, in the fens and the vast forests, the last of the Saxons had defended themselves against the bitter rule of Uther the Conqueror; then the words "Norman" and "Baron" had been equivalent to the modern word of "Sahib"; then Llewellyn ap Griffith's head,

in its crown of ivy, had mouldered on the clustered spikes
of the Tower; then you would have met the mendicants by
the roadside, mutilated men who carried their right hands
in their left, and the forest dogs would have trotted beside
them, also mutilated by the removal of one toe—so that
they could not hunt in the woodlands of the lord. When Arthur first came, the country people had been accustomed to
bar themselves in their cottages every night as if for siege,
and had prayed to God for peace during darkness, the good-
man of the house repeating the prayers used at sea on the
approach of storm and ending with the plea "the Lord bless
us and help us," to which all present had replied "Amen."
In the baron's castle, in the early days, you would have
found the poor men being disembowelled—and their living
bowels burned before them—men being slit open to see if
they had swallowed their gold, men gagged with notched
iron bits, men hanging upside down with their heads in
smoke, others in snake pits or with leather tourniquets round
their heads, or crammed into stone-filled boxes which would
break their bones. You have only to turn to the literature
of the period, with its stories of the mythological families
such as Plantagenets, Capets and so forth, to see how the
land lay. Legendary kings like John had been accustomed
to hang twenty-eight hostages before dinner; or, like Philip,
had been defended by "sergeants-at-mace," a kind of storm
troopers who guarded their lord with maces; or, like Louis,
had decapitated their enemies on scaffolds under the blood
of which the children of the enemy had been forced to
stand. This, at all events, is what Ingulf of Croyland used
to tell us, until he was discovered to be a forgery. Then
there had been Archbishops nicknamed "Skin-villain," and
churches used as forts—with trenches in the graveyards
among the bones—and price-lists for fining murderers, and
bodies of the excommunicated lying unburied, and famish-
ing peasants eating grass or tree-bark or one another. (One
of them ate forty-eight.) There had been roasting heretics
on the one hand—forty-five Templars had been burned in
one day—and the heads of captives being thrown into besieged castles from catapults on the other. Here a leader
of the Jacquerie had been writhing in his chains, as he was
crowned with a red-hot tripod. There a Pope had been
complaining, as he was held to ransom, or another one
had been wriggling, as he was poisoned. Treasure had
been cemented into castle walls, in the form of gold bars,

and the builders had been executed afterwards. Children playing in the streets of Paris had frolicked with the dead body of a Constable, and others, with the women and old men, had starved outside the walls of beleaguered towns, yet inside the ring of the besiegers. Hus and Jerome, with the mitres of apostasy upon their heads, had flamed and fizzled at the stake. The hamstrung imbeciles of Jumièges had floated down the Seine. Giles de Retz had been found to have no less than a ton of children's bones, calcined, in his castle, after having murdered them at the rate of twelve score a year for nine years. The Duke of Berry had lost a kingdom through the unpopularity which he earned by feeling sorry for eight hundred foot soldiers who had been killed in a battle. The youthful count of St. Pol had been taught the arts of war by being given twenty-four living prisoners to slaughter in various ways, for practice. Louis the Eleventh, another of the fictional kings, had kept obnoxious bishops in rather expensive cages. The Duke Robert had been surnamed "the Magnificent" by his nobles—but "the Devil" by his parishioners. And all the while, before Arthur came, the common people—of whom fourteen were eaten by wolves out of one town in a single week, of whom one third were to die in the Black Death, of whom the corpses had been packed in pits "like bacon," for whom the refuges at evening had often been forests and marshes and caves, for whom, in seventy years, there had been known to be forty-eight of famine—these people had looked up at the feudal nobility who were termed the "lords of sky and earth," and—themselves battered by bishops who, because they were not allowed to shed blood, went for them with iron clubs—had cried aloud that Christ and his saints were sleeping.

"Pourquoi," the poor wretches had sung in their misery:

> *"Pourquoi nous laisser faire dommage?*
> *Nous sommes hommes comme ils sont."*

Such had been the surprisingly modern civilization which Arthur had inherited. But it was not the civilization over which the lovers looked out. Now, safe in the apple-green sunset before them, there stretched the fabled Merry England of the Middle Ages, when they were not so dark. Lancelot and Guenever were gazing on the Age of Individuals.

What an amazing time the age of chivalry was! Everybody was essentially himself—was riotously busy fulfilling the vagaries of human nature. There was such a gusto about the landscape which stretched before their window, such a riot of unexpected people and things, that you hardly knew how to begin describing it.

The Dark and Middle Ages! The Nineteenth Century had an impudent way with its labels. For there, under the window in Arthur's Gramarye, the sun's rays flamed from a hundred jewels of stained glass in monasteries and convents, or danced from the pinnacles of cathedrals and castles, which their builders had actually loved. Architecture, in those dark ages of theirs, was such a light-giving passion of the heart that men gave love-names to their fortresses. Lancelot's Joyous Gard was not a singularity in an age which has left us Beauté, Plaisance, or Malvoisin—the bad neighbour to its enemies—an age in which even an oaf like the imaginary Richard Coeur de Lion, who suffered from boils, could call his castle "Gaillard," and speak of it as "my beautiful one-year-old daughter." Even that legendary scoundrel William the Conqueror had a second nickname: "the Great Builder." Think of the glass itself, with its five grand colours stained right through. It was rougher than ours, thicker, fitted in smaller pieces. They loved it with the same fury as they gave to their castles, and Villars de Honnecourt, struck by a particularly beautiful specimen, stopped to draw it on his journeys, with the explanation that "I was on my way to obey a call to the land of Hungary when I drew this window because it pleased me best of all windows." Picture the insides of those ancient churches— not the grey and gutted interiors to which we are accustomed —but insides blazing with colour, plastered with frescoes in which all the figures stood on tip-toe, fluttering with tapestry or with brocades from Bagdad. Picture also the interiors of such castles as were visible from Guenever's window. These were no longer the grim keeps of Arthur's accession. Now they were filling with furniture made by the joiner, instead of the carpenter; now their walls rippled doorless with the flexible gaieties of Arras, tapestries like that of the Jousts of St. Denis which, although covering more than four hundred square yards, had been woven in less than three years, such was the ardour of its creation. If you look closely in a ruined castle even nowadays, you can sometimes find the hooks from which these flashing tapestries were hung. Remember, too, the goldsmiths of Lorraine, who made shrines in the shape of little churches, with aisles, statues, transepts and all, like dolls' houses: remember the enamellers of Limoges, and the champlevé work, and the German ivory carvers, and the garnets set in Irish metal. Finally, if you are willing to picture the ferment of creative art which existed in our famous ages of darkness, you must get rid of the idea that written culture came to Europe with the fall of Constantinople. Every clerk in every country was a man of culture in those days —it was his profession to be so. "Every letter written," said a medieval abbot, "is a wound inflicted on the devil." The library of St. Piquier, as early as the ninth century, had 256 volumes, including Virgil, Cicero, Terence and Macrobius. Charles the Fifth had no less than nine hundred and ten volumes, so that his personal collection was about as big as the Everyman Library is today.

Lastly there were under the window the people themselves —the coruscating mixture of oddities who reckoned that they possessed the things called souls as well as bodies, and who fulfilled them in the most surprising ways. In Silvester the Second a famous magician ascended the papal throne, although he was notorious for having invented the pendulum clock. A fabled King of France called Robert, who had suffered the misfortune to be excommunicated, ran into dreadful troubles about his domestic arrangements, because the only two servants who could be persuaded to cook for him insisted on burning the saucepans after meals. An archbishop of Canterbury, having excommunicated all the prebendaries of St. Paul's in a pet, rushed into the Priory of St. Bartholomew and knocked out the sub-prior in the middle of the chapel—which created such an uproar that his own vestments were torn off, revealing a suit of armour underneath, and he had to flee to Lambeth in a boat. The Countess of Anjou always used to vanish out of the window at the secreta of the mass. Madame Trote de Salerno used her ears as a handkerchief and let her eyebrows hang down behind her shoulders, like silver chains. A bishop of Bath, under the imaginary Edward the First, was considered after due reflection to be an unsuitable man for the Archbishopric, because he had too many illegitimate children—not some, but too many. And the bishop himself could hardly hold a candle to the Countess of Henneberge, who suddenly gave birth to 365 children at one confinement.

It was the age of fullness, the age of wading into everything up to the neck. Perhaps Arthur imposed this idea on Christendom, because of the richness of his own schooling under Merlyn.

For the King, or at least this is how Malory interprets him, was the patron saint of chivalry. He was not a distressed Briton hopping about in a suit or woad in the fifth century—nor yet one of those *nouveaux riches de la Poles*, who must have afflicted the last years of Malory himself. Arthur was the heart's king of a chivalry which had reached its flower perhaps two hundred years before our antiquarian author began to work. He was the badge of everything that was good in the Middle Ages, and he had made these things himself.

As Malory pictures him, Arthur of England was the champion of a civilization which is misrepresented in the history books. The serf of chivalry was not a slave for whom there was no hope. On the contrary, he had at least three legitimate ways of rising, the greatest of which was the Catholic Church. With the assistance of Arthur's policies this church—still the greatest of all corporations free to learned men on earth—had become a highway open to the lowest slave. A Saxon peasant was Pope in Adrian IV, the son of a carpenter in Gregory VII. In those despised Middle Ages of theirs you could become the greatest man in the world, by simply having learning. And it is a mistake to believe that Arthur's civilization was weak in this famous science of ours. The scientists, although they happened to call them magicians at the time, invented almost as terrible things as we have invented—except that we have become accustomed to theirs by use. The greatest magicians, like Albertus Magnus, Friar Bacon, and Raymond Lully, knew several secrets which we have lost today, and discovered as a side issue what still appears to be the chief commodity of civilization, namely gunpowder. They were honoured for their learning, and Albert the Great was made a bishop. One of them who was called Baptista Porta seems to have invented the cinema—though he sensibly decided not to develop it.

As for aircraft, in the tenth century a monk called Aethelmaer was experimenting with them, and might have succeeded but for an accident in adjusting of his tail unit. He crashed *"quod"*—says William of Malmesbury—*"caudam in posteriori parte oblitus fuerat adaptare."*

Even in modernity, the ages of darkness were not so far behind us. At least they had some sparkling names for their fiercer cocktails: which they called Huffe Cap, Mad Dog, Father Whoresonne, Angel's Food, Dragon's Milke, Go to the Wall, Stride Wide, and Lift Leg.

The view from the window was delightful, though in some cases it was odd. Where we have hedged fields and parklands, they had village communities, moorlands, fens and forests of enormous size. Sherwood stretched for hundreds of miles, from Nottingham to the middle of York. The busyness that went on in the island, the bee-keeping and the rook-scaring and the ploughing with oxen: for these you must look in the Lutterell Psalter, where they are beautifully drawn. In those days, if you had been interested by peculiar things, perhaps you would have had the luck to notice a knight-in-armour riding past the window. You would have noticed his head, which was shaved round the ears and at the back: but on the top his hair rose up like a Japanese doll's, so that the skull looked like a cottage loaf. This top-knot made an excellent shock-absorber, under his helm. The next man to pass might have been a clerk, perhaps on an ambler, and the hair of this one would have been exactly the opposite of the knight's—for he would have been completely bald on top, because of his tonsure. When he had gone to the bishop to be made a clerk in the first place, he had taken a pair of scissors with him. Next, if you wanted some peculiar person to ride by, there might have come a crusader who had promised to deliver the grave of God. You would have expected the cross on his surcoat, no doubt, but you might not have realized that he was so delighted with the whole affair that he put the same symbol almost everywhere that it could be made to go. Like a new Boy Scout, transported with enthusiasm, he would have stuck the cross on his escutcheon, on his coat, on his helm, on his saddle, and on the horse's curb. The next man to pass the window might have been one sort of Cistercian lay-brother, whom you would have expected to be a learned man because of his cloth. But no, he was *ex officio* an illiterate. It was his business to stick the leaden seals on papal bulls, and, so as to preserve the Secrecy of the Pope, they used to make sure that he could not read a word. Now might come a Saxon wearing the beard and a sort of Phrygian cap, as a sign of defiance—now a knight from the

Marches of the Northern border. The latter, because he
lived by raiding during the night-time, would have borne
a moon and stars on azure in his coat. Here might be some
smoke in the landscape, rising from the bellows of an al-
chemist who was, most sensibly, trying to turn lead to gold
—an art which has remained beyond us to the present day,
though we are getting nearer to it with atomic fusion. There,
far away in the environs of a monastery, you might have
seen a procession of angry monks making a barefoot march
round their foundation—but they might have been walking
against the sun, in malediction, because they had fallen out
with the abbot. Perhaps, if you looked in this direction, you
would see a vineyard fenced with bones—it had been discovered, during the early years of Arthur, that bones made
an excellent fence for vineyards, graveyards, or even for
forts—and perhaps, if you looked in the other, you could
see a castle door that looked like a keeper's gallows. It
would have been completely covered with the nailed heads
of wolves, bears, stags, and so forth. Far away, over there
to the left, perhaps there would be a tournament going on
according to the laws laid down by Geoffrey de Preully,
and the Kings-at-arms would be carefully examining the
combatants, like referees before a boxing match, to see
that they were not stuck to their saddles. The referees at a
judicial duel between a certain Earl of Salisbury and a
Bishop of Salisbury, under the supposed King Edward III,
found that the bishop's champion had prayers and incan-
tations sewn all over him, under his armour—which was
almost as bad as a boxer hiding a horse-shoe in his glove.
Below the window-ledge a pair of constipated papal nuncios
might have been riding gloomily back to Rome. Such a pair
were once sent with bulls to excommunicate Barnabas Vis-
conti, but Barnabas only made them eat their bulls—parchment, ribbons, leaden seals and all. Following closely behind
them perhaps there would have strode a professional pilgrim,
supporting himself on a stout knobbed staff shod like an
alpenstock and weighed down with blessed medals, relics,
shells, vernicles and so forth. He would have called himself
a palmer and, if he were a well-travelled one, his relics might
have included a feather from the Angel Gabriel, some of the
coals on which St. Lawrence was grilled, a finger of the Holy
Ghost "whole and sound as ever it was," "a vial of the sweat
of St. Michael whereas he fought with the devil," a little
of "the bush in which the Lord spake to Moses," a vest

of St. Peter's, or some of the Blessed Virgin's milk preserved at Walsingham. After the palmer perhaps there would have prowled a rather more sinister figure: one of those who "sleep by day and watch by night, eat well and drink well, but possess nothing." He would be an outlaw, of whom they wrote:

"For an outlawe this is the lawe, that men hym take
    and binde
Wythout pytee, hanged to bee, and waver with the
    wynde."

But before he came to his last wavering in the wind, he would have lived a free life. His mate would be marching sturdily beside him, also with a price on her head—her hair shaven off before she took to the woods, and known as a weyve. She would glance back occasionally, alert for the hue and cry with which they might be hunted.

Here might come a baron with a hot pie carried carefully before him, because he had to bring such a pie to the King once a year, so as to let King Arthur sniff it in payment of his feudal dues. There might go another baron at full tilt after some dragon or other, and bump! down he might come, while the horse cantered away. But if he did so, one of his attendants would immediately mount him again on his own horse—just as we would do to a master-of-hounds today—because that was the feudal law. In the distance of the north, under the fading sunset, there might spring up the cottage light of some busy witch who was not only making a wax image of somebody she disapproved of, but also getting the image baptised—this was the operative factor—before she stuck some pins into it. One of her priestly friends, by the way, who had gone to the Little Master, might be willing to say a Requiem Mass against anybody you wanted to dispose of—and, when he came to the *"Requim aeternum dona ei, Domine,"* he would mean it, although the man was alive. Equally distant in the west, under the same sunset, you might have seen Enguerrand de Marigny, who built the enormous gallows at Mountfalcon, himself rotting and clanking on the same gallows, because he had been found guilty of Black Magic. The Dukes of Berry and Brittany, two decent men, might have been trotting along the road, in satin cuirasses which imitated steel. These two did not like to accept the advantage of armour, and, finding the satin cooler to wear, they were determined to be ordinary and brave. Lancelot might have done the same sort of thing. Above them on the hillside, but unobserved by them, might have sat Joly Joly Wat, with his tar-box beside him. He was the most typical figure of Gramarye, his tar being the antiseptic of his sheep. If you had said to him, "Don't spoil the ship for a ha'porth of tar," he would have agreed with you at once—for it was he who invented the adage, which we have translated from sheep into ships.

Towards the remoter distance perhaps a bankrupt might have been getting a vigorous whacking in some muscovite market-place—not out of ill-feeling toward himself, but in the fervent hope that if only he squealed loud enough some of his friends or relations in the crowd would pay his debts out of commiseration. Further south, towards the Mediterranean basin, you might have seen a seaman being punished for gambling, under a law of Richard Coeur de Lion. The punishment consisted in being thrown into the water three times from the mainmast tree, and his comrades used to acclaim each belly-flopper with a cheer. A third ingenious punishment might possibly have been inflicted in the market-place below you. A wine merchant whose wares were of bad quality would have been stuck in the pillory and there he would have been made to drink an excessive quantity of his own liquor—after which the rest would be poured over his head. What a headache next morning! In this direction, if you happened to be broad-minded, you might have been amused to see the saucy Alisoun who cried "Tee-Hee!" after she had been given the unusual kiss which Chaucer tells about. In that one, you might notice an exasperated Miller and his family, trying to straighten out the hurrah's nest which happened last night through the displacement of a cradle, as the Reeve tells in his tale. A schoolboy who had had the good luck and the initiative to shoot an Earl of Salisbury dead, with one of the new-fangled cannons, might be being idolized by his fellow scholars in the playground of yonder monastery school. Plum trees, only lately introduced like Merlyn's mulberry, might be shedding blossom under the light of eve beside the playground. Another little boy, this time a king of four years old in Scotland, might be sadly issuing a royal mandate to his Nannie, which empowered her to spank him without being guilty of High Treason. A disreputable army, who used to live by the sword as a trained band, might be begging its bread from door to door—a good fate for all armies—and a man who had taken sanctuary in that church away to the east there, might have had his leg cut off because he had taken half a step outside the door. In the same sanctuary there would be quite a congeries of forgers, thieves, murderers and debtors, all busy forging away or sharpening their knives for the evening's outing, in the restful seclusion of the church where they could not be arrested. The worst that could happen to them, once they had got their sanctuary, was banishment. Then they would have had to walk to Dover, always keeping to the middle of the road and clutching a crucifix—if they let go of it for a moment, you were allowed to attack them—and, once there, if they could not get a boat immediately, they would have had to walk into the sea daily up to their necks, to prove that they were really trying.

Did you know that in these dark ages which were visible from Guenever's window, there was so much decency in the world that the Catholic Church could impose a peace to all their fighting—which it called The Truce of God— and which lasted from Wednesday to Monday, as well as during the whole of Advent and Lent? Do you think that they, with their Battles, Famine, Black Death and Serfdom, were less enlightened than we are, with our Wars, Blockade, Influenza and Conscription? Even if they were foolish enough to believe that the earth was the centre of the universe, do we not ourselves believe that man is the fine flower of creation? If it takes a million years for a fish to become a reptile, has Man, in our few hundred, altered out of recognition?

# 4

*Lancelot and Guenever looked over the sundown of* chivalry, from the tower window. Their black profiles stood out in silhouette against the setting light. Lancelot's, the old ugly man's, was the outline of a gargoyle. It might have looked in hideous meditation from Notre Dame, his contemporary church. But, in its maturity, it was nobler than before. The lines of ugliness had sunk to rest as lines of strength. Like the bull-dog, which is one of the most betrayed of dogs, Lancelot had grown a face which people could trust.

The touching thing was that the two were singing. Their voices, no longer full in tone like those of people in the strength of youth, were still tenacious of the note. If they were thin, they were pure. They supported one another.

> "When that the moneth of May (sang Lancelot)
>  Comes and the day
>  In beames gives light,
>  I fear no more the fight."

"When," sang Guenever,

> "When that the sonne,
>  His daily course y-ronne,
>  Is no more bright,
>  I fear namore the night."

"But oh," they sang together,

> "But oh, both day and night,
>  My heart's delight,
>  Must one day leave foredone
>  All might, all gone."

They stopped, with an unexpected grace-note on the portative, and Lancelot said: "Your voice is good. I'm afraid mine is getting rusty."

"You shouldn't drink spirits."

"What an unfair thing to say! I have been nearly a teetotaller since the Grail."

"Well, I had rather you didn't drink at all."

"Then I won't drink, not even water. I will die of thirst at your feet, and Arthur will give me a splendid funeral, and never forgive you for making me."

"Yes, and I shall go into a Nunnery for my sins, and live happily ever after. What shall we sing now?"

Lancelot said: "Nothing. I don't want to sing. Come and sit close to me, Jenny."

"Are you unhappy about something?"

"No. I was never so happy in my life. And I dare say I shall never be so happy again."

"Why so happy?"

"I don't know. It is because the spring has come after all, and there is the bright summer in front of us. Your arms will go brown again, just a flush along the top here, and a rosy round elbow. I am not sure I don't like the places where you bend best, like the insides of your elbows."

Guenever retreated from these charming compliments.

"I wonder what Arthur is doing?"

"Arthur is visiting the Gawaines, and I am talking about your elbows."

"I see."

"Jenny, I was happy because you were ordering me about. That's the explanation. You were nagging about not drinking too much. I like you to look after me, and to tell me what I ought to do."

"You seem to need it."

"I do need it," he said. And then, with a suddenness which surprised them both: "May I come tonight?"

"No."

"Why not?"

"Lance, please don't ask. You know that Arthur is at home, and it is much too dangerous."

"Arthur won't mind."

"If Arthur were to catch us," she said wisely, "he would have to kill us."

He denied it.

"Arthur knows all about us. Merlyn warned him in so many words, and Morgan le Fay sent him two broad hints, and then there was the trouble with Sir Meliagrance. But he doesn't want to have things upset. He would never catch us unless he was made to."

"Lancelot," she said angrily, "I am not going to have you talking about Arthur as if he were a go-between."

"I am not talking about him like that. He was my first friend, and I love him."

"Then you are talking about me as if I were worse."

"And now you are behaving as if you were."

"Very well, if that is all you have to say, you had better go."

"So that you can make love to him, I suppose."

"Lancelot!"

"Oh, Jenny!" He jumped up, nimble as ever, and caught her. "Don't be angry. I am sorry if I was unkind."

"Go away! Leave me alone."

But he continued to hold her tightly, like someone restraining a wild animal from running away.

"Don't be angry. I am sorry. You know I didn't mean it."

"You are a beast."

"No, I am not a beast, and nor are you. Jenny, I shall go on holding you until you stop being cross. I said it because I was miserable."

Her muffled and restrained voice remarked plaintively: "You said you were happy just now."

"Well, I am not happy. I am very unhappy and miserable about the whole world."

"Do you suppose you are the only one?"

"No, I don't. And I am sorry for what I said. It will make me unhappy for having said it. There, please be a dear and don't make me unhappy for longer?"

She relented. The years had smoothed their earlier tempers.

"Then I won't."

But her smile and yielding only moved him afresh.

"Come away with me, Jenny?"

"Please don't start it all over again."

"I can't help starting," he said desperately. "I don't know what to do. God, we have been going over this all our lives, but it seems to be worse in the spring. Why won't you come with me to Joyous Gard and have the whole thing above board?"

"Lance, let go of me and be sensible. There, sit down and we will have another song."

"But I don't want to sing."

"And I don't want to have all this."

"If you would come with me to Joyous Gard it would be finished, once for all. We could live together for our old age, anyway, and be happy, and not have to go on deceiving every day, and we should die in peace."

"You said that Arthur knew all about it," she said, "and that we were not deceiving him at all."

"Yes, but it is different. I love Arthur and I can't stand it when I see him looking at me, and know that he knows. You see, Arthur loves us."

"But, Lance, if you love him so much, what is the good of running away with his wife?"

"I want it to be in the open," he said stubbornly, "at least at the end."

"Well, I don't want it to be."

"In fact," and now he was furious again, "what you really want is to have two husbands. Women always want everything."

She declined the quarrel patiently.

"I don't want to have two husbands, and I am just as uncomfortable as you are: but what is the good of being in the open? As we are now it is horrible, but at least Arthur knows about it inside himself, and we still love each other and are safe. If I were to run away with you, the result would be that everything would be broken. Arthur would have to declare war on you and lay siege to Joyous Gard, and then one or other of you would be killed, if not both, and hundreds of other people would be killed, and nobody would be better off. Besides, I don't want to leave Arthur. When I married him, I promised to stay with him, and he has always been kind to me, and I am fond of him. The least I can do is to go on giving him a home, and helping him, even if I do love you too. I can't see the point of being in the open. Why should we make Arthur publicly miserable?"

Neither of them had noticed, in the deepening twilight, that the King himself had come in as she was speaking. Profiled against the window, they could see little of the room behind. But he had entered. He had stood for the fraction of a second collecting his wits, which had been far away considering the Orkneys or some other matter of state. He had stopped in the curtained doorway, his pale hand with the royal signet gleaming in the darkness as it held the tapestry aside—and then, without eavesdropping for a moment, he had let the tapestry fall and disappeared. He had gone to find a page to announce him.

"The only decent thing," Lancelot was saying, twisting his hands together between his knees, "the only decent thing would be for me to go away, and not come back. But my brain didn't stand it the other time, when I tried."

"My poor Lance, if only we had not stopped singing! Now you are going to get into a state again, and have one of your attacks. Why can't we leave everything alone, and let your famous God look after it? It is no good trying to think, or do anything because it is right or wrong. I don't know what is right or wrong. But can't we trust ourselves, and do what does itself, and hope for the best?"

"You are his wife and I am his friend."

"Well," she said, "who made us love each other?"

"Jenny, I don't know what to do."

"Then don't do anything. Come here and give me a kind kiss, and God will look after us both."

"My sweetheart!"

This time the page clattered up the stairs with the usual noise, in the way of pages, bringing light with him at the same time. Arthur had ordered the candles.

The room glowed into colour round the lovers, who had released each other quickly. It began to show the splendour of its hangings as the boy put fire to the wicks. The flowery meads and bird-fruitful spinneys of the Arras teemed and rippled over the four walls. The door curtain lifted again, and the King was in the room.

He looked old, older than either of them. But it was the noble oldness of self-respect. Sometimes even nowadays you can meet a man of sixty or more who holds himself as straight as a rush, and whose hair is black. They were in that class. Lancelot, now that you could see him clearly, was an erect refinement of humanity—a fanatic for human responsibility. Guenever, and this might have been surprising to a person who had known her in her days of tempest, looked sweet and pretty. You could almost have protected her. But Arthur was the touching one of the three. He was so plainly dressed, so gentle and patient of his simple things. Often, when the Queen was entertaining distinguished company under the flambeaux of the Great Hall, Lancelot had found him sitting by himself in a small room, mending stockings. Now, in his homely blue gown—blue, since it was an expensive tincture in those days, was reserved for kings, or for saints and angels in pictures—he paused on the threshold of the gleaming room, and smiled.

"Well, Lance. Well, Gwen."

Guenever, still breathing quickly, returning his greeting. "Well, Arthur. You took us by surprise."

"I'm sorry. I have only just got back."

"How were the Gawaines?" asked Lancelot, in the old tone which he had never succeeded in making natural.

"They were having a fight when I arrived."

"How like them!" they exclaimed. "What did you do? What were they fighting about?" They made it sound as if it were a matter of life or death, getting the mood wrong because of their own.

The King looked steadily in front of him.

"I didn't ask."

"Some family affair," said the Queen, "no doubt."

"No doubt it was."

"I hope nobody got hurt?"

"Nobody got hurt."

"Well then," she cried, noticing that her relief sounded absurd, "that was all right."

"Yes, that was all right."

They saw that his eyes were twinkling. He was amused at their trouble, and the atmosphere was normal.

"Now," said the King, "need we talk about the Gawaines any more? Do I never get a kiss from my wife?"

"Dear."

She drew his head towards her and kissed him on the forehead, thinking of him as a faithful old thing—her friendly bear.

Lancelot stood up. "Perhaps I ought to be off."

"Don't go, Lance. It is nice to have you to ourselves for a little. Come: sit by the fire, and sing us a song. We shall be able to do without the fires soon."

"So we shall," said Guenever. "Fancy, it will soon be summer."

"Still, it is nice to sit by the fire—at home."

"It is nice for you in your home," said Lancelot peculiarly.

"But what?"

"I have no home."

"Never mind, Lance, you will. Wait until you are my age, and then start worrying about it."

"It is not," said the Queen, "as if every woman you met didn't chase you for miles."

"With a hatchet," added Arthur.

"Half of them actually propose."

"And then you complain about not having a home."

Lancelot began to laugh, and the last strand of tension seemed to have broken.

"Would you," he asked, "marry a woman who chased you with a hatchet?"

The King considered the matter gravely before he answered.

"I couldn't do that," he said in the end, "because I am married already."

"To Gwen," said Lancelot.

It was peculiar. They seemed to have started talking with meanings which were separate from the words they used. It was like ants talking with their antennae.

"To Queen Guenever," said the King, in contradiction.

"Or Jenny?" suggested the Queen.

"Yes," he agreed, but only after a long pause, "or Jenny."

There was a deeper silence, until Lancelot rose for the second time.

"Well, I must go."

Arthur put one hand on his arm.

"No, Lance, stay a minute. I want to tell Guenever something this evening, and I would like you to hear it too. We have been together such a long time. I want to make a clean breast about an old business to both of you, because you are one of the family."

Lancelot sat down.

"That's right. Now give me a hand each, both of you, and I shall sit between you like this. There. My Queen and my Lance, and neither of you is to blame me for what I am going to tell."

Lancelot said bitterly: "We are not in a position to blame people, King."

"No? Well, I don't know what you mean by that; but I want to tell you the story of something which I did when I was young. It was before I was married to Gwen, and long before you were knighted. Will you mind if I do that?"

"Of course we shan't mind, if you want to."

"But we don't believe you did anything wrong."

"It started before I was born, really, for my father fell in love with the Countess of Cornwall, and killed the Earl in order to get her. She was my mother. You know that part of the story."

"Yes."

"Perhaps you didn't know that I was born at rather an awkward date. It was too soon after the marriage of my father and mother. That was why they hushed me up altogether, and sent me off in my swaddling bands to be brought up by Sir Ector. Merlyn was the person who took me."

"And then," said Lancelot cheerfully, "you were brought

back to court when your father died, and pulled a magic
sword out of a stone, which proved that you were the right-
ful King born of all England, and lived happily ever afterward, and that was the end of that. I don't call it a bad
story."

"Unfortunately that was not the end."

"How?"

"Well, my dears, I was taken away from my mother the
moment I was born, and she never knew where I was taken.
Nor did I know who my mother was. The only people who
knew the relationship between us were Uther Pendragon
and Merlyn. Many years afterward, when I was already a
king, I met my mother's family, still without knowing who
they were. Uther was dead, and Merlyn was always so muddled with his second sight that he had forgotten to tell me,
and so we met as strangers. I thought that one of them was
clever and handsome."

"The famous Cornwall sisters," mentioned the Queen
coldly.

"Yes, dear, the famous Cornwall sisters. There were three
daughters by the former Earl, and of course, though I did
not know it, they were my half-sisters. They were called
Morgan le Fay, Elaine, and Morgause, and they were considered to be the most beautiful women in Britain."

They waited for his quiet voice to resume, which it did
without a falter.

"I fell in love with Morgause," it added, "and we had a
baby."

If either of them felt surprise, resentment, commiseration
or envy, they did not show it. The only surprising thing to
them was that the secret had been kept so long. But they
could tell from his voice that he was suffering and that he
did not want to be interrupted until he had purged his heart
in full.

They stared into the fire for the longest of their silences.
Then Arthur shrugged his shoulders.

"So, you see," he said, "I am Mordred's father. Gawaine
and the others are nephews, but he is my full son."

Lancelot saw by the eyes that he might speak.

"I don't think your story is wicked, even at that. You
didn't know she was your half-sister. You hadn't met Gwen.
And probably, knowing her subsequent history, it was the
fault of Morgause in any case. That woman was a devil."

"She was my sister—and the mother of my son."

Guenever stroked his hand.

"I am sorry."

"Besides," he said, "she was a very beautiful creature."

"Morgause . . ." began Lancelot.

"Morgause has paid for her share by having her head cut off, so we must leave her to rest in peace."

"Cut off," said Lancelot, "by her own child, because he found her sleeping with Sir Lamorak . . ."

"Please, Lancelot."

"I am sorry."

"I still don't think it was wicked of you, Arthur. After all, you didn't know she was your sister."

The King took a long breath, and began again more huskily.

"I have not told you," he said, "the worst part of what I did."

"What was that?"

"You see, I was young, I was nineteen. And Merlyn came, too late, to say what had happened. Everybody told me what a dreadful sin it was, and how nothing but sorrow would come of it, and also a lot of other things about what Mordred would be like if he was born. They frightened me with horrible prophecies, and I did something which has haunted me ever since. Our mother had hidden Morgause away as soon as it was known."

"What did you do?"

"I let them make a proclamation that all the children born at a certain time were to be put in a big ship and floated out to sea. I wanted to destroy Mordred for his own sake, and I didn't know where he would be born."

"Did they do it?"

"Yes, the ship was floated off, and Mordred was on it, and it was wrecked on an island. Most of the poor babies were drowned—but God saved Mordred, and sent him back to shame me afterwards. Morgause sprang him on me one day, long after she had got him back. But she always pretended to other people that he was a proper son of Lot's, like Gawaine and the rest. Naturally she didn't want to talk about the business to outside people, and neither have the rest of his brothers."

"Well," said Guenever, "if nobody knows about it except the Orkneys and ourselves, and if Mordred is safe and sound . . ."

"You mustn't forget the other babies," he said miserably. "I dream about them."

"Why didn't you tell us before?"

"I was ashamed to."

This time Lancelot exploded.

"Arthur," he exclaimed, "you have nothing to be ashamed of. What you did was done to you, when you were too young to know better. If I could lay my hands on the brutes who frighten children with stories about sin, I would break their necks. What good does it do? Think of all that suffering, and for nothing! And the poor babies!"

"All drowned."

They sat again, looking into the flames, until Guenever turned to her husband.

"Arthur," she asked, "why did you tell the story today?"

He waited, collecting the words.

"It is because I am afraid that Mordred bears me a grudge, poor boy—and rightly too."

"Treason?" inquired the commander-in-chief.

"Well, not exactly treason, Lance; but I think he is dissatisfied."

"Cut the sniveller's head off, and have done with him."

"No, I could never think of it! You forget that Mordred is my son. I am fond of him. I have done the boy a great deal of wrong, and my family has always somehow been hurting the Cornwalls, and I couldn't add to the wickedness. Besides, I am his father. I can see myself in him."

"There does not seem to be a great resemblance."

"But there is. Mordred is ambitious and fond of honour, as I always was. It is only because he has a weak body that he has failed in our sports, and this has embittered him, as it probably would have embittered me if I had not been lucky. He is brave, too, in a queer way, and he is loyal to his people. You see, his mother set him against me, which was natural, and I stand for the bad things in his mind. He is almost sure to get me killed in the end."

"Are you seriously advancing this as a reason for not killing him now?"

The King suddenly looked surprised, or shocked. He had been sitting relaxed between them, because he was tired and unhappy, yet now he drew himself up and met his captain in the eye.

"You must remember I am the King of England. When you are a king you can't go executing people as the fancy takes you. A king is the head of his people, and he must stand as an example to them, and do as they wish."

He forgave the startled expression in Lancelot's face, and took his hand once more.

"You will find," he explained, "that when the kings are bullies who believe in force, the people are bullies too. If I don't stand for law, I won't have law among my people. And naturally I want my people to have the new law, because then they are more prosperous, and I am more prosperous in consequence."

They watched him, wondering what he meant to convey. He held the look, trying to speak with their eyes.

"You see, Lance, I have to be absolutely just. I can't afford to have any more things like those babies on my conscience. The only way I can keep clear of force is by justice. Far from being willing to execute his enemies, a real king must be willing to execute his friends."

"And his wife?" asked Guenever.

"And his wife," he said gravely.

Lancelot moved uncomfortably on the settle, remarking with an attempt at humour: "I hope you won't be cutting off the Queen's head very soon?"

The King still held his hand, still looked upon him.

"If Guenever or you, Lancelot, were proved to be guilty of a wrong to my kingdom, I should have to cut off both your heads."

"Goodness me," she exclaimed. "I hope nobody is going to prove that!"

"I hope so too."

"And Mordred?" asked Lancelot, after a time.

"Mordred is an unhappy young man, and I am afraid he might try any means of giving me an upset. If, for instance, he could see a way of getting at me through you, dear, or through Gwen, I am sure he would try it. Do you see what I mean?"

"I see."

"So if there should ever come a moment when either of you might, well ... might give him a sort of handle ... you will be careful of me, won't you? I am in your hands, dears."

"But it seems so senseless ..."

"You have been kind to him," said Lancelot, "since he came here. Why should he want to harm ..."

The King folded his hands in his lap, seemed under his lowered lids to be looking on the flames.

"You forget," he said gently, "that I never managed to give Gwen a son. When I am dead, Mordred may be the King of England."

"If he tries any treason," said Lancelot, clenching his fists, "I will kill him myself."

Immediately the blue-veined hand was on his arm.

"That is the one thing you must never do, Lance. Whatever Mordred does, and even if he makes an attempt on my life, you must promise to remember that he is a sort of heir apparent to the blood. I have been a wicked man . . ."

"Arthur," exclaimed the Queen, "you are not to say so. It is so ridiculous that it makes me feel ashamed."

"You would not call me a wicked man?" he asked in surprise.

"Of course not."

"But I should have thought, after the story of those babies . . ."

"Nobody," cried Lancelot fiercely, "would dream of such a thought."

The King stood up in the firelight, looking puzzled and pleased. He considered it ridiculous to suppose that he was not wicked, but he was grateful for their love.

"Well," he said, "in any case I don't propose to be wicked any longer. It is a king's business to prevent bloodshed if he can, not to provoke it."

He looked at them once more, under his eyebrows.

"So now, my dears," he ended cheerfully, "I shall run along to the Court of Pleas, and arrange some of our famous justice. You stay here with Gwen, Lance, and cheer her up after that wretched story—there's a good fellow."

# 5

*When Arthur had said that he was going to arrange* some of his famous justice, he did not mean that he was actually going to sit. Kings did sit personally in the Middle Ages, even as late as the so-called Henry IV, who was supposed to have sat both in the Exchequer and the King's Bench. But tonight it was too late for law-giving. Arthur was off to read the pleas for the morrow, a practice which he followed like a conscientious man. Nowadays the Law was his chief interest, his final effort against Might.

In Uther Pendragon's time there had been no law to speak of, except a childish and one-sided kind of etiquette which was reserved for the upper classes. Even now, since the King had begun to encourage Justice so as to bind the power of Fort Mayne once for all, there were three kinds of law to be wrestled with. He was trying to boil them down, from Customary, Canon and Roman law, into a single code which he hoped to call the Civil one. This occupation, as well as reading the morrow's pleas, was what used to call him off to labour every evening, to solitude and silence in the Justice Room.

The Justice Room was at the other end of the palace. It was not as empty as it should have been.

Although there were five people in it, waiting for the King, perhaps the first thing which a modern visitor would have noticed would have been the room itself. The startling thing about it was that the hangings made it square. It was night, so that the windows were covered, and the doors were never uncovered. The result was that you felt you were in a box: you had the strange feeling of symmetrical enclosure which must be known by butterflies in killing-bottles. You wondered how the five people had been introduced into the place, as if it were a Chinese puzzle. All round the walls, from floor to ceiling in a double row, the stories of David and Bathsheba and of Susannah and the Elders were told in flexible pictures whose gay colours were in full tone. The faded things which we see today bear no relationship to the bright tapestry which made the Justice Room a painted box.

The five men glittered in the candle-light. There was little furniture to distract the eye from them—only a long table with the parchments laid out for the King's inspection, the King's high chair, and, in the corner, a raised reading-desk and seat combined. The colour of the place was in the walls and men. Each of them wore a silk jupon blazoned with the chevron and the three thistles, distinguished in the case of the younger brothers with various labels of cadency, so that they looked like a hand of playing cards spread out. They were the Gawaine family, and, as usual, they were quarrelling.

Gawaine said: "For the last time, Agravaine, will ye hold yer gab? I winna have airt nor pairt in it."

"Nor will I," said Gareth.

Gaheris said: "Nor I."

"If ye press on with it, ye will but split the clan. I have told ye plain that none of us will help ye. Ye will be left to yer ain stour."

Mordred had been waiting with sneering patience.

"I am on Agravaine's side," he said. "Lancelot and my aunt are a disgrace to all of us. Agravaine and I will take the responsibility, if no one else will."

Gareth turned on him fiercely.

"Ye were aye fit for work of shame."

"Thank you."

Gawaine made an effort to be conciliatory. He was not a conciliatory man, so the effort looked actually physical, like an earthquake.

"Mordred," he said, "for dear sakes, hearken reason. Ye'll be a brave hind and let it bide? I am the elder of ye, and can see what ill will come."

"Whatever comes of it, I am going to the King."

"But, Agravaine, if you do, it will mean war. Don't you see that Arthur and Lancelot will have to go for each other, and half the kings of Britain will side with Lancelot because of his reputation and it will be a civil war?"

The chieftain of the clan lumbered over to Agravaine like a good-natured animal doing a trick, and patted him with a huge paw.

"Tuts, man. Forget the wee blow struck this forenoon. There is a passion in every man, and, at the hinder end of it, we are but brothers. I canna see how ye may bring yourself to act against Sir Lancelot, knowing what he has done for us long syne. Dinna ye mind he rescued you, and Mordred to it, from Sir Turquine? Away, ye owe him for your lives. And so do I, man, from Sir Carados in the Dolorous Tower."

"He did it for his own honour."

Gareth turned on Mordred.

"You can say what you like about Lancelot and Guenever between ourselves, because unfortunately it is true, but I won't have you sneering. When I first came to court as a kitchen page, he was the only person who was decent to me. He had not the faintest idea who I was, but he used to give me tips, and cheer me up, and stand up for me against Kay, and it was he who knighted me. Everybody knows that he has never done a mean thing in his life."

"When I was a young knight," said Gawaine, "God forgive it, and fell into disputacious battle, I was used to backslide into passions—aye, and kill a body after he had yielded. And foreby I have killed a lassie. But Lancelot grieves no creature weaker than himsel'."

Gaheris added: "He favours the young knights, and tries to help them win the spurs. I can't see your grudge against him."

Mordred shrugged his shoulders, flicking his coat sleeve, and made belief to yawn.

"As for Lancelot," he observed, "it is Agravaine who is after him. My feud is with the merry monarch."

"Lancelot," stated Agravaine, "is above his station."

"He is not," said Gareth. "He is the greatest man I know."

"I have no schoolboy's passion for him . . ."

A door on the other side of the tapestry squeaked on its hinges. The handle grated.

"Peace, Agravaine," urged Gawaine softly, "hold off yer noise."

"I will not."

Arthur's hand lifted the curtain.

"Please, Mordred," whispered Gareth.

The King was in the room.

"It is only fair," said Mordred, raising his voice so that it must be heard, "that our Round Table should have justice, after all."

Agravaine also, pretending not to have noticed anyone coming, added his loud reply: "It is time that somebody should tell the truth."

"Mordred, be quiet!"

"And nothing but the truth!" concluded the hunchback with a sort of triumph.

Arthur, who had come pattering through the stone corridors of his palace with a mind fixed on the work in front of him, stood waiting in the doorway without surprise. The men of the chevron and thistle, turning to him, saw the old King in the last minute of his glory. They stood for a few heartbeats silent, and Gareth, in a pain of recognition, saw him as he was. He did not see a hero of romance, but a plain man who had done his best—not a leader of chivalry, but the pupil who had tried to be faithful to his curious master, the magician, by thinking all the time—not Arthur of England, but a lonely old gentleman who had worn his crown for half a lifetime in the teeth of fate.

Gareth threw himself on his knee.

"It has nothing to do with us!"

Gawaine, lumbering to one knee more slowly, joined him on the floor.

"Sir, I came ben hoping to control my brothers, but they willna listen. I dinna wish to hear what they may say."

Gaheris was the last to kneel.

"We want to go before they speak."

Arthur came into the room and lifted Gawaine gently.

"Of course you can go, my dear," he said, "if you wish it. I hope I am not going to cause a family trouble?"

Gawaine turned blackly on the others.

"It is a trouble," he said, drawing the old language of knighthood round him like a cloak, "that will aye destroy the flower of chivalry in all the world: a mischief to our noble fellowship: and all by cause of two unhappy knights!"

When Gawaine had swept contemptuously out of the room, pushing Gaheris before him and followed by Gareth with a helpless gesture, the King walked over to the throne in silence. He took two cushions from the seat and put them on the steps.

"Well, nephews," he said evenly, "sit down and tell me what you want."

"We would rather stand."

"You can please yourselves, of course."

Such a beginning did not suit the policy of Agravaine. He protested: "Ah, Mordred, come! Nay, we are not quarrelling with our King. There is no thought of that about it."

"I shall stand."

Agravaine sat on one of the cushions humbly.

"Would you care for two cushions?"

"No, thank you, sir."

The old man watched and waited—as a man who was to be hanged might submit to the hangman, but who would not need to help with the noose. He watched with a tired irony, leaving the work to them.

"Perhaps it would be wiser," said Agravaine, with well-made reluctance, "to say no more about it."

"Perhaps it would."

Mordred burst through the situation by main force.

"This is ridiculous. We came to tell our uncle something, and it is right he should be told."

"It is unpleasant."

"In that case, my dear boys, if you would prefer it, don't let us talk about the matter any further. These spring nights are too beautiful for us to worry with unpleasant things, so who don't the two of you go off and make it up with Gawaine? You could ask him to lend you that clever goshawk of his for tomorrow. The Queen was mentioning just now, how she would enjoy a nice young leveret for dinner."

He was fighting for her, perhaps for all of them.

Mordred, glaring at his father with blazing eyes, announced without preamble: "We came to tell you what every person in this court has always known. Queen Guenever is Sir Lancelot's mistress openly."

The old man leaned down to straighten his mantle. He twitched it over his feet to keep them warm, raised himself again, and looked them in the face.

"Are you ready to prove this accusation?"

"We are."

"You know," he asked them gently, "that it has been made before?"

"It would be extraordinary if it had not."

"The last time that rumors of this kind were circulated, they were produced by a person called Sir Meliagrance. As the matter was not susceptible of proof in any other way, it was put to the decision of personal combat. Sir Meliagrance appeeched the Queen of treason, and offered to fight for his opinion. Fortunately Sir Lancelot was kind enough to stand for Her Majesty. You remember the results."

"We remember well."

"When, finally, the combat took place, Sir Meliagrance lay flat on his back and insisted on yielding to Sir Lancelot. It was impossible to make him get up in any way, until Lancelot offered to take off his helm, and the left side of his armour, and to have one hand tied behind his back. Sir Meliagrance accepted the offer, and was duly chopped."

"We know all this," exclaimed the youngest brother, impatiently. "Personal combat has no meaning. It is an unfair justice anyway. It is the thugs who win."

Arthur sighed and folded his hands. He continued in the quiet voice, which he had not raised.

"You are still very young, Mordred. You have yet to learn that nearly all the ways of giving justice are unfair. If you can suggest another way of settling moot points, except by personal combat, I will be glad to try it."

"Because Lancelot is stronger than others, and always stands for the Queen, it does not mean that the Queen is always in the right."

"I am sure it doesn't. But then, you see, moot points have to be settled somehow, once they get thrust upon us. If an assertion cannot be proved, then it must be settled some other way, and nearly all of these ways are unfair to somebody. It is not as if you would have to fight the Queen's champion in your own person, Mordred. You could plead infirmity and hire the strongest man you knew to fight for you, and the Queen would, of course, get the strongest man she knew to fight for her. It would be much the same thing if you each hired the best arguer you knew, to argue about it. In the last resort it is usually the richest person who wins, whether he hires the most expensive arguer or the most expensive fighter, so it is no good pretending that this is simply a matter of brute force.

"No, Agravaine," he went on, as the latter made a movement to speak, "don't interrupt me at the moment. I want to make it clear about these decisions by personal combat. So far as I can see, it is a matter of riches: of riches and pure luck, and, of course, there is the will of God. When the riches are equal, we might say that the luckier side wins, as if by tossing a coin. Now, are you two sure, if you did appeach Queen Guenever of treason, that your side would be the luckier one?"

Agravaine entered the conversation with his imitation of diffidence. He had been drinking carefully, and his hand no longer shook.

"If you will excuse me, uncle, what I was going to say was this. We hoped to settle the matter without a personal combat at all."

Arthur looked up at once.

"You know quite well," he said, "that trial by ordeal has been abolished, and, as for doing it by purgation, it would be impossible to find the necessary number of peers for a Queen."

Agravaine smiled.

"We don't know much about the new law," he said smoothly, "but we thought that when an assertion could be proved, in one of these new law-courts of yours, then the need for personal combat did not arise. Of course, we may be wrong."

"Trial by Jury," observed Sir Mordred contemptuously, "is that what you call it? Some pie-powder affair."

Agravaine, exulting in his cold mind, thought: "Hoist with his own petard!"

The King drummed his fingers on the arm of the chair. They were pressing, flanking and driving him back. He said slowly: "You know a great deal about the law."

"For instance, uncle, if Lancelot were actually found in Guenever's bed, in front of witnesses, then there would be no need for combat, would there?"

"If you will forgive my saying so, Agravaine, I would prefer you to speak of your aunt by her title, at least in front of me—even in this connection."

"Aunt Jenny," remarked Mordred.

"Yes, I believe I have heard Sir Lancelot calling her by that name."

"'Aunt Jenny'! 'Sir Lancelot'! 'If you will forgive my saying so!' And they are probably kissing now!"

"You must speak civilly, Mordred, or you must leave my room."

"I am sure he does not mean to be presumptuous, uncle. It is only that he is upset about the dishonour to your fair fame. We wanted to ask for justice, and Mordred feels so deeply—well—for his House. Don't you, Mordred?"

"I don't care a damn about my House."

The King, whose face had begun to look more haggard, sighed and retained his patience.

"Well, Mordred," he said, "we had better not start wrangling about smaller things. I have no longer the resistance to be rude about them. You tell me that my wife is the mistress of my best friend, and apparently you are to prove this by demonstration, so let us stick to that. I take it that you understand the implications of the charge?"

"No, I do not."

"I am sure that Agravaine will, at all events. The implications are these. If you insist on a civil proof, instead of an appeal to the Court of Honour, the matter will go forward along the lines of civil proof. Should you establish your case, the man who saved you both from Sir Turquine will have his head cut off, and my wife whom I love very much, will have to be burned alive, for treason. Should you fail to establish your case, I must warn you that I should banish you, Mordred, which would deprive you of all hope of succession, such as it is, while I should condemn Agravaine to the stake in his turn, because by making the accusation, he would himself have committed treason."

"Everybody knows that we could establish our case at once."

"Very well, Agravaine: you are a keen lawyer, and you are determined to have the law. I suppose it is no good reminding you that there is such a thing as mercy?"

"The kind of mercy," asked Mordred, "which used to set those babies adrift, in boats?"

"Thank you, Mordred. I was forgetting."

"We do not want mercy," said Agravaine, "we want justice."

"I understand the situation."

Arthur put his elbows on his knees and covered his eyes with his fingers. He sat drooping for a moment, collecting the powers of duty and dignity, then spoke from the shade of his hand.

"How do you propose to take them?"

The bulky man was all politeness.

"If you would consent, uncle, to go away for the night, we should get together an armed band and capture Lancelot in the Queen's room. You would have to be away or he wouldn't go."

"I don't think I could very well set a trap for my own wife, Agravaine. I think it would be just to say that the onus of proof lies with you. Yes, I think that is just. Clearly I have the right to refuse to become—well, a sort of accomplice. It is not part of my duty to go away on purpose, in order to help you. No, I should be able to refuse to do that with a clear heart."

"But you can't refuse to go away ever. You can't spend the rest of your life chained to the Queen, on purpose to keep Lancelot away. What about the hunting party you were supposed to join next week? If you don't go on that, you will be altering your plans deliberately, so as to thwart justice."

"Nobody succeeds in thwarting justice, Agravaine."

"So you will go on the hunting party, Uncle Arthur, and we have permission to break into the Queen's room, if Lancelot is there?"

The elation in his voice was so indecent that even Mordred was disgusted. The King stood, pulling his gown round him, as if for warmth.

"We will go."

"And you will not tell them beforehand?" The man's voice tripped over itself with excitement. "You won't warn them after we have made the accusation? It would not be fair?"

"Fair?" he asked.

He looked at them from an immense distance, seeming to weigh truth, justice, evil and the affairs of men.

"You have our permission."

His eyes came back from the distance, fixing them personally with a falcon's gleam.

"But if I may speak for a moment, Mordred and Agravaine, as a private person, the only hope I now have left is that Lancelot will kill you both and all the witnesses—a feat which, I am proud to say, has never been beyond my Lancelot's power. And I may add this also, as a minister of Justice, that if you fail for one moment in establishing this monstrous accusation, I shall pursue you both remorselessly, with all the rigor of the laws which you yourselves have set in motion."

# 6

*Lancelot knew that the King had gone to hunt in* the New Forest, so he was sure that the Queen would send for him. It was dark in his bedroom, except for the one light in front of the holy picture, and he was pacing the floor in a dressing-gown. Except for the gay dressing-gown, and a sort of turban wound round his head, he was ready for bed: that is, he was naked.

It was a sombre room, without luxuries. The walls were bare and there was no canopy over the small hard couch. The windows were unglazed. They had some sort of oiled, opaque linen stretched over them. Great commanders often have these plain, campaigning bedrooms—they say that the Duke of Wellington used to sleep on a camp bed at Walmer Castle—with nothing in them except perhaps a chair, or an old trunk. Lancelot's room had one coffin-like, metal-bound chest. Apart from that, and from the bed, there was nothing to be seen—except his huge sword which stood against the wall, its straps hanging about it.

There was a kettle-hat lying on the chest. After some time, he picked it up and carried it to the picture light, where he stood with the same puzzled expression which the boy had had so long ago—looking at his reflection in the steel. He put it down, and began to march once more.

When the tap came on the door, he thought it was the signal. He was picking up the sword, and stretching his hand to the latch, when the door opened on its own account. Gareth came in.

"May I come?"

"Gareth!"

He looked at him in surprise, then said without enthusiasm: "Come in. It is nice to see you."

"Lancelot, I have come to warn you."

After a close look, the old man grinned.

"Gracious!" he said. "I hope you are not going to warn me about anything serious?"

"Yes, it is serious."

"Well, come in, and shut the door."

"Lancelot, it is about the Queen. I don't know how to begin."

"Don't trouble to begin then."

He took the younger man by the shoulders, began propelling him back to the door.

"It was charming of you to warn me," he said, squeezing the shoulders, "but I don't expect you can tell me anything I don't know."

"Oh, Lancelot, you know I would do anything to help you. I don't know what the others will say when they hear I have been to you. But I couldn't stay away."

"What is the trouble?"

He stopped their progress to look at him again.

"It is Agravaine and Mordred. They hate you. Or Agravaine does. He is jealous. Mordred hates Arthur most. We tried our best to stop them, but they would go on. Gawaine says he won't have anything to do with it, either way, and Gaheris was never good at making up his mind. So I had to come myself. I had to come, even if it is against my own brothers and the clan, because I owe everything to you, and I couldn't let it happen."

"My poor Gareth! What a state you have got yourself in!"

"They have been to the King and told him outright that you—that you go to the Queen's bedroom. We tried to stop them, and we wouldn't stay to listen, but that is what they told."

Lancelot released the shoulder. He took two paces through the room.

"Don't be upset about it," he said, coming back. "Many people have said so before, but nothing came of it. It will blow over."

"Not this time. I can feel it won't, inside me."

"Nonsense."

"It is not nonsense, Lancelot. They hate you. They won't try a combat this time, not after Meliagrance. They are too cunning. They will do something to trap you. They will go behind your back."

But the veteran only smiled and patted him.

"You are imagining things," he announced. "Go home to bed, my friend, and forget it. It was nice of you to come— but go home now and cheer up, and have a good sleep. If the King had been going to make a fuss, he would never have gone off hunting."

Gareth bit his fingers, plucking up the face to speak directly.

At last he said: "Please don't go to the Queen tonight."

Lancelot lifted one of his extraordinary eyebrows—but lowered it on second thoughts.

"Why not?"

"I am sure it is a trap. I am sure the King has gone away for the night on purpose that you should go to her, and then Agravaine will be there to catch you."

"Arthur would never do a thing like that."

"He has."

"Nonsense. I have known Arthur since you were in the nursery, and he wouldn't do it."

"But it is a risk!"

"If it is a risk, I shall enjoy it."

"Please!"

This time he put his hand in the small of Gareth's back, and began moving him seriously to the door.

"Now, my dear kitchen page, just listen. In the first place,

I know Arthur: in the second place, I know Agravaine. Do you think I ought to be afraid of him?"

"But treachery . . ."

"Gareth, once when I was a young fellow a lady came skipping past me, chasing after a peregrine which had snapped its creance. The trailing part of the creance got wound up in a tree, and the peregrine hung there at the top. The lady persuaded me to climb the tree, to get her hawk. I was never much of a climber. When I did get to the top, and had freed the hawk, the lady's husband turned up in full armour and said he was going to chop my head off. All the hawk business had been a trap to get me out of my armour, so that he would have me at his mercy. I was in the tree in my shirt, without even a dagger."

"Yes?"

"Well, I knocked him on the head with a branch. And he was a much better man than poor old Agravaine, even if we have grown rheumaticky since those bright days."

"I know you can deal with Agravaine. But suppose he attacks you with an armed band?"

"He won't do anything."

"He will."

There was a scratch at the door, a gentle drumming. A mouse might have made it, but Lancelot's eyes grew vague.

"Well, if he does," he said shortly, "then I shall have to fight the band. But the situation is imaginary."

"Couldn't you stay away tonight?"

They had reached the door, and the King's captain spoke decisively.

"Look," he said, "if you must know, the Queen has sent for me. I could hardly refuse, once I was sent for, could I?"

"So my treachery to the Old Ones will be useless?"

"Not useless. Anybody who knew would love you for facing it. But we can trust Arthur."

"And you will go in spite of everything?"

"Yes, kitchen page, and I shall go this minute. Good gracious, don't look so tragic about it. Leave it to the practised scoundrel and run away to bed."

"It means Good-bye."

"Nonsense, it means Good night. And, what is more, the Queen is waiting."

The old man swung a mantle over his shoulder, as easily as if he were still in the pride of youth. He lifted the latch and stood in the doorway, wondering what he had forgotten.

"If only I could stop you!"

"Alas, you can't."

He stepped into the darkness of the passage, dismissing the subject from his mind, and disappeared. What he had forgotten was his sword.

# 7

*Guenever waited for Lancelot in the candle-light of* her splendid bedroom, brushing her grey hair. She looked singularly lovely, not like a film star, but like a woman who had grown a soul. She was singing by herself. It was a hymn—of all things—the beautiful *Veni, Sancte Spiritus* which is supposed to have been written by a Pope.

The candle flames, rising up stilly on the night air, were reflected from the golden lioncels which studded the deep blue canopy of the bed. The combs and brushes sparkled with ornaments in cut paste. A large chest of polished latoun had saints and angels enamelled in the panels. The brocaded hangings beamed on the walls in soft folds—and, on the floor, a desperate and reprehensible luxury, there was a genuine carpet. It made people shy when they walked on it, since carpets were not originally intended for mere floors. Arthur used to walk round it.

Guenever was singing and brushing, her low voice fitting the stillness of the candles, when the door opened softly. The commander-in-chief dropped his black cloak on the chest and stepped across to stand behind her. She saw him in the mirror without surprise.

"May I do it for you?"

"If you like."

He took the brush, and began sweeping it through the silver avalanche with fingers which were deft from practice, while the Queen closed her eyes.

After a time, he spoke.

"It is like . . . I don't know what. Not like silk. It is more like pouring water, only there is something cloudy about it too. The clouds are made of water, aren't they? Is it a pale mist, or a winter sea, or a waterfall, or a hayrick in the frost? Yes, it is a hayrick, deep and soft and full of scent."

"It is a nuisance," she said.

"It is the sea," he said solemnly, "in which I was born."

The Queen opened her eyes and asked: "Did you come safely?"

"Nobody saw."

"Arthur said he was coming back tomorrow."

"Did he? Here is a white hair."

"Pull it out."

"Poor hair," he said. "It is a thin one. Why is your hair so beautiful, Jenny? I should have to plait about six of them together, to be as thick as one of mine. Shall I pull?"

"Yes, pull."

"Did it hurt?"

"No."

"Why didn't it? When I was small, I used to pull my sisters' hair, and they used to pull mine, and it hurt like fury. Do we lose our faculties as we get older, so that we can't feel our pains and joys?"

"No," she explained. "It is because you only pulled one of them. When you pull a whole lock together, then it hurts. Look."

He held down his head so that she could reach, and she, stretching up backward with a white arm, twisted his forelock round her finger. She tugged until he made a face.

"Yes, it still hurts. What a relief!"

"Was that how your sisters pulled it?"

"Yes, but I pulled theirs much harder. Whenever I came near one of my sisters she used to hold her pigtails in both hands, and glare at me."

She laughed.

"I'm glad I wasn't one of your sisters."

"Oh, but I should never have pulled yours. Yours is too beautiful. I should have wanted to do something else with it."

"What would you have done?"

"I should . . . well, I think I should have curled up inside it like a dormouse, and gone to sleep. I should like to do that now."

"Not until it is finished."

"Jenny," he asked suddenly, "do you think this will last?"

"What do you mean?"

"Gareth came to me just now, to warn us that Arthur had gone away on purpose to set a trap, and that Agravaine or Mordred was going to catch us out."

"Arthur would never do a thing like that."

"That's what I said."

"Unless he was made to," she reflected.

"I don't see how they could make him."

She went off at a tangent.

"It was nice of Gareth to go against his brothers."

"Do you know, I think he is one of the nicest people at court. Gawaine is decent, but he is quick-tempered and rather unforgiving."

"He is loyal."

"Yes, Arthur used to say that if you were not an Orkney, they were frightful: but, if you were, you were a lucky man. They fight like cats, but they adore each other really. It is a clan."

The Queen's tangent had somehow brought her back to the circle.

"Lance," she asked in a startled voice, "do you think they could have forced the King's hand?"

"How do you mean?"

"Arthur has a terrific sense of justice."

"I wonder."

"There was that conversation last week. I thought he was trying to warn us. Listen! Did you hear something?"

"No."

"I thought I heard somebody at the door."

"I'll go and see."

He went to the door and opened it, but there was nobody there.

"A false alarm."

"Bolt it then."

He slid the wooden beam across—a great bar of oak five inches thick, which slid into a channel deep in the thickness of the wall. Coming back to the candle-light, he separated the shining hair into convenient strands and began to plait them swiftly. His hands moved like shuttles.

"It is silly to be nervous," he observed.

She was still speculating, however, and replied with a question.

"Do you remember Tristram and Iseult?"

"Of course."

"Tristram used to sleep with King Mark's wife, and the King murdered him for it."

"Tristram was a lout."

"I thought he was nice."

"That was what he wanted you to think. But he was a Cornish knight, like the rest of them."

"He was said to be the second-best knight in the world. Sir Lancelot, Sir Tristram, Sir Lamorak . . ."

"That was tittle-tattle."

"Why did you think he was a lout?" she asked.

"Well, it's a long story. You don't remember what chivalry used to be before your Arthur started the Table, so you don't know what a genuis you have married. You don't see what a difference there is between Tristram, and, well, Gareth for instance."

"What difference?"

"In the old days it was a case of every knight for himself. The old stagers, people like Sir Bruce Saunce Pité, were pirates. They knew they were impregnable in armour, and they did as they pleased. It was open manslaughter and bold bawdry. When Arthur came to the throne, they were furious. You see, he believed in Right and Wrong."

"He still does."

"Fortunately he had a tenacious character as well as this idea of his. It took him about five years to set it on foot, but it was that people ought to be gentle. I must have been one of the first knights to catch the idea of gentleness from him, and I caught it young, and he made it part of my inside. Everybody is always saying what a parfit, gentle knight I am, but it has nothing to do with me. It is Arthur's idea. It is what he has wished on all the younger generation, like Gareth, and now it is fashionable. It led to the Quest for the Grail."

"And why was Tristram a lout?"

"Well, he just was. Arthur says he was a buffoon. He lived in Cornwall; he had never been educated by Arthur; but he had got wind of the fashion. He had got some garbled notion into his head that famous knights ought to be gentle, and he was always rushing about trying to live up to the fashion, without properly understanding it or feeling it in himself. He was a sort of copycat. Inside, he was not a bit gentle. He was foul to his wife, he was always bullying poor old Palomides for being a nigger, and he treated King Mark most shamefully. The knights from Cornwall are Old Ones and have always been hostile to Arthur's idea, inside themselves, even if they do get hold of a part of it."

"Like Agravaine."

"Yes. Agravaine's mother was from Cornwall. The reason why Agravaine hates me is because I stand for the idea. It is a funny thing, but all three of us that the common people used to call the three best knights—I mean Lamorak, Tristram and myself—have been hated by the Old Ones. They were delighted when Tristram was murdered because he copied the idea, and, of course, it was the Gawaine family who actually killed Sir Lamorak by treachery."

"I think," she said, "that the reason why Agravaine hates you is the old story of sour grapes. I don't think he cares a bit about the idea, but he naturally envies anybody who is a better fighter than himself. He loathed Tristram because of the thrashing he got from him on the way to Joyous Gard, and he helped to murder Lamorak because the boy had beaten him at the Priory Jousts, and—how many times have you upset him?"

"I don't remember."

"Lance, do you realize that the two other people he hated are dead?"

"Everybody dies, sooner or later."

Suddenly the Queen had swept her plaits out of his fingers. She had twisted round in the chair, and, with one hand holding a pigtail, she was staring at him with round eyes.

"I believe it is true, what Gareth said! I believe they are coming to catch us tonight!"

She jumped out of the chair and began pushing him to the door.

"Go away. Go while there is time."

"But, Jenny . . ."

"No. No buts, I know it is true. I can feel it. Here is your cloak. Oh, Lance, please go quickly. They stabbed Sir Lamorak in the back."

"Come, Jenny, don't get excited about nothing. It is only a fancy . . ."

"It is not a fancy. Listen. Listen."

"I can't hear anything."

"Look at the door."

The handle which lifted the latch of the door, a piece of wrought iron shaped like a horse-shoe, was moving softly to the left. It moved like a crab, uncertainly.

"What is the matter with the door?"

"Look at the handle!"

They stood watching it in fascination, as it moved blindly, in jerks, a sly, hesitating exploration.

"Oh, God," she whispered. "And now it is too late!"

The handle fell back into place and there was a loud, iron knocking on the wood of the door. It was a good door of double ply, one grain running vertically and the other horizontally, and it was being beaten from the other side with a gauntlet. Agravaine's voice, echoing in the cavern of his helmet, cried: "Open the door, in the King's name!"

"We are undone," she said.

"Traitor Knight," cried the neighing voice, as the wood thundered under the metal. "Sir Lancelot, now art thou taken."

Many more voices joined the outcry. Many joints of harness, no longer under the necessity of precaution, clanked on the stone stair. The door butted against its beam.

Lancelot dropped unconsciously into the language of chivalry also.

"Is there any armour in the chamber," he asked, "that I might cover my body withal?"

"There is nothing. Not even a sword."

He stood, facing the door with a puzzled, business-like expression, biting his fingers. Several fists were hammering it, so that it shook, and the voices were like a pack of hounds.

"Oh, Lancelot," she said, "there is nothing to fight with, and you are almost naked. They are armed and many. You will be killed, and I shall be burned, and our love has come to a bitter end."

He was cross at not being able to solve the problem.

"If only I had my armour," he said with irritation, "it seems ridiculous to be caught like a rat in a trap."

He looked round the room, cursing himself for having forgotten his weapon.

"Traitor Knight," boomed the voice, "come out of the Queen's chamber!"

Another voice, musical and self-possessed, cried pleasantly: "Wit thou well, here are fourteen armed, and thou canst not escape." It was Mordred, and the hammering was growing louder.

"Well, damn them then," he said. "We can't have this noise. I shall have to go, or they will wake the castle."

He turned to the Queen and took her in his arms.

"Jenny, I am going to call you my most noble Christian Queen. Will you be strong?"

"My dear."

"My sweet old Jenny. Let us have a kiss. Now, you have always been my special good lady, and we have never failed before. Do not be frightened this time. If they kill me, remember Sir Bors. All my brothers and nephews will look after you. Send a message to Bors or Demaris, and they will rescue you if necessary. They will take you safe to Joyous Gard, and you can live there on my own land, like the Queen you are. Do you understand?"

"If you are killed, I shall not want to be rescued."

"You will," he said firmly. "It is important that somebody should be alive to explain about us decently. That is the hard work which you will have to do. Besides, I should want you to pray."

"No. The prayers will have to be done by somebody else. If they kill you, they can burn me. I shall take my death as meekly as any Christian queen."

He kissed her tenderly and set her in the chair.

"Too late to argue," he said. "I know you will be Jenny whatever happens, and I must e'en be Lancelot." Then, still glancing round the room with a preoccupied look, he added absent-mindedly: "It makes no odds about my quarrel, but they did ill to force it on you."

She watched him, trying not to cry.

"I would give my foot," he said, "to have a little armour —even just a sword, so that they could remember."

"Lance, if they would kill me, and save you, I should be happy."

"And I should be extremely miserable," he answered, suddenly finding himself in intense good humour. "Well, well, we shall have to do the best we can. Bother my very old bones, but I believe I am going to enjoy it!"

He put the candles on the lid of the Limoges chest, so that they would be behind his back when he opened the door. He picked up his black cloak and folded it carefully lengthwise into four, after which he wound it round his left hand and forearm as a protection. He picked up the foot-stool from beside the bed, balanced it in his right hand, and took a last look round the room. All the time the noise was getting louder outside, and two men were evidently trying to cut through the wood with their battle-axes, an attempt which was frustrated by the cross grains of the double ply. He went to the door and raised his voice, at which there was immediate silence.

"Fair Lords," he said, "leave your noise and your rashing. I shall set open this door, and then ye may do with me what it liketh you."

"Come off then," they cried confusedly. "Do it." "It availeth thee not to strive against us all." "Let us into the chamber." "We shall save thy life if you come to King Arthur."

He put his shoulder against the leaping door and softly pushed the beam back, into the wall. Then, still holding the door shut with his shoulder—the people on the other side had desisted from their hewing, feeling that something was about to happen—he settled his right foot firmly on the ground, about two feet from the door jamb, and let the door swing open. It stopped with a jerk at his foot, leaving a narrow opening so that it was more ajar than open, and a single knight in full armour blundered through the gap with the obedience of a puppet on strings. Lancelot slammed the door behind him, shot the bar, took the figure's sword by the pommel in his padded left hand, jerked him forward, tripped him up, bashed him on the head with the stool as he was falling, and was sitting on his chest in a trice—as limber as he had ever been. All was done with what seemed to be ease and leisure, as if it were the armed man who was powerless. The great turret of a fellow, who had entered in the height and breadth of armour, and who had stood for a second looking for his adversary through the slit of his helmet, this man had given an impression of docility—he seemed to have come in, and to have handed his sword to Lancelot, and to have thrown himself upon the ground. Now the iron hulk lay, as obediently as ever, while the bare-legged man pressed its own swordpoint through the ventail of the visor. It made a few protesting shudders, as he pressed down with both hands on the pommel of the sword.

Lancelot stood up, rubbing his hands on the dressing-gown.

"I am sorry I had to kill him."

He opened the visor and looked. "Agravaine of Orkney!"

There was a terrific outcry from beyond the door, with hammering, hewing and cursing, as Lancelot turned to the

Queen. "Help with the armour," he said briefly. She came at once, without repugnance, and they kneeled together beside the body, stripping it of the vital pieces.

"Listen," he said as they worked. "This gives us a fair chance. If I can drive them off I shall turn back for you, and you will come to Joyous Gard."

"No, Lance. We have done enough harm. If you do fight your way out, you must keep away till it blows over. I shall stay here. If Arthur forgives me, and if it can be hushed up, then you can come back later. If he does not forgive me, you can come to the rescue. Where does this go?"

"Give it to me."

"Here is the other one."

"You were far better to come," he urged, struggling into the habergeon like a footballer putting on his jersey.

"No. If I come, everything is broken forever. If I stay, we may be able to patch it up. You can always rescue me if necessary."

"I don't like to leave you."

"If I am condemned, and you rescue me, I promise I will come to Joyous Gard."

"And if not?"

"Wipe the helmet with your cloak," she said. "If not, then you can come back later, and everything will be as it was."

"Very well. There. I can do without the rest."

He straightened himself, holding the bloody sword, and looked at the dead body which had killed its mother.

"Gareth's brother," he said thoughtfully. "Perhaps he was drunk. God rest him—though it seems absurd to say it."

The old lady turned him to face the candles.

"It means Good-bye," she whispered, "for a little."

"It means Good-bye."

"Give me a kiss?" she asked.

He kissed her hand, because he was armed and dirty with blood and covered with metal. They thought simultaneously of the thirteen men outside.

"I should like you to take something of mine, Lance, and to leave me something of yours. Will you change rings?"

They changed them.

"God be with my ring," she said, "as I am with it."

Lancelot turned away and went to the door. They were calling out: "Come out of the Queen's chamber!" "Traitor to the King!" "Open the door!" They were making as much noise as possible, to aid the scandal. He stood facing the tumult, with legs apart, and answered them in the language of honour.

"Leave your noise, Sir Mordred, and take my council. Go ye all from this chamber door, and make not such crying and such manner of slander as ye do. An ye will depart, and make no more noise, I shall tomorn appear before the King: and then it will be seen which of you all, outher else you all, will accuse me of treason. There I shall answer you as a knight should, that hither I came for no manner of mal engine; and I will prove that there, and make it good upon you with my hands."

"Fie on thee, traitor," cried the voice of Mordred. "We will have thee maugre thy head, and slay thee if we list."

Another voice shouted: "Let thee wit we have the choice of King Arthur, to save thee or to slay thee."

Lancelot dropped the visor over his shadowed face and pushed the door-bar sideways with his point. The stout wood, crashing open, showed a lintel crammed with iron men and tossing torches.

"Ah sirs," he said with a grimness, "is there none other grace with you? Then keep yourselves."

# 8

The Gawaine clan was waiting in the Justice Room, a week later. The room looked different by daylight, because the windows were uncovered. It was no longer a box, no longer that faintly threatening or deceitful blandness of four walls, no longer the kind of arras trap which tempted Hamlet's rapier to prick about for rats. The afternoon sunlight streamed in at the casements, illuminating the tapestry of Bathsheba, as she sat with her two round breasts in a tub on the battlements of a castle, which seemed to have been built from children's bricks—picking out David, on the roof next door, with a crown and a beard and a harp—rippling from a hundred horses, parallel lances, helms and suits of armour, which thronged the battle scene in which Uriah was killed. Uriah himself was tumbling from his horse, like rather an inexperienced diver, under the influence of a stroke which one of the opposing knights had delivered in the region of his midriff. The sword was half-way through his body, so that the poor man was coming in two pieces, and a lot of realistic vermilion worms were gushing out of the wound in a grisly manner, which were intended to be his guts.

Gawaine sat gloomily on one of the side benches placed there for petitioners, with his arms folded and his head against the arras. Gaheris, perched on the long table, was fiddling with the braces of a leather hood for a hawk. He was trying to alter them so that they would shut more firmly, and, as the interlacement of such braces was complicated, he had got himself in a muddle. Gareth was standing beside him, itching to get the hood into his own hands, because he was certain that he could set the matter right. Mordred, with a white face and his arm in a sling, was leaning at the embrasure of one of the windows, looking out. He was still in pain.

"It ought to go under the slit," said Gareth.

"I know, I know. But I am trying to put this one through first."

"Let me try."

"Just a minute. It is coming."

Mordred said from the window: "The executioner is ready to begin."

"Oh."

"It will be a cruel death," he said. "They are using seasoned wood, and there will be no smoke, and she will burn before she suffocates."

"So ye believe," observed Gawaine morosely.

"Poor old woman," said Mordred. "One can almost feel sorry for her."

Gareth turned on him fiercely.

"You should have thought of that before."

"Now the top one," said Gaheris.

"I understand," continued Mordred, in what was almost a soliloquy, "that our liege lord himself must watch the execution from this window."

Gareth lost his temper completely.

"Can't you hold your tongue about it for a minute? Anyone would think that you enjoyed watching people being burned."

Mordred replied contemptuously: "So will you, really. Only you think it is not good form to say so. They will burn her in her shift."

"For the sake of God, be silent."

Gaheris said, in his slow way: "I don't think you need to worry."

In a flash Mordred was facing him.

"What do you mean, he need not worry?"

"Of course he needna worry," said Gawaine angrily. "Do ye think that Lancelot willna come to rescue her? *He* is no coward, at any rate."

Mordred was thinking quickly. His still pose by the window had given place to nervous excitement.

"If he tries to rescue her, there will be a fight. King Arthur will have to fight him."

"King Arthur will watch from here."

"But this is monstrous!" he exploded. "Do you mean to say that Lancelot will be allowed to slip off with the Queen, under our noses?"

"That is exactly what will happen."

"But nobody will be punished at all!"

"Good heavens, man," cried Gareth. "Do you *want* to see the woman burn?"

"Yes, I do. Yes, I do. Gawaine, are you going to sit there and let this happen after your own brother has been killed?"

"I warnit Agravaine."

"You cowards! Gareth! Gaheris! Make him to do something. You can't let this happen. He murdered Agravaine, your brother."

"So far as I can understand the story, Mordred, Agravaine went with thirteen other knights, fully armed, and tried to kill Lancelot when he had nothing but his dressing-gown. The upshot was that Agravaine himself was killed, together with all thirteen of the knights—except one, who ran away."

"I did not run away."

"Ye survivit, Mordred."

"Gawaine, I swear I didn't run away. I fought him as well as I could. But he broke my arm, and then I could do no more. On my honour, Gawaine, I tried to fight."

He was almost weeping.

"I am not a coward."

"If you didn't run away," asked Gaheris, "how came it that Lancelot let you go, after killing the others? It was in his interest to kill the lot of you, because then there would have been no witnesses."

"He broke my arm."

"Yes, but he didn't kill you."

"I am telling the truth."

"But he didn't kill you."

What with the pain of his arm, and rage, the man began to cry like a child.

"You traitors! It is always like this. Because I am not strong, you side against me. You stand for the muscular fools, and will not believe what I say. Agravaine is dead, and waked, and you are not going to punish anybody for it. Traitors, traitors! And it will all be as it was!"

He broke down as the King came in. Arthur, looking tired, walked slowly to the throne and set himself on it. He motioned to them, to resume their seats. Gawaine slumped back on the bench from which he had risen, while Gareth and Gaheris remained standing, observing the King with looks of pity, to the background of Mordred's sobs.

Arthur stroked his forehead with his hand.

"Why is he crying?" he asked.

"He was for explaining to us," said Gawaine, "how Lancelot killed thirteen knights, but resolvit on his second thoughts that he shouldna kill our Mordred. It was by cause there was a fondness between them seemingly."

"I think I can explain. You see, I asked Sir Lancelot not to kill my son, ten days ago."

Mordred said bitterly: "Thank you for nothing."

"You don't have to thank me, Mordred. Lancelot would be the right person to thank for that."

"I wish he had killed me."

"I am glad he did not. Try to be a little forgiving, my son, now that we are in this trouble. Remember that I am your father. I shall have no family left, except for you."

"I wish I had never been born."

"So do I, my poor boy. But you are born, so now we must do the best we can."

Mordred went over to him with haste, with a sort of shamefaced dissimulation.

"Father," he said, "do you know that Lancelot is bound to come and rescue her?"

"I have been expecting it."

"And you have posted knights to stop him? You have arranged for a strong guard?"

"The guard is as strong as it can be, Mordred. I have tried to be just."

"Father," he said eagerly, "send Gawaine and these two to strengthen them. He will come with great force."

"Well, Gawaine?" asked the King.

"Thank ye, uncle. I had liefer ye didna ask."

"I ought to ask you, Gawaine, out of justice to the guard which is already there. You see, it would be unfair to leave a weak guard, if I thought that Lancelot was coming, because that would be treachery to my own men. It would be sacrificing them."

"Whether ye ask me or no, saving your Majesty, I shallna go. I warned the twa of them at their outsetting that I wouldna have to do with it. I have nae wish to see Queen Guenever burn, and I maun say I hope she willna, nor will I help to burn her. There ye have it."

"It sounds like treason."

"It may be treason, but I have my fondness for the Queen."

"I also am fond of the Queen, Gawaine. It was I who married her. But where a matter of public justice arises, the feelings of common people have to be left out."

"I fear I canna leave my feelings."

The King turned to the others.

"Gareth? Gaheris? Will you oblige me by putting on your armour, and strengthening the guard?"

"Uncle, please don't ask us."

"It gives me no pleasure to ask you, Gareth."

"I know it doesn't, but please don't force us. Lancelot is my friend, so how could I fight against him?"

The King touched his hand.

"Lancelot would have expected you to go, my dear, whoever it was against. He believes in justice too."

"Uncle, I can't fight him. He knighted me. I will go if you wish, but I won't go in armour. I am afraid that mine is treason too."

"I am ready to go in armour," said Mordred, "even if my arm is broken."

Gawaine observed sarcastically: "It will be safe enough for you, my mannie. We ken the King has bidden Lancelot not hurt ye."

"Traitor!"

"And Gaheris?" asked the King.

"I will go with Gareth, unarmed."

"Well, I suppose it is the best we can do. I hope I have tried to do what I ought."

Gawaine got up from his bench and tramped over to the King with clumsy sympathy.

"Ye have done more than e'er a body could expect," he said warmly, holding the veined hand in his paw, "and now we must look onward for the best. Let my brothers go, unarmed. He willna hurt them, gin he see their faces. I maun stay ben with you."

"Go then."

"Shall I tell the executioner to begin?"

"Yes, if you must, Mordred. Give him my ring and get the warrant from Sir Bedivere."

"Thank you, father. Thank you. We shall be hardly a minute."

The pale face, burning with enthusiasm and for the moment with a strangely genuine gratitude, hurried from the room. He followed his brothers, who had gone to join the guard, with blazing eyes and a nervous twitch of his mouth. The old King, left behind with Gawaine, sank his head upon his hands.

"He might have done it with a little more decency. He might have tried to show that he was not so pleased."

Gawaine put his hand on the stooping shoulder.

"Never fear, uncle," he said. "It will come to right. Lancelot will rescue her in God's good time, and nae harm done."

"I have tried to do my duty."

"Ye have striven to admiration."

"I sentenced her because it was the law to sentence her. I have done my best to see the sentence will be carried out."

"But it willna be. Lancelot will bring her safe."

"Gawaine, you are not to think that I am trying to get her rescued. I am the Justice of England, and it is our business now to burn her to the death, without remorse."

"Aye, uncle, and every man kens fine how you have tried. But that dinna alter the truth, that we both desire at heart she may come safe."

"Oh, Gawaine," he said. "I have been married to her all these years!"

The other turned his back and went to the window.

"Dinna disturb yerself. The coil will come to right."

"What is right?" cried the old man, looking after him with a face of misery. "What is wrong? If Lancelot does come to rescue her, he may kill those innocent fellows of the guard, which I have set to burn her. They have trusted me and I have put them there to keep him off, because it is justice. If he saves her, they will be killed. If they are not killed, she will be burned. But burned to death, Gawaine, in horrible, burning flames—and she is my much-loved Gwen."

"Dinna think about it, uncle. It willna happen."

But the King was breaking down.

"Why doesn't he come at once, then? Why does he wait so long?"

Gawaine said steadily: "He has to wait until she is in the open, in the square, for otherwise it would mean to storm the castle."

"I tried to warn them, Gawaine. I tried to warn them a few days before they were caught. But it was difficult to say the things in plain English, without hurting people's feelings. And I was a fool, too. I didn't want to be conscious of it. I hoped that if only I was not quite conscious of everything, it would come straight in the end. Do you think it was my fault? Do you think I could have saved them, if I had done something else?"

"Ye did the best ye could."

"When I was a young man I did something which was not just, and from it has sprung the misery of my life. Do you think you can stop the consequences of a bad action, by doing good ones afterwards? I don't. I have been trying to stopper it down with good actions, ever since, but it goes on in widening circles. It will not be stoppered. Do you think this is a consequence too?"

"I dinna ken."

"How horrible it is to wait like this!" he cried. "It must be worse for Gwen. Why can't they bring her out at once, to have done with it?"

"They will do so soon."

"And it is not her fault. Is it mine? Ought I to have refused to accept Mordred's evidence and over-ridden the whole affair? Ought I to have acquitted her? I could have set my new law aside. Ought I to have done that?"

"Ye might have done."

"I could have acted as I wished."

"Aye."

"But what would have happened to justice then? What would have been the consequence? Consequences, justice, bad deeds, babies drowned! I could see them about me, all last night."

Gawaine spoke quietly, in a changed voice.

"Ye must forget sic things. Ye maun summon up your powers to what is difficult. Will ye do that?"

The King held the arms of his throne.

"Yes."

"I fear ye must come to the window. They are for bringing her out."

The old man made no movement, except that his fingers tightened on the wood. He sat staring in front of him. Then he pulled himself to his feet, taking his weight on the wrists, and went to his duty. Unless he was present at the execution, it would not be a legal one.

"She is in a white shift."

They stood together quietly, watching like people who must not feel. There was a numbness in their crisis, which forced language into conversational levels.

"Aye."

"What are they doing?"

"I dinna ken."

"Praying, I suppose."

"Aye. Yon is the bishop in front."

They examined the praying.

"How strange they look."

"They are just ordinary."

"Do you think I could sit down," he asked, like a child, "now that I have shown myself?"

"Ye maun stay."

"I don't think I can."

"Ye must."

"But Gawaine, if she were to glance up?"

"If ye dinna stay, it willna be right at law."

Outside, in the foreshortened market-place under the window, they seemed to be singing a hymn. It was impossible to distinguish the words or melody. They could see the processional clerics busy about the decencies of death, and the twinkling knights standing motionless, and the people's heads, like baskets of coco-nuts, round the outside of the square. It was not easy to see the Queen. She was too much obscured in the eddies of the ceremonial, being led in this and that direction, being converged upon by small coveys of officials or of confessors, being introduced to the executioner, being persuaded to kneel down and pray, being exhorted to stand up and make a speech, being aspersed, being given candles to hold, being forgiven and being asked to forgive, being carried patiently onward, being ushered out of life with circumstance and dignity. There was nothing dingy, at any rate, about a legal murder in the Age of Darkness.

The King asked: "Can you see any rescue coming?"

"Nay."

"It seems a long time."

Outside the window, the chanting ceased, making a distressing silence.

"How much longer?"

"Some minutes yet."

"They will let her pray?"

"Aye, they will let her."

The old man suddenly asked: "Do you think we ought to pray?"

"If ye wish it."

"Ought we to kneel down?"

"I doubt it matters."

"What shall we say?"

"I dinna ken."

"Shall I say the Our Father? It is all I can remember."

"That will do fine."

"Shall we say it together?"

"If ye wish it."

"Gawaine, I fear I must kneel down."

"I will stand," said the laird of Orkney.

"Now . . ."

They were beginning their unprofessional petition, when the faint bugle sounded from beyond the market.

"Whist, uncle!"

The prayer fell at mid-word.

"There is soldiers coming. Horses, I think!"

Arthur was on his feet, was at the window.

"Where?"

"The trumpet!"

And now, clear, shrill, exultant, the song of brass was piercing the room itself. The King, shaking Gawaine by the elbow, with trembling voice began to cry: "My Lancelot! I knew he would!"

Gawaine forced his heavy shoulders through the frame. They were jealous for the view.

"Aye. It is Lancelot!"

"Look at him. In silver."

"The argent, a bend gules!"

"The bonnie rider!"

"Look at them all!"

Indeed, it was worth looking. The market-place was an avalanche, like a scene from the Wild West. The baskets of fruit were broken, so that the coco-nuts poured down. The knights of the guard were mounting, hopping beside their chargers with one foot in the stirrup, while each horse revolved about the axis of its rider. The acolytes were throwing away their censers. The priests were butting their way through the crowd. The bishop, who wanted to stay, was being bundled away towards the church, while his crosier came after him like a standard, carried high above the tumult by some faithful deacon. A canopy, which had been carried on four poles over somebody or something, was sinking with the poles askew, like a liner foundering in Atlantic. The onrushing tide, of flashing cavalry with clanking arms and brassy music, poured into the square with feathers tossing as if they were the heads of Indians, their swords rising and falling like a strange machinery. Abandoned by the cluster of ministrants who had obscured her as the last rites were being offered, Guenever stood like a beacon. In her white shift, tied to the high stake, she remained motionless in the movement. She rode above them. The battle closed about her feet.

"What spurring and plucking up of horses!"

"Nae other body ever charged like yon."

"Oh, the poor guard!"

Arthur was wringing his hands.

"Some man is down."

"It is Segwarides."

"What a mêlée!"

"His charges," stated the King vehemently, "were always irresistible, always. Ah, what a thrust!"

"There goes Sir Pertilope."

"No. It is Perimones. It is his brother."

"Look at the braw swords in the sun. Look at the colours. Well struck, Sir Gillimer, well struck!"

"No, no! Look at Lancelot. Look how he thrangs and rashes. There is Aglovale unhorsed. Look, he is coming to the Queen."

"Priamus will stop him!"

"Priamus—nonsense! We shall win, Gawaine—we shall win!"

The big fellow twisted round, grinning with enthusiasm.

"Wha' is We?"

"Very well—'they' then, you chucklehead. Sir Lancelot, of course. He'll win. There goes Sir Priamus."

"Sir Bors is down."

"No matter. They will horse Bors again in a minute. Here he is, coming to the Queen. Oh, look! He has brought her a kirtle and a gown."

"Aye, has he!"

"My Lancelot would not let my Guenever be seen in her shift!"

"He wouldna."

"He is putting them on her."

"She is smiling."

"Bless them both, the creatures. But oh, the foot-people!"

"It is finished, ye might say."

"He won't do more execution than he need. We can trust him for that?"

"We can trust the man for that."

"Is that Damas under the horse?"

"Aye. Damas had ever a red panache. I think they are for drawing off. How quick they have been!"

"Guenever is up."

The bugle music touched the room again, a different call.

"They must be away. That is the retreat. Lord, lord, will ye look at the confusion!"

"I hope there are not many hurt. Can you see? Ought we to have gone to their help?"

"There will be many stiff from this," said Gawaine.

"The faithful guard."

"Above the dozen."

"My brave men! And it is my fault!"

"I dinna see that it was the fault of any man particular: unless it was my brother's, and he now dead. Aye, there gangs the last of them. Ye can see the Queen's white gown above the press."

"Shall I wave to her?"

"No."

"It would not be right?"

"No."

"Well, then, I suppose I must not. Still, it would have been nice to do something, as she is going."

Gawaine turned upon him with a swirl of affection.

"Uncle Arthur," he said, "ye're a grand man. I telled ye it would come to right."

"And you are a grand man, too, Gawaine, a good man and a kind one."

They kissed in the ancient way, joyfully, on both cheeks.

"There," they said. "There."

"And now what is to be done?"

"That is for you to say."

The old King looked about him as if he were searching for the thing to do. His age, the suggestion of infirmity, had lifted from him. He looked straighter. His cheeks were rosy. The crow's feet round his eyes were beaming.

"I think we ought to have a monstrous drink to begin with."

"Verra guid. Call the page."

"Page, page!" he cried at the door. "Where the devil have you gone? Page! Here, you varmint, bring us some drink. What have you been doing? Watching your mistress being burned? And a very good sell for you!"

The delighted child gave a squeak and rattled down the stairs again, which he was half-way up.

"And then, after the drink?" asked Gawaine.

Arthur came back cheerfully, rubbing his hands.

"I have not thought. Something will happen. Perhaps we can make Lancelot apologize, or some arrangement like that—and then he can come back. We could get him to explain that he was in the Queen's bedroom because she had sent for him to pay the Meliagrance fee, as she had briefed him, and she didn't want to have any talk about the payment. And then, of course, he had to rescue her, because he knew she was innocent. Yes, I think we could manage something like that. But they would have to behave themselves in the future."

Gawaine's enthusiasm had evaporated before his uncle's. He spoke slowly, with his eyes on the floor.

"I doubt . . ." he began.

The King looked at him.

"I doubt ye will ever patch it up in full, while Mordred is on life."

Lifting the tapestry of the doorway with a pale hand, the ghostly creature in half-armour, its unarmed elbow in a sling, stood on the threshold.

"Never," it said with the bitter drama of a perfect cue, "while Mordred is alive."

Arthur turned round in surprise. He surveyed the feverish eyes, then went to his son with a movement of concern.

"Why, Mordred!"

"Why, Arthur."

"Dinna speak to the King like yon. How dare ye?"

"Do not speak to me at all."

Its toneless voice had stopped the King half-way. Now he pulled himself together.

"Come," he said kindly. "It has been a terrible carnage, we know. We saw it from the window. But surely it is better that your aunt should be safe, and all the forms of justice satisfied. . . ."

"It has been a terrible carnage."

The voice was that of an automaton, but deep with meaning.

"The foot-people . . ."

"Trash."

Gawaine was turning on his half-brother like a mechanism. His whole body turned.

"Mordred," he asked with a cumbrous accent. "Mordred, wha' have ye left Sir Gareth?"

"Where have I left them both?"

The red man began to ejaculate, making his words fast.

"Dinna ape me," he shouted. "Dinna cry like a parrot. Speak where they are."

"Go and look for them, Gawaine, among the people on the square."

Arthur began: "Gareth and Gaheris . . ."

"Are lying in the market-place. It was difficult to recognize them, because of the blood."

"They are not hurt, surely? They were unarmed. They are not wounded?"

"They are dead."

"Havers, Mordred."

"Havers, Gawaine."

"But they had no armour," protested the King.

"They had no armour."

Gawaine said, with frightful emphasis: "Mordred, if ye are telling a lie . . ."

". . . the righteous Gawaine will slay the last of his kin."

"Mordred!"

"Arthur," he replied. He turned on him a face of stone, insanely mixed between venom, blandness and misery.

"If it is true, it is terrible. Who could have wanted to kill Gareth, and him unarmed?"

"Who?"

"They were not even going to fight. They were going to stand by, because I told them to. Besides, Lancelot is Gareth's best friend. The boy was friendly with the Ban family. It seems impossible. Are you sure you are not making a mistake?"

Gawaine's voice suddenly filled the room. "Mordred, wha' killed my brothers?"

"Who indeed?"

He rushed upon the crooked man, towering with passion.

"Who but Sir Lancelot, my husky friend."

"Liar! I must away to see."

He stumbled out of the room, still rushing, in the same charge which had taken him towards his brother.

"But, Mordred, are you sure they are dead?"

"The top of Gareth's head was off," he said with indifference, "and he had a surprised expression. Gaheris had no expression, because his head was split in half."

The King was more puzzled than horrified. He said with wondering sorrow: "Lance could not have done it. He knew them. . . . He loved them. They had no helmets on, so that he could recognize them. He knighted Gareth. He would never have done such a thing."

"No, of course."

"But you say he did."

"I say he did."

"It must have been a mistake."

"It must have been a mistake."

"What do you mean?"

"I mean that the pure and fearless Knight of the Lake, whom you have allowed to cuckold you and carry off your wife, amused himself before he left by murdering my two brothers—both unarmed, and both his loving friends."

Arthur sat down on the bench. The little page, coming back with the ordered drink, bowed himself double.

"Your drink, sir."

"Take it away."

"Sir Lucan the Butler says, sir, can he have some help to bring the wounded men in, sir, and is there any bandage linen?"

"Ask Sir Bedivere."

"Yes, sir."

"Page," he cried, as the child went.

"Sir?"

"How many casualties?"

"They say twenty knights dead, sir. Sir Belliance the Orgulous, Sir Segwarides, Sir Griflet, Sir Brandiles, Sir Aglovale, Sir Tor, Sir Gauter, Sir Gillimer, Sir Reynold's three brothers, Sir Damas, Sir Priamus, Sir Kay the Stranger, Sir Driant, Sir Lambegus, Sir Herminde, Sir Pertilope."

"But Gareth and Gaheris?"

"I heard nothing of them, sir."

Blubbering and still running, the red, mountainous man was in the room once more. He was running to Arthur like a child. He was sobbing: "It is true! It is true! I found a man wha' saw it done. Poor Gaheris and our wee brother Gareth—he has killed them both, unarmed."

He fell on his knees. He buried his sand-white head in the old King's mantle.

# 9

*On a bright winter day, six months later, Joyous* Gard was invested. The sun shone at right-angles to the north wind, leaving the east side of the furrows white with frost. Outside the castle, the starlings and green plover searched anxiously in the stiff grass. The deciduous trees stood up in skeleton, like maps of the veins or of the nervous system. The cow-droppings, if you hit them, rang like wood. Everything had the colour of winter, the faded lichen green, like a green velvet cushion which has been left in the sun for years. The vein-trees, like the cushion, had a nap on their trunks. The conifers had it all over their funeral draperies. The ice crackled in the puddles and on the gelid moat. Joyous Gard itself stood up, a beautiful picture in the powerless sunshine.

Lancelot's castle was not forbidding. The old-fashioned keeps of Arthur's accession had given place to a gaiety of defence, now difficult to imagine. You must not picture it like the ruined strongholds, with mortar crumbling between the stones, which you see today. It was plastered. They had put chrome in the plaster, so that it was faintly gold. Its slated turrets, conical in the French fashion, crowded from complicated battlements in a hundred unexpected aspirations. There were little fantastic bridges, covered like the Bridge of Sighs, from this chapel to that tower. There were outside staircases, going heaven knows where—perhaps to heaven. Chimneys suddenly soared out of machicolations. Real stained-glass windows, high up and out of danger, gleamed where once there had been blank walls. Bannerets, crucifixes, gargoyles, water-spouts, weather-cocks, spires and belfries crowded the angled roofs—roofs going this way and that, sometimes of red tile, sometimes of mossy stone, sometimes of slate. The place was a town, not a castle. It was light pastry, not the dour unleavened bread of old Dunlothian.

Round the joyful castle there was the camp of its besiegers. Kings, in those days, took their household tapestries with them on campaign, which was a measure of the kind of camps they had. The tents were red, green, checkered, striped. Some of them were of silk. In a maze of colour and guy-ropes, of tent-pegs and tall spears, of chess-players and sutlers, of tapestried interiors and of gold plate, Arthur of England had sat down to starve his friend.

Lancelot and Guenever were standing by a log fire in the hall. Fires were no longer lit in the middle of the rooms, leaving the smoke to escape as best it could through lanterns. Here there was a proper fireplace, richly carved with the arms and supporters of Benwick, and half a tree smouldered in the grate. The ice outside had made the ground too slippery for horses. So it was a day of truce, though undeclared.

Guenever was saying: "I can't think how you could have done it."

"Neither can I, Jenny. I don't even know that I did do it, except that everybody says so."

"Can you remember anything?"

"I was excited, I suppose, and frightened about you. There was a press of people waving weapons, and knights trying to stop me. I had to cut my way."

"It seems unlike you."

"You don't suppose I wanted to, do you?" he asked, bitterly. "Gareth was fonder of me than he was of his brothers. I was almost his godfather. Oh, let's leave it, for God's sake."

"Never mind," she said. "I dare say he is better out of it, poor dear."

Lancelot kicked the log thoughtfully, one arm on the mantelpiece, looking into the ashy glow.

"He had blue eyes."

He stopped, considering them in the fire.

"When he came to court, he would not name his parents. It was because he had to run away from home, so as to come, in the first place. There was a feud between his mother and Arthur, and the old woman hated him coming. But he couldn't keep away. He wanted the romance and the chivalry and the honour. So he ran away to us, and wouldn't say who he was. He didn't ask to be knighted. It was enough for him to be at the great centre until he had proved his strength."

He pushed a stray branch into place.

"Kay took him to work in the kitchen, and gave him a nickname: 'Pretty Hands.' Kay was always a bully. And then . . . it seems so long ago."

In the silence—while they stood, each with an elbow on the mantel and a foot towards the fire—the weightless ash shuffled down.

"I used to give him tips sometimes, to buy himself his little things. Beaumains the kitchen page. He took to me for some reason. I knighted him with my own hands."

He looked at his fingers in surprise, moving them as if he had not seen them before.

"Then he fought the adventure of the Green Knight, and we found out what a champion he was. . . .

"Gentle Gareth," he said, almost in amazement, "I killed him with the same hands too, because he refused to wear his armour against me. What horrible creatures humans are! If we see a flower as we walk through the fields, we lop off its head with a stick. That is how Gareth has gone."

Guenever took the guilty hand with distress.

"You couldn't help it."

"I could have helped it." He was in his customary religious misery. "It was my fault. You are right that it was unlike me. It was my fault, my fault, my grievous fault. It was because I laid about me in the press."

"You had to make the rescue."

"Yes, but I could have fought the armed knights only. Instead of which, I laid about me against the half-armed foot-soldiers, who had no chance. I was cap-à-pied, and they were in cuir-bouillé, just leather and pikes. But I cut at them and God punished us. It was because I had forgotten my knighthood that God made me kill poor Gareth, and Gaheris too."

"Lance!" she said sharply.

"Now we are in this hellish misery," he went on, refusing to listen. "Now I have got to fight against my own King, who knighted me and taught me all I know. How can I fight him? How can I fight Gawaine, even? I have killed three of his brothers. How can I add to that? But Gawaine will never let me off. He will never forgive now. I don't blame him. Arthur would forgive us, but Gawaine won't let him. I have got to be besieged in this hole like a coward, when nobody wants to fight except Gawaine, and then they come outside with their fanfares and sing:

> Traitor knight
> Come out to fight.
> Yah! Yah! Yah!"

"It doesn't matter what they sing. It doesn't make you a coward because they sing it."

"And my own men are beginning to think so too. Bors, Blamore, Bleoberis, Lionel—they are always asking me to go out and fight. And when I do go out, what happens?"

"So far as I can learn," she said, "what happens is that you beat them, and then you let them off and beg them to go home. Everybody respects your kindness."

He hid his head in the crook of his elbow.

"Do you know what happened in the last battle? Bors had a tilt with the King himself, and knocked him down. He jumped off his horse and stood over Arthur with his sword drawn. I saw it happen, and galloped like mad. Bors said: Shall I make an end of this war? Not so hardy, I shouted, on pain of thy head. So we got Arthur back on his horse and I begged him, begged him on my knees, to go away. Arthur began to cry. His eyes filled with tears, and he stared at me and said nothing. He looks much older. He doesn't want to fight us, but it is Gawaine. Gawaine was once on our side, but I slew his brothers in my wickedness."

"Forget your wickedness. It is Gawaine's black temper and Mordred's cunning."

"If it were just Gawaine," he lamented, "there would still be a hope of peace. He is decent inside himself. He is a good man. But Mordred is always there, hinting to him and making him miserable. And there is the whole hatred of Gael and Gall, and this New Order of Mordred's. I can't see the end."

The Queen suggested for the hundredth time: "Would it be any use if I were to go back to Arthur, and put myself on his mercy?"

"We have offered it, and they have refused. It is no use going in the face of that. They would probably burn you after all."

She left the fireplace and drifted over to the great embrasure of the window. Outside, the siege works were spread below. Some tiny soldiers in the enemy camp were merrily playing Fox-and-Geese on a frozen pond. Their clear laughter came up, separated by distance from the tumbles which gave it rise.

"All the time the war goes on," she said, "and footmen who are not knights get killed, but nobody notices that."

"All the time."

She observed, without turning: "I think I will go back, dear, and chance it. Even if I am burned, that would be better than having the Trouble."

He followed her to the window.

"Jenny, I would go with you, if it were any use. We could go together, and let them cut our heads off, if there was any hope of stopping the war by that. But everybody has gone mad. Even if we did give ourselves up, Bors and Ector and the rest would carry on the feud—if we were killed. There are a hundred extra feuds on foot, for those we killed in the market-place and on the stairs, and for things through half a century of Arthur's past. Soon I will not be able to hold them, even as it is. Hebes le Renoumes, Villiers the Valiant, Urre of Hungary: they would begin revenging us, and everything would be worse. Urre is horribly grateful."

"Civilization seems to have become insane," she said.

"Yes, and it seems that we have made it so. Bors, Lionel and Gawaine wounded, and everybody raving for blood. I have to sally out with my knights and rush about pretending to strike, and perhaps Arthur will be urged against me, or Gawaine will come, and then I have to cover myself with the shield, and defend myself, and I mustn't hit back. The men notice it, and say that by not exerting myself I am prolonging the war, which makes it worse for them."

"What they say is true."

"Of course it is true. But the alternative is to kill Arthur and Gawaine, and how can I do that? If only Arthur would take you back, and go away, it would be better than this."

She might have flared up at such a tactless suggestion, twenty years before. It was a measure of their autumn that now she was amused.

"Jenny, it is a terrible thing to say, but it is true."

"Of course it's true."

"We seem to be treating you like a dummy."

"We are all dummies."

He leaned his head against the cold stone of the embrasure, until she took his hand.

"Don't think about it. Just stay in the castle, and be patient. Perhaps God will look after us."

"You said that once before."

"Yes, the week before they caught us."

"Even if God won't," he remarked bitterly, "we could apply to the Pope."

"The Pope!"

He looked up.

"What do you mean?"

"Why, Lance, the thing you said. . . . If the Pope was to send bulls to both sides, saying he would excommunicate us if we didn't come to terms? If we appealed for a papal ruling? Bors and the others would have to accept it. Surely. . . ."

He looked at her closely, as she chose the words.

"He could appoint the Bishop of Rochester to administer the terms of peace. . . ."

"But what terms?"

She had caught her idea, however, and was on fire with it.

"Lance, we two would have to accept them, whatever they might be. Even if they were to mean . . . even if they were bad for us, they would mean peace for the people. And our knights would have no excuse for carrying on the feud, because they would have to obey the Church. . . ."

He could find no words.

"Well?"

She turned to him with a face of composure and relief —the efficient and undramatic face which women achieve when they have nursing to do, or some other employment of efficiency. He did not know how to answer it.

"We can send a messenger tomorrow," she said.

"Jenny!"

He could not bear it that she was allowing herself to be
handed from one to another, no longer young, or that he
was to lose her, or that he was not to lose her. Between
men's lives and their love and his old totems, he was left
with nothing but shame. This she saw, and helped him with
it also. She kissed him tenderly. Outside, the daily chorus
was beginning:

> "Traitor knight
> Come out to fight.
> Yah! Yah! Yah!"

"There," she said, stroking his white hair. "Don't listen
to them. My Lancelot must stay in the castle, and there
will be a happy ending."


# 10


*"So His Holiness has made their peace for them,"*
said Mordred savagely.

"Aye."

They were in the Justice Room, Gawaine and himself,
waiting for the last stages of the negotiations. Both were
in black—but with the strange difference that Mordred was
resplendent in his, a sort of Hamlet, while Gawaine looked
more like the grave-digger. Mordred had begun dressing
with this dramatic simplicity since the time when he had
become a leader of the popular party. Their aims were some
kind of nationalism, with Gaelic autonomy, and a massacre
of the Jews as well, in revenge for a mythical saint called
Hugh of Lincoln. There were already thousands, spread
over the country, who carried his badge of a scarlet fist
clenching a whip, and who called themselves Thrashers.
About the older man, who only wore the uniform to please
his brother, there was a homespun blackness, the true, de-
spairing dark of mourning.

"Just fancy," Mordred went on. "If it had not been for the Pope, we should never have had this beautiful procession with everybody carrying olive branches and the innocent lovers dressed in white."

"It was a guid procession."

Gawaine's mind did not move easily along the paths of irony, so he accepted the sneer as statement of fact.

"It was well stage-managed."

The older brother moved uncomfortably, as if to ease his position, but returned to the same one from which he had started.

He said doubtfully, almost as if it were a question or an appeal: "Lancelot says in his letters that he killed our Gareth by mistake. He says he didna see him."

"It would be just like Lancelot to lay about him at unarmed men, without looking to see who they were. He was always famous for that."

This time the irony was so heavy that even Gawaine took it as it was.

"I ween it dinna seem likely."

"Likely? Of course it isn't. That was not Lancelot's line. He was the *preux chevalier* who always spared people—who never slew a person weaker than himself. That was the high road to Lancelot's popularity. Do you suppose he would have suddenly dropped this pose, to begin killing unarmed men regardless?"

With a pathetic effort to be fair, Gawaine said: "There seems to be nae reason why he should have killed them."

"Reason? Was Gareth our brother? He killed him as a reprisal, out of revenge because it was our family that had caught him with the Queen."

More carefully, he added: "It was because Arthur is fond of you, and he was jealous of your influence. He planned it fair, to weaken the clan Orkney."

"He has weakened himsel'."

"Besides, he was jealous of Gareth. He was afraid that our brother would poach on his preserves. Our Gareth copied him, which did not suit the *preux chevalier*. You can't have two knights without reproach."

The Justice Room had been prepared for the final pageant. It looked barren, with only two men in it. They were sitting in a curious way, one behind the other on the steps of the throne, which meant that they did not look each other in the face. Mordred looked at the back of Gawaine's head, and Gawaine at the floor. He said with a slight choke: "Gareth was the best of us." If he had turned round quickly, he might have been surprised at the intentness with which he was being watched. The younger face was at variance with the music of its voice. If you had looked closely, you might have noticed that Mordred's manner in the past six months had become stranger.

"Dear fellow," he said, "and to be killed by the very man who had his faith."

"It will teach me ne'er to trust the southron."

Mordred altered the pronoun with an imperceptible emphasis.

"Yes, it will teach us."

The old tyrant swung round. He seized the white hand so as to press it, speaking with confusion.

"I was used to thinking it was Agravaine's mischief— Agravaine's and yours. I thocht ye were over prejudiced against Sir Lancelot. I am ashamed."

"Blood is thicker than water."

"It is that, Mordred. A body may clatter about ideals— about right and wrong and matters of that ilk—but in the end it comes to your ain folk. I mind when Gareth used to rob the priest's wee orchard, by the cliff. . . ."

He tailed off lamely, till the thin man prompted him.

"His hair was almost white when he was a boy, it was so fair."

"Kay used to name him Pretty Hands."

"That was meant for an insult."

"Aye, but it was true. His hands were bonnie."

"And now he is in his grave."

Gawaine flushed to the eyebrows, the veins swelling at his temples.

"God's curse on them! I willna have this peace. I willna forgive them. Why should King Arthur seek to smooth it o'er? What business has the Pope within it? It is my brother that was butchered, none of theirs, and, God Almighty, I will have the vengeance!"

"Lancelot will slip through our fingers. He is an oily man to hold."

"He shallna slip. We hold him this time. The Cornwalls have forgiven over much."

Mordred shifted on the steps.

"Have you ever thought what the Table has done to Cornwall and Orkney? Arthur's father killed our grandfather. Arthur seduced our mother. And Lancelot has killed three of our brothers, besides Florence and Lovel. Yet here we are, selling our honour, to reconcile the two Englishmen. It seems cowardly?"

"Nay, it isna cowardly. The Pope may force the King to take his Queen, but there is nae word in his bulls about Sir Lancelot. We gave him sanctuary to bring the woman, and we will also let him go. But, after that . . ."

"Why should we let him escape us, even now?"

"By cause he has safe-conduct. Guid sakes, man Mordred, we are knighted men!"

"We must not stoop to dirty weapons, even if our enemies do."

"Aye, just. We will let the boar have law to run, and then pursue him to the death. Arthur is failing: he will do our will."

"It is sad," said Sir Mordred, "how the poor King seems to lose his grip, since all this business started."

"Aye, it is sad. But he kens the difference yet of right and wrong."

"It is a change for him."

"Ye mean, to fail his powers."

"You guess so quickly."

His sarcasms were as easy as teasing a blind man.

"He canna have it every way. He never should have sided with that traitor at the start."

"Nor married Gwen."

"Aye, the fault lies with them. It isna we who sought the quarrel."

"Indeed, it is not."

"The King must stand for justice. Even if His Holiness should make him take the woman to his bed, we have our right towards Sir Lancelot. Man, he has done strong treason when he took the Queen, as well as when he slew our brothers."

"We have every right."

The burly fellow took the other's hand again, the pale one in the horny sexton's. He said with difficulty: "It would be woeful sore to be alone."

"We had the same mother, Gawaine."

"Aye!"

"And she was Gareth's mother too . . ."

"Here comes the King."

The pageant of reconciliation had reached its final

stages. With trumpets blowing in the courtyard, the dignitaries of Church and State began to filter up the stairs. The courtiers, bishops, heralds, pages, judges, and spectators were talking as they came. The cube of tapestry, an empty vase before, began to flower with them. It flowered with bald-faced ladies in head-dresses which looked like crescents or cones or the astonishing coiffure worn by the Duchess in *Alice in Wonderland*. In bright bodices with their waists under their armpits, in long skirts and flowing sleeves, in camelin de Tripoli or taffeta or rosete, the delicate creatures swam into their places with an aroma of myrrh and honey —with which they had washed their teeth. Their gallants— young squires in the height of fashion, many of them wearing Mordred's badge as Thrashers—came mincing in with their long-toed shoes, in which it was impossible to walk upstairs. At the foot of the steps they had slipped out of them, and their pages had carried them up. The impression given by the young men was mainly of legs in stockings— it had even been found necessary to pass a sumptuary law, which insisted that their jacket should be long enough to cover the buttocks. Then there were more responsible councillors in extraordinary hats, some of which were like tea-cosies, some turbans, some bird wings, some muffs. The gowns of these were pleated and padded, with high ruff-like collars, epaulettes and jewelled belts. There were clerks with neat little skull-caps to keep their tonsures warm, dressed in sober clothes which contrasted with the laity. There was a visiting cardinal in the glorious tasselled hat which still adorns the notepaper of Wolsey's College at Oxford. There were furs of every kind, including a handsome arrangement of black and white lambs' wool, sewn in contrasting diamonds. The talkers made a noise like starlings.

This was the first part of the pageant. The second part began with nearer premonitions on the trumpets. Then came several Cistercians, secretaries, deacons and other religious people, all burdened with ink made by boiling the bark of blackthorn, parchment, sand, bulls, pens, and the sort of pen-knife which scribes used to carry in their left hands when they were writing. They also had tally sticks and the minutes of the last meeting.

The third instalment was the Bishop of Rochester, who had been appointed nuncio. He came in all the state of a nuncio, though he had left his canopy downstairs. He was

a silk-haired senior, with his cope and crosier, alb and ring
—urbane, ecclesiastical, knowing the spiritual power.

Finally the trumpets were at the door, and England came.
In weighty ermine, which covered his shoulders and the left
arm, with a narrower strip down the right—in the blue velvet cloak and overwhelming crown—heavy with majesty
and supported, almost literally supported, by the proper officers, the King was led to the throne on the dais, its canopy
golden with embroideries of the dragons ramping in red—
and there, the crowd now parting, Gawaine and Mordred
were revealed to meet him. He sank down where he was
put. The standing nuncio seated himself also, on a throne
opposite, hung with white and gold. The buzz subsided.

"We are ready to begin?"

Rochester's priestly voice relieved the tension: "The
Church is ready."

"So is the State."

It was Gawaine's rumble, faintly offensive.

"Is there anything which we ought to settle before they
come?"

"It is a' fair settled."

Rochester turned his eyes to the Laird of Orkney.

"We are obliged to Sir Gawaine."

"Ye are welcome."

"In that case," said the King, "I suppose we must tell
Sir Lancelot that the Court is waiting to receive him."

"Bedivere man, send forth to bring the prisoners."

It was noticed that Gawaine had put himself in the habit
of speaking for the throne, and that Arthur let him do it.
The nuncio, however, was less subdued.

"One moment, Sir Gawaine. I have to point out that the
Church does not regard these people as prisoners. The mission of His Holiness which I represent is one of pacifica-
tion, not of revenge."

"The Church can aye regard the prisoners as she pleases.
We are for doing what the Church has said, but we shall
do it in our ain poor fashion. Bring forth the prisoners."

"Sir Gawaine . . ."

"Blow for Her Majesty. The Court sits."

In the middle of music like a bad pageant, and of music
answered from outside, the heads turned round to the door.

There was a rustle among the silks and furs. A lane was
made with shuffling. In the archway, now open, Lancelot
and Guenever waited for their cue.

There was something pathetic about their grandeur, as if they were dressed up for a charade but not quite fitted. They were in white cloth, of gold tissue, and the Queen, no longer young or lovely, carried her olive branch ungracefully. They came shyly down the lane, like well-meaning actors who were trying to do their best, but who were not good at acting. They kneeled in front of the throne.

"My most redoubted King."

The movement of sympathy was caught by Mordred.

"Charming!"

Lancelot looked to the elder brother.

"Sir Gawaine."

Orkney showed him his back.

He turned towards the Church.

"My lord of Rochester."

"Welcome, my son."

"I have brought Queen Guenever, by the King's command, and by the Pope's."

There was an awkward silence, in which nobody dared to help their speech along.

"It is my duty, then, if nobody will answer, to affirm the Queen of England's innocence."

"Liar!"

"I am come to maintain with my body that the Queen is fair, true, good and clean to King Arthur, and this I will make good upon any challenge, excepting only if it were the King or Sir Gawaine. It is my duty to the Queen to make this proffer."

"The Holy Father bids us to accept your proffer, Lancelot."

The pathos which was growing in the room was broken by the Orkney faction for the second time.

"Fie on his proud words," cried Gawaine. "As for the Queen, let her bide and be forgiven. But thou, false recreant knight, what cause had'st thou to slay my brother, that loved thee more than all my kin?"

Both the great men had slipped into the high language, suitable to the place and passion.

"God knows it helps me not to excuse myself, Sir Gawaine. I would rather to have killed my nephew, Sir Bors. But I did not see them, Gawaine, and I have paid it!"

"It was done in despite of me and of Orkney!"

"It repents me to the heart," he said, "that you should think so, my lord Sir Gawaine, for I know that while you are against me I shall never more be accorded with the King."

"True words, man Lancelot. Ye came under safe-conduct and sanctuary, to bring the Queen, but ye shall go hence as the murderer ye are."

"If I am a murderer, God forgive me, my lord. But I never slew by treason."

He had intended his protest in innocence—but it was received at more than its face value. Gawaine, clapping one hand to his dagger, cried: "I take your meaning in that. Ye mean Sir Lamorak. . . ."

The Bishop of Rochester lifted his glove.

"Gawaine, cannot we leave this wrangling to another time? The immediate business is to restore the Queen. No doubt Sir Lancelot would like to make an explanation of the trouble, so that the Church may be justified in her reconciliation."

"Thank you, my lord."

Gawaine glared about him, till the King's tired voice prompted the proceedings. They were going forward clumsily, by a series of jerks.

"You were taken with the Queen."

"Sir, I was sent for to my lady your Queen, I know not for what cause; but I was not so soon within the chamber door when immediately Sir Agravaine and Sir Mordred beat upon it, calling me traitor and recreant knight."

"They called thee right."

"My lord Sir Gawaine, in their quarrel they proved themselves not in the right. I speak for the Queen, not for my own worship."

"Well, well, Sir Lancelot."

The ill-made knight turned to his oldest friend, to the first person he had loved with his poises. He dropped the language of chivalry, falling into the simple tongue.

"Can't we be forgiven? Can't we be friends again? We have come back in penitence, Arthur, when we needn't have come at all. Won't you remember the old days, when we fought together and were friends. All this wickedness could be smoothed out by the goodwill of Sir Gawaine, if you would give us mercy."

"The King gives justice," said the red man. "Did ye give mercy to my brothers?"

"I have given mercy to all of you, Sir Gawaine. I dare say I may speak without boasting, when I say that many in this room are indebted to me for liberty, if not for life. I have fought for the Queen in others' quarrels, so why not in my own? I have fought for you also, Sir Gawaine, and saved you from an ignoble death."

"Yet now," said Mordred, "there are but two of Orkney left."

Gawaine flung back his head.

"The King may do as he will. My mind was made six months ago, when I found Sir Gareth in his blood—unarmed."

"I would to God he had been armed, for then he might have withstood me. He might have killed me, and saved our misery."

"A noble speech."

The old fellow cried out passionately and suddenly, to anybody who would listen: "Why will you believe that I wanted to kill them? I knighted Gareth. I loved him. The moment I heard he was dead, I knew you would never forgive. I knew it meant the end of hope. It was against my interest to kill Sir Gareth."

Mordred whispered: "It was against our heart."

Lancelot tried one last effort of persuasion.

"Gawaine, forgive me. My own heart bleeds for what I have done. I know how you are hurt, because it has hurt me too. Won't you give peace to our country, if I make a penance? Don't force me to fight for my life, but let me make a pilgrimage for Gareth's sake. I will start at Sandwich in my shirt, and walk barefoot to Carlisle, and I will endow a chantry for him every ten miles in between."

"Gareth's blood," said Mordred, "is not to be paid for by chantries, we think—however much it might pleasure the Bishop of Rochester."

The old knight's patience broke.

"Hold your tongue!"

Gawaine was flaming on the instant.

"Keep civil, my murdering mannie, or we will stab you at the King's own feet!"

"It would need more . . ."

Again the nuncio intervened.

"Sir Lancelot, please. Let some of us keep due temper and decency, at any rate. Gawaine, sit down. A penance has been offered for Gareth's blood by means of which the war may be brought to an end. Give us your answer."

With the moment of expectant silence, the sandy-haired giant swam into the higher tone.

"I ha' heard Sir Lancelot's speech and his great proffers, but he hath slain my brothers. That I may never forgive, in chief his treachery to Sir Gareth. If it please mine uncle, King Arthur, to accord with him, then the King will lose my service and that of all the Gael. However we may talk of it, we ken the truth. The man is a revealed traitor, to the King and to masel'."

"There is nobody alive, Gawaine, who has called me a traitor. I have explained about the Queen."

"We have done with that. I make no insinuations about the woman, if it be proper not to do so. I speak of what airt your own judgment is to be."

"If it is the King's judgment, I shall accept it."

"The King is agreed with me already, before ye came."

"Arthur . . ."

"Speak to the King by his title."

"Sir, is this true?"

But the old man only bowed his head.

"At least let me hear it from the King's mouth!"

Mordred said: "Speak, father."

He shook his head like a baited bear. He moved it with the heavy movement of a bear, but would not look from the floor.

"Speak."

"Lancelot," he was heard to say, "you know how the truth stands between us. My Table is broken, my knights parted or dead. I never sought a quarrel with you, Lance, nor you with me."

"But can't it be ended?"

"Gawaine says . . ." he began faintly.

"Gawaine!"

"Justice . . ."

Gawaine rose to his feet, foxy, burly and towering.

"My King, my lord and my uncle. Is it the court's will that I pronounce sentence upon this recreant traitor?"

The silence became absolute.

"Know then, all ye, that this is the King's Word. The Queen shall come back to him with her liberty as it was, and she shall stand in nae peril for nothing that was surmised afore this day. This is the Pope's will. But thou, Sir Lancelot, thou shalt go forth banished out of this kingdom within fifteen days, a revealed recreant; and, by God, we shall follow thee after that time, to pull down the strongest castle of France about thine ears."

"Gawaine," he asked painfully, "don't follow me. I will accept the banishment. I will live in my French castles. But don't follow me, Gawaine. Don't keep the war forever."

"Leave that to thy betters. Such castles are the King's."

"If you follow me, Gawaine, don't challenge me: don't let Arthur come against me. I can't fight against my friends. Gawaine, for God's sake don't make us fight."

"Leave talking, man. Deliver the Queen and remove yer body quickly from this court."

Lancelot pulled himself together with a sort of final care. He looked from England to his tormentor. He turned slowly to the Queen, who had not spoken. He saw her ridiculous olive branch, her clumsiness and silly clothes. With a lifted head he raised their tragedy to nobleness and gravity.

"Well, madam, it seems that we must part."

He took her by the hand, led her to the middle of the room, translating her into his remembered lady. Something in his grip, in his step, in the fullness of his voice, made her bloom again—it was their last partnership—into the Rose of England. He lifted her to a crest of conquest which they had forgotten. As stately as a dance, the gargoyle took her to the centre. There, poising her flushing, the arch-stone of the realm, he made an end. It was the last time that Sir Lancelot, King Arthur and Queen Guenever were to be together.

"My King and my old friends, a word before I go. My sentence is to leave this fellowship, which I have served in all my life. It is to depart your country, and to be pursued with war. I stand then, for the last time, as the Queen's champion. I stand to tell you, lady and madam, in presence of all this court, that if any danger may threaten you in future, then one poor arm will come from France to defend you—and so let all remember."

He kissed her fingers deliberately, turned stiffly, and began to pace in silence down the long length of the room. His future closed about him as he went.

Fifteen days to Dover was the time assigned to any felon who had taken sanctuary. He would have to do it in the felon's way "ungirt, unshod, bareheaded, in his bare shirt as if he were hanged on a gallows." He would have to walk in the middle of the road clutching the small cross in his hand, which was the symbol of his sanctuary. Probably

Gawaine or his men would be skulking at his heels, in case
for a moment he should lay the talisman aside. But still,
whether in shirt or mail, he would be their old Commander.
He would walk steadily, without haste, looking straight in
front of him. As he passed the threshold, the look of endurance was already on him. People felt tawdry in the Justice
Room when the old soldier had left it, and many eyed the
red whips sideways, with a secret dread.

# 11

*Guenever sat in the Queen's chamber at Carlisle*
Castle. The huge bed had been re-made as a settee. It looked
tidy and rectangular under its canopy, so that you were
shy of sitting down. There was a fireplace with a little pot
warming beside it, a high chair, and the reading desk. Also
there was a book to read, perhaps the Galeotto one which
Dante mentions. It had cost the same price as ninety oxen,
but, as Guenever had already read it seven times, it was no
longer exciting. A late fall of snow threw the evening light
upward into the chamber, shining on the ceiling more than
on the floor, so as to alter the usual shadows. They were
blue, and in the wrong places. The great lady was sewing,
sitting rather formally in the high chair with the book beside
her, and one of her waiting women, sitting on the steps of
the bed, was sewing too.

Guenever stitched away with the half-blank mind of a
needlewoman, the other half of her brain moving idly
among her troubles. She wished she was not at Carlisle.
It was too near the north—which was Mordred's county—
too far away from the securities of civilization. For instance,
she would have liked to be at London—in the Tower perhaps. She would have liked, instead of this dreary expanse
of snow, to be looking out from the Tower windows at the
fun and bustle of the metropolis: at London Bridge, with
the staggering houses all over it, which were constantly
tumbling off into the river. She remembered it as a bridge

of great personality, what with the houses and the heads of rebels on spikes and the place where Sir David had fought a full-dress joust with the Lord Welles. The cellars of the houses were in the piers of the bridge, and it had a chapel of its own, and a tower to defend it. It was a perfect toy-town of a place, with housewives popping their heads out of windows, or letting down buckets into the river on long ropes, or throwing out slops, or hanging the washing, or screaming to their children when the drawbridge was going to be pulled up.

For that matter, it would have been nice merely to be in the Tower itself. Here, in Carlisle, everything was as still as death. But there, in the Conqueror's tower, a constant ebb and flow of cockneys would be livening the frost. Even Arthur's menagerie, which he now kept in the Tower, would be giving a comfortable background of noise and smell. The latest addition was a full-sized elephant, presented by the King of France, and specially drawn for the record by the indefatigable news-hawk, Matthew Paris.

When Guenever got to the elephant, she put down the sewing and began to rub her fingers. They were numb. They did not thaw so quickly as they used to.

"Have you put the crumbs out for the birds, Agnes?"

"Yes, madam. The robin was perky today. He sang quite a trill against one of the blackbirds who was greedy."

"Poor creatures. Still, I suppose they will all be singing in a few weeks."

"It seems a long time since everybody went away," said Agnes. "The court is like the birds now, it is so silent and heartless."

"They will come back, no doubt."

"Yes, madam."

The Queen took up her needle again, and pushed it carefully through.

"They say Sir Lancelot has been brave."

"Sir Lancelot always was a brave gentleman, madam."

"In the last letter it says that Gawaine had a duel with him. He must have been miserable, to fight him."

Agnes said emphatically: "I can't think why the King will go with that there Sir Gawaine against his best friend. Anybody can see that it is only out of blind temper. And then to lay waste the land of France, just to spite Sir Lancelot, and to do these terrible killings, and to say such things as them Thrashers do. It won't do nobody no good, to carry on like that. Why can't they let bygones be bygones, is what I ask?"

"I think the King goes with Sir Gawaine because he is trying to be just. He thinks that the Orkneys have a right to demand justice for Gareth's death—and I suppose they have. Besides, if the King didn't cling to Sir Gawaine he would have nobody left. He was prouder of the Round Table than of anything, and now it is splitting up and he wants to keep somebody."

"It is a poor way to keep the Table together," said Agnes, "by fighting Sir Lancelot."

"Sir Gawaine has a right to justice. At least, they say he has. And the King's choice is not free either. He is swept along by the people—by men who want conquest in France and have made a claim to it, or who are sick of the long peace he has managed to keep, or who are anxious for military promotion and a killing in return for those who died in the Market Square. There are the young knights of Mordred's party, who believe in nationalism, and who have been taught to think that my husband is an old fogey, and there are the relatives of the ones who were in the fight on the stairs, and there is the clan Orkney, with their ancient hatreds on their minds. War is like a fire, Agnes. One man may start it, but it will spread all over. It is not about any one thing in particular."

"Ah, these high and mighty matters, madam—they are beyond us poor women. But come now, what did it say in the letter?"

Guenever sat for some time, looking at the letter without seeing it, while her mind revolved the problems of her husband. Then she said slowly: "The King likes Lancelot so much that he is forced to be unfair to him—for fear of being unfair to other people."

"Yes, ma'am."

"It says," said the Queen, noticing the letter she was looking at with a start, "it says that Sir Gawaine rode in front of the castle every day, and called out that Lancelot was a coward and a traitor. Lancelot's knights were angry, and went out to him one by one, but he charged them all down, and hurt some of them badly. He nearly killed Bors and Lionel, until at last Sir Lancelot had to go himself. The people inside the castle made him. He told Sir Gawaine that he was driven to it, like a beast at bay."

"And what did Sir Gawaine say?"

"Sir Gawaine said: 'Leave thy babbling and come off, and let us ease our hearts.' "

"And did they?"

"Yes, they had a duel in front of the castle. Everybody promised not to interfere, and they began at nine o'clock in the morning. You know how Sir Gawaine can always fight better in the mornings. That was why they began so early."

"Mercy on Sir Lancelot, to have him as strong as three! For I did hear tell that the Old Ones have the fairy blood in them, through the red hair, you know, madam, and this makes the laird as strong as three people before noon, because the sun fights for him!"

"It must have been terrible, Agnes. But Sir Lancelot was too proud not to give the advantage."

"I wonder he was not killed."

"He nearly was. But he covered himself with his shield and parried slowly all the time and gave ground. It says he received many sad brunts, but he managed to defend himself until midday. Then, of course, when the fairy strength had gone down, he was able to take the offensive, and he ended by giving Gawaine a blow on the head which knocked him over. He could not get up."

"Alas, Sir Gawaine!"

"Yes, he could have killed him there and then."

"But he didn't."

"No. Sir Lancelot stood back and leaned on his sword. Gawaine begged him to kill him. He was more furious than ever and called out: 'Why do you stop? Come on then: kill me and finish your butchering. I will not yield. Kill me at once, for I shall only fight you again if you spare my life.' He was crying."

"We may depend upon it," said Agnes wisely, "that Sir Lancelot refused to strike a felled knight."

"We may depend."

"He was always a kind, good gentleman, though not what you may call a beauty."

"He was the chief of all."

They fell silent, shy of their feelings, and began to stitch. Presently the Queen said: "The light gets bad, Agnes. Do you think we could have the rushes?"

"Certainly, madam. I was thinking the same myself."

She began lighting them at the fire, grumbling about the

backward place and the naked, northern savages to have no candles, while Guenever hummed absently. It was the duet which she used to sing with Lancelot, and, when she recognized it, she stopped abruptly.

"There, madam. The days seem to draw out."

"Yes: we shall have the spring soon."

Sitting down and stitching away in the smoky light, Agnes resumed her catechism where it had broken off.

"And what did the King say about the business?"

"He cried when he saw how Gawaine was spared. It made him remember things, and he became so wretched that he was ill."

"Would that be what they call a nervous shakedown, madam?"

"Yes, Agnes. He fell sick for sorrow, and Gawaine had concussion, so they were bad together. But the knights are keeping up the siege."

"Well, it isn't a very cheerful letter, is it, madam?"

"No, it isn't."

"I remember having a letter once—but there, they say bad news travels the fastest."

"Everything is letters now—now that the court is empty, and the world split, and nobody left but the Lord Protector."

"Ah, that there Sir Mordred: I never could abide the likes of him. What does he want to go a-speechifying at the people for, and taking off his hat to make them cheer? Why can't he dress more cheerful like, instead of hanging about in that black, as if he were Holy Doomsday? He caught it from poor Sir Gawaine, I dare say."

"The uniform is supposed to be in mourning for Gareth."

"He never cared for Sir Gareth, that one didn't. I don't believe he cares for anybody."

"He cared for his mother, Agnes."

"Aye, and she had her throat slit for being no better than she should be. They are a queer pack, the lot of them."

"Queen Morgause," said Guenever thoughtfully, "must have been a strange person. It is common knowledge, now that Mordred is made the Lord Protector, so it doesn't matter talking about it. But she must have been a powerful woman to have caught our King when she had four big boys of her own. Why, she caught Sir Lamorak when she was a grandmother. She must have had a terrible effect on her sons, if one of them could have felt so fiercely about her that he killed her. She was nearly seventy. I expect she ate Mordred, Agnes, like a spider."

"They did used to talk at one time, about the Cornwall sisters being witches. Of course, the worst of them was Morgan le Fay. But that there Morgause ran her close."

"It makes one sorry for Mordred."

"You keep your pity for yourself, my lady, for you will get none from him."

"He has been polite since he was left in charge."

"Aye, that he has. It is the quiet ones that do the mischief."

Guenever considered this, holding her material to the light. She asked with some anxiety: "You don't think that Sir Mordred means to do wrong, do you, Agnes?"

"He is a dark one."

"He wouldn't do anything wrong when the King has left him to look after the country, and to look after us?"

"That King of yours, madam, if you will excuse the liberty, is quite beyond my comprehension. First he goes to fight with his best friend because Sir Gawaine tells him to, and then he leaves his bitterest enemy to be the Lord Protector. Why does he choose to act so blind?"

"Mordred has never broken the laws."

"That is because he is too cunning."

"The King said that Mordred would have to be the heir to the throne, and you could not take the King and the heir out of the country at the same time, so naturally he had to be left as the Protector. It was only fair."

"That fairness, madam, it will never come to no good."

They sewed away.

Agnes added: "The King should have stayed, if that is true, and let Sir Mordred go."

"I wish he had."

Later she explained: "I think the King wants to be with Sir Gawaine, in case he can moderate between them."

They stitched uneasily, the needles fusing through the dark material with a long gleam like falling stars.

"Are you frightened of Sir Mordred, Agnes?"

"Yes, madam, that I am."

"So am I. He walks about so softly lately, and . . . looks at people in a queer way. And then there are all these speeches about Gaels and Saxons and Jews, and all the shouting and hysterics. I heard him laughing last week, by himself. It was horrible."

"He is a sly one. Maybe he is listening now."

"Agnes!"

Guenever dropped her needle as if she had been struck.

"Oh, come now, madam: you must not take on. I was only having my joke."

But the Queen remained frozen.

"Go to the door. I believe you are right."

"Oh, madam, I couldn't do that."

"Open it at once, Agnes."

"Madam, but suppose he is there!"

She had caught the feeling. The hopeless rushlights were not enough. He might have been in the room itself, in a dark corner. She rose in a flutter, like a partridge while the hawk is over, and plucked at her skirt. For both women the castle was suddenly too dark, too empty, too lonely, too northerly, too full of night and winter.

"If you open it, he will go away."

"But we must give him time to go away."

They strove with their voices, feeling themselves to be under a black wing.

"Stand near it and speak loudly then, before you open."

"Madam, what shall I say?"

"Say 'Shall I open the door?' Then I will say, 'Yes, I think it is time to go to bed.'"

"I think it is time to go to bed."

"Go on."

"Very good, madam. Shall I begin?"

"Begin, yes, quickly."

"I don't know as I can do it."

"Oh, Agnes, please be quick!"

"Very well, madam. I think I can do it now."

Facing the door as if it might attack her, Agnes addressed it at the top of her voice.

"I am going to open the door!"

"It is time to go to bed!"

Nothing happened.

"Now open it," said the Queen.

She lifted the latch and threw it open, and there was Mordred smiling in the frame.

"Good evening, Agnes."

"Oh, sir!"

The wretched woman dropped him a fluttering curtsey, with one hand clutching at her breast, and scuttled past him for the stairs. He stood aside politely. When she was gone he stepped into the room, sumptuous in his black velvet, with one cold diamond beaming in the rushlight from his scarlet badge. Anybody who had not seen him for a month or two would have known at once that he was mad—but his brains had gone so gradually that those who lived with him had failed to see it. He was followed by his small black pug-dog, flirting its bright eyes and curly tail.

"Our Agnes seems to be in a nervous state," he said. "Good evening, Guenever."

"Good evening, Mordred."

"A little fine embroidery? I thought you would be knitting socks for soldiers."

"Why have you come?"

"Just an evening call. You must forgive the drama."

"Do you always wait outside doors?"

"One has to come through a door somehow, madam. It is more convenient than coming through the window—though, I believe, some people have been known to do that."

"I see. Will you sit down?"

He took his seat with an elaborate gesture, the pug jumping into his lap. In a way it was tragic to watch him, for he was doing what his mother did. He was acting, and had ceased to be real.

People write tragedies in which fatal blondes betray their paramours to ruin, in which Cressidas, Cleopatras, Delilahs, and sometimes even naughty daughters like Jessica bring their lovers or their parents to distress: but these are not the heart of tragedy. They are fripperies to the soul of man. What does it matter if Antony did fall upon his sword? It only killed him. It is the mother's not the lover's lust that rots the mind. It is that which condemns the tragic character to his walking death. It is Jocasta, not Juliet, who dwells in the inner chamber. It is Gertrude, not the silly Ophelia, who sends Hamlet to his madness. The heart of tragedy does not lie in stealing or taking away. Any featherpated girl can steal a heart. It lies in giving, in putting on, in adding, in smothering without the pillows. Desdemona robbed of life or honour is nothing to a Mordred, robbed of himself—his soul stolen, overlaid, wizened, while the mother-character lives in triumph, superfluously and with stifling love endowed on him, seemingly innocent of ill-intention. Mordred was the only son of Orkney who never married. He, while his brothers fled to England, was the one who stayed alone with her for twenty years—her living larder. Now that she was dead, he had become her grave. She existed in him like the vampire. When he moved, when he blew his nose, he did it with her movement. When he acted he became as unreal as she had been, pretending to be a virgin for the unicorn. He dabbled in the same cruel magic. He had even begun to keep lap dogs like her—although he had always hated hers with the same bitter jealousy as that with which he had hated her lovers.

"Do I feel a coldness in the air this evening?"

"It is bound to be cold in February."

"I was referring to the delicacy of our personal relationship."

"The Protector, whom my husband appointed, is bound to be welcome to the Queen."

"But not the husband's bastard, I suppose?"

She lowered her needle and looked him in the face.

"I don't understand your coming like this, and I don't know what you want."

She had no wish to be hostile, but he was forcing her. She had never been afraid of anyone.

"I was thinking of a chat about the political situation—just a little chat."

She knew that they had reached a crisis of some sort, and it made her weak. She was too old now to deal with madmen, although she still had no suspicion of his sanity. Only the cumbrous irony of his tone made her feel unreal herself—made her unable to put her own words simply. But she would not give in.

"I shall be glad to hear what you want to say."

"That is extremely generous of you . . . Jenny."

It was monstrous. He was making her into one of his fantasies, not speaking to a real person at all.

She said indignantly: "Will you be so kind as to address me by my title, Mordred?"

"But certainly. I must apologize if I have been trespassing on Lancelot's preserves."

The sneer acted like a tonic. It raised her stature to the royal lady which she was, to a straight-backed dowager whose rheumatic fingers flashed with rings, who had ridden the world successfully for fifty years.

"I believe," she said at once, "you would find some difficulty in doing that."

"Well! However, I am afraid I asked for it. You were always a bit of a spitfire . . . Queen Jenny."

"Sir Mordred, if you can't behave like a gentleman, I shall go."

"And where will you go?"

"I should go anywhere: anywhere where a woman old enough to be your mother would be safe from this extravagance."

"The question is," he observed reflectively, "where you would be safe? The plan seems bound to founder in the last resource, when you consider that everybody has gone away to France, and that I am the ruler of the kingdom. Of course, you could go to France . . . if you could get there."

She understood, or began to understand.

"I don't know what you mean."

"Then you must think it out."

"If you will excuse me," she said, rising, "I will call my woman."

"Call her by all means. Though I should have to send her away."

"Agnes will take her orders from me."

"I doubt it. Let us try."

"Mordred, will you leave me?"

"No, Jenny," he said. "I want to stay. But, if you will sit down quietly for a minute, and listen, I promise to behave like a perfect gentleman—like one of your *preux chevaliers,* in fact."

"You leave no option."

"Very little."

"What do you want?" she asked. She sat down, folding her hands in her lap. She was accustomed to a life of danger.

"Come now," he said, in high good humour, quite mad, enjoying his cat-and-mouse. "We must not rush it in this bald way. We must be at ease before we begin our conversation, otherwise it will seem so strained."

"I am listening."

"No, no. You must call me Mordy, or some such pet name. Then it will seem more natural when I call you Jenny. Everything will go forward so much more pleasantly."

She would not answer.

"Guenever, have you any idea of your position?"

"My position is that of the Queen of England, as yours is that of the Protector."

"While Arthur and Lancelot are fighting each other in France."

"That is so."

"Suppose I were to tell you," he asked, stroking the pug, "that I had a letter this morning? That Arthur and Lancelot are dead?"

"I should not believe you."

"They killed each other in battle."

"It is not true," she told him quietly.

"As a matter of fact, it isn't. How did you guess?"

"If it was not true, it was cruel to say so. Why did you say it?"

"A great many people would have believed it, Jenny. I expect a great many will."

"Why should they?" she asked, before she had caught his drift. Then she stopped, catching her breath. For the first time, she began to feel afraid: but it was for Arthur.

"You can't mean . . ."

"Oh, but I can," he exclaimed gaily, "and I do. What do you think would happen if I were to announce poor Arthur's death?"

"But, Mordred, you couldn't do such a thing! They are alive . . . You owe everything . . . The King made you his deputy . . . Your fealty . . . It would not be true! Arthur has always treated you with such scrupulous justice. . . ."

He said with cold eyes: "I have never asked to be treated with justice. It is something which he does to people, to amuse himself."

"But he is your father!"

"So far as that goes, I did not ask to be born. I suppose he did that to amuse himself, also."

"I see."

She sat, twisting her sewing in her hands, trying to think.

"Why do you hate my husband?" she asked, almost with wonder.

"I don't hate him. I despise him."

"He didn't know," she explained gently, "that your mother was his sister, when it happened."

"And I suppose he didn't know that I was his son, when he put us out in the boat?"

"He was scarcely nineteen, Mordred. They had frightened him with prophecies, and he did what they made him."

"My mother was a good woman until she met King Arthur. She had a happy home with Lot of Orkney, and she bore him four brave sons. What happened after?"

"But she was more than twice his age! I should have thought . . ."

He stopped her, holding up his hand.

"You are speaking of my mother."

"I am sorry, Mordred, but really . . ."

"I loved my mother."

"Mordred . . ."

"King Arthur came to a woman who was faithful to her husband. When he left, she was a wanton. She ended her life in a naked bed with Sir Lamorak, justly slain by her own child."

"Mordred, it is no good saying anything if you can't see . . . if you can't believe that Arthur is kind and sorry and in trouble. He is fond of you. He was saying how he loved you only a day or two before this misery began. . . ."

"He can keep his love."

"He has been so fair," she pleaded.

"The just and noble king! Yes, it is easy to be fair, when it is over. That is the amusing part. Justice! He can keep that too."

She said, trying to speak steadily: "If you proclaim yourself king, they will come from France to fight you. Then we shall have a double war instead of a single one, and it will be fought in England. The whole fellowship will be blotted out."

He smiled in pure delight.

"It seems unbelievable," she said, pinching the embroidery.

There was nothing she could do. For a moment it crossed her mind that if she humiliated herself to him, knelt down on her stiff old knees to plead for mercy, he might be soothed. But it was evidently hopeless. He was fixed in a course, like a ball in a groove. Even his conversation was, as it were, a spoken part. It would end according to the script.

"Mordred," she said helplessly, "have pity on the country people, if you will have none on Arthur or on me."

He pushed the pug off his lap and stood up, smiling at her with crazy satisfaction. He stretched himself, looking down on her, but not seeing her at all.

"I should, of course, have pity on you," he said, "if not on Arthur."

"What do you mean?"

"I was thinking of a pattern, Jenny, a simple pattern." She watched him without speaking.

"Yes. My father committed incest with my mother. Don't you think it would be a pattern, Jenny, if I were to answer it by marrying my father's wife?"

# 12

*It was dark in Gawaine's tent, except for a flat pan* of charcoal which lit it dimly from below. The tent was poor and shabby, compared with the splendid pavilions of the English knights. On the hard bed there were a few plaids in the Orkney tartan, and the only ornaments were a leaden bottle of holy water which he was taking for medicine, marked *"Optimus egrorum, medicus fit Thomas bonorum,"* together with a withered bunch of heather, tied to the pole. These were his household gods.

Gawaine was stretched face downward on the plaids. The man was crying, slowly and hopelessly, while Arthur, sitting beside him, stroked his hand. It was his wound that had weakened him, or else he would not have cried. The old King was trying to soothe him.

"Don't grieve about it, Gawaine," he said. "You did the best you could."

"It is the second time he has spared me, the second time in ae month."

"Lancelot was always strong. The years don't seem to touch him."

"Why canna he kill me, then? I begged him to have done with it. I told him that if he left me to be patched, I should but fight him fresh when I was mended.

"And, God!" he added tearfully, "my head sore aches!"

Arthur said with a sigh: "It was because you got both blows on the same place. That was bad luck."

"It makes a body feel shamed."

"Don't think about it, then. Lie quiet, or you will get feverish again, and will not be able to fight for a long time. Then what would we do? We should be quite lost without our Gawaine to lead the battle for us."

"I am but a man of straw, Arthur," he said. "I am but an ill-passioned bully, and I canna kill him."

"People who say they are no good are always the good ones. Let's change the subject and talk about something pleasant. England, for instance."

"We shall never see England again."

"Nonsense! We shall see England just in the spring. Why, it is almost spring now. The snow-drops will have been out for ages, and I dare say Guenever will have some crocuses already. She is good at gardening."

"Guenever was kind to me."

"My Gwen is kind to everybody," said the old man proudly. "I wonder what she is doing now? Going to bed, I suppose. Or perhaps she is sitting up late, having a talk with your brother. It would be nice to think that they were talking about us at this minute, perhaps saying admiring things about Gawaine's prowess: or Gwen might be saying that she wished her old man would come home."

Gawaine moved restlessly on the bed.

"I have a mind to gang home," he muttered. "If Lancelot hates clan Orkney, as Mordred says, why does he spare the laird of it? Mayhap he did kill Gareth by mischance."

"I am sure it was mischance. If you will help to end the war, we may be able to stop it fairly soon. It is your justice we are said to be fighting for now, you know. I and the others who want to fight would have to bow to that eventually. If you are content to make it up there is nobody who will be more happy than I will be."

"Aye, but I swore to fight him to the death."

"You have had two good tries."

"And taken a braw thrashing ilka time," he said bitterly. "He could have made the war end twice. Nay, it would look like cowardice to compound."

"The bravest people are the ones who don't mind looking like cowards. Remember how Lancelot hid in Joyous Gard for months, while we sang songs outside."

"I canna forget our Gareth's face."

"It was sad for all of us."

Gawaine was trying to think, an effort not made easy to

him by practice. On this dark evening it was twice as difficult, because of his head. Since the time when Galahad gave him concussion in the quest for the Grail he had been liable to headaches, and now, by a curious accident, Lancelot had given him two blows in separate duels, on the same place.

"What for should I give in," he asked, "because he beats me? It would be fleeing him to give in now. If I could fell him in a third engagement, maybe. And spare the chiel... It would be even."

"The fields," said the King thoughtfully, "will soon be king-cups and daisies in England. It would be nice to win a peace."

"Aye, and the spring hawking."

The figure twisted in its dim bed with a movement of remembrance, but froze as the pain shot through its skull.

"Almighty, but my head throbs sorely."

"Would you like me to get a wet cloth for it, or a drink of milk?"

"Nay. Let it bide. It willna help."

"Poor Gawaine. I hope nothing is broken in it."

"The thing that is broken is my spirit. Let us talk of other matters."

The King said doubtfully: "I ought not to talk too much. I think I ought to go away, and leave you to sleep."

"Ach, stay. Dinna leave me by mysel'. It irks me when I am by my lone."

"The doctor said..."

"Tae hell wi' the doctor. Bide a wee while. Hold my hand. Tell me of England."

"There ought to be a post tomorrow, and then we shall be able to read about England. We shall have the latest news, and there will be a letter from young Mordred, and perhaps my Gwen will write to me."

"Mordred's letters are cold cheer, some way."

Arthur hastened to defend him.

"That is only because he has an unhappy life. You may depend upon it there is a regular fire of love inside him. Gwen used to say that all his warmth was for his mother."

"He was fond of our mother."

"Perhaps he was in love with her."

"That would account for why he was jealous of ye."

Gawaine was surprised at this discovery, which had struck him for the first time.

"Perhaps that was why he allowed Sir Agravaine to kill her, when she had that affair with Lamorak ... Poor boy, he has been ill-treated by the world."

"He is the only brother I have left."

"I know. Lancelot's was a tragic accident."

The laird of Lothian moved his bandage feverishly.

"But it canna have been accident. I could jalouse it had they worn their helms, but they were bonnetless. He must have known them."

"We have talked this over often."

"Aye, it is vain."

The old man asked with tragic diffidence: "You don't think you could bring yourself to forgive him, Gawaine, however it happened? I am not seeking to abandon duty, but if justice could be tempered with mercy ..."

"I will temper it when I hold him at my mercy, not before."

"Well, it is for you to say. Here comes the doctor to tell me I have stayed too long. Come in, doctor, come in."

But it was the Bishop of Rochester who entered in a bustle, carrying packets and an iron lantern.

"It is you, Rochester. We thought you were the doctor."

"Good evening, sir. And good evening to you, Sir Gawaine."

"Good evening."

"How is the head today?"

"It grows better, thank you, my lord."

"Well, that is excellent news."

"And I," he added archly, "have brought some good news too. The post has come in early!"

"Letters!"

"One for you," he handed it to the King, "a long one."

"Is there ought for me?" asked Gawaine.

"Nothing, I am afraid, this week. You will have better luck next time."

Arthur took the letter to the lantern and broke the seal.

"You will excuse me if I read."

"Of course. We cannot stand on ceremony with the news from England. Dear me, I never thought I should become a palmer at my time of life, Sir Gawaine, and have to gallivant in foreign parts. ..."

The bishop's prattle died away. Arthur had made no movement. He had turned neither red nor pale, nor dropped the letter, nor stared in front of him. He was reading quietly. But Rochester stopped speaking, and Gawaine raised himself on one elbow. They watched him reading, open-mouthed.

"Sir . . ."

"Nothing," he said, brushing them away with his hand. "Excuse me. The news."

"I hope . . ."

"Let me finish, please. Talk to Sir Gawaine."

Gawaine asked: "Is there ill tidings . . . May I see?"

"No, please, a minute."

"Mordred?"

"No. It is nothing. The doctor says . . . My lord, I would like to speak to you outside."

Gawaine began to heave himself into a sitting position.

"I will be told."

"There is nothing to be upset about. Lie down. We will come back."

"If ye go without telling me, I shall follow."

"It is nothing. You will hurt your head."

"What is it?"

"Nothing. It is only . . ."

"Well?"

"Well, Gawaine," he said, suddenly collapsing, "it seems that Mordred has proclaimed himself the King of England, under this New Order of his."

"Mordred!"

"He has told his Thrashers that we are dead, you see," Arthur explained, as if it were some sort of problem, "and . . ."

"Mordred says we are dead?"

"He says we are dead, and . . ."

But he could not frame it.

"And what?"

"He is going to marry Gwen."

There was a moment of dead silence, while the bishop's hand strayed vaguely to his pectoral cross and Gawaine's clenched itself in the bed clothes. Then they both spoke at once.

"The Lord Protector . . ."

"It canna be true. It will be a jest. My brother wouldna do a thing like yon."

"Unfortunately it is true," said the King patiently. "This is a letter from Guenever. Heaven knows how she managed to get it through."

"The Queen's age ..."

"After the proclamation, he proposed to her. She had nobody to help. The Queen accepted his proposal."

"Accepted Mordred!"

Gawaine had managed to swing his legs over the side of the bed.

"Uncle, give me the letter."

He took it out of the limp hand, which yielded it automatically, and began to read, tilting the page to the light.

Arthur continued to explain.

"The Queen accepted Mordred's proposal, and asked for permission to go to London for her trousseau. When she was in London with the few who remained faithful, she threw herself suddenly into the Tower and barred the gates. Thank God, it is a strong fort. They are besieging her in the Tower of London now, and Mordred is using guns."

Rochester asked in bewilderment: "Guns?"

"He is using the cannon."

It was too much for the old priest's intellects.

"It is incredible!" he said. "To say we are dead, and to marry the Queen! And then to use cannon ..."

"Now that the guns have come," said Arthur, "the Table is over. We must hurry home."

"To use cannons against men!"

"We must go to the rescue immediately, my lord. Gawaine can stay here ..."

But the Laird of Orkney was out of bed.

"Gawaine, what are you doing? Lie down at once."

"I am coming with ye."

"Gawaine, lie down. Rochester, help me with him."

"My last brother has broken his fealty."

"Gawaine ..."

"And Lancelot ... Ah God, my head!"

He stood swaying in the dim light, holding the bandage with both hands, while his shadow moved grotesquely round the tent pole.

# 13

*Anguish of Ireland had once dreamed of a wind*
which blew down all their castles and towns—and this one
was conspiring to do it. It was blowing round Benwick
Castle on all the organ stops. The noises it made sounded
like inchoate masses of silk being pulled through trees, as
we pull hair through a comb—like heaps of sand pouring
on fine sand from a scoop—like gigantic linens being torn
—like drums in distant battle—like an endless snake switch-
ing through the world's undergrowth of trees and houses—
like old men sighing, and women howling and wolves running. It whistled, hummed, throbbed, boomed in the chimneys. Above all, it sounded like a live creature: some monstrous, elemental being, wailing its damnation. It was
Dante's wind, bearing lost lovers and cranes: sabbathless
Satan, toiling and turmoiling.

In the western ocean it harried the sea flat, lifting water
bodily out of water and carrying it as spume. On dry land
it made the trees lean down before it. The gnarled thorn
trees, which had grown in double trunks, groaned one trunk
against the other with plaintive screams. In the whipping
and snapping branches of the trees, the birds rode it out
head to wind, their bodies horizontal, their neat claws turned
to anchors. The peregrines in the cliffs sat stoically, their
mutton-chop-whiskers made streaky by the rain and the
wet feathers standing upright on their heads. The wild
geese beating out to their night's rest in the twilight scarcely
won a yard a minute against the streaming air, their tumul-
tuary cries blown backward from them, so that they had to
be past before you heard them, although they were only a
few feet up. The mallard and widgeon, coming in high
with the gale behind, were gone before they had arrived.

Under the doors of the castle the piercing blasts tortured
the flapping rushes of the floors. They boo'ed in the tubes
of the corkscrew stairs, rattled the wooden shutters, whined

shrilly through the shot windows, stirred the cold tapestries in frigid undulations, searched for backbones. The stone towers thrilled under them, trembling bodily like the bass strings of musical instruments. The slates flew off and shattered themselves with desultory crashes.

Bors and Bleoberis were crouching over a bright fire, to which the bitter wind seemed to have given the property of throwing out light without heat. Even the fire seemed frozen, like a painted one. Their minds were baffled by the plague of air.

"But why did they go so quickly?" asked Bors complainingly. "I never knew a siege to be raised like that before. They raised it overnight. They went as if they had been blown away."

"They must have had bad news. Something must have gone wrong in England."

"Perhaps."

"If they had decided to forgive Lancelot, they would have sent a message."

"It does seem strange, sailing away at a moment's notice, without saying anything."

"Do you think there can have been a revolt in Cornwall, or in Wales, or in Ireland?"

"There are always the Old Ones," agreed Bleoberis numbly.

"I don't think it could be a revolt. I think the King was taken ill, and had to be carried home quickly. Or Gawaine might have been taken ill. That blow which Lancelot gave him the second time, perhaps it perched his brain-pan?"

"Perhaps."

Bors banged the fire.

"To go off like that, and never say a word!"

"Why doesn't Lancelot do something?"

"What can he do?"

"I don't know."

"The King has banished him."

"Yes."

"Then there is nothing to do."

"All the same," said Bleoberis, "I wish he would do something."

A door opened with a clatter at the bottom of the turret stairs. The tapestries swirled out, the rushes stood on end, the fire gushed smoke, and Lancelot's voice embedded in the wind, shouted: "Bors! Bleoberis! Demaris!"

"Here."

"Where?"

"Up here."

As the distant door closed, silence returned to the room. The rushes lay down again, and Lancelot's feet sounded clearly on the stone steps, where before it had been difficult to hear his shout. He came in hastily, carrying a letter.

"Bors. Bleoberis: I have been looking for you."

They had stood up.

"A letter has come from England. The messengers were blown ashore, five miles up the coast. We shall have to go at once."

"To England?"

"Yes, yes. To England, of course. I have told Lionel to act as transport officer, and I want you, Bors, to look after the fodder. We shall have to wait until the gale blows itself out."

"Why are we going?" asked Bors.

"You should tell us the news . . ."

"News?" he said vaguely. "There is no time for that. I will tell you in the boat. Here, read the letter."

He handed it to Bors, and was gone before they could reply.

"Well!"

"Read what it says."

"I don't even know who it is from."

"Perhaps it will say in the letter."

Lancelot re-appeared before they had taken their researches further than the date.

"Bleoberis," he said, "I forgot. I want you to look after the horses. Here, give me the writing. If you two start spelling it out, you will be reading all night."

"What does it say?"

"Most of the news came by the messenger. It seems that Mordred has revolted against Arthur, proclaimed himself the Leader of England, and proposed to Guenever."

"But she is married already," protested Bleoberis.

"That was why the siege was broken up. Then, it appears, Mordred raised an army in Kent to oppose the King's landing. He had given it out that Arthur was dead. He is besieging the Queen in the Tower of London, and using cannon."

"Cannon!"

"He met Arthur at Dover and fought a battle to prevent the landing. It was a bad engagement, half on sea and half on land, but the king won. He won to land."

"Who wrote the letter?"

Lancelot suddenly sat down.

"It is from Gawaine, from poor Gawaine! He is dead."

"Dead!"

"How can he write . . ." began Bleoberis.

"It is a dreadful letter. Gawaine was a good man. All you people who forced me to fight him, you didn't see what a heart he had inside."

"Read it," suggested Bors impatiently.

"It seems that a cut which I gave him on the head was a dangerous one. He never ought to have travelled. But he was lonely and miserable and he had been betrayed. His last brother had turned traitor. He insisted on going back to help the King—and, in the landing battle, he tried to strike his blow. Unfortunately he was clubbed on the old wound, and died of it a few hours later."

"I don't see why you should be disturbed."

"Listen to the letter."

Lancelot carried it to the window and fell silent, examining the writing. There was something touching about it, the hand being so unlike its author. Gawaine had hardly been the sort of person you thought of as a writer. Indeed it would have seemed more natural if he had been illiterate, like most of the others. Yet here, instead of the spiky Gothic then in use, was the lovely old Gaelic minuscule, as neat and round and small as when he had learned it from some ancient saint in dim Dunlothian. He had written so unfrequently since, that the art had retained its beauty. It was an old-maid's hand, or an old-fashioned boy's, sitting with his feet hooked round the legs of a stool and his tongue out, writing carefully. He had carried this innocent precision, these dainty demoded cusps, through misery and passion to old age. It was as if a bright boy had stepped out of the black armour: a small boy with a drop on the end of his nose, his feet bare with blue toes, a root of tangle in the thin bundle of carrots which were his fingers.

*Unto Sir Lancelot, flower of all noble knights that ever I heard of or saw by my days: I, Sir Gawaine, King Lot's son of Orkney, sister's son unto the noble King Arthur, send thee greetings.*

*"And I will that all the world wit that I, Sir Gawaine, Knight of the Round Table, sought my death at thy hands—and not through thy deserving, but it was mine own seeking. Wherefore I beseech thee, Sir Lancelot, to return again unto this realm and see my tomb, and pray some prayer more or less for my soul.*

*"And this same day that I wrote this cedle, I was hurt to the death in the same wound which I had on thy hand, Sir Lancelot—for of a more nobler man might I not be slain.*

*"Also, Sir Lancelot, for all the love that ever was betwixt us . . ."*

Lancelot stopped reading and threw the letter on the table.

"Here," he said, "I can't go on. He urges me to come with speed, to help the King against his brother: his last relation. Gawaine loved his family, Bors, and in the end he was left with none. Yet he wrote to forgive me. He even said that it was his own fault. God knows, he was a right good brother."

"What are we to do about the King?"

"We must get to England as quickly as we can. Mordred has retreated to Canterbury, where he offers a fresh battle. It may be over by now. This news has been delayed by storm. Everything depends on speed."

Bleoberis said: "I will go and look to the horses. When do we sail?"

"Tomorrow. Tonight. Now. When the wind drops. Be quick with them."

"Good."

"And you, Bors, the fodder."

"Yes."

Lancelot followed Bleoberis to the stairs, but turned in the doorway.

"The Queen besieged," he said. "We must get her out."

"Yes."

Bors, left alone with the wind, picked up the letter with curiosity. He tilted it in the failing light, admiring the zed-like g, the curly b, and the curved t, like the blade of a plough. Each tiny line was the furrow it threw up, sweet as the new earth. But the furrow wandered towards the end. He turned it about, observing the brown signature. He spelled out the conclusion—making speaking movements with his mouth, while the rushes tapped and the smoke puffed and the wind howled.

*"And at this date my letter was written, but two hours
and a half afore my death, written with mine own hand,
and so subscribed with part of my heart's blood.*

*Gawaine of Orkney."*

He spelled the name out twice, and tapped his teeth.
Gawaine. "I suppose," he said out loud, doubtfully, "they
would have pronounced it Cuchullain in the North? You
can't tell with ancient languages."

Then he put down the letter, went over to the dreary
window, and began humming a tune called *Brume, brume
on hil,* whose words have been lost to us in the wave of
time. Perhaps they were like the modern ones, which say
that

> Still the blood is strong, the heart is Highland,
> And we in dreams behold the Hebrides.

# 14

*The same wind of sorrow whistled round the King's*
pavilion at Salisbury. Inside there was a silent calm, after
the riot of the open. It was a sumptuous interior, what with
the royal tapestries—Uriah was there, still in the article of
bisection—and the couch strewn deep with furs, and the
flashing candles. It was a marquee rather than a tent. The
King's mail gleamed dully on a rack at the back. An ill-
bred falcon, who was subject to the vice of screaming,
stood hooded and motionless on a perch like a parrot's,
brooding in some ancestral nightmare. A greyhound, as
white as ivory, couching on its hocks and elbows, its tail
curved into the bony sickle of the greyhound, watched the
old man with the doe-soft eyes of pity. A superb enamelled
chess-board, with pieces of jasper and crystal, stood at
checkmate beside the bed. There were papers everywhere.
They covered the secretary's table, the reading desk, the
stools—dreary papers of government, still bravely persevered
in—of law, still to be codified—of commissariat and of

armament and of orders for the day. A large ledger lay open at the note of some wretched defaulter, William atte Lane, who had been condemned to be hanged, *suspendatur,* for looting. On the margin, in the secretary's neat hand, was the laconic epitaph "susp.", suitable to the mood of tragedy. Covering the reading desk there were endless piles of petitions and memorials, all annotated with the royal decision and signature. On those to which the King had agreed, he had written laboriously *"Le roy le veult."* The rejected petitions were marked with the courtly evasion always used by royalty: *"Le roy s'advisera."* The reading desk and its seat were made in one piece, and there the King himself sat drooping. His head lay among the papers, scattering them. He looked as if he were dead—he nearly was.

Arthur was tired out. He had been broken by the two battles which he had fought already, the one at Dover, the other at Barham Down. His wife was a prisoner. His oldest friend was banished. His son was trying to kill him. Gawaine was buried. His Table was dispersed. His country was at war. Yet he could have breasted all these things in some way, if the central tenet of his heart had not been ravaged. Long ago, when his mind had been a nimble boy's called Wart—long ago he had been taught by an aged benevolence, wagging a white beard. He had been taught by Merlyn to believe that man was perfectible: that he was on the whole more decent than beastly: that good was worth trying: that there was no such thing as original sin. He had been forged as a weapon for the aid of man, on the assumption that men were good. He had been forged, by that deluded old teacher, into a sort of Pasteur or Curie or patient discoverer of insulin. The service for which he had been destined had been against Force, the mental illness of humanity. His Table, his idea of Chivalry, his Holy Grail, his devotion to Justice: these had been progressive steps in the effort for which he had been bred. He was like a scientist who had pursued the root of cancer all his life. Might—to have ended it—to have made men happier. But the whole structure depended on the first premise: that man was decent.

Looking back at his life, it seemed to him that he had been struggling all the time to dam a flood, which, whenever he had checked it, had broken through at a new place, setting him his work to do again. It was the flood of Force Majeur. During the earliest days before his marriage he had tried to match its strength with strength—in his battles against the Gaelic confederation—only to find that two wrongs did not make a right. But he had crushed the feudal dream of war successfully. Then, with his Round Table, he had tried to harness Tyranny in lesser forms, so that its power might be used for useful ends. He had sent out the men of might to rescue the oppressed and to straighten evil —to put down the individual might of barons, just as he had put down the might of kings. They had done so—until, in the course of time, the ends had been achieved, but the force had remained upon his hands unchastened. So he had sought for a new channel, had sent them out on God's business, searching for the Holy Grail. That too had been a failure, because those who had achieved the Quest had become perfect and been lost to the world, while those who had failed in it had soon returned no better. At last he had sought to make a map of force, as it were, to bind it down by laws. He had tried to codify the evil uses of might by individuals, so that he might set bounds to them by the impersonal justice of the state. He had been prepared to sacrifice his wife and his best friend, to the impersonality of Justice. And then, even as the might of the individual seemed to have been curbed, the Principle of Might had sprung up behind him in another shape—in the shape of collective might, of banded ferocity, of numerous armies insusceptible to individual laws. He had bound the might of units, only to find that it was assumed by pluralities. He had conquered murder, to be faced with war. There were no Laws for that.

The wars of his early days, those against Lot and the Dictator of Rome, had been battles to upset the feudal convention of warfare as foxhunting or as gambling for ransom. To upset it, he had introduced the idea of total war. In his old age this same total warfare had come back to roost as total hatred, as the most modern of hostilities.

Now, with his forehead resting on the papers and his eyes closed, the King was trying not to realize. For if there was such a thing as original sin, if man was on the whole a villain, if the bible was right in saying that the heart of men was deceitful above all things and desperately wicked, then the purpose of his life had been a vain one. Chivalry and justice became a child's illusions, if the stock on which he had tried to graft them was to be the Thrasher, was to be *Homo ferox* instead of *Homo sapiens*.

Behind this thought there was a worse one, with which he

dared not grapple. Perhaps man was neither good nor bad, was only a machine in an insensate universe—his courage no more than a reflex to danger, like the automatic jump at the pin-prick. Perhaps there were no virtues, unless jumping at pin-pricks was a virtue, and humanity only a mechanical donkey led on by the iron carrot of love, through the pointless treadmill of reproduction. Perhaps Might was a law of Nature, needed to keep the survivors fit. Perhaps he himself . . .

But he could challenge it no further. He felt as if there was something atrophied between his eyes, where the base of the nose grew into the skull. He could not sleep. He had bad dreams. Tomorrow was the final battle. Meanwhile there were all these papers to read and sign. But he could neither read nor sign them. He could not lift his head from the desk.

Why did men fight?

The old man had always been a dutiful thinker, never an inspired one. Now his exhausted brain slipped into its accustomed circles: the withered paths, like those of the donkey in the treadmill, round which he had plodded many thousand times in vain.

Was it the wicked leaders who led innocent populations to slaughter, or was it wicked populations who chose leaders after their own hearts? On the face of it, it seemed unlikely that one Leader could force a million Englishmen against their will. If, for instance, Mordred had been anxious to make the English wear petticoats, or stand on their heads, they would surely not have joined his party—however clever or persuasive or deceitful or even terrible his inducements? A leader was surely forced to offer something which appealed to those he led? He might give the impetus to the falling building, but surely it had to be toppling on its own account before it fell? If this were true, then wars were not calamities into which amiable innocents were led by evil men. They were national movements, deeper, more subtle in origin. And, indeed, it did not feel to him as if he or Mordred had led their country to its misery. If it was so easy to lead one's country in various directions, as if she was a pig on a string, why had he failed to lead her into chivalry, into justice and into peace? He had been trying.

Then again—this was the second circle—it was like the

Inferno—if neither he nor Mordred had really set the misery in motion, who had been the cause? How did the fact of war begin in general? For any one war seemed so rooted in its antecedents. Mordred went back to Morgause, Morgause to Uther Pendragon, Uther to his ancestors. It seemed as if Cain had slain Abel, seizing his country, after which the men of Abel had sought to win their patrimony again for ever. Man had gone on, through age after age, avenging wrong with wrong, slaughter with slaughter. Nobody was the better for it, since both sides always suffered, yet everybody was inextricable. The present war might be attributed to Mordred, or to himself. But also it was due to a million Thrashers, to Lancelot, Guenever, Gawaine, everybody. Those who lived by the sword were forced to die by it. It was as if everything would lead to sorrow, so long as man refused to forget the past. The wrongs of Uther and of Cain were wrongs which could have been righted only by the blessing of forgetting them.

Sisters, mothers, grandmothers: everything was rooted in the past! Actions of any sort in one generation might have incalculable consequences in another, so that merely to sneeze was a pebble thrown into a pond, whose circles might lap the furthest shores. It seemed as if the only hope was not to act at all, to draw no swords for anything, to hold oneself still, like a pebble not thrown. But that would be hateful.

What was Right, what was Wrong? What distinguished Doing from Not Doing? If I were to have my time again, the old King thought, I would bury myself in a monastery, for fear of a Doing which might lead to woe.

The blessing of forgetfulness: that was the first essential. If everything one did, or which one's fathers had done, was an endless sequence of Doings doomed to break forth bloodily, then the past must be obliterated and a new start made. Man must be ready to say: Yes, since Cain there has been injustice, but we can only set the misery right if we accept a *status quo*. Lands have been robbed, men slain, nations humiliated. Let us now start fresh without remembrance, rather than live forward and backward at the same time. We cannot build the future by avenging the past. Let us sit down as brothers, and accept the Peace of God.

Unfortunately men did say this, in each successive war. They were always saying that the present one was to be the last, and afterwards there was to be a heaven. They were always to rebuild such a new world as never was seen. When the time came, however, they were too stupid. They were like children crying out that they would build a house—but, when it came to building, they had not the practical ability. They did not know the way to choose the right materials.

The old man's thoughts went laboriously. They were leading him nowhere: they doubled back on themselves and ran the same course twice: yet he was so accustomed to them that he could not stop. He entered another circle.

Perhaps the great cause of war was possession, as John Ball the communist had said. "The matters gothe nat well to passe in Englonde," he had stated, "nor shall nat do tyll every thyng be common, and that there be no villayns nor gentylmen." Perhaps wars were fought because people said *my* kingdom, *my* wife, *my* lover, *my* possessions. This was what he and Lancelot and all of them had always held behind their thoughts. Perhaps, so long as people tried to possess things separately from each other, even honour and souls, there would be wars for ever. The hungry wolf would always attack the fat reindeer, the poor man would rob the banker, the serf would make revolutions against the higher class, and the lack-penny nation would fight the rich. Perhaps wars only happened between those who had and those who had not. As against this, you were forced to place the fact that nobody could define the state of "having." A knight with a silver suit of armour would immediately call himself a have-not, if he met a knight with a golden one.

But, he thought, assume for a moment that "having," however it is defined, might be the crux of the problem.

I have, and Mordred has not. He protested to himself in contradiction: it is not fair to put it like that, as if Mordred or I were the movers of the storm. For indeed, we are nothing but figureheads to complex forces which seem to be under a kind of impulse. It is as if there was an impulse in the fabric of society. Mordred is urged along almost helplessly now, by numbers of people too many to count: people who believe in John Ball, hoping to gain power over their fellow men by asserting that all are equal, or people who see in any upheaval a chance to advance their own might. It seems to come from underneath. Ball's men and Mordred's are the under-dogs seeking to rise, or the knights who were not leaders of the Round Table and therefore hated it, or the poor who would be rich, or the powerless seeking to gain power. And my men, for whom I am no more than a standard or a talisman, are the knights who were leaders—the rich defending their possessions, the powerful unready to let it slip. It is a meeting of the Haves and Have-Nots in force, an insane clash between bodies of men, not between leaders. But let that pass. Assume the vague idea that war is due to "having" in general. In that case the proper thing would be to refuse to have at all. Such, as Rochester had sometimes pointed out, was the advice of God. There had been the rich man who was threatened with the needle's eye, and there had been the money changers. That was why the Church could not interfere too much in the sad affairs of the world, so Rochester said, because the nations and the classes and the individuals were always crying out "Mine, mine," where the Church was instructed to say "Ours."

If this were true, then it would not be a question only of sharing property, as such. It would be a question of sharing everything—even thoughts, feelings, lives. God had told people that they would have to cease to live as individuals. They would have to go into the force of life, like a drop falling into a river. God had said that it was only the men who could give up their jealous selves, their futile individualities of happiness and sorrow, who would die peacefully and enter the ring. He that would save his life was asked to lose it.

Yet there was something in the old white head which could not accept the godly view. Obviously you might cure a cancer of the womb by not having a womb in the first place. Sweeping and drastic remedies could cut out anything—and life with the cut. Ideal advice, which nobody was built to follow, was no advice at all. Advising heaven to earth was useless.

Another worn-out circle spun before him. Perhaps war was due to fear: to fear of reliability. Unless there was truth, and unless people told the truth, there was always danger in everything outside the individual. You told the truth to yourself, but you had no surety for your neighbour. This uncertainty must end by making the neighbour a menace. Such, at any rate, would have been Lancelot's explanation of the war. He had been used to say that man's most vital possession was his Word. Poor Lance, he had broken his own word: all the same, there had been few men with such a good one.

Perhaps wars happened because nations had no confidence in the Word. They were frightened, and so they fought. Nations were like people—they had feelings of inferiority, or of superiority, or of revenge, or of fear. It was right to personify nations.

Suspicion and fear: possessiveness and greed: resentment for ancestral wrong: all these seemed to be a part of it. Yet they were not the solution. He could not see the real solution. He was too old and tired and miserable to think constructively. He was only a man who had meant well, who had been spurred along that course of thinking by an eccentric necromancer with a weakness for humanity. Justice had been his last attempt—to do nothing which was not just. But it had ended in failure. To do at all had proved too difficult. He was done himself.

Arthur proved that he was not quite done, by lifting his head. There was something invincible in his heart, a tincture of grandness in simplicity. He sat upright and reached for the iron bell.

"Page," he said, as the small boy trotted in, knuckling his eyes.

"My lord."

The King looked at him. Even in his own extremity he was able to notice others, especially if they were fresh or decent. When he had comforted the broken Gawaine in his tent, he had been the one who was more in need of comfort.

"My poor child," he said. "You ought to be in bed."

He observed the boy with a strained, thread-bare attention. It was long since he had seen youth's innocence and certainty.

"Look," he said, "will you take this note to the bishop? Don't wake him if he is asleep."

"My lord."

"Thank you."

As the live creature went, he called it back.

"Oh, page?"

"My lord?"

"What is your name?"

"Tom, my lord," it said politely.

"Where do you live?"

"Near Warwick, my lord."

"Near Warwick."

The old man seemed to be trying to imagine the place, as if it were Paradise Terrestre, or a country described by Mandeville.

"At a place called Newbold Revell. It is a pretty one."

"How old are you?"

"I shall be thirteen in November, my lord."

"And I have kept you up all night."

"No, my lord. I slept a lot on one of the saddles."

"Tom of Newbold Revell," he said with wonder. "We seem to have involved a lot of people. Tell me, Tom, what do you intend to do tomorrow?"

"I shall fight, sir. I have a good bow."

"And you will kill people with this bow?"

"Yes, my lord. A great many, I hope."

"Suppose they were to kill you?"

"Then I should be dead, my lord."

"I see."

"Shall I take the letter now?"

"No. Wait a minute. I want to talk to somebody, only my head is muddled."

"Shall I fetch a glass of wine?"

"No, Tom. Sit down and try to listen. Lift those chessmen off the stool. Can you understand things when they are said?"

"Yes, my lord. I am good at understanding."

"Could you understand if I asked you not to fight tomorrow?"

"I should want to fight," it said stoutly.

"Everybody wants to fight, Tom, but nobody knows why. Suppose I were to ask you not to fight, as a special favour to the King? Would you do that?"

"I should do what I was told."

"Listen, then. Sit for a minute and I will tell you a story. I am a very old man, Tom, and you are young. When you are old, you will be able to tell what I have told tonight, and I want you to do that. Do you understand this want?"

"Yes, sir. I think so."

"Put it like this. There was a king once, called King Arthur. That is me. When he came to the throne of England, he found that all the kings and barons were fighting against each other like madmen, and, as they could afford to fight in expensive suits of armour, there was practically nothing which could stop them from doing what they pleased. They did a lot of bad things, because they lived by force. Now this king had an idea, and the idea was that force ought to be used, if it were used at all, on behalf of justice, not on its own account. Follow this, young boy. He thought that if he could get his barons fighting for truth, and to help weak people, and to redress wrongs, then their fighting might not be such a bad thing as once it used to be. So he gathered together all the true and kindly people that he knew, and he dressed them in armour, and he made them knights, and taught them his idea, and set them down, at a Round Table. There were a hundred and fifty of them in the happy days, and King Arthur loved his Table with all his heart. He was prouder of it than he was of his own dear wife, and for many years his new knights went about killing ogres, and rescuing damsels and saving poor prisoners, and trying to set the world to rights. That was the King's idea."

"I think it was a good idea, my lord."

"It was, and it was not. God knows."

"What happened to the King in the end?" asked the child, when the story seemed to have dried up.

"For some reason, things went wrong. The Table split into factions, a bitter war began, and all were killed."

The boy interrupted confidently.

"No," he said, "not all. The King won. We shall win."

Arthur smiled vaguely and shook his head. He would have nothing but the truth.

"Everybody was killed," he repeated, "except a certain page. I know what I am talking about."

"My lord?"

"This page was called young Tom of Newbold Revell near Warwick, and the old King sent him off before the battle, upon pain of dire disgrace. You see, the King wanted there to be somebody left, who would remember their famous idea. He wanted badly that Tom should go back to Newbold Revell, where he could grow into a man and live his life in Warwickshire peace—and he wanted him to tell everybody who would listen about this ancient idea, which both of them had once thought good. Do you think you could do that, Thomas, to please the King?"

The child said, with the pure eyes of absolute truth: "I would do anything for King Arthur."

"That's a brave fellow. Now listen, man. Don't get these legendary people muddled up. It is I who tell you about my idea. It is I who am going to command you to take horse to Warwickshire at once, and not to fight with your bow tomorrow at all. Do you understand all this?"

"Yes, King Arthur."

"Will you promise to be careful of yourself afterward? Will you try to remember that you are a kind of vessel to carry on the idea, when things go wrong, and that the whole hope depends on you alive?"

"I will."

"It seems selfish of me to use you for it."

"It is an honour for your poor page, good my lord."

"Thomas, my idea of those knights was a sort of candle, like these ones here. I have carried it for many years with a hand to shield it from the wind. It has flickered often. I am giving you the candle now—you won't let it out?"

"It will burn."

"Good Tom. The light-bringer. How old did you say you were?"

"Nearly thirteen."

"Sixty more years then, perhaps. Half a century."

"I will give it to other people, King. English people."

"You will say to them in Warwickshire: Eh, he wor a wonderly fine candle?"

"Aye, lad, that I will."

"Then 'tis: Na, Tom, for thee must go right quickly. Thou'lt take the best son of a mare that thee kinst find, and thou wilt ride post into Warwickshire, lad, wi' nowt but the curlew?"

"I will ride post, mate, so that the candle burn."

"Good Tom, then, God bless 'ee. Doant thee ferget thick Bishop of Rochester, afore thou goest."

The little boy kneeled down to kiss his master's hand—his surcoat, with the Malory bearings, looking absurdly new.

"My lord of England," he said.

Arthur raised him gently, to kiss him on the shoulder.

"Sir Thomas of Warwick," he said—and the boy was gone.


The tent was empty, tawny and magnificent. The wind wailed and the candles guttered. Waiting for the Bishop, the old, old man sat down at his reading desk. Presently his head drooped forward on the papers. The greyhound's eyes, catching the candles as she watched him, burned spectrally, two amber cups of feral light. Mordred's cannonade, which he was to keep up through the darkness until the morning's battle, began to thud and bump outside. The King, drained of his last effort, gave way to sorrow. Even when his visitor's hand lifted the tent flap, the silent drops coursed down his nose and fell on the parchment with regular ticks, like an ancient clock. He turned his head aside, unwilling to be seen, unable to do better. The flap fell, as the strange figure in cloak and hat came softly in.

"Merlyn?"

But there was nobody there: he had dreamed him in a cat-nap of old age.

Merlyn?

He began to think again, but now it was as clearly as it had ever been. He remembered the aged necromancer who had educated him—who had educated him with animals. There were, he remembered, something like half a million different species of animal, of which mankind was only one. Of course man was an animal—he was not a vegetable or a mineral, was he? And Merlyn had taught him about animals so that the single species might learn by looking at the problems of the thousands. He remembered the belligerent ants, who claimed their boundaries, and the pacific geese, who did not. He remembered his lesson from the badger. He remembered Lyo-lyok and the island which they had seen on their migration, where all those puffins, razorbills, guillemots and kittiwakes had lived together peacefully, preserving their own kinds of civilization without war—because they claimed no boundaries. He saw the problem before him as plain as a map. The fantastic thing about war was that it was fought about nothing—literally nothing. Frontiers were imaginary lines. There was no visible line between Scotland and England, although Flodden and Bannockburn had been fought about it. It was geography which was the cause—political geography. It was nothing else. Nations did not need to have the same kind of civilization, nor the same kind of leader, any more than the puffins and the guillemots did. They could keep their own civilizations, like Esquimaux and Hottentots, if they would give each other freedom of trade and free passage and access to the world. Countries would have to become counties—but counties which could keep their own culture and local laws. The imaginary lines on the earth's surface only needed to be unimagined. The airborne birds skipped them by nature. How mad the frontiers had seemed to Lyo-lyok, and would to Man if he could learn to fly.

The old King felt refreshed, clear-headed, almost ready to begin again.

There would be a day—there must be a day—when he would come back to Gramarye with a new Round Table which had no corners, just as the world had none—a table without boundaries between the nations who would sit to feast there. The hope of making it would lie in culture. If people could be persuaded to read and write, not just to eat and make love, there was still a chance that they might come to reason.

But it was too late for another effort then. For that time it was his destiny to die, or, as some say, to be carried off to Avilion, where he could wait for better days. For that time it was Lancelot's fate and Guenever's to take the tonsure and the veil, while Mordred must be slain. The fate of this man or that man was less than a drop, although it was a sparkling one, in the great blue motion of the sunlit sea.

The cannons of his adversary were thundering in the tattered morning when the Majesty of England drew himself up to meet the future with a peaceful heart.

EXPLICIT LIBER REGIS QUONDAM
REGISQUE FUTURI

THE BEGINNING